"His characters are not just real, they are also capable of esoteric thought and bursting turgid feelings.....I found it irresistible... *The Evangelist* is at the top of my must-read book list this year."
—Claire McNabe, A.B.M, Literary Critic
Author of *Confessions of an Ex-Catholic*

"*The Evangelist* is a splendid tale, filled with hauntingly accurate recollections of the Second World War, as seen through a child's eyes, classical references and intelligent conversations.... This is a must read for every Greek-American."
—Elias C. Grivoyannis, Ph.D., Yeshiva University

"From the Greek islands to the American South, this is the story of a man displaced by circumstance and haunted by his past.... Historical references add color and depth to this beautifully constructed narrative."
—Berch Haroian, Ph.D., William Paterson University
Author of several texts

"Mr. Georgalis's *Evangelist* is a triumphantly perceptive achievement. He has aptly fathomed the ethereal substance of la femme sans the provocative polemics typical with other authors. This book is a brilliantly executed tour de force that shall delight the selective readers of creative and avant-garde world literature.
—J.M. Woodward, C.E.O., Marika's Designs

THE

EVANGELIST

At the Left Hand of God

By
Frank Georgalis

This book is a work of fiction.

Names, characters, places and incidents are either a product of the author's imagination or are used fictitiously and any resemblance to actual persons, living or dead, events, or locales is entirely coincidental.

Dedication

This book is dedicated to my life long heroes, my mother and father, Athina and Louis Georgalis. They are both my true and larger than life heroes who, in the middle years of their life, made the sacrifice of leaving their home, their land, family and friends to come to America for the betterment of their children.

"Dad, Mom, please hear my thanks and smile as kind fate and God have smiled upon me. If I have neglected to tell you that I love you, I am telling you now. The efforts and sacrifices you had made for your children were not in vein. Dad, your words of belief in me, even at times of failure, kept my spirit up and closer to God's wishes. I can still recall the words you often spoke in times of disaster or distress: 'Λοιπον, παμε καλα,' "Well, we're doing good." Mom, I can still see you gazing at me with pride on your lovely face; no other woman has ever looked at me that way."

I now know why this country is so great; sensitive children of immigrant parents felt their parents' pain and did their best to please them. These are the happiest of times, but an obscure sadness lingers on. One of my books is about to be published and I am happy to thank you, my heroes, but I am saddened by your not being here to thank in person. Although you are no longer with us, I want you to know your sacrifice has fulfilled your child's dream.

Acknowledgements

The author is immensely grateful for the continued support and encouragement that was offered him throughout the creation of this book by his sister Peggy and her husband, Larry Quick, both educators. It was Larry who boasted to his friends and colleagues of his brother-in-law's abilities and kept them updated on the stages of this book's progress, not unlike following a favorite professional athlete. It can be said that a writer is like a mountain climber who could easily slip and fall if not for the attention, concern and support of those on his team.

Thanks go to Larry Marro, a thirty-year friend of the author who, with his great knowledge of Greek mythology, poetry and history, was always ready and willing to help the author in his search for the proper mythic symbolism and poetic reference.

Thanks too go to the author's brother, Tom, who played the devil's advocate throughout this work's creation. By using reverse psychology, he urged the author to move forward towards completion.

Thanks to Dr. G.J. Tzannetakis, Ph.D., Dr. Berch Haroian, Ph.D., Professor Elias Grivoyannis, Ph.D., Yeshiva University and George Handrinos, a friend for over thirty years, all of whom took the time to read excerpts from the manuscript and offered comments that added immensely to the finished work.

A special thanks goes to Dr. Elias Lignos, who kept a safe guard on the original screenplay manuscript for many years and at whose urging the play became a novel.

Thanks goes to David Malta for his contribution to the design of the cover, to Jonathan Gullery for the professional print layout and to Ron Pramschufer, publishing consultant, all of whom were invaluable in the publication of this novel.

Finally, thanks go to Frank Gee, the author's reckless, forever young, devil may care alter ego for his tolerating the discipline and control required to complete this work by Frank Georgalis.

Prologue

Erik Karas began life in a fishing village on the Ionian coast of Greece shortly before the Second World War. In the 1950s, when he was a teenager, his family immigrated to the United States in search of a better life. It was in their new homeland that his father began to implant his hopes, dreams and ideals, always reminding his son of other Greeks that had found both fortune and fame in the land they so proudly called "the land of the free and the home of the brave." Erik subsequently was programmed to climb a lonely mountain, hearing his fathers words, "You cannot climb the mountain of life without love and pain. You must go on, my son, the sun will shine after the rain." Even after has father had passed on, his hopes and prayers lived on deep in his son's psyche until suddenly, in Erik's middle years, they bubbled to the surface. It was at breakfast with his wife and son, in their Westfield, New Jersey home, that he announced his mission and his destiny. This is the story of the Erik's mission, his love, his pain and his destiny.

Part I

CHAPTER 1

The family breakfast

The June morning sun darted its beams reproachfully into the kitchen where three people sat at the table to eat breakfast. Erik, his wife Susan and their son Randy celebrated the end of the week with a hearty morning meal prepared by Susan while they listened to humorous stories of by-gone days, told by Erik who, all through the week, looked to sit and enjoy this ritual after having spent the week with the tasks of an insurance salesman. This morning, however he seemed restless; he rose from the table, walked to the opened kitchen window and stared at the horizon.

Although accustomed to her husband's wandering spirit, Susan sensed something new brewing in his unpredictable and often changing moods. She had married him not for his wealth, which he never had much of, but for his good looks. She liked running her fingers through his thick curly hair and never tired of admiring his Grecian statue-like body, which he consciously kept in good form. From the first day she met Erik she was amused by his humor and enchanted by his impulsiveness; one minute he would be sitting at a café romancing a cup of coffee and suddenly he would insist on her going with him for a cup of Greek coffee several miles away.

He was a remarkable man and his telling of stories to his wife Susan, about his mother country Greece, would appear to have infused a considerable portion of his restless and inquiring soul into her breast and to have awakened in her mind the insatiable thirst to hear more. It was obvious to her that although he had a sharp and quick mind, at times it went the wrong way.

His aspiration for success, inspired by his background, seemed, at times, as idle dreams to others but to him was a reality that instilled more than a little fear in Susan's mind as to the ways her very intriguing man would go about achieving his goal. Erik's parents were middle aged when they immigrated to the United States with their three youngsters, two boys and a girl, aged fifteen to eleven. His father was his hero who, with sparse knowledge of the English language, little money and not a solid promise of security from anyone, left his friends and relatives and ventured to a new land with the desire in his heart and the purpose in his mind of giving his children a chance to reach their potential.

Erik knew and understood his father's sacrifices and ambitions and as this spirit guided him, it also hindered him. He often appeared to be striving to realize his father's dream and to be bigger than this giant of a man, his father.

Erik at times realized the classic Greek lesson of Alexander the Great who begrudged his father for having so many triumphs that he left merely a few battles for his son to fight.

After Susan and Erik married, he carried the full load of providing for his family which now grew to three with the arrival of their son Randy. Her husband, security and Randy, now five years old, were Susan's main concerns. Wealth and fame were beyond her thoughts and imagination.

In their household was a deep running love, but not a smooth current of existence, with many loud disputes between husband and wife. Most of those incidents were originated by a phrase or word thrown by Susan and picked up by Erik that developed into a war of words lasting less than one or two hours, while the child, Randy, listened intently but never stopped loving either one of them, as often revealed by his words and actions. Erik, with his devil-may-care attitude, a forever optimist, a spoiled husband and vibrant and differently handsome man with great charm and intimidating charisma occasionally would find comfort, peace and satisfaction in other women's arms on a temporary basis.

Susan was fairly convinced, by innumerable examples, that her husband loved her and cared for her and their child with all his heart and effort, so she refused to scrutinize his actions or look to find evidence of infidelity or immorality in him.

"Erik," said Susan looking at him intently. "Aren't you going to eat your eggs?"

Erik turned and looked at Susan as if he were elsewhere attending to a different matter. He walked back to the table slowly and sat on the chair without uttering a word.

"Go ahead and eat them. They are getting cold," remarked Susan, looking at him with an anticipating manner.

"I had another of those horrible dreams last night," said Erik, looking away.

"Again? Let's have it. You'll feel better afterwards. You always do," said Susan, reaching over and touching his hand.

"Tell us another war story, Daddy. I like to hear them," said Randy, who was intently employed with his pleasing task of eating.

"Okay, Big Guy," said Erik, caressing the little boy's dark brown hair.

"But don't say anything while your father is telling the story," interjected Susan, with a calm voice.

"I had a dream of the day my father was taken away by the Germans and my dream was almost as real as when it happened more than twenty five years ago," said Erik. He then paused, considered, pulled out a cigarette, lit it, took two or three short puffs and in contemplation of what he was about to say, a painful smile mantled on his face.

He hadn't forgotten that day but with the last night's dream his memory received a very disagreeable refresher on the subject.

"The entire population of the town, about two and half thousand," started Erik, "were awoken early in the morning and escorted to the town's main square where we were made to stand and face the big church that stood on the west side of the square. I remember the men were separated from the women and children, but I sneaked in the ranks with the men while I held my father's hand. We were made to stand there in the hot June sun for many hours and after a while I saw the German soldiers moving around hurriedly, as if something important were about to take place. Suddenly I saw a big truck stop between the church and the crowd and the soldiers began to unload machine guns; they were displayed in front of us facing the crowd.

Upon this, the women burst into loud and dismal screaming, and rushing to gather their children, flung their arms around them to preserve them from danger. I felt my father's hand tightened around mine and I heard nothing but screams and confusion resounding from all sides.

Eventually the screaming and the noise subsided. There were rumors told in low voices around me; one of the rumors I heard, while I was in the middle of the crowd of men, was that the Germans were going to execute us all like they had done in another town called Kalavrita on December the thirteenth of the past year when one thousand nine hundred and fifty-six teen aged boys and men were put to death by machine guns. Eleven men survived the massacre and most of them were wounded. That story didn't affect me very much because I was holding onto my father's hand and I knew that he wasn't about to allow something like that to happen to me."

Erik stared with unutterable ferocity for a long moment, fixing his eyes into space. He proceeded to tell his wife and child how three German soldiers broke the ranks and grabbed his father, breaking him away from his father's grasp and pushing him with such force, Erik fell on the ground. He remembered seeing how the Germans took his father by the arms and hair, never releasing their hold or allowing him to stop until they reached the old building across from the square where they made him stand up facing the wall with another fifty or so men. As they did that, Erik could hear the shouts of the populace who were witnessing the removal of additional men from the main ranks, they too were dragged into the old open three-wall building. Erik charged towards the building, where his father was made to stand with his hands raised high at arms length, but he was stopped and pushed away by another German soldier.

Erik thrust against the soldier, screaming and cursing his existence. Pouring out those screams and accompanying them with violent motion, he threw himself single-handedly upon the man who pushed him. The intensity of his energy and the unexpected suddenness of his assault caught the soldier by surprise, bringing him down heavily on the ground.

The soldier and he rolled on the ground together and Erik showered him with punches but the soldier responded with some light slaps around the face.

The contest was too unequal to last long. Erik slid away from the German's grasp, stood up panting and, striving to hold back his tears, noticed the battalion commander and three other high ranking officers standing and looking at him from the balcony of Petalas' house, the largest house in town with pure marble steps situated on the side of the square; it was being used by the Germans for their headquarters. He then saw two angry soldiers coming to him from across the street. They kept at the very top of their speed until they reached where he was standing, still panting and now thinking to run away. The screaming from the women and the yelling from the men were renewed upon seeing the two soldiers heading for the boy. The nearest voices took up the cry and hundreds echoed.

Of all the terrific yells that ever fell upon mortal ears none could exceed the cry of that infuriated throng. Some spent their breath in impotent curses, others cried shaking their clenched fists while becoming more and more excited as they yelled. Erik, after a vast quantity of hitting, kicking and struggling managed to escape from his captures. The fears and the anxiety of the spectators were temporarily relieved on seeing Erik climbing to the top of a small sycamore tree that was just big and strong enough to support the boy's weight and high enough to keep him out of harms way. The German soldiers, looking up angry and bemused, yelled and motioned for the boy to come down. "I wasn't about to come down," continued Erik, puffing on his cigarette, "I stood on top of the tree, looking around the crowd below to catch a glimpse of my mother, sister and brother, but I wasn't able to see them. I then scanned the area for a way out of the tree and noticed the big sycamore, rooted in Mr. Magginas' courtyard, with its branches spreading all around, one branch reached very close to where I was standing. I was familiar with the tree, the courtyard and the gate that led to the other side of the house that was near the foot of the mountain. Some times I delivered milk from our goat for Mr. Magginas' wife who was either always sick or liked the taste of our goat milk."

"I stood there and thought that if I could only make it to the other tree, I would jump into the courtyard and then would head for the mountains and it would take half of the German army to find me."

"It wasn't impossible to jump. My friends had done it plenty of

times before but they were a little older than I. They had jumped
to get into Mr. Magginas' property to steal fruits. We used to steal
grapes in the summer time and oranges in the winter months. I said
we, because I was with them sometimes, but I stayed outside; I
was told that I was the look out man and when they came out
loaded with fruits they would give me some for being the lookout
man," said Erik, gazing at his son who was paying keen attention
to his father, "They called me the lookout man. I felt good. I was a
man. Yes, I was a man," said Erik, laughing and hammering his
chest with both hands.

"Daddy, you are telling us a sad story and you are laughing," said
Randy.

"Sonny, I want you to remember that Monday's tragedy is
Tuesday's comedy," said Erik caressing the young boy's hair. "I
stood up there and it looked to me as if I were on top of the world,
but while the crowd was screaming at the Germans, the Germans
were screaming at me and the branch of the tree looked as if it
were distancing itself from me; I felt that I was at the bottom of the
world. All I wanted to do at that time was to get to where my father
was, find my mother, sister and brother and go home. I then
suddenly thought that if I could only jump I would make it into Mr.
Magginas' courtyard and then I would sneak around and get to
where my father was impounded. Blinded by my desire and intoxicated by the thought of saving my family and restoring my world
back to its pleasant and normal existence, I jumped. I jumped but
I didn't make it across because I missed the branch of the big tree
and fell, but my ankle got caught between two 'Y' shaped branches
and I hung upside down about fifteen feet off the ground and
remained there, dangling like a piece of meat on a butcher's hook.
Looking at the world upside down sent fear through my veins and
my heart began to pump blood at a high speed. I heard and saw the
German soldiers below me jumping up trying to catch me but I
was too high up. I then saw an army jeep pulling up and it came
underneath me. The soldiers jumped on the Jeep and took me
down with all the carefulness and precision of men in the business of saving lives rather than taking them. Once I was down they
made me sit on the back seat and one of the soldiers eyed me
intently from the bottom of my feet to the top of my head, without

the slightest alteration of his face to reveal any feelings. This survey lasted a long time and just when I expected some outbreak of anger from him, he went and sat behind the wheel, looked up at the balcony and I saw the battalion commander giving him a sort of a signal, he then drove away with me sitting in the back seat and the other soldier sitting next to me talking in his native language, as if he were speaking on the most ordinary family domestic topic."

"I was driven through the main deserted market and I was dropped off at the harbor. I ran to get back to my father but the German guards had the street leading to the square blocked off."

"There I roamed with a wilted heart. While I was pacing around the harbor meditating and casting dark evil looks at the German guards and figuring my possibilities and methods of invading the square, I felt torn by my fears on one hand and my anxiety on the other. I did that for almost two hours, as close as I can recall, I then saw the guards leaving their post and several men, familiar fishermen, were coming down from the square, heading for their boats in a complete silence. I realized that the Germans had let everybody go. I darted and headed straight for the square, hoping to catch up with my family and my father, thinking while I was running how wonderful it would be for all of us to go home and to gather around the fireplace and listen to my father telling us stories of the bygone days while my mother was making delights for all of us. I reached the square with throbbing breast but much to my disappointment, I found the square virtually empty."

"Without any further delay, pause or a moment's consideration, without once turning my head to the right or left, raising my eyes to the sky or lowering them to the ground but keeping them straight ahead with a strange desire and unnatural anxiety, I rushed towards my house as fast as if a dozen wolves were at my heels. I held my headlong course not slowing down nor relaxing a muscle until I reached the front door. I opened it softly and on entering I found my mother sitting by the dining room table with her head buried in her hands crying and my sister Poppy and my brother Nassos standing next to my mother looking sad."

"Where is Father?" I asked.

"The soldiers took him to jail and they are going to kill my Papa," cried my sister, with tears coming down from only one eye because the other looked dark and swollen.

"What happened to your eye?"

"A German soldier hit me when I went to see my Papa in jail," she cried and rushed to me.

Although I was sometimes unkind to my sister and brother, as most big brothers are, she always found comfort standing next to me in her moments of distress; my little brother on the other hand would keep away from me for days.

"Shh! They are not going to kill him. Don't cry!"

"Taki," said my mother, raising her head and looking at me with a stream of tears coming down her face, "your father is gone. You must now be the man of the house."

"Hearing those words from my mother, I must confess to you Susan and Randy, broke my heart," said Erik, looking at them with an earnest glance. "Being the look out man was a game. But now, I wanted to cry like they all did, but I couldn't. I had to be the man of the house and men don't cry. Some say that they have lost their childhood. I lost my years of crying. I have never learned how to cry."

"You are right," said Susan "I have never seen you cry."

"Another confession I must make to you at this time," said Erik, lighting another cigarette.

"The day they captured my father we were all scheduled to die. I t was to be another Kalavrita massacre. Something happed to the motorcycle that was bringing the orders back from the higher ups in another town. So what they did, they chose seventy-seven men to die including my father, but before they set up the machines guns to kill the men another motorcycle came urging the local commander to send those seventy-seven men to be executed in another town. They loaded them on trucks but the guerillas blew up the highway, so by the time they were transferred to the other town the schedule of execution had already taken place. They then were ordered to send them to Athens to be executed, but the train to Athens was derailed because of sabotage and finally the men were sent to Germany. My father survived and after the war he came home. I listen to his story of being a hostage in Germany and I realized he escaped death and was kept alive for some unknown reason. I also escaped death plenty of times, during the war when

I was a young lad and later in life." Erik stopped and looked around nervously, "Somehow, down through the years, I learned that I was destined to come to America. You may call it an omen."

Susan looked at her husband with both love and pity in her glance. "Don't you feel better now that you've vented out?"

"Yes. Like you said, I always feel better after telling my dream, but to go on and to leave the past, I must tell you that I have some good news and some bad news," said Erik, digging his fork into his food with no apparent desire to eat, "which do you want to hear first the bad or the good?"

Susan carefully placed her fork down and fixed her eyes on him as if she were clearly expecting something bad and fearing the worst. "This good and bad news has nothing to do with your last night's dream?"

"Yes and no."

"Good news and bad news, yes and no... Say whatever you have to say."

"Which do you want to hear first? The good or the bad news?"

"The good news first, Daddy, the good news," said Randy, with much delight in his voice, "I don't like bad news " continued the little boy, "bad news always make me cry."

"Randy, when was the last time that you heard bad news and cried? " asked Erik, grinning.

"The last time was when I told you that I was in love with Ellie, Mrs. Fletcher's big daughter, and I told you I wanted to marry her, and you told me if I would marry her I had to leave home"

"That's it? That's the bad news?"

"Wait! I'll tell you. I'm not finished yet," replied the little boy.

"Okay, okay. Take your time, big guy, take your time," said his father.

"You told me when you were a little boy in Greece, you were only six and you were in love with a Gypsy girl, she was nine, and lived with her family in a big tent, near your house. You said you got up one morning and you ran to her tent, as you did since you met her, and the tent was gone and the whole family moved away and took her with them. You told me you were very sad and you cried, but later on you told me you found somebody better, my mommy, but I still cried."

"Why did you cry?"

"I cried because you told me that you haven't seen her since then. I thought it was very sad and that's why I cried."

The boy glanced at his father with a quivering lower lip and flooded eyes.

"I understand," said Erik, caressing the boys head, "and I love you very, very much. This news is not as bad as that news"

"Mommy, were you in love when you were six, like my daddy and me?"

"No, honey. Your father and you are early risers."

"The early bird gets the worm, they say," rejoined Erik, smiling.

"You should be very tired, but you are not," said Susan soberly.

"Why? For getting up early?" asked Erik, still smiling.

"No, for eating all those worms," replied Susan, "lets have the news. We have heard enough of your sunrise conquests. We all know you are a hot blooded Greek"

"Me too, Mommy?" asked the little boy anxiously.

"Unfortunately yes, my son," replied Susan, still looking at her husband and waiting for a response to her first inquiry.

"It gives me great pleasure to pass on to you that as of yesterday, I became a free man. I quit my insurance job," said Erik almost in one breath, fearing that during that recital he would have lost his ability to breath.

Susan looked at her husband, but there was no message in her glance.

"Where is the good news?" she asked.

"I am free," said Erik, leaning back, smiling as if he were proud of his accomplishment.

"Now, what are we going to do?"

"You will do nothing but sit back, enjoy the New Jersey sun in the summer and the snow in the winter, like you have been doing for the last ten years," replied Erik.

"How about money to live on? Where are you going to get a job as good as the one you had in that insurance office? The only other things you know how to do is what you've learned in the army, jumping from planes and shooting pistols and they're only good for robbing banks or hijacking planes."

"Susan," said Erik, becoming very somber in face and in manner, wishing his statement to appear as solemn as possible, "I swear to both of you that I will do something so rare and so big it will leave a mark on this here earth. I need your help."

Susan dropped the fork into her plate of eggs, raised her eyes towards the clouds as he was making the above appeal and assumed a look of fear that showed in her face how terrified she became at the idea of her husband's reflexivity in pledging himself so emphatically. "You scare me when you talk like that."

"Susan, I told you that I was destined to come to America. I don't hear voices in my head. Oh, no. I believe that everybody has a mission in life. My mission is my destiny. God, Zeus, Allah, an invisible spirit is hiding my mission somewhere here in America and I must find it. I was kept alive long enough to find it, to accomplish it, and then I will be taken away," said Erik, emphatically.

"It sounds as if you went off your rocker," remarked Susan.

"My dear lady, any new and bright idea seems amusing and laughable to the common mind," said Erik, with as much celebration and dignity as if a king were announcing his immortality.

"Pardon me sir, you sound as if this new, rare and big something is locked in the bag."

"No. I carry no bags. It's locked in my head and in my heart. It's been there for the longest time. I simply didn't let it out."

"Are you sure it's the right time to let it out, Erik? Aren't you afraid that it might harm someone?"

"I'm sorry you find it so amusing"

"Amusing? It's terrifying. You are giving me no hint. The only hint you are giving me is that you are ready to be committed to the New Jersey Institute for the Insane."

"I'll give you a hint, Susan. I am going to be a movie star!" said Erik.

Susan's astonishment was too real and too evident to escape her husband's observation; he therefore proceeded, "or a writer, or a singer - any of the three." Having delivered that message with a very sage and mysterious air he looked profoundly around and then at his wife and child with an air of authority and accomplishment.

Susan who had had the time to deliberate upon his answer, "What?"

"Do you want me to repeat the answer?" replied Erik, with much indifference in his tone.

Susan's astonishment turned into very loud laughter and Randy giggled along with her.

She took as much time to deliberate the contents of his statement as she had done to deliberate the answer. She suddenly turned serious and composed.

"You mean you believe that you were kept alive through wars and other close call events so you could become an actor? Are you serious?" asked Susan.

When the laughter from the astonishment stopped, the situation seemed to be more serious. Erik looked at her as severely as she had looked at him.

"I am dead serious, Susan. Quit playing games with me as if I don't know what I am doing or saying. It is only the beginning," responded Erik sternly. "I said that I wanted to do something big and different."

"You want to be a movie star or a writer or a singer. Is that what you're saying? Is this why you left the security of your job, Erik?" There she stopped and looked at him, partly to think and partly to hear something from him.

But Erik remained serious and stared at her indifferently.

"Erik, you were an actor, you were a singer, you were a writer and a poet and nothing came out of it," said Susan, letting her eyes rest on him. He now felt the necessity to say something.

"That's funny, I was all those crazy things and that's why you fell in love with me. Do you remember? Do you remember saying to me, ' I love you, Erik, because you are a poet a singer an artist and many other things,' all those things you loved about me, those are the very same things that make you dislike me now. There is an old Greek saying. 'A woman marries a man and is hoping to change him, but when a man marries a woman he is hoping that she doesn't change.'

"I don't want you to change, Erik, you are my husband and I love you. I am just disappointed that you haven't grown up yet! Grow up, Erik. Grow up!"

Rising rage and extreme bewilderment had swollen the noble breast of her husband, almost to the point of bursting everything

in sight, after the delivery of his wife's defiance. He stood, transfixed on the spot, staring at her with a harsh look. The dropping of
Randy's spoon on the floor recalled him to himself.

"You don't want me to change. You say grow up like the rest of
us. Leave the world of imagination and enter the world of reality.
The unbearable world of reality. Drop your dreams! At least hide
them like the rest of the sane world." There he stopped as if he
were out of breath but filled with a lot of anger, looking at her,
"grow up, Erik, you say to me. Acting, singing, writing books are
children's games. That's what you are saying to me, Susan. But tell
me why do the grown ups pay to see an actor on the screen? Tell
me why are you grown-ups spending big bucks for books? Tell me,
Susan, why do you grown-ups spend big bucks for musical
cassettes? You are not telling me to grow up, you are telling me to
enter your world of reality and be as miserable as most of you
because misery loves company. I am sorry to have placed you in
this difficult situation. Allow me to suggest that the best way to
avoid such difficult situations in the future is to be more selective
in the choosing of a husband," he continued, taking out another
cigarette and lighting it with nervous hands.

"Mommy, I don't understand a word Daddy is saying," said
Randy who had been silently listening to the familiar war of words
between his father and his mother.

"He is going to be a movie star, honey, and he is practicing
Shakespeare," replied Susan as if she heard nothing of what her
husband had recited.

Erik gazed at his wife as if he heard nothing from her, but he
was convinced that there was no quantity or quality of words that
would penetrate the invisible shield by which she was covered,
and that more importantly, in her mind, she felt protected and
therefore she allowed nothing new or extraordinary to enter it
enabling her to see things his way. He put out his cigarette and
proceeded to eat his cold eggs; it seemed that harmony had
prevailed once more around the breakfast table. The lingering irri-
tability appeared to have found a temporary resting place in Erik's
breast. The breakfast was not about to be concluded in harmony
because neither heard what the other was saying.

"I don't believe this, " said Susan in a low voice breaking the temporary silence of that ceremony.

"What? Is it safe to say that you don't have the ability to understand my feelings or is it more proper to say that you are not compassionate enough."

"I can't see how a man forty five years old with a family is dropping everything to follow a dream that's been dead for years."

"You are wrong, Susan!" returned Erik, with a hidden delight thinking that the conversation would wind up in his favor once he was given the opportunity to state his plans, something that he was denied from the beginning. " My dreams never died. I had them hidden deep in my soul. That is the way and the reason I have lived this long," concluded Erik with a voice tremulous with emotion. He suddenly reached over, grabbed Randy's chair and directed his attention at the young lad. "Son, I wish to take the time to tell you why your mother is so cynical. Everyone who is at all acquainted with theatrical matters knows the existence of those hopefuls or dreamers, who are striving to achieve their dreams, and so often are stricken with poverty and disappointment. One can walk and browse around the streets of big cities and observe a host of shabby looking men and women not regularly engaged as actors, singers, writers or instrument players, roaming and looking for something to eat as if they have forgotten why they've gotten there in the first place."

"Mommy," cried the boy, "Daddy is practicing Sneakpete again."

"It's Shakespeare, honey, he was a great writer from England," replied Susan with a wide smile on her face.

"Do you know, Randy, why Shakespeare was such a great writer, he was not married to your mother," said Erik humorously. "Anyway, let me continue to explain to you, in a lighter tone, how I am going to be a movie star, because your mother is not in any favorable state of mind to listen to me, and later you can explain to her."

"Yes, Daddy, yes."

"First I want to tell you that no matter what route I will take, I will not allow anyone to stomp and pound on me because I will always remember what I'm after. Do you understand, Randy?" exclaimed the father knowing his wife was listening carefully.

"Yes, Daddy I understand everything," returned the little boy, with great interest.

"This next and last part of my plans is easier for me to explain because I have rehearsed it in my mind a thousand and five times." There he stopped for a moment, "Are you still with me, I don't want to loose you, Randy."

"No, I'm still with you Daddy, I understand everything you are saying."

"Good. When I was five years old, your age..."

"I'm six, Daddy, I am six years old."

"You are five," announced his mother unexpectedly.

"I am six."

"You were born in December and now we have June," insisted the mother.

"What's the difference, that's a small detail. We don't bother with the small stuff, do we, Daddy?"

"No! We don't bother with the small stuff," said the father with pretence.

"You said, small stuff is for women and small guys. Didn't you, Daddy?" concluded the boy in the same tone as his father.

"Yep! That's what I said," responded the father.

"Two peas in a pod," remarked the mother.

"Now, where was I at? I forgot."

"I remember. When you were my age, " said the boy smiling.

"Oh! Yes. When I was your age... six years old, I used to love to hear my father telling me stories of the war. War stories, you know."

"But this is not a war story, Daddy, is it?"

"Maybe yes and maybe no."

"I know! This can be a war story between you and Mommy. A war with words. No guns."

"No! No guns and no fists. Just words. Because if your mother were as good with guns as she is with words, I'd be dead long time ago," said the father.

"Look who's talking? The pot is calling the kettle black," returned the wife.

Erik was visibly happy, not so much for the amusing conversation he was holding with his son but hoping his wife was paying zealous and unremitting attention to him.

"Let's go on with our plans," started Erik.

"Yes, lets go on," replied the child, feeling and acting older than five.

"First I will go to photo shop and have my picture taken, then I will take one hundred pictures and send them to one hundred producers and directors in New York and Hollywood. Do you understand?"

The boy nodded vigorously.

"With every picture I will send a note, saying that I would like to be given a part in their next movie and in an exchange I will invest five hundred thousand dollars. Out of the hundred, ten will get in touch with me and from there I will begin to learn the movie business.

"Great! Daddy, that's great," yelled the little boy so full of excitement, grabbing his father's hand and shaking it vigorously and speaking so loud that the exertion imparted a crimson hue to his benevolent face. "Then you will be in the movies."

"Where are you going to get five hundred thousand dollars Mr. Big shot? You don't even have five hundred nickels," declared his wife with a frown on her face.

At that statement Erik thought that he had tried all kinds of methods of amusement to get to his wife, the serious, humorous, offensive, defensive or inoffensive. The words;

"Mr. Big shot", offended him. The tone by which those words were spoken elevated his blood pressure and the grimacing look on her face awakened the beast in him. Realizing this was the first occasion he was being put to the test, he shrank back from the trial beneath her eye, reminding himself that the only way he would win was that if he didn't regard her judgment.

"You didn't understand, did you?" asked Erik calmly. "I said that I would be given the opportunity to learn the film business"

"Listen to me, son," said Erik

At that time Susan, whether she wanted to interrupt that delightful conversation between father and son or to tell the world, her world, that her insides were on fire, it is unknown; she let out a deep and loud sigh.

Erik turned to her with fire in his eyes and wrath on his face. "Don't sigh, Susan! Just breathe! Do you know how to breathe without making any noise? Just breath!" Erik turned to his son with calm features, "Then, that's how I will learn the film business..."

"Learn, learn, and learn. When are you going to learn that you have responsibilities?" uttered Susan angrily, "people can go hungry learning."

Erik stood up and faced her with the same anger she was showing to him.

"Are you hungry, Susan?" His voice became loud to the point of yelling. "Have you ever been hungry in your life, Susan?" saying this he stuck his fingers in his plate and came up with a fist full of running eggs. He mashed them in his hands and then he threw them on her plate. "Eat goddamn it! Eat and shut up! Eat if you're hungry."

Susan rushed out of her chair grabbed her son and headed for the back door picking up speed and anger on the way there. She wasn't fear stricken; she was stricken with a feeling of revenge.

Erik charged after her in person and in wrath took her by the elbow and hissed like a snake, "somehow you have always managed to wake up the beast in me. You are going out and I'll do the same but when I return I better find you here with my son. If you aren't here, I'll find you and when I do, God help you."

Susan jerked her arm away from him and rushed out of the door, dragging their son behind her.

Erik stood in the middle of the floor with his eyes wandering around the room, as if he were searching to find an exit. He heard the car door slamming outside and the car pulling away. He roamed around the house for a while. By the way he moved about the house it became evident that he had mixed reality with his dreams and lost the ability to separate the two given the strange confusion to which they had evolved. He clenched his fist and teeth and hit the wall. He looked at his hand and it was bruised with drops of blood trickling down; he felt his pride wounded. He took a suit jacket, departed the house like the wind and drove away like a thief, taking the direction his wife had gone a few minutes earlier.

CHAPTER 2

The appearance of a sitting duck

He must have driven for miles because now the sun had reached and passed the middle mark in the blue cloudless sky. He parked his car in a desolate but crowded parking lot. He walked alone through some shady lanes and sequestered footpaths and just when he was almost inclined to regret the expedition, he found himself on the main street of a recreated town that resembled the old west. He stood on the principal street of this illustrious town and gazed with an air of curiosity, not unmixed with interest in the objects around him.

There was an open square for the flea market and in the center of it was an old refurbished inn with a signpost in front. Within sight were an old auctioneer's and fire agency office, a linen shop, a bakery, a warehouse having been also appropriated for the diffusion of western hats, bonnets and other wearing apparel. There was a medium size red brick house with a small paved yard in the front. A number of people were walking and browsing around that little town while some shopkeepers had come outside for a breath fresh air and to bring in some new customers. Erik avoided the flea market and walked along the red brick paved street, until another weathered house came into sight; a signpost in front revealed its use, which was a saloon. Erik headed for the place and walked right in. The saloon was very busy with people either eating a late lunch or an early dinner. The vast deal of talking and rattling of knifes, forks and plates made the place irritating to his ears and mood, so he proceeded to the bar, a quieter spot, and took a seat where none took heed of his existence. While waiting for the bartender to serve him, Erik watched the three ponderous waiters running about with speed and zest. It seemed that those patrons who got up to leave had smiles on their faces and some burped and petted their bellies with pride and joy that told the beholder that they had plenty to eat. As soon as a table was empty the bus boys and the waiters removed the tablecloth, bottles and glasses and readied it to set up for the next hungry bunch.

He took a special notice of the table next to him, which was encircled by a family of nine people. In the middle of the general hum of mirth and conversation that ensued, there was a very striking girl with long black hair, a beautiful sculpted face and vague smile that made her look as if she had only come along for the ride. She wore a light blue blouse, buttoned on the third button from the top, divulging a well-built body that filled her well-tailored and fitted clothing. Erik noticed the young man sitting next to the attractive girl was quiet and bored, though it seemed that he had accompanied the girl. Occasionally, the young man would look around and survey the herd around the table. When the conversation slackened he appeared to be contemplating putting something heavy into it, and now and then he would burst into a short fake cough to attract their attention, but that was always in vain.

The girl with unfathomable beauty looked at Erik and threw a flirting glance, but by now he was getting anxious for a drink and oblivious to all happenings.

"Can I help you?' asked the bartender who was dressed like he was working in some old Kansas City Gun Smoke saloon.

"Yes," returned Erik. "Six beers and six whiskies. Line them up," said Erik drawing an invisible line, with his hand, on the bar indicating how he wanted them to be set up.

"Are you expecting company?" asked the bartender.

"I hope so," said Erik, roaming his eyes around the eating and noisy crowd. His wandering eyes fell upon another table, not too far from where the beautiful girl was sitting. At the head of that table was a stocky man who had been eating, drinking, and talking without a pause. With every good stroke he administered to his steak, he expressed his satisfaction and approval of the eatery in a most condescending and patronizing manner, which could not fail to have been highly gratifying to the waiter. At many times a lady who was sitting next to him, apparently his wife, attempted to attract his attention by poking him in his well-insulated ribs with her right index finger. Resenting this indignation, he would respond with a scowl for being distracted from his tasks.

The bartender stood there and waited for Erik to look at his direction.

"Did I tell you what I want?" asked Erik, seeing the bartender looking at him curiously.

"Yes, I got your order," replied the bartender coolly.

"Is there something wrong, or you're waiting for me to give you proof that I am old enough to drink?" inquired Erik, seeing the odd look of curiosity in the man's face.

"Nothing wrong," replied the man, walking away to pursue his commission.

"It's a funny order. That's all," said the bartender filling up the glass on the first part of the order.

"If it's so funny, you should be laughing," remarked Erik.

"It's not funny for laughing."

"How about crying?"

"Cry if you want. We have enough tissues," mumbled the bartender.

The bartender finished delivering his order without uttering another word and Erik deposited his money onto the counter.

"Do you have a gun back there, behind the counter?" asked Erik when the last glass of the spirits was set before him.

"What kind of stupid question is that? Why are you asking?" demanded the bartender with features now distorted, thinking he had been much abused by Erik.

"You are behaving as if you are under the protection of a gun and you truly believe that you are working for Miss Kitty in the Gun Smoke Saloon," exclaimed Erik, looking him in the eye.

The bartender contorted his face into the most fearful and astonishing of grimaces. He then straightened himself up, threw his chest out, closed his mouth and audibly, visibly and deeply inhaled enough air to empty a tractor tire and said through clenched teeth,. "I don't like foreigners. And you sound like one." As the bartender uttered those words, he put himself very temptingly within the reach of Erik's fist. There was little doubt that Erik could have answered the bartender with a blow to his mouth but didn't, first out of respect for where he was and secondly, the interposition of a customer, who upon hearing the bartender's words, called upon the bartender to serve him immediately. The bartender seeing Erik's apparent indignation, attended the sitting customer without the slightest delay. When he returned immediately thereafter, he stood a little farther back and away from Erik's reach while looking harshly into his face. The contortions of his features had no affect on Erik.

"I don't like clam diggers and you smell like one. You must have been a clam digger before you got this job," expounded Erik to the bartender.

"I was. And I'm damn proud of it," declared the bartender loudly.

"How would you like to go back to clam digging?" asked Erik grinning, with his eyes fixed on him.

"Who is going to send me there? You?"

Erik reached down, picked a full whiskey glass and very quickly and subtly thrust the contents of it on the bartender's red shirt missing his face intentionally. He did it so discreetly and so quickly nobody noticed it and before the bartender had time to see, do or say anything, Erik said calmly, "me! Now, can I see my cousin, your boss, Theo Vasilis?"

The bartender, surprised, took a step forward.

"Theo is your cousin? Why didn't you say something?" uttered the bartender throwing his arms out as if he wished to embrace him. "There is Theo now," said the bartender pointing behind Erik while speaking in a much humbler tone of voice.

Theo, a short stocky but very nice looking man, recognized his cousin and darted forward, disregarding customers and personnel, speeding to where Erik was standing by the bar stool, waiting. They both threw their arms around each other and kissed each other on the cheeks.

"Let me see you!" shouted Theo, stepping back and examining Erik from head to toe. "You look good. You son-of -a-gun! How are Susan and Randy?"

"Good. Good, very good, they both are. How long have you had this place?

"Two nice months"

"This is the first time I've seen it. I just strolled in here like a wanderer. How did you know that I was here?"

"I didn't see you. Being in this business you always look at the bar to see if the bartender takes care of matters. I saw six and six, that's your mark. Then I knew that it had to be you," said Theo. "I was going to surprise you but dumb Ralph, the bartender, pointed me out to you. Ralph!" Turning to Ralph who was standing behind the counter pretending to be busy, "This here good looking Greek is my cousin, Erik Karas. We had the same name, a long last name. We split it, he took the first half and I took the second half. Because he is older than me."

"Older than you? You old wolf," returned Erik

"Not much older," joked Theo, winking at the bartender, "His money is no good here. You hear?"

"We met, boss. He asked for you when he came in."

"What happened to your shirt? Go change it! I don't like sloppy personnel," said the boss to Ralph. "Erik, let me finish what I was doing and I'll be back," concluded Theo, turning around to leave. "Incidentally, this six and six, still works on the women?"

"I always catch something," replied Erik.

"Do you still call them, 'Duck Decoys'?"

"Still. And I only drink two. As always," said Erik.

"We will see," remarked Theo, leaving with a hearty and loud laugh.

After he had taken a few steps still laughing, Theo returned as if he remembered something important.

"Erik, the bartender said that you asked for me, how did you know I was here?"

"While I was talking to Ralph I noticed the half-burnt Greek flag you always have by the register."

"Gosh! You still remember that? The first thing that I do when I buy a new place, I bring the half-burnt flag and set it next to the register. Do you know why?" asked Theo.

"Knowing you, you probably got angry with the Greek politicians and tried to burn that flag," commented Erik

"No! No, nothing like that. Not that I don't get angry with the stupid Greek politicians; it's something else. Do you remember Nick and Alec?" asked Theo.

"Sure, the convicts."

"Yea! The convicts. They had a diner on Route Nine, north from here. They kept it open twenty-four hours a day, even if they would had have kept it open thirty-six hours a day they wouldn't have made it. Anyway, one Sunday they decided to burn the place down to collect the insurance money, look how stupid those two guys were. They closed the place on Sunday and they set fire to it on the same day, Sunday afternoon. After they set the fire in the kitchen with rags soaked in gasoline, they got in their car and sped down Route Nine to get home. They didn't live far from there. They figured by the time the fire department calls them, they would be home to answer the phone. They thought they were establishing their alibi."

"How stupid," remarked Erik.

"No! That's nothing. They were driving one hundred and ten miles an hour, according to the police, when the state trooper stopped them. The state trooper, being a wise ass himself, asked them, 'why are you going so fast, where is the fire, men?' The poor stupid Greeks, at least one of them, Nick, didn't speak very good English, and misunderstood the question and said 'I didn't set the fire he did,' pointing at Alec. Alec got angry and hit Nick. While they were fighting in the car, the trooper got word on his radio that the diner was on fire. The trooper put two and two together and took them in. They were convicted and sent up the river for a nice long vacation," concluded Theo with a big smile on his face.

"The flag, Theo, the flag, why the half-burnt flag?" inquired Erik impatiently.

"Wait. I'm getting to it. I bought the diner from the State. I held it three weeks and resold it. The only thing I took from there was the half-burnt Greek flag and I put it next to the register in every place that I buy to remind me that no matter how bad business gets not to set fire to the joint." Concluding his story and expressing an earnest wish for Erik to wait until he returned, he backed away, waved a provisional good-by and left hastily, laughing.

Erik took back his stool and romanced his drinks. He thought of Theo, how well he had done for himself and how conservatively he lived his life, whereas, Erik thought of himself as a man, with no sense of family, duty or civic obligation, as his wife had stated earlier. He thought how he would act if Theo's wealth was poured upon him, how he would riot in pleasure. He felt, even with all his cunning, that he was deceived. He wasn't deceived by the law—the eagle-eye of the law itself, or society; he was deceived by none other than himself. Being deceived by himself was as severe as if he were handed over to a thousand madmen's hands. He thought how his wife had dedicated herself to him for love and only love, which he had thrown away so many times. That is why, plenty of times before, he thought that his entire surroundings would have been in better shape if he were to be placed stiff and cold in a dull leaden coffin. All those things passed rapidly though his mind as he sat there, shifting his eyes around with a vacant look. He felt very justly and properly indignant with himself that his cousin, with fewer abilities, was in a better station in life and was going higher, while he, Erik Karas, thought of himself as being deadlocked. One thing that kept him alive was his ability to switch, at the drop of a coin, from the unbearable misery to jauntiness, especially at the sight of a pretty woman. Erik gazed at the table where the beautiful girl had been sitting. Much to his surprise and to his disappointment, the table was empty and was undergoing a face-lift by the waiters and the bus boys. He sat there drinking and pondering about the earlier dispute that he had with the sharer of his troubles and cares, his wife. Suddenly a sweet female voice, coming from next to him, greeted his ear favorably.

"You're thirsty, aren't you," echoed the voice belonging to none other than the beautiful girl he had eyed earlier.

Erik's style was not to exhibit any kind of excitement when being picked on by a beautiful member of the opposite sex; he only gazed with an indifferent manner.

"I'm not thirsty, I'm hungry," Erik stated coolly, without taking the time to look at her.

She could already have guessed that the man was not about to pour out gratifying and flattering statements, as most men do when they are approached in that manner.

"You should be eating then, instead of drinking," remarked the girl with the same even tone in her voice.

"I am not hungry for food, I am hungry for excitement."

"What do you do for excitement?"

Erik turned slowly and gazed at her with a vague smile and said, "I make love."

"This must be your appetizer," said the girl applying as much effort to answer as he did.

"No. These are my duck decoys"

"Are you looking for ducks?"

"Not just ducks, sitting ducks."

"Why not flying ducks?"

"Flying ducks are too restless to settle and too wild to tame. Besides they tend to land in other people's lakes."

"Is this your lake?" asked the girl.

"No. This is just a hunting lake."

"Do you do this very often?"

"I hunt when I have the time," replied Erik with a smile.

The girl returned the smile, "I can tell that you are a hunter. Do you hunt here often?"

"No. This is my first time."

"What kind of ducks are you looking for, the ones that taste good or the ones that have good taste?"

"The ones that have good taste," returned Erik, breaking into a wide smile.

"Have you eyed any sitting duck yet?" asked the girl, looking around.

Hearing this, Erik looked at her with a grin on his face and said, "come to think of it, yes!"

"Where is she?"

"Right here. Sitting next to me," said Erik, pointing his index finger at her ribs.

"Oh, do you think I have good taste, or you think I taste good?"

"I don't know if you taste good, but I know you have good taste because you landed next to me."

"It is a very noble ambition and I feel flattered, but at the same time insulted that you think I am a sitting duck waiting to be picked, plucked and potted by you or any other cowboy who comes along. Besides, I am a flying duck, too restless to settle and too wild to tame," said the girl without revealing the slightest indication of being indignant. "I may fly away any minute now."

"You can't fly away now that you have landed in my hunting

lake."

"Just because I landed here, makes me a sitting duck, cowboy?"

"You are my sitting duck," said Erik.

"Are you always in the habit of counting your ducks before they hatch?"

"Are you always in the habit of repeating someone else's words?" asked Erik.

"Whose words am I repeating?"

"My mother's" he said grimly before he broke into a wider smile.

"You must have been jumping the gun since you were a little boy," interjected the girl prudently.

"I'm an optimist. Do you see it as a problem?"

"You are a dreamer," noted the girl, cleverly overlooking the rest of his comment.

"Do you have a problem with that?"

"You know, I don't even know your name; I've known you for less than three minutes and I find you to be egotistical, obnoxious, loathsome and intolerable," said the girl as if she were delivering a compliment.

"Does that mean that sleeping with you tonight is out of the question?"

"Besides being obnoxious, loathsome, intolerable and egotistical you're also a fool."

"But I find you very interesting," said Erik.

"How is that?"

"The fact that you haven't flown away."

"That makes me a fool," replied the girl in an almost regrettable tone of voice.

"Then, you and I have one thing in common," said Erik.

"Yes? What's that?"

"We should be able to get along just fine, because we are both fools." There he stopped for one moment and paused. To place emphasis on his following statement he raised his index finger and said very softly and solemnly. "Interesting fools, though. Bear in mind there are many types of fools,"

"Your efforts to be easy and graceful with me, you think are gratifying, but I find them insulting," said the girl, becoming a little more spirited than before.

"You are very kind, ma'am," said Erik, knowing he was approaching what could be a dead end with the girl; he decided to take more cautious steps.

"Did you take that as a compliment?"

"What else? You realized that I am trying very hard to be gracious, but in the meantime I don't want to turn this into cookie baking discussion that will remove me from my objective."

"And your objective is? As if I don't already know," remarked the girl.

Erik, hearing this, turned his act into a theatrical presentation.

"Oh, dear, dear girl, how long I have anxiously been waiting to hear that question uttered from your lips. Dear girl, I wished to go home with you, to do your floors, to clean your windows, to iron the ironables and to finish the unironed, to cook your edibles and polish and shine your unedibles, to bow before you, every time your eyes fall upon me and I promise, my lady, I will not shrink the distance between me and you to less than six feet. And when the clock strikes eight P. M. I will bid you good-bye and I shall stay away, even if I have fallen madly in love with you I repeat I will stay away until you call upon me again to render my humble services to you and to yours. My lady, I promise you, I will allow you to treat me like a dog and like a dog I will obey you." Saying this, he touched her face gently. "Have I forgotten anything, my lady?" concluded Erik.

"Oh, yes, washing of the car. Second thought, the car goes with the in-edibles. Right?"

"Perfect!" exhaled Erik

"To you and to yours?" asked the girl with astonishment, looking for a sensible answer.

"That's a legal term."

"In what book? Boy, did I ask for this," said the girl.

"The book of love," replied Erik soberly.

"You must have written it," commented the girl.

"No. I only read it,"

"You are, no doubt in my mind, the biggest bullshit artist in the world,"

"I see you as being very feisty," said Erik displaying feigned amazement.

"I am Italian, that makes me aggressive."

"I must confess to you that you are the most beautiful girl in here and I had my eyes on you since I saw you sitting next to that young man. Was he… is he related to you? Or am I being out of line, in what seems to the bare eye, trying to get into your private life?" said Erik with his words carefully chosen.

"You are funny, not comically funny, just funny," said the girl, coming out with a sweet smile on her face, "You talk as if you are dying to get into my pants, but very timid to get into my private life."

Erik nodded assent and coughed, whether he did that to attract the attention of the bartender, who was standing behind the bar with a clean shirt or to cut that line of conversation; it is unknown.

"Yes Mr. Karas, What can I do for you, sir?" asked the bartender graciously.

"See what the lady wants,"

"Nothing for me, thank you, I had enough for one day," replied the girl.

"You, sir, you look that you are well supplied." Said the bartender and made a military about face and marched away like a soldier.

"You are not ready to set up a pup-tent and break bread with me yet," commented Erik displaying a little disenchantment.

Hearing the delivery and seeing the sad look on his face, the girl burst into boisterous laughter.

"You looked like a little boy saddened by a rejection. You should see your face, Mr. Karas."

"Please call me Erik. Not Mr. Karas. That makes me feel old," said Erik softly.

"I was only trying to make a joke by calling you Mr. Karas, besides you never gave me your name."

"You never gave yours," complained Erik, a little louder than normal.

"My name is Sophia," said the girl smiling, as she handed him her hand in a most dignified manner. Erik took it, shook it gently and it let it go.

She looked at him with a sweet smile again, "I liked that," she said. "Liked, what?" asked Erik.

"The way you took and shook my hand, and you didn't kiss it. Some men are show offs. They take your hand and slobber over it.

Just to tell you that they know chivalry."

"I understand. Some men really want to show off," said Erik in a very serious way.

"Erik."

"Yes?"

"You are the biggest show off that I have seen in my life," said the girl, staring at him for a very long moment. "I can't explain it. But you really don't come off as a show off, though," continued the girl leaving her eyes nailed on him, while maintaining her smile.

"Do you know why it seems that way?" asked Erik

"Why?"

"Because I never conquer, I always surrender," declared Erik and not allowing her time to deliberate on his statement, he said, "you have the sweetest smile that I have ever seen. Not that there are bitter smiles, but some smiles are sweeter than others. Yours is the best"

"Erik!"

"Yes, sitting duck"

"Do you want me to tell you about the guy that I was sitting with at the table?"

"If it doesn't hurt you very much," said Erik, pegging his eyes on her and waiting to hear something funny.

"Hurt me you asked, stranger?" uttered the girl in such a pretentious and dramatic way that it could have made Betty Davis eat her heart out. "He was, I mean he still is the love of my life," said the girl, making believe that she wiping tons of sweat from her forehead with the back of her hand. "I shall never find anyone else, Erik, my unfortunate friend, that I can love so much!"

"Compose yourself, my dear unfortunate girl, compose yourself. Your tears are thick, thick enough to pierce the heart of a stone," said Erik, pretending to wipe her forehead with a napkin. "Take it from me, dear girl, they are piercing my heart, even though it's made out of brick according to some members of the opposite sex."

"Help me, stranger, please help me! In a passion of grief, I will faint and fall into your arms. Shall I find comfort there?" said the girl, looking up discreetly at Erik's face.

"You shall, my dearest one, you shall. You'll find them to be more comfortable than a Seely Posturepedic mattress, with no springs attached," uttered Erik with a great degree of compassion.

"No springs attached, you said?" returned the girl, with an astonishing smile that was on the verge of bursting into boisterous laughter.

"Oh! You are cured of your ills already," said Erik seriously.

"No springs attached cured the hell out of me," said the girl. "No springs attached," she mumbled as if she were talking to herself, wiping the tears that were brought on with laughter.

"He is a bore," declared Sophia abruptly.

"Who?"

"That young man who was sitting next to me."

"I'm sorry," said Erik.

"Why are you sorry?"

"I don't know. I just feel bad when things don't work out between people."

"Now, I know why you are so very timid about getting into people's private lives," said Sophia.

"Why?"

"Don't ask me where we are going and I won't ask you where you've been," said Sophia, with her eyes fixed on him as if she were waiting for an answer. "That's your motto, isn't it? I bet you, you have made love to women and that you never knew their names,"

"I am not that good with names, I must admit," answered Erik.

Sophia suddenly reached over very hastily, took Erik's hand and said in a very low voice as if she were whispering. "Come with me. I want to introduce you to some people that you will enjoy talking to and then we'll go somewhere else, as you call it, to set up a pup-tent. Go on, finish your drinks and take your money then we'll go."

"I never finish my drinks. Remember? They are my 'duck decoys."

"I forgot. Now that you've got your duck, screw the decoys," returned the girl, pulling his arm and insisting that he get up. "The money?"

"I'll leave the money to the bartender for calling him a clam digger earlier." Saying this, Erik stood up and stared at the girl for a long moment. Then he turned and looked at his duck decoys and said dismayingly. "If I had drank all these there would be some bad consequences,"

"What kind of bad consequences? Erik," asked the girl inquisitively.

"Not what you are thinking, if you are thinking of anything bad. If I had drank all that, it would have left me with only a vague recollection of being with you, walking with you about the streets, browsing with you while holding your hand and talking with you. These are the joys of life that we must remember."

"My God. Now I know why you have made love to women and never got their names. You got them so worked up they couldn't wait to get you to bed."

"Are you trying to tell me that I was deceiving them, Sitting Duck?"

"Spellbinding is the word. And I might add that you are doing it without any intent."

"But I must confess to you that I have deceived many of them," said Erik, letting her hand go and stepping back one pace to look at her.

"It's just as easy to deceive as it is to be deceived," retorted Sophia. Then she vigorously grabbed his hand and exclaimed. "Let's go. With all the deceiving you have done, if you cannot blame it on love, blame it on physical attraction."

Sophia was leading the way out and Erik, seeing the sort of fascination that she took in him, followed and hoped in the meantime that his cousin wouldn't see him leaving with the girl, not wanting to supply him and the rest of his friends and relatives with any more ammunition to criticize him with, knowing that they always referred to him as the spirited one, but what they really meant was that he was a rebel. He knew that he had been strong willed, rebellious, resented by some but envied by others for having the courage to be different. He had that spirit, that different spirit burning inside of him that, like a porter's knot, was strongest when challenged by heavy loads, but he also knew that as a porter's knot so easily breaks, his spirit could break and his worldly cares and troubles would be too heavy to bear and then he would sink beneath them.

He was following the girl, with his eyes roaming over her body, examining her from head to toe, viewing her every gesture and the movement of her every muscle and bone and concluded she was one degree above perfect.

The girl, who was leading him somewhere, showing so much care and interest in him, would wish to set a pillow upon his face and squash the life out of him without remorse, if she were ever to discover that he had a wife and a child.

Those thoughts and parts of other guilty feelings raced rapidly through his mind. He then pulled his eyes away from the girl as he realized that the rope of attachment to his wife and child was stronger than his desire to share time with this perfect creature.

They finally emerged outside to a sunny day. Everything looked different to him than it did before, when he was alone. They stood there in the sun and gazed at each other like two unsplit friends.

"I want you to meet my mother and father," said Sophia, straightening out his jacket, "you'll like them. I know they will like you. They live here and they own a store around the corner."

Erik did entertain considerable misgivings in the very lowest recesses of his heart, but ignoring her kind invitation could have placed a thought in her mind to suspect something was not exactly right and proper, therefore he replied with great stamina, "certainly, I will enjoy it." She continued, "You will meet a lot of my relatives. They have come down from the north to attend an engagement affair for one of my cousins who still lives down here with her parents. I was born in this town but when I finished college I moved to North Jersey for a better job," said the girl with a certain degree of regret in her voice and tone.

She drew in a deep breath as she gazed around while realizing what she left behind. She missed the town, the hundreds of perfumes from the gardens that stretched in front of every house nestled there beneath the scented air, the deep green meadows shining in the morning as the dew glistened on every leaf that was trembled at the sunny dawn by the slow and gentle breeze that came from the sea like a wandering pauper. She missed the times of the birds' morning songs when all the flowers opened their colorful eyes and stretched out their multihued ears to look and listen to the new day as the sun came up slowly from behind the tall trees to awake and renew the mission of every living thing. The smallest leaf, the minutest blade of grass, the toiling ant, the butterfly fluttering in the summer sun, myriads of insects spreading their transparent wings and reveling in their brief but happy existence, all were bursting with life. She missed them all. She also realized what she had then and what she has now. How could anyone, she thought, live to gaze from day to day at the bricks, slates and concrete blocks, who had once felt the influence of such natural beauty? How can anyone continue to exist where there are no cows, no crops but only a bounty of bricks and cement?

"You missed being here? Didn't you?" asked Erik gently, looking around with melancholy, after seeing the nostalgia in her eyes.

"Yes, very much" replied Sophia.

"Where do you live up north?" asked Erik

"In Jersey City, in an apartment, on North End Avenue. Do you know the street?" asked the girl. She appeared disposed to add more but the melancholy choked the delivery of her words.

"I understand. Sometimes we shoot at the crow but we kill the pigeon." She looked at him, astonished, for one long moment.

"You know, Erik, I just realize that you have green eyes," said the girl now thoroughly relaxed.

"You just saw them? I've had them for a long time."

"How long?"

"Oh, since before you were born," returned Erik with a loud laugh.

"What did you do from then up till now?"

"Do you want to hear my life story, Sitting Duck?"

"Something like that"

"I'll tell it when we set up a pup tent and break bread," replied Erik, smiling.

"What will it cost me?"

"Nothing."

Sophia, hearing the answer, burst into loud laughter and said, "now I know why they say, 'beware of Greeks bearing gifts'"

"Why?" asked Erik, smiling.

"You surrender in order to conquer."

"You know, Sitting Duck, you are half my age and you know twice as much. How did this happen?"

"I am an Italian," said the girl, taking him by the hand " Come on, I'll have you meet some more smart Italians."

There were several families browsing around the area and Erik and Sophia strolled amongst them. Sophia had passed her left arm through Erik's right and continued at the pace the crowd allowed them. They turned the corner and her parents' store came into sight with a signpost in front identifying it as the MILANO GROCERY. Erik and Sophia walked right in holding hands and sharing smiles.

Several family members, who were assembled in the large store to greet the guests, rose to greet Sophia and her newfound beau. During the performance of the ceremony of introduction, with all the due and proper formalities, Erik had time to observe the appearance of the characters and speculate on the nature and pursuits of those people by whom he was surrounded.

"That old lady is my father's rich sister. She can't sit, she can't walk, yet she can make demands and everybody is catering to her, waiting for her to die, hoping to inherit some of her wealth, " whispered Sophia, while looking away from the old lady. "I can see you like to study the people's temperaments. We have enough of all kinds here to keep you busy. Let me go say hello to some that are not worth the trouble of your meeting them. I'll be right back."

Erik discreetly peered at the aunt and the two young ladies who were paying keen and constant attention to her. They crowded around her wheel chair and shot ferocious looks at anyone who made any slight attempt to threaten their status. One was holding a peeled and sectioned apple in a small dish for the old lady to eat, if and when she chose to. The second young lady, who apparently was the sister of the one with the apple, was mostly engaged with patting and punching the pillows that were placed on the wheel chair for the old lady's support and comfort.

There was another well-fed lady standing a few paces away, who looked as if she were approaching the big three quarters of a century mark. She was holding an orange in one hand and what looked like a small bottle of smelling salts in the other and her eyes were intently fixed on the lady in the wheel chair, waiting for an opportunity to assist with the caring. The lady in the wheel chair seemed to be happy when there was an abundance of helpers around her but when she thought that she was not the main concern, responsibility and focus of everyone's attention, she would change her attitude and begin to sob. With increasing vehemence she would sound alarming manifestations of an approaching fainting spell. That was her way of keeping all around her on an alerted status. On the opposite side sat a middle-aged man with a benevolent face; he wore a white collar that indicated to the world he was a man of the cloth. His face had expanded under the influence of good living and its bold fleshy curves had extended beyond the limits originally assigned to them. His chin, for the same cause, had acquired a companion that is commonly known as a *'double chin'.* The color of his skin, pinkish, could only be seen on men of his profession, definitely not the outdoor types, who nourish themselves on meat and potatoes. Next to him sat a lady who never stopped talking or touching the priest's hand and would now and then leave her hand there a few moments more than necessary and would only remove it when the priest pulled his away. The jolly lady of words looked well skilled in cooking and, judging by her stoutness, one could say that she was also very well skilled in eating. There was another lady, skinnier than a stair spindle, standing close to Erik, her belly appearing ready to deliver a bundle of flesh and bones and who seemed delighted to pour out information on her own domestic affairs. She straightaway proceeded to report to the lady who was standing next to her that she was the mother of seven and in two months she was nearly ripe and ready to present her husband, John, with the eighth. The other lady responded most earnestly that her sister was the mother of nine siblings and all were girls. The skinny pregnant woman upon hearing this, moved away slowly. Whether she moved away for not being able to top that story or she moved away for having nothing else to report, it is unknown. Erik followed her with his eyes. He saw her stopping and planting herself next to another idle lady and beginning the same story.

Although Erik was too far away to hear the stuffing of her one-way discussion, he saw her touching and caressing her belly very proudly. Two or three older gentlemen and several ladies sat bolt upright and motionless on their chairs staring very hard at Sophia.

While Erik turned his head in another direction looking to pin his eyes on another interesting subject, he felt Sophia's hand wrapping around his.

"Come with me!" said Sophia proudly pulling Erik by the hand and walking towards her mother and father who were behind the counter catering to the bunch.

On the way, as Erik was almost being dragged he nodded his head and smiled at the people acknowledging their presence with genuine politeness.

"He said hello to you as he went by, " whispered a young lady, poking with her elbow the ribs of an older lady who appeared to be her grandmother.

"Ah?" exclaimed the older lady, "It don't matter. He don't care for an old lady like me. He is too young for me, anyway. Besides he has Sophia who is half his age." Then she paused and looked hard at him as he and the girl were passing by. She turned to her grand-daughter and said, "I never thought that I would live long enough to say that a forty five year old man is too young for me. I don't know if I should cry or laugh"

"What did she say? What did she say?' asked another older lady who was also sitting next to the granddaughter. She was deaf and like many deaf people, less deaf to a number of things, but in this instance, she didn't seem to realize the fact that other people could hear what she was saying a lot clearer than she did, declaring "I may be too old for him but he is not too young for me." A burst of laughter and some applause came from more than a dozen people who heard her. She was oblivious to all the attention but then, seeing their stares, their laughter and their applause directed at her, she turned away in bewildered wonder. Then, not knowing how to bear it, she too burst into loud laughter, and went one step further, slapping her legs with both hands.

A universal wave of laughs fell upon that entire surrounding bunch, but Sophia and Erik were unaware of that event. They kept on moving slowly away from the sitting crowd.

There was a younger man standing and leaning with his back on the wall. The heaviness of his body was resting on his left foot while the right knee was extending outwards with his leg bent and the bottom of his shoe almost glued to the white wall, a position that Erik found to be uncouth and insensible. He was closely looped by more than a half dozen young females who, to all appearances, spoke to him in a non-stop fashion, while he gently and slightly nodded his head in token assent.

"That man standing and talking to the women is my cousin. He is a doctor," said the girl with her mouth close to his ear and her eyes upon the doctor. "Let's go and see him."

"That man with the bottom of his shoe resting on your father's clean white wall?" asked Erik. Before Sophia had time to comment he said, "He is a doctor? I am not sick. I don't have to go to see him," whispered Erik into her ear the same way as she had done.

"Erik," expressed the girl a little louder, "you are becoming obnoxious again."

"I am obnoxious? Your cousin, the doctor, is obnoxious and thoughtless and insensible. Besides, you don't even know what I do to make a living. I may be another doctor for all you know."

"I know what you do. You are a gynecologist. You heal the wounds of young women," said Sophia smiling.

"Did I heal your wounds?"

"I wasn't wounded. You were wounded," returned the Italian girl.

"How do you know that I was wounded? Are you a doctor too?"

"I saw you licking your wounds behind your duck decoys. They weren't duck decoys, they were the wall hiding you from society. I will probably be wounded by you later" saying this, she stood and looked into his eyes steadfastly.

"Thank you for the compliment, my dear lady."

"What compliment?"

"That I am good enough to wound you," uttered Erik, with a humorous smile.

"Only if I choose to play the game of love with you."

"Have you been wounded?"

"Do you want me to tell you my life story?"

"Something like that" replied Erik.

"When we set up a pup-tent and break bread, then I'll tell it."

"Are you anxious?"

"I am more careful than anxious."

"Why?" asked Erik.

Sophia looked deeply into his eyes and said, "love and war have many things in common. Somebody is bound to get wounded."

"Only if we are not careful," returned Erik.

"That's why I said that I am more careful than anxious," said the girl earnestly, "Anyway, I'm not going to force you to do anything. I must say hello to him. I will be right back," said Sophia as she left.

Erik followed her with his eyes as she walked away and then he turned and looked around again.

Aside of the study that he was conducting of the people, he took time to survey the store, its décor and contents. He described it as a big and long store with a rich hardwood floor, a ceiling garnished with hams, sides of prosciutto, ropes of onions and braids of garlic, heads of cheeses and hanging wicker bottles of Italian wines and spirits. The walls were decorated with many bridles, a saddle, hunting whips, and a grandfather clock that stood in one corner, solid and sedate in demeanor as it ticked gravely away.

"Excuse me!" Erik heard a female voice coming from behind him. He turned and faced the person who addressed him and saw a bony woman in her fifties, straight all the way down, with long brown hair and a pointed jaw, wearing a green dress that marked her waist two inches below her armpits.

"I must tell you that the girl you came in with is my son's fiancée. My son is not one to tangle with," said the woman with a grin that agitated Erik's countenance from head to toe.

"Lady, tell your son to come and see me, in person!"

"Are you in the habit of taking other men's girls?"

"Were you sent here or did you come of your own accord?" exclaimed Erik in a storm of indignation.

"I came to advise and tell you that he has a gun," said the woman without taking any time for consideration.

"Tell your son, the gun he has will only be fired if the bullet goes through him. It's up to you to find out whether he wants the shot to go through the right or the left eye, in the meantime if he comes to me with something other than a gun, I will transform him into a four-footed companion for you to share the rest of your life with." Saying this he turned away feeling the most unmitigated disgust.

"Don't say, I didn't warn you," said the woman softly, following slowly at his heels.

"Lady, what do you want from me?" asked Erik, stopping and turning to face the lady who was pursuing him in such a strange way.

"I'm sorry if this seems odd to you. I know I used the wrong method of approach. But what I have told you is true. I don't wish anything bad to happen to my son because of a girl. I hear him all through the night walking around the house since she broke up with him nearly two weeks ago. I went to her and begged her at least to go to dinner with him and some other friends and relatives; she did it for me. For that I respect her and am grateful. This whole day he has been following her and you and I am truly afraid he may do something crazy and I will lose him. He is the only thing I have and I know no other way to handle this," concluded the woman with tears running from her eyes. She inserted an end of a white handkerchief into the corner of each eye, one after the other, and began to weep copiously.

While Sophia, who was busy talking with the doctor and his admirers, looked towards Erik walking away from the woman whose son she was supposedly engaged to, she saw her following closely behind him. Sophia rushed to the scene and by the time she arrived Erik had already stopped and turned to face the woman once more, and when he was about to make a remark, Sophia grabbed the lady gently by the arm and said, "Mrs. Rega, what are you doing here?"

"Leave me alone!" uttered the lady with a distorted face and fiery eyes, jerking her arm away with such speed and strength, she poked someone behind her in the stomach so severely that he let out a low toned howl.

Coincidently, that someone was Mrs. Rega's son who was just approaching the trio unnoticed.

Mrs. Rega realizing what she had done and to whom she had done it, turned with the same vigor that she had administered the accidental blow, threw her arms around her son and screamed. "My son, my boy, did I hurt you?"

"Mom," said that young man, who earlier that day was sitting with Sophia in the restaurant. "You didn't hurt me you only stunned me. Relax, calm down," continued the good son, peeling her arms gently away from his neck and body.

The rest of the invited guests, including the deaf, were startled, shocked and surprised and a universal stillness and pure silence fell on the whole establishment. The only sound that survived was the rattling and banging of the dishes at the far end of the place as they were being picked and gathered by two Mexican boys who were oblivious to the event.

"I'm sorry," apologized the young man, directing his feeling to Sophia, "I only caught the tail end of the feud between my mother and your friend."

"That's okay, Danny" said Sophia calmly.

"Let's go home, honey. Let her be with whomever she wishes. You will find somebody else better than her. I know you will," pleaded the mother.

"Mom! She is not and never has been my girl friend. We are only good friends," said Danny, desperately trying to appease his mother.

The entire guest roster, including the healthy and the ill, the far and near sighted, the deaf and the hearing, the proud and the humble, the fat and the skinny, the high and the mighty, that perfect sampling of our society, although all different from one another, harmoniously resumed their activities of talking, commenting, bragging, demanding, eating and drinking.

"Mom," said the young man very soothingly, "I said, I was happy being in her company and I wished she had felt the same, but you cannot insert love in anyone's heart. It has to be there," concluded the young man and taking his mother by the arm began to escort her outside.

Erik, who listened to this in silence and sensing that mother's torment, felt some sadness in his heart and followed them with traces of grief on his face.

Sophia looked upon Erik's face and saw his lips compressed in a dogged pain as they quivered and parted involuntarily. His face had turned pale and drops of sweat appeared on his forehead as he virtually staggered along behind mother and son.

"Erik! Are you all right?" asked the girl.

"She is not crazy, she is a mother," remarked Erik, looking in the lady's direction.

"I didn't say she is crazy," objected Sophia.

" I know you didn't, but that's what I thought at the beginning. Now I realize that she is that kind of a mother who only wishes for her son's happiness. I have seen plenty of them during the war in Greece."

Erik told Sophia of when he was a very young lad, growing up in Greece during WWII, seeing many similar spectacles of a mother's stress every time an enemy soldier arrested a young man and marched him through the town to his place of execution. He saw them first in transport, and then in mental anguish as the suffering mothers would throw themselves upon their knees at the feet of the German soldiers, fervently begging them to execute them and spare the lives of their sons. The struggle to save their sons and the everlasting grief succeeded in breaking their hearts eventually. He remembered a particular mother who, while her son was held in a prison camp waiting for his execution day, went to see him but was not allowed by the soldiers to get closer to him than fifty feet. Every day she went there, eagerly and feverishly attempting, with piteous lamentations, to soften the hearts of his captures enough to allow her to speak with him. It was all in vain. She stood in the sun for hours, holding onto a bag containing some food and water for him that she wouldn't consume, waiting to see him and thinking that each day would be the last for her. Even when she fell ill, her spirit of endurance that had for so long upheld her was able to contend against bodily weakness. She dragged her tottering limbs from the bed and went on to visit her son once more. While waiting, her strength failed her and she sank power- less on the ground and the soldiers forbade anyone to go near her, hoping that she'd die there and it would be the end of a nuisance. She was not dead. In a little while she half stood up attempting to make one last effort to reach her son but fell again and the Germans mocked her feeble efforts. She was removed at night by some towns- people. Erik heard a few days later that her soul vacated her torn and sick body. He was a young boy and he remembered that he cried when he heard of her death. He got on his knees and thanked God for taking her soul and prayed and hoped that she finally found eternal happiness and rest.

"Mothers are engulfed throughout their lives in the happiness and welfare of their children. They are mothers. They are not crazy," remarked Erik.

Sophia observed Erik's sadness, feeling a part of his sorrow and having a soft and tender heart, she shed a tear visible to him.

"I think, I am in trouble," remarked Erik, touching the young girl's face and wiping away the tear.

"Why are you in trouble?" asked Sophia, wiping away another tear with the back of her hand.

" The shedding of tears is contagious, my lady."

"You made me cry. Come on!" said Sophia, grabbing Erik's hand with a certain and sudden sparkle in her eye. "You have to meet my mother and father," and dragged Erik like a little boy behind her; he followed her like one. She walked fast. She didn't look to the right and she didn't look to the left, only straight ahead and didn't stop until they reached the place where her mother and father appeared as if they were waiting, appearing anxious to greet him.

"Mom! Dad!" said Sophia with gleaming eyes and a dazzling tone in her voice. "This is my friend, Erik Karas. He is Greek."

They both came out from behind the counter and greeted him with noticeable delight as they turned and gazed bewildered at their daughter's beaming face.

"How long have you known each other," asked the father with smiling eyes that matched perfectly his wife's enchantment.

"It seems forever," said Sophia timidly.

"We can only guess from this, that the two of you are having a good time," said the mother who had straight black hair, combed back, with a face providing evidence she was Sophia's mother.

"I'm really enjoying myself tremendously, thanks to your daughter who is being such a good hostess," responded Erik, looking at the girl affectionately.

"It's good to be a good hostess, but what makes it better is that also has her mother's good looks," said the father looking at his wife.

"He always flatters me," replied the mother.

"On the contrary. Instead of good looks he should use the word 'beautiful'," said Erik gazing on each of them with a conservative smile.

It was becoming an increasingly difficult task for Erik to leave and forget the entire family from whom he had received so much kindness and so much hospitality. He knew that the whole event was growing more surreal to him. It started as a simple game, something he was accustomed to. It was turning into a dream that he feared might spin into a nightmare. If he were single and free, he might have infused a lot more warmth into the presentation.

"Mom, Dad, it's a nice day outside; I would like to take Erik for walk around the town for a while. I'll stop and see you before I go back up north," said the daughter, taking Erik by the arm.

"Why do you have to go back up there; this is your home," said the mother with a saddened tone of voice.

"Mom! We have been through this before," said Sophia thoughtfully.

"Please come back and see us again, Erik," said the father shaking Erik's hand once more. Very eager to leave, Erik gave both of them a bow accompanied by a hint of a military salute and followed Sophia outside.

They began to walk in silence, detached from one another, but close enough to be observed as a couple. They walked under the shady trees cooled by the light wind that gently rustled the foliage. Songbirds, perched upon the boughs, enlivened the natural setting. Ivy and moss crept in thick clusters over rows of small houses and tall trees and green turf covered the ground like a soft mat. Shadows of some clouds were thrown on the ground and raced across the red brick roads and green lawns like running thieves. Shoppers, in bunches, lingered around the stores. There were also some larger herds that had been dropped off by a tour bus on the outskirts of the town and they hastily and vociferously scrambled into the market.

"My intentions were not to pass you off to my relatives as the love of my life. I just wanted to show my mother and father that even though I live away from home I have found happiness," declared Sophia, stopping Erik in the middle of the main street.

"I am used to being used, " said Erik, glancing away, his face now coated with a trace of sadness.

Her laughter was the loudest ever when she heard that statement and saw his face smeared with that sullen look. "Erik," said the girl, turning sincere, "I'm really happy being with you, even if it's for a day."

"I'm just a nice guy," said Erik still sullen.

"Right now and for now, you are my nice guy."

"Nice act. You shined, sparkled and shimmered in there."

"Erik, my boy, let me tell you something," said Sophia turning to him soberly, " I am a woman and most women don't only see with their eyes but they can also hear. When, as you said, I shined, sparkled and shimmered, I saw a great deal of apprehension in your face. Now you think the whole thing was an act and that makes you sad. Erik! I am not an actress. I feel what I show."

"Your mission has been accomplished. Just tell me when to leave town and I will," said Erik sullenly as if he understood nothing of what she had said.

"Erik, you are not going to conquer me by surrendering. You've got to wrestle," remarked Sophia.

Erik looked at her in a funny way and asked softly, "will I win? Will I win if I wrestle?"

"I take nothing on a silver plate and I hand out nothing on a silver platter."

"I understand. I'm just a nice dreamer to you. That's how you see me," said Erik sadly, looking away as if to hide something he felt had fallen upon his face.

"Erik! Erik!" exclaimed Sophia with a hearty laugh, "you should see your face. I have never met anyone in my life who can switch from being the most humble man to the most arrogant bastard at the drop of a hat. Your face is covered with such sadness, a dozen virgins would wait in line to surrender themselves to you just to cheer you up if they saw your face like that."

When she finished laughing she put her arm through Erik's and said, "I want to show you something."

"The dozen virgins?"

She laughed again, "No, silly. Come on!"

They started walking away from the market place and into the more residential area. They walked through the village and down the hill with passion, as oftentimes true-lovers do.

The weather was warm. Some people were sitting at their doors and some were strolling in their yards and vegetable gardens. All of them seemed to enjoy the serenity of the day and a respite from their jobs. She hadn't been in that part of the town since she was a little girl. There were strange faces in almost every house and she realized how fast her world had changed.

"I was born in that house," said Sophia letting out a deep sigh, pointing at a small yellow cape cod style house.

They stood in front of the house and gazed at it. It was the house of her infancy for which her heart yearned with passion and affection. It had a fence and was surrounded by many lilac trees. How well she remembered the fence when it seemed then to be much higher. She remembered that there were more bushes and many more vibrant and happier flowers than what she saw now. There was the oak tree under which she sat thousands of times when she was tired of playing in the sun with the rest of the neighborhood children or when she was angry with her mother. She sometimes would go there just to be missed.

She saw her old neighbor, Mr. Veleccio, who was sitting on his chair in front of his house. Now he is a feeble and frail old man but she remembers him as a sound and sturdy laborer. He looked and studied her face from afar, but she was unknown to him as she was to many others in the vicinity. As she made a further search of her passed days she remembered being a young girl, clinging to her mother's and father's hands while peacefully going to church.

Erik looked at her face and observed nostalgia and sadness as a tiny tear found its way down her lovely face. He pushed back her wind-rustled hair and said, "You should see your face and how sadness has shrouded it. You remind me of me when I was a little boy, when things didn't go my way I would be sad and my mother would bend down towards me, nail her blue eyes on me with a pretending distorted face and would say, 'I shall remain like this until I see the sadness fly away from your face and a nice smile planted.' Then I would burst into hearty laugh and I was glad I did."

Sophia reached out, took his face in her hands, kissed his lips softly and said tenderly, "Erik, how long is a clock's hour. Is it an hour long, a minute a day or a year? Erik, it must be a year because I feel that I have known you for four and a half years."

"I only hope that knowing me all those years hasn't curbed your appetite for me," joked Erik.

"Erik," yelled Sophia, "why is it when I get serious you become silly and when I get silly you become serious?"

"Sophia!" yelled Erik back, at the same level of sound. "Haven't you heard? Opposites attract."

"Erik, why aren't you married?" asked the girl suddenly in a very low voice as if she feared the worst.

Erik returned no verbal response. He gazed into her eyes with a vacant look, then took out a cigarette, lit it and blew the smoke out very slowly looking away for a long moment. If Erik Karas would entertain the most remote and most distant idea to say he was not married, he knew that he would betray his wife and child and would deceive the young lady who seemed to be as vulnerable and tender as any newborn creature. If he evaded the question she would think the worst. The worst was the whole truth for which he felt he had no defense. Here and now he realized what a terrible and loathsome character he was. They say love is blind, but the other five senses are alive and well. But love at first sight, as in this case, was not only blind but had distanced itself from the rest of the senses. Did he or did she lose their senses? Erik thought about her earlier observation of him - he was, from a young age, in the habit of 'jumping the gun'. Moreover, evading the answer at this point would be the best solution for him but such avoidance was difficult unless something more important was to be said, heard or done.

He then began to roam his eyes about, as if he were searching to find an interesting topic to which to change the subject. Nothing was surfacing and time was running out. He observed the expression on her face and realized that she was ready to ask the question in a more stern fashion. If she persisted, the game was over. Hoping for the best but expecting the worst, he had worked everything in his favor and the most he could have lost was one night's pleasure. What vile beds we make and lie in for one night's pleasure, he thought.

Suddenly Sophia rushed to him, threw her arms around his neck and kissed him passionately for a long moment. This was done without any considerable resistance from him. He felt certain inward misgivings, but the sweetness of her kiss, the feeling of her embrace and the smell of her womanly fragrance abolished all misgivings, guilty or otherwise.

"Let's go to a restaurant out of town, pitch a 'pup-tent' and break some bread," said the girl looking up into his eyes with a winning smile. "I am dying to hear your life story."

Erik looked straight ahead over her head; his eyes caught someone resembling Danny, her ex-boyfriend, rushing swiftly from one building to another. Erik remained wholly unmoved by that suspicious sight. His right hand slid into his pocket and felt the revolver, that most of the time he carried out of habit. With his thumb, while the revolver was still in his pocket, he pulled back the hammer and set it, ready to fire if the time came. Then he thought that possibly his eyes and the unfavorable thoughts implanted in his head by Danny's mother might have joined together to play tricks on him.

"One thing I must ask and you must do," said Erik, without removing his eyes from the spot where the unknown man had appeared and disappeared so quickly.

"Yes?'

"We'll get into my car and we'll go together wherever you want to go, and then we'll come back here and you'll take your car,"

"Erik, I have no car here, my cousin brought me down. I was to go back with her again. Okay?" responded Sophia, "you sound so strange. Is there something wrong?" inquired Sophia in a soft tone of voice.

"Why are you whispering, Sophia?" asked Erik in similar tone. "There is nothing wrong, sweetheart. I just want you to get in my car because I don't want to lose you so early in the day."

She broke into a loud and sweet giggle, as she usually did, "Sweetheart," said Sophia when her laugh had to some degree subsided, "you are not going to lose me. I'll do as you say." Saying this she kissed his lips tenderly, released him and pulled back.

Erik took the time, after carefully surveying the area, to reply with a tender gaze and a smile.

They began to walk close together in their usual way with Sophia's left arm inserted into Erik's right arm. They worked their way though the crowd hastily past Theo's place, where they had met just a few hours earlier and gazed at each other with smiles as if recounting their recent past. As they walked out of the shopping area into the woods along shaded lanes and pebbled paths, their conversation turned to the delightful scenery by which they were surrounded on every side. They listened to the birds singing as they fell into an enchanting and delicious reverie. The girl walked along by his side with her head resting on his shoulder, as a dreaming lover often does. A loud greeting brought them back to their other selves. They stopped and looked to the left and then to the right with wandering eyes but saw no one standing, sitting or lying down. They suddenly heard an imposed cough and saw a kind face belonging to a tall older man wearing army fatigues.

"How are you?" asked the man who was out of breath and looked as if he were running to catch up to them, "I'm glad to see you. I thought you would be leaving a lot later with the rest of the visitors," the man said.

"Oh, yes?" replied Erik, not being quite certain what the man wanted.

"Someone visited your car," said the man, with a whispering voice and quite manner, drawing closer and directing his observation to Erik "A woman was browsing around the parking lot and stopped when she came to yours. She closely inspected the car as she walked around it, then put a note on the windshield and vanished in the parking lot. She did that very fast like she didn't want anybody to see her." said the man, pausing after that and looking around as if he were being watched by someone other than the people he was talking to. Both of the visitors looked in silent wonder.

"Have you ever seen that woman before?' asked Erik, with considerable concern in his voice.

"No!" replied the man earnestly, "I went home to get my glasses to see her better, hoping that she would still be around the parking lot, but by the time I came back she was gone. I went to the car to look for the note and it was gone too. The reason I did all that is I thought it was some kind of emergency, from the way the lady was behaving."

"Did you happen to notice if she were with someone?' asked Erik, emphasizing the "with", and exhibiting a mild alarm in his question.

"I didn't see anyone else, but I think I heard her talking to someone when she left. You see at my age, I can't hear well and I can't see that good either," said the old man grinning.

"What did the woman look like?" asked the girl sounding less alarmed than Erik.

"I am sorry, Miss. I told you I couldn't see very well. The only thing I know is that it was your car," turning to Erik, " and the reason I know that's your car is because I saw the Greek flag on your bumper when you drove in. I thought that you had gone to Theo's place. That is where all the Greeks go when they come here and they are alone. I know the Greek flag because I was in Greece in the army during the WWII. It was really after Germany lost. I only stayed there a few days waiting for the ship to take us home. I saw that all the Greeks love their flag." There he stopped for a long moment. He looked down and then, "Thinking of it now it seems like it was yesterday, but it was some time ago…almost thirty years ago. I was nearly fifty years old. Looking at me now you can't imagine that I was a soldier. I was a career soldier. I was a sergeant. When I was in Greece it was my last year in the army. Young people think when they look at older people, that the old people were born old." Saying this, he shook his head mournfully.

"I know, it's sad, but it's true," agreed Erik.

Erik expressed his appreciation in a very delightful style. Both Erik and Sophia thanked him again as they bid the old soldier good-by and headed for Erik's car.

"Erik, do you know who that woman can be?" asked the girl.

"No! Somebody who knows me and knows my car," said Erik without showing much concern. At this point he was not about to elaborate on his thoughts or divulge the conversation he had with Danny's mother a few hours earlier.

"Maybe one of those women that you never got the name of is coming back for a second serving," remarked the girl with an amusing delivery.

"Maybe a jealous wife of a husband you drove crazy," said Erik.

"How dare you say something like that to me?" fumed Sophia in a rage such as would have scared a snake out of its skin. She stopped and stood still on that spot as if she were demanding that the case should be heard right then and there. "Do you think that I am the type to go out with married men?"

"I'm sorry! I'm sorry, I was only kidding," apologized Erik most earnestly, "it's possible that a married man could have sneaked up in your life."

"None that would stay with me long enough to be driven crazy and have his jealous wife after me."

"I'm sorry again, " said Erik turning towards her and looking seriously into her eyes. I now believe that one thoughtless word spoken tends to taint one thousand kind words that have been said. I only misstated something that was meant to be humorous. "Besides, me being an immigrant, I tend to make mistakes as I speak."

Sophia placed her hand on Erik's face and slid it slowly down to his chest and said with simplicity. "I forgive you, immigrant. How many times have you used that immigrant stuff? It's probably a part of your regular apologies when you know you are wrong," said Sophia softly, still stroking his chest with the tips of her fingers. "I must tell you that I keep all the kind words and things you say close to my heart and the thoughtless ones I thrust aside as if they are bad apples, after all, they are thoughtless."

If there were only seven times in his life when Erik felt that it was better for him to keep quiet, this was one of them.

"I am very sorry for getting angry with you. But I don't think I can stay angry with you very long. I don't think there is anyone who could be angry with you for long," said Sophia.

"I have nothing else to say or to take back, so let's go and have a nice dinner in a nice place and we will call it, like the news man, Paul Harvey, says 'Page Two'," said Erik touching her face.

She stood there and kept on gazing at him even when he walked away and neared his car, as if she were trying to continue her comments.

"Are you coming or am I to go alone?" asked Erik

"Erik!"

"Yes, sitting duck"

"I liked you, from the very first moment I saw you sitting at the bar with those bottles and glasses in front of you. I wanted to talk to you then. Your duck decoys, as you refer to them, puzzled me," confessed Sophia, "I wanted to know more about you and you duck decoys."

"Theo!" Erik yelled, raising his voice to its loudest pitch and looking around him like a crazy man. "Theo! It still works, you son-of-a-gun." Erik yelled again, shaping his hands into a blow-horn as if he were trying to reach someone miles away.

Seeing this outrageous display, Sophia rushed over to Erik and threw her arms around him as if she wished to be a part of that glorious revelation.

"What works? Where and who's Theo? Is it something I said that created this great event? Please tell me, Erik!" persisted the girl with an expression of delight.

"Theo is the owner of the restaurant," responded Erik calmly now.

"What restaurant?"

"Where we met."

"Do you expect Theo to hear you from here?"

"I'll pretend that he heard me, telling him that it still works," said Erik in a more tamed voice.

"What works?" . "It's something I saw," he said, touching her face with some crazy joy.

Sophia tilted her head sideways to feel the smoothness of his hand.

Erik and Sophia having worked their hearts into a galloping state and their blood into over active circulation embraced each other with heated desire.

"People are watching us, Erik," said the girl, pulling away from him with a crimson face, "we are acting like two teenagers."

"Now I understand, " said Erik, walking towards the driver's door.

"You understand, what?" said Sophia, holding him back by his arm.

"I understand that I must play the birth certificate act."

"What's that?"

"I must open my wallet take out my birth certificate, read the date of my birth and act according to my age. But one thing you must bear in mind, my dear lady, is that we don't all grow old the same way. I have a friend who is a few years older than I am and he and his wife went out the other day looking to buy a cemetery plot. He had the guts to invite me to find one for myself. I gave him a dirty look and he called me irresponsible for not wanting to look for a cemetery plot."

Hearing this, Sophia burst into a laugh and strolled away from him. " I only said that we just can't stand in the middle of a parking lot, in front of people, behaving like two teenagers in heat and you gave me a sixty-four dollar speech." There she stopped and looked at Erik seriously, "maybe your friend is sick and he thinks he is dying."

"He is sick all right. He's sick in the head, like a lot of people are. I don't have a birth certificate. I don't want to know how old I am. I even scratched out my birth date from my driver's license. I will act as I damn well please and when the time comes that I feel old, I'll grab myself a pick and shovel go out find a spot, buy it and dig my grave." He stood there and looked at the girl, "Come here!" he said, grabbing her with energy and bringing her close to him, he kissed her passionately. "Now. How old do you feel you are?"

"Young. Young and foolish," whispered the girl.

"There is still some hope for you yet," said Erik getting into his car.

Groups of people who were either coming or going to the town gazed at the car and its occupants while Erik drove slowly out of the parking lot. The car made its way onto the main road and rolled past the fields and orchards that bordered the road. Farther down, where the road was skirted with corn and tomato fields, small groups of laborers, who were picking and gathering ears of corn and placing them in a trailer rigged to an idling tractor, paused for an instant from their labor while shading their sun-burned faces with their browner hands in order to peer at the slow moving car. There were some children belonging to the farm workers, too small to work and too mischievous to be left at home, playing in the middle of the road who stopped and waved to attract attention each time a passenger car went by. Erik cast a look behind him as he slowed to turn a curve in the road and saw that the laborers returned to their picking and the children had resumed their play.

The influence of a scene like that was not lost in the pair's minds, the wandering of their eyes and the pleasant expression on their faces vividly showed the pleasure they derived from observing rural life.

CHAPTER 3

They break bread

There is no month of the whole year in which nature wears a more beautiful appearance than the month of June. A mellow softness appears to hang over the whole earth. Blue skies, green fields and sweet smelling flowers are everywhere and the snow, the ice and bleak winds are gone from view and consequently have faded from everybody's minds and plans, as if they had disappeared from nature's schedule for ever.

The car entered a different scene and cruised slowly through the well-paved streets of a thriving handsome little town, eventually stopping in front of the restaurant of a large hotel with circular driveway.

"Staying over or just dinner, Sir?" said one of the valet boys who rushed over to the car, standing by the driver's door with his hand on the doorknob.

"Attend to the other door and assist the lady," said Erik sternly.

The valet sped over to the passenger's side, opened the door and assisted Sophia out by giving her his hand.

"Dinner only," said Erik loudly for the girl to hear, walking around the car, waiting for Sophia, with one hand extended in her direction while giving a bill to the boy with the other.

The boy took it, glanced at it quickly and stood aside stiffly, then bowed to the girl as she passed by for Erik's hand.

They walked in leisurely and in silence. They were greeted graciously by an attractive blond hostess and were immediately ushered to a nice table with a view of the sea.

Pleased with the table and the elegance of the hostess, Erik placed a bill in the blond lady's hand. She thanked him genuinely

and went away with a smile. It appeared that was the best arrangement that could have been made, as it was certified by the pleasing look on Sophia's face and the twinkling in her eyes.

"That's funny," began Erik, with a slight smile on his face, as he
sat across from the girl who already had taken her seat.

"What's funny?"

"When man came down from the trees he searched the ground
for food and found plenty, he was better off than spending his life
up in the tree, but he wasn't satisfied. When he started living in a
cave away from the rain the snow and all the bad weather, he still
wasn't satisfied. When he discovered fire and could eat hot food, he
still wasn't satisfied and when he built his first house and lived
there with his own family, still not satisfied. When he built hotels
like this with all the conveniences in the world, still not satisfied.
In my opinion, one thing is definite, is that the man from the beginning of his life builds like there are a million tomorrows but he
takes and takes like there is no tomorrow."

"Are you looking for an answer or was it a random statement?"

"I'll listen to a logical answer if you have one."

"When you die, will all of you die, Erik?" asked the girl, with a
look as serious as Erik's was when he recited his thoughts, and
without giving him time to answer she said, "we don't completely
die, Erik, we always leave a part of ourselves behind. Children, for
instance, are the continuation of our selves. That's where your
million tomorrows come in." Erik glanced with amazement on
hearing a girl, who he thought shouldn't be concerned with
anything else in this world except looking pretty, responding with
thoughts that had come from deep introspection.

"I said it to you before and I'm going to say it again. You are half
my age and you know twice as much. How did this happen, sitting
duck?"

"You said that the Italians are smarter than the Greeks and I am
Italian."

"Don't push your luck, sweetheart!" said Erik, lifting his index
finger for more emphasis,

"I said that I thought the Greeks were smarter than the Italians
and then I said that I thought I was wrong. I didn't say that the
Italians are smarter than the Greeks."

"Erik, my dear boy, I don't want to be smarter than you, I just want to be as smart," said the girl, leaning over and placing her hands on the table top.

"Just don't get ahead of me!"

"How could I?" replied the girl with a smile wider than a mile, "I'd be lost."

Erik gave her a satirical look and said nothing.

Sophia returned the same look followed by a giggle. She stopped and looked at him again seriously this time, "lost Erik, just lost, not wounded."

"You're bad," mumbled Erik, lighting up a cigarette and glancing around as he usually did. First he looked to his left where the sea stretched out starting as a blue-gray boundless sheet and extending far away as a dainty and bewitching spirit. He then turned to his right. The hum of many voices, the sound of feet, vague piano music and loud laughter were perfectly bewildering. Lights shined and jewelry sparkled, faces beamed, brilliant eyes lit up with pleasurable expectations and gleamed from every side. A piano bar was at the far corner but in a perfect view from where the couple sat. A number of ladies and gentlemen hovered around it, oblivious to the piano playing, appearing to be discussing different subjects interesting and delightful perhaps only to themselves. Lounging near the door in a remote corner was a group of silly young men displaying a variety of classless and humorless performances trying to amuse themselves and joyfully thinking that they were the objects of general observation and praise by somber and serious people. At the most distant corner, seated at a large round table, was a group of ladies, appearing to Erik as divorced or single who had just passed their prime and were unable to attract the hand and admiration of tall, dark and handsome gentlemen, but who deeply refused to accept that truth and were laughing loudly as they were exchanging daily scandals and gossip; to all appearances they all had just a little more to drink than the good Lord allows to still be of sound and of logical mind.

A young man brought and carefully placed a basket of hot bread covered with a white napkin and a small tray of butter on the table.

"Let's break bread!" said Sophia, wrapping her long slim fingers around a small loaf of bread as with some effort she broke it in two. She kept one piece and handed the other piece to Erik, with a smile of accomplishment on her face. Erik, who was lost in the contemplation of his observation of the entire surrounding scene, missed the struggle that Sophia had undergone to break the bread.

"Erik! You wanted to break bread with me and set up a pup-tent. Here is your bread, I already broke it with my own two hands."

"Thank you," said Erik taking the bread with a smile and looking at her "when do we set up a pup-tent?"

"Still not satisfied" replied the girl as she stopped buttering her bread.

"You seem to remember everything I say," commented Erik.

"I do. I hope you remember everything I say."

"Oh, I do."

"What do you remember that I've said to you?"

"Let me see," there he stopped for a moment; he was really waiting for her to make a comment, "you said that you were born in this area,"

"Come on, come on, Erik you can do better than that," she interrupted, while shooting her piercing green eyes at him with a very serious expression on her face as if a different persona had surfaced.

"Don't look at me like I am on some kind of a trial" said Erik, as serious as she was.

"Come on, Erik, repeat what you heard from me!"

"You don't take anything on a silver plate and you don't give anything on a silver platter," said Erik, hoping that all doubt surrounding the subject would be removed.

"That's my boy!" remarked Sophia, leaning back and relaxing her features with a smile.

Erik took the menu and began to read with keen interest.

"Do you know how most Italian men know when they've had enough to eat?" asked Erik, looking at Sophia over the menu.

Sophia looked at him with a smile and said, "Tell me how!"

"They sit on the chair with their stomach three inches away from the table and begin to eat and when their stomach touches the table, they know they had enough food and that's when they stop".

"Very funny, very funny" said the girl, with a hesitant smile, "how about the Greeks?"

"Tomorrow at breakfast, I will tell you."

Sophia did not allow that statement to pass unheeded. She raised her eyes from the menu and zoomed them on his.

Erik at the same time looked up to test the waters.

"I can't wait to hear this," remarked Sophia without a hint of feelings or thought.

That statement, to which neither a reply was needed, nor was one readily available in Erik's head, was allowed to perish, without further comment. It only perished from the table but not from their minds. It was like one was trying to hide the donkey but its ears were showing.

"I know what I want," said Sophia, putting the menu down and beginning to play with the fork after a brief silence.

"I know what I want and I know what I am going to have," followed Erik, putting the menu down.

"You know, Erik, with the little experience I have with men, after all I'm very young, anyway, I have discovered one thing,"

"What's that?"

"There are four different types of men. There is the smart man, the wise man, the smart-ass man and the wise-ass man. The smart man talks with humor but listens with his eyes, the wise man talks while thinking and listens with his ears, the smart-ass man, thinks he's a wise man and the wise-ass thinks he's smart," said the girl anticipating a comment from Erik.

"Tell me about that guy, Danny!" said Erik.

"Why do you want to know?"

"I have a reason."

"You spoke to his mother?"

"Yes"

"His father left them when he was a little boy. He grew up without a father and became a very nasty boy. Not too long ago he broke somebody's windshield for passing him on the highway. He always carries a pistol. You carry one too. But he flaunts it and you don't. You don't think I've seen your pistol, but I did."

"Does it bother you?" asked Erik.

"Not with you. But with him yes," said Sophia, "I have a pistol too."

"Do you know how to shoot it?"

"I'll do what I have to do if I have to do it," replied the girl smiling.

Erik made no other comment about the subject. He only gazed at her and grinned.

A great many more subjects of similar nature and others that had been disclosed were discussed during dinner and neither of the two was holding out any signs of meaning to leave.

The major part of the conversation was confined to one-liners with a touch of humor and current light philosophy.

Both of them were easily persuaded into having another glass of wine and when it came time for the third glass, Erik looked out and realized that it was getting dark. He emptied his glass to the last drop and flicked the ashes from his cigarette into the ashtray with poise.

"When are you going to tell me when the Greeks know they've had enough to eat?" asked Sophia.

"At breakfast"

"What do you have for breakfast?"

"Depends on where I have breakfast and with whom."

"At my apartment and with me," answered Sophia with a smile, knowing that she unleashed an immeasurable pleasure in his heart.

"I'm Greek, don't you remember?' said Erik standing up and gesturing to the waiter, who was standing nearby, ready to place the check on the table.

"I remember, but what does that mean?" asked Sophia

"That means I know how to cook. I'll cook breakfast," declared Erik.

"Be my guest. I will go powder my nose and will meet you outside," said the girl, rising.

She left and went away as if she were familiar with the path to the powder room.

Erik lingered around the table for a moment, waiting for his change to come back, then headed for the exit door. On his way there his eyes encountered the sight of Danny, mingling with the rowdy group of youths in a remote corner. Danny's eyes fell upon Erik the moment Erik's were upon him. Danny did not show any visible surprise and that led Erik to the utmost point of indignation. Erik gestured sternly to Danny to meet him outside. Danny appeared somewhat hesitant at first but then turned and whispered something to one of his friends, who in turn looked at Erik with a distorted look in his face. Danny proceeded alone and with confidence to where Erik had pointed.

When Danny arrived outside, he realized he had lost sight of Erik and, stricken with fear, was about to go back in when a hand suddenly grabbed him by the sleeve and jerked him behind some tall thick bushes. He recognized that hand belonged to Erik and the face he was looking at was Erik's too and it depicted nothing more than severe indignation. Without any further ceremony, Erik, knowing that they were away from all eyes and ears, slapped Danny across the face with the palm of his right hand as he held him up with the left hand to almost a tip- toe position. He then quickly imparted another slap with the back of his hand and immediately followed those with another blow to his face. He then reached into his pocket, pulled out the revolver and pressed it against Danny's mouth.

They both remained still for some seconds, Erik panting and Danny blowing wind in and out of his lungs with increasing difficulty.

"I'm going to search you and if I find a gun on you I will shoot you right here and now in self defense. Tell me punk! Do you have a gun? Move your stupid head left and right, if you don't have one. If you have one, move your stupid head up and down!" demanded Erik. Danny stayed motionless for a few seconds. Erik, with his thumb, gently and slowly cocked the revolver. Danny, seeing the rage on Erik's face, not knowing whether he was sane or insane and feeling the cold steel pressed against his mouth, started to move his head vigorously and uncontrollably from left to right. He did that several times, making sure that Erik had gotten the signal while his eyes became flooded and tears began to flow down his face. Erik, viewing the pouring of tears and thinking that the entire incident could have been a mistake, professed his heartfelt regret and begged to know whether he could do anything to alleviate the sorrow and pain of that suffering young man. He put the gun back in his pocket, leaving his hand in with it.

"No, nothing," murmured Danny, wiping the tears off his face. When that pitiful act was completed and after he somewhat composed himself, he turned and looked hard into Erik's eyes and uttered with clench teeth, "you bastard!" and jumping out of the bushes and running for the door of the hotel, crashed into Sophia who was just coming out. The impact caused Danny to lose his balance and fall on the steps.

"Danny!" yelled Sophia.

Danny, without waiting for the usual exchange of ritual greetings, ran inside.

Erik leisurely strolled out from behind the bushes, his direction unnoticed by Sophia.

"Did you see him?" she asked, seemingly bewildered by the rude encounter.

"See, who?" asked Erik as if unaware of her reference.

"Danny Rega," voiced the girl.

"He is your boy friend not mine," said Erik, while moving to the middle of the driveway and waiting for his car.

"He is not my boy friend, he has never been nor will he ever be one. Boy, you make me angry, Erik, when you accuse me of something that I know nothing about," protested Sophia with audacity. "I have better taste in men than that."

"I'm sorry," said Erik going over to her and offering his hand. "Sometimes I tend to sound like a smart-ass."

"Really," said the girl, hesitating whether to give him her hand or not, but thinking of that charming apology, she did.

"I know how it feels to be falsely accused of something that you are completely innocent of. Forgive me," said Erik, forcing his hand on hers and shaking it with the utmost chivalry, while declaring she possessed a noble spirit that he held in high regard and that he too sought her forgiveness.

In the meantime his green car arrived; the valet boy opened the door for her as Erik walked over to the driver's side, once seated, they drove away.

A visibly disturbed Danny, who evidently was monitoring the whole scene from the window of the restaurant, watched as the car pull away.

CHAPTER 4

A little boy's dream, a mother's nightmare

The car rolled along the wide quiet road under the light of a full moon in South Jersey.

Meanwhile, North Jersey was being beaten by a merciless rain, vigorous wind and blinding streaks of fire that shot from the sky, almost touching the top of Erik's house and exploding with blasts that sent Randy, stricken with an innocent pure fear, into his mother's arms.

"When is Daddy coming home, Mommy?' cried the little boy, hiding in his mother's embrace, listening to the roar of thunder and seeing the blinding lightning that brightened the universe and shook the house on its foundation. The widows quivered as if their teeth rattled and their bones screeched striving to get away from nature's madness.

"Mommy, I'm scared," said the boy trembling.

"That's alright, honey, it will go away soon," said the mother soothing the little boy, "your Daddy will be home soon," said Susan with a quivering lip and hesitating voice desperately trying to hide the tear that had suddenly trickled down her face.

Erik, driving the car, listened to Greek music and reveled in the full luxury of the beginning of an affair. Sophia slid over and planted a kiss born of great affection on his cheek, which act apparently caused him to stop the car on the shoulder of the road. She thought this was a very accountable behavior and that he had stopped the car to throw his arms around her and to kiss her passionately; but the fact was that Erik stopped the car, climbed out leaving his door open and the music blasting to high heaven, went around to open the passenger door and assisted Sophia out.

"Come here, sitting duck, dance with me," he said, giving her one end of a white handkerchief while holding the other and raising his left hand that held the handkerchief shoulder high, snapping his right hand fingers to the rhythm of the song. He moved his body and side stepped his feet gracefully and Sophia followed the performance. They did a Greek dance in the moonlight. At times Erik would bounce up gently, according to the Greek music and dance, at other times he would rest his right hand on his waist and raise his head high. In the course of that dance, after more than a few twists and rounds without stopping, he reached into his pocket, came out with the revolver and fired two shots into the air, sending fear through Sophia's heart. She made a feeble attempt to run away but Erik pulled her closer to him and said loudly, "Let us be happy even if it's only for one night. In Greece they break plates, in America we shoot guns."

"Erik! You are going to be arrested!" she cried piercingly.

"Triumph brings happiness. That cannot be arrested. Life, my dear, is a joke when you are seeing it from up here. The ancient Greeks got rid of the creator and embraced Zeus who was like them, a fun loving god," uttered Erik loudly, continuing his dance.

"Erik! Please put the gun away," pleaded Sophia.

"Come up to me! Enter my heart and stay there forever, lost in the stars and sky up above and be like a free spirited Greek, always in love."

The thunder and the lighting storm in North Jersey had subsided. Susan was standing by the window in the living room looking at the rain beating the trees, shrubs and flowers while Randy was a few feet way watching the TV intently.

"Mommy, when is Daddy coming home?"

"Soon, honey, soon," whispered Susan without taking her eyes from the rain.

"Mommy!"

"Yes," replied Susan a little louder.

"Grown ups always ask me what I'm going to be when I grow up. Can I tell them that I'm going to be like my Daddy?"

Susan turned her head to look at her little boy and saw that his question was serious to him and from the look of his eyes demanded an answer. She walked over to him, sat on the couch with perfect gravity, placed her hands on her knees and looked into her son's face with an expression of true concern that showed that she had not the remotest intention of allowing his question to be lost and said to him with pride and passion. "Sure, honey, your father is a good man."

This young wife whose duty was to preside over a house and family, rendered herself useful in a variety of ways, particularly in the departments of waiting, aiding and supporting every wish and inclination presented by her husband whose immature ways and actions were making her life more difficult with each day that came and went. There was a question in her mind whether she could go on any further. Invaded by these puzzling thoughts, Susan placed her face in her hands and sobbed so violently that the young lad, affected by that sight, moved closer to her, placed his little arms around her and touched her face, desperately trying to ease his mother's noticeable pain. While this was taking place in Erik's home, he was a full hundred miles to the south of his wife and child, in the company of a gorgeous young female, still dancing on the shoulder of the road, smiling with a bland dignity that sufficiently testified he was in the state of mind where dreams take over and reality vanishes. He felt every note he heard, he lived every word that was sung, he sensed no land beneath his feet, only clouds, the descended pockets of hovering white mist. He danced as if he were celebrating an event of gravely bad news that had suddenly turned out to be good news. He was clutching the pistol in his right hand and with his left was still holding onto the handkerchief.

Sophia, having let go of it, stood and watched him in astonishment and fear. "Erik!" yelled Sophia in her loudest pitched voice, to overcome the sound of the music that was blasting from the car radio, "let's go! You are going to be arrested."

"Here," said Erik handing her the gun, "I fired three shots, there are three more bullets. Fire them into the air and then we'll go."

She took the gun, trembling with fear and feeling the crimson rush to the crown of her head, closed her eyes and pointed the gun up and to the right and her face down and to the left. She squeezed the trigger with one hand three times but the last time, on the third round, she lowered the gun and the bullet hit the right head light of the car, the light went dark and glass was scattered all over the land.

"Oh! My God, I can shoot the pistol," Sophia shrieked, " but I killed your car!"

"No! You didn't kill it; you only poked out one of its eyes. It can still see where to go. Let me have it!" said Erik taking the gun from her hand and placing it in his pocket, "you have nothing to fear. It's empty," he concluded opening the door for her to get in.

"Aren't you upset?" asked the girl with a tone of bewilderment.

"No! I'm not upset. In fact I'm glad," remarked Erik holding the door open.

"Glad? Are you glad you said?"

"Yes, I'm glad it wasn't my eye," replied Erik humorously, closing the door after she entered the car.

Many favorable feelings about this man swept swiftly through her mind. One thought though, that stood out vividly, was that he said he fired three shots, but she had the recollection of his firing only two. Not being sufficiently acquainted with guns, she let that thought flee from her head faster than it had entered.

They got into the car; Erik, leaving the music loud, sped away.

Sophia, still excited though confused by that unusual performance from a grown man, sat next to him in silent apprehension After a little while, as if wishing to descend down to reality, she began to employ herself in the usual manner by turning the light on to adorn her face. Erik, who already had been touched by reality, was now calm and thinking how basely human and happy they were in the careless hours of the open unguarded space of time. But he wondered if the warmth and cordiality would continue once they reached her apartment. The snugness and merry conversation they enjoyed as they were traveling towards their destination was abruptly interrupted by a burst of rain that came down from heaven as if it were ordered by some spirit with the intent to stop them from reaching the end of the two hour trip to Sophia's apartment.

It was a matter of wonder Erik thought, that he, a man almost passed the prime of his life with no great accomplishments, a mediocre income and with little chance of climbing to a much higher station in life in the near or far future, could acquire the hand and heart of such a gorgeous, young, well educated girl with all the makings to attract younger and wealthier men. A prettier face, a happier heart, a sweeter smile and a sexier body than Sophia's never walked the face of the earth, and she, with sparkling eyes, a joyous sound to her voice, a merry laugh and clever mind, could, with the nod of her head, destroy hearts and ruin lives or could have opened doors to homes for herself that men the likes of Erik Karas could only view from a tourist bus riding through her neighborhood. The situation might have been awkward, but he thought it to be enviable.

"Make a right at the next corner," said Sophia, while Erik was struggling to see through the rain.

The car rolled on to the right for one block, pulled in and stopped in a parking lot.

"That's my building, over there," said Sophia pointing and squinting her eyes to see.

"Let me pull up there to let you off. I'll park the car and I'll be right with you."

"Are you thinking of coming in?" asked Sophia.

"I have to, if I am going to cook breakfast," said Erik puzzled.

"I couldn't eat breakfast now if my life depended on it."

"I can cook lunch, late dinner, snack, anything your heart desires," said Erik, sounding almost desperate.

"I like breakfast, but in the morning. Come back in the morning and cook. I am dying to hear about when the Greeks have had enough to eat," suggested the girl in an earnest tone of voice.

"You mean you want me to leave and come back tomorrow morning to cook breakfast?"

Sophia nodded looking away.

"What am I, a traveling cook?" said Erik sarcastically.

Sophia looked at him seriously and said, " You should see your face…"

"Don't start with the dozen virgins again," interrupted Erik, " I feel like a wet cat and there isn't one drop of water on me and I see you like the cat that ate the canary. If I had another bullet in my gun I'd pull it and kill myself."

"Why? Because I don't want to have breakfast at nine o'clock at night."

"Somehow you manage to bring out the little hurt guy in me," said Erik softly.

"You, silly little boy, I wouldn't miss showing you my apartment for the world," murmured the girl while stroking his face gently.

"I wouldn't miss seeing your apartment for the world."

"Then you might as well come up."

Erik turned and paused with a smile which he abandoned after she bestowed a wink and a wider smile.

"Let me park the car," he said, shifting gears and preparing to move the car.

"Aren't you going to let me out? I'll wait for you under the canopy."

"No! You show me where to park the car. Besides, a bird in the hand is better than two in the bush. You're my bird and you are in my hand now," said Erik, allowing the car to move slowly ahead.

"I thought I was your sitting duck"

Erik looked at her, smiled, drove away and parked the car within sight of her apartment's window as she indicated to him.

"Stay here!" said Erik, rushing to the back of the car. Opening the trunk, he pulled out a beige raincoat. He came around, opened her door and as soon as she got out, threw that coat over her, covering her head, and together they headed towards the door.

She thought that there was nothing that could subdue the native politeness evidenced in that assistance. They both ran, keeping at their top running speed to escape the rain, until they reached the glass double doors of the building. Without any further ceremony she led the way to an elevator that was waiting with the door open.

Sophia knew that she had allowed herself to reach the unalterable point of no return. The apartment door was but a few steps from the elevator. She led the way in silence and he followed her with uneasy and cautious steps. When the door opened she gestured for Erik to proceed before her; he entered and glanced around for a split second then paused as she came from behind him, embracing him and kissing his neck.

"This is where I live," said Sophia softly.

"I must admit this does resemble the heaven I've seen in my

dreams," said Erik softly.

Sophia kissed his neck again without uttering a word.

"This is heaven because I feel an angel's touch," said Erik in the same tone, reaching behind him, taking her by the arms and bringing her before him," isn't it?"

She gazed up at him with sober eyes and said in a caressing voice, "Erik, tell me what do you want from me?"

That question was posed with an expressive look on her face and a tender sound in her voice, but Erik looked as if he had suddenly found himself under a cloud of sadness. Whatever reply Erik might have had entertained in his mind never came to pass because it was speedily diverted by Sophia, thinking that she might have pressed him into an uncomfortable position, she abruptly said, "can I make some coffee?"

Not making an attempt to undo herself from his arms.

"Don't you want to hear the answer to your question?"

"Don't embarrass me, Erik," said Sophia shyly.

"When a girl meets a boy she has three things in mind: love, security and eventually marriage. When a boy meets a girl he only has one thing in mind and that is to take her to bed," said Erik

Sophia looked at Erik without a sign of any thought or judgment.

"Now can I make some coffee?" she asked, as if to avoid any acknowledgement of or comment on his answer.

"Do you have to leave my arms to make coffee?"

"No! We can go to the kitchen together like Siamese twins."

"Go! I'll wait for you, then," said Erik, turning her around to the direction of the kitchen and giving her a gentle push. Sophia bestowing upon him one of her sweetest smiles, walked gracefully away from him, leaving him in the state of admiration of her charms, both physical and mental. In her absence he carefully studied the apartment and found it interesting that nothing was scattered about. Everything was in a perfect order and the white carpet looked as if it hadn't ever been stepped on. He sat on a comfortable chair, one that matched the pale green couch. He got up again and tried another chair. He could tell that Sophia was well acquainted with domestic duties and she did everything with an admirable regulation. Cleanliness and order reigned supreme throughout the apartment, or as much of the apartment as could be seen from where he was sitting in proper posture, as if he were about to have a photo portrait taken. He noticed that there were several pictures and portraits of family and friends carefully placed on the off-white walls at eye level. Two round glass lamp tables with brass stands matched the coffee table. At last his train of thought was interrupted by Sophia's entrance. She carefully carried a silver tray laden with coffee, cookies and water and cautiously placed it on the coffee table very close to Erik. Due to the curious arrangement of the furniture and the station in which Erik chose to position himself, the only way left for Sophia to apply the last touch to the tray and its contents was for her to bend forward, but that bending caused her skirt to be raised an ample distance above the back of her knees and her buttocks to extend out pointing at Erik, a view for which he had no qualms.

"How do you like it?" asked Sophia, still bending forward.

"I love it," said Erik, staring at her backend with a countenance greatly mollified by that unexpected presentation.

"Everybody who has seen it loves it."

"That I believe, " responded Erik altering neither his glance nor the expression on his face.

"Do you want to buy it?"

"Is it for sale?"

"Everything is for sale at the right price,"

"Everything?" asked Erik, astonished and very much perplexed by Sophia's statement.

"Well, almost everything."

"What do you like about it?" asked Sophia still occupied with the tray.

"It's nice and round," uttered Erik, smiling again. Sophia straightened herself up, turned and looked at Erik without the smile on her face one might have expected.

"Round? You said ? This room is not round," then, after what seemed to be a brief meditation, she burst into loud laughter.

"Oh! My God "declared Sophia covering her mouth. Then she stared at him for one long moment. "It's round, you said?'

"Nice and round I said," corrected Erik.

"Are you trying to be a wise-ass guy? First I must tell you that

I live all alone and certain habits I've developed because there is no one to see me, second I must get even with you," said the girl approaching him with a theatrical pose, in a conspicuous and positive manner, implying she was set to strike at a moment's notice. "I was asking you about my apartment and you were looking at my butt."

"I'm bad," said Erik, laughing loudly while raising his arms to protect his face in case of an attack, "it's my fault that I couldn't see the forest for the tree. The beautiful tree."

"I still find you to be arrogant, egotistical, obnoxious and selfish," said the girl in a suggestive tone with her mouth close to his and her hands around his face and neck.

"Does that mean...?"

"Shh.... Don't say it..." whispered Sophia, sitting on his lap and kissing him softly at first then grabbing his hair with both hands she began to kiss him passionately.

He threw his arms around her, picked her up and effortlessly carried her into the bedroom where he placed her on the bed without interrupting their kiss. Once he was sure that she was comfortably positioned on the double bed and feeling the passion and will of a woman yearning to be possessed, his right hand began to unbutton her blouse then his lips slid down her neck and stopped when they touched her right breast. Suddenly a vivid flash of lighting brightened the ill lit room, it was followed by a peel of thunder that crashed and shook the building to its core, then another flash of lightning followed with another thunder louder than the first and then down came the rain; the two lovers forced by desire and empowered by nature's madness struggled to conquer one another. There was pure silence, except for the roaring echo of the thunder as it faded to the distance, tender moaning from both lovers and Sophia's breathless gasps that set the pace for their lovemaking.

At that very moment, in another town not too far from that lovers battle field, Randy, Erik's little son, awakened by the lightning and thunder and terrified by those sights and sounds got up and rushed into his mother's and father's bedroom. Finding no one there he screamed in a high-pitched voice and ran into the living room where Susan, Erik's wife, was lying on the couch. She jumped up and grabbed her little boy who flew into her arms still screaming.

"It's only thunder. Don't be afraid, honey" said Susan, drying his tears with a handkerchief that looked like it was used not too long before for the same purpose.

"I'm not so afraid of the thunder. I had a dream. I saw a woman coming into the house looking to kill you," cried the little boy while struggling to catch his breath.

"It was only a dream; it will go away," replied Susan soothing his face with her hand. It didn't take long for the youngster to fall asleep again. She picked her son up and took him into his bedroom where she tucked him in with care and adoration. She then went back to the living room and sat on the couch. In her agonies of rationalizing her husband's attitude and absence, she looked sometimes at the carpet, sometimes at the ceiling, sometimes at the wall; when neither the carpet, the ceiling, nor the wall, offered her any consolation or any small bit of inspiration, she got up, went to and stood looking out of the window. She saw the rain shinning in the light like long silver needles hitting the ground and breaking into small pieces that jumped in different directions before hiding under the grass. Her heart found home when she saw a pair of headlights pulling into the driveway, but her heart sank and then accelerated when she noticed that two men came out of the car and ran towards her door. She rushed to open the door with a horrified look on her face.

"Something happened to my husband," she cried out.

"No!" said one of the men fixing a grin on his face to make her feel better, seeing the terrifying look on hers. Soon after she heard the message she backed off and gestured the two men to come in. She leaned against the wall, still holding on the doorknob, closed her eyes and took a deep breath.

"We are the police," said one of the officers still wearing a pleasant grin.

"I know." said the lady of the house walking towards the easy chair. "I saw your car with the light on the top. Sit down please," suggested Susan, taking a seat for herself.

"No, thank you ma'am. I assume your husband is not here."

"No! He is out," replied Susan without much emphasis on her statement.

"We received a report from the Tuckerton police that a man

driving your husband's car pulled over on the shoulder of the road and fired a pistol in the air. Someone saw him, took his license plate number and called the police."

"It sounds like my husband. He gets into some kind of weird mood when he listens to Greek music and fires his pistol. He has a recreational permit to carry one. He is an expert with the pistol."

"We know," replied the officer.

"Did he break any law?" asked Susan with a little more life in her question.

"No, ma'am. It's not against the law to fire a gun in the forest," replied the same officer.

"We don't know that, Mrs. Karas," interjected the other officer who was heavy and a lot shorter than the other, "you see, ma'am, I know your husband,"

"Then you should know that my husband never breaks the law," added Susan, with a more definite tone in her voice.

"Did he ever threaten you with the gun?" asked the fat officer, disregarding her statement.

"No!" declared Susan showing traces of agitation on her face and in her voice.

"Did he ever threaten anyone else, that you know of?" persisted the officer, determined to investigate the matter to its very bottom.

"No!" She said sternly.

"Did he ever hit you with his hand or something else?"

"Officer what is you name?" asked Susan, waiting to hear his name.

"Officer O'Rielly. Did he ever hit you?" asked the officer again, oblivious to her feelings and visible agitation.

"Did I ever call the police for help," snapped the wife smartly.

"That doesn't mean anything, ma'am. Sometimes when American women marry foreigners they suffer from physical violence by their husbands, because those people have different ideas about women."

"O'Reilly!" warned the other officer. "Let's go!"

"Shut up, Gary, this is my case!" said O'Reilly, looking into the other officer's eyes with a poisonous look on his. "Where were you, ma'am, about two hours ago?" inquired the fat officer, standing with his legs far apart and shifting his weight from one to the other, as was his habit.

The wife remained speechless though visibly angered.

O'Reilly threw his eyes around the room aimlessly, then turned to her and gazed upon her with a grin. "It has been reported that your husband was accompanied by a woman,"

"What do you mean by this, officer O'Reilly?" demanded the wife with great indignation and rapidity in her speech. "Now I know what your problem is. You are a chauvinist. I don't like you, officer O'Reilly; I don't dislike you because you are bald and fat. I don't like your character or your attitude. You are exactly what American people hate about policemen. Now you heard it from an American, who is paying your salary. And I wish you would leave at once, before I ask this officer to take you in on a citizen's arrest based on the complaint that I'm about to file against you for harassment. Do you hear me, O'Reilly?" screamed Susan, bursting with anger.

"Let's go! O'Reilly," demanded the other officer taking O'Reilly by the arm.

"Leave me alone!" hissed O'Reilly, feeing his arm with a forceful movement, and walking away slowly enveloped in visible frustration.

The tall officer followed but when he reached the door, stopped, turned and said with a sincere smile. "Ma'am, you are a good woman. I like the way you defended your husband."

Susan only nodded and locked the door when both officers were in their car. She threw herself on the easy chair, wrapped in the contemplation of her indefinite future. Then she began to sob. She sobbed violently and wiped the tears off softly with the same handkerchief she used to wipe her son's tears earlier. She carried out that feat with sadness and dexterity. Then she leaned back, tilted her head to the left, sighed deeply and closed her eyes, striving to steer herself through that turbulent sea of reality, with an empty chart once drawn by dreams.

The birth of a new day glimmered in the sky while the rain continued coming down, pounding on Erik's car, that was parked outside the apartment building where it was left the night before.

Erik lay in bed, his eyes open and directed towards heaven with Sophia next to him, her head on his upper arm. He felt the guilt of betrayal. He felt he was a wretched man and wished he could get down on his knees and ask God to admonish him for his horrible sin. He would promise a forever devotion to his wife and child, and ask that his hatred of himself be undying and inextinguishable and haunt him through all his life, if he could only find peace of mind at that terrible moment. He heard the thick drops of rain pecking on the window as if trying to get in and saw flashes of lightning filling the room with cold unflattering fire.

Then he remembered having a dream while sleeping in the arms of the girl. He dreamed that he was traveling the high seas in a boat with people that he didn't know. Suddenly the sea turned into an angry mass of roaring water. Huge waves burst onto the deck from all sides and every minute a wave would jump on board, on its way out dragging somebody overboard as if to feed the fuming and hungry sea beneath the ship. The sails fluttered in ribbons and the boat was going downwards fast and coming up slowly with the bilge filling with foaming seawater. The boat toiled and labored in the howling storm. He was the captain but had lost control of the ship. In the midst of the turbulent sea's rage, an enormous wave struck the vessel on it's stern. That loud crash, in his dream, caused Erik to wake up and lie there next to a stranger, listening to the thunders roaring one after the other, echoing and re-echoing as if one were chasing another that other strove to elude its grasp. He stirred, trying carefully to maneuver himself away from the girl without disturbing her.

Although Erik was not one of the most modest and delicate minded of mortals, to exhibit his naked body to the young girl, even though he knew she was asleep and had made love with him a few hours earlier, was not one of his favorite performances. He suddenly stood up, tip toed into the bathroom where he opened the shower door and got underneath the water. He scrubbed himself vigorously in one last attempt to wash away his sins. It was not unusual for Erik to spend the night away from his home, in some other female's bed, but this time there was something unusual about it for him. The recollection of the marriage vows he had made to his wife never left him for a moment. Scenes were created and recreated before his eyes; one event followed another and all were connected in some way to the girl that he had spent the night with. He finally came out of the bathroom dressed, carrying his shoes in his hands with his suit jacket over one arm, heading quietly for the door when he heard,

"You are married aren't you?" said the girl who had awoken and evidently was waiting for him, as they had planned the night before, to make breakfast.

Startled by that unexpected sound, Erik dropped both of his shoes on his toes with a crash and went quietly and slowly to sit next to her on the edge of the bed, looking devoured by her question.

"How did you arrive at that delightful conclusion?' asked Erik, pushing her hair back caringly.

"Where would a free and single man go at 6 o'clock on Sunday morning?" said Sophia softly and sullenly.

"Church?" answered Erik, hoping that statement would plant a smile in the girl's heart and on her face.

"Oh, yes, you are as religious as I am an angel," responded the girl, turning her face away from him and pushing his arm away from her face, "Now you are leaving. Will I see you again?" asked the girl as she turned to face him once more, but now with a tear in her eye.

Erik, seeing the tears on her face and feeling her pain, spoke softly, almost in a singing voice, as if to avoid answering the question directly, that being Erik's style. "If ever I would leave you, it wouldn't be in summer..."

"Don't play mind games with me, Erik!" interrupted the girl, sitting upright and pulling up the front of her pink nightgown, as decent girls often do to cover their breasts. From the expression on her face and the look in her eyes, it became apparent Sophia was not desirous of undergoing an additional trial of patience, realizing that the man she had spent the night with was concealing his past and now was making a joke of her feelings.

Erik, who had a good notion of his eloquence, paused for a reply. But her words '**mind games**' captured his thoughts and he said very soothingly. "In America love is a game. In Germany it's a duty. In France it's an art, in Greece, my dear lady, love is a tragedy.

Hearing that delivery of words, Sophia raised herself to a full sitting position, disregarding the drape of her gown and the exposure of her breasts.

"Let me tell you something, smart ass, love in America is not a game. A woman in America gives her body to a man for his love. Last night I gave you my body and today you give me cheap Greek philosophy." At the end of her outburst, she raised her right hand and slapped Erik across his face.

Erik involuntarily stood up, shrank back a pace or two and stood still, gazing wide-eyed on the unexpected scene before him, remaining perfectly motionless from amazement and confusion. Hoping to smooth matters between the angry girl and himself, he broke into a forced smile, trying to put an end to that embarrassing and distasteful incident. "I'll shoot you!" screamed the girl, rising from the bed and charging against Erik. She pounded on his chest with speed and strength that was fueled by the scorn and wrath that is normal in enraged females, and then, twining her hands in his black hair, tore out enough to make a toupee. Erik stood there, taking the pounding like a horse in the rain, knowing neither what to do nor where to go. He kept his eyes closed, not wanting to see the fire and hate in her eyes where love had peaked and preened only a few hours earlier, now believing that the worse kind of hate is the one that starts as love.

Having completed the punishment she staggered back and, being a woman of both high emotions and delicate feelings, instantly fell on the bed, face down, sobbing violently. Erik knew that the worst kind of pain is the one that comes from a broken heart and shattered dream, and he thought how lucky are the ones who have never loved and never lost.

"I don't know what to say," said Erik, approaching and standing close to her, still holding his coat over his arm and his shoes still in the middle of the floor. He reached out with the intention of touching her face, but since her face was sunk into the bed covers, he stroked her hair.

"Get out of here, Erik, before I shoot you," growled Sophia, feeling his hand on her hair. She stood up and with her distorted face pointed at Erik; "Get out!" she screamed in a loud piercing shriek, then darted for the door. She opened the door and holding it open, waited for him to get out.

"Last night I was a Greek god, today I am a goddamned Greek. That is the way the world turns," said Erik in defeat and distress as he walked towards his shoes, and trying to save time, put on his coat as he walked along. When he bent over to gather his shoes, the girl came upon him from the other side, shoved him into the hallway and locked and bolted the door behind him while his shoes remained inside on the floor. She then leaned her head back on the door; streams of tears ran down her cheeks. She shortly noticed the shoes, but did nothing about them, thinking that she was at least imparting some unpleasantness upon him.

Whatever grounds Erik might have had to feel relieved in escaping that awkward situation were quickly overcome when he found his present position by no means better. He was standing out there, wanting to go home, hearing the rain coming down and he was with no shoes. Because of the rain it was still dark outside; he thought that going out in the dark he could very well step on something sharp and cut his feet to ribbons. To knock on the door asking for his shoes was a difficult decision, remembering the fury on her face and recalling the words 'Get out of here or I'll shoot you.' He knew and feared that he stood a very good chance of being shot or perhaps killed by some other weapon, but the worst would have been the tale that she would tell the world afterwards that it was in self defense and that he was a stalker. That he thought was not a very dignified way to leave this earth. His horror was suddenly converted into an uncertain joy, when he heard a knock coming from the other side of the door.

"Erik?" sounded the girl from behind the door.

"Yes?" He replied dimly.

"Do you believe in God, Erik?"

"Right now to me He is like a cop; where is he when you need one?" declared Erik softly.

"Can't you ever give a straight answer, Erik?" asked the girl a little louder.

"That's the best I can do for now and from here; standing in front of your door like a pauper begging you for a pair of shoes."

"I pray to God, that I will never become another sitting duck for a one-night stand for anyone. And for you, my love, I will pray to God that you have a nice life."

"Sophia?" said Erik, placing his ear against the door and listening for a reply. He heard nothing. "Sophia!" he repeated with a light knock on the door. He still heard nothing. He then realized the anger was rapidly teaming up with revenge. He had no other option but to go on. Chancing all sufferings, he went away like a kicked dog with his tail between his legs and bare-footed, running like one, stepping in water in some places, mud in others; he didn't stop until he was in his car. There he sat, shivering from the cold water on his feet and the chilling rain on his back. He looked up and saw her standing by the window, looking more like a phantom than the beautiful creature he had seen and held for the last fourteen hours in their brief existence together. He then looked in the mirror and on seeing himself, said with clenched teeth, "God, do I hate you!"

CHAPTER 5

The tragedy

In retrospect, he thought that even if his character appeared to be flawed, the love and the deep devotion he had for members of the opposite sex should plead some slight excuse for his performance. It is to be noted that every self-respecting traitor should have a favorable mind for rationalizing, and whether Erik was born with this type of mind or acquired it while still in the cradle, is unknown. He thought that women were like stunning scented flowers whose beauties and fragrances were to be enjoyed by those who loved and cherished them. If some women had taken the love and admiration he had for them as being captured and conquered, it was entirely their problem and they had to deal with it. Erik, not allowing himself to sit and listen to any more critical opinions of himself and without any further reflections on passion, started his car, hastily left the area and sped down the road heading for his home, where he thought there was an abundance of love but very little compassion and understanding. For now, he thought, he could try to live with one and without the other. He also knew that once he reached his home he was destined to undergo another trial of character examination, then prosecution promptly followed by an execution and he would be wholly unable to plead any justification, having been convinced that he was as wrong as a left shoe on a right foot and, thinking of shoes, where was the explanation for the absence of his? No matter what would be the outcome of that trial, which was approaching as fast as the car was rolling though that non-stop rain, he would be satisfied to be found guilty of a breach of the promises of marriage and would accept the judge's and the plaintiff's, one in the same- his wife's, decision on whatever punishment was to be passed down to him. An anxious half hour had passed since he left Sophia's apartment thought Erik, as he looked at the car clock. He comprehended that he was approaching his destiny fast and surely. In Erik's head were not only the trouble that was waiting for him ahead at home but also the disaster that he left behind. There was no punishment to fit his crime, because any punishment that would be imposed on him would be punishing the plaintiff simultaneously. He thought the only thing he rightly deserved at this time was pity. Have some pity for Erik Karas, he thought. Have some pity for the man who wants love, romance, understanding and compassion in a world such as this. Pity for him, pity for wanting it all instead of settling and accepting what was available at hand and trying to live from day to day, like most of the men in this world do. Pity he should be given, pity garnished with a good dose of contempt.

Arriving home, Erik drove into the driveway, parked the car and, without shoes but with plenty of apprehension, ran into the house.

He closed the door behind him very carefully and stood still in the middle of the living room. He was soaked from the top of his head to the bottom of his rolled up pants. He really looked like someone who was far too occupied with his pursuits to take any great notice of or regard for his personal appearance.

These tokens of Erik's appearance were not lost on his son, who burst out of the kitchen and ran to greet his father but stopped when he came near him, noticing the deplorable condition he was in. "Daddy! Daddy! You look wet and awful. What happened to you? Mommy! Daddy is here," yelled the little boy with as much keenness as surprise. "Don't worry, Daddy, you have more shoes and you have other clothes that are not wet. Everything will be alright, Daddy."

Erik didn't move a muscle but looked inattentively down at Randy for a moment and with the same thoughtless look on his face took off his coat and placed it on the chair near where he was standing.

Susan walked slowly from the kitchen into the living room and looked at Erik. All the quarrels, all the ill will and bad blood rose to her face and planted themselves in such a distasteful and distrustful visage that any husband on this earth would kill to avoid seeing it.

"You should see yourself," said Susan, in the condescending tone that ordinary folks use on little people.

Erik stood with both bare feet planted firmly on the carpet.

"You will be okay, Daddy, once you dry off," said the little boy as he took Erik's jacket and half dragged it across the room looking for a place to hang it. Erik totally disregarded the reassuring words of his son, and finding it was of no use to discuss anything with his wife, headed for the bedroom in silence and distress like a wet cat.

The little boy went to the closet holding his father's coat with both hands and jumping a few inches off the floor with both feet while nailing his attention on the revolver with both eyes, tried to hang up the coat with a determined look on his face. "Daddy, I can't hang up your coat," yelled the little boy, looking around for help. The father entered from the bedroom wearing fresh clothes, took the jacket from the boy, hung it and then walked towards the kitchen.

The little boy stayed behind, his eyes still nailed on the gun. "How many years will it take for me to grow tall enough to hang up your coat?"

"Months not years. Only a few months," responded the man of the house on his way into the kitchen.

The little boy patted the gun as he bid it good-bye and then he too went into the kitchen.

"Daddy, did you bring me a toy?"

"I always bring something for my little guy," remarked the father getting closer to the mother.

"When can I have it?" asked the little boy, sitting down with a bowl of dry cereal in front of him.

Susan was standing by the kitchen window looking outside and listening to the pouring rain.

"If I say I'm sorry about yesterday would that be enough for you to talk to me or must we have a cold war that will go on for days?" asked Erik standing behind her, close enough to touch her.

"I have no intentions of carrying on a cold war," said Susan abruptly; she hastily went out of the kitchen and into the living room resuming her stance by the window.

Randy's ears perked and his eyes opened wide with alarm seeing his parents' disposition.

Susan would have said much more but her voice was heard to be breaking during the utterance of her last words as if grief were choking her.

Erik appeared struck by the way and the tone in which those words were dispensed. He walked over and stood in the living room staring at Susan's back for a long moment before moving near her, reaching out to touch her hair. Susan, feeling his approach, slid away and went back into the kitchen.

The moment Susan walked into the kitchen and stood by the window, the boy looked at her and seeing the apathy on her face figured the coast was clear to take another look at the gun and went straight to the closet where the coat was hanging.

He took the gun from the pocket and looked at it. Realizing that it was the real thing and being overcome by fear, he put it back quickly and turned to his father who was still standing by the window looking out,

"Can I have my toy now, Daddy?' asked the boy, approaching his father carefully, stopping by his side and looking up at him.

Whatever displeasing thoughts circulated in Erik's head were quickly abstracted by the boy's voice. His face relaxed as he looked down at his son. He took his son by the hand and guided him to the light green couch and gestured for the boy to sit down.

The boy sat there with a happy face looking up at his father. Whether he thought that his father was about to hand over a toy, or if he anticipated a hearty talk with his father, as he often enjoyed, it is not known.

"Do you love me?" asked Erik, kneeling in front of the boy.

"Yes, Daddy," replied the little fellow, smiling and slapping his lap with both hands.

"You know, Randy, Mommy and I love you too," said the father, caressing the boy's hair with his right hand, and laying his left hand gently and compassionately on his arm. "Don't pay too much attention to the way your Mommy and I fight. We don't fight very often. You know that," said the father soothingly.

"But why do you fight?" asked the boy in a low and timid voice.

"Oh, because I make some stupid mistakes sometimes."

"But Mommy tells everybody that you are very smart."

"Yea! I'm a genius," muttered Erik, removing his eyes from the youngster for a moment. "No matter how smart one is, he can make mistakes if he is not thinking right."

"Daddy, will I fight with my wife, when I get one?" asked the boy a little louder.

"Of course, you will if you love your wife and you care what she says or thinks. Now, go into the kitchen and eat and when you are finished I'll give you your toy," directed the father, helping the boy up from the couch and tapping him on his back. The boy left, pleased as if they had struck a bargain.

"Daddy?" asked little Randy, stopping by the door to ask something else, "Where were you last night?"

"I was out of town working. Go have your breakfast," urged the father without taking anytime to consider a better answer.

"Daddy!"

"Yes, Randy."

"Can I go with you out of town next time?"

"Yes."

"That should be an interesting sight to see," interjected Susan who was in the kitchen preparing breakfast.

The boy took his chair, searched with his eyes around the table and pretended that he didn't hear his mother's remark.

"Maybe we should both go to hear your father's sales pitch," spouted Susan, directing that statement to her son, but by the way it was delivered it was really intended for her husband to hear.

Having heard that unnecessary remark and understanding that the cold war was about to turn into a hot battle, Erik entered the kitchen slowly, stood by the door and waited to hear the follow up, knowing that there had to be one.

"Breakfast is waiting," announced Susan still not looking at her husband.

"Husband on one side, wife on the other and son in the middle, a beautiful view and wonderful accommodations too," noted Erik.

"It's a unique observation, " responded Susan.

They sat down to breakfast, but it was evident, regardless of the husband's satirical comment, the wife was harboring considerable anxiety within her chest.

"Why don't you ask your father to tell you where he really was last night," said Susan with heated sarcasm, "Why don't you?"

"Why don't you shut up?" retorted Erik immediately and softly, digging into his food.

"Never! I will never shut up from now on as I has been doing," returned Susan loudly with greater energy, now standing up and looking hard at her husband.

"You have no idea when to talk and when to shut up, do you?" said the husband, still softly.

"I may have formed some new ideas about the subject. Last night, I had a whole night filled with thoughts and I want to share them with you now," snapped Susan, besieged with agitation.

"Then I should feel most obliged to you, for any advice that you may come up with," said Erik, with the profound solemnity that few men could muster during situations like these. "But, my lady, could this wait till after breakfast, away from small ears and small eyes?"

"Oh, Erik, you have such a way with words," said Susan after a long moment's silence. She suddenly darted out of the kitchen and into the living room.

Erik, looking at the boy who was eating his cereal and appearing to have turned a deaf ear to the whole scene, took a few more bites of the food his wife had prepared, stood up, stroked the boy's hair and went out of the kitchen into living room where Susan was standing by the window, looking out with her arms folded before her. Erik neared her and looked outside in the same manner as she did. They both remained for some time absorbed in their own meditations, while their boy, in the kitchen mechanically eating his breakfast, cast an anxious look from time to time towards the living room, disturbed by inward misgivings regarding his parents' arguments.

The sky was gray; the rain pounded on the roof of the house and hammered violently on the bushes and flowers setting an uneasy mood in Susan's heart.

"Why Erik? Why are you punishing me? What sin am I guilty of? What have I done to you so terrible to deserve such punishment from you, Erik?" cried Susan, turning around to display a thousand drops of tears rolling down her face and over her quivering lips; with trembling uncontrollable hands she attempted to wipe them away.

"Susan," said the husband reaching out to touch her.

"No! Please Erik," said Susan, turning her face and her body away. "Please, tell me Erik, is spending one night with a strange woman worth killing me? Why don't you take that pistol you always carry and shoot me, Erik? Stop my suffering. Please do that for me. I want to die, Erik, don't you understand that? Didn't you ever think of my dying rather than suffering the way I do? I don't have the courage to do it myself, Erik. You do it for me. I am already dead inside. All my dreams have turned into nightmares and now even they are gone and I am left without any good or bad feelings. Since I lost the dream of waking up in the morning and looking at my husband and believing that he loves me, I don't wish to live anymore. You loved me once, I know you did"

"I still love you," asserted the husband taking her in his arms and wiping the tears off her face, looking at her through his own tears.

"Please Erik tell me why you stopped loving me," she pleaded with a shattered voice.

"I haven't stopped loving you, sweetheart," insisted Erik, trying to make her believe it.

"Is it because I'm a burden on you, Erik?" Susan went on, as if she heard nothing of what he said.

The boy, listening to his mother crying and hearing his father pleading with her, got down from his chair and stood for a long moment looking like a distressed grown up then went out of the kitchen.

"Erik, I have always tried to make you happy. I did. I always have done what was expected of me. Tell me if it's not true."

"Honey, you are my life," whispered Erik caressing her doleful face.

"Let me go in the kitchen for something to wipe some of my tears away," said Susan softly as she disengaged herself from her husband's arms and went into the kitchen.

Erik without the slightest delay followed her there.

"I know I have been a burden on you, Erik," repeated the wife.

The boy stood in front of the closet listening to his mother and father arguing in the kitchen.

"I know, Erik," said the wife, turning to face her husband who had his back to the window; "I have stopped you with my nagging and my need for security from becoming someone more important than you are. I'm sorry. I'm sorry, Erik," chattered Susan; placing her face into her hands, she sobbed violently.

"You didn't stop me, honey, I stopped myself," said Erik, tenderly attempting to sooth her pain and trying to dry the tears off his wife's face with a tissue.

"I have been a chain around you neck, Erik. I know. You could have been an actor, a singer, a writer, but I stopped you. I didn't give you any support, I know it and it's eating me alive," admitted Susan.

"No! No! You are my golden chain that adorns me, sweetheart," said Erik, caressing her face. "Please listen and look at me!" said Erik, holding his wife by the shoulders. "I have neither the courage nor the heart to stand before you and confess my sins to you, but I promise you right now, that I will sin no more."

"Mom, Dad," called the boy holding the gun with both hands and pointing it at both of them.

"The gun!" screamed Susan as she darted towards the boy.

"It's empty," yelled Erik, dashing towards the boy too.

Both parents sped towards the young lad. The boy pulled the trigger and the gun didn't fire. He immediately turned the gun to himself to see why it didn't go off, closed one eye and pulled the trigger again. The parents were only inches away when they saw the gun jump in the boy's tiny hands. The gun shot explosion erupted, blood splashed on the wall and Susan shrieked like wounded wild beast and with a mother's energized rage, in an act of desperation and suffering for her child's pain, went down on the floor to break her son's fall.

Erik grabbed the boy as he was falling, let him down easily on the floor and threw the white tablecloth on his severely damaged face. The cloth was instantly soaked with blood and the little boys body was moving violently as if he were trying to stand up and then it was only trembling beneath the tablecloth. Susan, screaming, came to her feet for one short moment and then dropped herself on top of the little boy's trembling body. She threw her arms around him screaming louder, calling his name over and over.

Erik moved her away, picked the body up and placed it the on the kitchen table.

"He is still alive, Erik! My Randy is still alive. Do something,

Erik!" Susan kept screaming while Erik was holding her back.

The little boy's body stopped moving.

Susan, covered with the boy's blood, face and body, screamed when she saw that the little body had stopped moving. "Our boy is dead, Erik. He is dead, Erik." She placed her face on the bloody cloth and sobbed violently and then she said, "We have no more boy, Erik. I have no little friend anymore to talk to." saying this she went down. She fainted. Erik picked her up, carried her into the living room and opened the front door for some air to revive her. Even though she had fainted her maternal pain brought her back to her consciousness. She barely opened her eyes, and said dimly, "Sit me up, Erik." He did so and collapsing beside her, he covered his face with his hands and sobbed loudly.

Three days later, on a misty early-summer day the funeral procession mournfully rolled down the highway headed for the cemetery. From the long queue of cars one could see that the Karas family had a lot more friends than anyone could have anticipated. The grieving parents in the black limousine, their eyes sunken in their skulls, sat motionless as if the slightest move would cause their bodies to collapse. There was no figure of speech or method of communicating to describe the ache and the grief in their hearts. As the limousine continued the journey, Susan suddenly caught a glimpse of an abandoned bridge and began to sob violently sending an additional dose of anxiety into her husband's already troubled mind. He reached to touch her hand with his and gently pulled her towards him. She rested her head on his chest and slowly lifted her eyes towards the bridge again. She recollected happy times with Randy when he would coax her to lift him up so that he could better see the glistening water and sometimes the faint reflection of the two of them bending over the railing. She would point out to him the pleasure boats cruising up and down in the huge lake not far from the bridge. As the youngster became more familiar with the setting, he would gather twigs, drop them in the river's flowing waters then run to the other side of the bridge to watch them drift downward and eventually disappear in the tumultuous lake.

She recollected his light heart, his merry laugh and his sparkling eyes looking at her for approval and applause for what he had done.

Sometimes the father, taking off a few hours from his job, would join them. They used to gaze upon their only child and feel each other's cheerful hearts, happiness, hopes and dreams. She recollected one time, that she was reading a book while leaning on the guardrail of that unused bridge and Randy went to the side of the bridge, stuck his head through the rails and leaned outwards as far as he could without overbalancing himself, endeavoring with great perseverance, to spit on the twigs he had dropped on the other side of the bridge. Besieged by fear she screamed, ran and pulled him gently by the seat of his short pants. The young boy brought in his head and shoulders with absolute swiftness, stood back, looked at his mother's panic-stricken face and laughed with a full heart. She knew that she would never forget his bare knees and belly laughs. She remembered how she and her young companion had sat at the bridge watching the patient fishermen in their very tiny boats let the hours go by without a yank or a bite from the inhabitants beneath the rolling waters. Realizing that those pleasant events would never come again, she felt frail, disheartened and looked as if she were sinking, weighted down by the combined effects of physical illness and the mental torment brought on by her son's untimely death.

The entire caravan of over thirty vehicles followed the hearse as it passed through the double-gated entrance to the cemetery, under an arched sign **SUNSET CEMETARY** that welcomed the visitors.

The motorcade was directed by a cemetery official pointing to the location of the grave. The cars parked along the winding cemetery road and the hearse, flower car and limousine stopped close to the little boy's final place of rest.

First, all the flowers were unloaded and carefully arranged around the grave by four somber individuals. Susan stepped from the limousine, dressed completely in black with a black veil pulled covering her face, walked on slowly with her head down and with her right arm in Erik's left, leaning on him. The doors of all the other cars opened almost simultaneously and the mourners poured out heading for the grave. They approached and stationed themselves close to where Susan sat on a chair. The people that had gone to witness the burial of the little boy gathered around and stood still by the gravesite.

The little coffin was borne slowly forward on the shoulders of six men. A dead silence soaked the mourning crowd broken only by birds' caroling, audible lamentations of some women and the shuffling steps of the bearers on the grass. They carefully and slowly placed the coffin near the grave.

The priest, from Holy Trinity Greek Orthodox Church, accompanied by a cantor and an alter boy assumed their places at the grave. He held the Holy Bible close to his chest with his left hand and from his right hung the censer with burning incense. He began the Service of the Burial with reverence and homage, chanting and swinging the censer back and forth in front of him while revolving to face the mourners. From time to time he handed the censer to the alter boy freeing his right hand to cross himself as well as to bless the people with the sign of the cross. The alter boy stood attentively for fear of missing the cue to return the censer to the priest who, with the cantor, alternately chanted from the **Trisagion Hymn,** "Holy God, Holy and immortal have mercy on us.... **Alleluia.... alleluia.... alleluia....** As the smoke of the incense wafted up thus may our prayers ascend to heaven and be acceptable to God...."

Those of the same faith accompanied the priest in singing softly, "May his memory be in our hearts forever...Alleluia... alleluia...alleluia.... Glory be to God... Amen."

Susan reached behind her veil and with trembling hands wiped her tears while Erik glanced at her with his eyes flooded. One could see there weren't many dry eyes fixed on the little coffin. The mourners' heads bent downward their hands clasped before them. Since the eulogy was conducted in the Greek language, only those of the Greek Orthodox faith were able to understand and chant along. The priest crossed himself again, and in imitation of that, all of the mourning men, women and children followed.

The priest gestured for the censer; the boy respectfully handed it to him, kissed his hand again and shrank back one pace. The priest, swaying the censer and voicing the chant of another verse, held the last note longer than usual and threw a quick glance at the tall, well dressed cantor who was standing next to him, who gladly assented to the priest's gesture, and continued the chanting of the hymn in a voice and style that echoed as if that chanting were coming from on high, in celebration of the little boy's departure from earth and his arrival in Heaven. It was apparent that the cantor had spent his entire life making sorrowful events pleasing to the ear and implanting kind expectations in the hearts of the sad beloved ones with his voice. The priest, affected by the sound of that magnificent chanting, moved slowly over and planted himself closer to the little coffin, swinging the censer, whispering a part of the ceremony with inaudible words that had apparently come from the Holy Book and that he had learned, verbatim.

This went on for a while, the cantor singing hymns and the priest whispering prayers and swinging the censer. The priest handed back the censer to the alter boy in the manner he had done before, and the cantor finished his hymn at that very precise moment. A short silence followed that was only to be broken by the priest, who raised the Holy Book to his lips and gave it a reverent kiss. He raised the Holy Book higher than his head, looked down at the coffin and chanted, "May his memory live forever," and then raising his head high, he brought the Holy Book down, pressing it against his chest, closed his eyes and said, "Amen."

He handed the big book to the cantor who placed it behind him on a folding table that had been set up earlier. The priest, although being one of nature's most even tempered creatures and being well trained and habituated to control his emotions, took a white hand-kerchief from his pocket, removed his spectacles and wiped some tears from his eyes. He turned and faced the mourners and said in English, "I'm not accustomed to saying farewell to youngsters, so I am at a loss for words for the first time in my public life. The only thing I can say is that I pray that God may enlighten the hearts and souls of little Randy's father and mother to believe that Randy is in good hands, in God's hands," continued the priest. Turning his attention to the little coffin and taking a single rose in a God fearing way, with a trembling hand he placed it on the little coffin, "Randy, I hope some day I will come to be in the same place you already are, next to God." Then he turned and gazed at the mourners and said a little louder, "Sorrowful and sudden events such as this cause me to remember to truly be what I am, God's servant" He then slowly turned and walked over to Randy's father and mother who were sitting; he bowed to the mother. She stood up with her husband's aid, looking at the priest from behind a veil. The priest said in a very choked and weak voice. "God be with you, Mrs. Karas, as your son is with God." Having recorded his feelings with those words in an intelligible but cheerless tone, he gave Erik an awkward fleeting look, shook his hand in silence then walked away, taking out his handkerchief to wipe tears from his eyes, as the alter boy followed at his heels. The cantor, repeating the priest's presentation, as he often did by tradition, expressed his condolences in stronger and louder terms and headed the way the priest went, he too wiped away tears that he held back all through the eulogy.

After that Susan, with her husband's assistance on one side and another lady's on the other, slowly approached the little coffin that was poised to be lowered into the earth. She suddenly disengaged herself from her two helpers and ran towards the coffin, dropped herself on her knees, embraced the coffin and cried out loudly, "Randy! Randy! My baby. I don't want you to go. Don't go, Randy. What am I going to do without you, Randy?"

While the mother was wailing those sad lamentations, Erik, hearing those affecting words and not being able to endure the pain any longer, disregarded all the mourners, turned and hastily walked away until he came upon a tree a few yards away. He placed his head on the tree trunk and sobbed heartily, grasping his skull with both hands. He could still hear his wife's cries, now mingled with the weeping of others.

He remembered how their child sat patiently at his and Susan's feet for hours, listening with his little hands folded in front of him and how his thin face rose upwards to them with a smile of child-ish cheerfulness. They watched him grow bigger from day to day, while answering his many curious questions. How happy they were then, in those moments filled with the joy of his childish dreams.

He couldn't fathom that their son was gone from them forever and had moved to a final peace and place of rest. He was Randy's father and he knew his loss would sink deep in his soul. He thought that death for himself would be the only exit from this adversity and trial, but unexpectedly, at that moment, the tapping of a hand on his back brought him back to reality. It was the hand of Sophia. He turned and saw she too was dressed in black. Her eyes were sunk into a face that looked gaunt, as if wasted with famine.

"I'm sorry, Erik, I am truly sorry for the loss of your son. I only wish, I could share your pain. I wish I could lift some of the burdening pain off your heart and place it onto mine. But I must confess to you that I share a part of the guilt you are feeling," said the woman he had referred to as the 'sitting duck'. He saw her lips quivering and he heard her voice, broken.

"No, you had nothing to do with my son's death. It was my fault; it will remain within me for ever."

"Just remember, Erik, now you are passing through a storm. The storm will be over some day, hold on to anything you can, because after the storm is over, anything you held on to will be priceless and invaluable to you," said Sophia, ending her statement with the touch of an encouraging smile.

"Kind lady, I'll try my best."

"Good bye, Erik, my friend," said the girl, giving him her hand. He took it and gently rang it, then gently kissed it and let it go.

Sophia looked at her hand and the spot he had kissed then gave him another inspiring smile.

"I didn't leave any lip prints," said Erik, trying hard to smile back.

"Maybe not on my hand, but in my heart you did, Erik, have a nice life," said Sophia, turning her face away to wipe a tear from her eye with the corner of a handkerchief she was holding all along.

Without looking back at him again, she strode away hastily.

He briefly looked at her as she departed and in his crowded, tired and confused psyche found a drawer to load and lock away yet another thought of her. He thought of the character she possessed, offering sympathy and hope in his time of need when everything deserted him; without any personal profit for herself, she endeavored to bring him comfort and express true affection, those things that no wealth can purchase or power can bestow.

Sleep didn't come easy to Erik that night, or to his wife who had taken the couch in the living room. He heard her tossing and turning throughout the night and in the early hours when she visited their son's bedroom and sobbed. Erik finally fell into a state of partial unconsciousness in which the mind wanders uneasily from scene to scene, from place to place without the control of reason yet unable to divest itself of vague senses, in his case, suffering.

His mind at last anchored on something steady and solid, a dream. He dreamed that he was walking through the graveyard where his boy had just been buried. In his endeavor to find the site of the boy's grave, he ran all around the cemetery; it was very dark without a ray of light anywhere near or far. Suddenly he heard and saw a group of children jumping out of a freshly dug grave, tripping across the road looking and mocking him as they passed. Then he turned and saw half a dozen silver-headed little children crowding around him, briefly shining their piercing eyes on him. He brought his arm up before his eyes to block their brilliant glances as all the children seemed herded down and away into a grave a few yards from where he was standing, stricken with horror.

He ran to find the exit gate and was still running when he heard voices coming from the bottom of an old grave. He stopped, taking time to catch the breath that his running and horror had for the moment taken from him.

Then all sound seemed to freeze. There was no sound anywhere, not even the rustle of a leaf. The profound stillness that enveloped that solemn landscape made him question his ability to hear.

Abruptly, a million echoes of voices poured from the end of the cemetery. Those voices became louder but more distinct and gradually elevated to ethereal singing sounds, as if they were coming down from Heaven.

"Daddy! Daddy!" a lone voice echoed out from another place, but the source and the place were invisible to him and the chorus had stopped.

"Randy?" replied Erik "Randy, where are you, honey?"

"I'm here, Daddy, you can't see me."

"Why boy? Why?"

"I have no face, Daddy. I lost my face before my soul left me. I am going to Heaven Daddy. I'll be in Heaven in a little while." Then silence again returned.

Suddenly after that farewell, Erik saw a brilliant ball of illumination speeding across the cemetery a few feet off the ground; leaping over the high tombstones, it quickly disappeared in the sky.

CHAPTER 6

The collapse of the family

The dawn had already broken when Erik awoke and found himself lying full length on the bed without his wife next to him, something very unusual due to the fact he was an early riser and she was in the habit of sleeping late. Then he realized that after the burial of their son, she had chosen to sleep on the couch in the living room. At first he couldn't bring himself to believe the reality of it all, but when he heard no one in the house he was assured of the bitter truth. While lying there he thought of his wife's state of mind and distress. He assessed, in his own mind, as a token of consolation, that women, the most tender and most fragile of nature's creatures, were probably able to withstand sorrow, adversity and distress better than men, because they held in their hearts an inexhaustible running spring of affection, patience and devotion for the infants they carried and brought to life and for whom nature enables them to live longer and to be stronger survivors than men, in order to care for those new lives.

As for himself, Erik wallowed in unkind thoughts of his own selfishness, thoughtlessness and reckless behavior and felt that he had caused his family an irrevocable catastrophe. Man or God should impose harsh and continuous punishment on him, he thought. Since no man's law was broken, God alone should inflict the punishment.

He should be allowed to live to a very old age and the balance of his life should be nothing but a miserable existence from now until his last hour. He should be condemned to walk the cold, lonely, loveless and merciless streets searching for but never finding a kind eye directed his way. He should live without any hint of good in his memory, and every eye of a merry face should change and glare at him with a deep scowl of malice and ill humor as he passes. The holidays should be his loneliest days, having no one to bid a fond wish or a glad tiding to him; he should be cursed to walk alone in the snow and freezing wind only to see the cheerful lights of blazing fireplaces, to hear the loud laughs and the joyful shouts of those who gathered to wish each other the best for the holidays, to smell the many savory scents steamed up from their kitchen windows, with no one to speak to or anywhere to go, but to a desolate corner away from all eyes and ears to pass the holy nights, alone.

Finally, after a meaningless existence, his insignificant body should be found by ravenous stray dogs and torn to pieces before humans have a chance to bury it. Sentenced by those adverse thoughts and hostile feelings, he felt like a condemned man.

A quick thought came to his mind that his wife may need him, so he got out of the bed, cleaned up, dressed, and headed for the kitchen where he stood by the door. He noticed a large suitcase sitting on the floor, a long black umbrella leaning on the wall and the car keys on the table next to a cup of steaming coffee.

Susan sat there still dressed in black, looking like an altered woman; those observations suggested that she had decided to go, hoping to shake off some of her grief, to seek and find bread and shelter elsewhere. She knew it wouldn't be easy, having misplaced her confidence for the last few years with Erik, so she tried to feel as wise as she could, coaxing herself to believe what her husband told her many times before, 'the universal law was not created to stop the strong from winning but only to stop the weak from losing.'

Still standing by the door that led to the kitchen and seeing Susan in that attitude, he paused long enough to realize that another unexpected event was happening, the end of a marriage. That thought was sending a cold chill down his spine, along with the indescribable feeling of a greater loss than he could imagine. At that moment Erik thought there might be something he could do to stop the destruction of his family, what family was left. He slowly and timidly went down on his knees at Susan's feet and with a pitiful broken voice said, "You are not leaving me, sweetheart, are you?"

"It's very hard for me to leave you, Erik, but it's God's will, and you must bear it for my sake. God has taken our boy! He had a reason. He is happy now, I know Randy is in God's hands, but he is not here with me. What will I do without him Erik?"

"You must stay. Susan, you must stay here with me," pleaded the husband, as he stood up, stepped back a few paces, and running out of his last traces of hope, pulled his hair lightly with both hands as if he thought an enlightening thought would be invoked and speak out in his defense in an attempt to convince his wife to grant him another trial. He got down on his knees again, embraced her legs and added more calmly, "be yourself, be merciful, my dear wife, stay with me, I need you more than ever. Don't let all the love we felt and still feel for each other drown and die in sorrow."

"Never again, Erik, never again," she said with a string of tears running down her face, "I shall leave this dreadful place. I can't stay here another minute or I shall die."

"I'll go with you," said Erik, getting on to his feet with some enthusiasm.

"No Erik, no, my love. I have to go alone."

"No! Susan, not alone. What will I do? What am I going to do without you Susan? Where will I go?" I've burnt all my bridges behind me and if you leave me, I'll be lost. I cannot live here in this cursed house without my Randy and you. I caused God to take Randy, don't let yourself take you away from me."

"Erik," said Susan, caressing his face, "Go on! Live your life. Find another love, Erik. You must have love in your heart to live."

"How can I live? You are taking my life, how can I love? You are taking my heart. I am sorry for all the bad things I've said and done to you, my dear Susan," cried Erik sinking his face into her dress and sobbing violently.

She gazed upon his head and wiped away the teardrops that streamed plentifully from her eyes, after hearing his weeping and feeling his heart and spirit breaking.

"Erik, you said one time to me that everything in life is temporary; happiness and sadness, neither are permanent," said Susan, caressing and looking down at his hair, "please. Erik, let me go peacefully. I have no more strength to defend my actions. Don't place more guilt in my heart, God knows it's full already."

After an extended silence and thought, Erik stood up and looked down at his wife. "It's too late for us, isn't it?" exhaled Erik, with a deep sigh.

She shook her head in sullen assent and looked away to hide her emotions, seeing no further reason to plant a greater grief in his heart.

The great loss, the deep despair and the want for his wife cut fierce ravages on his face and form in those few minutes, causing his face to go deadly white and his body to stoop forward as if stricken with old age. Thoughts of desperation entered his mind and pierced his heart, bringing both to a state beyond repair. He looked at her for some long moments, not one more tear or sound of despair escaped from him. He sat on the chair and faced the bloody spot on the wall, his boy's blood, leaned his body forward, rested his arms on the table and gazed vacantly straight ahead. He was about to be left all alone in the world he thought, the world he had so many chances of clenching his teeth upon to chew, devour and enjoy so much, if it weren't for his enemies, but the worst enemy he could point his finger at was himself.

Susan stood up and walked to the window, stared out for a few moments, then walked

towards the door. She stopped and looked at Erik who had his eyes cast away from her.

Feeling her glance upon him, he turned to look at her; their flooded eyes met. They stared at each other in silence. She broke her gaze, bent down and picking up her umbrella and suitcase, walked to the front door.

He could see her from where he was sitting, standing by the door with one hand on the doorknob, the other holding the suitcase and umbrella.

She put down her suitcase and turned her eyes to him, still holding onto the doorknob; his face had already turned away. She looked up towards the clouds and then very slowly turned the door-knob, picked up the suitcase and went out of the door, closing it behind her as methodically as she had looked up.

Erik, hearing the door close and not knowing whether she left or stayed, turned hastily around, but seeing nothing, closed his eyes and kept them shut until he heard the car door slam. Shortly thereafter, he heard the car engine start and then he said lowly, "Have a nice life, Susan." Saying this and without any further thought or delay, he turned his face towards the bloody spot, placed his head in his hands, and knowing he was away from all eyes and ears, wept intensely.

He passed the whole day there without moving a hand or a foot, in silence and in desolation.

At length, Erik, displaying the most definite symptoms of having been convicted, cursed, condemned and severely sentenced, stood up and went into the bathroom. There he studied himself in the mirror, noticing the thickness of his whiskers, a testimony to the accuracy of his state of mind, but caring not about his personal appearance in this sad hour of his life, out of habit splashed cold water on his face, combed his hair and strapped on the holster holding his gun and having checked its readiness, walked into the living room. The front door flew open and the big stomach of officer O'Reilly appeared, closely followed by his face and the rest of his body. The officer stood there staring with a calm eye and a fixed grin, switching his weight from one leg to the other, as he often did, in a steady and certain way.

"Are you okay, Mr. Karas?' asked the officer.

"I'm okay, officer O'Reilly," replied Erik, in a tone thick with ferocity. " I'm fine, sir."

"Oh, very well," said the officer advancing a few paces.

"I believe there is no man anywhere who can say that I am not alright," said Erik, placing his revolver into its holster.

"I understand, sir."

"State you business, O'Reilly and then get the hell out of here."

"Oh, are you going to shoot me, too?" said the fat officer, raising his eyebrow.

"O'Reilly, never mess around with a man who has nothing left to lose," said Erik, advancing a few steps towards the officer whose face was beginning to pale.

"Are you threatening me, sir?" interposed the fat man, in a voice that rattled in his throat.

"No, I'm advising you, sir; I'm only giving you friendly advice," said Erik, turning and walking away from him.

"In my opinion, sir," said the officer, now speaking a little louder and unbuttoning his coat to show his armor, "it was not an accident."

"I don't really give a shit about your opinion," said Erik, suddenly turning around sharply and imparting a blow that hit the officer under the chin with such unerring aim and force the officer tripped backwards. First his body, then his feet hesitantly followed as he fell back with a part of his rear end landing on the floor and the rest on the couch.

Upon this, Erik rushed to him and jerking out his revolver planted it on the officer's temple.

"You thought I was crazy before, now you have the chance to really see me. I told you, don't screw around with a man who has nothing to lose! There is an unwritten rule of nature's way that a man who has come to lose his friends, home and happiness acquires the freedom to behave recklessly. In plain English, he doesn't give a shit about anything. Do you understand O'Reilly?" uttered Erik, pressing the gun harder into the fat man's face, "and if I were a stray dog, dying alone in some ditch in the woods, I couldn't be more forgotten or unheeded than I am now. I am a dead man, dead to all and to myself."

The excitement that had cast an irate look on Erik's face while he spoke subsided as he concluded, and then he suddenly yanked the revolver back from the officer's face and shoved it into its holster.

The fat officer, coming to his feet with great difficulty, massaged his face and chin where he had been hit and where the gun had left an imprint.

Following their confrontation they stood and fixed on one another. The officer was obviously affected and the two men stared at each other, not with ferocity or contempt, but with discernable signs of sympathy and misery that spoke more of their feelings and their state of mind than two hours of verbal explanation could have.

"I want to tell you, off the record, that I came here of my own accord and more or less to warn you."

"Warn me?" interrupted Erik loudly with indignation, not necessarily directed at the officer but at the idea and whoever was behind it.

"Wait!" said the officer, raising his hand as to be allowed to continue with his appeal. "This is a lousy world we live in, take it from me, because I am right smack in the middle of it. Half of the people are breaking down the doors to get in jail, the other half are being pushed out by Captain Benson. Your wife was questioned, as you well know, just like you were, but with her Benson was trying hard to put words in her mouth. He has no case against you. He can't make one, but he can make your life miserable, because he is miserable. God, I know what you are going through. Forgive me for approaching you so recklessly; I wanted to make one last attempt to verify the truth that I already know." said the officer. "Go with God! Erik, forgive me for what I have done to you," said the officer, endeavoring to discharge his true feelings in an upright manner and giving him his hand to shake. While his hand was in Erik's he added, "Erik, find a reason to live, because there is no prize for dying." Saying this, the officer, acting in an honest spirit, turned as fast as his fat body allowed him to and headed for the door. There he stopped and turned once more, this time only twisting his head. He looked benignly at Erik and said, "I'll take care of the rest. Go before tomorrow morning, Erik! A reason to live is better than a prize for dying." Thus repeating his statement, officer O'Reilly turned away again, fixed his gun belt and hat with great precision and left abruptly, closing the door behind him.

That scene was an impressive one, well calculated and well delivered to strike sense in Erik's heart and mind. O'Reilly's earnest entreaty did not penetrate to Erik's thoughts, those having been laden with all the disastrous recent events. His disheartened visions were beyond repair, his courage was lost and he could not go on without his wife and child. His mind was blurred with shadows and a perpetual darkness hovered around him. He could see no light at the end of this real nightmare. He was in the middle of a storm with no twirling winds, no sparks of lighting, no sounds of fury, no ray of hope; neither the breath of life nor the threat of death was anywhere near or far. He stood there in the middle of the floor with no rebellious feelings, no anger to vent, no strength to think, no aspiration to leave and no plan to stay.

In this hopelessness he bent his steps towards the kitchen aimlessly, approached then stood by the window and looked out with no purpose or intent. He just gazed into the flowering garden that his wife had created and cared for, where she had spent all the mornings of the spring planting flowers and half the evenings of the fall picking up their remains and cleaning their beds. There she devoted her time toiling and spending the little money that she had accumulated from ingenious and honest ways, as many women of fair mind do, instead of dispensing it on her personal adornment. It was a garden to please her son's and husband's eye. The sky was cloudless and the sun shined out bright warm beams. The birds' caroling and the hum of the myriad of summer insects filled the air all around as far as the eye could see and the ear could hear. The garden, crowded with flowers of every rich and beautiful tint, sparkled in the morning dew like a bed of glittering jewels with some tucked away and some scattered about in various corners and circles taking on the forms of petunias, impatiens or sweet peas. The roses were looking down on them and the snapdragons looking up, while the cicada's song certified that summer was here, but Erik neither heard nor saw any of those natural wonders. He had only a vague and nostalgic recollection of himself coming home from work, being received with a storm of delight by his wife and child. He turned away from the window, walked to and sat on that same chair. Resting his eyes on the bloodstained wall, he fell into very deep thought. He was not thinking of his future's greatness, but wracked his memory to find someone somewhere he could call upon for some words of guidance, wisdom or gentle consolation. He sat there for hours, never moving a hand or a foot, with his whiskers getting thicker, his vision more blurred, and his mind even more perplexed. Finally he fell asleep with his head resting on the edge of the table. After what seemed a short eternity he opened his eyes and perceived the birds waking up, getting ready to welcome the new day. Eventually raising his head, he looked about trying to gather up an organized thought or a tad of strength. He tripped into the bathroom where he splashed handfuls of cold water on his face and hair. He returned to the kitchen looking as if he were half ready to find his destiny. He stayed there surveying that room as if he hadn't seen it for a long time. He then walked off into his boy's room and with flooded eyes and quivering lips examined it closely. Reaching into his pocket he took out the toy he had intended to give his boy, a harmonica, he held it tight, then carefully placed it on the boy's pillow. He turned hastily and walked sadly back into the kitchen. Erik opened the back door and gazed far beyond the garden into the darkness ahead. He saw far off lights twinkling and dancing in the damp atmosphere. The air felt cool and a mist rolled along the ground like a dense cloud of smoke. He started to walk towards those flickering lights and quickly disappeared in the soft darkness. He walked on, the grass was wet and the low places were filled with water. The damp breath of the wind soothed languidly by with a hollow moaning sound, but Erik walked on, insensitive to it call. After a short while rain began to pour and the wind became sharper, piercing as if it were in a hurry to reach other distant lands, then the birth of a new day glimmered faintly in the sky. The objects that looked dim and blurred in the darkness grew more defined and gradually were resolved into their familiar shapes as he came upon them then passed them by. He was staggering and creeping, almost mechanically, with his head drooping on his breast as he was drawing space between himself and his home.

He suddenly heard sirens in the distance and police cars squealing their tires, human shouts of anxiety and anger, dogs barking with purpose and fury; they were all coming from where he had left, looking for him and he knew well that it was Benson's pursuit. Looking back, Erik saw men silhouetted against the lights, climbing the fence of the field in which he was standing; dogs were running ahead of them, barking and looking for blood, he realized it was his blood they sought. He dashed off at full speed laying as much distance as the Lord allowed between him and the pursuing team of angry men and mad animals. That was the arm of the law, he thought, the real arm of the law with unyielding hearts, strong legs, one-way narrow minds, unbending convictions and clenching teeth. The tireless animals and their striving masters were tightly focused on catching and grasping to unleash their pent up angers and frustrations on their prey.

Erik darted to the left and stumbled in a swift running creek where he struggled, crawled, ran and swam in that cold, unkind body of water, knowing that the dogs might loose his tracks. Exhausted, he coiled himself under a bush in the rushing stream of murky water and hid there panting and shivering.

Ultimately the shouts of men and the barking of dogs became indistinct as the party of hunters distanced itself from him. Wet, tired and drained he made it out of the little river and headed away, still loping and pressing onward in the same wild disoriented manner. Washed of all energy, he finally emerged onto a street and shortly thereafter found himself nearing a small deserted park. Upon reaching the park, feeling a little safer, he stopped running and shifted to a fast walk. He abruptly stopped in the middle of the park after he noticed a slow moving train leaving town. Summoning up his strength for one last trial, he ran and reached the railroad tracks at the very precise moment the train was passing. With his last ounce of strength, he ran alongside an open door of a boxcar and kept pace with the train that was running alongside the creek. He finally managed to grab the side of an open door and pull himself into the boxcar.

The day had broken already and Erik could see that half of the boxcar was loaded with huge reels of telephone wire, stacked two reels high, the other half was dirty and empty. Erik, panting, slowly went to a corner. He sat there looking straight ahead, his face distorted and pale, his eyes red and blood shot. He looked less like a man and more like a frightening phantom freshly arisen from the grave, empowered by an evil spirit. He slowly leaned over and lay down coiled up on the wooden floor. His eyes, for an instant, were directed towards the open door, he then focused them on the floor. Raising his trembling right hand to his lips, absorbed in the agony of his thoughts, he began to bite his fingernails. He lay there, while the train carried him slowly towards a hidden destiny, listening to the monotonous rhythm of the tracks crackling beneath him. After the passing of ten or so minutes, Erik had caught his breath and heard what he thought was the sound of low voices coming from behind the huge reels. Throwing his glance towards the sounds, he saw two heads slowly appear, coming up from behind the cargo and looking straight at him.

Erik never moved a bone or a muscle, but tensed with alarm as he watched the heads rising to full view, followed closely by the bodies of a pair of men, one young and one older.

The younger man climbed and sat on top of a reel, while the

older one came and stood close to Erik, who by this time had slid his revolver out of its holster and held it concealed under his wet coat. Their attire was clearly telling the eyes of the beholder that these two belonged to the well-known society called **hobos**. The young one went down behind the reels and fetched two dirty bundles, the kind that hobos often carry with them. The older one stood squarely in front of Erik effortlessly balancing his weight on his long legs and studied him while a scowl deepened on his face.

"It's going to cost you to ride with us on this train," threatened the older man and after a brief pause, not allowing much time to lapse in order to make himself understood and be taken as a serious minded person, he growled again. "Did you hear me?"

"I smelled you a lot more than I heard you," responded Erik, calmly and serenely, without moving a hand or a foot.

"What did you say?" shouted the man.

"I said you need a bath. I don't like your underarm deodorant or your cologne," informed Erik in the same calm tone.

Hearing Erik's response, the younger hobo who was sitting on the edge of the reel, jumped off and with an extraordinary demonstration of agility threw a somersault, which landed him very close to Erik, thus planting himself in a threatening attitude.

Erik swiftly jumped to his feet with the revolver in his hand and fire in eyes said, "Come on you queer looking throw-aways. Start something if you want to die right here and now."

The younger one, seeing the gun and sensing Erik's soberness and anger, sank back and fell into the other's arms. They both stood there afraid and astonished, looking like two kid gloves folded into each other.

Erik, still holding the gun in a manner that demonstrated he knew what he could do with it, made it clear to the hobos that he was just as used to handling a gun as they were to being thrown off trains.

"Take your Samsonite suitcase and your Pierre Cardin suits and get out! This is your stop," said Erik, kicking their soiled bundles of rags and remnants. "Move!" Shouted Erik, pointing the gun and advancing two paces towards them.

The two lost souls were so startled and scared they stood there nailed to the floor like two lampposts and held on to each other knowing there was nobody else on earth who could help them now.

Erik paused, waiting for them to move, but when nothing happened, said "okay, leave your pantyhose here but you're getting off. I'll air mail them to you when you reach your destination." At the conclusion of that statement, Erik approached the pair of refugees from the lost and found of human remnants and, to save time, changed the gun from the right to the left hand while the right came up and hit the little guy several times across the face faster than a little barking dog.

"Didn't you say that it's going to cost me to ride with you? Do you want to get paid?" said Erik, preparing to impart another dose on the other guy who, covering his face and head, stood waiting to receive his share of the reward.

"No, Mister I was only kidding," cried the man.

"Yeah, yeah, yeah I believe you. You're a mean pair of nothings. If I didn't have a gun or stand up to you, you would have thrown me off the train without giving it a second thought," said Erik.

"No, Mister, I wouldn't. Please don't hit me," pleaded the older man.

"Why is it that a Monday's hero is a Tuesdays a dead man or Wednesday's coward?" Asked Erik calmly.

"I don't know, Mister, I don't know," cried the same man again.

"You!" said Erik turning to the young man, "Who do you want to be? Tuesday's dead man...?"

Before Erik finished his words the young man let out a shriek so loud and piercing it could have blown the crust off a loaf of bread.

Without waiting one more second, Erik pushed and hit hard, until the terrified hobos reached the door and while they were at the very edge, waiting for the right and safe moment to jump, Erik pushed both of them out of the boxcar of that slow moving train.

The unfortunate creatures, hitting the ground in silence and fear, rolled right into the running creek. Erik threw out their belongings behind them and yelled, "I said, you needed a bath." With this, the hint of a smile broke out on his face.

The ill-fated hobos, still holding onto one another, wet, scared and cold, and making demonstrative vulgar gestures towards Erik while pouring out loud declarations, mixed with anger, threats and curses and protesting that they were not in the habit of being thrown off moving trains, hurried out of the brook. Shaking off some water and mud from themselves, they hastily picked up their surviving gear and started running to catch the train, but they eventually gave up when they felt that air wasn't flowing in and out of their lungs as fast as they were running and their hearts were beating faster, as if trying to get away from them. Then, to make matters worse, the train suddenly picked up speed, disappearing around the bend with Erik waving at them, a broad smile now on his face. They were left there, with that awful feeling that they were a mile behind, a day late and a dollar short.

PART II

THE RECOGNITION

CHAPTER 1

A stranger in a strange land

A night of repose in the shallow silence of the boxcar, breathing the Virginia open meadows fresh and fragrant air, brought some relief to Erik's chest as he sat by the door of the boxcar with his feet dangling over the side. He was by no means recovered from the effects of his recent catastrophe; a cloud of sadness seemed to hang on his face as he still was wholly at a loss. Looking around him, Erik realized he had the company of some men who must have boarded the train while he was fast asleep.

Erik cast his eyes on the figure of a man who was sitting in the far corner of the boxcar with his head tilted on his shoulder, sleeping peacefully. The man's hair hung over his face; his features looked as if they had been changed by suffering or drained by famine, he looked like nothing more than an old bundle of flesh and bones, more bones than flesh.

Near him, leaning listlessly against the wall, stood a lean rugged looking man dressed in an ill worn country western outfit. There was a rusty spur on his right boot and once in a while he would jerk his spur into a cardboard box and with his lips puckered up, would make the sounds of a rider encouraging his horse to gallop.

On the other side of the boxcar an old man was seated on a small wooden box, his eyes riveted on the floor, his face settled into an expression of the deepest and most hopeless despair.

There were three or four more hobos congregated in a little knot in the middle of the floor talking loudly amongst themselves. Such was the scene in that boxcar and those were the objects that Erik viewed with an indifferent attitude. After taking the time to observe, out of curiosity, his fellow travelers, he edged himself away from the door and as close as possible to the opposite door, beaming forth looks of unfriendly countenance. Erik's mind, like those minds of men who have been up and have been down life's trails, was open to conviction, powerful reasoning and quick decisions. He now understood and believed that his son was gone forever, concluding that the little boy was held safe in the hands of some super spirit and his wife, wherever she was, was happier there than being with him; after all, she deserted him, he didn't abandon her.

He spent the whole day revolving those and similar thoughts around in his mind until the train began to slow down and finally stopped. He dismounted and started walking in the same direction as the train, thinking that there had to be a town ahead of him. He walked on alone with fresh strength and new courage while a small fire within him was making a wretched attempt to brighten his cheer but it was dimmed beneath the dispiriting influence of his catastrophe. He didn't hope to recover his peace of mind or happiness, for they both had fled forever, but only to restore his prostrate energy.

He finally arrived in a town, but dim and dark shadows of the summer night had fallen all around by the time he reached its center. Once he entered the small city, his first consideration was to find a place to eat and therefore he entered the first restaurant that came into sight along the main street in the middle of the main shopping block. It was a long narrow place with a counter and stationary stools on the left, several booths on the right and a dining room occupying the furthest end of the establishment. There were many customers sitting in the booths, at the tables and on the counter stools. The music was soft and low, low enough to hear footsteps, now and then clear merry laughter and low gentle voices. Erik sat on the counter stool across from the kitchen's entrance door. He grinned when he looked at the register and saw a partially burnt Greek flag as he had seen at Theo's place and then the figure of a man coming from the kitchen, resembling Theo in height, pounds and years. The man was sprucely attired and looked like someone who'd run up a high tailor's bill, get invited to a lot of parties and live with his family in the richest part of town where domestic help did the cooking and the serving. Gazing around he smiled complacently, as often owners of establishments do, bowing obsequiously to some new comers and nodding familiarly to others being ushered to their seats by a tall young lady, whose body could be the envy of women and the fantasy of men.

His eyes fell on Erik who beckoned for him to approach. When the man came and stationed himself in front of Erik, he fixed into a searching look and spoke in a low but distinct emphatic tone.

"What can I do you for?" asked the man with a familiar accent, seeing Erik in a deplorable disheveled condition.

"BlacoV eisai," said Erik, with a smile, hearing his accent and guessing the man's origin.

"Hey!" uttered the man loudly and enthusiastically, "You're Greek!" giving Erik his hand and shaking it feverously, he lapsed into a series of broad and unmitigated grins while manifesting other demonstrations of being in a highly enviable state of inward merriment.

"There are not too many Greeks around to say hello to. Are you a real Greek?"

"Proeferwn to rw katarerotereumenon," responded Erik, still grinning.

"My God!" exhaled the man, "that phrase is familiar only among learned Greeks, it was what the ancient great orator Dimosthenis uttered to the Athenians when, after a long and difficult struggle, he was able to pronounce the Greek letter 'R' at its most perfect pitch. Yes? That phrase has six hard Rs in it. You *are* Greek."

"True Greek, wrapped in the American flag," replied Erik.

"Me too, a true Greek wrapped in the American dream," said the man, still grinning from ear to ear.

"PwV edw palikari?" asked the man.

"I'm passing through."

"Are you going to stay long in our town."

"It depends. But I will stay long enough to get some clothes and clean up. What's the name of the town?" asked Erik.

"The name is, Richville, I call it in Greek, B*lacocwri,* (farmers' town)," said the man with an air of pride, "what we have here is a lot of farmers and cattle ranchers."

"Apo pou eise? " inquired the man.

"I am from Astako, Xupomerou," responded Erik.

"Ti leV, mwre, egw eim' ap t'n Arta" said the man, in his native dialect.

"Arta? Then I was right when I said you are *BlacoV*," remarked Erik smiling.

"I'm proud being *BlacoV, alla cwriV probata,* but a shepherd without sheep, I feel like a fish out of the water," complained the Greek, finishing with a very loud laugh.

"I know what you mean."

"No. I'm only kidding I like the restaurant business; it's almost the same. What's your name?"

"Erik Karas."

"Mine is George Papas. I have shortened my name like you've shortened yours," said the man giving his hand to Erik one more time and shaking as vigorously as he had done at first.

"You have a politician's hand shake," remarked Erik with a grin on his face.

"Yes, I'm glad you noticed it. In this business you have to be a politician, you have to be a good cook and you also have to be a good manager, like a good shepherd. I'm going to tell you a short story. I'm going to say it in English," saying this he lowered his voice to a whisper and proceeded, "I'll come around." George rushed around from behind the counter went to sit on the other side next to Erik and looking at him in full face, he continued, "The reason I try to speak English is because some of the customers don't like to hear a foreign language. They think we talk about them," said George.

"I don' t blame them."

"Me neither. I'm going to tell you why I said that this business is the same as being a shepherd and why I like it better. I'm going to kill the same bird with two rocks."

" No," interrupted Erik touching the man's hand kindly. "You're going to kill two birds with one stone, you want to say."

George looked at Erik with a delighted expression on his face. "I have finally found an educated Greek, in this town you are educated! Huh?"

"Enough to know the difference in that saying."

"You see I never went to school here. I learned English in the kitchen. I also learned Spanish in the kitchen, because most of the people I have working in the kitchen are from Mexico. They always speak Spanish. Either they don't like English or they can't learn it, I don't know. Anyway, one day, one of the customers asked me why the Greeks are in the restaurant business and most of them are successful. I told him that most of the Greeks, who come here, to America, are hungry and the first place they go is somewhere to eat. There they find a job washing dishes and after a while they buy the joint. Most of us, who came here, were shepherds in the old country. A good shepherd likes one thing; he likes to see his goats eating well, because goats and sheep are very finicky eaters. He likes to see his goats feeding on fresh mountain sage and the sheep grazing in the meadows. The more they eat, the more milk they produce, the better the wool and they become heavier for the butcher. We use all kinds of tricks to make the animals eat and we keep them a secret, like a good meat loaf recipe, and so here we are, we have all these people who come around to eat. We love to see them eating. Before we look at their faces we look to see if they ate all the food on their plates. If the food goes in the garbage, that means the food is no good; so we tend to them as we tended to our animals. Being a shepherd, I love to see my animals eating. This guy, I was telling him this story, he got angry and hit me in the mouth. He hasn't come back for a long time; he probably thought I called him an animal. Maybe my English is not that good." There he stopped and looked at Erik waiting for him to add something and when Erik said nothing, George continued. " I wish I liked people as much as I liked my animals," said George looking down as if he were talking to himself. "Do you understand and do you agree with me? First you have to understand."

"One hundred percent; I understand and I agree, George. I couldn't have said it better myself," replied Erik with a wide smile on his face. "Something else you could have added to your reply, that doesn't take anything away from what you said to him."

"Oh, yes? What 's that?"

"At the Olympic games, when the participants and spectators came, the local residents would prepare food and sell it to them."

"They were the first vendors," replied George.

"Precisely"

"I always say that in all of the universe we have the three (S's)," said George with a brilliant smile.

"What are those?"

George holding onto his smile extended his right hand outwards and began to recite, counting with his fingers. "Soup, sex and shelter. If you have those three things you should be very happy. I provide the soup for my customers. I provide the one of the top three necessities. Good?" said George with heroic firmness. "The rest they can go someplace else to get."

Erik nodded in assent and grinned.

"I told this to one of my customers. You understand these are my thoughts. They can be wrong, as wrong as selling horsemeat for beef. He is educated, he is American. The reason I say American is because if I say that to a Greek he'd try to find something wrong with it. Like the Italians used to say during the WWII, if you have four Greek soldiers, it is like having five captains. Anyway, Erik, this customer came back one day and said to me that he read his wife her rights. He said that every night she had a headache; so he said to her in a very loud voice that there are the three Ss in life; soup, sex and shelter. 'I provide the shelter, George provides the soup and you have to provide the sex, otherwise tomorrow there will be no soup from George and no shelter from me'. George started to laugh and added that the wife gave him sex, but now, she doesn't want to cook, she wants to come here for her soup. I talk a lot, don't I?" asked George.

"I like people who talk a lot. I don't like people who only listen or pretend they are listening. They are what I call buyers; they don't sell. They only take but they don't give," said Erik.

"We, the Greeks talk a lot," said George

"No, not all Greeks. The Greeks who have money don't talk a lot. The more money they have, the less they talk. They feel they don't have to say anything, because they let their money do the talking."

"Erik, you are right. I know this Greek who lives in this town and he has a lot of money. Many people say he does. He comes here once in a while by himself, sits down and says nothing except 'how are you' and when he gets up to go, he has a whole bunch of silver in his pocket and he always rattles it like goat bells. He only drinks coffee, nothing big, and when he goes to the register he always pays with a dollar bill, so he can add more silver to his already full pocket. I don't like him. Now I just found out from you why I don't like him. Erik, I feel I know you for a long time. I'm going to ask you a question but I don't want you to feel insulted," said George "Go ahead, shoot!" replied Erik.

"If you don't have any money, tell me, because here they have a law that you must have at least five dollars in your pocket, and if you don't look so clean, they take you to jail. They say this is a free country. But here they can put you in jail for less than five dollars. Evidently this country was made for the rich and the ones who try to get rich. Don't get me wrong," said George touching Erik's arm passionately, " I love it here. This is where I will leave my bones, most likely in a grave all by myself. You see, I've been here in this country long enough to be married three times." There he stopped and glanced at Erik with a wandering look. "Being married three times, in your opinion, does that make me bad?"

"It doesn't make you good or bad, I think it makes you a little different, if not a little crazy."

"You think so?" asked George.

"You sound as if you like your freedom and yet you got married three times. Why?"

"First I am going to answer the last part of your question. Why three times. That's what I call the tattoo syndrome. At the time of tattooing it sounded like a good idea but then later on you realize how stupid it was. First part of the question is, if you like freedom why get married?" said George pausing, partly to think and partly to study Erik. "You see being married to a woman you are not losing your freedom, you are really gaining strength. I don't have much education but what I learned, I learned from living with the creatures of nature in the mountains of Greece, you know. I like a woman who respects me as a man and I love them and cherish them as if they are flowers. You see? Respect for the man and love for the woman. That's my motto. I want my woman to ask me if I like her dress. If I don't like it, I don't care if she wears it all day and all night long, but you must remember the important thing, Erik, she asked me." There he stopped for a moment, partly to gaze around at his establishment and partly to think of his next comment. "I like her to ask me how I like her hair and the paint on her fingernails, that means that she is thinking of me when she does all those things and that gives me strength knowing that someone else besides me is thinking of me. I also like her to tell me what necktie to wear and what color shirt. Does that sound stupid to you?"

"No. Not to me. We are from the same school."

"You were a shepherd too?" asked George, with amazement on his face.

" No. My beginning in life is the same as yours. We don't go too far away from our beginnings. I learned it from my grandfather, he was a shepherd."

"Okay, then. I am what they call a romanticist. Did I say it right?"

"No. The word is romantic," replied Erik, with a smile.

" Romantic! Boy, the English language is hard. Do you know they say the Greek language is hard?"

Erik nodded in assent.

"You know, the English language has a lot of Greek words."

Erik nodded again.

"So, if the Greek language is hard, then the English is hard for having so many Greek words, but they pronounce them different," said George and looking at Erik for a moment, "romantic, you said?"

"Yes."

"Being romantic," continued George, "I like to walk in the rain with my woman hanging on to me under an umbrella. I walk feeling strong and she walks feeling safe. I know a lot of husbands and wives, when they get up in the morning, they don't even look at each other and when they go out in the rain they have two umbrellas. What is the fun in that? My house is a one-umbrella house, Erik. When I come home and I see another umbrella in the corner, I say to myself, something is wrong and I'm right. A little while later, she says that she wants to be independent. And I say okay. So I go out and I find a partner for my umbrella. I get caught. I get divorced, and so on and so forth and that's how the world turns around me. They all come as one-umbrella women, but they leave with one umbrella for themselves only. Like I said I learned it from nature. You should see the way the animals, the goats and the sheep, the way they behave. You see, Erik, I believe that animals are closer to God than humans because animals are not smart like we are, so God still whispers into their ears what to do and where to go to survive. Erik, You should see the male goat standing in the rain with his head straight up and the female goat goes and puts her head underneath his to get away from the rain. Did your grandfather ever mentioned that, Erik?"

"No."

"Good. Anyway, he stands there primped and proud taking the rain, but he doesn't mind it. I don't mind working until I have no more need for air and no lungs to carry it in. I'll take the pressure of running a business as long as she is under the same umbrella with me. The animals get along just fine. You will never see a male goat beating up a female goat. Some people say that we are not animals. Oh, yeah? We, the humans are not as good as animals and the shepherds are as soft as their animals. I have known shepherds bigger than two big donkeys and stronger than mules, with knives bigger than swords on one side and pistols bigger than a horse's jaw on the other, who never ate meat in their lives and went behind a rock and cried with tears as big as **kombologia** (worry beads) for losing one animal from the herd or selling it to the butcher. Huh? What do you think?"

"I don't know George. I left the old country when I was very young and I have never been a shepherd, said Erik, jokingly.

"Oh, yeah? I have been to your hometown, AstakoV, it's a goat town, too," said George smiling.

"George, I enjoy hearing what you are saying"

"I know, I sing like a bird. But the birds sing in the morning being happy to see the new day, I sing at night being happy to see the day gone with all its problems and that's when I go home to sit next to my woman. Anyway, I started this whole speech when I asked if you have any money. I don't want you to go to jail because of that stupid law."

Erik looked at him, smiled, placed his hand on George' s shoulder and said, "That's the vagrancy law, George. I have money. Thank you, George. I have money, not a lot, but enough for me to roam around for six months without having to work."

"That's good!" said George, "But why are you dressed…?"

"Like this?" interrupted Erik "It's a long story, George, I don't want to go into it right now, but I'm going to give you a hint. I could have taken the passenger train from New Jersey and come down here, but I chose to take the freight train, but not due to the lack of money."

At that point a slight commotion was heard at the front door and George turned to see about ten customers arriving together. They entered and said that they wished to be seated for dinner. The full splendor of the scene burst upon George's face. He stood up, advanced a few paces, greeted them with a deep bow and asked them to wait one moment for the tables to be set up. It was intensely interesting to observe the manner in which George, a former goat shepherd, performed his part in the welcoming ceremony of the newcomers. A waitress and two busboys sped at George's cue and abruptly put together a couple of tables in the middle of the dining room; they immediately covered the tables with white table clothes. Upon these were laid the knives, forks, spoons, white dinner napkins and enough cups and saucers to correspond with the number of guests. One of the dinner guests took the liberty and advanced ahead of all the rest; he was a stout gentleman who looked as if the major part of his income was devoted to his only pleasure, that being eating. He was wearing a white shirt, a green sports jacket and a very thin necktie. His shirt was so tightly wrapped around him that, as he walked, his belly threatened, at any moment, to break the buttons and escape into the open for a breath of fresh air.

The entire assortment of men and women took their seats and immediately burst into loud laughter. George returned to Erik and in a very low voice and looking away from the bunch, he said. "You see that heavy-set bastard with the green sport jacket and the skinny tie?"

Erik looked in that direction and nodded in assent.

"He, Bob, is the one who hit me in the mouth; he always makes trouble for me in here every time he comes in." George, saying this, walked over, bowed again as he normally did and asked if the seating accommodations were in a satisfactory order. Everybody nodded and mumbled out their satisfaction.

"No, not everything," shouted the fat man. .

"Bob!" interposed one of the gentlemen in his company, "you really didn't have to come with us and if you want to go, you are free to." At the end of that gentleman's remark the entire group laughed heartily.

"In my opinion this place stinks. It should be a corral for goats. You heard that George?"

General alarm rang in the ears of most customers, but they all just looked at one another with glances filled with contempt for the orator.

Even though Erik was busy with and exhausted from his own thoughts, that man's unkind remark greeted his ear unfavorably, causing his eyebrows to rise. He deplored his attitude, like most patrons of the restaurant had.

"Did you hear what I said, gorgeous George?" repeated the fat man, the last part of his statement being loaded with sarcasm.

Erik heard the remark and his feelings of gallantry were roused, mostly by observing George, who now was acting as a stranger in his own place and was accepting those cruel remarks in a humble manner. Holding himself to be a daring man of nerve and guts and a defender of the weak and the humble, Erik rose from his seat and hastily went into the kitchen.

"Some day, Bob, you will find your match," said another gentleman from the group who was sitting close to Bob, wearing a red sports jacket.

Bob glared a long moment at the man who made that statement, "I'd like to see him," returned the fat man.

"Here I am, at your service" declared Erik, bowing especially to Bob and then turning to the man with the red jacket. Erik evidently had gone into the kitchen, put on a white coat, buttoned it up to his chin, carefully placed a starched white cloth dinner napkin over his arm, and looking like an authentic waiter of the first class, came out to redress the unfair, "I'm very much obliged to you, ladies and gentlemen, for your patronage and also for your recommendations and I shall be your humble servant for this evening and whatever additional assistance in serving you is required I hope, ladies and gentlemen, will be met with your satisfaction."

"He sounds like a damn foreign professor," said Bob loudly, as if the thrill of hatred struck his heart.

"We are all foreigners, sir, in this country whether we came on the Mayflower or came later on, we all took the same route, sir," recited Erik, turning to Bob. "I'm certain your ancestors did what most of us did. Don't you hold any reverence for them and don't you bear any respect for them in your heart or head either, sir. We are not all the same though, sir; some of us are a little less tolerant and more violent than others. I, sir, do my job to the best of my ability and I don't expect to be tolerated by anyone, because sir," Erik went very close to Bob, looked him in the eye and continued, "I don't tolerate anyone's arrogant manner. Do I make myself clear to you, sir, or do you wish that I move on to my plan B, which I'm very certain you don't want to witness." That statement could have made some men's faces grow pale and induce some women to faint, had it been delivered with a manner matching its meaning and with one or two more emphatic words added, but it was delivered without the slightest resonance of indignation and with the most complete simplicity and equability of style that it left the rest of Bob's fellow diners bewildered. After a moment's pause, Erik turned away, as if to proceed with his commission.

"He thinks he is a tough guy," stated Bob, rather faintly, but loudly enough to reach Erik's ears.

"Not tough, but I am right," said Erik, turning and facing Bob with the same calmness as he had held onto up till now and continued, "please remember, sir, being right, the law of nature provides you with greater strength to protect yourself from the unfair. If you think you're right, sir, act upon it! I'm here to assist you in any way that I can."

Bob looked at Erik with mild fear on his face but broke his gaze by picking up a menu and pretending to study it. Erik's mild and confident manner appeared to have conveyed something alarming to Bob and, even though he seemed preoccupied with reading the menu, he still looked puzzled, embarrassed and frightened for a few more seconds but the expression on his face suddenly changed to a forced smile and a long glance around the table, so as not to appear a reckless coward.

"Let's eat! That's what we came here for, isn't it?" announced Bob loudly, turning his face back to the menu, trying to avoid eye contact with Erik who stood there still, half turned and glaring at him.

It was evident that Bob had realized plan B, as was presented by Erik, was not an invitation to Erik's birthday party, but a definite suggestion for him to get up and challenge his antagonist on the spot. Feeling Erik's presence, Bob raised his head once more and looked at Erik, "Never mind, sir," said the fat man, bending his head downwards as he started reading the menu again.

Hearing the phrase, 'Never mind, sir,' Erik comprehended Bob's cowardly and repulsive character, then turned and walked away without saying another word while Bob raised his head and let his eyes follow.

There is often something special about the phrase 'never mind, sir' and Bob must have been aware of it. He could not recollect witnessing a fight starting in a bar where one of the arguing persons said 'never mind, sir;' nor could he recollect any brawl in the street, parking lot or any other public place to have begun after the phrase 'never mind, sir' was uttered. He felt that there might be something magical hidden in the phrase of 'never mind, sir', that reduces the indignation in the breast of the addressed much more than any other earnest apology.

Bob's obvious retreat was not lost on the gentleman with the red sport jacket. He settled his spectacles more firmly on his nose and sensing Bob's feelings said, " it was not my wish for you to be embarrassed or hurt, but to warn you to be careful."

Bob raised his eyes to look at the gentleman, tried to smile, but a grave look washed across his face again, he said nothing and went back to reading the menu.

At that precise moment the arrival of two police officers brought a wide smile of relief to George's face. He welcomed them, showed his gratitude by immediately escorting them to the counter, where they were evidently accustomed to sitting like most men who haven't much time to spare, and ordered the waitress to serve them at once.

"Let's eat!" said George, with a grateful bow to Erik; taking him gently by the arm he escorted him to the furthest corner booth, away from all eyes and ears, where they would feel more comfortable.

"Sit here and we will eat together," said George, pointing to the booth. With this friendly remark that was delivered in an animated and earnest manner, Erik took a seat then bounced up and down a couple of times not to test the seat's comfort but to show George his gratitude as George took the seat across from him.

"What are we going to eat?" asked Erik

"Oh, I have the best leg of lamb, just fresh out of the oven, and potatoes and Retsina wine. We will eat like two rich men and will feel like we are on top of Mount Olympus where the Greek Gods used to eat. I have already told the cook and the food will be here any moment."

Hearing the description of the meal that was about to come their way, Erik smiled and bowed abstractedly, nursed his right leg with his right hand and waited for George to proceed.

"First I must thank you for intervening, that was very helpful to me, because being in this business means that sometimes you have to turn a deaf ear. I want you to know, Erik, I am not a coward. I am not one of those who say, 'It's better to be a live coward than a dead hero.' Oh, no, not me. I don't mind dying as long as I know that there may be something in it for somebody. But I think you are a man who is on the side of the underdog," said George, pausing for a long moment and staring at Erik.

"Yeah, I'm a regular **Don Quixote,**" mumbled Erik sarcastically, a statement mainly directed to himself that was possibly lost in route to George's ear.

"But tell me, Patrida, (countryman), what was plan B?"

"I had none. I would have probably gotten my ass kicked. The only way out at that moment was to bluff," said Erik smiling.

A sudden look of astonishment blossomed on George's face. He broke into a loud laugh and threw himself back into his seat. "I would have helped you, you know?" said George, after his thrilled laugh had subsided.

"No, it wouldn't have been proper, you are the owner. You have to have more sense than that. I was just the crazy waiter," said Erik soberly.

The food arrived by waitress and busboy and after some gentle preparations they made many assurances that it would taste as good as it looked. The preparations were on the most delightful scale, fully realizing George's prophetic anticipations. The servers displayed it proudly before them with the utmost graciousness and care.

"Let's eat and drink!" said George, pouring the wine into the two tall glasses.

Erik needed no second invitation to induce him to yield full justice to the meal.

"Drink!" said George, touching Erik's glass with his own and saying. "St'gia maV, and every other good thing your heart desires and deserves"

"Sthn ugeia maV, patrida," added Erik, winking with the eye that was not concealed by the glass he had raised to his lips and drank with such zest as that private get together deserved.

"Delicious" said George, the satisfaction of whose countenance, after drinking, bore testimony to the sincerity of his remark, "do you like the lamb, Erik?"

"Very, very good," added Erik, continuing the occupation of emptying his plate with his fork and the knife, paying very little attention to anything else, nevertheless, it was still evident that fragments of sadness lingered in his heart and showed on his face and in his gestures as he was eating; they were followed, now and then, by some shallow sighs.

"Did you say, that horrible Bob would have beaten you?" asked George, putting down his fork, mindfully as if that question surfaced after some thought had been loitering in his mind.

"Huh, huh," replied Erik without taking time off his task.

"I don't think so."

"Why don't you think so?"

"Kalio na nogaV, para na dunesai. Do you understand?"

"Yeah! That's an old Greek saying, 'it's better to have skill, it is mightier than physical strength,'" answered Erik, as he raised his head, looked up and smiled. "What makes you think that I have the skill to win the battle?"

"I see the way you move your hands with the knife and the fork. You have a great skill."

"Cutting up the meat?"

"Yeah.

"But George, this is dead meat. It doesn't fight back."

"He is dead meat too. He only talks loud and a lot. That reminds me of what my grandfather used to tell me when I was a young boy in my hometown, Arta. I used to get a little cocky, looking to get into a fight by threatening someone. My grandfather, God bless his soul wherever he is, hell or Heaven, he would warn me with pity in his voice, 'some day, you are going to find 'To maliarokolo,' he would say to me. You know the word Maliarokolo? " asked George with a smile.

"Yes, George"

"How do you say Maliarokolo, in English?"

"Hairy-ass, or Hairy –butt, George," replied Erik, continuing with his task of eating.

"Hairy-ass," said George softly, as if talking to himself, "Hairy-ass, doesn't sound as good as MaliarokoloV. Any way, that went on for years but I never understood what he meant by that; so I asked him to tell me what that saying meant. Back in the old days the men, where I come from, used to wear FoustaneleV, white FoustaneleV, like pleaded short skirts,"

"I know what a Foustanela is, George," snapped Erik, still eating.

"How old are you Erik?"

"Let's say forty, forty five," answered Erik, swinging his fork in the air for George to proceed with his story.

"Is it forty or forty five?"

"What's the difference? Put down forty."

"I'm not trying to find out how old you are, I'm only trying to find out if you remember anyone in your hometown, Astakos, wearing a **foustanela.** I am fifty, I remember some men wearing them," said George.

"I remember them too. I also remember to Silaci, do you remember that?" asked Erik, now smiling. "Yes, oh yes, to Sliac, " snapped George, in his native dialect, revealing his origin again while letting his emotions denote that he was greatly amused with something that he had never thought of hearing in this country. "Looked like the old money belt. The men used to put everything in there, from tobacco to mustache wax." exclaimed George, picking up his glass and looking at Erik who did the same, then he rang Erik's glass, saying with some nostalgia, "Let's drink to **foustanela, siliahi, Arta, Astakos, hairy-butt** and **goats, sheep** and may all of them live forever in our hearts. Anyway," said George, after they both drank and he returned his attention to the telling of his story, "they never wore any underwear under those white skirts, you know."

Erik nodded in assent.

"My grandfather had a cousin who always kicked and beat on guys smaller than him. His father told him the same thing my grandfather kept telling me, that there would be a day when you are going to see 'The hairy-butt'. One day, this gallant young man went into town, but this time, he picked on the wrong man at the wrong time. He picked on someone with more strength and greater talent than him. This one took my grandfather's cousin's head and stuck it between his legs, under his white skirt, and started pounding his ass brutally, accurately with both hands. While the imparting of those merciless punches was taking place, my grandfather's cousin, in a desperate trial to get out from underneath that odious place, looked up and saw, as you called it, the other man's hairy-ass. Whether he broke away or he was let go, it is unknown, but he went home like 'teleutaioV kai kataudromenoV'. How do you say it in English? Oh, yes. Like the man in the race, 'soaked with sweat and last,' all beaten up on the ribs, ass and face, almost crying he told his father how and what he saw under the foustanela."

George, at the conclusion of his story raised his glass again and said, "I will tell you my philosophy of life. You must live life with apathy." George stopped, looked at Erik, raised his glass a little higher and said solemnly, "Erik, my friend, let's drink to apathy for life and some hairy-ass for Bob."

"To the house with one umbrella," said Erik, raising his glass a little higher than George. They both drank, before George plunged into a laughing fit, with the shield of delight on their faces for wishing and predicting Bob's unavoidable fate. Erik thought, for just and instant, that place and that moment offered him a light of a slim hope in his dark and dreary world. Even so, the passing happy moment created a guilty feeling in his soul and he wished he could leave, go out into the open fields where none could see or hear him cry and indeed cry until the air was filled with his tears and sorrow. He could not avoid casting an anxious look around the place, reflecting on what he felt was the absurdity of any happy time. The interior of the place now looked to him ill lit and poorly ventilated; he asked his friend to point the way to the restrooms and away he went. George's eyes followed him as he was walking away and he thought the man's face bore traces of sorrow, suffering and great despair; his observation added a sizeable portion of melancholy to George's soul. To George, Erik looked like a man who once upon a time brightened celebrations, rioted in pleasure, mended sad hearts and brought hope and belief to the dispirited. He thought along those lines while Erik was out of view.

The sight of Erik restored George to his original contentment and that sight imparted on the countenance of his guest some new courage.

"Have another glass of wine," stated George, pouring more wine into Erik's glass.

"We can't dance we can't sing and it's too wet to plow; we might as well get drunk," said Erik, with a new tone and passion depicted on his face.

"Erik, I see you as a man of sense, humor and talent," said George, "I am very happy I have met you and that you came here to break bread with me and share a glass or two of wine in my humble place."

"And I, George," returned Erik, "feel deeply honored by this expression of your opinion and kind words."

"Erik, one thing about us Greeks is that we are very sentimental people. Some would say that we are sentimental slobs because we think a lot with our hearts. If we think only with our heads then our hearts will die from not being used. Erik, you think with your heart like a true Greek and that's what makes you better than most people."

"Allow me to tell you that I am not what you see."

"Nonsense, Erik. You are forgetting that I was brought up in the open fields of Greece, where you learn to read the unwritten, you learn to see the invisible and you learn to feel the change of the weather before nature's decision. I must inform you that I have read a lot in my life, from comic books to the Odyssey. With this background don't you think I can feel there is suffering and sorrow in your heart? Don't you think that I knew when my animals felt good or bad? Don't you know that I felt their pain and their suffering? They don't talk. If I can feel the pain in the animals who don't talk, smile or cry, don't you think I can sense it in you?"

It was not clear to George whether Erik was paying attention to him, had sunk into his own thoughts and had locked everything and everyone out, was contemplating some type of defense or a simple answer for him or was simply satisfied with the peaceful repose of that exclusive get together. George stopped, looked and listened with his eyes, as often many smart men do, waiting for Erik's comment.

"Sometimes when you are in the middle of a rain storm you feel not only can you not think of sunshine but that you will never be dry and fit for service again. I have been blown down by the wind already and right now I don't think I have the strength or the desire to stand up and submit or commit myself to the same process again," said Erik.

"Staying in the rain, my friend, will not wash away your sins, whatever sins you think you are guilty of. God could never send that much rain down to wash them away. Just remember, we Greeks, because of our decent upbringing from the very beginning of our lives, tend to magnify our guilty feelings. No matter how many thousands of miles you travel you cannot get too far away from your beginnings. You are staying in the rain not just to wash your sins and guilty feelings away; you are also staying away to punish yourself and that will eventually happen; you will either die or go crazy, if you don't allow someone to get you out of the storm. I noticed something, earlier; I have this beautiful hostess and there is no male from nine years old to ninety who doesn't look at her, and you, you just went by as if she never existed in your sight."

"Maybe I'm gay," said Erik grinning.

"No, you are not. They too go by and glance at her, wishing they could look like her," said George.

"George, I will remember the things you've said and will put them in my head and work on them during the night, but first you must allow me to pay for the damages here, then I will ask you to point me to a hotel and a place where I can go to buy some clothes," said Erik.

"First, remember I gave you some outside advice and that advice is no good unless it is acted upon, second, you owe me nothing. The whole thing was a pleasure and third, the stores are open till 10 p.m. tonight and two or three clothing stores are within walking distance of the hotel at the end of the block. I hope to see you tomorrow for breakfast," uttered George very solemnly.

As he looked and studied his new friend, Erik, though ragged and squalid, was not quite so hollow as before. He murmured some broken expressions of appreciation and muttered something about having been saved from starving. "I told you that the whole thing was an unexpected pleasure for me, Erik," replied George, patting him on the back as he went away and disappeared outside.

The night had matured and the time was ripe for Erik to get some rest. After having completed his personal shopping, he entered his hotel room. Closing the door behind him and surveying the room briefly, he sat on the bed still holding his shopping bag in his hands. Looking around the room, he felt as if he was there neither to prepare himself for the next day and look for his destiny, nor to get away from his past but only to remove his thoughts from the present in order to avoid a fresh quarrel with himself and to get some much needed rest.

He found the room rather large, as if it were built to accommodate a whole boarding school, to say nothing of the two large dressers that would have held the clothes of a small army.

He undressed slowly in front of the bed, took the handgun out of his pocket and held it as if he were studying its purpose and strength before putting it down. He then crawled under the covers, although it wasn't cold, and went to sleep almost immediately. He wasn't asleep more than fifteen minutes when he fell into a dream. He dreamed his wife and son were back in their home. His son was running around with his mother standing close by, holding a package that she was about to hand over to him. Erik jerked up, looked around, startled and confused, until he realized he was all alone and away from his home. He closed his eyes, squeezed his eyelids tight together and tossed from side to side, trying to fall asleep. No use. He stayed half awake most of the night.

CHAPTER 2

The parade and the political debate.

Finally the morning came and greeted Erik's ears with a mingling of commotion and human voices sounding as if the entire population of Richville had awakened with the intent of starting a revolution. There was a low roar running through the crowd that usually announces the arrival of whatever it has been waiting for. Erik went hastily to the window of his second floor room, looked outside down to the street and viewed several acres of ground covered with people, all their faces turned to the right and all their arms waving in that same direction. The roaring shouting anxious humans, the army of American flags fluttering merrily in the air and the fields of balloons held by every living soul of that town and probably those that surrounded it, glistened brightly in the sun and portrayed the beginning of a celebration. There was a grand band of trumpets and drums of all sizes marshaled four abreast, solemn and stern, especially the drummers. There were groups of policemen marching, committeemen shuffling, a mob of voters yelling for their favorite candidate who was seeking reelection, whose name, as much as Erik could tell, was written on several signs bearing 'John Lambright.' There were policemen on horseback and policemen on foot. A Cadillac convertible came rolling slowly along in the middle of the tumultuous street.

The honorable Mayor of Richville, John Lambright, sat up on the top of the back seat of that white Cadillac with four others, smiling and waving to his beloved voters. There were four more white Cadillac convertibles of the same year occupied by his friends and supporters.

The flags were rustling vigorously and the band was playing

loudly, while more policemen were marching past and the local dignitaries, looking like real authors, who had written whole books and published them afterwards, were strolling along. Men of commerce and trade, men of law and men of order and many more with large bank accounts and many other self appraised house-holders and geniuses of the town also walked on with their heads up high, and the mobs of people were shouting and the horses were drumming their feet onto the ground, blowing air in and out of their huge lungs and foaming from mouth and body. The large flag carriers were perspiring, and everybody and everything assem-bled there was done in the honor of and hope for mayor John Lambright.

Erik rushed into the shower and after a little while he appeared outside all spruced up and dressed for the occasion, with a bright blue jacket, white shirt, black shoes and pants. He went down to where the action was and stationed himself near the podium. He stood there leaning against a tree trunk, casting his attention on the surrounding people and their activities when he suddenly felt a soft tap on his shoulder. Turning around he saw his new friend George, who was also well dressed, standing before him all lit up with a happy smile, preening like a peacock.

"How did you find me?" asked Erik loudly, to overcome the roar of that mixed bag of givers and the takers.

"The desk clerk told me; her eyes followed you all the way here."

"The one with the blue eyes?" asked Erik humorously.

"Did you notice her?"

"No, but everybody has blue eyes here in this town," said Erik.

"There are only Anglo-Saxons here in this town."

"What's going on?" asked Erik, engrossed in the activities.

"The two hopefuls for Mayor are to have a debate in the open before all these people. The incumbent is John Lambright, who was born and raised here in this town and the challenger, Harry Sharkey, came here only a few years ago. No one anticipated this size crowd!" exclaimed George.

A sudden burst of loud shouting and cheers came from the other side of the throng when the challenger, Harry Sharkey, arrived, unloaded himself from his convertible and went to the center of the stage, stopping a few feet away from John Lambright.

The crowd pressed on with a burning desire to see their man, the challenger, Harry Sharkey. During the melee, Erik was pushed away from George by ferocious groups of men and women, who, he felt were all strong in body but weak in mind. He was pushed up to the wooden steps that led to the stage, acquiring a poke in the head in the process. From where he was standing, Erik could see that the right side of the stage was marked and reserved for the honorable Mayor, his staff and followers. The left was reserved for Harry Sharkey and his combatants. Between these two groups of true believers and those others faithful to their own candidate was a fat man well in possession of a huge bell that he kept ringing vigorously, calling for silence.

John Lambright, was a tall distinguished looking man, with gray hair, more salt than pepper, wearing a dark blue shark skin suit, exuding an aura of confidence and assuredness; on the other side was a tall but skinny Harry Starkey whose hair was brownish with more on the sides and back than on the top. They both stood side by side with their right hands upon their hearts and their lefts holding a traditional hat, both bowing with the utmost affability toward the troubled sea of heads that inundated the open space in front, from where a storm of groans, shouts, yells and hooting was coming that would have done honor to an earthquake.

Every one of the men, women, boys, girls and babies who were assembled to see their favorite candidate, screamed with delight and ecstasy as both men of power, hope and ambition walked around solemnly and proudly. Loud and long were the cheers and mighty was the rustling of the flags as a strong wind rushed through them, trying furiously to grab anything that wasn't held on or tacked down. Following at times was a cloud of dust with the same attitude and speed, trying to catch up with the wind, while the tall trees bent their branches pointing the way the wind went.

Suddenly a huge sign bearing Harry Sharkey's name was blown off, a part of it hit on the head and shoulders of a number of his staff, with no serious injuries. The other part went with the wind and the cloud of dust that followed close behind, as if to cover the wind's tracks, the flight of the sign and the other objects that joined in the flying parade. The crowd burst, first into astonished screams and then seeing no one injured, into cheering and laughter.

Harry Sharkey, feeling that man and nature betrayed him, shook his fist with anger; whether he shook his fist at man, heaven or the honorable Mayor, was unknown. He bestowed a look of excessive disgust on his opponents, and if he could have, he probably would have hurled some dreadful and evil curse on their heads and bodies. His staffers, seeing the wrath of nature in their master, held on to him. Whether they held on to him to keep him safe, to prevent him from flying after his sign, or to keep him from going after his opponents, who far outnumbered his supporters, was not clear.

The honorable Mayor, inspired by the incident, believing it was symptomatic of victory, glory and strength, and was put forth by man and nature for his benefit, felt that the gust of wind that passed and captured his opponent's sign had come from heaven. He put on his hat, paused, considered, and in the middle of the gratifying shouts from his supporters, his eyes beaming with cheerfulness and gladness, he stepped down from the stage and began to shake hands and kiss babies faster than a thief in a watermelon patch. The Mayor, melodramatically, but in clear words, followed by respectable gestures and bows, testified to the crowd his ineffaceable obligations to the town of Richville that he was willing and able to meet.

There was a moment of great suspense when his challenger for the throne of the Mayor, Harry Sharkey, suddenly realizing his opponent's splendor, frowning with majesty and boiling with rage, yelled to his officers that what the Mayor was doing was not on the agenda. Then, wasting no further time, with violent effort Harry Sharkey disengaged himself from the grasp of his loyal supporters and plunged down into the crowd on his side of the stage; he moved around quickly, with his feet about three feet apart, as the crowd set into another loud round of cheers. He shook hands and kissed babies faster than his opponent, which triggered another cheer, much louder that the previous one in support of the Mayor. It was most interesting to see the manner in which Mr. Sharkey performed his role, acting in that ceremony, with the torture of anxiety painted on his face, viewing and figuring his opponent was gaining on him. There were people everywhere, up on the roofs of the buildings, in the trees and standing at windows. The stage was closely packed with as many persons as could manage to stand upright on it. John Lambright came up on the stage again and took the microphone in his hand. The bell rang into everyone's ears, demanding silence to come, but unfortunately, for John Lambright, in that place silence was deaf.

Harry Sharkey looked at the Mayor, and feeling he was being left behind, hissed and made some threatening gestures to the incumbent. The honorable Mayor only gazed with delight on his face, without responding in words or gestures, as often strong and confident men do.

The challenger rushed onto the stage, struggling for breath he stood there, not knowing how to occupy himself. Sensing that there were a thousand eyes upon the Mayor and only two upon him, those of his wife, who was standing a few heads away desperately trying to catch his attention to tell him to calm down.

"Ladies and gentlemen," shouted the Mayor, as loudly as he could force his voice, "ladies and gentlemen, I am here today to express my beliefs, goals and the sacrifices that I am willing to make for our town to bring pride, prosperity and an even higher level of recognition which this town and its wonderful people, you, deserve. You deserve the best and the best is yet to come - with me at the helm for another four years."

"How is the lumber business?" cried a voice from the crowd, interrupting the Mayor's heartfelt speech, " Are you making a lot of money building useless sheds for the city?"

That loud outcry was received with a storm of jeers and cheers, with again the bell ringing out for silence. The Mayor kept up his verbal output but the microphone was turned off, rendering the remainder of the speech inaudible. Finally, as the microphone was turned on towards the end of his speech, the Mayor was heard boasting that he was the best man for the job and that the past three and half years was not enough time to finish what he had started.

Next, the tall, skinny and hopeful Harry Sharkey took the microphone in his hands and boasted to the crowd that he was the most fit and proper person for the job of Mayor in their beloved town. The crowd applauded long and loud for him while the Mayor's people groaned with equal duration and volume. Between the jeering, cheering, groaning and hooting, more hooting than cheering, and other natural and unnatural sounds and noises, the tall man could have sung the Greek national anthem and would have been heard and understood about the same and probably would have had more fun just singing it than trying to penetrate, with skillful words, the skulls of that noisy, excited and confused crowd. Harry Sharkey finished his speech with a question in his and his supporters' minds as to whether he had finished his speech or finished his political career; according to the groaning crowd on the honorable Mayor's side, Sharkey's career could very well have come to an end.

Almost spontaneously, another serious-minded gentleman, double his proper weight, swimming in sweat, clearly confusing the meaning of the two old American proverbs, 'Strike while the iron is hot' and 'If you can't stand the heat get out of the kitchen,' sped forward, apparently to testify and verify that whatever Harry had said was true and correct.

Erik, taking a second look at the fat man, recognized the physiognomy of Bob with whom he had the brief encounter in George's restaurant the previous evening. Erik smiled and looked around to catch a glimpse of George's face, but he was nowhere to be seen. With the gloomy reception that Harry was being given, Bob, the fat man, stood steadfastly by his side; he wasn't about to abandon ship yet, and most of all, he didn't wish to give up on Harry Sharkey's career because Bob's career was tied to his master's and therefore he was willing to fight to his last drop of sweat. Very few people, only those who have tried, know what a difficult process it is to convince people to listen when they've already made up their minds not to because they don't believe what they are about to hear. After a few sentences of figurative expressiveness, the fat man became enraged, denouncing those who had the nerve to interrupt him while he poured out magnificent expectations for and the remarkable talents of his leader, exchanging defiance with them and anyone else who rejected his presence and performance. The uproar of the opposites rose louder and was joined by others who roared but didn't have the slightest idea of what they were doing, except they knew they were roaring. This phenomenon reduced Bob to the necessity of expressing his feelings with a series of vulgar gestures. Finally, after a long struggle with words, realizing that he was losing big time, he ran for his life and limb as the opponents took an ugly, mean and aggressive stance.

Erik, seeing Bob running, smiled, remembering George's story of the hairy butt. His anticipated nonexistent plan 'B' was about to emerge and be put into execution by the crowd if Bob were not as fast and as free with his feet as he had been with his mouth.

Seeing this, the honorable Mayor, thinking that the cards were being stacked in his favor, commanded the band to commence playing his theme song, stronger and louder than before.

The command, like all the mandates of emperors, judges and other great potentates of the earth, was forthwith obeyed.

That notion was brutally rejected by the challenger's party, and struggling, pushing and fighting started. The Mayor, being a true politician, making laws and not thinking of their consequences, never anticipating a vicious battle between opposing people of the right and left parties to take place, did what was within his power by issuing imperative orders to the chief of police to seize the ringleaders of both sides, amounting to more than two dozen, and to put them in a barricaded enclosure away from the main body of the crowd until after the debate. But the chief of police, being accustomed to being shown both the hanger and the nail it's hanging from, didn't separate the trouble makers, but kept them together as if they were old friends and so when they reached the barricaded area, much to his surprise and not to anyone else's, a small war erupted among those ringleaders fueled with even more fury and fire than before, even though the police were present. If there were a one-eyed man looking at the police and the fighting men, his other eye would have gone bad too. To be more specific, some of the police were looking on with an indifferent expression on their faces, some yawned from boredom and all of them attempted to do nothing because, the truth be told, they had no one to lead them, because the mayor's brother in law, the chief of the police, couldn't divide hay between two donkeys without getting confused. The struggle went on for several minutes and at the end, some lost blood, several lost teeth, others got pretty well bruised and some got black and blue swollen eyes.

The fighting bunch finally stopped of their own accord, when they all had their fill of beating and being beaten.

The butcher benefited more than anyone else that day, because the beef steaks he had brought along to sell to the spectators cooked rare, medium or well done, before, during and after the debate, instead were sold raw to the wounded in order to lay on their bruises and puffed black and blue eyes. The number of hurt was greater than the number of steaks the butcher had brought. However, that event brought a storm of delight to the butcher's breast and a proverb came to his mind, from a similar incident, a long time ago, that is, **one man's meat is another man's poison.** The butcher, after selling the entire stock of his raw meat and being one of the many moneychangers of the town, cast all his attention to his steam table that was loaded with hot dogs, polish kielbasa, chili sauce and tons of sauerkraut.

The crowd was displeased and most of the voters showed contempt and scorn for the Mayor in allowing the fistfight to happen, and of course the Mayor placed all of the blame on his brother in law, the chief of police.

"Are you stupid?" asked the Mayor, whispering to the Chief but smiling at the angry and disappointed crowd. "Don't you have any brains in your stupid Irish head?"

"You told me to put them away from the main crowd," replied the chief, fearing his boss's words and dreading the consequences.

"I'm going to lose the damn race because of you. Look at that reporter from the Home Town News waiting to start interviewing the voters. The bastard hates me and now he has a way of burying me. I'm going to lose the race, I'm telling you!"

"No, you are not. Your beating Harry Sharkey is a piece of cake," said the chief.

"A piece of cake? Shit, I couldn't even beat the town gravedigger now, even if I shook fifteen hundred hands and kissed one hundred and five babies per minute, I couldn't win, stupid. Why did you put them together?"

"I couldn't tell who was who." said the police chief, with a fake smile on his face.

"How about those keystone cops you got out there?"

"They couldn't either."

"I feel like taking your gun right now and blowing off your goddamned head, I would say your brains but you ain't got any." said the Mayor, with the same tone and the same smile on his face, without stopping for breath or any other consideration. "Look at those guys; they look like they came out of the Battle of Gettysburg," said the Mayor, appearing as if he had reached the highest pitch of his excitement and was about to vent his grief and wrath in another way.

There they were, those gallant men of the fist war, holding the steaks on the sores. Some of them were standing, some sitting and some walking around suffering with pain and madness.

The suffering of the two dozen or so men, the idling of the chief's keystone cops, the hooting and the cheering were all carefully and intently observed by Erik, who was very close to the stage and very close to Harry Sharkey who was also standing, accompanied by his friends and supporters, with counterfeit manners, deploring the events, while enjoying the ill reception of the crowd towards the honorable Mayor. Erik's eyes fell on the domestic dispute between the two top town officials, the chief of police and the Mayor. John Lambright, the honorable Mayor, like most politicians who think they can govern everything including their patience, flew into a frightful rage.

If anything else could have been added to that amusing scene, it would have been the Mayor chasing his chief of police with a baseball bat to impart some blows on the Chief's butt and head. The mayor grabbed the chief by the collar and shook him brutally, shouting, but Erik and the crowd could not hear the words. The Chief, with a violent effort, shifted himself away from the Mayor's grasp and in doing so administered an unintended blow to the Mayor's shoulder with such accuracy and force the Mayor fell on top of a baseball bat that a young boy was holding. The Mayor, without any consideration or further thought, came to his feet with a distorted face, holding the bat with both hands ready to strike at the Chief, who upon seeing the Mayor in such an insane condition, sped away like a jackrabbit, jumping off the stage like a paratrooper, flying over the chairs and some little old men and ladies like a runaway dog with the Mayor at his heels. The Chief, turning back while running to see if the space between him and his brother-in-law was expanding or shrinking, smacked wildly against the butcher and with a loud crash the butcher, the chief and the Mayor fell heavily down, taking with them the butcher's steam table laden with hot dogs, catsup mustard and sauerkraut. Most of these campaign staples landed on the butcher's stomach and he lay there on his back, too wise to move. Erik ran to that jumble of men garnished in food, went down on his knees next to the Mayor and Chief and advised both of them to get up and pretend that the whole thing was a joke.

"Who are you?" asked the Mayor, pulling sauerkraut away from his face and hair.

"I'm Nick Polis and I'm the guy who is going to save your ass. Do as I say! Start eating some hot dogs! Hurry! Pick them up from the butcher's belly and laugh, damn it, laugh!" With those words, Erik fled onto the stage. He looked around at the sea of laughing faces and took the microphone in his hands.

"Ladies and gentlemen," shouted Erik, ringing the big bell with all the strength he could muster. As he looked ahead of him into the crowd he thought that he had never seen such a sea of white faces, yellow heads and earnest blue eyes. All looked up and hoped that he would be the one to calm the waters.

"Ladies and Gentlemen, let's give a big hand to the mayor and the chief for that ingenious stage act they so skillfully performed." The echo of his voice rang in George's ears who had stationed himself a few ranks of people away from the frenzy, by a tree trunk. He looked at his friend with the widest smile that nature allowed anyone to exhibit.

"I am Nick Polis and I must admit that I am the creator of that whole scene; the fight between those gallant men was not designed to go that way, it got out of hand. Give them a hand any way, " continued Erik.

The crowd responded with a round of applause that caused Harry Sharkey to shrink by at least a foot, if not more.

"Ladies and gentlemen I'm the new entertainment director for the city of Richville."

"I thought I was the director, " said a small middle aged man softly, standing in front of George and looking as if his main meal for the day had consisted of no more than a chicken sandwich and a glass of milk.

"Shut up!" said George, administering a feeble slap on the head of the little man, "You are not the director."

"No, I'm the director," protested the man, looking back to see who slapped him.

"I said shut up. The next thing I'll do is hit you with my **Tsarouci,** (shepherd's boot)," uttered George calmly and forcefully.

"What's that?" asked the little fellow with a squeaky voice.

"You'll find out when it goes up your ass."

The little man looked behind him once again and started to move away quickly, but George's arm was quicker, so he grabbed and pulled him back to his original station and said emphatically, "Stay here! Are you going to be quiet or are you going to growl like a hungry stomach? Your mother told me to keep my eye on you. I don't want you to get lost," said George, with his eyes directed and riveted firmly on Erik.

"My mother? My mother is dead," replied the director full of bewilderment.

"She died already? Poor woman. She was such a nice woman,"

"No, she wasn't, she was a tramp," said the little guy angrily.

"You see? That's why I knew her. Anyway, your mother told me this before she died. Now shut up and listen to the man!"

"You're pulling my leg."

"When I pull your leg, you'll know it because I'll be pushing on the other and making a wish," said George more emphatically.

"Ladies and gentlemen the mayor knows that happiness is laughter and laughter brings happiness. Look at your Mayor!" said Erik, observing that all the heads turned to look at the Mayor who stood there dividing his time in small alternate allotments between eating, smiling and waving.

"He is happy and you know he is a happy person. Show me a happy person and I will show you a winner. Show me a miserable one and I will show you a loser. No offence to you, Mr. Sharkey, and your loyal follower Bob, wherever he is," said Erik, turning to Sharkey with a smile and waving at him.

Being a serious and distinguished looking gentleman, Mr. Sharkey displayed a striking smile, taking it as a joke, but his friends and supporters around him displayed something of the opposite.

The beaming faces of the crowd cheered with uncountable energy and zeal.

"The Mayor, ladies and gentlemen, was born and raised here. He is a proud citizen of this town. This is his hometown. This is his home and any fair-minded man cares for his home. Mr. Sharkey was born and raised in another town. Do you people want a stranger to run your town? If his hometown was any good, he would have stayed there and been its Mayor."

The Mayor stopped chewing and started to preen as if he were the only rooster in the hen house. Turning to look at the butcher, the Mayor saw his face, head and shoulders emerging from beneath the smorgasbord of food; he rushed to his aid and gave him his hand until the butcher was restored to a standing position and then the chief began to clean the butcher as if he were the butcher's mother, while in the meantime Erik was conducting a seminar on the mayor's behalf.

"Send the bill to the city," said the Mayor brushing off the bewildered butcher, "and do you know how the butcher got rich?" asked the honorable Mayor.

The butcher, having his mouth full of an unwanted mixture of food, only nodded negatively.

"The butcher got rich by saying to his customers, 'it's a little bit over.' Do you understand?"

The butcher, with all his problems, managed to smile and nod vigorously.

"Do that! Fatten up the bill, the city will pay," said the Mayor, picking a long piece of sauerkraut from the butcher's hair.

The butcher's smile turned wider and he nodded more vigorously, knowing that he could charge more than what he had lost.

"Ladies and gentlemen, I must tell you that you can grow old in harmony with your friends and relatives. You must overlook their bad side and triumph on their good side. Mayor John Lambright has been a friend of the city and a friend of yours throughout his life," said Erik. He stopped and looked around him with an air of wonder, then took out his handkerchief and slowly wiped the sweat off his face.

Dismay and anguish were depicted on every face around the

challenger.

"I personally do not know the challenger, Mr. Harry Sharkey. He may be a wonderful husband, father and he may also be a wonderful grandfather. He might turn out to be a good Mayor too. But he may also be the opposite of that. That's the chance you are taking if you are going to vote for the challenger, Harry Sharkey. The honorable John Lambright, on the other hand, you know well, better than I. He may not be perfect, but is it so bad for someone not to be perfect in an imperfect world such as ours? What would he be if he were perfect? If he were perfect he would be a lonely man with no one to talk to. A lonely man is miserable. Would you, ladies and gentlemen, like to have a miserable man as Mayor? We were made from the beginning to be perfect.

Adam and Eve were perfect, but bounded by and locked in the goodness of the Creator, they were miserable. They had no knowledge of anything bad. Then the serpent came along and convinced Eve to eat the forbidden fruit. The serpent did not deceive Eve but, to the contrary, enlightened her, and through her, all mankind. The serpent was not an enemy of Eve, but rather, her best friend. The Greek idea was that, far from being the seducer of the race, the serpent was our first schoolmaster by teaching us to choose between good and evil. Imagine going through life in a monastery under the rule of a suppressive Creator with no adventure, no excitement, no gain, no loss, no reward, no punishment, no joy and no sorrow. But when we learned the other side of good, all of the above came to light; that's why the ancient Greeks called it the enlightenment of the serpent because, most of all then, we acquired the right to choose. Here, ladies and gentlemen, you have to choose between two imperfect men. They both have some good and some evil in them, like most of you out there. Some of you have more evil than good and some of you have more good than evil. You have lived with the honorable John Lambright, therefore you know him. He is more good than bad. Mr. Sharkey on the other hand, you don't know, he might be more good then evil or he might be more evil than good." Cheering filled the air and the Mayor's heart so much so that he almost choked on his hot dog. While Erik was speaking, the crowd looked on with interest, beaming faces and lit up eyes, waiting to applaud at the first opportune moment. George was looking on, overtaken by the thrill of association and the Mayor and the Chief were occupying themselves with the cleaning of the butcher, who didn't seem to care about his personal appearance, but only the condition of his little ruined empire.

The Harry Sharkey gang stood around looking as helpless as little kittens sinking on a broken raft in the turbulence of a river's rushing waters.

"That son-of –a-bitch is good," remarked Harry Sharkey to his friends, with anger on his face. "He's smart. He's getting into the people's hearts with that stupid Mayor, bypassing their heads. He's an actor."

"Ladies and gentlemen, I stand here before you and God, and I am saying to you if something is not broken don't try to fix it! We, my dear new friends, see breakups everyday in our lives. We see the breakup of families where the husband, the wife and the children go their separate ways; the painful break up of happy friendship groups; the breakup between an employee and an employer; a change of fortune that brings the breakup of a business. Most of these breakups didn't need fixing. They only broke up because someone tried to fix something that was not broken in the first place. Maybe it wasn't perfect, but it was not broken. I am asking you, at this important moment, ask yourselves and let God be your witness if your relationship with your honorable Mayor, John Lambright, is broken before you try to fix it. John likes to see you happy. I know he does, he went through hell and almost killed himself and the poor butcher in a desperate effort to put smiles on your faces. The magic words for today should be 'make someone happy,' and you will be happy too. My dear friends, get up in the morning, try to make someone happy and then you'll see, you'll be happy too. That's what the Bible says, Give and you shall receive."

There was another wave of applause stronger than the previous one.

"No matter what we think of those public servants, commonly known as politicians, they are people of a special breed, they are people who love people. They like to see people happy. John!" shouted Erik, "Come on up here and say a few words, John. Don't be shy!" There was a great storm of laughter accompanied by an avalanche of applause. John, stricken with glory and pride, rushed towards the stage, gathering strength and confidence as he approached.

Erik stopped, partly to wait for John and partly to enjoy the ongoing applause.

"John," said Erik, when the Mayor came and stood by his side, "I want you to know that you probably won't see me again. My work as the director of entertainment was only for one day. John, my brief friend, you don't have to lead the town anywhere. You don't have to lead the people; the people know what to do by themselves. Just give some help to the needy; keep the taxes down; keep the streets clean and safe and keep the parks green. And be humble, John. Our lord Jesus Christ was humble, John, and look how many people are following him. Go with your heart, John, not just with your head. The heart, John, is stronger than the head. So long, John, I must go." Erik turned, wiped some sweat from his face and rushed off the stage hastily. There was a surge of applause. The young, the old, the sick, the healthy, men and women all stood up, applauded and waved with energy and passion.

"Ladies and gentlemen – no, I will not call you ladies and gentlemen, if I'm permitted by you, I will call you my friends. My friends, I am here ready to debate my challenger, Mr. Harry Sharkey. I will debate with all my heart."

Erik moved between the spectators as they made room for him to walk through, looking at him while clapping their hands and bidding him goodbye.

Then George fought his way through, unnoticed and unrecognized, rushing to catch up with his new friend. It was later and away from the crowd when George caught up with him.

"Erik!" shouted the former shepherd with a full lungs and strong voice. Erik was heading out of town, towards the hotel and moving fast, as if he had to go somewhere important and was running late.

"Erik!" yelled George, forming his hands in the shape of a blow horn. Erik turned and seeing George running his way, stopped and waited for him to approach. "Where are you going so fast?" asked George, out of breath and out of time, grabbing Erik by the arm. "You move like you are trying to get away from the bad to catch up with the good."

Erik smiled faintly.

"I am going to pick up my utensils from the hotel, knowing that the election is still weeks away and seeing there are a great number of voters whose ears weren't greeted with too many positive ideas and whose hearts weren't filled with favorable and convincing arguments from either side, they remain undecided. My plans to stay in this town are not going to be extended for that or any other reason; so I'm leaving the battlefield of the givers and takers, the haves and the have-nots and I'll be heading out."

"Where are you going?" asked George, calmly now that he had caught his breath.

"Like I said, I was going to go back to my hotel room to pick up my utensils."

"You told me that. By the way what's utensils?" interrupted George.

Erik looked at George and smiled, then his smile shrank, "utensils are the same thing as eating and cooking tools or remnants or odds and ends or belongings. If you knew my life story you would have accepted that as my 'leftovers'."

"I've got it. Where are you going now?" asked George.

"Oh, I don't know, away."

"No! We'll have breakfast and we'll talk," said George, still holding on to him as they started to walk away. "What happened back there? I heard that there was a riot," he continued, hoping to keep Erik from going, leaving the most serious matters for the breakfast table.

"Not a riot, a battle like that of the Olympic Gods and the Titans"

"That bad?"

"Worse. More warriors here."

"Who won?" asked George.

"The Gods won. They killed all the Titans except Poseidon," said Erik, stopping his walk.

"I know, they made him the God of the seas," interrupted George, "come on, with me," urged George steering Erik in the direction of the restaurant.

"Wait a moment George!" said Erik, pulling his arm out of the grasp as gently as George was holding it. "I must be going right now, without sounding like an ungrateful snob, I must tell you that I have to go."

George appeared struck by Erik's remark, "Go? Go where?"

Erik looked at his new friend as if he were prolonging a response.

"Where will you go?" asked George, with a little more energy and a lot more concern in his question.

"I'm a lost man, George," answered Erik speaking softly, looking away. "I lost everything within minutes less than a week ago. George, I am not talking about love and fortunes, I am talking about something more dear to life than life itself. When you are lost you must find a reason for living or a prize for dying, whichever comes first. But with you, I enjoyed talking and listening. I will value our brief visit and it will be a long friendship. I must go to do what I have to do. If I'm ever in need of a piece of bread or a word of encouragement, I will call upon you, my friend. I had a one-umbrella house, but I loused it up."

"Erik, or Nick? " there he stopped for one long moment and waited for Erik to talk. Erik's head was facing downwards; he only lifted his eyes and smiled.

"You were at the park, weren't you?"

"Yes, I saw you and I heard you."

"My real name is Erik Karas, like I told you before. I wasn't about to declare my real name knowing that I wasn't going to be around very long."

"I talk a lot but staying in the rain will not wash away the sins and the guilt we Greeks are known for. Walking in boots with no toes, and working in gloves with no fingers will not do it," said George, "don't get lost Erik. You have the talent of bringing the lost out from the dark into the light. There are too many lost people out there who need to be found. If the Government ever decides to open up a lost and found department for humans, they will fill two Yankee stadiums in every large city in America. In Greece you don't have to try to be better in order to be good; here the moment you stop trying to be better you are no longer good. Here, it is a race everyday of the week, throughout the year. If you lose you are lost. In the old country there is no race, therefore, there isn't any winning and there is no losing. If your father left you with sixty-five goats and you leave your children with seventy, then you are successful. Here, if your father leaves you with sixty-five limousines and you don't try to make them one hundred forty, you are going to end up with two limos and four flat tires. I told you that this country is for the rich and for those who are trying to be rich. The rest will fall behind and get lost like lovers who followed their hearts and lost their heads or investors who followed their heads and lost their hearts or women who lost their hearts and heads to find themselves. Those who are trying to find solid proof of God's existence, end up worshipping idols; they are lost. There are singers who don't sing anymore, there are actors who don't act, there are lovers who can't love, there are mothers who can't mother anymore and husbands who have no wives. They are good people who no longer know how to be good. Those are the people who failed the race. They need help. They need you to talk to them. You don't have to be a saint to teach the word of God. The reason I am telling you all this is because I know what you are, Erik. Find those lost people. They are dead but not buried under the ground. Find them, Erik, talk to them and bring them back to life."

"Talk is cheap," said Erik.

"Do you know why they say that 'talk is cheap'?"

"Why?" asked Erik.

"Because it costs you nothing to talk," said George, looking at Erik intently, "but, my God, it's priceless to the people who need it. As for you, my dear and unforgettable friend, you have the gift of passing on ten-cent words for one hundred dollar bills, just because you have a way of shaping them together into arrows that restart the heart of the lost."

There was a moment, heavy with awful suspense, as George waited to hear something from Erik.

Erik seemed rather pleased with George's compliments and having nothing else to say to him, he straightened his tie and buttoned his new blue sport jacket, for the sake of appearance. He then told George he was ready to move out, shook George's hand vigorously and turned away. George stood there, planted like a lamppost, on the same spot, watching his adamant friend disappear into the fields beyond the town limits on his way to the hotel to pick up his leftovers, as he had put it.

CHAPTER 3

The attempted robbery

Erik walked for two days and almost two nights with the sunrise behind him and the sunset ahead. The night was closing in with a dark angry sky ripe and ready to open its cataracts to irrigate the earth. He gazed at the sky but went on, with the hidden pain inside of him and the bundle of his belongings on his back, not a bit wiser or happier than before.

Suddenly the rain began to fall, accompanied by strong gusts of wind, blinding flashes of lighting and crashing thunder, as though Mother Nature wished to thin down the earth's solid soil rather than refresh its life. The rain didn't come straight down, but the wind sent it across the road hitting Erik on the side of his face and body. For a moment the rain would die down and Erik would begin to deceive himself into believing that the worst was over, then he would hear it growling and whistling again, rushing over the trees and the hilltops, gathering sound and strength as it drew nearer to dash with fury against him, as if he were the target of its madness. Driving the sharp needles of rain into his muscles and its cold breath into his bones, the storm passed him, screaming and scowling with a conspicuous roar, as if ridiculing his weakness and celebrating its own strength and power. He felt personally offended by nature's unkind attitude. The mired and the muddy road, the heavy pouring of pure water and being on the road, on foot for better than two days, left Erik weak and fearing the imminent danger of fainting. He suddenly saw a bridge ahead and gathering the last drops of his strength, he made it off the road to seek its shelter. He sat there trembling from lack of will and energy. He opened up his bundle with shaking hands, took out a piece of bread and with much difficulty, gently placed it in his mouth, hoping to revive some leftover power.

He finished his bread, remained as still as a dead log for five or so minutes and then began to feel alive again, not alive and well, just alive; even though his body felt heavier, it still had more strength than his mind.

The rain had stopped and the lighting and thunder were now triumphing far away. He stood up, leaned against the foot of the bridge to test his strength and finding it adequate, walked up the hill and took to the road again. Finally he came to a two-lane black-top highway. With no mud or water under his feet, he hastened his steps; a couple of cars and an eighteen-wheeler zoomed by, but none stopped to lend him a hand. He walked on and after a while, he grinned as his spirit was lifted a little when he saw, a few hundred yards ahead, an old two-story building with some cars parked out front. He threw a quick glance at the upper part of the structure as he put on his jacket, somewhat dried from the many hours in that summer night's heat after the rain. The unusual structure in that odd place was lit up like a Las Vegas casino with strong lights shooting out of the windows and shedding bright rays on the road, some which even lit the hedge on the other side. Making these brief observations with his head and eyes roaming around, he walked two steps up and entered what seemed to be a bar and restaurant with sleeping accommodations on the second floor. He walked to a booth, and sat opposite the bar, his back to the open door. His eyes fell on the pretty waitress who was working a few tables away from him, laying a fresh cloth on a big round table. At times she found it necessary to stoop over, in order to reach the table's farthest edge. The move caused her dress neckline to dip allowing the upper parts of her large breasts to pop out, but they seemed undecided whether they were going to come out, stay tucked in, or just hang around looking ahead, as if mocking their beholder.

This picture of negligence had no effect on Erik but at the bar there was a stout man with a red face whose eyes were severely nailed on the scene, as if he had made up his mind to see the most he could of her. If Erik were a little closer, he would have seen the man's mouth watering. Erik gazed away and around, surveying the establishment. He saw a delightful and charming display of hanging hams, Virginia hams that is, with jars of pickles and preserves together with many liquor bottles arranged on the shelves behind the bar, presenting a delicious collection of food and spirits that would enhance the appetite of any reasonable man. At the end of the bar sat a middle age lady with a contented face, wearing a white apron, and from her gestures and the confident attitude she exhibited, she was obviously the owner and ruler of those pleasing-to-the-eye possessions. On the next barstool sat a man about her age properly dressed and engaged in parley with her. It didn't require too much thinking to conclude that the man was endeavoring to persuade her to be his sharer of troubles and cares for the remainder of the night or his natural life, whichever she preferred the most.

The woman, not being sufficiently enlightened by the man's words or actions, and not knowing whether he was trying to get into her heart, her place of business, her pants or all of the above, stood up, and while walking away, said, "I had one good husband."

The lady voiced those words loudly and clearly enough to be heard by anyone who had his eyes and ears pointed at her direction. "He died and I will not be attached to anyone else unless he is as good if not better than my late husband and that I find to be improbable, if not completely impossible." She concluded her recital with an air of secure independence, letting that man know, in front of witnesses, that she was as much in favor of him as his height and the man was not very tall, in fact, he was kind of short, thus she continued her short journey into the kitchen.

The man looked bruised and disappointed realizing all those affectionate familiarities he tried to pass on the widow instead were passed down the drain. He remained there still and quiet, holding onto the only thing that was at his disposal at that moment, that being his glass of spirits.

The waitress with the large breasts came to Erik, took his order and hastily tripped into the kitchen.

While waiting for his hot meal to come, Erik looked outside and saw the lightning, heard the thunder and observed the rain coming down again with the wind blowing strong enough to make every timber in the old house creak and groan as though they were crying for help.

When his hot food arrived, Erik looked at the dinner the widow had hurled up for him with her own hands; without losing a second he went to work on it and gobbled it up in no time at all. He finished his wine, knitted his hands on the back of his head and stretched backwards, feeling his body had been through long service and hard usage.

After a little while, the widow came out of the kitchen, stood at the end of the bar with her left elbow resting on the rail and her right hand on her hip, gazed intently at Erik and thus created yet another rejection for the unfortunate love seeker.

Erik's constitution was able to endure a considerable amount of trial and fatigue but the combination of attacks from Mother Nature, being battered by the storm and parched by the summer heat, caused him to feel drained and drowsy. He stretched out in the booth with his head tilted back, relaxing to the best of his ability. The well-dressed man with the widow's rejection in his head, the glass of spirits in his hands and his ego ripped to shreds beyond repair, divided his gaze between the widow and Erik, feeling very justly and properly indignant that Erik, who looked as if he had won first place in a worst dresser contest, was about to be called upon by the widow herself to keep her company. He was deliberating whether he had a perfect right to pick a fight with Erik for contriving to get into her good graces. The other man, whose mouth was watering from looking down the waitress' dress, took a hint of how much the well-dressed man was suffering, how much damage had been inflicted on his manly pride and divided his gaze between Erik and the man with the broken heart.

The widow had planted herself by the bar and was looking at Erik. The well-dressed man felt ill used and persecuted in so much as he was properly dressed and well mannered but had been rejected by the lady. The stout man, acting a little funny from feeling the effects of his drink, was rubbing the knee of his right leg, applying more force than normal, and was dividing his gaze between Erik and the well-dressed man.

Erik, who was stretched out looking at the ceiling, feeling relaxed and tired, saw that a situation was brewing where anything could happen and even though he was by far not the main cause, he was right smack in the middle of that evil twist of fate where dilemmas could flare up into something with serious consequences. According to some well-informed and well-read theological students, God, and or fate, is monitoring critical situations, and this situation should have qualified as a critical one. At that precise moment when both men at the bar turned their gaze to Erik and the looks on their faces changed to distortion and anger, Erik, feeling their stares, moved slightly and placed his hand on his gun. As the drama was about to unfold and could easily have turned into an OK coral shoot out, whether God was monitoring that moment or fate willed it, suddenly two well armed police in full uniform walked into the place.

The widow abandoned her flirtatious glances at Erik and turned to face the police. Seeing that both men at the bar returned to their drinking, Erik removed his hand from his gun.

"What can I do you for, big boys?" asked the lady of the house in a sexy tone of voice, "Hello, Bob, what are you doing big fellow?"

"Anybody I can and the good ones twice," replied Bob loudly and confidently.

With those words, that he repeated with great emphasis and violence, Bob, one of the two officers, dashed his hat upon the bar in a most unusual show of excitement and then, grabbing Pam with both hands by the shoulders, brought her close to him, looked firmly and fixedly in her face, and said "You're the only woman who snuck and coiled herself into my poor and hurting heart."

The waitress who was setting the tables, hearing those words of sycophancy, cast her eyes on that overplayed scene, looked around with a vinegary smile and turning back to her work, moved her hands sadistically, as if to wring a neck.

Pam playfully disengaged herself from him and backing off a couple of paces said, in the same manner, as she broke away, "I have never known bricks to hurt, they're hard and cold."

"Pam, those words have reduced this two hundred and twenty pound statue to nothing, so much nothing it can be knocked over by a feather," said Bob, hitting his chest with both hands, "you mean to tell me that I have a hard cold brick for a heart?"

"What a bull shit artist," mumbled the waitress in a low voice, but loud enough for Erik to hear, as if she were venting her anger.

Staring at her for one long moment, Bob said more affably than before, "I've a little something to trouble you with, Pam. Come into the kitchen for a just a moment."

Pam slowly led the way into the kitchen; Bob and the other officer followed. As this happened, the man with the red face rubbed his knee again, stood up and moved out limping; the well dressed man followed very calmly but cautiously. Erik maintained his original position of relaxing.

Seeing the two men walked out together, Erik surmised that they were old pals but had sat separately so the one of them could make a move on the widow, though their leaving as soon as the police arrived and moving out with a calm cautious manner created a suspicious feeling in Erik's mind but he remained visibly unaffected.

After a little while both police officers walked out of the kitchen with the lady leading the way. The trio stood behind the counter for a moment with the two officers exhibiting the appearance of discipline and looking as if they truly belonged to that learned profession of police officer.

The questions and answers were completed to everyone's satisfaction and the two officers walked away hastily, as all busy men with purpose typically do. Suddenly Bob stopped, turned, looked at Pam and said, "You can bring a horse to water, but you can't make it drink." Then he grinned and continued, "I wish you would drink from my pond."

"I'm not thirsty yet. When or if I get thirsty I'll jump in your pond. But don't keep it empty just for me. There must be plenty of mares around who'd love to play in your pond."

Picking up his hat, placing carefully on his head, he imparted a wink, turned and walked away quickly trying to catch up with the other officer.

Seeing them disappear out of the front door, the widow first looked at Erik, then gazed around with a searching eye and walked over to him. He, out of keen courtesy, restored himself to a proper sitting position and stared at her with a vacant look on his face.

"What happened to lover boy?" asked the lady, nodding her head towards the door as if she already knew that he was gone.

"They went out together."

"Together?" asked the lady with more concern in her question.

"Yes they were together, friends, you know."

"How do you know?"

"I'm telling you something, those two were friends. They only separated in here so one could hit on you" said Erik in a serious and much solemn manner.

"May I sit down?" asked the lady, exhaling a revolting sigh. "Linda!" yelled the lady, apparently to the waitress," bring me a cup of coffee, Honey. Do you want anything? I'm buying."

"No, thank you ma'am. The food was delicious I meant to complement you earlier."

"Thank you, stranger."

"Call me Erik"

"Hello, Erik. My name is Pam. Pamela Flood," said the lady, offering him her hand with a smile.

"I'm glad to know you, Pamela Flood," replied Erik, shaking her hand gently, "All the rain that fell the last two days, you must have a lot of floods down here," said Erik humorously.

"No relation to the floods created by the rain, only related to the real Floods."

"I am sure that they feel honored to be related to you. Anyone would be delighted, no matter what the nature of the relationship is," replied Erik, with a grin on his face.

"Smooth, very smooth," returned the widow Flood, "are you going to try to hit on me too, stranger?"

"No ma'am. It's not my style. Nothing personal. Humor is my cup of tea."

The waitress, with the low neck line, whose half exposed breasts had made the other man's mouth water without her knowledge or concern, brought the coffee and gazed at Erik out of curiosity, but much to her surprise he didn't return a glance.

"Anything else, Pam?" asked the waitress, looking at Erik who still didn't oblige her.

Pam only shook her head negatively.

"How about you, sir?" asked the waitress.

"No thank you ma'am" returned Erik, with a grin and quick glance. The two remained silent until the waitress disappeared in the kitchen.

"Aren't going to ask me what the police were doing here at this hour of the night?"

"You just called me stranger. What kind of a stranger would I be if I'd tried to learn your business?"

"You have a funny way of answering questions with a question."

"I told you that humor is my cup of tea."

"You're right. I remember you told me that. They are looking for two men. I have a number of people who are sleeping upstairs but none of them are connected with each other."

"Now that you made it my business, why are the police looking for them, did they say? I am curious."

"They tried to hold up a convenience store outside Richville. Do you know where Richville is?"

Erik smiled and said, "I know Richville, I left there the day before yesterday."

"I'm from Richville, I was born there. I got married there, my first marriage. The second, my husband died, accident. My first husband is still there."

"I hate to interrupt your autobiography, but tell me about those two men," asked Erik seriously.

"What are you? A justice seeker?"

"No, that's the police, they're the justice seekers, I'm just curious."

The widow looked at him for a long moment and then grinned. "The police didn't have much on them. The owner of the convenience store said that he only saw them running. He saw them from the back. Oh, one was slightly...."

"Limping?" interrupted Erik.

"Yes. How did you know?" asked the lady, concerned.

"Very interesting, " mumbled Erik, looking downwards.

"What's very interesting?" inquired the widow.

"Very interesting," repeated Erik in the same way.

"What's interesting?" asked the woman in a louder voice, "You are driving me crazy."

"Never mind," said Erik, looking away.

"What do you mean, never mind, after you planted something in my mind?" stated the lady.

"Look and listen to me. Do you have a gun?"

The lady didn't respond; she only stared at him with deep concern showing in her eyes.

"Look, the police came and told you that they are looking for two bad guys. The bad guys are here."

"Were here, you mean."

"No! They are still here. They will be back. That I know."

"Why will they come back?" asked Pam, terrified.

"They forgot to say good night to you. Why will they come back?"

"To rob the place?"

"By golly, you've got it. I asked you if you have a gun."

"What am I going to do with a gun?"

"Shoot them," responded Erik, harshly.

"Me? I can't shoot anybody."

"I can," returned Erik, reaching into his pocket, "here is my gun permit. My name is Erik Karas."

"You're Greek?" asked the widow with surprise, as she looked at the document in astonishment.

"Yes, You sound as if being a Greek is some kind of a rare animal," said Erik hurriedly.

"My first husband is Greek"

"Good," interrupted Erik again, quickly and politely, "we'll talk about your husbands later. Now, do you have a gun?"

"Do you?" she asked emphatically.

"Yes, but I have to have two. One to show and one to hide."

"Why are you talking this way? I think there is something wrong with you," said the widow, getting up, "I think I'm going to call the police."

"Okay," said Erik, pulling on her white apron gently, "sit down and I will explain everything to you. Then you can do anything you want. Then you can call the priest, your aunt, your uncle or the chief of police...Sit down please."

Having her eyes fixed firmly on his, the lady sat down, slowly and carefully.

"The guy you were talking to, his friend has a bum knee. I thought I saw something suspicious on my way in here. I saw a car facing the street. That's a getaway position. These guys need something. These are the guys the police are looking for. They're still out there, somewhere near."

"You said they need something. Is it money?" asked the girl.

"I don't think so," said Erik, scratching his head, "If they wanted to rob the place they would have done it before I came in, while the place was empty. They wouldn't talk to you as if they were old pals of yours."

"What are they looking for?"

" I don't know. I don't know what you have in here," responded Erik.

"I have nothing but what you see, and some money that I've taken in since I came back from the bank this afternoon," said Pam, with fear both in her voice and on her face.

"They're going to hit tonight. They'll wait until I leave. If they see that I am not leaving they'll hit anyway. They don't know who I am."

"They probably think you're a hobo," said Pam, smiling a little.

"Thank you, Pam."

"A handsome hobo," returned Pam, smiling more.

"Who's staying upstairs?"

"Six people. I know all six of them. One is Mr. Beaty, who comes here after an argument with his wife. Mr. Nash gets drunk and goes to sleep because he doesn't want to drive home..."

"Okay, okay, you don't have to give me the whole roster," interrupted Erik.

"Do you want me to lock the door?" asked the woman.

"If I were in my right mind, I would say yes. Lock the door after I leave. They would break the door down or would come back tomorrow," said Erik, looking at her intently as if he were thinking of some additional comment.

All his remarks and answers were said in a low voice as if they were hints calculated to awaken suspicion in Pam's mind and put her on guard.

"What do you think?" asked the widow, "you don't think they're going to try to break the door down, do you?"

"That is a consideration, Pam," replied Erik, now looking around.

"I don't like it, Erik"

"No kidding?"

"What are we going to do?" asked the woman, horrified.

"That's what I'm trying to figure out, can't you see I'm thinking?"

"Thinking what?"

"I'm thinking of singing the Ethiopian national anthem," said Erik sarcastically, "if I knew what I was thinking, I wouldn't be thinking anymore."

"You don't know what you're thinking and I don't know what to do, we are in one hell of a mess." said the widow, more terrified than before, "What are we going to do? I think I should go and lock the door."

"No, because if they try to get in and can't, they'll break a window and come in shooting. Where is the gun? Go get it!"

"Aren't you making this a little bigger than what it is? Come in shooting is like the old west"

"Look! My mother used to say, watch out for the unexpected! Now, go get the gun!" ordered Erik.

"I have it here. It's under my apron. I put it under my apron when the police told me what they were looking for."

"You see, you are a little suspicious too. Do you know how to shoot a gun?"

"It's easy. Isn't it? Just point and pull the trigger."

"You've seen too many John Wayne movies. Just give it to me under the table very discreetly!"

"Why discreetly? There's nobody in here except Linda, the waitress," questioned Pam.

"Then take it out, swing it around for five minutes and then hand it over to me," said Erik. "They might be looking in, Pam."

The lady passed it to him with a slow hand and a galloping heart. Erik felt it in his hands and smiled with surprise.

"I love it, it's a forty five. The best pistol ever made for my hand. It's a G.I. issue."

"How do you know that?"

"I was in the army."

"Which army?"

"Venezuelan," said Erik, without a grin.

"American army what do you think?"

"How would I know that? You Greeks are spread all over the world like horseshit, pardon my French," replied the woman, "can I go to call the police?"

"No!" said Erik grumpily, "How far is the police station from here?"

"Next town, about fifteen miles; Erik, I am scared," whispered the horrified lady.

"That's natural. Try to relax," rejoined Erik soothingly, "you see, Pam, by the time the police get here it will be over. If the police get here before these guys attack..."

"Attack?" she interrupted, filled with fear.

"No, they are going to come in with a pizza," said Erik sarcastically again, "of course, attack. If the police get here before these guys attack, they are going to look around. They'll find nothing and they are going to leave. The bad guys will come back knowing that the police will mark it as a false alarm. Second calls on false alarms are placed on the back burner. These guys know where the police station is," said Erik.

"What are we going to do?"

"We are going to lie down and die, I am sure we will receive a proper burial."

"Here we are in big trouble and you're joking. What are we going to do?"

"If you ask me again, what we're going to do, I'm going to smack you."

"Oh, you like to smack women around?"

"No. I have never done it before but there's always a first time for everything," said Erik sternly. "But you are a very pretty lady; it would break my heart to hurt your face."

"With those words you're not going to make me fall for you," said Pam.

"You mean to tell me, that when I leave, you are not going to give me your heart and soul to take with me?" asked Erik.

"I will give them to you, if you stay here by my side so I can see what you are doing with them."

This statement was delivered in a demeanor originated in an increased sense of safety, being with Erik, whom, though she knew for only a short time, felt was on her side.

"I'm scared, Erik."

"Don't panic! Just stay calm. Excessive confusion will bring horrible results. Listen to me carefully. I am an expert with a pistol; these men haven't a chance against me. I have the training and the know-how to kill them before they have a chance of pulling off their first shot. So, be calm! I don't want you to worry."

The lady submitted to this piece of practical advice and smiled, "you sound like Billy the Kid."

"Billy the Kid was a killer and crazy; I'm neither. Do you understand?"

She nodded in assent.

"The best thing is, these guys don't know I have a gun or how good I am with one. But they are also stupid. Stupid people are unpredictable."

"How do you know they're stupid?"

"No, they're geniuses," replied Erik, "most crooks are stupid. They'll come in recklessly. I don't want to kill them. I don't want to kill anyone. So, if you don't want them dead, do as I say!"

"Have you ever killed anyone?" asked the lady, trembling.

"We'll talk about that later when we talk about your husbands," said Erik, hastily. "The reason they haven't come in yet is because they want to give the police time to distance themselves from here. Every difficult situation is concocted like a religious ceremony. First comes the prayer, then the sacrifice, then the waiting for an answer."

"What kind of sacrifice?"

"We'll sacrifice your bosomy waitress to Zeus, the ancient Greek god."

"What?" shrieked the widow.

"Shh! Stop it, I'm only kidding. You do the praying, I'll make the sacrifice and we'll both sit and wait," said Erik.

"You have a weird sense of humor," replied Pam, scratching her head with both hands, "besides, you may be in cahoots with the other two to rob this place."

"What, am I stupid? Does it take three men to rob a widow?"

"I don't know. You said that most crooks are stupid," returned Pam.

"My dear lady, you are a charming and delightful creature,"

said Erik, touching her hand, "and you have only one fault that I know of. You don't trust people."

"Do you know what I have gone through in my life, Erik?" said Pam, setting her teeth together and speaking like a savage warrior who feeds on raw meat.

"Do you know how many times Prometheus had his liver eaten by vultures?" asked Erik.

"Who's Prometheus, your cousin?"

"No," returned Erik laughing, "Prometheus was the guardian of fire. Zeus, the supreme God of the twelve Greek gods, didn't like Prometheus because he favored the mortals, so Zeus tied him up and left him in a forest on a mountain of Caucasus where the vultures ate his liver."

"God Zeus did that? What a nice god he must have been." Murmured Pam.

"Your God still does the same thing now. Look around you, girl."

"You Greeks always go back to your mythology. My ex-husband George did that."

"Let me correct you. It's not mythology. The Christians and the Jews gave it the name mythology because they wanted people to follow their Bible. Greek mythology, as you call it, is both Greek religion and Greek philosophy and it's very similar to Genesis. The ancient Greeks believed that the serpent wasn't Eve's enemy; it was her best friend and enlightened her. The serpent gave her food for thought," said Erik.

"My God, my God, now I know why," exclaimed Pam, hammering the table with her fist lightly.

"Why, what?"

"You see, Erik, this place here, a long time ago, was owned by a Greek and its name was 'THE SERPENT' everybody knew it by that name. He sold it to a Polish man and he didn't like the name so he put up a big sign in the front of the building, 'ABRAHAM LINCOLN' and under that sign he put ' ***Better known as 'THE SERPENT.'*** After the passage of the civil rights act the NAACP came here and made him remove the sign, saying that it was referring to Abraham Lincoln as a snake," said Pam, sighing deeply as if she had just finished a difficult task.

"Leave it to the Greeks and Polish, they are both capable of lousing up a junk yard," said Erik, with a vague smile. "Any way, back in the farm, we have a problem here now and we must solve it," he continued earnestly.

"Tell me about it, as if I don't know."

"In three minutes I want you to go into the kitchen and take the girl down to the basement. Hide, and don't come up unless I call you or the police call you, which is likely if I get killed"

"Killed? You're getting killed? My God, I feel like screaming"

"Don't! I'm not planning on getting killed," replied Erik, in an effort to calm her down, seeing the panic in her face. "Talk to me about your husbands."

"You're talking about getting killed or killing and you want me to talk about some stupid husbands." The lady seemed to be much affected; a great fear passed over her frame as she convinced herself that she was destined to become an animated target. She began to think it was high time to cry, so she took the edge of her apron and before she wiped her eyes she looked at Erik from behind her tears.

"Shh! " said Erik, touching her hand affectionately, understanding that he had alarmed the poor widow sufficiently, he decided to change the ground of discussion, "Talk about them, it will make you feel better!"

"Which one?" cried the lady, wiping the tears off her eyes with edge of her apron. The entire conversation took place at a very fast pace and in an almost confidential tone

There was no more visible confusion on the lady's or Erik's face. All that time, Erik's eyes were wandering around discreetly.

"I don't care. How many have you had?"

"Husbands?"

"No dogs," returned Erik comically, trying to convince her he wasn't scared, "we were talking about dogs. Don't you remember?"

"Boy, you are rough. Do you always treat women like they're horses?"

"Precisely. Haven't you heard the old saying? 'Treat a lady like a horse and a horse like a lady'," said Erik, grinning.

"That must an old Greek saying."

"Then you've heard it. You said your first husband is a Greek," remarked Erik.

"Oh yes, my first husband's name is George. He has a restaurant in Richville."

Erik's eyes opened wide with astonishment, "George Papas?"

"Do you know him?"

"I know him well. I just left George. I told you, I was there two days ago. He has been married three times."

"I was his second wife. Did he say anything about me?" asked the widow, scanning Erik's face with a worried leer, as if it were the first time she laid her eyes on him.

"George with the one umbrella house, right?"

"Right. He is a sweetheart. He is a romantic fool," said Pam.

"He is a great dresser. Go now! We'll talk about George later."

"When are you going to see George again?" she asked, with the same tone and smirk on her face.

"In a couple of years," replied Erik, without too much emphasis on his answer, as if he were hiding a question inside him.

"I've got an idea, when they come in, I'll turn all the lights off," said the widow with a sudden bright feeling that she had just discovered something good, after hearing that Erik wasn't about to see George any time soon.

"Don't!" uttered Erik, "I'm not going to play the mysteries of blind-man's bluff. Just go and hide somewhere!"

"Go and hide somewhere?" returned the lady, "what an awful way of putting it. It sounds as if I've done something wrong and I am about to be punished" After that remark, Pam Flood stood up, planted an encouraging smile on her face, waved good-bye and off she went.

Erik leaned back and gradually blended into his seat, holding a pistol in each hand hidden under his jacket.

Suddenly, the front door to squeaked open and two men appeared standing in its shadow. The well-dressed man advanced slowly, looking around intently, while the red-faced man stayed behind by the door, closing it carefully, as if he were the sentinel.

Erik didn't move a hand or a foot; he only turned his head and looked at the well dressed man who was now behind the bar looking around with the scrutinizing eye of a landlord, as though thinking all this was his property. He was standing there behind the bar with his hands folded behind him, feeling quite at home. He grinned vacantly, as if he wished Erik to see his white teeth.

"Where is the boss woman?" he asked with a diabolical sneer; and then, without pausing for an answer, he added, "I want to talk to her."

"I think she and the girls went upstairs for something. She asked me to watch the place until they come down. She should be coming down any moment. You seem to know her, pour yourself a drink."

"Who are you?" asked the same man sternly.

"Me? I am a humorous, homeless, harmless hobo who has very little to do and expecting to do less."

"You talk funny."

"I already said I was humorous; don't you understand English?"

"You're also silly," returned the man. Both men laughed spontaneously, then the man behind he bar stopped laughing; he signaled something to the red-faced man who immediately pulled out a pistol but before he had time to aim or fire, Erik shot at the doorknob and jumped to his feet, holding his aim.

"Now, put your gun down! The next shot will be planted between your eyes, ugly. Don't try to run like you ran before because I'll shoot you in the back. I said, drop it!" shrieked Erik, looking furious and aiming his gun at the red face man, ready to fire. If the building they were standing in had suddenly got up and walked across the street, both men wouldn't have been as stunned as they were seeing Erik, the hobo, standing before them ready, willing and able to shoot them down. They both realized, by his words and actions, that he was a serious man of business, leaving no time for foolishness and no room for play.

"I will not ask again!" growled Erik, further verifying their impression of him.

"No, Mister! Don't shoot! We only came in for a drink," said the man petrified, sliding the gun over towards Erik while his eyes remained fixed on him.

"Lover boy, if you move one inch, I'll take two inches off your height, something no short man can afford to lose. Come out from behind the bar, you've had your day back there, and we'll see just how funny I am. Keep your hands behind your back like a whore looking for a trick. Move!" yelled Erik. At that moment the red-faced man made a run for the door but the doorknob was missing.

"No doorknob?" said Erik, seeing the man's desperate attempt to escape and the uncomfortable scene he had created for himself.

"No door knob," repeated the red-faced man, with a scared grin.

"It's all gone?"

"It's all gone," replied the man, shrugging his shoulders.

"That means, don't get into anything you can't get out of. Pretty soon we'll say the same thing about your balls. They're all gone. That's the only thing you seem to have."

"No, Mister!" pleaded the red-faced man. "That's not all I have. I have no balls. I mean, that's not all I have."

"You have no money, do you?"

"I have some money."

"How much money do you have, ugly?"

"About fifty dollars."

"That's no money."

"No."

"The only thing you seem to have is a gun and a pair of balls. That's all you have to have to rob people. You gave me your gun and now I think I'm going to take your balls, so you'll never rob again."

"No, Mister, please, that's not all I have. I have a wife and three kids at home, Mister," said the red-faced man, whose mouth was watering earlier while staring at the waitress' large breasts. Looking at him now, much to his surprise and with fate being unkind, his eyes began to water from seeing two full drawn pistols aiming straight at him.

"You worry about your kids and wife?" asked Erik without the slightest degree of sentiment in his voice.

"Yes, yes," cried the man.

"You see, you are not so lucky after all, if you had met me a long time ago and if I had done then, what I'm going to do now, you wouldn't have to worry about a wife and kids.

Do you understand, stupid?" Erik paused for one long moment, and then turned to the well dressed-man.

"How about you, lover boy? Do you have a wife and kids?"

"Yes, sir," uttered the other man on the verge of breaking down into a sobbing fit. "I have the same and I love them."

"Go, and stand by where I was sitting and no monkey business."

"No sir, no sir! " they kept repeating as they went and stood by the booth.

"When I say, sit, then you sit, " said Erik looking at them with angry eyes, still pointing his pistols with steady hands.

"Sit!" ordered Erik. They both sat facing across from each other and instead of looking at one another they hung their heads down, staring at the tabletop.

"Let me go and find Pam. I'll be right back. I can see you from wherever I am. Pam! Come on upstairs!" he was heard saying. "I haven't made up my mind what I want to do with you two," said Erik, placing a hand on the table and leaning heavily on that arm, "let me see what happened to Pam and the girls," said Erik, heading off for the kitchen. He entered the kitchen, stayed there for one long moment, then carelessly walked out and headed back to the table, but on the way back he picked up the red-faced man's gun and put it in his pocket.

The kitchen door opened almost immediately and Pam appeared holding a rifle aimed at the two bandits.

"Here I am," uttered Pam, slowly approaching while still aiming at the two characters.

"Put that away Pam! Those are not the guys the police are looking for. I mistook them and I damn near killed them," said Erik, turning to the bandits, "Sit quiet and relax, both of you."

Erik, after a few minutes of silence, stood and stared at them with an angry look on his face.

"You should all be ashamed of yourselves, fathers and husbands of probably nice people, who are depending on you to do the right thing. Your wives and children would rather eat live snakes than be eating food that came from a place where you could have been killed or got caught for armed robbery. Whether you are stupid or crazy or both, I don't know. You are giving a chance to the police and prosecutors to make a name for themselves by catching you and sending you to jail, that is pure stupidity to me. I would rather scrape the surface of the earth, looking for food, with my bare hands until I have no more flesh on them, than steal and give some jerky judge the chance to pass out years in jail for me, like he was throwing biscuits to his dogs. If you can't find love in yourselves for your wives and children, then find hate for the people who are looking to put you away. Hate them, to the point that you will deny them the opportunity to put you away. Don't give them the chance to thrive on your sickness, misery and death.

Next time the notion of robbing someone or some place enters your mind, consult your conscience and your feelings about the ones you are going to leave behind who will be too ashamed to speak your name or reveal your link to them and if you find that favorable, then do it! Then you'll know you have no conscience and no feelings. Let your wives find other husbands and other fathers for your children because you are not good enough for them. I want you two to know that I don't know what to do with you. If I let you go and I don't turn you in, eventually you'll be caught and sent away and you'll never breathe air outside prison walls for the rest of your lives. You will live there the rest of your days without any prospect of liberation. There is no mistaking the facts that someday you will kill someone with the gun you carry and your remaining loaves of bread in the free society are numbered and few.

After saying this, Erik stopped and looked hard at them, from one to the other, for a few seconds, as if he were debating some matter within himself, still resting his body with his hand on the tabletop. He then rose from the table, walked away a few paces, stopped, turned his head and said. "I'm going to call the police," directing his attention to the well-dressed man who he asked sternly, "Have you ever been arrested and convicted for a crime?"

"No, sir" responded the man.

"You think I should call the police?" asked Erik.

"No. We are the police," said the well-dressed man, getting to his feet and showing his badge to Erik who looked at it carefully.

"I am lieutenant Charles McKay," the policeman continued, "the one you called ugly is my partner Patrick Newsome. We are here investigating the disappearance of Jerry Strucker who was Pam's second husband."

Pam, numbed for a few minutes by the lieutenant's words, thrust her body towards the officer, and as she came close to him, said in a loud complaining voice, "It's about time somebody is doing something about my husband."

"You've been calling yourself a widow since the day after he disappeared," said the lieutenant sternly.

"I knew he was dead the day after he didn't come home. My husband would not have gone anywhere without telling me. He loved me. He was not a liar or a sneak. I know he had an accident. There she stopped and a malignant scowl passed over her face as she drew closer to officer McKay, "I told the police to search but they ignored me; they ignored him as if he were not a member of the human race," replied Pam angrily.

Having recorded her feelings in these intelligible terms, she sat on the chair, placed her head on the table and sobbed violently, while the officers looked at each other in awkward silence.

"Did your husband carry a handgun, Mrs. Strucker?" asked McKay softly, touching her shoulder.

At this inquiry, Pam raised her head and looked at McKay, surprised, then she looked at the other officer and returned her eyes back to McKay, "Why are you asking me that question?"

"We've found your husband in the lake, not too far from here." said the officer, stopping to listen for a response.

Pam came up with a smile of sadness, then turned pale and fainted in Erik's arms.

"Get me a lemon!" yelled Erik, while he and officer McKay lifted her to a booth and helped her stretch out.

Linda, the bosomy waitress, ran to Erik with two lemons in her hands; he took one, scratched the peel lightly, passed it around a few inches under Pam's nose, who after smelling the lemon, began to regain her power of speech.

" Floating in the lake, you said?" asked Pam faintly.

The officer nodded in assent.

"He loved fishing. I always worried about him going there, to the lake, alone, fishing," murmured Pam as her senses faintly came back to her.

"Do you have life insurance on him?" asked McKay.

"He didn't believe in insurance. He thought the insurance companies were nothing but rip offs," responded the widow, now staring at the ceiling.

"Had you ever gone fishing with your husband in that lake?" inquired McKay.

"Which lake? There must be at least ten small lakes around here," replied Pam, raising her eyes and gazing at the inquirer coldly.

The officer returned Pam's gaze of stone and, out of habit, proceeded to make the most he could of her answer; the most, however, was nothing at all; so after a profound silence of some seconds' duration he asked,

"When did you realize that your husband was missing?"

The widow winced beneath the gaze of the officer. She made a desperate struggle to screw up enough strength to reply, and although it was coming unscrewed again, she managed to respond.

"He left early in the morning to go to work, but when he didn't come home at his normal time, six o'clock, I began to worry and I called his job and they told me he didn't go to work that day. Sometimes he skipped work to go fishing, but he would always tell me. He never said anything to me that day."

At that moment, Linda, the bosomy waitress, who was standing and listening to the whole dialogue asked softly, "Can you tell how long the body had been at the bottom of the lake?"

There appeared nothing unusual in this question, 'At the bottom of the lake,' but the way it was asked and the look that accompanied it, plus the fact 'At the bottom of the lake' was not mentioned by the police, produced a question into Erik's mind, but he withheld it for a better time.

The waitress' question was never answered by the policeman who, by now, had his mind set in a different direction. "When did you call the police, Mrs. Strucker?"

"I think the following day," said the widow, raising her head to face her interrogator, "Let me set the record straight," continued the woman, wiping tears off her face with the edge of her apron. "I really thought, way down deep inside, that he left me. I thought that he went away and started a new life for himself. I thought he meant to call me but after a while got into some kind of accident and died before he had the chance to call. That's why I was telling everybody that my husband died in an accident; and it wasn't right after his disappearance, it was way later when I began to refer to myself as a widow. He had a friend who he only called RDR. I never met RDR. He told me that he was a policeman in town and he wanted to go to Australia. Linda!" said the widow, turning her attention to Linda, "you told me that you had a policeman boyfriend, whatever happened to him?"

"That was a long time ago. I don't want to talk about it," replied Linda, turning her eyes towards the empty bar.

After that answer Erik, studying her troubled countenance, detected signs of fear. But fear without basis at times is common among people who have had bad experiences with judicial authority or the police force. Often they have guilty feelings unrelated to the present matter, fear of skeletons in closets that might be exposed by police inquisitions, as some people think, whether they are right or wrong, of the police as malicious, ill disposed, spiteful, vindictive creatures with hardened hearts. Erik was unable to put a finger on the source or type of fear that was depicted on her face.

"Let me get you some coffee," said Linda, as she left without waiting for a response.

"The other thought was," continued the widow, "that he sold his car and he and his friend RDR went to Australia. I thought if there were a car accident his car would have been found and I would have been notified. All these thoughts and ideas lingered in my head for the past two years and the police department offered me no help. I bought this place from Mr. Ritter and Linda, who was working here, stayed on with me and has been a tremendous help for which I thank her."

"Who are you, sir?" asked the red face man, turning to Erik.

"My name is Erik Karas, sir," replied Erik.

"He is my ex-husband's, George's, friend," added Pam.

"George Papas from Richville?" inquired the same officer.

"Yes, do you know him?" asked Pam with surprise.

"We did our homework before we came here," said officer McKay; turning to the stout man, with a bad knee he continued "Keep the waitress behind the bar, while I'm speaking to Mrs. Strucker."

Waiting for the coast to clear, McKay watched the waitress go behind the bar to prepare coffee for all.

"We're here from the Richmond homicide department and we're investigating the murder of your husband, Mrs. Strucker," began the officer.

"Murder?' exclaimed the widow.

"Yes," continued officer McKay, "we didn't want to reveal our identity for reasons I can't disclose at this time, but thanks to Mr. Karas, our cover was blown. Two years ago, three days before you reported your husband's disappearance two men snatched two bags full of money, about two hundred thousand dollars, from a payroll truck in Richmond. One of the police who guarded the payroll truck was officer Patrick Newsome, my partner with the bad knee," said the officer pointing at the red face man, "and the other officer was Jay B. Frost. One of the bandits was your husband, Mrs. Strucker," said officer McKay, pausing and staring at Pam with a vacant look on his face, "the other man, Edward Daily, was apprehended three weeks ago and is now locked up waiting trial on murder one."

Erik looked at Pam who turned suddenly pale, Pam looked at Erik, the officers looked at each other, and Linda's hands froze on the coffee cups, her eyes doweled directly straight ahead away from everybody while the warm blood in her body tingled up into the tips of her ears.

Erik, noticing the waitress' strange behavior, not knowing exactly what to think or say, turned his head quickly towards the bar and merely exclaimed, "Linda!"

Linda, hearing her name called right after the word 'murder' uttered by the officer, was visibly startled.

"Is the coffee ready, sweetheart?" asked Erik, in an attempt to avoid any confrontation between the officers and the waitress.

"Yes," shouted back Linda, employing her hands again and, without looking in Erik's direction, she continued, "it will be there in a moment," in a now softer voice.

"Never mind the coffee yet," yelled the officer, looking at Erik who added nothing.

The officer with a preparatory cough proceeded, "But I don't believe Daly is guilty."

Then he beckoned Erik and Pam to follow him to the next table, a little farther from the bar.

"Daly said that your husband had help from another police officer who was to get one third of the heist and the only name he had was RDR. The deal was, according to Daly, RDR was to arrange

for one of the police guards to create a commotion once the bandits
snatched the money, so they could get away. One of the officers on
the payroll truck was my partner Newsome and the other was
Frost. RDR made the deal with Frost. That's exactly what happened.
Strucker and Daly grabbed the two bags and ran, when my partner,
Newsome, was close to tackling one of them, Frost shot him from
behind and hit him in the back of the knee. That's why you see him
limping. Frost's testimony was that it was a pure accident. We, the
police, believed him. Six months later he was found dead in his
car with two bullets in his head. Now I believe that RDR is the
killer. RDR would most likely be initials of a full name, but we
checked and found no one in the police department with those
initials. We're going to conduct an investigation in all the police
departments in the area and I'm sure we'll come up with something, now that we know that RDR is in this area.

"How do you know my husband was murdered? He could have
gone there fishing and fell in and drowned," offered Pam.

"Your husband was found at the bottom of the lake, strapped
behind the wheel of his car with a bullet in his head. We believe he
was murdered elsewhere. We also believe that where he was
murdered is where the money is hidden," replied the officer.

Perceiving the sight created by those horrible words, the widow
burst into painful sobbing then wept loudly with growing anguish.
The widow's tears continued to gush forth until she gained a little
time to think the matter over. She then raised her head and looked
at the officer from behind her tears and said, "At least my husband
wasn't a murderer, he wasn't a violent man with hate inside of him,
only a needy adventurer who chose the wrong way to make things
right for him and me. I miss him terribly and I will always love
him."

When the ceremony of mourning was over, officer McKay
approached the widow timidly and said, "I am truly sorry, Pamela."

"RDR killed my husband, took the money, ran away and he
now lives in luxury in some country like Argentina," said the widow
with a deep sigh.

"RDR was or still is a policeman. No policeman from any department around here, or even farther out, has left or retired and lives,
in or out of the country, in luxury. Like I said, we did our home-

work. We all believe the money is hidden where your husband was murdered."

Immediately after the officer finished his words, Erik, with a serious face, stepped forward towards the officer in charge and asked loudly, to put emphasis on his request, "I beg you pardon, officer, may I have a few words in private with Mrs. Strucker?"

"A private conversation with Mrs. Strucker in the middle of my investigation procedure?" asked the officer in amazement.

"Yes, sir, a private conversation with Mrs. Strucker, unless she is a target of the investigation," replied Erik, rather firmly.

McKay turned and looked at his partner, Newsome, who now was standing by the bar, watching Linda preparing the coffee and didn't respond.

"Patrick!" repeated McKay.

Patrick Newsome still remained silent.

"Hey, you," yelled the officer.

Newsome turned around abruptly, looked at McKay with a curious eye and said nothing.

Staring at Newsome with a frown, McKay asked angrily, "Karas wants to speak with Pam in private, do you think it will be okay?"

Patrick Newsome shrugged his shoulders and screwed up his face, as if he didn't care one way or another.

"You are a lot of help, Patrick," mumbled McKay, turning to Erik, "go ahead, have it your way," said McKay in a loud stern voice.

Gesturing for Pam to follow him, Erik walked a few paces closer to Linda on the other side of the bar, stood there facing the waitress, and seeming to debate the matter within himself for a few seconds, said in a whisper just loud enough for Linda to hear,

"Pam, I know you know who RDR is; just don't give a hint to the officers of whatever you're thinking. Let them find him and let them arrest him.

Pam nodded in assent.

"You have a good idea where RDR is, don't you?"

Pam nodded negatively with a vigorous shake of her head.

"Good. Don't say anything. Keep it to yourself," said Erik, pretending that Pam's shaking of the head, was a positive one, knowing the waitress was monitoring the situation.

"I know that you know where the money is hidden," whispered

Erik, as if those words were spoken softly for Pam's ears only, but Linda heard a few of them.

Pam's face was overtaken with confusion and having not caught on to Erik's game, she was about to protest when he imparted a wink and pointed at Linda with his index finger, discreetly.

Hearing some of Erik's words 'know-money-hidden', the waitress, with a thoughtless impulse, turned her head in his direction. They exchanged a brief glance; there was nothing but worry and anxiety in her eyes that could not be mistaken. Realizing she had revealed her ability to hear some of what was said, she turned her head away abruptly and continued with her task. Though feeling nervous and confused by her own speculations, she continued to listen inconspicuously.

Erik seemed pleased that Linda appeared to exhibit a great deal of awareness and more interest than would be ordinary; he was convinced that she was somehow connected to the subject. He was especially glad that she heard what was meant for her to hear.

"Be careful Pam, RDR is a smart and a tough bird, but he'll be grabbed by tomorrow night. He'll be sent to prison and then you can take the money and run like hell."

"How did you guess all that," she asked, after having caught on to Erik's game.

"Shh! Behave! Lets go back to the policemen."

Erik walked towards the officer in charge, who was still standing in the same place, contemplating his next move.

"Red, who's going to pay for Pam's door knob?" asked Erik, turning and heading for the front door with Pam following behind him.

"You are Karas. Good thing you stopped with the door knob otherwise now you would have to pay for shooting my balls off," returned the officer humorously.

"You would have gotten from me the same thing you lost," replied Erik, with a hearty laugh as he made a display of showing her the doorknob.

"I don't know how to fix this," said Erik, shooting his eyes towards Linda and when he couldn't see her he frowned, particularly when he noticed that the telephone was missing from its place and the wire was leading into the kitchen.

"Linda is on the phone," whispered Erik.

"She is probably calling her brother to pick her up. She gets off in a few minutes," said Pam, "you're suspicious of everybody."

"I told you my mother used to say, watch out for the unexpected," whispered Erik, "I will pretend that I am leaving in a few minutes. Take your gun from my pocket while I'm amusing myself with fixing the door; put it under your apron. When everybody is gone, be on the extreme alert. Anyone who comes in here, that you or Linda knows, may very well be the man, RDR; don't let him close to you, no matter what he says. If he insists on advancing towards you, even in a friendly manner, shoot to kill! Empty the gun on him! Then run out. I won't be too far from here."

"My God! Erik, kill him?" cried the widow.

"No, hug him and kiss him, of course, kill him. If you were a good shot, I would say, cripple him, but if you try to just cripple him, I'd bet you a dollar to a donut you'll miss altogether. Don't panic now, I told you, I'll be around. What I just told you is plan B. Plan A is that I will be in here with you. Lets get back to the policemen!" whispered Erik.

"Gentlemen, if I'm free to leave, I'd like to leave now," said Erik, on his way to them.

"Come over here first and have your coffee. We have to go soon too," said McKay, "Linda, bring that coffee now, please."

"It's four o'clock. The day will break in an hour and I have to go get some sleep," said Linda as she delivered a pot of coffee and four cups to the table.

"Do you drive?" asked Erik.

"No, I only live less than a mile from here; sometimes I walk and sometimes my brother picks me up. I just called the house and there was no answer. He's probably spending the night with his girlfriend," responded Linda.

Pam poked Erik's rib discreetly with her elbow, indicating to him that she was right when she told him that Linda was calling her brother to pick her up.

Erik thought different; he heard the waitress talking to somebody for a lot longer than to simply leave a short massage, but he chose to say nothing to Pam.

"Do you live east or west of here?" asked Erik again.

"I live east. Why do you ask?"

"I'm going west, I thought I would walk with you," replied Erik.

As soon as the coffee was consumed, the two police officers bid everyone goodnight and left by the side door.

Pam seemed to breath more freely when they were gone, but Erik's relief was far greater, besides the constraint he felt being around police, he felt helpless and at a disadvantage in not being able to aid the widow. He also felt a deep sorrow for that lady who he had just met this day and only spoke with for the past several hours; he imagined she must have faced a hard fight through the world and continued to struggle, as if there weren't enough space on this earth for an insignificant woman, not to get to the top, but to simply prevent herself from getting squashed at the bottom. He wished he had the tools and the talents to mellow the bitterness of the disappointment she seemed to suffer.

It was curious and interesting for Erik to be standing there, with very little money in his pocket, not well dressed and without any prospects in his life or even the will to live, feeling sorry for that lady and not for himself.

Erik bid the two women goodbye and headed for the side door. He was not encumbered with much luggage, having only his bag with a minimum of survival gear dangling from his back, but was burdened by head filled with trouble and unfinished business. He hurried out the door on his self-imposed mission and when outside, he stood and looked around him to gather his thoughts and find his bearings in the dark end of the night. He made a left turn and after a few paces came to the top of a knoll and saw the main road. Hurrying along the road for a few more steps, Erik abruptly turned and hid behind the bushes, waiting for Linda to come out. He stood in that position for about five minutes when he suddenly heard the side door open. Linda appeared, walking up the hill and heading for the same road rather hurriedly. Reaching the road, she crossed it and began to walk west, the opposite from what she told Erik. She moved in solid hasty steps, eagerly looking about, as though in quest of some expected object and taking no heed of Erik, who watched her closely. The road, deserted and dark with trees and other free grown tall bushes on either side, rose heavy and dull from the dense mass of vegetation that looked down sternly upon its black top. A mist hung over the road, blurring the bright light shooting from a service station less than a half a mile ahead; only a glimmer shone feebly upon Linda's path. Erik slunk along in the deepest shadows he could find, staying a good distance behind her, adjusting his pace to hers, stopping when she stopped and moving again when she moved, but creeping stealthily on, never allowing himself to gain upon her footsteps.

Linda finally reached the well-lit service station, stopped less than a hundred feet from its center and waited impatiently, taking a few restless steps back and forth, all the while being closely watched by Erik, who had advanced and hid within hearing distance of her.

Suddenly, two headlights appeared heading in her direction; they stopped abruptly close to Linda, who hurried and stood by the driver's side.

"Hurry! She's all alone. The Greek is gone. There's no one upstairs. The hotel rooms are empty. She was lying when she said she had six people in the rooms. Hurry! Please! The front door is broken; you are not going to get in. Here's the key to the side door," said the girl.

"I have the key," said the driver, a voice unknown to Erik, he then motioned to Linda to step back, so he could move, "Will you be OK?"

"I'll be alright. I'll walk home. Be careful!" replied Linda, tapping the car gently.

Linda backed off; the car squealed its tires and sped towards Pam's place. Linda started to walk back in the direction she came from.

The car arrived at Pam's place, turned to the right, stopped a few yards from the road and hid in the bushes. The car door opened and Bob, the policeman who had gone to see Pam earlier, stepped out in full uniform. He stood there across the street from Pam's place and looked hastily around. When he saw nothing moving, he ran across and planted himself against the wall, as there seemed no better place of concealment, then waited and studied his surroundings. He was at the very point of emerging from his hiding place and regaining the foot path leading to the side door when he heard the sound of footsteps, and, directly afterwards, the sound of whispering voices.

He drew himself straight upright against the wall and, scarcely breathing, listened attentively again. The footsteps stopped, the voices went silent and Bob waited.

In the meantime, down the road from him, Linda was being followed closely by Erik, who burst out of the bushes, grabbed Linda by the arm and said, "don't run girl, you have some things to explain."

Linda, startled by Erik's unexpected appearance, shrieked but Erik slapped his hand over her mouth and said softly, "Behave, "I'm not here to harm you, I'm here to save you," then he slowly removed his hand from her mouth.

"Save me from what?" cried Linda.

Linda was now being confronted by Erik; Bob down the road, was still standing firmly and solid against the wall and Pam, inside her place, was sitting in a booth holding, with both hands, a cup of coffee, her eyes fixed upon the front door.

Suddenly she heard the side door open and, turning her face and body in the direction of the sound, saw Bob enter. He stooped over and urged her, with hand motions, to sit and be silent, placing his index finger on his lips.

Pam, disregarding Bob's signals, stood up and watched him crawl behind the bar.

"Pam, are you alone?" whispered Bob. He listened for a response and when he didn't get it, remained quiet and hidden for a few seconds. He then raised his head and saw Pam standing next to the booth aiming a pistol at him.

The pistol kicked up in her hands; Bob fell down behind the bar and the many shots she fired caused the liquor filled shelves to fall on top of him. The building rang with the sounds of that angry thunder. Pam ran to examine the disaster she created and, on her way there, saw McKay and Newsome, the two policemen, standing by the door with wide grins on their faces.

"I killed Bob, I killed Bob the policeman," cried Pam, placing her face on the bar.

"I know, I know," said McKay, removing the gun from her hand and placing it on the bar gently, "he must have known you know where the money is."

"But I don't know where the money is," replied Pam, raising her face and looking at the cop in astonishment.

"Quit lying lady, quit the goddamn lying," shouted the officer, raising his hand ready to slap her at a moment's notice.

"But I'm not lying," yelled back the widow, moving away from him.

"Don't lie to me goddamn it," growled McKay, grabbing her hair and shoving her face down on the bar.

"I swear, I don't know where the money is," cried the widow, her face glued to the bar.

"Don't swear to me!" returned the officer, with his teeth now clenched as he raised her head up by the hair and pounded it down on the bar again, hard.

"What kind of a policeman are you?" screamed the widow.

"I'm not a cop, you dumb bitch; I'm RDR, your smart husband's partner. He tried to cheat me out of my share. Take us to the money, before I slice your throat and throw you in the lake like I did to your ugly husband. Do you understand that?" snarled the mad man, bringing her blood covered face up by the hair with his left hand, while imparting several hard slaps across her jaws with his right.

As this drama was unfolding in the bar, Linda explained to Erik what was taking place while they rushed down the lonely highway towards Pam's place.

"Daly is not in jail. As I've told you, he just got out of jail after two years for something else. RDR is Daly's partner. RDR is the one who killed the other cop, Frost. Bob knows all that but has no evidence to convict him on," exclaimed Linda rushing behind Erik.

"One thing," said Erik breathlessly, "I told Pam to shoot anybody who goes to her if she knows them. I'm afraid that Pam might shoot Bob."

Meanwhile, Pam, in the hands of those two mad men, was trying to endure the ruthless punishment she was receiving from the brutal McKay.

"If you're smart, you'll take us to the money and we'll let you go unharmed. We're leaving the country tonight, because Monday I go on trial and that's when all hell will break loose. Do you understand? you dumb broad."

"I told you I don't know where the money is,' cried the widow faintly.

Erik and Linda were approaching quickly.

"In less that five minutes, we'll be there," said Erik, moving as fast as he could."

"The reason Bob believes they are going to hit tonight is because he spread the word around that Pam knows where the money is," said Linda, trying hard to keep up.

"When we get there, go though the side door and keep your distance from them if they're there. I'll come in through the front door. I left it open. I hope Pam didn't close it," explained Erik, without slowing to look or think.

"Okay, okay," said Pam, "I'll take you to the money. But first tell me why you waited two years to come for it?"

"You really want to know why?" asked RDR, a grin blossoming on his face.

Pam nodded in assent.

"This dumb partner of mine," said RDR, pointing his finger at Daly, who didn't take it so well, "was in jail. Your husband told him that he had hid the money in here somewhere, because he didn't want to pay out my share."

"It's in the cellar. I'll show you, if you promise not to harm me," cried Pam.

"We don't have any reason to harm you, do we Daly?' asked RDR, without removing his eyes from the widow.

Daly nodded negatively.

"Let me have some time to breathe," begged Pam.

"Take your time now, old girl," said the mad man softly.

"Can I have a couple thousand from that two hundred thousand? I really need it," said the Pam faintly, with tears in her eyes.

"Oh sure, oh sure," said RDR, pushing her blood soaked hair away from her face, "oh sure. It's okay with you isn't it Daly?"

"Oh sure, oh sure," repeated the man with the bad knee.

"Okay then. Let's go. Follow me," exclaimed the widow, now with a weak grin on her face.

"Stay here!" ordered the well-dressed man, following the widow, "You see how easy it was?"

The red faced one with the bad knee gazed around for a long time, then with a fulfilled look in his face, went behind the bar, looked where Bob was sprawled on the bottom of everything that had come down from the shelves, opened the refrigerator door, took a cold bottle of beer and began to drink. From the expression on his face, Newsome felt the pure joyful reality that the time had finally come for him to be reunited with the money. He strolled into the kitchen thinking how wonderful it was to be rich - rich enough to enjoy the beach in another country, far away from the arms of the American legal system that pursued him for the biggest part of his life.

Strolling out of the kitchen and entering the dining room, he saw Linda standing by the door, proceeding to enter.

"Where's everybody at?" inquired Linda, sauntering in with a nonchalant attitude, advancing to the middle of the dining room.

"Stay where you are!" growled Daly, aiming his pistol at her.

"What happened?" asked Linda startled.

"Never mind. Stay there or I'll shoot you down like a dog, bitch," ordered Daly.

"What's happening? Where's my boss, Pam?" asked Linda, horrified.

"She'll be around. She's showing RDR where the money is," said the convict, a wide grin now blooming on his face.

"What?"

"You heard me," said Daly,

"Where is Bob?" exploded Linda.

"Bob?" asked the convict calmly, "You knew Bob was coming down here. I think you're all in cahoots."

"Where is Bob?" repeated Linda, with the same force, her eyes searching, terrified.

"Bob is gone," replied Daly in a satisfied manner, pointing at the ruins with his gun, "Your boss killed him."

The panic-stricken woman started to go where he pointed his pistol to look for Bob.

"Hold it!" screamed the convict, " don't make a move, or I'll shoot you now."

"What are you going to do with her after you get the money? Are you going to kill her too?"

"Never mind about her. I'll hate to waste you though. You're a beautiful woman with a body too good to waste. It'd be a shame to off you too. But business is business," said the man with the bad knee, pointing the gun at her.

"Are you crazy?"

"Never mind about me being crazy, " said Daly, moving closer, "Worry about yourself if you don't do what I want. Start taking your clothes off, and go and lay on that big table."

"Okay. Will you spare our lives if I'll agree to that, officer?" questioned Linda, beginning to unbutton the top of her blouse,

"Officer? I'm no cop, I'm Daly," he said, aiming the gun at her as though he were preparing to fire, but moving closer to her and staring with hungry eyes, "I'm not making any bargains with you for a piece of ass, I'll have enough money to buy ten like you, and better."

Suddenly Erik burst in, hurried towards him and, without wasting a second, fired twice. The bandit went down and Erik ran for cover behind the bar

"Linda run for cover," yelled Erik, from his hiding place.

The bosomy waitress ran and ducked next to Erik behind a knee-high wall that held some flowerpots.

"You son-of-a-bitch, you killed me," cried the man coiled on the floor, holding his bleeding right leg with his left hand.

"You should have shot before you talked, " said Erik, from behind the wall, "you only talk before you make love, stupid! I didn't want to kill you. I shot the hand that held the gun and the good knee. Where are Pam and your other half?"

The man said nothing; he only moaned and held onto his wounds.

"Don't play games with me. It's not hurting you that much, yet. The real pain will come soon. You better tell me or I'll shoot your balls off," growled Erik through clenched teeth.

"In the cellar," cried the wounded man.

"How do I get there, Linda?"

"Through the kitchen you'll see an open door," replied Linda, trembling.

Erik crawled into the kitchen, then stood up and headed quietly and vigilantly for the cellar. He stopped on the cellar steps when he was half way down, gazed about with the revolver ready in his hand, hiding as much of himself as possible, and listened for a sound. He then descended another three steps, very slowly. The steps creaked beneath his feet. He looked around carefully for a long profound moment. The cellar was ill lit, but ahead of him, behind a wall, a bright light was beaming. He finally came all the way down and hid behind the steps. After listening for a few seconds he began to walk towards the beaming light. As he drew nearer to the bright light, a feeling came over him that he was being watched. He then heard splashes of thick water.

"Pam?" whispered Erik, rushing away from where he was standing. He placed himself against the wall.

"Erik?" shouted Pam, "I'm in here. Come right in. I've got everything under control, Erik my dear," shouted Pam, from the well-lit room.

Erik rushed into the room and saw Pam standing above a black water hole, off to one side of the room, watching the detective from Richmond rolling around in the oil filled well, splashing in a fruitless effort to escape.

"What happened here?" asked Erik, looking at the battered lady, "What happened to your face, Pam?"

"The scum that you see floating in the grease trap did all this. You know who and what he is, don't you?"

"I know, I know, Linda told me all about it. Where is Bob?"

"I think I killed him, Erik. I did what you told me to do. I emptied my gun on him and he is laying behind the bar," returned Pam, now beginning to cry.

"Oh! No! Lets go see him," said Erik, running upstairs with Pam following closely.

"Erik, the reason I shot him is because it suddenly dawned on me that his last name is Ritter. He's the brother of the previous owner," explained Pam, running behind Erik, " his first name is Robert. I thought that his middle name started with D. Then RDR made sense to me.

When they came out of the kitchen, they saw Linda tending to Bob who was sitting down with his back leaning on the inside of the bar.

"You are alive?" screamed Pam, falling on her knees next to him.

"You are under arrest, Pam Strucker," said Bob, wiping some of the spilled liquor from his face and clothing.

"What's the charge?" asked Pam, without too much worry.

"Attempted murder."

"I didn't know what I was doing," replied Pam with a grin, " you don't know how happy I am that you're still alive. Are you OK?"

"OK enough to haul your ass in."

Erik picked up the pistol from the bar, removed the magazine, examined it and said,

"You mean to tell me you emptied the gun on him and never hit him once?" in great amazement.

"I never hit him once? I Just pointed the gun, thinking that he was RDR, and pulled the trigger as hard as I could," stated Pam, jerking the pistol from Erik's hand," let me have that. No weapon no charges," saying this she dropped the pistol between her breasts, looked at Bob and smiled like a dog that stole the meat from the butcher's hook and swallowed it.

"I don't care if you put it where the sun don't shine, I'll find it," uttered Bob.

"You should be thankful that I'm a good shot and you're not dead," returned Pam, turning to Erik she whispered, "You were right when you told me not to try to cripple him, that I would miss altogether, that's what really happened."

"Call the police to make a report," said Erik.

"I am the police, don't you people remember?" uttered Bob, getting onto his feet.

"If I were you, I wouldn't tell anybody that this woman beat you to the draw," said Erik, smiling, "Let's go get that guy out of the oil pit, before he drowns," as he then headed for the cellar, " And call an ambulance for this guy here before he bleeds to death," pointing at Daly, who was still moaning in the middle of the floor.

"Why in hell do you have a well in the cellar?" asked Erik on the way to the oil well.

"It used to be a septic tank. I made it into a grease trap for the restaurant," replied Pam, following Erik.

"A septic tank inside the building?"

"Evidently it wasn't always inside but when they expanded the building, they built another septic and left this inside. The former owner cleaned it out and turned it into a grease trap for the restaurant."

"How did he fall in?"

"The scum beat the shit out of me so I'd tell him where the money is. I don't know where in hell the money is, but he didn't believe me," explained Pam. "He said he was going to kill me. Then I thought of the open tank down here. The tank is three feet across, seven feet deep and has over five feet of kitchen grease in it. It had a rotten wood cover, but I had that thrown out and was going to put a new one on. I had the tank covered with a canvas. When we came down here, I pointed at the wall and told him that the money was stashed behind there. He got excited, ran to the wall, stepped on the canvas and the rest is history. I was really stalling for time, knowing that you were coming back. If I thought you weren't coming back, I think, I just would have let the scum kill me. You see, Erik, you saved my life."

"You're a smart and lucky lady, my dear," said Erik, laughing.

"Are you going to help me out of here?" asked the formerly well-dressed man, seeing the couple approaching.

"I'd like to shoot you first, " said Pam. Grabbing Erik's pistol from his belt, she pointed it and shot; it went off, hitting the wall above his head. A huge beam let loose from behind the wall and water burst out spraying everything around, including the man in the oil pool.

"My God, how did that happen?" asked Pam, looking at the gun.

"I know," said Erik, taking the gun from Pam, "You just squeezed the trigger without knowing."

"The water is coming out of the wall, I must have shot the well water pipe. We must break open the wall to get behind there. There was an opening outside, but before I bought the place the old owner plugged it up to keep out the squirrels. Erik, we have to do something. It will flood the basement. I have a lot of equipment here. Please, Erik, help me!" shrieked the widow.

"Do you have a sledgehammer? If you do, I'll help you to break down the wall," said Erik.

"I have one," answered Pam, leaving to get a sledgehammer.

"What I should really do, lover boy, is let the water fill up the basement until you drown," said Erik to the man in the pool, while waiting for the sledgehammer.

"No, please Mr. Karas, no!" cried the well-dressed man in the oil pool.

RDR looked up into Erik's face, as if he were making a mute appeal for mercy. He stood there in the glare of the light, on the bottom of the filthy cesspool, with one hand holding on the edge of that pit and the other moving slowly around to balance himself upright, so he wouldn't slip in the oil and drown. He darted his head upwards with trembling lips, as his unkind luck unfolded and his bad deeds came back to haunt him; to make matters worst, the water from the broken pipe was pounding on him without mercy.

Beyond these manifestations of hopelessness and anxiety, he stirred one hand and one foot.

Erik asked why a sentence of death should not be passed upon him. He only looked intently upon Erik's face while the question was asked. His haggard face was still upwards, his lower jaw hung down and his eyes bulged out before him, as Pam came in holding the sledgehammer.

"Turn your face the other way while I break open the wall, if you don't want to go blind for the rest of the short life you've designed for yourself," said Erik, taking the sledgehammer from Pam.

The man gazed incoherently around him for an instant but then obeyed.

"This is too heavy, my dear lady," said Erik, balancing the sledgehammer in his hands. " I'm afraid I'll do more damage to the pipes behind the wall. Let me have a hammer."

"I don't have a hammer, my dear man, you know I'm not a carpenter, but there's a trunk in the bottom of a closet where there might be some tools," replied Pam, walking away and towards a dusty cabinet that stood against the wall like an old forgotten wooden Indian in front of a cigar store.

Erik placed the sledgehammer by the grease trap and said, while he walked towards Pam, " RDR, you touch that sledgeham-mer and you'll be playing cards with the Angel Gabriel before the day is over."

RDR, exhausted by the ordeal, could barely keep his mouth above the grease.

"Here it is," said Pam, bending down, "I found this trunk here when I bought the place. Who knows, there might be a hidden treasure in here," she continued, pulling the left side handles.

"Let me help you with the hidden treasure," said Erik, grasping the other side.

The trunk looked heavy but felt lighter as they carried it over and set it beneath the light near the grease trap.

Erik bent down to open the trunk. "Stay back!" he said.

"Why?"

"There may be a snake in here. That's why the Greek called this place 'THE SERPENT'."

"You're funny," returned Pam, her eyes fixed on the trunk.

Erik slowly opened the lid and pulled out an old pair of men's pants.

"Those are my husband's old pants," screamed Pam, getting down on her knees and pulling out a flannel shirt. She walked a few paces away, held her husband's pants close to her chest and cried bitter tears.

Meanwhile Bob, reaching the bottom of the cellar steps and hearing Pam's screams, stopped and yelled, "What's happening down here?" Then he heard another scream louder and more terrifying than the previous one and identified it as coming from the same person. Bob, being a true policeman with a suspicious mind, unable to detach himself from expecting the worse from the unexpected, began to move slowly towards the scene of that commotion with his eyes and ears at their full employment. He suddenly stopped when he saw Pam standing in a bizarre manner in the middle of the cellar, underneath the bright light. Overcome by confusion, fear, bewilderment and every other human passion that is brought to light by the unexpected, Bob rushed to the trunk, knelt down and looked in. His mouth drooped open and his jaw hung loose; he dipped his huge hands into it and began turning around bundles of money that Erik and Pam uncovered while looking for the hammer.

"What 's happening down here? " asked Bob pathetically. He then began picking up bills, raising them high and let them go, watching them land softly back in the trunk.

Linda, who just arrived in the cellar, saw the spectacular display of green money and brought her hand to her mouth to prevent herself from screaming.

"We evidently found the money, " replied Pam, trembling with fear and anxiety.

"You found it or took it from RDR?" asked Bob, coming to his feet, looking around suspiciously. "Now I know why you shot at me, Miss Flood." Turning to Pam, and without saying another word, Bob took out his gun and ordered both Linda and Pam to raise their hands high and move towards the wall.

"Where is the Greek?" asked Bob sternly.

"You have been straddling between heaven and earth," said Erik, who was now standing behind Bob with his pistol pointed at him.

Bob suddenly turned and, seeing the gun pointed at him, said nothing but only turned pale.

"Like I said, you've been straddling between heaven and earth ever since you realized the money was hidden in here. You are the devil's angel, Bob. You seem to be ready, willing and able to shoot and kill people for money. You are a creature of warped mind and soiled soul and now you are fluttering between life and death. I feel you belong in that bright light where so many gifted creatures like you have winged their early flight. Drop your gun and move backwards!" commanded Erik, holding his gun on him.

"You're wrong," protested Bob, in a loud voice.

"Tell me!"

"I just realized the money was hidden in here somewhere so I called the station and told the chief to send down a team to search for it. I thought you and Linda and Pam were all involved," exclaimed Bob.

"How's that?" asked Erik.

"I don't know. I see everything from the other side of right. That's what makes a good policeman," he answered.

"How do you know that we are not?" asked Erik, still holding the gun on Bob.

"I don't know, I guess it's a policeman's intuition. But I called in for a team to come down to look for the money," replied Bob.

"He is telling the truth, Mr. Karas, I heard him calling the police," said Linda.

"I'll be dammed," said Erik, putting his gun in his pocket and turning his head away from them all, "I have never been wrong so many times as I have since I came to this place. Maybe I'm just stupid."

"No, you haven't been wrong. You guessed these two clowns were up to something no good. You're the only Greek I ever met though who said he might be stupid. All Greeks think they're smart," said Bob.

"Did I say that I'm stupid?"

"Yeah," replied Bob.

"You see, I am wrong again," replied Erik.

"Tell me again that speech you gave while you stood behind me," said Bob, now with a smile.

"It was not a speech, it was a eulogy," replied Erik, with a serious face, "but you didn't seem to be scared. Tell me why?"

"I knew you weren't going to shoot, because you told Daly 'don't talk first, just shoot'," replied the officer of the law, "you only talk first before you make love."

"You were alive, well and conscious under all that rubble, you son-of-a-gun," uttered Erik in amazement.

"No, I was resurrected."

"What are we going to do with this here money?" asked Pam.

They all looked at each other for different reasons.

"Because of this money, I am a widow," returned Pam earnestly.

"Pam," said Bob, "The insurance company didn't kill your husband. Your husband got killed because he stole the money from the insurance company. The police will take it and turn it over to the courts. The court will hand the money over to the insurance company and you will probably receive a small reward from, after they receive the money from the courts," explained Bob earnestly.

"Pass out the bread, here comes the bologna. I will probably receive a small reward, you said? Can't you see, I'm the victim here?" asked Pam.

"You are not the victim, Pam," returned Bob, looking around with the air of a person who earned some slight support from his listeners.

"Who is the victim then?" asked Pam, looking around the very same way that Bob had at the conclusion of his spoken words.

Hearing nothing in return, she proceeded, "Who is the victim then? The payroll company got their money back from the insurance company and the insurance company is going to get back their money that I just found. In this case we have nothing but villains and no victims."

"We can say your husband is a victim," said Bob, softly being uncertain of his statement.

"Can you repeat that, please," requested Pam.

"I don't know what I've said. You need a lawyer," replied Bob, more emphatically.

"I don't need a lawyer, I need a gun to take this here money and ride into the sunset, me and the money my husband gave his life for. Then you will have a victim. The insurance company."

"This whole conversation is stupid," said Bob, "Let's go upstairs and wait for the police."

As he spoke those words and indicated with his hand the direction in which he wished them to proceed, Erik stepped forward.

"Wait a moment, please. How long will that take?" asked Erik.

"What?" asked Bob.

"For the money to be returned to the insurance company," said Erik.

"Probably a month," replied Bob.

"Pam, " said Erik, softly, as he walked and stood near her, "The reward is not because you are a widow, the reward will be for finding the money, which obviously you did. You, on the other hand, have the right to create an obstacle in court that will prevent the judge from handing the money over to the insurance company immediately. You should get a lawyer and have him sue the insurance company, the payroll company and the Richmond police department for having a crooked cop guard the money. An honest policeman would have prevented your husband from stealing the money and that is negligence on their part.

"The police department didn't know the cop was crooked," interrupted Bob, moving his body forward like a proud strong officer of the law.

"Et's not my yob, mon," said Erik, with a mocking foreign accent, "the police should have known that cop was crooked because he had done something improper before then and the police brass failed to find it or to do anything about it."

"Who said that?" asked Bob, preparing himself for an argument.

"Her lawyer, if he is any good, will find that out," replied Erik, looking at Bob with a self- satisfied grin.

"Never mind," said Bob, and Erik smiled wider upon hearing the phrase, 'never mind'.

"That way it will stop the insurance company from receiving the money so quickly. If you file a suit against them it could take almost seven years for the case to be heard. With that in mind, the insurance company will come to you with the hope that you will agree on a reward far more than what they had in mind of giving you. When you go to court it's almost certain that you will lose, but there is a slight chance that your lawyer can convince the jury that your husband was the victim and therefore you are a victim too. The jury may feel sorry for you. That's what insurance company lawyers are afraid of," said Erik, standing there with his eyes fixed on Pam until she jumped, threw her arms around him and screamed with joy.

"You may be wrong again," said Bob.

"Bob, I am used to being wrong in this place, that's why I've got to get the hell out of here very soon," said Erik, disengaging himself from Pam.

"Not so fast," returned Bob.

"Why not so fast?" asked Erik.

"Mr. Karas you just shot a man and he is probably bleeding to death upstairs. The courts must decide your innocence."

"How long?"

"Four, five days," replied Bob, heading for the stairs.

So five days glided away while Erik waited for his name to be cleared by the courts for shooting Daly; five days which, in the life of most blessed and favored mortals, would have been filled with happiness. But in Erik's troubled and cloudy mind, all his days were trances and his nights were filled with restlessness and gloomy dreams. With the purest and most amiable hospitality from Pam, it was a little easier for him, but the lingering fire within him to run away from everything was not going anywhere. The sad thoughts and feelings from the loss of his family were not budging, they were only mixed with the present challenging events that were enough to occupy only a portion of his mind and drive out some self consideration from his memory.

At length, early one evening, when Pam and Linda were serving the dinner crowd,

Erik entered the dining room, with some hesitation, and asked permission to bid them both goodbye.

"Who are you, Erik Karas? Where do you come from and where are you going?"

"We'll talk about it later when we talk about your husbands."

"I know one thing, Erik Karas, wherever you are going, it will be an adventure and I wish I could go with you," said Pam, as she zestfully threw her arms around him and kissed him farewell with the greatest affection.

Erik moved away hastily, his survival gear on his back and good feelings in his heart, heading for the side door. When he reached there, he grabbed the doorknob, opened the door, stopped, and looked back, "Remember the doorknob, Pam. Never get into a place where you can't get out," said Erik, with a smile.

"Oh, I promise you, dear Erik, I'll never enter any room that has a door with a doorknob and no window, just in case," replied the widow, with a hearty laugh.

Imparting a smile and the hint of a military salute, Erik stepped out and disappeared into the night.

CHAPTER 4

Meeting a strange man

The rich smell of raspberry bushes rose up to join the hundreds of perfumes from the little wild flowers that bordered the railroad tracks where Erik was walking, his bundle on his back and sorrow in his heart, some days after he left the widow and the bandits. He stopped and sat on the rail tracks, partly to catch his thoughts and partly to see nature at her best behavior.

The meadows shimmered all around him with drops of morning dew resting on every leaf; the birds sang as if every sparkling drop of dew was a fountain of inspiration to them. Erik, having cross-examined loneliness, using the most approved precedents at considerable length, turned his head around and gazed, as though he were searching for an exit from solitude or an entrance to a world of peace, a place to rest his troubled mind. With some remaining remnants of hope in his heart and a feeble fragment of self-preservation in his head, not yet defeated by guilt, he stood erect and headed west along the railroad tracks.

He walked on all day long with a dead silence pervading the wilderness, broken only by the audible lamentations of a lonely dove. He came upon a piece of desert-like land and he traveled on, passing alone through the scorching sand. After some long hours' walk under the hot summer sun, the wind began to build and rush though with force and fury. The sand blinded him as the wind lifted its grains and carried some away to distant lands and foreign places. The sun came down like living fire, burning every inch of him without mercy. The bones of lost animals lay scattered at his feet, warning him not to proceed, but to turn back. Being a man of great nerve and true grit, Erik steadfastly proceeded into that hell, where only fools would think of going. The scorching sun, the burning earth and the whipping wind would not relent, as though nature were trying to tell him to turn back, but it is a known fact that no one can tell a man what to do if he doesn't want to live, so Erik kept on. Eventually the wind reduced him to a mindless beast, lost in a forbidden land. After some time, he realized his last breath of life was very near. Then, in a sudden fluttering moment, torn between life and death, Erik felt the sweet smell of life coming to him and now he wanted to live, so as to be born again; he went on with some stroke of power and another slice of strength. Even though his tongue and throat were dried and brittle, with his bundle hanging from his back and new hope tucked deep in his heart, he rushed forward, armed with thoughts of living again. But then his tattered strength began to dwindle, his vision reduced to blindness; he could only feel the hot soil beneath his feet. Exhaustion, fatigue, thirst and hunger caught up with him and he fell, senseless, on the burning sand with his heart beating faintly, languidly holding his soul in place. He lay there devoid of thought or strength.

At last the hot sun faded, the night crept in and stretched out, all over the sand, spreading some coolness and comfort to his parched and burning body. The morning finally arrived; birds were heard to be singing far, far away. Suddenly he heard a bird caroling close to him. He heard another, a little further off, and when the singing stopped for a moment, the trickling of running water greeted his ear, seeming to come from not too far away. The thought of fresh water's fragrant coolness revived him and he stood up to see the clear stream of babbling water running into a small pond, just a few yards from where he was and had spent the night. He stumbled and fell, then crawled slowly with only the traces of strength that hunger and thirst had failed to lift from him. He crept on with his face dragging in the sand and his body trailing behind, moving one limb one inch at a time. Thirst and hunger caught up with him again, he then stopped moving and only lay there, hearing the water trickling a few feet ahead and realizing that he was either a few breaths away from that spring of life or one breath away from the gates of death. Saving his breath would mean losing his strength.

What a curse for a blessed man and what a blessing for a sinful one that circumstance was. Removing his face from the sand, he rolled onto his left side, coiled himself and listened to the silence of the deserted land.

The profound stillness of that scene was broken by heavy footsteps coming his way. He looked without being able to move a limb, but was only able to vaguely see a black horse going for the water, unconcerned about his presence.

The horse drank vigorously while Erik was tilting away from life slowly but surely.

After a long while the horse lifted his head from the water pond and looked at the dying man. Without any hesitation or further consideration, the horse walked towards Erik and stopped almost above him, looking down, the animal dripped fresh water on Erik's face. Feeling the fresh water, the man, who was about to cross over from this world to the other, slowly moved his right hand and shoved some of that dripping water into his own mouth.

Trying to smell the man, as most kind animals do, the horse brought its muzzle closer to him and dripped more water on Erik's face.

By those drops of water from the horse's mouth, Erik was revived and segments of energy were dimly restored to his body and mind; he rolled on his back and breathed deeply.

The horse, standing between him and the small clear pond and seeing the man moving, backed off one full length; it looked and waited as if to see the results of its good deed. With the beginnings of newborn strength, Erik started to crawl towards the pond and the horse stepped aside once again to allow him to pass.

Reaching the clear water, he threw his limbs into the stream and drank deeply.

Having had enough to drink and being satisfactorily refreshed, Erik strolled out of the clear running stream, landed on the bank, rolled on his back, looked up at the sky and breathed deeply again. He heard a train whistle blowing, but it was far from him. He realized that during the night's darkness and the sand storm, he had lost his direction and distanced himself from his path, along the railroad. Knowing there was not much he could do about it at that time, except to strengthen himself, he turned on his side, grabbed his bundle, opened it, took out a piece of dried bread and a tin cup, filled the cup with water, crushed his bread in it and stirred it with a twig. It came out soupy and with a trembling hand he brought it to his lips and nourished himself with the fuel of life. Looking at the cup of cold bread soup, after his first sip, he said aloud, raising the cup high, "George, here is to your three Ss, soup, sex and shelter. One out of three, George, it isn't so bad. I will survive." Saying this, Erik finished his cold bread soup, leaned back and smiled, as if moved to a delightful trance. He sat there for a long while, now and then raising his head to watch the flight and landing of some birds by the stream. Carrying his eyes along the path of the glorious crimson sun that was coming from where he had left several days ago, "One reason for living is to see and feel life all around," he mumbled.

Seeing the man had finished his drinking, the horse returned to the pond and began to drink again.

Erik's strength now was sufficiently restored; he stood and walked towards the beautiful animal with the intent to thank and befriend his life's savior. Taking cautious steps with the bundle in one hand and his shoes in the other, he came very close to the horse. The horse stopped drinking, raised its head, looked at the stranger for some time, shook its head violently, then snorted and blew out a huge amount of air and water. Because of his background, being more sufficiently acquainted with donkeys than horses, Erik turned and ran away, thinking the snorting was a warning sign before an attack on anyone who came too near.

The horse, puzzled with the man's strange behavior, looked on with an indifferent attitude and continued to drink. Erik, standing there, looking at the creature while it drank peacefully, contemplated gathering another burst of courage with which to approach the mysterious beast once more. He dropped his shoes and bundle on the ground, thinking that if he had to run again the survival gear would only be a burden. He went off again to negotiate with the horse, but when he came close enough to almost touch it, this time Erik began to speak in a gentle voice.

"Come on horse, I need your help to catch a train."

The horse, whether sufficiently acquainted with the polite tone of the human voice, or intrigued by the word 'train' that held forth the chance to travel to other lands, did not make a move, or shake its head, snort or run away, but it only stood there, with its ears perked, listening to Erik. Having heard enough human talk, the horse started slowly and gently towards him, and Erik, not knowing what to make of the horses' whole attitude, turned and hastily headed for his belongings. The horse followed, then paused when Erik stopped a few feet away. What appeared to be his new friend, the black beauty, planted its four feet firmly on the ground, nailed his big eyes on him and waited for instructions.

Erik took off his belt and extended it along with one of the ropes that held his bundle tacked and rolled, tied his shoe strings together, threw them over his shoulder and then carefully tossed the belt around the horse's neck. He waited to see its next move, but the horse didn't move a muscle. However, when Erik attempted to mount the creature, it darted back a full length.

"Whoa," said Erik, "good horse, nice horse" he repeated. But that was misguided flattery. The closer he tried to get to that horse, the more it horse sidled away; the more Erik coaxed and wheedled, the less the horse listened. The man and the four legged mortal beast went around and around several times until finally the animal came to its horse sense, as if it knew it was fighting a losing battle; it stopped, stood still and allowed Erik to mount.

The horse immediately started to behave strangely; whether it felt it had just found a new playmate and was desirous of having a little fun, or it had just occurred to the creature to test the man's ability, it bolted up on its hind legs, then came back down to the ground with them, and then, realizing the man's talent as a rider and his persistence, it picked up its ears, extended its tail outwards, and took off at a gallop, heading for the railroad tracks.

A little more than a mile was left between the galloping pair and the tracks when the train whistle blew in the distance, telling the world that it was coming through. Erik shaded his eyes with his hand, looked in the direction of the shrill whistle's sound and saw the train coming towards them, slowly. Once horse and man came close to the point of departure, Erik guided the handsome stallion to a lower level of the terrain in order to hide from the train's engineers. When the train engine passed, Erik spurred the horse's belly with his bare heels once again and the horse, having the horse sense he inherited from his mother and father, rushed onward, ran parallel to a boxcar for a while and slowed down when it saw an open door that would be easy for his friend to jump in. After throwing his bundle in the boxcar, Erik, with an acrobatic move, leaped right in, taking with him his shoes and his belt. The horse kept on at a gallop with its tail out, its neck stretched forward and its ears pointed upwards, as if it were mocking the train's confinement to the tracks, and triumphing in the consciousness of its own freedom and speed; it passed the train and headed towards the stream.

Erik surveyed the boxcar with a nonchalant attitude and gazed at an unusually large square crate sitting in the far corner; he moved to the left of it, away from the open door. As he sat there removing his shoes from around his neck and starting to pack them into his bundle, he gazed at the crate again without any thoughtful intent. Suddenly as he looked at it, the crate began to move sideways. Seeing the large wooden crate moving in a strange manner somewhat astonished him. The crate stopped for no obvious reason. Suddenly an old shriveled human face appeared to be rising from it, followed by the figure of a tall slim older gentleman that came to a standing position and faced Erik, smiling. His coat looked as if it were made of loose remnants handed down from the lost and found department of another era.

"Good morning," said the old gentleman, rubbing his chin with the left hand and holding a dilapidated hat with the other, "Are you going my way, young fellow?"

"Looks like it. We both paid the same fare," replied Erik, unmoved by the uncommon stance of a man.

"Do you happen to have a drink for this man here?"

"No! I don't" answered Erik, still trying to put his shoes in the bundle, as he was preparing for a good day's rest.

"How can you travel first class without a drink on you?"

"First class is the next car over. Would you like me to help you get over there?" asked Erik, without stopping his preparations.

"How's that?" asked the poor old chap.

"Tell me yes, and I'll show you how."

"Show me first, and if I like it, I'll tell you yes."

"Look, go to sleep, old fellow, because that's what I intent to do," said Erik, beginning to grow a little indignant.

"Come on. That's not the way to address an old man. You have less respect for me than if I were a hobo."

"I didn't mean to treat you with disrespect, sir," said Erik, stopping with his chores for a moment.

"Well maybe yes, maybe no. But I know a lot about you, young fellow."

"I'm sure you do," said Erik, proceeding with his chores.

"I do, I'll tell you if you want."

"No! I've already had my palm read by two experts, on the last train."

"I don't read palms, I read faces. I've read yours already."

Waiting for some response and hearing none, the old man looked around in silence for some time and then sat down in his crate again, but with half of him out.

"You are not poor, you're poverty stricken," remarked the old man.

"What's the difference? Poor, broke, poverty stricken, they are all the same," returned Erik, without much emotion.

"Poverty stricken and broke are temporary, being poor is permanent," said the old man as he stopped abruptly and looked at Erik with a soft glance, "Maybe you don't have a lot of money, but you are not poor."

"I know," returned Erik, stopping his task; he stared at the old man curiously.

"I know you very well, I said."

"What do you know about me, old man?" asked Erik, now with a hint of indignation in his manner, "I'm kind of tired to listen to your nonsense."

"I told you, you have no right to speak to me with disrespect, didn't you hear me, boy?" voiced the old gentleman sternly, raising himself farther up from the crate as if he were preparing for a violent challenge.

When the old man said this he looked so fierce that Erik felt his face redden from embarrassment and replied softly, "I'm sorry, old man."

"And don't call me old man! It sounds, as if you are trying to insult me."

"I'm sorry, again."

The old gentleman stared at Erik a long time, but Erik took no significant notice of it. The old hobo slowly shrank back into his crate and while doing so never once altered his gazed from Erik.

"You are a very nice young fellow, " remarked the hobo after a while, "I was young and handsome too, once. You can't tell by looking at me now, but I was held in great favor among women in my day. That's funny; I thought then that those days would last forever. Have you heard the saying, 'only the good die young?'"

"I think I heard it before."

"Do you know what that means?" asked the old man smiling, keeping his eyes pinned on Erik and waiting to hear a response.

"It means what it says, that's all."

"Do you see me now?" sad the old man, standing up, stretching over six feet high, "aren't I something repulsive to look at?"

"Not really, you look okay," uttered Erik, "you don't look like a young stallion, but you look okay, but don't put too much on me, men are not my specialty, women are."

"I know that."

"How do you know that?"

"I told you that I know you," said the old gentleman with a smile. "Here!" said the old man, handing him a picture, "that's a picture of me when I was in my prime."

"Very handsome, I must say," said Erik, looking at the picture earnestly and long enough to recognize him.

"I never wanted to grow old and look like this. People who knew me then, when they see me now, after many years, are astonished. 'My God, John, what happened to you?' they say to me."

He stopped, took his picture and carefully put it back into his inside coat pocket.

"If God liked me, He would have taken me when I was young, so nobody would see the unkind and ungodly change in me. Apparently He didn't like me, because I wasn't very good. I have no more friends, I have no more sweethearts, I have no one to caress my body or touch my hair and face, no one who cares for my well-being. So don't put salt on the wound by calling me, old man."

"I'm sorry. That will never happen again," said Erik, sighing involuntarily.

"You and I have one thing in common."

"Yes, I know, we are both rich but we play the game of being hobos just for the fun of it," said Erik, sarcastically.

The old man burst into a fit of laughter and when that was done, restored himself back to a serious posture, and said, "We don't believe that we belong anywhere right now. We don't believe that we are entitled to anything in this life except punishment. I don't know what you have done, but whatever it is, to you, it is very bad." Then the old gentleman walked away slowly, stood by the boxcar's open door and gazed outside. He stood by the door looking at the forest as it passed by a little faster than before. There he stood, perfectly motionless, his eyes staring blindly, without even the slightest expression on his face of anything that could have resembled astonishment, curiosity, sorrow or any other known passion that agitates the human breast.

"When I was younger, I used to hear the words 'Burnt out' I didn't understand them then. Now I do," said the old gentleman, as he turned to face Erik who was standing a few paces away from him, listening with some interest.

"I have no more fires left inside me. They're all gone. That's what they meant by 'burnt out.' You know, worse than not having a horse, is having a horse that you can't ride," said the old man, looking at Erik now with sorrow on his face, "do you understand what I'm trying to tell you?"

"Not really" replied Erik, looking at him with a greater interest.

"You know what I am saying but you're looking for a second opinion. That's what most smart men do," said the hobo.

Erik lowered his head and grinned.

"If you knew me, you would have understood," said the old gentleman, thrusting his hand in his pocket as if to stop it from trembling, then turning half-around to look outside, "having a horse and you cannot ride is a punishment, and I am being punished for the bad things I have done in my life." Looking at Erik as if he wanted to add something else, "Dale Carnegie said, 'To die when you're poor is normal, but to die when you're rich is a punishment.'" concluded the old man.

"That's not exactly what he said," remarked Erik.

"Then that's what I said," interrupted the old man.

"What have you done, if I may ask?" said Erik, advancing a few steps towards him.

"I killed my son when he was only fifteen," murmured the old gentleman in a soft broken voice, just loud enough to overcome the rattling of the moving train and for Erik to hear him.

Erik opened his eyes and ears wider when he heard those words.

"My God! How dreadful that is. I don't have to tell you, sir, how sorry I am to hear that," said Erik, looking at the old gentleman, his face awash with pity, "how and why?"

The old fellow paused for a few moments, apparently struggling with his feelings and emotions, and then said, "About twenty-five years ago, my wife and I went on vacation to Europe, I had two sons, John and Teddy. John was the older and my junior, you see my name is John, and he was in college and Teddy, only fifteen, was in high school. Teddy didn't want to go to Europe with us because he had a lot of friends and was something of an important figure in sports. My wife didn't want to go without him, but I did. We went on my command and six days later, while we were in Switzerland, we received a phone call and were told that our son had drowned." At this moment, he burst into a storm of tears, crying with a full heart.

Erik kept his distance, thinking there was nothing he could to console the old gentleman.

"My wife blamed me and I blamed myself for what I had done. She and I never went anywhere since then. She never again left our home but she was there only in body. That hurt me more, when the only person that should know you, in this whole world, doesn't want to know you. She passed away way before her time. I worked and worked to fill my days. Now I am a hobo, not out of necessity but out of the wish for punishment."

The whole time he spoke his eyes focused downwards toward the floor, with one hand holding onto a rail and the other remaining in his pocket.

"So, if it wasn't for my selfishness, my son would still be alive today, because I would never have allowed him to go swimming in that lake of death. Do you understand what I'm saying to you, stranger?"

"God, do I."

"Now tell me, what's eating you?"

Erik took a lot of time to answer the old gentleman, but when he spoke he only said, "My mother used to say that every piece of wood has a termite that's eating it." Saying this, he walked away and headed for his bundle.

"Sometime this afternoon we'll be in Myrtle Beach. That's where we get off," said the old gentleman, wiping the tears and sweat off his face with his sleeve.

"Do we get off?" asked Erik, without much emphasis to his question.

"There are no more trains from there. You must go to another railroad yard. Now get some rest. You'll be my guest for tonight "

"More first class accommodations?" asked Erik, grinning.

"We'll take whatever we can get," returned the old man, smiling.

Eventually, later on that afternoon, the train came to a dead stop, both men jumped out and walked away with the old gentleman leading the way. He seemed to be as quick on his feet as he had been with his mouth. They finally made their way out of the train yard and headed towards the beach, still in formation. The old gentleman was leading, with his bundle on his back and Erik followed, with his over his shoulder. One thing Erik noticed to be out of the ordinary was that the old man knew where he was going and was moving discreetly, as if he cared who would see him, which is something unusual for hobos. They passed that illustrious main street of Myrtle Beach, crossed it and the ocean came into sight. The lanky old gentleman bent his steps to the left, once in a while looking back to see if Erik was following and then would gesture to him to speed up. They came to the side of a high-rise hotel, **THE LAMBRIGHT INN**. There was one small door on the side, like a delivery door. John stopped there, thrust his right hand into his pocket, and bringing out a number of keys, opened the door and beckoned Erik to follow him.

"What, are you crazy?" warned Erik, pulling the old man back and restraining him from entering the luxurious hotel.

"What's the matter?" exclaimed the old hobo, disengaging himself from Erik's grasp "are you afraid of first class accommodations? What's your name?"

"Erik"

"Erik? I thought it was....Nick or John?" said the old gentleman, showing a degree of surprise.

"No! Erik. Yours is John?

"Oh, that's where I got the name John. Let's go!" said the old man, taking Erik by the arm, "I'll show you something."

As soon as they entered the building, in what appeared to be the basement, the old gentleman made a right turn and led the way to an ill-lit passage, still looking back to see if his friend, Erik, was following close at his heels. Passing a wide staircase, he stopped at what seemed to be a freight elevator with a heavy cage door, pushed the button and in a few seconds, the elevator arrived. The doors opened automatically and John, with a look of accomplishment, motioned for Erik to get in.

"What floor do you want to stop on?" whispered John, waiting to push the button for the elevator to move.

"Basement for me, next to the heating and air-condition unit. That's the only place that I would feel safe and sound in a building like this," said Erik, looking around uncomfortably.

"Relax!" said John, pushing the penthouse button "nobody knows we're here."

The elevator stopped at the penthouse floor, the doors opened and John urged Erik to hurry out of the elevator and immediately conducted him to the first door on the right. There, John stopped to dig for something in his pocket, while Erik was looking at him anxiously. John drew from his pocket the same set of keys that he used to get in, looked at Erik, grinned expressively, then unlocked the door and threw it open, pulling Erik in with a gentle touch on his arm.

Erik hesitantly went in and gazed about like a peasant lost in the big city.

"Welcome to my hotel" said John, stepping forward and making a left turn. He opened a closet door and threw in his bundle and his coat, which he had been in the process taking off on his way there.

Erik, still looking lost but now also bewildered, stood in the middle of the floor, after placing his bundle by the side wall, and took a survey of the whole penthouse. The room was huge and beautiful with the beach stretched at its feet and a view of the horizon that was only a little short of that from the Rock of Gibraltar. The elegant living room furniture was perfectly matched, skillfully displayed and accented by some, of what seemed to be, original paintings carefully placed on the walls.

"I am Lambright, the owner of this magnificent structure," said John, with a wide and conceited smile on his face, his eyes flashing with pride and joy.

"I don't know whether to congratulate you, hug you or bust you in the mouth," said Erik, surveying his surroundings in awe.

"I deserve none of that. In a way, I'm lucky. Everything I do is without intent and most things come out right. You want a drink?"

"No, thank you."

"Don't you drink?"

"I don't have to carry a bottle with me."

"What do you mean?"

"I drink wine socially or sometimes I drink to show off."

"I am the same way," said the old gentleman.

"Why did you asked me for a drink on the train?"

"I wanted to know if you drank," said John, with a smile.

"Boy, you are full of surprises, Mr. Lambright, sir."

"How is that?"

"How is that? First you show up dressed as a hobo, second you said you have no friends and then you come up as a millionaire. You've got more secrets than the CIA."

John smiled, "There is a reason for my behavior. Your behavior is not so different from mine. Think about it!" said John, nailing his eyes on him.

"I'm not a millionaire," said Erik, walking away in a painful effort to conceal his hurt.

"If I gave you what I have, would you be happy, Erik? What's eating you cannot be cured with money," replied John.

On that unexpected reply, Erik turned and looked at John with a long stare.

"Would you?" asked the old gentleman, loudly and firmly.

"I am not trying to built an empire like you have," returned Erik, closing his eyes for enough time to count to five; when he opened them, they were fixed on John.

John pulled up a chair, sat and carefully untied his boots. He took them off and placed them under a desk, all the while staring at Erik.

"These are my possessions, but a lot of the time I live like a hobo," said the old man, commencing in a loud voice, and ending in a faint one. "I didn't build this. I owned the land here and some more land a little further up from here. A group of investors came to me, we made a deal, they built this and I remained a majority stockholder. I bought this land after my Teddy's death. I bought it to go broke but it turned out that it made me a rich man," said John, "I feel happier living like a tramp. Living like a tramp is a punishment per se; it's an escape from extravagant living and after what I've done, I don't deserve any luxuries. Living as a hobo, I don't feel guilty. I don't have to impress anybody or set pace for anyone." Saying this, John looked at Erik intently, "does any of this make sense to you?"

Erik shook his head mournfully for a long time, looking down at the floor, "you're crazy, John," said Erik, raising his head to look at John with a vacant stare.

"I know," replied John, sighing involuntarily. "After my Teddy's death, my brain tilted to the right or to the left, and stayed there like that. I left it like that, it felt comfortable, but I realized with all my suffering and all the time I sacrificed, my Teddy didn't come back and he won't come back, ever," said John, getting up and walking towards Erik. "The other day I heard a man, I don't know how wise he was, but what he said was wise, 'Open up your day by making someone happy, and you'll be happy too.' He went on to say 'as the Bible says, 'give and you shall receive.'" John stopped and smiled, "I'll try to make somebody happy."

Erik looked at him, smiled and said, "You were there, you old bastard, that's why you called me Nick. You weren't sure of my name."

"Being punished, for all this time, is really miserable," said John, bypassing Erik's statement for a moment, "I was there dressed as a hobo, what I really am, at heart. Mayor John Lambright...."

"Is your son, your other son," interrupted Erik.

The old gentleman smiled and nodded in assent.

"Does John, the mayor, know how you spend your days?"

"No! Nobody knows, except you."

"Then you're a nice target for blackmail," said Erik, smiling appropriately.

"Then you're a nice target for rifle practice," said John, seriously.

"I see you're a tough old boy."

"To make millions and survive as a hobo you have to be tough, particularly when you look weak."

With his hands in his pockets, Erik leaned against a dresser, nodding his head up and down and producing a succession of bland and benevolent smiles, being moved by John's last comment. John looked on him with a great degree of pride, but then noticed that Erik began to take on a hopeless image, portrayed in every line of his expressive face.

"What's eating you, Erik? I asked you that question on the train and you gave me no answer. I can understand that, seeing me dressed like a hobo, thinking that I had nothing, you took me for being stupid, like most people do when they meet me as a hobo. But now seeing that I have a lot of things, you probably think I'm smart, like most people do."

"What are you driving at, John?" asked Erik, going towards the window to stare out at the ocean; he said nothing more.

"What are your plans, Erik?" asked the old gentleman, breaking that silence.

"I have no plans."

"I thought so," said John, sighing involuntarily. "I know no matter what I say or do, I can't help you, but I'll say something anyway."

"Go ahead. Fire when ready!"

"Do you believe in God, Erik?"

"That question was asked of me once before, not long ago, but my answer will be different now than it was then. I believe that there is a God, but I don't believe in Him," said Erik, looking at John as if he were waiting for an answer. When he heard none, he continued "do you understand what I just said?"

"Yeah, I understood perfectly what you said. You're telling me that you don't have a prayer with God. You're also telling me, with the same answer, that you're angry with Him. I'm telling you that I know you're angry, period. You know, Erik, going around and living with hobos, I learned that those hobos have one thing in common. They all believed in someone; that someone never delivered, in accordance with their high expectations, so they finally gave up. They're suffering. Take it from me, Erik, suffering is no laughing matter. You have the talent to make people believe in what you believe. I heard your speech. They will take the bull by the horns and will do better for themselves and will be better people."

A burst of laughter slipped out of Erik, as he walked away.

"Don't walk away from me, boy, when I am talking to you."

Erik turned very slowly, faced his new friend and said softly and calmly,

"John, I'm not traveling for my amusement or to find myself or to find a way to instruct other people how to live their lives. Another thing, John, I never thought I would ever get to a point where God, man, death or the devil don't scare me any more," concluded Erik, now coming closer to John, staring intently.

"I didn't yell at you to scare you, I yelled to wake you up."

"Wake up. That's the thing that bothers me the most. Opening my eyes after sleeping, I don't care whether God or the devil takes me, neither one scares me one bit, but life does scare me, a lot. Going through this..."

"Suffering, Erik, suffering is the word you want to use. So many people are suffering," said John loudly, "get out while you can. Get out!"

Hearing those words, Erik fell into an instant trance, where the soft light of a different hope appeared burning feebly in his lost soul, not like one that comes and goes, but lingering, with the vague promise to stay lit and grow, but he, unable to grasp its terms and demands, turned and looked back at the old gentleman with vacant eyes.

"I lived with your kind of hurt for almost twenty five years, until it became a habit for me, a hurting habit," continued John, seeing the small change in Erik's face, "I would get up in the morning and go down to the bridge, stand and look down at the ocean water and it seemed to me that it was muttering an invitation of repose and rest. One leap, I used to think, a splash, a short struggle, and gentle ripple above my head as the water would close over me, locking out all my sorrow, misfortune, misery and guilt, forever. Did it ever strike you that putting yourself to sleep in a bed of deep water would bring happiness and peace?" asked John, with excitement flashing on his face as he spoke. But it subsided quickly, when he saw Erik studying him with a curious eye and saying nothing, as if deploring the mental image that was drawn.

"Get out of it, while you can. You are smarter than I am. At least you have an open mind, something that I lacked and still do. Plus, my dear friend, you have something else I don't have .You have the talent of speaking, not the speaking everybody has, but the kind that inspires people to listen. It was indeed a noble and brilliant sight to see you up there talking to the crowd," said John, coming closer to Erik, looking at him more intently than at anytime before, "while you were speaking to the people," said John in a solemn voice, as if a fiery burst of poetry, harbored in his breast, was about to erupt, "While you were speaking to them, their faces beamed, not with warlike ferocity that I saw before. Their eyes flashed with a civilized gentleness, the soft light of humanity and intelligence that was a picture every painter would give his right kidney for the opportunity to capture with his brush. They were listening to you as you poured out your words of simple, common and everyday wisdom. Do you know how the walls Jericho fell?"

Erik shook his head negatively.

"By the trumpets blowing," said John, leaving his eyes tacked on Erik.

Whether Erik turned a deaf ear to John Lambright, as he had done with George Papas or whether he heard everything but let it penetrate his loaded head and sit there to be called upon another day, he showed no change of heart; he only gazed at the old gentleman and walked towards his bundle. He picked it up, swung it in the air and as it landed on his shoulder, he turned, looked at John and said with anger, "I'm just a bullshit artist, John, and I've harmed a lot of people; I broke hearts and homes with my, what's you called, common and everyday wisdom; it's pure bullshit, can't you understand that? I would have to spend the next one hundred and seventeen years doing nothing but good to undo all the harm that I've done up till now. I loused up all the dreams that I had for myself and that other people had for me; the only thing I've accomplished is jumping from one broad's belly on to another's." The excitement that cast an unwanted light on his face while he spoke did not subside for one moment but grew stronger along with his voice, as he went on, "Now I am down," continued Erik, "nobody has to worry about me going down or taking anyone else with me. You didn't suffer, John. You told me that you suffered. You played a game. You took a vacation. Instead of going into the woods to rough it up, you rode the trains with a whole bunch of lost souls and that made you feel good because they were lost and you weren't. When the game was over and you had enough you came back to this overgrown playpen."

"Wait a moment, boy!" interrupted John, showing his indignation, "Why have you turned your guns on me? You think you have all the answers, but you don't even have the questions."

"Go ahead, John, fire when you're ready," rejoined Erik, grinning on seeing John's indignation, "Where am I wrong?" he asked.

"How do you know how I felt?" said John, inspecting Erik from the crown of his head to the lowest string of his shoes.

"How you felt? How you felt? I know how you felt because I feel now how you felt then, John. Do you hear me? Do you see me?" yelled Erik, emphatically.

"Here!" yelled John, taking the keys from his pocket and hammering them on the desk, with features distorted and eyes flowing, not far different from an insane man, "I'll give you all I have, including this overgrown playpen, as you called it; will that make you happy?" John stood tall and angry in front of Erik, waiting for some kind of answer.

Erik, at first, looked at him with a forced grin, as if to reduce the man's anger, then slid his bundle off his back and placed it by the wall. "No, John. That would not make me happy. Nothing will make me happy anymore," continued Erik, with a soft voice, "You misunderstood me. I don't think you are completely happy, but you are not suffering as much as you pretend. Please believe that I understand, no matter what you have, your life will never be complete, John, without your son."

"What makes you so high and mighty?" returned John, losing his communicative disposition, as if Erik's words had awakened and brought to life some of his deepest secrets.

Erik turned away from John, walked a few paces, turned back his head and gazed at John, "You said that I have the talent of bringing out the best in people, well, I also have the talent of bringing out the worst in people."

"It doesn't take talent to bring out the worst in people, any angry idiot can do that. You are an angry young man. Your anger has fermented into feeling sorry for yourself. I didn't say you have the talent of bringing out the best in people, I only said that you have the talent of inspiring people to listen to what you have to say and they believe you. I also said that there are an awful lot of people who need some help. Blow your trumpet, Erik! Bring down that wall of Jericho."

"My little boy killed himself the morning after I came home from shacking up with some broad," said Erik, in a voice that rattled in his throat. "After that my wife left me. How can I stand in front of people and tell them how to run their lives when I can't run my own, only a fool would think that," said Erik, grimacing. "If you really care about people, take your money and open up a soup kitchen, but you don't have enough money because there are too many people out there who are hungry that God has forgotten. God is only for the good, the strong and the humble. They are His children. He wants to eliminate the weak, He doesn't give a damn about them. God is somewhere up there protecting his favorite people. If I were good and strong, why in hell would I need him or anybody else?" said Erik, in a soft voice that grew in volume as his thought progressed. "God to me is the same repressive creator he was for Adam and Eve. 'You can have anything' he said to Adam and Eve, except the apple. It was easy for him to control them. They had no knowledge except of good, which is no knowledge at all, unless you have some knowledge of the other side of good. The snake came along and showed them the tree of knowledge, the apple tree, and they ate the fruit. They learned to choose. It became a little more difficult for Him to control them and He became more oppressive. He is now like the ruthless husband who only cares for his wife as long as she is devoted to him. She has to cook for him, clean his house, care for the children and be good in bed. God forbid if she can't do all that. Did you hear what I said, John? I said, God forbid. That's when all hell breaks loose. The devil can't do anything without God's permission. That's God for me, ruthless and strict. First He sent down Moses with the Ten Commandments and then,

He wasn't satisfied with that, He sent down His son with fifty more commandments. The law making politicians issued another one hundred thousand rules, laws and regulations. It's come to the point where, between God's commandments," he stopped and turned to attract John's full attention, "did you hear what I said, John? I said commandments, I didn't say suggestions, John, they are called commandments, which, as you know, comes from the word 'command'. For instance, John, listen to this, 'Thou shalt love thy neighbor'. How in hell can you be commanded to love someone? How in hell can you love the neighbor who lives in the apartment above you, has six children, he had no business having more than one in the first place, the rest are a perfect nuisance to society and they play all nightlong, basketball, football or even hockey and don't care about you downstairs, while you're trying to get some rest, so you can go to work in the morning. You are commanded to love that neighbor? That's just stupid, but," continued Erik with a softer manner in his voice and gestures, "in the first Bible, that was translated into Greek from Hebrew, they are not called Commandments, they are called 'Entoles' which means, authoritative warning, or authoritative advice, and The Anglicans, to make it more emphatic and more threatening, translated the word into 'commandments', which, in reality, means 'Do or Die', orders from God."

"Anyway, it has come to the point where we can't even open our eyes from sleep and breath more than three minutes, without violating some rule, breaking some law or committing some kind of sin. Some of those laws are stupid. Did you know there's a law in some town in Indiana that's illegal for a woman to kiss a man who has a mustache? Do you know there's a law in New Jersey, that you can't plow the ground using elephants to pull the plow? Do you know they spent two million dollars in New Jersey to make a law that you can't have sunny side up eggs? You can only eat them over and well done? Between God's Sixty Commandments and man's one hundred thousand laws, I said and I am saying again, you can't breath more than three minutes of free air without getting into some kind of trouble. Now get it? They might as well give us all a lobotomy, John. Do you know what a lobotomy is, John? A Lobotomy is cutting into the brain to alter its functioning. You know what most of the people say? 'I don't care if a man can't kiss a woman if he has a mustache; I don't have a mustache; I don't care if I can't plow with an elephant, I don't have an elephant; I don't care if I can't eat sunny side up eggs in a restaurant, I like mine well done and over.' But if you let the politicians get away with those, the next thing will be a lobotomy for anyone who goes off the track just a little bit. Then, my dear friend John, we will have a nation or a world of Zombies. Pretty soon, John, there will be a law against smoking around people who don't smoke."

"I saw a sign on bus saying 2,343 people died last year from second hand smoke. The government paid for this sign. Where did these people die, in the bus? In a hospital? In a town or a city, in Buzzard's Breath, Wyoming? Where? In Dog Patch, Arkansas? Are these 2,343 people world wide out of seven billion? Besides, how does anybody know that those people died from second hand smoke? Did somebody ask them? 'Why are you dying, lady?' 'My husband was smoking around me,' the dying lady would respond with a half a breath. 'But your husband is still alive, lady, don't die.' Help me to find God they say. What do you want me to do, John? Help them to find God? At least down here where I am, I have no fear. I said that I had a fear of life. No. I don't even fear that anymore. I am free from fear, because I don't give a damn. Down here is the furthest down you can go."

"Some of us don't want to live down there."

"Good. Then read and obey the sixty commandments that Moses and God's son handed down and then the one hundred thousand laws of man."

"You know Erik," said John, approaching as if though to make certain that he heard what he was about to say, "You're not angry with God, you're angry with people. I also know, at least, you are not an Atheist," declared John, perplexed by the summary disposition of his acquaintance's character and thoughts.

"You're right. I believe in God, I believe in Christ, I believe in Mohammad, in Buddha, in Allah. I even believe in Voodoo. I believe in all of them. There's no difference in any of them. They're just like the Republican and the Democratic parties. Is there any difference in them? No! You're right, John, I 'm not a nonbeliever. Not only that, I don't care what you believe in or don't. I will never start a religious war."

"Erik," said John, breaking into a faint grin, "You did a good job telling me the ills of the world, as if I was born yesterday and I didn't know them. There's an old American saying 'If you can't beat them, join them." John stopped and stared at Erik until his faint smile faded away. He was beginning to feel that Erik's breast was not only filled with anger, it was also abundantly supplied with a wild desire to awaken people, "You don't have to help people find God, just help them endure and overcome their ills and be strong. God is like a ruthless husband you said," continued John, trying to pick up some pieces.

"I don't know what I said, John, I only know what I believe, and that changes all the time too," said Erik, the slight grin returning, demonstrating his talent of blending humor and anger.

John, to whom those observations were addressed, only looked at Erik, puzzled, but said nothing else and appeared taciturn and thoughtful. On seeing that there was nothing else for Erik to say and noticing him becoming restless, John descended to the common business of life and said, "I'll call the bellboy to bring you to your room, a room that I have always kept for special guests such as my son who comes down to see me once in a blue moon."

"Okay, I think I need the rest," returned Erik.

"I will also instruct the boy to go buy you some clothes. Don't say anything, Erik, this is not a gesture of charity this is only a gesture of friendship. I want you to be my friend for life. I haven't met many people who call things as they see them, without getting angry," said John softly, "Erik, I hear you knocking to come in, I understand you because I know where you come from and where you've been."

Erik looked at John for a long moment with surprise and said, "Sure. Empty barrels make more noise than full ones, one of my high school teachers told that me when I was being a smart ass."

"Also, a cannon blasts louder than a BB gun," returned John, "Be ready, in a couple of hours, we'll eat downstairs in the dining room with some of the best known hotel guests, mostly golf nuts," said John stopping to observe Erik's reaction, but when he saw none he continued. "Do you like golf? I have a lot of friends who play golf. I lied to you on the train, when I told you that I have nobody to care for me. That's what I like to think, that I have nobody. I have a lot of friends but something happens to me at times, regardless of what you say and think, I suddenly feel guilty and I leave to take to the road again," said John as if he had finished talking about his feelings and the past, "I asked you if you like golf, " he added.

"The first job I had when I came to America was a caddy. I used to get two dollars for eighteen holes; it was the hardest money I have ever made," said Erik, bursting into a loud laugh.

"My God, I did that too, during the depression. I only made fifty cents, how did you manage to get two dollars?" returned John, with a sudden light-hearted attitude.

"John, when you were a caddy, butter was a nickel a pound and when I was a caddy butter was a dollar, " said Erik, humorously.

"Where in Greece?"

"No, Chicago."

"Oh, yes? Was there a prohibition on butter too?"

"No, it was an open market."

"Look, if you are trying to say that I'm old, you did a good job when you said butter was a nickel a pound when I was a caddy. One thing I don't like about you is that you always bring my age into light, like I've forgotten it."

"I'm sorry, John, I'm not perfect," said Erik, still with a smile.

"I know, you said that in your speech to me," said John, returning the smile. "We were talking about golf. Do you like golf?" repeated John.

"Not really."

"I think it's the dumbest game in the world."

" Did you have golf in Greece when you were there?"

"We had something a little more exciting, it's a mixture of golf, baseball and hockey it's called, Gourounoula, (Gourounoula) and it really means, **female pig,** I think we can call it Pig's eye. It's not a national sport or anything like that. It's a kids' game."

"Tell me more about it I'm interested in knowing about other cultures. How do you play it?"

"It's not a competitive game. Like a friend of mine put it, in Greece there is no race of any kind, therefore there are no winners or losers. There are not many competitive games," replied Erik.

"In Greece? Isn't it where the Olympic competitions started?"

"Yes, but those competitions were on a one to one basis. Greeks don't make very good teammates. Besides, there's an old Greek saying, 'a hungry bear can't dance'."

"Please explain that to me, Erik."

Erik smiled, and proceeded with another anecdote of his childhood. "Back in the old days when I was a kid, I remember the Gypsies would roam around the country doing odd jobs, from playing the clarinet to making horse shoes. Entertaining people was one of their prime tasks. They would bring around exotic animals, like parrots, monkeys and others. One that stuck in my mind was the dancing bear. A gypsy with a huge muzzled bear and a bongo drummer would roam into town. The bongo player would start playing in the middle of the street and the bear was trained to stand up and dance. The bear would stand up for a brief moment and we would see a sign hanging from the bear's neck, saying 'a hungry bear cannot dance.' The bear stood up long enough for us to read the sign and then it would drop down to its four legs. The man would yell, 'a hungry bear cannot dance, make a donation to feed the bear.' While he was holding the bear's chain with one hand, he would pass around his hat with the other and the bongo player kept beating his drum. So, John, my dear friend, wars revolutions and natural disasters kept the modern Greeks hungry and they couldn't dance. No sports, John. Remember! 'A hungry bear will not dance," concluded Erik with a smile.

"Very interesting, Erik, very interesting. Talking about hunger, this bear here," said John pointing to himself, "is hungry, let me get the bellboy up here to take you to your room, so you can get ready for dinner," saying this, old gentleman rang the bell captain by phone, accordingly.

After a very short while a bellboy appeared and Erik was escorted into his room where he changed into clothing that was promptly brought to him by another bellboy.

Erik came downstairs wearing a new suit that fitted him well. He was ushered into the dining room where John and two other well-dressed men were waiting for his arrival before ordering dinner. The exchange of cordialities with his host and his two friends was even more hearty and long-drawn-out than he had anticipated.

"Gentlemen, as I was saying to you, my friend, Erik Karas, is a superb speaker, an antagonist and a student of the Bible," declared John solemnly, as the quartet sat down.

Erik laughed very loudly, "Knowing, '***Give and you shall receive***,' doesn't make me a student of the Bible, John, with all due respect," replied Erik, taking his napkin and laying it on his lap. In this opinion, both other guests expressed their concurrence and having been directed by the host to drink up, they all raised their glasses in a harmonious toast. Everyone ordered according to his appetite; the food arrived and quickly disappeared, which verified the testimony to the excellence of the food and wine. The conversation during the festivity was about food, golf and local news to which Erik, not being a cook, a golfer or interested in local affairs, contributed little and his manner became somewhat abstemious and resolute.

"Let me ask you, Erik," said one of the golfers, by the name of Jack, "How was Greece during the war; were you old enough to remember anything? I have never met anyone before who has lived with the enemy," said Jack with a great degree of interest, glancing around at his friends and directing his gaze from one to another until he felt he was heard and understood. "Do you remember anything?" repeated Jack, who was about Erik's age and a well-groomed man with thick red hair, a crimson face and a bushy mustache.

"The war? The war you want to know?" asked Erik.

Jack nodded in assent.

"I remember it very well. I was too old to be called a kid and too young to be called a man," said Erik, taking a cigarette and lighting it; all the eyes of the host and guests were cast upon him, as if they were admiring sport fans.

"First, I remember the Italians entering Greece, then a couple of years later they were followed by the Germans and then some years later by the communists. Until I came here, to America, I don't remember a time or a place I had been where there wasn't some kind of war or I lived without some kind of fear. My hometown, Astakos, which means Lobster, is built at the foot of a gray mountain called Beloutsa, (Veloutsa) and at the edge of the flat and the relatively calm blue Ionian Sea, directly across from lower

Italy. It was thought of, in those days, as a small fishing village and now it is a resort town of some three thousand inhabitants that are mostly fishermen and small farmers, too smart to be just peasants and not skilled enough to be called men of commerce. Most of them own their own homes that have been handed down to them from generation to generation. The wine is inexpensive due to the fact that almost everybody has enough acreage for vineyards and they make a supply of wine for the entire year. There is no minimum drinking age but I can recall only two habitual drinkers all the time I lived there, the first fifteen years of my life." There he stopped and looked around the table with obvious melancholy.

"When the Italian soldiers came, as troops of occupation, they confiscated some of the tallest buildings in town, to live in - — the tallest was only three stories high, because of the constant threat of earthquakes. Most were built out of stones from the mountains and almost all of them had marble stairs from marble that came from across the bay, less than five kilometers away. As I was saying, about the Italian occupation, often the soldiers took possession of some private homes too. I remember some of the lower ranks lived in the house across from mine. They loved the young children of the neighborhood and would do anything for them. They used to split their rations with us, knowing we were hungry."

"In the early part of the war, they pulled their heavy cannons with great big Clydesdale horses that were kept in a stone stable, almost across from my house, at the edge of the town and a few hundred yards from the Ionian blue bay that ended with a sandy beach."

"Early in the morning, the Italian soldiers would place troughs in the middle of the gravel street and they would fill the troughs with shiny long-grain oats for the two-dozen huge horses. There was also one domestic horse, the color of gray, I remember, they called it 'Greco'. We, the young children, about a dozen of us, differ-ent ages, from six to ten, would wait, standing around the horses holding in our hands small homemade brooms and dust pans, hungry and cold in the winter months, hot and sweaty in the summer; we waited a few paces away from the troughs for the horses to finish and then we would rush and scoop up whatever oats the horses spilled or left, to feed to our chickens. I was told that the less fortunate children would take the oats home and their mothers would make a meal out of it for the family's lunch or dinner. I remember the Italians, most of them, seeing us standing by, barefooted with skinny legs and sunken faces, would interrupt the horses' meal by pulling the horses away, pretending that the animals had enough to eat, so we could scoop up the left over oats. That went on for many months, if not a couple of years. I remember we used to be afraid of those big horses and the soldiers used to pick up the youngest of the neighborhood kids and sit them on the horses' backs for a ride. The horse called Greco was worthless, but was treated like a pet. Then one day, after many months, Greco was missing. That day, the soldiers and all the young children had a feast of soup with meat, a very rare commodity for all. Later on we learned the meat for the festivities came from the horse called Greco.

"Then the Germans became our new conquerors and the Italians, whom by now we had grown accustomed to and thought of as our friends, were sent away to some prison camps or slaughtered after a brief battle with the Germans. The Germans took over the same horses and when they got up in the morning, they stretched the troughs out in the middle of the street as the Italians had done before, but the Germans made certain that the horses ate all the oats and walked away with full bellies. Then the German soldiers would empty the troughs in the middle of the street, kicking the oats to mix in with the gravel so we, the young ones, couldn't scoop up any oats.

"As the horses went away we'd rush, dropping ourselves on the gravel street with bare knees to glean whatever we could with our hands and the little brooms. The Germans stood back; oh, how many times I saw them and I can still see them watching us, with ironic grins on their pale faces, while we were down on our knees trying to pick up whatever was left; they would laugh, I saw them looking and laughing at us and as if we were little animals. I saw them laughing heartily and mocking our feeble efforts. What bad luck for us and what a disgrace for them." Erik stopped, took the edge of his napkin and wiped his eyes. "I remember a couple of the children, being blinded by hunger or filled with revenge or stubbornness, plunged themselves towards the troughs near the end of the horses' breakfast, and then the German soldiers beat them with the ropes, mercilessly. My God, one of them was named Stathis, two years older than I, big for his age and more courageous than the rest of us. He was hit by a German soldier on the head with a thick rope and Stathis turned and charged against him with fire, fury and with the strength of a grown man. Another soldier came from behind and hit him on the back of the head with the butt of a rifle. Stathis went down headfirst, his face dropped into a water puddle and remained there motionless.

"The rest of us dropped our dustpans and brooms and ran away to hide behind walls, tree trunks or bushes from where we could still see Stathis' fate...

"After a little while, two Germans dragged Stathis from the water puddle by his bare feet and tossed him to the side of the road. Stathis did not die but he never communicated with words or gestures again, with anyone, not even with his mother. Every morning he would go and stand on top of a hill and gaze at the sea for hours, without ever moving a hand or a foot. He would stand like that until his poor mother would come and take him home. I learned some years later that Stathis was committed to an insane asylum, in Athens, for the remainder of his life; he eventually died there from malnutrition, because he had lost his ability to swallow food."

Erik stopped for a moment and sipped from his glass of wine, "Don't mind me, gentlemen, these are painful subjects. I have endured these things for many years and I try to resist venting my feelings, but sometimes I find it difficult if not impossible."

"I'm sorry," apologized Jack earnestly, "I wouldn't pry on your feelings for the world."

"No, Jack, don't worry, I'm not so fragile as to break by telling a story," said Erik, touching Jack's arm gently.

"Another time, I remember we were playing outside my house and two German soldiers, one was an officer, forced themselves into the house next door. They came out, after a few minutes, dragging the man who lived there; he was a fisherman and the father of seven young children. They made him stand against the wall in front of his own house, with his children a few feet away from him screaming and crying but too scared to go near him.

One of the soldiers, the officer, took his out Luger, aimed, fired and shot the poor fisherman in the head. The father of the seven children went down like an empty burlap sack; as he was sliding down along the wall, he left behind him a wide line of blood and all his children ran to his aid, but he was dead. I saw the one who did it. He was a young man with a deep old gash on the left side of his face. They both walked away, not smiling not laughing and not even a bit remorseful for what they had just done," continued Erik, speaking in voice tremulous with emotion, turning his glass around tensely as if in a trance.

"I'm sorry," said Jack, touching Erik's arm softly.

"I am much obliged to you, for your condolence on what you think is a painful subject.

"No, no," returned Jack, "not one more word; it's a painful subject, I can see."

"It is good for your soul to vent your bad feelings sometimes. Unless, you people find it uncomfortable."

"No, no," said John, "I find it fascinating."

"I am going to tell you something that even now, when I tell this true story, gives me goose bumps all over my body," continued Erik, with scornful grin. "As I remember, it was that summer when my father was captured by the Germans and sent away to another town, about sixty kilometers from my home town. My mother went away to find him, thinking that she would try to convince his captors to let him go. We three, my younger brother, sister and I, were taken to live with our aunt Margo. I was old enough to under-stand that my aunt didn't have enough food for us plus her two young sons, so I used to leave her house in the morning and go away to a secluded area, away from all the people, natives and foreigners, and wrap myself in gloomy thoughts. I would most often wander along a narrow path beneath the frowning gray cliffs, to a wild and lonely spot; where I would sit myself on some fallen fragments of the mountain and bury my face in my hands, as if I wished not to see or hear anybody; I would remain there, some-times until the night had completely closed around me and the long shadows of the cliffs above had cast a thick black darkness on every object near there.

A few hundred meters from that place of solitude was a lonely monastery ***ProfhthV HliaV*** (Profit Elias), built on top of a plateau above a cluster of rugged cliffs overlooking the sea. I often went there with our family goat, which provided us with the milk of the day. One day, as I was at the bottom of the hill assisting my goat to indulge herself in feeding from the thick green bushes, I saw about forty German soldiers, on foot, heading for the monastery and I, with my four-footed friend, decided to carefully follow them, staying out of their sight. I knew what I was doing. I thought if I got caught on those mountains I would tell them that I was caring for my goat. Anyway, the soldiers reached the monastery, scattered and looked around the courtyard with their weapons ready to fire at a moment's notice. I tied my goat to a small bush and climbed a tall almond tree behind the church. I sat there with a perfect view of the whole courtyard and the little church. The area was formed into an oval platform, bounded by a two-foot stonewall and large enough to make a good tennis court. The little church stood in the middle of this flat piece of land, with a fantastic view of the sea and my hometown below it. On the other side of the wall there were the steep cliffs, with over a one hundred-foot drop to the bottom of the mountain.

"Suddenly I saw the soldiers bringing several monks out into the courtyard, all the while kicking them savagely and pushing them, without a hint of mercy. I heard the soldiers order them to stand up along the short wall with the sea and the cliffs behind them. Then I saw the platoon leader, with the rank of a captain displayed on his uniform, bring out a little boy, by the hand. I was close to the whole thing, so close I could hear the rustling of their arms and smell their sweat with the aid of the gentle breeze that came from the sea. The little boy began to cry.

'Don't cry,' said the captain.

The little boy stopped and looked up at the captain, rubbing his eyes with the knuckles of his hands, as often, young children do when they are in tears.

'What is your name, little boy?' asked the captain in Greek, with a German accent, once he brought him out into the open air.

'Yianni,' murmured the little boy, looking down on the ground.

'You must speak a little louder. I can't hear you. You are down there and I am all the way up here,' joked the captain, who was tall and slender and, as far as I could tell, in his middle to late twenties in years.

'Yianni,' said the boy, a little louder.

'Good. How old are you?'

'Eight.'

'Where is your father?'

'I have no father. He has been killed.'

'Who killed your father?'

'The soldiers.'

'What soldiers?'

'The Italian soldiers, he was fighting in Tapeline,' said the boy, as if he had known that Tapeline was the famous battleground between the Greeks and the Italians in the year of 1940.

'Ahem. Where is you mother?'

'She is killed too.'

'Who killed her?'

'The soldiers.'

'What soldiers?'

'The German soldiers,' said Yianni, looking up to him.

'I'm sorry,' said the captain, then reaching into his pocket he brought out a coin and showed it to the little boy, as if he wished to pay damages to the boy for the loss of his mother, 'do you know what this is?'

The boy shook his head negatively, still rubbing his eyes with the knuckles of his hands, 'No, sir'

'This is money. Do you know what money is?'

The boy shook his head again, negatively, 'No, sir,'

'When the war is over, you can use this money to buy chocolate. Do you know what chocolate is?' asked the captain, squatting down next to the boy, to hand over the coin. The boy examined it closely and kept it in his hand.

'No, sir,' replied Yianni, looking at the captain and holding the coin tightly in his right hand.

The officer stood up, reached into his pocket and brought out a small chocolate bar.

'Here! Take the wrapper off and eat it!'

Yianni took the candy bar, examined it for a short time and tried to put it into his pocket and with his right hand tried to hand back the coin, but the captain gently told the boy to keep the coin too.

'No! Don't put it in your pocket. Eat it now!' said the captain, with a visible amount of patience, seeing the boy attempting to put both the candy and the coin in his pocket.

The boy, with trembling hands, slowly and timidly, as if he were afraid of making a mistake, unwrapped the candy bar and looked at it closely, smelled it, and looked up at his donor, the captain. The captain smiled down at him.

'Go ahead eat it!' said the captain, with his eyes resting on the boy.

Yianni bit off a small piece of it, chewed it for a short time and then, liking the taste, put the rest in his mouth and looked at the captain again, this time with a winning smile.

The monks, the German soldiers and I watched with a great degree of curiosity, waiting to see what was going to happen next.

The captain waited patiently for the boy to finish chewing, 'You finished?'

Yianni nodded in assent.

'Did you like it?'

Yianni nodded more vigorously and said, 'Yes, sir' looking up at him once more.

The monks grinned and I, a little older than Yianni, remembered that before the war I had tasted chocolate and seeing that captain's generous act of giving away a chocolate bar, I was about ready to abandon my point of observation and go down there and ask the captain for a candy bar too, when all of sudden I saw the captain take out his pistol from the holster and press it on the boy's temple. I froze with fear, shrank back and coiled as much as I could." Erik stopped for a moment and looked vacantly around him as he took a sip from his wine.

"I remember Yianni tried to move, but the captain seized the boy and made a stern gesture for him to stay put. Then he stretched out his left arm, looked at his watch and addressed the monks with a firm tone of voice and a stern face. 'I will give you ten seconds to come forward and tell me where the guerrillas are hiding in these mountains and if you don't come up with an answer, I will pull the trigger and blow out his brains' said the German captain;

looking at his watch, he began a count down.

"The monks turned around and looked at each other; some with an indifferent look, not completely able to grasp the situation, some out of astonishment, some out of despair, but they all eventually looked at the captain and listened to his count down. When the officer finished and heard no one speak to him and saw no one move his way, he slowly walked away, about three steps, still holding the gun in his hand. Then, just as Yianni looked relieved, thinking that the worst was over, the captain quickly turned, aimed and shot the boy in the head. The blast of the gunshot sent all the birds away and echoed around the mountain, as if the little boy's soul was looking for a place to land and if it landed it must have landed far away because the echo faded and never stopped... God, my God, I saw the boy fall down. His right hand, the hand that held the coin, attempted to reach his head as if to pull out the bullet, but the hand went down and his feet kicked violently, almost in a complete circle, around his bloody head. The captain waited until the boy settled down, then went over to the dead boy, bent down, opened the boy's hand, took the coin and threw away the wrapper. All the monks shrieked and they all threatened to use violence and screamed in Greek:

'*Germanoi, skulia. FwniadeV tou kosmou. Na caqhtai! FwniadeV* !' 'German dogs, killers of the people. May you disappear from the earth, murderers!'

"As the captain walked away hastily with his head down, he yelled an order to his men in German that I couldn't understand. I then saw about half of his men follow close behind; the other half stayed back, suddenly turned and fired at the monks. The monks went down, torn with bullets from the German guns, one after the other, and some, with blood spurting out of them like faucets, that went mad. The captain kept on walking down the hill at a fast pace and his soldiers ran to catch up with him." Erik stopped and looked at the wall ahead of him for one full minute, in silence, until a teardrop came down his face. "I heard their equipment rattling and I saw their faces, calm and cool, as if they had done something like that many times before, so many times, it finally turned into a habit for them."

During the entire time of Erik's story, John Lambright exhib-

ited an expression of the most overwhelming and absorbing astonishment that the imagination can portray. After looking from Larry
to Jack, and from Jack to Larry, who both sat in a profound silence,
John softly uttered the words, "I'll be damned. I'll be damned."

"The monks were dressed in black robes," continued Erik, "and
I remember those robes turned a dark shiny red with their blood.
I heard them moaning and saw a number of them, forced by their
instinct to live, feebly attempt to dig into the ground with their
fingers, as if they were looking for a place to hide under the soil.
Shortly thereafter they stopped their weak and pathetic attempts;
their strength abandoned their bodies, but their eyes remained
opened, backed only by nature's will to survive. I saw some of those
eyes staring ahead; they never blinked, they never closed and they
never moved in any direction.

"That night and many nights after, I found it very difficult to
sleep. I used to toss, first on one side then on the other, then, I
perseveringly used to close my eyes, as if to coax myself to sleep.
It was no use. My thoughts kept on reverting, painfully, to those
grim pictures where the scar-faced young German soldier went up
against an unarmed, weak and hungry weather-beaten fisherman,
the father of seven. The picture of the fisherman going down,
leaving behind the stain of his own blood on a white wall, and the
little boy, his body wriggling with convulsions, then shaking to its
core as if his soul was caught and trapped by some invisible evil
spirit, then stopping dead on the spot, made my nights long, longer
in the years that followed. None knew my suffering," continued
Erik, as his countenance resumed its usual benign expression.

"My father was captured by the Germans, as I stated before,
and I, the oldest of the three, had being urged by my mother to be
the man of the house and take care of my brother and sister. I
couldn't show them I was afraid, so on the nights that I couldn't
sleep, I went to hide in some lonely corner and spent the weary
hours feeling the progress of the fever that was consuming my
brain. After the war was over, my father was freed in Germany,
where they had taken him. He came back and vowed that he would
never allow his family to undergo the trials of war again and he left
his estate, friends and relatives and we immigrated to America. At
last and finally I became a man. I became an officer in the United

States Army and of all the places in the world that I could have been sent, I was sent to Germany," said Erik, his face suffused with a happy crimson glow. "What a thrill for me, I felt, what a victory for the world and what a crushing blow for the Germans, losing the war they had started, the war they were so certain that they were gong to win. I then realized that God was not on our side, we were on the side of God. I roamed the streets of Frankfurt and I looked at the German men and now wandered how I could have feared them for such a long time. I was in their world now and I could laugh and shout at the best of them with no consequences. I could hug myself with delight when I thought of the fine trick that God played on them. I eventually became a part of that trick, but secretly inside me, I dreaded that one day I might become like them. I kept that secret inside me and went on laughing, not for joy, but to show them that I was there. When I spoke to those German men who used to be ruthless, mean and hateful, they were now yielding, respectful and humble in their own country, I could have screamed with ecstasy. Sometimes, when I dined out and sat next to them, I wondered, how much lower than humble they would get if they knew that I was one of their victims who had escaped and had become like a mad man sitting next to them. Now I was holding the shiny sharpened knife and now I had the power, and half the will, to put it in their hearts and sit there, pressing on with my meal, watching them die slowly, as they had done all over the world, not too long ago. I felt like a powerful man, that riches and treasures had fallen upon me," continued Erik, with a beaming face.

"As I mentioned before, I only had half the will to plunge my bright glittering knife into their hearts, thank God, for I still had the decency that I had inherited from my parents. I was a restrained mad man, not an uncontrolled crazy creature. I had to be sane and sound in mind because I was a proud member of the American Seventh Army. I had my father, mother, a sister and a bother back in the United States of America, tucked away in American life, safe and sound, waiting for me to return. Most of all, I wasn't about to let my father think how false I had grown. I felt I was given riches and treasures. I was given the right to be in America. I had to live for the future and not the past. But, my friends, that is easier said than done. I tried not to live in the past, but, beyond my powers, I lived with the past. I roamed the streets of Frankfurt with the freight of madness on my back and hatred in my heart, remembering those German soldiers who showed nothing but contempt for those young lives. The killing of the orphan, Yianni, the kicking of the oats, those and other obscene memories showed on my face with every glance I threw at them. The Germans knew, when they saw me, what I had in my heart. There were many men from other countries, who had also suffered at the hands of the Germans, who felt as I did. I was not the only scorned and mad man in their country, and they kept their distance, in the same manner I had hid from them in the place of my birth.

"One day when I was in Frankfurt, loitering inside the train station while waiting to catch the train to go to my base about ninety five miles east from there, I saw a man standing at the entrance of the station and from all appearances, he was working there as an information person. I felt a streak of burning fire run up my spine and I began to tremble when I looked at him and saw the gash on his face. I knew what I was seeing. I knew that he was the soldier with the gun; he only looked a little older; it was twelve years later. That was the man who had aimed, shot and killed the poor fisherman when I was just ten years old. He was the man who had taken the life of a poor fisherman for no good reason or course. I wanted to kill him, but I didn't want to kill him by a simple method. I wanted to take him somewhere far away from all the ones who could help him, so no one could have come to his aid. I wanted to take him far away, to hang him by his feet in the middle of an old house, to hear him crying and begging for his life, to look into his face and when I saw the last ray of hope leaving the pupils of his eyes, then I would have loved to set the house on fire. I wanted to see him swinging in the wind. What a fine sight I thought it would have been to see the house burning with flames shooting up like long, angry, hungry red tongues licking the skin of his body; he would be swinging and I would be standing there, watching his body smolder away to cinders. At that time I thought of killing him right there and then going after and killing his offspring, if he had any, to stop them from handing down his madness to his following generation or generations to come. I stood there looking at him and felt the madness mix in my blood and in the marrow of my bones. I stood a few feet away from him and looked. In spite of the confusing madness in my mind, although sprinkled with some mercy, the feeling of hate domineered my thinking. I despised his country and I hated its splendor. In my mind the fisherman's seven young ones flashed quickly as I had seen them then, gathered around their father, screaming, poking his body, caressing his face and rubbing his hands, desperately endeavoring to bring him back to life. I saw the despair on their faces and I heard their cries again in my head, although many years later and thousands of miles away.

"This was one of the men who had been one of Hitler's instruments of destruction; that was the image of the one who was well engraved in my mind, and there I was, holding his life in my hand. I hesitated, taking time to think of my next move. I deceived myself in thinking that he would stay there for me to make up my mind how, where and when I was going to kill him. I removed my eyes just for an instant, casing the area, as all good and smart thieves and criminals often do, and when I brought my eyes back to where he was standing, he was no longer there. I hastily scanned the crowd looking for him, in an almost panic. I ran headlong into some people in my desperate effort to find him, making some of them angry, but their faces and forms I couldn't see as I was so blinded by my wrath. I suddenly spotted him standing motionless, still in a corner of the train station; my blood, even now, chills my heart as I remember him. For a moment, his eyes fixed their gaze on me as if he had recognized me. But I knew that he couldn't have, in a million years, he couldn't have guessed, who I was and how I was linked to him. I walked around and kept my eyes carefully on him, trying to think what to do. I didn't want him to see me looking at him. Seeing me at that moment, he would have noticed the light of madness gleaming from my eyes like an inferno; his guilt would have made him run. I stood there and I watched him. He went a little ways from there, pulled up a chair and sat down, gazing leisurely at the passengers. I stopped and stood, where he couldn't see me, to study his face. It was the kind of face where his mouth never moved to smile or frown or become distorted from anger, as the faces of most mad men do. But the time had come for me to smile. To smile! To laugh out loudly and clearly, for the whole world to hear, and to roll on the ground with shrieks of joy for I finally found the killer. There was an empty chair next to him. I went and took it. I sat next to him and he looked at me with a vacant nonchalant look on his face, but he seemed to be wondering what I was all about.

There I was sitting next to the man who entangled my young brain and kept it ensnarled for many years after seeing the fisherman go down, leaving his seven children behind and a streak of blood on the white wall, as he slid down and away from life. I turned my eyes upon him. I could not help it. We sat in silence for a few minutes. He looked at me again and threw a searching eye on my attire; although I wore civilian clothes he knew that I was an American soldier because of my spit-shined black shoes. He said nothing, but I could feel the contempt he had for me for being an American. It's tough shit for him, I said to myself. Looking at him and remembering the past, I felt I was surrounded by a thousand demons pushing me to kill him right there and then. I shook my head knowing the results of my young energies. The madness I harbored inside of me for such a long time would have led me into a thoughtless riot where the consequences could have never been repaired. He looked at me once again for one brief second, now with a grimacing look on his face. It's tough shit for him again, I thought, his country wasn't big enough for both of us; I was there to stay and he was to go. The whole thing, the whole occasion felt like a secret within me and I knew that my secret had to be made known to him. I could not hide it anymore.

"Do you speak English?" I spoke first.

"No!" replied the ex-Hitler soldier, softly, without the slightest indication of being alarmed but sounding very arrogant.

'MilaV Ellhnika?' I asked him (do you speak Greek), I knew if he were in Greece he would have understood that.

"I saw the blood rushing to the top of his head. He closed his eyes for one brief moment and turned to me with a counterfeit smile on his face.

"Bita?" (please) he asked.

I hastily took a piece of paper from my pocket and wrote the name of my hometown in Greek, **AstakoV** I shoved it in his hand

and asked him in English 'Do you speak Greek?'

He looked at the paper. I knew then that he recognized the name of the town. I saw the sudden change that came upon his gaze and face. The color faded from his face and he drew back his chair. I dragged mine closer to him.

'Thank God, comrade, that in life you don't always get what you deserve, but eventually you get what you need. What I'm going to do to you now is what you needed a long time ago.' I said, almost whispering with clenched teeth, as I wanted to put a cutting edge on my words. I remember,...I remember that I smiled, trying to bring him back around to speaking with me. I felt the madness rising within me. I could tell he understood what I said and I could tell that he was still arrogant and yet afraid. I knew it was he. There was no doubt in my mind. He looked around him, hoping for someone to come to his aid, but help for him in that confused place was deaf and blind. I saw his hand grasp the chair, getting ready to attack.

The fury he saw in my eyes stopped him from moving, hoping that I would retreat. But it was too late for talk.

"I found you! You bastard! I found you in your own country.' I murmured in a low threatening voice.

"Qumasai ton yarra, deile, pousth. Qumasai to ftwco yarra?" (Do you remember the poor fisherman, coward) I was not talking anymore. I was screaming everything in Greek, as if I had forgotten the English language. He grasped the chair and hurled it at me, but missed; I darted against him and threw my arms around him and we both went down with a heavy crash. I was on top of him and he was down on the concrete floor. I remember, I dug my fingers into his hair and hammered the concrete floor with his head with all my might and wrath; I noticed stains of blood being left on the floor where his head had struck. Then I used my fists and pounded his face violently. I first gave him two or three for me, then two or three for the fisherman. I felt as if I were a vessel of power and madness. He was strong, fighting for his life and I was a powerful mad man thirsty for justice, ready to destroy him. I knew no strength could equal mine. I wanted to destroy him for burning my house, I wanted to destroy him and make him pay for all the atrocities his comrades committed in the place where I was born; I wanted to destroy him for all the children they left orphans. I was growling and he was moaning. His feet were moving violently, hammering the floor with his heels in a useless effort to get away from me. He was struggling and fighting back and gasping for air, but air for him was thick, he knew he was losing and I was winning. What an awful feeling for him and what a triumph for me. His attempts to get away from me grew weaker. I knelt upon his chest. I grasped his healthy thick neck firmly with both hands, I squeezed my hands together with his flesh and bones in between, trying to push out his soul .His face grew purple and his tongue jumped and stayed out, as if he were mocking me His struggles grew fainter until they wholly ceased and his eyes stayed open. The crowd rushed around me, screaming with fear and fury. The screams and shouts did not have any effect on me; my task of squeezing his cursed soul out of his odious body was greater than my desire to live. Suddenly I was pulled back. I wasn't harmed because they knew I was a foreigner and they were afraid of foreigners, for they knew what their leaders and followers had done to foreigners, now the foreigners were doing to them. They only held me back and stopped me from finishing what he had started twelve years before. I struggled for principal, pride and freedom. I stood on my feet, I freed myself from my assailants and rushed to him again, but he was out cold. I remember I kicked his head with a vigorous stroke and I saw his face pale as if it were lifeless, his tongue still sticking out and his eyes still open, they never winked or even closed when I kicked him. I was grabbed again by four strong arms and as I was held back, I saw a man coming at me holding a straight razor in his hand and showing it to me; I disengaged myself from them, I ducked and threw my left arm up in the air to protect my face, then I was hit in the arm with the razor. I saw the blood rushing down my sleeve," continued Erik. "I gained more courage and strength after that and kicked the man who had knifed me and he, after the blow I dispensed where it counts the most, below the belt, looked stunned, with a vacant look, into the crowd, holding his insides, as if to stop them from spilling out, and fell heavily to the floor. I cleared my way through the crowd with my healthy arm, as if I had an ax in my hand.

    I jumped over a banister and smashed the door open and in an instant I was out on the street. I ran; and when the people saw me running they stepped aside—- that made me feel good. I heard sirens in the distance and I ran as fast as my legs could carry me and as far away as possible from that scene. As I ran and distanced myself from there I noticed the crowd was getting thinner, the shops were fewer with the sirens gradually faded out. I finally turned to the right and I found myself in a deserted alley. There I felt weaker and I felt I was about to faint and suddenly I fell heavily upon the brick-paved street. My next recollection was looking up, through my blurry eyes, at many people gathered around me, looking at me with pity and care and not with contempt for they knew not what I had just done a few miles from there. I remember closing my eyes and when I opened them again I was in a hospital room surrounded by a bunch of young pretty nurses. American nurses." Erik stopped, grinned, took a sip from his wine glass and gazed around at the faces of his new friends, with a melancholy look, then pulled up his sleeve and showed them the scar from the cut, on his left arm. It was along scar starting from right above the wrist up to the elbow. His friends looked at it carefully with contempt on their faces.

"Did you kill him?" asked Jack, while the other two waited with held breaths to hear the answer.

Erik said nothing; he only lit a cigarette and looked around the dining room, but even the most unskillful observer could have detected in his troubled face that the answer to Jack's question had a tremendous impact on him. The question went away without being answered, and his new friends glanced at each other with fields of pity and sympathy.

"I went back there," said Erik, breaking that long profound silence, "several times to find him or something connected to him, but I found nothing. I was hoping to find him alive and have that talk I wanted in the first place; I wanted to know from him if he remembered what he had done and why."

"Weren't you charged with any crime?" asked John.

"No."

"If you had killed him, you would have been charged with the crime," said Larry, who was the youngest of the three.

"Not necessarily," replied Erik, putting out his cigarette in the ashtray and looking as if his whole attention was on that insignificant task.

"What do you mean, not necessarily" asked Jack.

"I was in Germany a few years after the war. The war they started. There was the American army, the English army and navy, the French. They all remembered and hated the Germans for what they had done to the world. There were many civilians from other countries who had snuck in there looking for revenge. It was not uncommon for a German to get murdered and no one complained. The Germans believed in the old Greek saying 'If you are a thief and somebody steals from you don't complain.' I was questioned by the American authorities as to how I was knifed and I told them that couple of guys jumped me."

"Did they believe you?" asked jack.

Erik sat back on his chair, looked at Jack for a long moment, scarcely breathing and said softly, "Why are you asking me this question, Jack? Are you trying to find out whether I am a killer or not?"

"No! No, Erik. I want to know, as every body would like to know, if the son-of-a-bitch got what he deserved," responded Jack, without taking anytime to reconsider his question

Looking into Larry's face and sighing involuntarily, and said, "They didn't say they didn't believe me. I know the company commander didn't believe me. He told some of my officer friends, that he didn't believe my story."

"What did he believe?" asked John, as if to remove the burden of questioning from his friend Jack

Erik turned and looked at John with a smile on his face, "He believed that some husband caught me in bed with his wife and tried to kill me," said Erik, smiling and looking around the three-some. "But the other guy who knifed me and I kicked, I think he's now singing soprano and will for the rest of his life."

"Did you regret what you did?" asked Jack softly.

"Regret kicking the soprano in the balls?" asked Erik.

"No. Killing the scar face?"

Erik looked at Jack with a wandering glance. He turned away, seemed lost in thought for a long moment, and said to Jack as he turned to face him again, in a calm, soft and almost tremulous voice, " First of all, I didn't say I killed him. If he died, he killed himself, because all I wanted to do was talk to him. I never learned their language, not even a word. I wasn't about to honor them in that way or any other. I still go through some long sleepless nights and have some dreadful dreams. I still see the German soldiers as large husky forms bent over my bed at night and I still see the light of madness gleaming from them like fire, tempting me to insanity. I drive my fingers into my ears, but the voices scream into my head till the room rings with their threats and I wake up soaked with cold sweat. When everything was fresh in my young mind I used to stay up and shudder with fear, hearing the horses' heavy footsteps galloping and the cannons shrieking as they were dragged behind them and listening to the horrible music of the guns' firing and people's screaming, from the first shades of dusk till the first morning light. Jack, I have a million stories in my head about my life as a boy in the war. They are like bad spirits. They visit upon me several times a year. Not as much now as they did before." said Erik, looking into Jack's eyes, " Jack, you seem to be a fair minded and red blooded American man, would you have had any regrets?" asked Erik.

"I am glad that I am in America, fair minded or red blooded or not. To answer your question, I would not have had any regrets," replied Jack passionately.

"But I must thank them, secretly, because what I have seen them do to my former country and its innocent people, only helped me to grow up to be a sensitive, compassionate and caring human being. I have nothing but contempt for them as a race and as part of mankind," said Erik, leaning forward towards Jack and looking him in the eye," Jack, no fair minded man can take a human life, even if it's justifiable, without regret. One of the ways to avoid hurtful regrets is to make yourself think that you didn't do it."

"Like you said, Erik, I think I am fair minded but killing some-body like him, I wouldn't have any regrets," said Jack emphatically, without taking any time for consideration.

Leaning back, knitting his hands behind his head, Erik smiled for a long moment and then his face turned serious as he said. "I felt bad. I wanted to know whether he left a wife and children behind and I spoke with my best friend Lt. Larry Newton. He screamed at me for telling him, and made me promise that I would-n't repeat the story to anyone. After a while, when he gained his composure, knowing how I felt, he said softly to me 'we were sent here because we were trained to kill, not to dance.'"

"Do you still hate the Germans?" asked Larry.

After watching John fill the glasses with wine, Erik took his full glass, raised it to his lips and with a gentle and almost unno-ticeable gesture, tilted it into the air and drank without a pause or stopping to draw a breath.

"Well? Do you still hate the Germans?" repeated Larry, with a lot more emphasis in his question.

"I made love to their women after that incident," replied Erik, with a serene look on his face.

"What does that mean?" asked Larry.

"I found them to be sensitive, generous, sincere, loving and soothing, like most of the women in the rest of the world. I didn't find them to be mothers of dogs or lions. If their sons became some-thing bad then somebody else must have brought them up, not them, and in short, the answer to your question, you may be surprised, is no. I don't hate them anymore. It was the war, Jack. Read about the Civil War in America, you will realize what Americans did to Americans. In Greece, after that war, they had a civil war and what the Greeks did to other Greeks was the same, if not worse."

"But, why? Does anybody know why?" asked Larry, shaking his head in sympathizing manner at this juncture.

Erik felt that he was expected to say something; he said "Ah!" and looked restlessly around.

"Ah?" echoed Larry, with a long-drawn sigh, directing his eyes on Erik. "Do you have an answer?"

"I have no answer, I only have an opinion."

"Let's hear it!" suggested Larry, while everybody's head bent forward as if they were waiting to hear a serious confession.

"Why is everybody looking at me?" asked Erik, leaning back with a cool on his face, desperately trying to avoid answering.

"Why?" asked John, "because you are different from us, you are an unusual man, Erik"

"Living through the war makes me unusual, John?"

"Maybe, or maybe not. You see, Jack and Larry are thinking of winning golf tournaments and I'm thinking of making money and you…" There John stopped and stared at Erik and seemed as if he were totally at loss.

"And I, my friend, you think that I am thinking of remodeling the world with words, you want to say," added Erik, soberly.

John stared at Erik and smiled, "you see?"

"See? See what? I didn't say shit," declared Erik, bursting into laughter. Erik, while laughing, looked to read their faces. He realized he was the only one who laughed, and the rest still had their eyes focused on him, still expecting an answer. "I forgot the question, that's how smart I am."

"The question," replied Larry, immediately, "was, why do they act like animals in the war."

Erik looked around with a restless glance, as he often did, "in my dictionary, there is no word bad. The bad comes from the exaggeration of the word **good**. In my opinion every bad thing in life starts as **good**. We the people are made to defend ourselves against danger; that's the will and advice of nature, which is good; we finally realized that the best defense is a good offence. So all these atrocities we commit, during war, are acts of defending, but they exaggerate into the bad acts of offending." said Erik, then he quickly commented, "I don't know if that makes any sense to you although it makes sense to me, but I really don't care, because I didn't charge you a damn dime for hearing it," he concluded, smiling and looking at his glass.

"It makes sense to me," said Jack, shaking his head and looking around at the others.

"Good," said Erik, "I'm glad, because I don't really know what I said. I just opened my mouth and put my teeth in gear and away I went."

"Erik, all kidding aside, that made a lot of sense to me. I may add something else to your theory, that greed and anger has a lot to do with your idea of 'offence for defense," said John, in a very business like manner.

"What happened to the captain?" asked Larry, "not to change the subject, but I find it just a little too deep for me."

"And the deepest you'll go is in the hole to pick up your golf ball, right Larry?" remarked John.

"No, wiseass. If I hit you in the mouth right now I will be doing something good; I will be stopping you from insulting me, which is self-defense. But knocking your teeth out is bad. So I understood and I agree with Erik that everything starts for the good and some time ends up bad," returned Larry, taking a drink in a similar manner as Erik had done.

"Not bad, not bad, by Golly, you've got it," said John, glancing around to see the other's reaction to that. "As I told you before, playing golf is what makes you look stupid."

"Never mind, never mind," replied Larry, pushing the air with the back of his hand, "tell me, Erik, about the captain who killed the little boy."

"Oh God!" spouted Erik, startled by the suddenness of that question "His name, I found out way later, was Rudolph Rands" He stopped and made a gentle gesture at John to fill his glass.

For some strange reason, Erik believed, at that moment, that he had lowered himself in the opinion of his new friends by his confession of the incident, in Germany, that may have revealed a savage attitude and the outrage in his feelings; however, he thought he had to find a way to reinstate himself to their good opinion. He thought that talking about his past and allowing some of the anger that was still harbored inside him to escape would only make them look at him as the last angry man, but the more he thought about Captain Rands, the more he convinced himself to tell them the story instead of saying 'I simply don't know'. He then looked perplexed, took his glass and tilted some wine into his mouth. He only paused once, to draw a long breath, and without taking his eyes from the glass he held it up again and drank without losing a drop.

"Now," said Erik, with a new vigor, deeply inhaling and then exhaling, "about the first week of December in the year of 1943, one hundred German soldiers were slaughtered by Greek guerrillas near the town of Kalavrita. Upon learning of the slaughter of those soldiers, the German high command, that was based in the city of Tripoli, about one hundred fifty miles from Kalavrita, ordered Captain Rands to take a full company of one hundred and sixty soldiers to that town, punish the guilty and teach a lesson to the rest of the three thousand souls that lived there. The Captain and his troops arrived by way of a German military train on December the 10th and camped in the middle of town. The day before the Germans arrived, the Greek underground forces had notified the inhabitants and all the able-bodied men had flown for cover in the sounding rugged mountains. The German detachment stayed there with what appeared to be a very good attitude and excellent intentions. They fed the hungry people and took care of the sick as if they were their own. Then they began to announce through loud speakers that the Germans were there as friends and not as enemies. They were there to protect the town from the brutal communist guerrillas and pleaded for the men to return to their homes to live with their families in peace, under their protection.

Learning of the Germans good intentions, the men began straggling into town and the Germans welcomed them. On December 13th, a few days after the Germans had arrived in town and once they had made certain that all the men had returned home, they proceeded with their secret plan. At five in the morning, the first rooster crowed, waking up the people from their peaceful repose. The church bells rang in celebration as the German soldiers scattered among the houses and knocked on the doors, not with rifle butts as they normally did in other towns, but with the knuckles of their hands. They announced that all the townspeople were invited to the town square for pre-Christmas festivities."

"Why are you saying with their knuckles and not the butts of their rifles?" asked Jack.

"There were over three thousand Greeks in that town and only one hundred and sixty Germans. Do you think that the outnumbered Germans wanted to make all those Greeks angry or suspicious?" replied Erik.

"Okay, I understand now," admitted Jack.

"They woke everybody up and the houses were searched; a lot of the inhabitants were suspicious, other were confused, some afraid, but all of them were quiet and calm, believing the reason for being escorted by armed soldiers was, according to what the Germans had said, to protect them from a guerrilla attack. Gradually they were escorted to their town square where machine guns were displayed in readiness, with belts of bullets hung from their bellies, set on the tripods and pointing to where the people were being gathered. It was a gloomy and dark day and the smoke from the fireplaces lingered around the chimneys of the houses, slightly above the roofs, as if it lacked the strength to rise. The clouds hung low under the gray sky as if they too lacked the spirit to let the rain loose.

In short, the dawn that broke upon the peoples sight was not at all calculated to elevate their spirits or to lessen their fears. The air was damp and raw; the streets were wet and sloppy. A rooster in the stable, deprived of every spark of his accustomed animation, feeling guilty, thinking he was the one who had called upon such a dismal day, balanced himself sadly on one leg on a short fence and stayed silent; a donkey, moping with his ears hanging from his drooping head, under a shed roof, appeared sad and miserable as if he were contemplating suicide. That was the mood of everything that lived in that town on that particular morning.

All the people finally had been herded into the square. Captain Rands, whom no one knew, either by face or reputation, stood stiff and straight, in the manner of an absolute authority, his eyes sharp and restless, as if announcing to the world his great confidence in himself and his consciousness of immeasurable superiority over all the people, domestic or foreign. As the hours passed, the townspeople, doing nothing but standing in the middle of the square on that cold winter day, showed signs of anxiety and restlessness, so then the Germans separated the men from the women and children. They escorted all the men and the boys over fifteen, about one thousand six hundred and eighty all together, to the top of Kapy Raxy, a hill next to the cemetery. Once they reached there they were told to relax, tea and coffee would be served very shortly. The balance of the population, consisting of over one thousand five hundred women and children, were benevolently escorted into a very large schoolhouse on the other side of town. They kept the men herded on the hill, without tea and coffee, until 1 p.m. Some of the men in that herd predicted something bad was going to take place but, facing the loaded machine guns on the hill, found it in vain to protest their treatment and feelings, so they stood there with the spirit of indignation.

"One man, who was there, told this to me when I visited the

town twenty years later. Captain Rands took the loud speaker and addressed the men on behalf of the Germans' good intentions, citing the good German character and deploring the communist guerrillas who, according to his speech, endeavored to destroy the good and honest feelings the Germans held in their hearts for the Greeks who were accepted and respected for being the founders of western civilization. Rands explained that his soldiers were going to demonstrate the firing of the machine guns and he apologized again for the inconvenience and assured their cooperation and their silence was truly appreciated. He asked the men to make a semicircle to see and to observe the mechanics of the fifteen heavy machine guns. The machine guns were set aimed at the mountain, away from the town and the men. The gunners and their assistants sat behind the guns; captain Rands stood back and gave the order to commence firing.

According to the man I spoke with, the guns suddenly swung around, aimed towards the Greeks and commenced firing. The men shrieked and screamed as the bullets blasted the hapless townsmen. Flesh, bones and body parts flew all around and filled the air. They fired until all the guns were empty, reloaded and fired again at the same targets. The blood of men and boys streamed downhill, painting the rocks and soil red.

"When everything was over and all the firing had stopped and the moaning of the wounded and dying filled the ear and the fragments of human parts covered the earth and filled the eye, one of the Greeks stood up, screamed **FuniadeV, Atumoi** (Killers, Disgraceful) and charged against the gunners. He was shot down instantly. The captain ordered his men to finish off all of the dying with their bayonets.

A team of soldiers fell savagely into the dying flock of humans and with zest, enthusiasm and excitement worked their hearts out knifing bodies, cutting heads and dismantling parts of those luckless men and boys, until their arms became tired and their backs were ached from fatigue. The man I spoke with was only twenty-three years old on that horrible day and was buried under many bodies, including his dead father and two younger brothers.

"Thirteen men managed to survive and one thousand six hundred fifty six were murdered.

Then the soldiers left the hillside and hastily headed for the school, where the women and children were locked up. Captain Rands gave orders to spray the whole school with diesel fuel and to set fire to it with everybody inside. Once the fire was set, the captain and his soldiers quickly boarded the waiting train, knowing that there were over five hundred Greek guerrillas in the surrounding areas. When the train began to move, one German, of Austrian descent, jumped off the train, ran and opened the doors for the women and children to escape, but when he tried to return to the to catch the slow moving train, the Germans shot him and there he was left, dead. I don't recall the man's name, but his statue has been erected and is standing in the middle of that town." Erik, deeply saddened, stopped and looked at Larry. "I learned when I was there and spoke with some women who were in the school house, that there were a tremendous number of girls and young women who had been living in an Institution for the Insane in that town." There he stopped and took another drink. "How big is your stomach, Larry, you have room for more? The overflow will eventually go into your brain. Everything is in my brain, Larry, I was very young, and I had a little stomach. My stomach couldn't take it all." Larry never made a sound. He only gazed down and looked as if he was suffering from guilt, being of German descent, as he stated later.

The German command, after The Kalavrita incident, knowing that half of the Greek guerrillas would be looking for Captain Rands, transferred him to eastern Greece, that's where I was born. When he arrived there, Captain Rands kept a low profile, but according to a Greek saying, 'you can hide a donkey but his ears will eventually surface'. He evidently took his mad self with him and that's when he went to the monastery and killed the little boy Yainny and the twelve monks. There was a thirteenth monk who was blind in one eye and was called Patchy, because he wore a patch.

Patchy survived the execution of the twelve monks and little Yianny by hiding in a secret well. Patchy, after the massacre, lost faith in God, left the church and became another Geronimo, you know, the American Indian renegade.

" Patchy fought and killed Germans and also killed a lot of Greeks who didn't want to join his pack of warriors," continued

Erik. "He finally captured Rands alive. He removed his eyes and pulled him along the mountain trails, like a dog, for almost a year, until the Greek communist guerrillas killed Patchy. The communists handed Rands to the Russians.

Captain Rands died at the ripe age of thirty-eight, in a German prison camp in USSR, in the year of 1952. That is also documented."

There's even more to the story. When I visited the town of Kalavrita, some years later, I saw a sign that was erected where the massacre took place and it read: 'This, a sight of German atrocities during WW II.' I found out, later on, the sign was changed read: 'Atrocities committed by the conquering army.' Isn't that a crock of shit?"

Erik looked wistfully into their faces, one by one, as though to see which face was more affected. John touched Erik' shoulder and briefly rubbed it with great affection.

At length there was a cry of silence and breathless looks from everybody towards Erik.

"The way you told and the way I heard those stories, we people in America take many things for granted," remarked Jack, shaking his head from side to side producing an expression of hopeless misery and mournful feelings, and although he was a man of play and pleasure, no word or thought said or imparted by Erik passed by him.

There weren't any remarks made after that story was told. Everything became still and silent, as if the world stopped turning.

Erik broke the thread of silence by asking to be excused for the remainder of the night and expressed his sincere hopes to see them again, perhaps in the morning for breakfast. The host and the guests stood up to wish him goodnight and, with a few more lamenting remarks passed around, they broke up the gathering with hearty handshakes.

Erik walked towards the beach instead of his room. He stood between the hotel and the beach and gazed at the tranquil sea. The hotel grounds looked almost secluded and the stream of people he had seen earlier had disappeared, warning him that the majority of them had gone to their rooms for the night. After walking the dividing line between the sea sand and the grass for a little while, he made a right turn, climbed two pairs of steps and found himself on the main avenue. He observed that everything was closed except for a tavern, a favorite place to many, with a flow of people going in and out. Every time the tavern door opened to let a party out, the next party made a violent rush to get in. There was much noise coming from that crowded place of spirits and good times that the customers seemed to enjoy. The dialogue that passed between the people waiting to get in was not making much sense to Erik so he left and headed for the hotel to spend one more night.

CHAPTER 5

Erik finds a four-footed friend

The gathering of that first night was repeated the next evening, and on the three evenings next ensuing. Early in the morning on the fourth day, Erik, descending deep into to his lowest spirit, went downstairs and from there, without speaking to anyone or trying to find any of his newly acquired friends, knowing that they had their own business to attend to, left by the front door and headed south, on foot. He came upon a small bridge not far from the beach and stood there, watching the sea and the water lovers who swarmed the beaches. The river under the bridge flowed slowly and noiselessly, a fisherman's oars dipped into the murky waters heading downstream looking for a favorable place to anchor and fish. He looked behind him saw that on both sides of that river the land was covered with corn fields and pastures stretching out as far as his eyes could see, showing off the rich landscape, rendered more attractive as the shadows of the few clouds moved across it, changing the lands colors under the morning sun. He suddenly heard a train whistle blow and without the slightest hesitation, started a rapid walk towards that sound. Erik walked with no spare time to observe anything that passed on the road, one-way or the other, with all his faculties being concentrated on catching that freight train. It was mid morning by the time he reached the railroad tracks and, not being sufficiently acquainted with the train schedule and anticipating a long wait, he walked off the road, went some hundred yards into the green fields and sat under a shady tree, concealed from most eyes that sped by in their cars some hundred yards away on the road he had just left.

A few hours passed and there was no sight or sound of any

train. It was late in the afternoon when he noticed a big dog turning into the path leading to where he sat. Erik stood up, alarmed by that animal's daring attitude and definite purpose, and looked around for something to protect himself from an unprovoked assault. The dog continued to approach and coming closer, seeing Erik hastily looking for something, it stopped less than ten feet from him. The dog looked at Erik with his mouth open, his tongue hanging out, blinking with both eyes and waving his tail so slowly it appeared that the feeble wind, that lingered in from the nearby sea, was swinging it. Erik stopped, looked back at the dog in a similar manner and noticed the dog had suffered a long gash, evidently administered by another dog with more talent and strength.

"What do you want, big fellow?"

The dog began to wag his tail with a visible thrill, jumped up a few inches from the ground with his front legs several times then, without advancing an inch towards Erik, sat on that spot and looked at him intently, showing only love and not a trace of fear or doubt.

"Look, Huck Finn, I am destined and prepared to starve for a while, are you committed to that?"

The dog tilted his head to the right a few degrees, put his tongue in, to show his respect and attention and continued to wink with both eyes, as he had done all along.

"Look! Two can live as cheap as one, if one doesn't eat."

The dog stood up and moved closer to Erik, with what seemed politeness. At that point Erik, looking in the direction of the train tracks and neither seeing nor hearing anything, walked over to a large tree, sat down with his back leaning on the trunk and gazed at his four-footed friend.

"If you were a smart dog you would have gone to The Lambright Hotel and hung around there for some bones with meat. Or has society rejected you too, for not being able to conform as a dog?" asked Erik, grinning. "Now go!" yelled Erik, but the dog didn't move; he only closed his mouth and growled gently at the order, not at the one who gave it.

After a little while, the dog picked himself up and nudged closer to Erik. He sat down with his front legs stretched out in front of him and rested there with his head on his feet and his eyes on his new friend, not his master. From his attitude, it was apparent the dog rejected authority but welcomed friendship and from his previous growling, it was also apparent the creature was not going to allow anyone to treat him like a dog, as he certainly would not obey like one.

"Huck Finn. Do you have any family? No? You must have some brothers and sisters somewhere, but they have their own families. They are probably smarter than you, because they have conformed to the rules and regulations of the world they live in. I can see you love your freedom. You don't mind starving as long as you're doing it in liberty. I see you don't have a license. Me neither. No license for you or me."

Erik turned, gazed at the dog and said, "I have a poem for you. I didn't write it, I read it somewhere:
The world lies down, flat at your feet.
Each option mapped out, like a paved street.
Though you are free, just to roam,
There is a place for you, in every home.
Erik opened up his bundle and brought out a nice loaf of bread. The dog looked but never moved a paw. Erik, with a long knife fished from his bundle, cut two pieces off the loaf, handed one to his sitting friend and kept the other for himself. At that moment the dog took the bread as gently as it had been given to him and looking at his friend, he realized that Erik was the personification of the human kindness of the world. He then carefully moved away a few paces, sat and began to eat his tidbit as peacefully as his donor, but chose to face away from Erik.

"Huck Finn, what you did is not very polite."

The dog, whether realizing what he had done, or thinking he was destined to receive another piece of bread, it is unknown, but he stood up, taking his lunch with him, went back to his original place, sat and continued eating.

"Now, you are a nice dog. You must be a collie. I know you are not a pit bull. Pit bulls are like the human police. They get a hold of you and will not let you go until they see your blood oozing out from every pore, and even then, they still they hold onto you."

While the birds were gainfully employed in singing their songs and his four-footed friend was occupied with his own task of eating, Erik, chewing and talking his heart away, kept his ears devoted to the chance of a train's sound. After a short while, that revelry of birds, man and dog was broken, as are all good things in life, by a crash of a distant thunder, following a strike of lightning that shot down from the sky. According to Erik's guess, it landed somewhere a few miles west. Thick clusters of dark clouds were closing in, making the earth dark. The wind became strong and if the rain were to come down, as strong as the thunder threatened, it would be in torrents. It would be impossible to stay here, thought Erik, and to survive against such obstacles, united.

"You know, Huck Finn, the morning of each day and the beginning of each life are so much alike. This morning the sun was bright and splendid, it promised to stay that way for the rest of the day by the manner in which it chased the clouds away. It was as beautiful as a page from a romantic novel. The beginning of life, like the morning of the day, starts out with plenty of promises and plans. God! What I wouldn't give to have my childhood days restored, or to abolish them from my mind, forever," uttered Erik, with his eyes flashing brightly as he spoke, as if what he had hoped for, would come to pass. But that momentary excitement quickly subsided and he turned calmly away and said,

"Huck Finn, even though my young days were filled with sadness, losses and fears, they were brightened by my happy dreams, now they're all gone too, like young love," mumbled Erik, casting his eyes downward he continued, "I think we should go under that bridge, if we don't want to drown right here, pardon my expression, like two cats in a pond." Suddenly a blade of lighting flashed and the thunder echoed, closer than before.

"Do you hear that thunder?" asked Erik, getting onto his feet, as the dog followed his move.

"That thunder is nature's announcement that the rain is coming." Another crashed, as if to verify the previous thunder's warning.

Both creatures started on their short journey to the bridge and the prospects before them.

The lighting, the thunder and the darkness of the sky were by no means encouraging, but the dog followed his friend with perfect confidence, stopping when he stopped, walking when he walked, running when he ran and jumping when he jumped; they both moved on mostly running without any admonitions. As soon as they reached the main road, a car rushed upon them, stopped and the back door flew opened.

"Jump in! Jump in!" cried a voice from inside the car, belonging to a young man sitting in the passenger seat. And before Erik knew precisely what was going on, he felt himself forced in the door by someone pulling his arms, and another who had come around from the driver's seat, pushing him from the back. Erik sprawled in; the dog was left out.

"My dog! My dog!" screamed Erik, looking behind him and seeing the dog following them in its top speed.

"Take it easy mister! Take it easy man! We'll stop down the road and wait for the dog," said the driver, who was as young as the other, with long hair that rested on his shoulders.

Erik looked behind, wiped the rear window with his sleeve and saw the dog running, but it was left way behind and the rain was coming down in sheets. The car was moving fast. They traveled at the unbelievable speed of more than one hundred good and solid miles per hour, without any definite purpose, from what Erik could tell, for almost five minutes. Fields, trees and hedges seemed to rush by, with the velocity of a tornado.

Erik planted himself in a seat corner, as firmly as he could.

"Here they are!' yelled the driver.

"Go on man! Go on faster!" shrieked the other young passenger. Erik looked ahead and saw a red car swerving along the road, as though it were playing a game. The red car, curtailing none of its speed, went on, sometimes in the middle of the road, sometimes on the right of the pavement's shoulder, sometimes on its left. The car Erik was riding in, without his benefit of choice, slowed only slightly.

"What do you want from me?" screamed Erik.

"We just pulled a job. They spotted the car, only this car. The car ahead of us, they're our friends, the four guys in that car. There'll be a roadblock ahead. They'll be looking for two guys. You'll be driving. We'll be tucked in the back seat, pointing a gun on you. You'll pass through. Nobody will stop you. They're not looking for an old guy like you. After that, we'll drop you off and you can wait for your dog," said the passenger, sternly and loudly as if he meant business.

"You seem bright! But you picked on the wrong guy." said Erik. "Pull over!" he yelled, foaming with rage and excitement "Pull over!" he roared again, grabbing the young passenger by the hair and pulling him back with a mighty rush of strength.

"Are you crazy?" screamed the driver. "Man, you're gonna kill us!"

A sudden jolt flung Erik all way from the back seat to up against the windshield, then a sudden smack—a loud crash under the car, then a scraping on the side; a wheel rolled away. The car ran off the road to the left, flew into the air and tilting to the right while airborne, came down on its side, landing in the sand near the water. It rolled upright, then on its side and settled on its roof, with the remaining three wheels still spinning furiously. After a few seconds of disorientation and bewilderment, Erik saw the red car they were chasing backing up towards their wreck; from it, two young men rushed to the scene. They fished out the two thieves, the driver and passenger, and secured them on their feet.

"Are you okay?" asked the young driver of the wreck, squatting down by Erik's side and seeing him lying there on his back. Erik, before having had enough time to check himself out or give an answer was interrupted by another man from the red car who grabbed the young driver of the wreck and pulled him aggressively, "Lets go!"

"The man, he may be hurt," protested the young driver, pointing at Erik.

"You're going to get real hurt yourself, if you don't go now!" yelled the other guy. They all scurried, got in the red vehicle and sped away. Erik was left in the wreckage; he extricated his head from the seat belt and other items that had fallen on him. He gained the use of his right leg and tried to remove his left, but found it difficult, because it was trapped between the twisted steering wheel and the dashboard. Overwhelmed by confusion, Erik tried to think his way through what seemed at first a simple job, but it turned out to be a complicated state of affairs, particularly when he noticed the tide creeping in like a liquid snake that could swallow the car and its only passenger. To make matters worse, he realized the car was concealed from the road, because of the low terrain where it was resting. He could hear the traffic above racing by. He tried violently to free his leg from its trap, but every attempt was in vain.

Through the damaged windshield, he could see the rain had stopped and the clouds were rushing away, as if they had already accomplished their mission. The day was preparing to shut off its lights and say goodnight to all, and Erik thought, "Will I see you tomorrow?"

Erik recollected John's thoughts, while standing by the bridge in the morning, being depressed after losing his son; 'One leap, a splash, a brief struggle and then the water closes above and locks out all troubles and misfortunes.'

Here, Erik thought, it will not be one leap, or splash, it will be a long struggle, gasping for air. The air will come at first and then will come mixed with water and as the water trickles in slowly, like a bad spirit, it will embrace the body and then the head. It's an uphill battle with the forces of nature against only me, he thought. It was a situation that would have most definitely disheartened the spirits of most men, but Erik, not being a member of the group that most men belong to, said out loud and emphatically,

"Erik, you are a beaten man," with a sudden smile on his face, as if the probability of escaping from the dreadful situation had lit a light in him.

"I may be beaten, but not destroyed, " he continued, turning around hastily, looking to find his bundle. He finally located his bundle and, with great speed, searched inside and came up with a huge knife in his hands. He took it into his hand and balanced it, as though he was marking its purpose and designing its task.

"I told you, I may be beaten, but not destroyed," he said to himself as he looked at the height of the water in the car, now nearly a foot deep. He carefully slit his pants from above the knee to as far as he could reach, which was a few inches above the ankle, exposing the knee to view. He took the rope, the same rope he had used to catch the horse, made a knot and twisted it around his leg above the knee, creating a tourniquet, then took the pistol, inserted it under the rope and began to tighten it by turning. He stopped for a moment, checked the depth of the water in the car again and saw no significant change.

"I have a little time yet. There is nothing new in a case like this; animals chew their feet off to get free from a trap. There is a little problem with this whole thing. What happens if I faint? How do the animals do it? The animals can only concentrate on one thing at a time. They don't have the mental power to think and imagine. So I will just think of getting free from this trap and I will not imagine anything else beyond that. If I do it fast enough and delay my imagination, it will delay the impact of the pain and I will be free." There he thought for a while; scratched his chin and suddenly turned his head towards the clouds. He seemed to have nailed his eyes as if looking for an instrument with which to free himself or another way out.

"God!" said Erik loudly, as if he wanted God to hear him in Heaven, far away. "Do you keep track of how many times you have beaten me? Why is it when a day comes that I feel happy, the next day you make something bad happen, so I can suffer? Do you do that with everybody or with only a few? Am I one of the few, God? Am I one of your chosen?" he kept his eyes and head up for a long moment.

"Is my mission on this earth to show the world that a man can survive nature's fury and your scorn?"

"Let me go," said Erik softly, throwing his right arm up and bending his head down, "Let me figure out how to get out of here without your help, I don't wish to speak to a God who is deaf not deaf and dumb, just deaf."

He turned and studied the water situation. He dunked his left arm all the way down to his ankle and felt around there for a while. He then looked and wondered what possible temptation could have induced a fly to come into a sinking car, when it had the choice of so many airy places, he thought, as a tiny fly circled around looking for a place to land.

"Fly, what are you doing here? Are you crazy too?" The fly flew and danced all around him and then settled on a safe spot.

"Fly, what makes you so happy? Your life expectancy is less than forty days. What do you think you can accomplish in forty days? I have been here over forty years and I haven't accomplished a damn thing. Why are you dancing around?" Erik moved his hand slowly towards where the fly was sitting and once his hand approached, the fly hopped over and sat on the back of his hand.

When he tried to bring his hand towards him to examine the little creature more closely, it flew and landed on the knife.

"There you go again. Even though you have less than forty days left, you are still trying to stay alive. Look who's talking, fly, I have less than four hours left and I am still making plans. I am not talking long term plans. I just put my hand down where my leg is trapped, I rubbed it for a few minutes and let it go, promising that I will do that again in fifteen minutes. Go away fly!" said Erik, waving his arm to scare the fly away. "Go away! I said. The fly flew and settled by the window. "You don't want to see a grown man drown. Drowning is not like dying. Dying is easy. You drown before you die. When you are drowning the world closes around you and you are cut off from everything, slowly. You know you are entering a world where you are not welcomed. You are being pushed out and you are looking to grasp onto something, something as insignificant as a straw, to enable you to stay in that new world, thinking you may able to adapt. You look for peace of mind, but peace doesn't come." The fly flew out.

"I see you got scared. I'll see you up there in forty days."

He looked around, and as there were no better prospects in that wrecked car that came to be his trap, or in his mental vision of his imminent death, he began to ruminate on a plan of escape. His features became pompous and threatening, his manner peremptory; his eyes sharp and restless and his whole being bespoke a feeling of confidence in himself and a consciousness of his cerebral dexterity.

"I will show you, God, that a man can be beaten but not destroyed. I have a twenty-five percent chance of not fainting, I also have a twenty-five percent chance that somebody will find me and I have a twenty-five percent chance that the tide will stop before it gets over my head. In other words, I have a seventy-five percent chance of surviving. That's not bad odds. In Las Vegas, they gamble on a fifty-fifty chance," saying this he took the knife in his hands raised it to the clouds and said, "I am provided with three choices. Each and every choice has a priority over the other. Now I must maintain a healthy and sound mind to sort out my priorities. Remember, half a loaf is better than none; likewise, a one-legged man is better than none. That takes care of one option.

Waiting for the tide to come in and hoping that it will not go over my head must be the last. Waiting for someone to come to my aid is the first option that I must exercise. Wait a moment! What the hell is wrong with me? I have another option. I am almost underneath the motor." Saying this, he began to poke with his knife above him very anxiously," I'll try to find a hose. A car has seventeen hundred hoses from different places to other parts; a two-foot hose will do it. When the time comes I'll breathe through the hose until the tide goes out again. That increases my survival chance, with all the options before me, to almost one-hundred per cent," he said, full of anticipation.

Suddenly, his four-footed friend appeared, coming down towards the car at the speed of light. The dog, completely disregarding obstacles, flew into the car, embraced his drowning friend and covered him with licks and kisses.

"Where have you been, Huck Fin?" said Erik, astonished.

The dog dashed to see his leg, noticed the exposed knee, rushed out of the car into the surrounding water, splashed around the car barking with madness, and then headed for the road. The dog was running from one side of the road to the other, as if trying to catch someone. Cars zoomed by him but the dog continued to furiously leap and bark at them. Some of the cars slowed down but sped away again, leaving the dog behind barking. Some of the cars swerved around the dog, some blew their horns in anger, but none stopped. This performance lasted a long time, with no favorable results. The water was filling up the car slowly but surely and had reached the lower part of Erik's knee. The dog, being in possession of the same spirit as his new friend, persisted with his impossible task, while Erik controlled his anxiety by talking to himself.

"I will wait another five minutes then I'll cut my leg off," uttered Erik, with fully inflated hope. "Do you hear? God do you hear me? I know you're up there. I believe you are there, but I don't believe in you, God! What else do you want from me? I know this is your domain and I'm only one of your subjects, not a humble subject I must admit, and that's what probably makes you angry. Am I to you what Prometheus was to Zeus? Are you afraid that I may turn the mortals against you, God? Are you angry because I have embraced the wisdom of the serpent? You took all I had. I cannot be one of your humble subjects and still be angry with you. It's between you and me, God. You don't want to help me. Then destroy me! Destroy me, God! God damn me."

He then, lowering his face in defeat, glanced in the mirror on the floor that reflected his whole face. He paused for a long moment to look at himself and the more he looked the more distorted his face and features became.

"You bastard you!' exclaimed Erik, on seeing his reflection, in an altered, deep, unrecognizable voice and grimacing tone.

"You wronged me, you bastard. You have been wronging me all my life. You always go the wrong way and you take me with you, and I follow you. You caused God to take my son. He did it just to punish you. One of this days I'll walk away from you and I will be different man without you," he said to his reflection. He then turned his head upwards and cried loudly, with tears in his eyes, "God, I just saw the man who lives inside me. Because if him, you took my child. My son died before his mother and father's eyes, to be more agonizing and painful for his parents. He didn't grasp for a breath of air, like I am going to grasp for air in a little while; he didn't struggle for life. You want revenge? Take my life! You got the wrong man, God. Bring back my son, take me and throw me in the sea and there I will die. I promise you that I will not stir a hand or foot to hold myself back from drowning. There will be no agitation from this drowning man, no rippling waves, no shouts and no pleas for help. The spot where I'll go down to my early grave will be undistinguishable from the surrounding waters."

Erik lifted his face and looked around him for one more long moment, then he turned his face downward, looked at his reflection again and said in his normal soft voice, "you can't bring my son back. I will do what I have to do, because there is one more reason for living and it's the prize of seeing you suffer on this earth." He turned his head to heaven, "God, I'll help myself now, I will give you my leg," he said softly, "I'll cut it off and send it to one of your churches. Then the world will see traces of suffering and despair, if that's what your wish is." Overwhelmed by the unalterable conviction that his only way out of that trap was to leave half of his leg behind him, he burst into a loud sobbing.

He took the knife in his right hand, held it firmly, and hastily began to tighten the tourniquet with his left, under the water that had already risen above his shoulders.

"Just, don't let me faint. I know you can do that much."

It was at that moment that he heard a siren coming his way, fast and definite. It was less than a minute later when he heard the siren stop near him and the dog barking not with anger, but with joy.

"Tom Sawyer" yelled a voice. "What's the matter boy?" said a middle aged man with a yellow raincoat, going to the dog, but the dog barked, jumped and ran to the car that was already filled with of water. Erik's eyes flashed with new hope.

"Here I am! I am down here!" Erik yelled out.

The dog jumped into the car and barked and barked again. Erik heard splashing steps coming his way and a man's face showed in the window, looking in.

"My god! Are you in there? Are you hurt?" asked the man.

"I'm not hurt. It's worst. I'm trapped, and about to go under," responded Erik, with tears in his eyes, tears of both joy and sorrow.

"The tide is coming in, but we'll get you out; I'm a fireman and this here trained dog is mine. Somebody drove by, recognized my dog and called to tell me that my dog was about to get run over about fifteen miles south of Myrtle Beach. Then they hung up, without any further explanation. I'm not going to take the time to ask you what happened. Let me call for help, they'll be here in less than five minutes."

"How high does the tide get here?" asked Erik, now with a grin on   his   face.

"About six feet."

"Six feet, huh? My head is about three feet from the bottom. That's nice. I would have been only three feet below the water line. That's better than six feet under the dirt," said Erik smiling.

"I see you haven't lost your sense of humor."

"You want to hear something my mother used to tell me?"

"I'd love to," said the fireman.

"When life around you is getting to be less certain than a rumor,

The best thing for you to do, my son, is to keep your sense of humor."

"How true, how true," said the fireman, as he ran to his truck with his dog following him.

"Six feet, " murmured Erik, "there goes my first twenty-five per cent down the river," endeavoring to loosen his leg tourniquet. Unable to locate his bundle under the water, he held the pistol and the knife in his hands, turned his eyes up to the sky and said softly, "I knew you were up there. I was right. I said that I didn't want to talk to anyone who is deaf. At least I believe one of your angels knows how to use the phone, or do you? You may convince me yet, to believe in you. It's still between you and me. Keep on trying. You will either make me humble or crazy."

A few minutes later, a second and a third fire truck had sped to the scene and almost a dozen firemen were working around Erik to set him free. He was carried from the car and the water onto the road, and was made to lie on a stretcher for a while, where he gave a detailed report to the police.

"Are you allergic to anything?" asked a young man in white coat with a stethoscope dangling on his chest, seeming, to all eyes, to be a doctor.

"Oh, yes," replied Erik, "I'm allergic to poverty;" with those words he passed out.

"Take him to the hospital. Anxiety and fatigue will result in dehydration," announced the young doctor to anyone who was listening and monitoring Erik's condition.

While he was being put in the ambulance, he opened his eyes for one short moment.

"Do you have any family?" asked the doctor, placing his hand on Erik's hand compassionately, holding up the process for a moment.

Erik's eyes widened, his face became sullen and then he closed his eyes again, retreating to nature's demands. It was obvious that the bodily powers of Erik Karas had been impaired and his mental energies had been exhausted but neither was gone. Even if the annoyance of his recent adventure had vanished from his mind, his thoughts of where he was and what he was doing, what he had and what he had lost, turned over and over in his mind at the same speed as his lingering heart beat in his chest; both were still there. On the way to the hospital, as the ambulance screamed through traffic, Erik opened his eyes two or three times and closed them without uttering a word. When he saw his arm attached to an intra-venous bottle, held by a young woman with long blond hair, a crimson face and gloomy expression, sitting at his side, he left his eyes open.

"Did I die and go to heaven?' asked Erik, grinning and attempt-ing to move his fingers closer to her dress.

"No. You didn't die and you're not in heaven," said the girl, straightening his pillow and pushing his hand away.

"Having an angel sitting next to me, I thought I was in heaven."

"No, I'm sorry to disappoint you. This is not heaven and I'm not an angel. But I think you may be a devil."

"Me?" asked Erik, in a feeble voice.

"You," replied the girl, grinning.

"That's funny, in my prime, I was referred to as a Greek God."

"Looking like a Greek god can make you a devil," said the girl, pushing his hand away again and placing a part of the blanket between her leg and his hand, "I see you feel better."

"The sight of a beautiful girl revives my heart and speeds up my blood circulation."

"That's what we're here for."

"I believe that. If it weren't for the sight of beautiful girls like you, men would die long before their time, having no reason for living."

"I see he's feeling better," remarked the ambulance driver, turning around carefully.

"I feel better and he feels better," replied the girl, soberly.

"If I would have seen you before they put me in the ambu-lance, I would immediately have felt so much better, you and I could have walked the fifteen mile stretch to the hospital."

"Without stopping?" asked the girl, humorously.

"Oh God! There are so many beaches from there to the hospi-tal. It's so hard to pass them up."

"Eventually, we'd have to get to the hospital," said the girl.

"For a check up?" asked Erik.

"No! For a blood transfusions for both of us," said the girl, break-ing into loud laughter, so loud and so clearly laden with height-ened pleasure, that the driver became troubled.

"Are you sure, you want me to take him to the hospital or you want me to stop by your apartment?" asked the driver, full of frustration.

"He's jealous," whispered the nurse, bending down close to Erik's ear. "He's been trying to put the make on me for the longest time, but he's using bait instead of finesse."

"I know. Some men can't tell the difference between a fish and a sitting duck."

"Do you think I'm a sitting duck just because I'm sitting next to you?"

"No. To me, you're a hummingbird. Too restless to settle and too wild to tame," said Erik, touching her hand passionately.

The nurse studied his face and expression for a moment, "I knew you were a devil the minute I laid my eyes on you."

The ambulance pulled into the hospital's emergency driveway. The driver got out and went around to open the door.

"Here's my name and telephone number," said the nurse, in a whispering voice, "you hummingbird you. Remember the song? 'Hummingbird, hummingbird, fly right on by! If I'll cut your wings will that make you mine?"

"Then I'll be a sitting duck," replied Erik, soberly.

When Erik was rushed into the emergency room, it looked like a snug little party consisting of two males, looking like doctors, and three romping and joking sun-tanned nurses. He was immediately placed on a hospital bed with everybody participating in the process and the girl, who had accompanied him there and whose name was Diana, paid special attention to him, to the point that the other nurses began to give her dirty looks and the driver, who was standing a little further from his bed, was drowning in jealousy and righteous anger.

"Will you call me?" asked Diana, getting close to his ear, pretending she was fixing his pillow.

"Your sparkling eyes and your girlish frolic drives every man crazy and every woman angry," said Erik.

Right after he finished his remark and Diana was about to return a comment or pose a question, the figure of the distinguished old gentleman, John Lambright, appeared standing at the bottom of Erik's hospital bed, grinning and shaking his head mournfully.

"Didn't you realize the world is bigger than you?" said John to

Erik.

"Granddaddy" yelled Diana, running into his arms, "What are you doing here?"

Erik didn't only turn pale from bewilderment but also speechless.

"I came to see my friend. Erik, this here beauty is my granddaughter, Diana. She is John's daughter. This, honey, is my newest and best friend, Erik Karas."

"How do you do," said Erik to her.

"Oh, stop it!" said Diana to Erik, in a confident manner that told that she lived and basked in the light of her grandfather's name and figure. "Granddaddy, he and I met. I was the one in the ambulance. I've already given him my phone number. He is quite fresh."

"Oh, yeah? It's easier for the sun to hold onto the morning mist, than for you to hold on to him."

"Is that bad?"

"Worse."

"How did you meet my granddaddy?"

"We both flew first class from Richville to Myrtle Beach?" said Erik, grinning.

"How do you feel?" asked John, advancing a few steps, with his granddaughter still clinging on to him.

"A little weak. Staying in that water for a few hours would only be first class accommodations for seals. Why are you here? I mean, how did you know that I was here?"

"The police called me. Evidently, when you gave them the report you mentioned my name. They got those young thieves."

"Why did they take me with them like that?"

"They had just robbed a gas station and they took off. They knew the police were looking for two youths and having you with them, they figured would fool any patrolman."

"How about the two in the other car?" asked Erik.

"Somehow they were all in the game."

"They aren't bad kids, only misguided," returned Erik.

"Here we go again, Father Flanagan; there are no bad boys. I'm with W.C. Fields; anybody who hates kids and dogs, can't be all that bad," said the old gentleman.

"Stop it!" interjected Diana, tapping her grandfather's hand,

"That's no way for you feel."

"Talking of dogs and kids, the dog saved my life."

"I know. That dog belongs to the fire department and is trained to do just that. His name is Tom Sawyer. I heard from the fireman that you called the dog Huck Finn, Why? "

"We met by the river and he and I shared something."

"What's that?"

"Being out to see the world," said Erik, imparting a faint grin.

"Oh yes, Mark Twain's, Huckleberry Finn."

"Your granddaughter is a chip off the old block," remarked Erik.

"Her father's?"

"Not my father's?" interjected Diana.

"I don't know your father very well. But I know your grandfather, and you're very much like him."

"Can we all have a nice dinner tonight granddaddy?" asked Diana.

At that point a doctor came in and asked the two visitors to leave and allow him to examine the patient.

Diana and her grandfather walked away with her arm wrung through his and, with her very bright eyes looking up to him, she asked her grandfather again about having dinner; it was then he took the time to tell her the story of Erik' son. As John told it, with a trembling voice, remembering the loss of his own son, he cast his eyes down and they met those of his granddaughter. They were light bright eyes and though they were tearful now, their influence was, by no means, lessened as she pleaded again with him to convince Erik to have dinner with them, but he knew better, from his experience, what state of mind Erik was in, and, not really wanting to impose on his friend, he turned his head away, as if to avoid being persuaded by them.

"We'll come back later on to see how he feels," said the old gentleman.

"Thank you, granddaddy, I'll see you then," said Diana, stretching upwards, giving him a kiss on his cheek and saying, "I love you." She left at once, almost running.

Two hours later Diana, dressed up, walked back into the hospital to see Erik, but the bed he had occupied was empty and ready to receive the next patient. She stood and stared at the bed, seemingly disappointed and lost, then turned and hurried towards the information desk.

"He signed himself out, about an hour ago," said the desk nurse.

After a brief pause, looking down the girl said, "may I use the phone, please!"

"Yes," said the nurse graciously, "Please take my seat," then the nurse went away to allow her some privacy.

Diana waited anxiously for the phone to be answered.

"Hello. Granddaddy... He's gone. He checked himself out," she said and then listened for a moment. "I understand, granddaddy. I feel so sorry for him." She listened again and said, "I know. He seems to be going through life, spilling humor from his lips to hide the suffering in his heart." She paused to listen again. "That's what makes me so sad. Granddaddy, he reminds me of you. Do you think he'll ever come back?" she asked intensely. "I'll have dinner with you tomorrow night then. Thank you, granddaddy." She paused to listen one more time. "I'll be all right. Love you." She concluded her call and walked away with her head down, laden with disappointment, saying softly to herself, with a grin "Hummingbird, hummingbird, fly right on by."

PART III

CHAPTER 1

A promise to a
dead woman's family

Two weeks after his release from the hospital, Erik was sitting on a bench in front of a train station, below a hanging sign stating the location was Portersville, Louisiana. He waited apathetically for the arrival of the passenger train heading west. His newfound friends, John and Diana, were left to their own styles of living and to their own amusements. Erik, in compliance with some inner pressing drive, continued west.

Suddenly a group of men, publicly drinking and half intoxicated, trickled by and stopped in front of him. At first, unaware of his existence, they drank, talked, joked and laughed loudly. Erik thought their sayings and deeds were amusing only to themselves. One of them offered his southern hospitality by presenting Erik with a small paper cup, gesturing for him to hold it out to be filled and to drink. It was not the habit of Erik to descend to the common level of ordinary minds. On this instance, however, to avoid any physical confrontation with them, he relaxed and stepped down from his pedestal, walked among them and adapted his remarks to the comprehension of that inebriated bunch; he appeared to be one of them.

His demeanor in this instance did not correspond with his thoughts or spirit, so unnoticed, he walked away with his bundle on his back and his head drooped to his chest. It was late morning. Before long, he found himself walking quickly down railroad ties, in the middle of winding tracks; the ties passed beneath him as fast as time itself. He was thinking of the men who had laid them down such a long time past. Their eyes have since been closed in the grave, but the manifestation of their deeds, the solid tracks and ties, were still there, triumphing, with no death in sight for them. Those men had worked their fingers to unbendable shapes with no hope of release from their toil and no prospect for freedom. Their blood and sweat has since dried and disappeared, but the atrocities of their dashed hopes and dreams are still buried under every single wooden railroad tie, imaginable enough to the skilled observer to give a rise to images of occurrences of bleeding limbs and sunken hearts. Seventy years ago they were there, day after day, as surely as the sun came up. Despair soon comes long after misfortune kills the dreams. They came, they saw and they were conquered. It was rather odd for Erik to think of what happened seventy years ago, but he couldn't stop thinking of those unschooled creatures laying down those tracks of steel in a such a disciplined manner, it being a such a long and difficult process, indeed.

Suddenly he heard the train coming and he rushed off the tracks. He waited until the train passed then grew positive and a bit cheerful on hearing it stop, not too far from where he was. He sped to catch it, but it was too far away from him and it only remained there long enough to load or unload one person.

Eventually the small station came into view. Erik walked there and sat on a bench, as he had done before at the previous station. He remained in that position for some time and then looking at the sun, realizing that that the day was passing by, he stood up, let out a heavy sigh and began to walk again, to the west, the way the train went, listening to the birds' midday caroling.

He shuffled along on the side of the railroad tracks for some time. His face was red and flushed from the heat when he stood with his jacket thrown over his shoulder, exposing his pistol in its shoulder holster. He looked around intently and saw he was standing on top of an old wooden trestle. He heard water howling just below him, turned left and headed down towards the foot of the trestle until he came very close to the river's gentle rushing waters. He looked as if he sensed a new plan and, from the frown on his face, appeared as if he wished to grant the river the pleasure of swallowing him, rather that fighting life's struggles, loneliness and pains. He turned his head away, to avoid being persuaded by the river's silent and splendid invitation to join it, and saw, not too far from where he was standing, a solitary house in ruin and decay. There were two windows on each side of a dilapidated entrance door, faded and unpainted. The house was one story, sitting on stilts, dark and dismantled, hidden in a cluster of wild and forgotten trees and bushes and, to all appearances, unfit for human shelter. Suddenly the door to the house was thrown open and a little girl, not more than six, with long and neglected light blond hair, came out, rushed to the edge of the river, near what appeared to be an outhouse, threw something solid in the river and ventured back at the same speed. When she was half way into the house, she stopped, turned and stared at the stranger for a long moment.

"You, come here! Come here, I said," yelled Erik sternly, thinking the girl was a young runaway.

The young girl remained unmoved, stared at him with an indifferent look on her face, turned and went in, leaving the door open, as if she were inviting the stranger to follow her. Right after the girl disappeared into the dilapidated house, Erik became troubled and alarmed, more so, when he heard muffled sounds and shouts mingled with threats and promises of revenge and terror. Dreading something bad and fearing the worst, he put on his jacket, took out his pistol, held it in his hand, ready to fire at a moment's notice and tripped towards the house with cautious steps. He then ran to the left of the house, stood near a small outbuilding and listened for a moment, intently. He rushed to the main house, placed his back against the wall and his eyes and ears on extreme alert. There he planted himself near the entrance, waiting and listening.

"Drink your milk, honey, and then you can do the dishes," said the same voice he had heard before, but now it was peaceful and gentle. The voice he heard bore a slight French accent. Erik then realized that he was in Cajun country. Suddenly, a young man poked his head out of a side window and looked around, but Erik was concealed behind a bushy short tree that stood between him and the man.

"Emma would like to have some milk too, so please don't drink it all" said a voice that belonged to an elderly woman.

Erik put his gun back in the holster, walked to the doorway and tapped with the knuckle of his forefinger—gently at first, then more audibly. After repeating this process a couple of times without effect, he ventured halfway into the house and cautiously peeped in. There, he saw a big room with a closed door leading into, evidently, another room. The room he was briefly surveying was long with very low ceilings; the walls were painted an off-white color. At one end was what resembled a kitchen, with some utensils hanging from the ceiling and a large round table positioned in the corner, covered with a blue plastic tablecloth, surrounded by four chairs. It appeared that organized and orderly people lived there. On one side of the room was a worn but clean couch, above it, a white wall clock hung between two picture prints. An aged well-fed lady was sitting on the couch, looking straight ahead. He saw two little girls sitting on either side of her; the one he had already seen, whose eyes now were swimming in tears, her face covered with sadness. The other little girl, not more than four, sat on the other side of the old lady, her head resting on her shoulder, she appeared frightened. At that moment the door from the other room was hastily thrown open, and as hastily closed, announcing the entrance of the man who had poked his head out the window. He strode on the creaking wooden floor majestically towards Erik, thrusting aside his proffered hand, and, grinding his teeth as if to put a sharper edge on what he was about to say, exclaimed in a frog like voice, "What are you doing here?" He surveyed Erik from head to foot and then he asked the question again, adding the words 'in hell' after the word 'What.'

"What?" asked Erik, startled.

"I'm asking you to tell me what you're doing here," repeated the man for the third time, raising his voice.

Erik threw a searching look at the man who was tall, slim, with brown hair, blue eyes, in his early to middle thirties and wearing red shirt buttoned to the top.

"I was passing by and I saw the little girl running in and then I heard screaming and I thought that someone in here may need help."

"I don't believe you."

"Well, you better believe me. I'm not here looking for a dance partner. That's for sure," said Erik, with a motion of his hand indicative of his ability to take out his gun and pistol-whip the angry man in front of what seemed to be his family.

"Stop it Morgan! Can't you see the man came in here to help?" said the old lady; while speaking, she looked straight ahead, which was away from both men.

"Thank you, ma'am,' said Erik, turning and bowing to the woman.

The six year old girl, with the tears in her eyes, rushed from the couch to the door from where Morgan had come, opened the door, hastily ran back to the couch and sat again next to the old lady in the same spot as before.

Hearing the old lady's words of advice and seeing the little girl's manner, Morgan slowly turned away and went to a wall, rested his head against it and began to sob, silently.

Erik walked towards the door that the little girl had opened and cautiously entered the room. There was a single bed on which a young lady was laying, face up, her hands folded. Erik approached slowly and reverently touched the young lady's forehead.

"Leave her alone! She's dead," said Morgan, who was standing behind Erik.

Erik, taken off guard by that deep and unexpected voice, pulled back his hand as cautiously as he had reached out.

Finding it unnecessary at that point to pour piteous lamentations on that poor man, Erik surveyed the dead young lady with his eyes, in silence. He thought that even death, which had landed in that room, did not dare change the young lady's beauty. She looked as if she were sleeping and had just lost her hold on earth, that her clouds of trouble had passed, leaving heaven's way clear for her to go up to her rest.

"That's my wife," said Morgan, with quivering lips and flooded eyes, looking at Erik who had already turned away from her and was facing him, sullen.

"That's my wife. They killed her, Mister; they killed her, "repeated Morgan, yelling with anger. "They killed her, do you understand? They killed her."

"Wait a minute, who killed her?" returned Erik, "Tell me who killed her. Stop raving! Tell me, man, who is **they**?" continued Erik, lowering his voice in this last statement.

"They killed her, I'm telling you," repeated Morgan, in the same tone.

"If you don't calm down, I'm walking out of here and you can call the police and tell them who killed her," said Erik, walking a few paces away, then turning to see if his words had sunk into Morgan's thick, confused and angry head. His face was suffused with a crimson glow while he stood and stared in a fearful pause, as Erik presented him with his intentions.

"Look," said Erik, seeing Morgan's changed attitude and advanced towards him, "my name is Erik Karas. What is your full name?" he asked, giving out his hand to shake, as the wonton lines of momentary passion that had ruled his face and brow gradually melted away and his features resumed their benign expression.

"I am Morgan Dante," said the man, shaking Erik's hand.

"Now, please tell me what happened to your wife."

"Michelle, honey, tell the gentleman what happened to your mother"

"Why can't you tell me?" asked Erik.

"I wasn't here when it happened," retuned Morgan, letting out a deep sigh.

The little girl jumped off the couch, ran to and stationed herself in front of Erik, knitted her hands before her, bent her head downwards and waited.

"Tell me, sweetheart, do you know what happened to your mother?' asked Erik, squatting down to her level.

"Two days ago or four days ago, my mother got very sick, and was getting sicker everyday. She had a lot of pain and she was screaming. Yesterday morning I ran down to Mr. Jonas's house and told him what happened," there the little girl stopped for a moment for want of air, "and Mr. Jonas and his wife Millie,"

"Who is Mr. Jonas, honey?" asked Erik.

"Mr. Jonas and his wife, Millie, are our neighbors. They live on Foxtail Road," said the little girl.

"Mr. Jonas and his wife Millie are our neighbors and they live down the road a piece from here and they both have been a big help to my family," said Morgan softly.

"I don't like Mr. Jonas," exclaimed the other little girl, boldly.

"Emma, honey! Mr. Jonas is very nice man," explained the old lady, poking the little girl, Emma, gently on the ribs with her elbow.

"Why don't you like Mr. Jonas, honey?" asked Erik, turning to her for a moment.

"He smells like beer all the time, " replied the little girl, now in a timid way.

"Mr. Jonas likes his beer, and sometimes becomes loud, obnoxious and nutty, but Millie sets him straight, real good," added Morgan, to make sure that Mr. Jonas was not going to be misrepresented by anyone, young or old, from his family.

"I understand, Morgan, some people behave differently when the are drinking," said Erik, hearing the explanation from Morgan, "then, what happened, sweetheart?"

"Mr. Jonas and his wife Millie took my mother and me to the hospital," hearing this, Michelle began to cry, wiping the tears off her eyes with the knuckles of her right hand.

Overtaken and bewildered, Erik stood up and looked around him. Morgan advanced towards his daughter; she embraced him as soon as he squatted next to her as he began to wipe her tears with the corner of his shirt and a trembling hand.

"She's scared and upset," said Morgan.

"Are you scared of me, honey?" asked Erik softly.

The little girl nodded her head up and down several times in assent.

"Why?" asked Erik

"She thinks that you're a policeman," returned Morgan.

"What makes you think that I'm a policeman?" asked Erik, again.

"You have a gun," murmured the little girl, turning her head up and looking at him.

"This gun is for hunting, honey," sad Erik.

"No…" sang out the little girl. "Mr. Jonas has a gun for hunting, it's long and he calls it a shotgun. What you have is a policeman's gun and it's for shooting people."

That little girl's statement rang like a bugle in Erik's head and woke up all the old ill thoughts and feelings that he carried with him since his son's death, but he soothed them to rest for a while, though he immediately turned pale and despondent.

"You're right, Michelle, honey," said Erik, with a broken voice, squatting in front of her, "but I am not here to harm you or anyone else," he continued, recovering his power of speech. "Just tell me what happened to your mother. I want to help you and your father, if I can."

"We went to St. Vincent's Hospital, in New Orleans."

"When you went to the hospital, what did the doctor say about your mother?"

"She didn't see a doctor, only a nurse. Mr. Jonas told us we couldn't see a doctor because we didn't have any money or insurance to pay for him. Mr. Jonas brought us back here and told my mother that the nurse told him that she would be okay, she only had a twenty four...." the little girl stopped there and stuck the tip of her finger in her mouth, as often little people do when they are lost for words.

"A twenty-four hour virus?" asked Erik.

"Yes, That's what Mr., Jonas said. My mother was in a lot of pain and she was crying all night long. She couldn't sleep."

"What happened then?"

"Early in the morning, she stopped crying and we stayed out here, quiet, so's not to wake her up. A little while later, my grandma told me to go see how my mother was doing and I went in there. She was on her side, looking at the wall. I touched her face to see if she had a fever and it felt cold, so I covered her more. I told my grandma that my mother felt cold and was sleeping with her mouth and eyes open. My grandma told me to hurry up and take her in there. I took my grandmother in there; you see my grandma is blind. My grandma went in, touched my mother's face, tried to wake her up, but couldn't and she put her ear on mother's chest and listened. My grandma told me to leave the room. I left the room but I left the door open and I saw my grandma turning my mother on her back. She closed my mother's eyes with her fingers and folded her hands on her stomach and then my grandma came out and told my little sister and me that our mother passed away. My little sister, Emma, didn't understand what that meant and my grandma explained to my sister that our mother went to Heaven. My little sister started to cry. She wanted to go to see my mother but my grandma and me held her back from going in. Then, in a little while, my father came home." The little girl's words trickled from her mouth in a such a singularly heartbreaking way that Erik, being much affected by that little girl's recital of the worst thing that could happened to any little girl, just stared at her for the longest time and she, either embarrassed, sad or afraid, never returned his glance. Erik let out a deep sigh, stood up and looked at Morgan, who was standing there, desperately trying to hold back the pouring of tears that lingered in his eyes.

"Where were you last night?" asked Erik softly.

Morgan, instead of giving an answer, sighed first and then he said, "One year ago.."

"I don't care and I'm not interested in one year or one month ago."

"My daddy was in jail when my mother passed away. He was in jail for one year, he was just let out a few hours ago and he came straight home and found my mother dead. I told you that," interrupted the little girl, with more courage than before on hearing Erik raise his voice to her father and, thinking with her little head, the shouting was unfair. She came to his aid, as often little girls do for their fathers.

At the conclusion of the child's address, which sounded like a grown woman's scorn, Erik, not knowing which of the two, father or daughter, to direct his apology to, scratched his temple lightly, nodded benignly to Michelle and turned to Morgan.

"Why were you in jail Mr. Dante?"

Morgan had many reasons to shed tears though had held them back in the corners of his eyes, but his daughter's short speech in his defense pushed him over the edge; the gates broke open, the tears came down and Erik waited, in gloominess and silence, until Morgan was finished venting the sorrow Erik was so familiar with.

"One year ago, I went into town and stopped in a restaurant looking for work." there he stopped to wipe some tears, "I had worked in that place before. I'm a cook. I worked for Linda Lynn, the lady who owns the restaurant. I had quit Linda Lynn's place and I got a job in another place in another town that paid better. It didn't work out with that place, so I went back to Linda Lynn to get my job back. She saw me standing there; she looked but didn't come over, pretending to be busy. Her son, who I knew, went to the register and took a twenty-dollar bill. He saw her looking at him when he took the money. He panicked and ran out but on his way, he stuck the money into my jacket pocket. I did nothing. I just stood there waiting for her to come over. Three minutes later the police arrived. They searched me, found the money and too me to jail. Two days later I appeared in front of the judge who listened to my story, then he listened to her and her son's stories, which were not true. He believed them and didn't believe me. It was a first offence and the judge gave me a whole year. I just got home a few hours ago, after spending eleven months and six days in prison."

"Why did she call the police for a lousy twenty dollar bill?" asked Erik.

"She was still angry for me leaving her, but she never thought the judge would send me up for that long. She told everybody afterwards that she was very sorry," said Morgan.

"I see."

"Anyway, I came back and found my wife dead and I have no money to bury her. What kind of a man am I, Mr. Karas? My wife took care of my family better than I did."

"Stop blaming yourself, son, it ain't your fault; you did good before they took you away," said the grandma. "Please son, think of your daughters; they need you now more than ever."

It was a heart-tugging spectacle to see the blind woman, eagerly but calmly, by affection and entreaty, attempting to sooth her son's pain, unable to see his face, only feeling his torture.

"How is this lady related to you?" asked Erik, pointing at the lady.

"She's my mother," replied Morgan.

"She's my grandma. Aren't you grandma?" said the little girl, Emma, throwing her arms around her grandma and caressing her face.

"Yes, honey, I am your grandma."

Erik turned, looked at the clock on the wall and saw that it was twelve thirty.

"I must go. What was you wife's name?"

"Louisettte," said Morgan, feebly.

"That's a very pretty name. Is there a town near here?"

"Yes, there's a small town, a couple miles down the road, called Choctawville."

"I'll be back later, " said Erik, nodding good-by at everyone and bowing to the old lady, before heading for the door. He paused at the door, turned slowly and looked at Morgan. "Now I know who 'they' are," said Erik, thrusting his hand outwards to tap his fingers with his thumb, "the president, the vice-president, the senators, the congressmen and all the other politicians who allowed the lawyers, the judges and the doctors to get away with these things." He paused, looked away then turned back again to address Morgan.

"Allow me to speak with you, Morgan! Out here!' said Erik, walking out hastily.

Morgan went outside where Erik was waiting.

"We will give your wife a proper burial. Where do you want her to be buried?"

"Heaven's Gate Cemetery, just outside New Orleans, that's where her mother and father are buried," stated Morgan, without the slightest hesitation.

"Done," said Erik, firmly.

"Are there many men like you out there Mr. Karas?" asked Morgan, shaking Erik's right hand with both of his.
"I don't know, but I'm going to find out soon," said Erik. He then left hastily.

Morgan stood looking until Erik disappeared beyond the bridge, then turned and went back into his house. With his bundle on his back, Erik walked in the direction of the town.

CHAPTER TWO

Erik teams up with Peddler

The June sun was high on the horizon and the silence pure. He heard birds singing their midday songs, the cicada's call, the lonely dove's coo, the woodpecker's knock. Rippling water hastened his footsteps as he tripped along the riverbank on a dirt road. After a while the river and Erik decided to go their separate ways. He hurried up a hill and sped down the other side. Emerging from a stand of trees, he came in front of a large church at the edge of a sleepy town sprinkled with several homes, those having a quiet and secluded appearance, all detached from each other and separated by green well-cared for yards. Anyone being tired and busy with his own thoughts probably would not have taken notice of the church, but Erik did. He stopped and gazed at the old forgotten church and its surroundings. The sky was bright and pleasant and all the living things around seemed to be flourishing. The church's walls were broken in many places and huge clusters of ivy climbed up, over and upon the jagged and pointed corners, trembling in every breath of wind. Some bushes and trees leaned mournfully on the walls, as if trying to hide that God-forsaken place from being embarrassed or disparaged by the passer-by. The roof, leaders and gutters, kicked, punched and whipped by the many winds and rains through the years, seemed to be hanging on only by their nails, though were still devoted to their mission. The steeple where the church bell once hung, although crumbling now, still stood as a symbol of its proud past, might and strength. Going back in time, the beholder could imagine the bell ringing and flocks of people, colorfully dressed, laden with good and plentiful food, strolling along the dirt roads, pouring in from every direction, headed for the happy feasts and revelries at that center of small town life.

Erik continued down the paved road, without seeing or hearing a human soul, a horse, a cow or even a dog, as one might have expected. He felt better once he turned the sharp curve in the road and saw a ***Cafe-Restaurant*** sign on the sidewall of a small, wooden, free-standing structure, surrounded by a number of parked cars and a blue station wagon.

Erik walked up the two front steps of the café, opened the wooden screen door and stepped in. The front of the establishment was empty; its principal features were the fresh sand and dirt on the floor that had been carried in on the customers' shoes and boots, the stale odor of tobacco and smoke coming from cigars and pipes. The rest of the place, towards the back, was crowded with several tables, round and square, and chairs of different colors and styles. Some of those tables, in the middle of the parlor, were covered with table-cloths of different ages and dates of washing, arranged to look as much related as circumstances would allow. On those tables were laid enough knives, forks and spoons for each surrounding chair. On the left was a long counter with stationery short stools. Cajun music was heard playing through a pair of old loud speakers.

Behind the counter and close to the wall, on the left, was a huge black potbellied stove, with no fire, encircled by a bunch of tough and curious-looking fellows. One was a slim and rather strong looking man in rust stained jeans and a flannel shirt; another was a stout, burly person, dressed in the same apparel. There were several who looked like they were related to one another by blood, deeds or creed. They were just there, loitering around the stove, some tapping to the rhythm of the music, some drinking coffee from large brown mugs and some, with their hands behind them, now and then with anxious countenance, whispering something in the ears of the others who would break into a smile or laughter while others would only shake their heads mournfully.

Erik drew himself into an obscure corner, took a chair and looked curiously around the place and its occupants. The longer he looked the more curious he became, as he wondered what profession these loungers could belong to. There was a middle-aged man standing near the pot-bellied stove, holding a long heavy crowbar, keeping time with the rhythm of the music by striking the base plate of the stove with that four-foot bar just a few inches from his sandals; it was an undisputable miracle that the man had the same number of toes he was born with.

Another of those loungers was a young man, barely twenty-one, holding a beer bottle in one hand, a paper cup in the other, a cigar in his mouth and, judging from his dried and grayish coloration, he had devoted the most recent years of his life to drinking and smoking.

On the opposite side of room, away from the loungers, stood a coarse vulgar young man, in his early thirties with a sallow face and harsh voice, displaying a freedom of speech normally exercised only among the lowest classes. He was playing pool with another man and on his every fruitless attempt at sinking a ball in the proper pocket and at his every failure to hit the cue ball squarely, he would launch into a dissertation aimed at the table, calling it crooked, lopsided and other accusations that seemed to establish him, in the opinion of all around, as a most excellent and possibly the best player in the whole artful mysterious game, blaming the table and the owner of that establishment for allowing such a crooked table to sit in the middle of the floor, deceiving all who played on it.

Behind the counter was a beautiful young girl, not more then twenty-two, speaking with an air of confidence, to one of the three customers who chose to sit at the counter rather then the tables. Once in a while, during her conversation, she would throw a glance Erik's way, acknowledging his arrival. Once her chat was finished, she went to Erik, placed a menu before him graciously, followed it with a courteous smile and the words 'good afternoon,' then planted her feet on the floor, her blue eyes on him, a pencil in her right hand, an order book in the left and without altering her smile, waited to take his order. While this was happening, the vulgar man came over; he had the appearance of either being a bankrupt farmer or an out-of-work hired hand.

"Mary Lou!" he called loudly, "Let me have a bottle of beer, a piece of paper and a pen. I'm going to write my father a letter and I need a drink, so as to give it to the old boy straight, with the right words that'll tell him just how much I hate him and his new wife."

"Leroy! Go away for a moment! I'm taking an order? Can't you see? Besides, you already had enough to drink."

"Mary Lou! What I have to do can't wait. That guy can wait; he has nowhere to go. Do you Mister?" trickled the words from his mouth as he looked intently at Erik on the last part of his statement. Erik, feeling disgusted with the dialogue, as well as with the air and manner of that man, was about to suggest the waitress take the time to accommodate him, when three men noisily entered the café. Everyone's attention was cast upon the newcomers, more particularly on one of the three who was a light skinned black man, about sixty-five years of age, who everyone called Peddler. The one they called Peddler wore dusty old pants and a threadbare coat, yet carried himself with a genuine air of importance and was received by the loungers in a likewise manner. The loungers, most of whom were obviously farmers and his customers, received him in a celebrating manner, yelling requests for items from barbed wire to plow blades. It appeared, however, that their orders were not about to be filled as speedily as they would have it, because the peddler asked to be excused for a little while so he could have a late lunch. Shaking some hands and patting some backs, the peddler walked to and sat at the furthest end of the counter, on the last stool, far from the loungers but near Erik.

"Come on, Leroy," said Mary Lou, taking advantage of the situation, "Sir, I'm sorry, would you mind if I go for a moment to tend to him? I'll be right back. Let me take care of him."

Erik politely agreed to her request with a grin on his face and a nod of his head.

It was not very long before Mary Lou returned to Erik. He then, without looking up at her, placed his order and handed back the menu; the waitress rushed into the kitchen that was in back of the counter.

It did not escape Erik's attention that a large, full bearded man, wearing a brown straw hat, who he previously observed slinking about the potbellied stove, crossed over, got behind the peddler and remained stationary, staring at the back of his head. Erik saw something suspicious in the big man's visit. The man proceeded to tap the peddler on the back.

"Please, leave me alone, I want to eat in peace" said the peddler loudly, in reply to that tapping, without looking back. At that moment the waitress placed a basket of thick brown bread in front of the peddler.

"Do you want to bring me some of that blackened redfish? And have the cook rush it, I'm operating under some time strains," said the peddler, touching Mary Lou's arm gently.

Mary Lou, knowing that there was no time to waste, cast a vacant look at the bearded man, nodded at the peddler and left for the kitchen.

"You took my seat," yelled the bearded man, suddenly.

The entire café became silent, all eyes and ears turned in the direction from where those words had come, all the numerous dialogues, which had been passing between those loungers, stopped. Erik's full attention drawn to that scene of the peddler sitting and the large man standing behind him.

The peddler turned and looked up at the large man and without any malice, anger or bewilderment showing on his face, only a fake grin, he stood up and moved away a couple of stools, taking his bread basket with him, then sat down and stared ahead, as though nothing had taken place.

Erik pinned his eyes on the bearded man who sat down on the peddler's seat and was beginning to rock back and forth vigorously.

"Hey, nigger, you broke my seat," shouted the man, looking at the peddler who remained calm, still showing no evidence of ill feelings towards his abuser.

All the farmers, the loungers and the rest of the idling souls moved languidly closer to that villain and his prey. All those eyes stared but revealed nothing more than watchfulness.

Erik came to his feet slowly and vigilantly, still holding his eyes on the large man. The man, as if impregnated with another burst of revelation, apparently striving to show the others his boldness and courage, and liking the sound of his own voice and the contents of his first statement repeated it again, louder, "Hey, nigger, I said you broke my seat." Saying this, he turned around, gazed about and looked for applause or other approval from the spectators.

Peddler turned and faced the bearded man with perfect composure.

"I want that seat. Do you hear me, boy?" screamed the bearded man, standing up slowly and going to where the peddler was sitting. He stood again behind him as he had done before.

The peddler turned and looked firmly in his eyes.

"I want your seat. Don't you have no respect for the white man no more?" uttered the large man, shaking the peddler and his seat violently.

"Do you hear me, boy? For two cents I'd break your ass."

At that time a coin flew over, landed and bounced on the counter; it was accompanied by Erik's voice, "here's a quarter, keep the change, blubber mouth."

Erik shoved a small table to the side and with the speed of a rattlesnake and hissing like one, he planted himself in front of the bearded man.

The bearded man, seeing the fury in Erik's eyes and feeling his ruthlessness, backed off and stationed himself in the middle of the floor.

"Who are you, Mister?" he asked.

"I'll let you know who I am before I'm done with you," replied the indignant stranger, moving carefully and slowly towards the bearded man. "I'll teach you some manners that you should have learned a long time ago," continued Erik, his eyes nailed on the villain.

"I've done nothing to you, Mister. What do you want from me?"

"I want you to sit on the seat you said was broken"

"Okay, okay," said the bearded man, backing away with his hands half way up to indicate his surrender. The man reached the seat and sat with his back to Erik, in the position the position the peddler had been before.

"Turn around and face me, blubber mouth!" ordered Erik, in a low voice, clenching his teeth and standing behind him.

The man spun around without delay or consideration and looked at Erik with fear in his eyes.

"What do you want from me?" he asked, gutlessly.

"Take your hat off when you speak to me! Don't you have any respect for a white man any more?" With this, Erik, in a dexterous manner, knocked the bearded man's hat to the other side of the room.

The bearded man reached up quickly and touched his head with both hands, as if to check if his head was still there or had gone with his hat.

"I see you have a gun," said the bearded man, in a broken voice.

"Do you want it?" asked Erik, taking it out to show it to the man.

Sounds of astonishment came from the crowed, on seeing Erik hand the gun to the villain.

The man looked at the gun briefly, turned around, looked away and said loudly, "I don't know how to shoot a pistol, I'm up from the north. We don't have guns up there. I'm a man of peace,"

Hearing that, the farmers, the loungers and anyone else who had gone there to eat, drink or to play burst into loud laughter.

"Why are you laughing? I am from up north, North Carolina," shouted the bearded man, looking at the crowd, while another burst of laughter filled the café.

At that moment, someone brought back his hat and handed to him. The bearded man looked at it, thinking if he were to put it back on his head, it would be knocked off again, he placed it on the counter.

"You know how to shoot your mouth off though, don't you?"

"That I know how to do well, but only when I'm drinking. Today I'm drinking," said the man grabbing his hat and putting on; he looked at Erik in defiance.

"Kill me if you like. Go ahead, big man with a gun, kill me! You'd like to, but you don't dare," exclaimed the bearded man, tempting fate.

"No, I won't kill you. You're not worth the trouble, I'd rather teach you some manners," said Erik, as he placed his pistol back in its holster and prepared for a fight. Then Peddler called out loudly

"Leave him alone, stranger! Just let him be!"

"Thank you, Peddler" uttered the big man, benevolently.

"Okay, Mr. Jonas. Are you okay?" asked the peddler, from his seat.

Erik stepped back a few paces, staring at the bearded man, bewildered, then remembered Morgan's high opinion of Jonas' humane side and the little girl's 'smells like beer' complaint.

Jonas turned away from Erik's gaze and, placing his head on the counter, seemed as if he were going to sleep. Several of the spectators came to move him to a comfortable place, among them was the young man, the one Erik observed earlier holding a beer in his hand and a cigar in his mouth; while helping the others to remove Jonas, he studied Erik with a distorted face and mumbled some insults and perhaps threats. Erik, who chose to ignore him, having had enough excitement for one day, just walked over to where Peddler was sitting.

"Join me at my table!" said Erik, in an imperious tone. Turning around sharply he returned to his table, looked back to see Peddler unmoved but staring at him with curious eyes. Erik raised his eyebrows and imparted a demanding look on the black man that produced the intended effect. Peddler, right after that look, picked up his breadbasket, strolled slowly and sat across from Erik.

"You must be very proud of yourself for allowing me to make an ass out of myself," said Erik, softly.

Peddler said nothing; he only occupied himself with the deliberate buttering of his bread, as Erik stared at him, waiting for an answer.

"What are you looking at? Am I supposed to thank you for thinking you saved my hide?" asked the peddler.

"No, I just want to know if you're proud of yourself."

"Yes. I'm proud of many things, first I am proud of the color of my skin..."

"Just don't wash it off," interrupted Erik.

"It doesn't wash off and it doesn't rub off!" returned Peddler, "sometimes some white rubs off on me. Please understand that doesn't make me Uncle Tom," continued the peddler, pausing his buttering efforts.

"Are you going to perspire for no good reason? Perspiring for no good reason is no good for you," said Erik, with a grin.

Peddler looked down for a long moment, thoughtfully, and asked, "Are you in the habit of fighting other people's battles?"

"No! I was defending the law of 'disturbing the peace' it was my peace, my peace of mind."

"I detect that you speak with an accent. Do you think with one too?" cajoled Peddler, grinning.

"I never think," returned Erik, abruptly.

"That makes sense. Is that why you're so touchy?"

"Not touchy, spirited."

"Pulling a gun on some drunken bastard, you call that spirited?"

"I was defending the law, that takes a gun."

"Are you a policeman?"

"I have citizen's rights."

"In what country?"

"Louisiana." returned Erik.

"No, Louisiana used to be French, but now it's American, or you haven't heard?"

"No!" said Erik with pretence, covering his mouth with his hand, as often embarrassed people do.

"Yes!"

"What are they going to think of next," stated Erik, solemnly.

"Next thing we're going to hear, would be freeing of the slaves," said Peddler.

"I think they did that already, up north," replied Erik, in a casual tone.

"Oh, yeah?"

"Yes, haven't they heard that down here?" asked Erik.

"No, man, no."

"Well, they say the southerners are a little slow in learning."

"No, we're not. We only learn what we want to down here," remarked Peddler.

"I know one thing, Mr. Jonas hasn't learned it," said Erik. "Talking about Mr. Jonas, I didn't know he was drunk."

"That's right. He can walk and talk as if he didn't have a drink, but he's loaded. And when he's loaded he picks on anybody, Indians, Cajuns, Creoles, even Colored People, just like he did with me," said Peddler.

"What I can't understand is why you allowed me to go on?" asked Erik.

"Why?"

"Yes. Why?" replied Erik.

"Two reasons. First, I wanted him off my back; second, I was hoping that somebody would teach him a lesson, but you became too rough with the guy. He's not a bad guy when he's not drinking. The others put him outside in his station wagon to sleep it off."

"Station wagon you said?" asked Erik, eagerly.

"That blue station wagon that's parked outside, it's his."

"Good, I'd like you to do me a favor," said Erik, nicely.

"Don't be so nice to me, I'm not used to it. I'd think you were trying to con me."

"Don't say that, Peddler, I saw all the people who were nice to you when you first came in. But as for me, this is the last time I'll be nice to you; I'll even buy you lunch."

"Well, as long as you're buying, let me change my order to something more tasty," said Peddler, turning to locate the waitress who was standing behind the bar and staring ahead without any expression on her face.

"Miss! Do you work here?" asked Peddler.

"No. My father is a millionaire on Long Island and sent me down here for my summer vacation," teased the waitress, as she immediately headed for their table, followed by "I see you two lost souls are in need of my help," on coming closer.

"Did you say lost souls, girl?" asked Peddler, looking at her while she dropped the menus playfully, one by one, with her eyes focused on Erik.

"I guess, I did," she replied.

"Do we look like losers to you, Miss?" asked Peddler.

"No. You look like a pair of winners. One of you beat up on poor Mr. Jonas and the other stood and watched."

"She's nuts," said Peddler, turning to Erik.

"And she is also beautiful," he returned, with his eyes on her.

"Your bodyguard has good taste in women," responded the girl, playfully.

"He also likes to show off. He is the one who went after Mr. big man Jonas, protecting this old colored guy," said Peddler.

"Look I didn't come to your aid because you're a colored man. I'm not here to take over what Abraham Lincoln started. I'm only buying you lunch. Old Abe himself would not have done that for you and as long as I'm buying, I'll order for you, just to show you that my heart is in the right place," announced Erik. He then turned to Mary Lou, "I am going to take the liberty and order fried chicken and watermelon for my new friend. If he doesn't like it, I'll eat it."

"Tell him that he's walking on thin ice. I'm going to take the liberty and order roast goat meat and rice pilaf for this immigrant friend of mine," said Peddler, looking up at Mary Lou.

"Tell my newly acquired friend," stated Erik, "that goat meat with rice pilaf is a Turkish meal and I'm not a Turk, I am Greek. Then tell him, when he understands the first part, that I am not an immigrant, I am imported because I was brought here by my father and mother when I was very young and had no choice."

"He said that goat meat with rice pilaf, is a Turkish meal, "returned Mary Lou, pointing her pencil at Peddler and lifting up her body on her toes with every word she uttered "and he said he is not a Turk, he is Greek, do you understand? And he also said that he's not an immigrant, he's imported."

"Ask him, if he hadn't been brought to America, what would he be in Greece, a shepherd for goats or sheep?" said Peddler, looking at the waitress.

"Never mind that, just bring him his fried chicken and the watermelon," replied Erik.

"Tell him that I know why he ordered fried chicken and water-melon, he thinks those two are colored folks food, but he's wrong. Actually, English kidney pie and Yorkshire pudding are my favorites," remarked Peddler.

"He says that fried chicken..... Oh, to hell with you guys, you heard what he said. But I say the only thing we have of all the stupid things you mentioned is fried chicken"

"No watermelon?" asked Peddler.

"Yes! We have watermelons, in the fields, in back of the restaurant" said Mary Lou, turning to leave, "When you all get hungry, you all can call me, anytime; but don't snap your fingers!"

"You see what you've done?" complained Peddler.

"Me?" protested Erik.

"You started the whole thing, with the fried chicken."

"I was only trying to make you happy. You said you wanted something more tasty," declared Erik.

"I don't know why I am sitting here trying to have lunch with you," said Peddler.

"I know why. First I'm buying and second you like my company."

"From what I've seen up till now, I'm probably the only one who likes your company," responded Peddler, looking around for the waitress.

"I have some friends," said Erik soberly.

"Oh, yeah? How long are they up the river for?"

The odd couple stared at each other for a long moment and then they both burst out in laughter; it was over in a short time.

"Are you going to do me that favor?" asked Erik, seriously.

"I suppose I owe you one, not for fighting my battle with Mr. Jonas... "

"For buying you lunch?"

"No. For knowing what I like to eat." replied Peddler.

"I know, English kidney pie and Yorkshire putting," said Erik.

"Hell, no. Fried chicken and watermelon," returned Peddler, bursting into hearty laughter.

"Let's be serious for a moment, Peddler." said Erik in a normal manner.

"Let's be serious, Curly."

"My name is not Curly, my name is Erik Karas."

"My name is not Peddler, my name is Stephen Spencer, but you can call me Peddler."

"Good. Now, I want you to help me bury a woman," said Erik.

"Shh! Not so loud . You mean to tell me you killed a woman?" whispered Peddler, leaning closer to Erik, before he gazed cautiously around.

"No. I ran into her on the way here."

"With a car or a truck?" asked Peddler, still whispering.

"You don't have to whisper," whispered Erik, with a grin. "Now you got me whispering too. I was walking," said Erik, louder.

"You ran into her while you were walking and she died?'

"Yeah. I was walking pretty fast and I stepped on her."

"Hard to believe. But I believe it. I saw how you jumped over the table going for Mr. Jonas," said Peddler.

"Good. If you believe that, give me a deposit, I'll sell you back the Louisiana Purchase."

"Slow down! Explain to me what happened," said Peddler.

Erik's explanation, having been partially told, was soon concluded, but neither during the course of his story nor afterwards did Peddler make any comment; Erik noticed the trace of sadness on Peddler's face.

"We will do whatever we can," said Peddler, inhaling with a deep sigh, looking around for the waitress, in an attempt to avoid showing the effect the story had on him.

"Thank you, Peddler."

The peddler didn't reply, he gazed at Erik and then withdrew his eyes, searching for the waitress again.

"Just don't take advantage of me!" said Peddler.

"How do you mean that?"

"This is a white man's world," he replied.

"Oh, I see," said Erik, smiling, his face then became serious, "I see you as a person, and if you can see yourself as I see you, we'll be okay," said Erik, casting his eyes on Peddler as if waiting for a comment from him.

"You have some spirit about you. You sound like you have seen something of life," said Peddler.

"Peddler, it's not only what you see of life, it's what you learn."

Peddler looked around and found the place to be deserted. All those good loungers had gone to the aid of Mr. Jonas and, once they had tucked him safely into his station wagon, had gone home to their farms and ranches, leaving him, his new friend Erik, Mary Lou and whoever else was in the kitchen, to amuse themselves.

"Mary Lou!" shouted Peddler, "do you think we're entitled to some service around here, or will we have to come back next week, when things are better?"

That was all Mary Lou needed to hear to set her off to practice her life long dream of becoming a professional actress.

"Do you suppose, Mr. Peddler, that I have nothing better to do but occupy myself with a couple of fellows, lazy and idling fellows, who have nothing else to do but lounge around when they ought to be glad to turn their hands to something that's called work." Suddenly, arresting her rapid torrent of speech, she addressed Erik alone. "And you, sir, a new face and late comer for lunch in the bargain, you sit there, amusing yourself while I toil."

"Poor guy didn't say nothing and you're picking on him," said Peddler.

"You, sir," continued Mary Lou, turning to Peddler, " you should confine yourself to selling shovels and chicken wire from your oversized milk truck to your Cajun friends and you should not interfere in other people's business; there may be some person here who's willing and able to make you to do just that."

"Stop talking like a nagging wife!" mumbled Peddler.

"What did you call me, sir? Will you repeat what you called me?" exclaimed Mary Lou, with the overplayed expression of a silent movie star.

"I called you a nagging wife," returned Peddler, turning his head away from her and winking at Erik.

"Yes, of course you did," said Mary Lou, backing gradually towards the kitchen door while raising her voice to its loudest pitch for the owner of the place to hear.

"Yes, of course you did!" she continued in the same loud tone, "Everybody knows that they can insult me while my boss is sleeping in the back. If I had a husband, he wouldn't allow his wife to be treated like this and be called a nag by a couple of idling men. My husband would come out and do to the city sleeker, what he almost did to poor Mr. Jonas, but it would be his head instead of his hat," said Mary Lou, with her ear nailed to the door, keenly listening for a response from inside the kitchen

"Her boss is madly in love with her. The only time he comes out is when he thinks she's being abused by the customers," whispered Peddler to Erik.

"My husband wouldn't be afraid, he wouldn't be a yellow bellied chicken." She paused again to listen if the repetition of her grievances had affected her boss. Finding that it had not been successful, she proceeded with a burst of sobs, that grew to a fit of weeping interspersed with moaning, until the door opened and her boss, a small man with a ferocious look on his face, holding a rolling pin firmly in his hand, came to her aid.

"Who's bothering you, Mary Lou," asked the boss, trying to lower his high-pitched voice, so as to sound tough.

"Now Barney, nobody did nothing to her," pleaded Peddler, coming to his feet.

"Was it Peddler, Mary Lou?" asked the little fellow.

Before Mary Lou had the chance to respond, Peddler grabbed Erik and pulled him up to a standing position.

"Now Barney, there are two of us and six more waiting outside who'd fight on our side and give their lives for us; you ain't gonna kill us all, are you, Barney?"

"Kill them, Barney, kill all of them!" shouted Mary Lou, mimicking the act of a woman in pain, at the same time she turned to Erik and winked at him.

Barney seemed frightened at the thought of facing two men, let alone killing anyone. He would probably have been just as frightened if he had been holding a machine gun in his hands.

"No one shall die!" yelled Peddler. "I will apologize to you, Lady Mary Lou, for referring to you as a 'nagging wife.' You have never been a wife, nor will you ever be one, but you will always be the lady of the house. Accept my apologies my Lady," concluded Peddler, with a deep bow.

"You are forgiven, my humble servant," returned Mary Lou, and then, turning to Barney,

"let them live, my Lord, let the lost souls live," appealed Mary Lou, planting herself in front of Barney who stood there, now released from fear and filled with pride and power.

"If you know what's good for you, Peddler..." threatened the little man, shaking the dough roller at Peddler.

"Oh, I know, that rolling pin can create a lot of damage on somebody's head, particularly on a colored man's, which by nature is not as hard as a white man's," stated Peddler in an appealing manner.

The little man stood for a moment, preened with satisfaction, turned abruptly, pushed Mary Lou, who was clinging on him, aside and went into the kitchen. The trio, after a short time, making certain that Barney was out of sight and sound, burst into hearty laughter.

"Mary Lou!" shouted Peddler, "we're going to celebrate, my new friend and I. Bring us two orders of fried chicken, mashed potatoes and gravy."

"Make it grits for me, instead of the mashed potatoes," said Erik, sitting down, grinning.

"Grits?" asked Peddler, surprised and amused.

"I'm trying hard to be one of you southerners. Like they say, 'when in Rome do as the Romans do',"

"Don't start that again!" said Peddler.

"I told you, I will only be nice to you just once," returned Erik, with a serious look.

The food arrived after a little while and was happily displayed before them as they attacked their plates with hungry eyes, idling ears, rushing hands and busy forks. Peddler paused for a moment to pour enough black pepper on his chicken to set any half dozen men with ordinary noses off onto a sneezing fit for seventeen hours.

CHAPTER THREE

The funeral and Erik's eulogy

Two days later, in the morning, just as the clocks of New Orleans were striking nine, outside the city, in a cemetery, the birds, for their own pride, peace and pleasure, sang their morning songs in the trees and bushes around and above, blissfully ignorant of death or the end of life. It was a fine morning; the hedges, trees, meadows and moorland offered every eye their ever-varying shades of deep rich green, blanketed by a cloudless sky. The graves, crowded with flowers of a million shapes and colors, sparkled in the heavy dew, and the birds' singing, the insects' humming, the butterflies' playful plummeting from plant to plant, the light wind caressing the leaves of the trees and the green blades of the grass, impressed a stamp of life onto that land of the dead. In the middle of that nature's celebration of life lay Louisette, in a wooden coffin next to an open grave, surrounded by her two bewildered little girls, her sorrow stricken husband and his mother, Mr. Jonas and his wife Millie, four or five neighbors, Peddler and Erik.

Sorrow and despair were depicted on every face and whether sorrow lived under the ceiling of the heart or beneath the roof of the mind, it shrouded all hopes and happiness, particularly those of the husband, who looked as if the steel teeth of sorrow had gnawed him down to skin and bones. Having lost all that was dear to him, tears rolled down from his eyes and landed on his quivering lips.

Erik cleared his throat to let everybody know he was about to utter some ceremonial words of comfort, when his eyes caught another burial taking place a few hundred feet away. He softly asked to be excused for a moment, left abruptly and headed for that burial.

He reached the other service at precisely the moment the minister had finished his eulogy for the dead. Erik approached the minister, whispered something into his ear and all the gathered eyes fell upon him. The minister nodded in assent, the musicians raised their instruments to their lips but the minister raised his hands in a gesture for them not to start.

He walked a few paces from Erik, turned to the crowd and said, "My dear friends, I have just been told a sad story of an unfortunate young woman, named Louisette. I would like to ask you to look beyond your own loss to the grief of another. I want you to reach out to her husband and the two little girls she left behind. Will you come with me to say a prayer for her?"

The minister raised his head and scanned the mourners and upon realizing that they were ready and willing to abide by his request, he headed, with Erik by his side, for Louisette's grave, followed close behind by the forty or so mourners and musicians. The good minister stationed himself near the grave, the musicians took their respective places while the rest of the people, who had come to witness a burial and say a prayer, as the minister had requested, gathered around and stood still by the grave. A dead silence soaked everything around the burial site. The minister moved one step towards the grave and one pace ahead of Erik. He opened his book, read a four-minute eulogy in a mournful style and when he finished, turned and asked Erik if he had anything to add.

"Yes I do, Reverend," answered Erik, softly stepping next to him. "Do you have any Bibles?" asked Erik of Peddler, in a very low voice.

"Yes I do. I've got cases of them, they're my best sellers in the colored folks sections," whispered Peddler.

"Please bring me one," said Erik, in the same whispering manner.

Peddler hurriedly headed for his truck while Erik cleared his throat one more time, looked first at the little girls, then at Morgan and then surveyed the crowd of gloomy faces.

"My dear friends, we have gathered here today to bury our beloved sister, wife and mother, Louisette," began Erik, and at that particular moment, Peddler placed a box of Bibles in front of him; the whole scene seemed as if it were planned and rehearsed.

"My friends, our sister, daughter, mother and wife, Louisette Dante died, but she is not dead. God has decided to take the body that Louisette's soul occupied, while alive here on earth, her soul, my friends, will be suspended while waiting for the judgment day. God has taken her away at a tender age. She is leaving behind two young daughters. It seems to me unfair to have to grow up without a mother or a father. As you can tell, I have lived on this earth many years and my eyes have witnessed many human tragedies and I have asked God many times, sometimes in anger, if He really believed that His people, especially the young people, were made out of stone in order to bear so many troubles and abuses."

Erik, bent his gaze downwards in front of him and seeing the box of the Bibles, allowed his mind to enter another dimension; he turned and looked at Peddler as if to congratulate him for an unexpected job well done, picked up a brand new Bible and held it carefully and respectfully with his left hand against his chest. "God never gave me an answer. But he pointed me to read His Bible," declared Erik, stretching his hand outwards holding the Christian text. "The answer to all life is written in this book. This man here," said Erik, pointing at Peddler with his hand and looking urgingly into his eyes, "will pass out the Bibles and you take this Holy Book home and read it, mark it, bend it, and carry it with you, wherever you go. You may make a small donation. I assure you the money will go to one who needs it and not to a rich person."

Peddler heard the message, understood and loved its meaning, rushed into the crowd and began, in haste, passing out the Bibles and collecting donations that he graciously accepted, returning many cordial words of thankfulness and respectful bows.

"Let us open the casket to view, for one last time, the young lady," said Erik, gesturing to Jonas and another man to proceed with opening the wooden coffin.

As the boards were lifted, sounds of astonishment were heard rising from the crowd on seeing such a beautiful young lady in the state of eternal rest.

"She looks like one of the few of nature's faces, that when stricken with death, can continue to gladden the beholder with their beauty," declared Erik, his eyes directed on the face of Louisette. "Here she lies, peaceful and sad, as if she understands that those who knew her, in happy times and troubled times, in childhood and as an adult, will come to kneel at the side of her coffin to mourn her and sense the spirit that was sent down to claim her. Let us get down on our knees and pray."

The entire crowd, without any obvious hesitation or even a slight consideration, knelt and bent their heads downward.

"Lord," voiced Erik, "please, understand that none of us are ready to be judged. When the time comes for her to be judged, please take into consideration her sufferings while here on earth. Please, Lord, have one of your angels watch and keep her company; she will be missing her two young daughters, her husband, Morgan and the rest of her family and friends. We know, Lord, she is your child, like we're all your children; please forgive her like a father. I know you had your reasons for claiming her so early in her life, find a reason to make her comfortable, as I know you will show mercy for her little girls and her husband, so they can live without her, as if she will always be there for them."

Erik, finishing his brief eulogy, came to his feet and gestured the others to do the same.

"Ladies and gentlemen, the moment we are born we are born with three fates; one fate, according to the ancient Greeks, is named Clotho, who spins the thread of life, one is named Lachesis, who measures it and the last, Atropos, cuts that thread of life. We are born with many designs and the most important of them all is that we know one day we all must die.

After death we will go somewhere and we will be judged for all we have done on this earth. That is why we all have to be prepared, not only to die, but also to be judged. The Bible will guide us not only to live here on earth, in peace, but also to be ready to be judged on Judgment day. I stand here before you and I must tell you, the most important victory is when we defeat ourselves. I must confess to you that many times, in my days of living, feelings waged war within my breast, as if someone evil inserted unhealthy ideas, unkind thoughts and bad habits, but I have overcome them, because I opened the Bible and I found how; I found the way, His way.

The Bible is not going to tell you how to create great wealth and accumulate a lot of riches, so you can live the life of luxury, but the Bible will teach you to live comfortably and happily with what you have and that is better than living in luxury. It is not a sin to be rich, but it is a sin when you deprive others of a safe and comfortable living so you can live in luxury. It is a sin when you look down upon others for not having what you have; it is a sin when you are eating and others around you are starving and you do nothing to help them. There are many sins that we commit everyday, and we will be judged and are being judged everyday, whether we know or not on, first on our sins and then on our good deeds. It has scientifically been proven that the ones who help other people live longer. Why? Why does this happen? Because, ladies and gentlemen, God needs you to help him help others. If you give something to the man who is passing out the Holy Books, you'll go home and I know you'll feel better and feeling better, my friends, you'll feel healthier. You will feel better, knowing you have helped someone in need."

Erik stopped for a moment, took out his white handkerchief, wiped his face and continued with a new tone of voice.

"There was a king, of a small kingdom in Greece, at the dawn of civilization, who, seated on top of his throne, in full council, rose in the exuberance of his feelings and commanded his troops to go out and take from his subjects, the best wines, the best fruits and all the lambs and pigs for the celebration of his son's engagement to a beautiful princess from another kingdom. Nothing was heard in the entire royal palace for three days and three nights, except the sounds of feasting and revelry, and his poor subjects stood outside, waiting for some food to be thrown their way. The King laughed and danced, thinking the best was yet to come for him and his royal family. Some days after that royal triumph, bad news hit the Kingdom— the illustrious Prince became afflicted with leprosy on his way back from visiting his fiancée, the beautiful Princess. You will read this in the Bible, 'Give and you shall receive' That also means, 'take and you will pay back' The ancient Greeks had a saying very much related to taking, 'Ta kakvV sunagvmena eiV kakaV apoqhkaV' which means, 'The ill-gathered will be ill-spent'," Erik turned his face about in all directions, gazing at the people for a moment, "So, God judges while we are still here on earth, as He does in Heaven. God bless you, my friends, and may He stay with you."

CHAPTER FOUR

Erik and Peddler, a friendship develops

"Mr. Erik Karas did a nice job with the prayer," said Jonas, who was driving the station wagon down a two-lane road, with his wife sitting next to him and the Dante family in the back.

"He is probably some kind of a preacher," said Millie, Jonas' wife, "don't you agree Morgan?"

"He has to be, not only for the way he spoke but for what he did for Louisette," replied Morgan, as down the road the wagon went.

The two little girls sat quietly, one on her grandma's lap and the other between the grandma and her father, Morgan. Their father felt as if he were in a tunnel, holding a small lantern that only threw a little light on the path immediately ahead but had the effect of rendering the other surrounding objects rather dark and unrecognizable images; it seemed, as he sat there looking straight ahead with traces of tears on his face, that he had no plan for what he was going to do next.

"Morgan, we will go to my house to get something to eat. Millie has invited the rest of the neighbors there," said Jonas.

"I want to go home to see mommy," cried the little girl, Emma, who was sitting on her blind grandma's lap.

"Honey! Mommy is in Heaven with the rest of the Angels," said the grandmother, caressing the little girl's hair.

"Then I want to go to Heaven, too," murmured the little girl.

"Heaven is far away, Emma," said the other little girl, Michelle.

The grandmother continued caressing Emma's hair and face, imparting a variety of words, trying to sooth the little girl's visible pain and anxiety.

"Jonas, that story about the leper," said Morgan, "was that to instill the fear of God in us so we behave, is that the way you understood it?"

Before Jonas could reply, the low sound of a car horn was heard; Peddler's milk truck pulled along side Jonas' wagon and reduced its speed to stay abreast of it.

"Do you people want to go with us for something to eat?" yelled Peddler, putting his head out of the window.

"No thank you, Peddler, we are going to my house, we have some other neighbors joining us," yelled back Jonas, "you and the preacher are welcome to come."

"Did you hear that? He called you a preacher," said Peddler to Erik, as he pulled his head in, and Erik, who was driving the truck, did not look, did not speak, but only drove on with an indifferent countenance.

"Would you like to join them?" asked Peddler.

"No. Let's go see Mary Lou, " said Erik, grinning, as he stepped on the gas.

"The driver has to go to see someone, it's important," yelled Peddler, waving his hand in the air to say good-by.

"I said that he called you a preacher, did you hear me?" asked Peddler, looking at Erik intently.

"That's nice," returned Erik, almost sarcastically.

"You have nothing else to say?"

"Nothing!" replied Erik, still looking ahead with an indifferent look on his face.

"Boy! I wish I had somebody call me a preacher," said Peddler, as if he were making a wish.

"Okay! Preacher!" remarked Erik, with a grin.

"I don't want anybody to call me what I haven't earned."

"That makes sense. We'll go find another funeral and you can step up there and do what I did."

"Curly, I don't have the flair or nerve to do that. You have a calm expression of eloquence, either you been trained or it's a natural gift from your birth. I don't have that," reflected Peddler, looking away and using hand gestures to describe his feeling, "where did you learn to give a short and sweet eulogy like that?"

asked Peddler, turning and looking at Erik.

"It wasn't a eulogy, Peddler, it was a speech of persuasion."

"Okay. A speech of persuasion; did you go to school for that sort of thing?"

"Did I go to school? What kind of stupid question is that?" replied Erik, showing a bit of indignation.

"I'm only trying to find out whether you went to some kind of theological school," said Peddler, hesitantly.

"No! Not a theological school," responded Erik with a laugh, "I went to a girl's school."

"Girls school?" exclaimed Peddler with astonishment, "You must be pulling my leg."

"No!" returned Erik, still laughing, "I don't pull legs, I only caress them if they are girls' legs and I kick them if they're men's legs."

"Why a girls' school? Couldn't you find something with boys and girls together?" asked Peddler, still astonished. "I have never met a man who said he went to an all girls' school, unless of course, he is one of those who's a boy that wants to be a girl."

"Homosexuals, you mean."

"Yeah, something like that."

"Do you think that I am a homosexual?" asked Erik, for the first time looking straight at Peddler.

"No! I don't think that because I saw how you looked at Mary Lou."

"Everything I've learned in life, I learned from women. I even learned the English language from girls, from going out with them, " exclaimed Erik, in a calm tone.

"From women?" exploded Peddler, with a high pitched voice, "they are the most unpredictable creatures on earth and you learned from them?"

"That's where you're wrong." said Erik, when he had time for reflection, "Women are not unpredictable; we men don't know how to figure them out and we don't know how to treat them. Women are like horses. When a horse gets restless, what do you do to calm it down? Do you kick it?" asked Erik. He waited for Peddler to answer.

"I don't know," replied Peddler, timidly, "I guess you pat it."

"Good! That's the way, you soothe it and you talk to the horse.

Even if the horse had no reason to get restless and wild and to start kicking, the horse will eventually settle down. Then you ride it again. You can ride the horse anywhere as long as you pull the reins lightly and you spur its belly gently. But if you jerk its reins and you bloody its belly with your spurs, it won't take you anywhere except to your death, trying to get rid of you."

Erik suddenly began to recollect his past trials and troubles, abandoned his current thoughts and with a melancholy frown on his face, remained silent as if absorbed in his own meditations. He felt that if he closed his eyes for just one minute he would have seen his wife, Susan, and his son, Randy, smiling and waving at him as they stood on the side of the road, waiting for him. He shook his head violently to get rid of that unexplainable and unnatural vision while remnants of past glories that lingered in his heart turned in his head.

Peddler cast an anxious look, from time to time, towards Erik.

"Now that I've learned everything about horses, when am I going to hear about that speech of persuasion?" asked Peddler.

"Hold your horses, Peddler, " said Erik.

"Okay, I'm holding them."

"Do you remember, a couple of days ago when we first met, when you made the comment that the way I came across I must have seen a lot of life?" asked Erik, gloomily.

"I remember, sure I remember. You said that it is not how much you see of life, but the trick is how much you learn," replied Peddler, very quickly.

Erik swiftly turned and faced Peddler, an astonished grin on his face, "You son-of-a-gun, you remembered."

"Of course I remembered, just because I'm a colored peddler, you thought I was stupid?" Erik grinned and then all at once his grin turned sour and he looked at Peddler crossly, "see if you can remember this; you must see yourself as I see you, because if you won't, I won't like the way you see me!" There he paused and looked at Peddler, hard, for a long time, in alternate glances between him and the road. "You will do that now, before you get any older," saying this, Erik turned slowly to look at the road whilst Peddler looked at him, with hungry eyes and greedy ears.

"You're right, Curly, it's a habit," cried Peddler, realizing the intent of the advice was true and sincere, even though it was so sternly delivered.

"A habit can easily be turned into a crutch," said Erik, using the same method of delivery to penetrate Peddler's skull.

Peddler looked ahead with a sullen face, though he was a man of words and had the power of persuasion, he said nothing to excuse or defend himself.

"Let me finish what I was about to say, before I was interrupted," said Erik, after a little while, now with a desperate calmness, as if he had just returned to consciousness, "it is not what you learn in life, it's how you use it." Erik became silent for a long moment, but by the way he ended his sentence, it was obvious he had not finished his thought and Peddler held his eyes on him. "I misused my knowledge," said Erik melancholically.

"How's that?" inquired Peddler, in a normal tone, as if the previous exchange had not taken place.

"Peddler," said Erik, followed by a deep sigh," you are looking at a man who had more opportunities knocking at his door than they're church bells in Rome, and they all rang as many times, sometimes collectively, sometimes separately, but I always answered and opened the wrong door." There he stopped, lit a cigarette and took a long drag, as if he just discovered its flavor, "The bells are still ringing, but my opportunities stopped calling, because there was nobody home. That's sad, Peddler, that's very sad," saying this, he took another healthy puff on his cigarette, "the whole story of my whole life reminds me of the story where the bells rang for days, in a small European kingdom, on the orders of the king, to let his people know that faucets running pure cream and pure honey would be turned on at the palace for three days and nights and that everybody was welcomed to fill their containers. This man heard it, but he rested under the thick shade of a sycamore tree, enjoying himself, thinking he had all the time in the world. He fell asleep and only woke up after the offer was over, then he picked up two pitchers and ran to the palace, got down on his knees and tried to gather with his trembling hands, what was left, on the marble steps. When he almost had them filled, the prince, who standing on the balcony and watching the man struggle with the leftovers, began to laugh loudly. The man heard the sound of laughter coming from above, looked up and saw the prince laughing and holding a large stone, with both hands, directly over the pitchers. The man said nothing, but the prince said sternly,

"You heard the bells ringing, you heard of my father's generosity. You did nothing about it. So go, be gone with you!" With those words the prince dropped the stone and broke both of the man's pitchers. The man walked away sad, sorry and angry with himself and lost himself into the wilderness, not because of his loss of cream and honey, but because he missed the call of the bells. It's been said, the man fled from that spot and plunged into the thick woods, from there he wandered on, night and day, under the burning sun and the cold moon, under the pounding rain and the freezing snow, up the lofty mountains and down the green valleys; eventually he faded away in nature's merciless abyss, leaving no tracks behind.

"Why are you telling me all this?" asked Peddler, as if he were looking to dispute something in Erik's story.

"Why, why! Why is because I like to hear myself talking," returned Erik, in a rather snappish manner.

"That's not it."

"What is it then? Nassos?" asked Erik, loudly.

"Nassos? Who's Nassos?"

"My brother. No matter what I say, he thinks of something else. He also thinks he can predict the future. Can you predict the future too?" asked Erik.

"Sometimes."

"Oh, God!" exclaimed Erik, bending forward and looking through the windshield at Heaven, "did I have to run into another Nassos thousands of miles away?"

"You see? You see?" uttered Peddler, pointing his finger at Erik, "you see, I am not the only one you fight with, you even fight with your own flesh and blood, your brother."

"Bull!"

"That's not bull, that's the truth," returned Peddler.

"What makes you so damn smart? Did your mother have a normal birth, Peddler, when she had you? Hell no! The doctor picked you up and instead of popping your ass, he popped you on the head. That's what probably happened to my brother. You both have warped minds."

"For your information, wise guy, there was no doctor, a midwife delivered me," yelled Peddler.

"Really? Oh, really, Peddler? No doctor?" said Erik with pretentious astonishment.

"No doctor, only a midwife."

"How sad," observed Erik, turning and looking at Peddler, "who in hell do you

think delivered me, Dr. Kildare?" returned Erik, raising his voice on the latter part of his statement.

"You? What doctor delivered you? It wasn't Dr. Kildare, it was Dr. Frankenstein, second thought, I know, it had to be a shepherd. A goat shepherd, that's why you act like a ram."

At that point, Erik, looking at Peddler seriously, for one long moment, burst out in loud laughter.

"Why are you laughing?" asked Peddler.

"I'm laughing because you know shit about goats and sheep. A ram is not a goat, stupid, a ram is a male sheep, a capricorn is a male goat.

Peddler turned his head and rubbed his neck, not knowing how to occupy himself, but with a timid grin on his face said, "what do I know about horses, goats or sheep? I only know about dogs and cats. That's what the civilized people know."

Meanwhile the truck rolled, without slackening, on its journey to where Mary Lou was working.

CHAPTER FIVE

The meeting of the minds

Erik and Peddler sat together, at the same table they had two days earlier, when Erik attacked Jonas in Peddler's defense. While they were waiting for service, they discussed food and prospects and eventually the conversation turned to the sharing of the profit that was realized from selling the Bibles at Louisette's funeral. Peddler reached into his pocket, brought out a roll of money and handed it to Erik.

"This is your share of the profits," said Peddler.

Erik took the money without looking, thinking or considering anything, put it into his shirt pocket and gazed to his left with a vacant look.

"Aren't you going to count it?" asked Peddler, with a serious look on his face.

Erik uttered no response.

"Aren't you going to count it to see if I cheated you?"

Erik stared at Peddler, said nothing, but looked as if he had something on his mind.

"I cheated you," repeated Peddler.

"I know it," said Erik, looking away.

"You know it and you were not about to say anything, as if you don't care?"

"Look, Peddler, you didn't try to cheat me out of greed, you were searching to find out how careful I am and how serious I am about the whole thing. But if you really want to know my thoughts; as long as I'm making a profit from being bad, I don't care if I'm cheated a little," said Erik, looking away as if he didn't wish to elaborate any further on that matter.

"You mean to tell me that you were being bad back there? How were you bad? Please tell me, Curly!" asked Peddler, holding his eyes on Erik.

"Look, what's the difference?" said Erik, turning and looking back a split second, then turning his eyes away again. They were both silent for one long moment.

"Look," said Erik, breaking the silence and turning to Peddler, "I lured those people to witness the burial and when I saw they were an easy target, after I noticed your Bibles, I gave them a sixty-nine dollar speech and I took their money. Does that make me good or bad, Peddler? I used to sell insurance, health and life insurance. I used to go to the people's houses and I used to, with words, back up the ambulance seven times at their front door, before they bought the policy. Was that good or bad?" There he stopped and looked partly to think and partly to read Peddler's mind, "For me it was bad, because," there he began to speak very slowly, "because I didn't believe in what I was doing. Let me tell you something for you to remember. A man becomes a man when he believes in what he is doing and a woman becomes a woman when she does what she believes, what I'm trying to tell you, I wasn't happy then, I felt that I was bad, but I had to do it, to make a living." said Erik, looking around with a grin of relief, "Now, make up your mind, Peddler, do you want me to be good or bad?"

"Didn't you believe in what you said at that burial? You were being bad? I really thought, the way you spoke, you're a man of God," said Peddler, in a most professional voice.

Erik didn't respond; he only took a cigarette, lit it slowly, inhaled deeply and then let the smoke pass out of his lungs without any effort, help or hurry and said the same way, "Peddler I've asked you a question, do you want me to be good or do you want me to be bad?"

"I don't want you to be good, I don't want you to be bad, I just want you to be smart. Let's forget about what is good or what is bad, let's talk about money," said Peddler, after a careful and long consideration.

"Let me tell you about my feelings for money. When I don't have it, it means something, when I do have it means nothing, that's why I spend it so fast." said Erik, in a very cut and dry way.

"Be smart! You don't have to be good and you don't have to be bad, there is something in between," said Peddler.

"What's that, in between?" asked Erik, curiously.

"It's what they call **smart.**"

Erik looked at Peddler a long moment, as if studying the man, "you mean, smarten up? I am sorry, I am not smart enough to smarten up."

"You are very smart."

"I am tired of people telling me that I'm smart," said Erik, interrupting Peddler, "If I am so smart, why don't I have something to show for it?"

"You're a story teller and I'm also a story teller. Maybe I can't paint my stories like you do, but some people understand them. Do you read me, Curly?"

"Loud and clear. Fire when you are ready."

"Now, I'll tell you a story. Two smart executives, from Wall Street, went to Minnesota to go ice fishing. There they were, fishing for three whole days, never caught a damn thing. They felt stupid and disgusted, particularly when they saw a young lad, not too far away from them, catching fish like crazy. They went to see what the young lad was doing so right and they were doing so wrong. They asked that boy to tell them what he was doing right. The boy looked at them and then he reached into his mouth and pulled, out of his mouth, a live warm and he said, with a mouth full of them, 'you've got to keep the worms warm.' Then they realized they were using the bait wrong," said Peddler, nailing his eyes on Erik firmly, "do you understand that, Erik Karas?" Peddler paused to ascertain what effect his story had produced, and, seeing a smile, took Erik's burning cigarette from the ash tray, drew a deep puff, trying to imitate Erik's style, and put it back, "you see I can smoke too."

Erik stared at him as a smile blossomed on his face.

"Yesterday, at the cemetery, I sold more Bibles than ever before in my entire life. People didn't buy Bibles, they bought what you had to say and the way you said it. So, my new friend, I will make you smarten up and I will make you rich."

"You'll make me crazy, that's what you are going to do," said Erik, soberly.

"That too."

"Let's see. You'll make me smarten up, rich and crazy," said Erik, putting out his cigarette carefully and politely, looking at Peddler, "just out of curiosity, I'm going to stick around to see which one is going to come first. The chicken or the egg," concluded Erik, recovering his spirit. Just at that moment, before Peddler had the opportunity to say something, Mary Lou appeared at their table.

"Speaking of chickens," said Peddler, looking at Mary Lou.

"Is there something wrong, Peddler?" asked Mary Lou, staring at him and then altering her glance to throw a flirting look at Erik. "Are you hungry today? You're late for lunch and early for dinner, as usual. But you're both dressed to kill," there she stopped for a moment, threw her weight on one leg, put her pencil playfully in her mouth gazed at Erik for one whole minute, she then turned to Peddler and added,

"I must inform you and your bodyguard that we have no fried chicken, no watermelon, no goat meat, not even rice pilaf. We only have what is in the menu," and then, turning to Erik, with a serious look, "coffee, tea and not me. Did I cover everything?"

"Good job, what time do you get off work tonight?" asked Erik, soberly.

"Why?" she asked.

"I want to take you home."

Mary Lou turned to Peddler and after an imposed sigh said, "your bodyguard not only talks funny, he also thinks funny," then she abruptly turned to Erik, "I'm engaged."

"To be married?" asked Erik.

"No, to go cotton picking."

"Don't say that!" quipped Peddler, "it gives me the chills."

"Why, Peddler? You never picked cotton one day in your whole life," returned Mary Lou.

"No, but I know someone who did." said Peddler, with a sigh.

Erik looked at Peddler very hard, again, to remind him of something.

Peddler looked down and then looked away with a slight grin.

"Anyway, like I said, I want to take you home," said Erik, with all his attention directed to her.

"Whose home, mine or yours?"

"Does it matter?"

"Yeah, it matters. You live in a motel. I don't like motels," returned the waitress.

"Yours then."

Mary Lou, with a funny face, looked at the stranger. "Mine then. But the only thing I can offer you is coffee at my house."

"Good. I like homemade coffee and..." inserted Erik.

"I'm sorry, no **And,** just coffee. If you agree with that proposition, come here at eleven p.m." asserted Mary Lou, giving her head a toss in the air to throw her shoulder length natural blond hair backwards, away from her face, as she often did, like a palomino filly.

Erik looked at her, grinning, and said to Peddler, "Now you can go ahead and order."

"Good thing she's easy, otherwise we would've been here all day."

"Easy, Peddler?" asked Mary Lou in a tone of defiance.

"I'm sorry, what I meant to say was that you're easy to understand and get along with," said Peddler, in an earnest voice.

Mary Lou took the order and rushed into the kitchen, in her usual harried way.

"Are you happy now?" asked Peddler.

"Happy for what?"

"This is your third day here and you set up a date with one of the prettiest girls in town."

"There's an old Greek saying 'Never sing a trapezium song unless you had your supper first," said Erik.

"What is a trapezium song, if I may ask; I guess it's my turn to learn some Greek"

"On happy occasions, in Greece, relatives, friends and neighbors get together for supper, to celebrate, and after they've had a nice meal, there is another reason to be happy and they sit around, drink wine and sing ballads. Those ballads are called 'trapezium songs'. Do you understand?" asked Erik, with a pleasant smile.

"I understand; it makes sense," returned Peddler, nodding his head, "I suppose, they begin to sing when everything goes according to plan."

"Yeah."

"In that department, you'll do well and soon," returned Peddler.

"What does that mean?" inquired Erik, turning his eyes on him with a look somewhere between curiosity and eagerness.

"I meant, since she's waitress, she serves fast," replied Peddler, with a low and timid voice.

Erik looked at Peddler very hard, but he saw him getting embarrassed so he softened his features, "was that nice?"

"What did I say? I only said she serves fast," said Peddler, in his defense.

"Look Peddler, remember this!"

"Don't give me too many things to remember or I'll forget all of them," declared Peddler, desperately endeavoring to cover up something he said that even he thought was improper and out of order. "I know what you meant. One bull-shitter cannot bull-shit another bull- shitter. Can you remember that?"

Peddler looked embarrassed. "Really, I am embarrassed for saying that about her."

"I know," remarked Erik, as seriously as Peddler delivered the apology.

"How do you know?" asked Peddler.

"You blushed, I saw you blushing," said Erik.

"You see, we blush, too."

"I know, I know, I have seen it with my own two eyes, you probably bleed, too."

"We bleed, too, red blood," said Peddler, maintaining his seriousness.

"You bleed red blood?"

"Yeah, I ain't lying to you."

"Will you personally bleed red if I cut you right now?" asked Erik, picking up the knife.

"Take my word for it. You don't have to cut me. I bleed red blood."

"I thought, only American Indians bleed red. You must have some Indian blood in you."

"Sure, I have Cherokee blood in me,"

"Those Cherokee Indians must have been good lovers," said Erik.

"Why do you say that, Greek?"

"Because most of the Americans claim that they have Cherokee blood in them. Yes sir, those Cherokee men must have been some kind of mean Italian stallions."

"No, Indian stallions," remarked Peddler, "now there's something for you to remember too, Curly, Indian Stallions."

"Thank you, Peddler. I always say, live and learn."

"Do you want to learn something else?" asked Peddler, seriously.

"Go ahead, Peddler, fire when ready."

"Why do you always say, fire when ready?" asked Peddler.

"That's an army saying. It came from the firing range when the officer in charge gives the order to the troops to fire their weapons. He says, ready on the right, ready on the left, commence firing or fire when ready," explained Erik.

"Like you said, live and learn," responded Peddler, "We were talking about Indians

"Cherokee Indians," returned Erik.

"What I'm about to tell you is serious."

"Do I have to wear my foustanella?" asked Erik.

"What the hell is that?"

"A white pleaded short skirt, the men wore, and it's a serious attire. You said you want me to be serious."

"I don't care if you listen to me bare ass," interjected Peddler.

"If I would wear my foustanella, I'd be bare ass, because they didn't wear underwear with it."

"No. Listen to me, as you are," said Peddler. "I'll tell you something about all the Indians. You may know it and you may not. When the whites came to America and settled here, there were nine million Indians and five hundred different tribes, in less than two hundred and fifty years, there were only two hundred fifty thousand Indians left," said Peddler.

"Are you trying to tell me that the whites killed all those Indians, Peddler?"

"No. God, no." replied Peddler, "I know better than that. The disease the whites brought over here from Europe killed a lot, some of Indians killed each other, the whites killed a lot of them, the blacks killed some, the change of the environment caused by the European settlers driving them off their land that led to their starvation did in a lot of them, but most of all, they died because they didn't have a king."

"A king?"

"Yes a king. They didn't have anybody to unite them and to guide them. You see, a king unites people, democracy, unless it's a limited democracy, divides them. What makes one a king is a kingmaker. I want to be a kingmaker and I want to make you a king," exclaimed Peddler, excitedly.

"A king of whom? The Indians, you know I'm not an Indian," said Erik.

"No not the Indians, they don't need a king anymore, they're Americans and have a democracy," returned Peddler.

"I know, I can be the king of Gypsies, that would suit me."

"No, no, I want you to be a king of a ministry," said Peddler, now seriously.

CHAPTER SIX

Erik and Mary Lou get together

A few hours after the meeting of the two humorous minds, Erik's and Peddler's, the night came to an end and the two went their separate ways. Erik found himself walking in the middle of a trailer park's narrow street with Mary Lou clinging to his right arm, while staring at him, seeming pleased with what she saw. The clouds were drifting slowly over the round moon, at times fully obscuring the moon and then pulling away, allowing it to show its face in full splendor and shed its soft light on the objects all-around; the clouds would playfully hide it again, shrouding the world with darkness. Trailers were parked on both sides of the street, throwing their shadows on the rough pavement and making the dark night even darker. Most of the trailers were set upon short foundations and required three or four steps to enter them. The lamp-posts were randomly scattered and threw their light on the trailers, revealing their time–stained fronts and windows that seemed to have shared the lot of mortal eyes, grown dim and sunken with age. The night seemed settled in silence and the silence was pure, except of the two friends' footsteps.

"The moon, simply refuses to light up the night for us," remarked Erik, looking upwards.

"It's not the moon that refuses, the clouds are to blame. But you see, Erik, you are the perfect man," said Mary Lou, still hanging on him.

"Am I perfect?" asked Erik, a bit taken back.

"No, Erik, I didn't say that you're perfect, I said you are the perfect man, always putting the blame on the wrong place."

Erik stopped and looked at her with a surprised curious eye.

"Who cares about the moon, we know where we are going without the moon," giggled Mary Lou.

"Do we?" asked Erik.

"At least I do," said Mary Lou, looking at him with glimmering eyes and a slight smile. "Leave it up to me!" disengaging herself from him, she rushed ahead a few paces and went up on the first of the three steps that led into a well cared for but modest trailer. "Here is where I live," said the blond girl, with a sparkle in her eyes, "this is my home. Do you like it?"

Erik, who was moving towards her with an aristocratic manner, remarked, "Better than mine."

"Everything I have is better than yours."

Erik went forward and stood in front of her, she was still one step up.

"I am also taller than you," she said.

"I can see that, but I'm still growing," returned Erik.

"That's another thing I like about you, Erik. You are an optimist." Having said that, suddenly Mary Lou reached over, took hold of his head by his hair and brought him close to her, "kiss me goodnight, Erik."

"Kiss you goodnight? What happened to the homemade coffee I was promised?" he asked, stepping back to better focus on her.

"I've changed my mind. I see in your green eyes that you want coffee and . . ."

At that moment the clouds opened, allowing the moon's brightness to escape; it's glow on her face and hair made her image more splendid than the moon itself.

"That's funny," whispered Erik, getting closer to her "I see the same thing in your eyes."

"That's the bigger problem."

"What I see or what you show?"

"What I feel," replied Mary Lou, in a soft voice.

Erik reached over to her with both hands and wrapped them around her face, pulled her face towards him and kissed her tenderly, he then he pressed her head backwards, as if to take a wider look of her and held that pose for a long moment.

"You look like a goddess, in the moonlight," said Erik, softly, "how does a goddess see the world?"

"I am neither a goddess, Erik, nor an angel. I'm just a waitress with dreams that I know will never come true," whispered the girl, seriously, she then cast her eyes downwards in a sullen and grave manner.

Erik slowly took her hands and rubbed his face with them, although they were a waitress' hands, they were very soft. "Dreams, my lady, are true as long as they are alive. If they are dreams, don't let them die," said Erik, as softly as the feeling of her hands on his face.

Mary Lou suddenly disengaged her hands from him, threw her arms around him and kissed him, passionately. On the moment of that lover's ceremony, a man's fist hammered the back of Erik's head. Erik staggered back and found himself face to face with Leroy, who according to Erik's recollection, was that vulgar ill tempered pool player who asked Mary Lou to bring him a paper and pencil with which to write a letter to his father telling him how much he hated him and his new wife.

Erik struck Leroy with his fist and Leroy hit the ground. Erik charged against him with fire and fury, but Mary Lou held him back, with all her might, screaming for help. Leroy had time to restore himself to an upright position, backed a few paces away from Erik, his small eyes filled with water and his form writhed with anger.

"Come on you bastard!" uttered Leroy; appearing as if his mind was telling him to charge, but his heart was telling him to retreat. Leroy, like most losers, listened to his heart and ran away. When he felt safe, he stopped, turned and made a vulgar gesture to Erik.

"I'll kill you! Remember! I'll kill both of you!" yelled Leroy, as he stood and looked at both of them, from a distance. Then suddenly, as if impregnated by a burst of courage and infused with a new dose of strength, he rushed back and stationed himself a few paces from Erik, visibly struggling to summon his courage. It did not heed the call and on taking a closer view of Erik, he turned around again, sped down the street and disappeared.

Erik, seeing some lights in the neighboring trailers go on, said, "your screaming woke up the neighbors."

"I know, and most of them are old folks," remarked Mary Lou.

"I see the lights are going out again as fast as they came on," he observed.

"The poor old folks were probably startled from their sleep. They must have turned their lights on, laid awake, trembling in bed, till everything went quiet again and when they felt safe, they covered themselves back up and went to sleep," explained Mary Lou, quietly.

"How do you know what happened," asked Erik.

"I'm their neighbor, Erik. Sometimes, in a disturbance, I stand outside watching and waiting for the lights to go off. If the lights don't go off, I go knock on their doors to see if everything is all right. When I'm satisfied, I go to sleep. Remember, Erik, some of these folks are all alone. Their children have gone away, to make a living elsewhere, or search for the end of the rainbow," said Mary Lou.

"My angel," remarked Erik, humorously, pushing her hair back away from her face.

"I'm sorry, Erik, I didn't know he was hanging around here, " apologized Mary Lou, dusting Erik's coat, which didn't need it, "I suppose he's still carrying a torch for me."

"He's carrying a torch for you but he's also carrying a sword for the anyone who touches you."

Mary Lou turned, unlocked and pushed the door open, then, suddenly turning towards Erik, she grabbed his hand and pulled him into the trailer. This was done in such an unreserved manner that Erik thought she acted as if she felt a heart to heart conversation with him would be the remedy for the stressful situation, even if it were only for a change of pace.

Leroy, standing at a corner a few doors away, saw Mary Lou pull Erik into her trailer, it fueled the fire inside him, but the anger was like a lemon without juice; he turned and walked away.

When Leroy reached an open street he sat down on a doorstep for a few moments wholly bewildered and unable to go on. Suddenly he came to his feet and hurried away, quickening his pace gradually until coming to a full run. After completely exhausting himself, he stopped to catch his breath, and, if suddenly recollecting himself and deploring his inability to do something, he sat on a different doorstep, wrung his hands and burst into tears.

Erik stood a few paces in from the door as Mary Lou poked her head out to see if Leroy was around, and seeing nothing of him, closed and locked the door and headed for her room.

It was somehow necessary for her to go arrange her hair and put on fresh lipstick, before she could think of presenting herself to Erik for the long anticipated visit. Erik looked around at the small two-bedroom trailer and found it to be clean and orderly, with many pictures hanging on the walls.

While Mary Lou was in her trailer, Leroy was sitting on a doorstep a few blocks away. It might have been his tears relieved him, or he felt the full hopelessness of his condition, but for whatever reason, he turned back. Hurrying with nearly as great a rapidity in the opposite direction as to keep pace with the violent current of his thoughts, he soon reached the house where he was a boarder. He rushed upstairs, opened the door hastily, went in and flung himself on the couch, panting.

The room in which he resided was a short distance from Mary Lou's trailer. It was a poorly furnished room, decorated only with Mary Lou's picture hung on a wall and a rifle, with a telescopic sight, next to her picture. A small window that opened onto a dirt lane ventilated the room. His quarters did not indicate that Leroy had sunk down in the world recently; they indicated he was always there.

After the preparatory ceremony, Mary Lou glided into the room where Erik stood, and without saying a word, took him by the hand and guided him to a chair at the kitchen table. "Please" she said, "have a seat and I'll make what I promised you," and off she went to perform her domestic duties, bestowing many smiles on Erik, in the process.

"Your homemade coffee," announced Mary Lou, after a short while. Bringing the coffee and carefully placing the cup in front to of him, she continued, "incidentally, I'm sorry for dragging you in here so suddenly after I told you to go home and kissed you good night."

"Sure, I look as if I hated every minute of it. It has been and still is my pleasure. Besides, this is what I was promised in the first place, coffee and."

"Erik!" warned Mary Lou.

"That's funny, the bump on my head from your ex-boyfriend

didn't make me forget the **and**," said Erik in a humorous tone, rubbing his neck.

"No problem for the coffee and," replied Mary Lou, standing close to him.

"No?" asked Erik with a surprise.

"No. I have a lot of cookies," returned Mary Lou with a grin, turning away.

"I dislike cookies as much as I dislike ex-boyfriends.'

"He is not now and never has been my boy friend; you can see that he's a little off in the head," said Mary Lou, cleaning some dishes, "but," she continued, leaving the dishes, wiping her hands with a small clean white towel as went closer to Erik, "you shouldn't leave here so soon, he might still be out there."

"I wouldn't think of leaving you here all alone. He'll probably be gone by sunup," returned Erik, smiling and looking up to her standing close to him

"No, Erik, he'll leave way sooner than that or I'll walk you home."

"I wouldn't think of it," he said, taking her by the waist and drawing her to him. She sat on his lap with her head resting on his chest and her face looking up. He looked down at her hair trailing over his arms, her beautiful light eyes fixed themselves upon his face and he felt pleasantly uneasy and nervous, but who can look into a sweet pair of bright eyes without feeling a bit nervous.

"Because your mouth looks so beautiful when you lean down here, I am afraid I'd be rude if I kiss it; I don't want to spoil its beauty."

The young lady put her hand on his mouth, as if to caution him not to do so, she said nothing, she didn't smile, she didn't blink, and she stayed there motionless breathing through her mouth as if waiting for it to happen.

He felt the warmth of her body, saw the passion in her eyes, heard the throbbing of her heart and sensed her desire; she was ready to surrender and he was there to accept her, on any terms. He touched her lips with his, dug his hands into her hair and pulled her back firmly but yet gently. He kissed her forehead and gently bit her neck and she slid down before him, on her knees, and with hasty movements she unbuttoned his shirt and kissed his chest.

What a feeling he received and a what a thrill she gave. She kept nothing for herself nor stored anything for another day. He brought her breasts out and composed himself for a moment, to look at them. Near them, they poked out to show off their firm shape, attesting their stubbornness and swearing to their purpose. He kissed one and then the other; then kissed them again, as if praying to their secrecy and worshiping their dignity. Erik suddenly stopped, stood up, walked away and stared out the window as if looking for a place to run.

Mary Lou looked after him, still kneeling in front of his chair. "Green eyes always fool me," she said, getting to her feet and buttoning her blouse, "you look as though you've changed your mind, I know," said the girl, coming close to him, "I know. I've never been so forward in my life. I figured, you being from the city, you'd like me to be sort of aggressive. Besides, I feel as if I've known you for a long time. I feel as I've been with you before, and I waited for you to come back, and you came back; isn't that weird?" said Mary Lou, turning and walking away. She then stopped, looked back and said, "I think I've tried too hard to be a city girl and to be your friend, Erik. I'm thankful for what and who I am and I can find my own way through my tiny world, without being beholden to anyone. Don't ever think that I'm a plaything for you giants, because I am not, and I will never allow myself to be one."

"Why have you turned on me? Do you think I've rejected you?"

"Yes, Erik. You pulled away from me, as if I were begging to your burden for the rest of my life," yelled Mary Lou.

"It's not you. It's me," said Erik, turning to face her, " part of my past came back to me. I'll explain it to you later, if we are still on speaking terms."

"Erik, sugar, I'm sorry for the way I've behaved. I have to confess," began Mary Lou, "after you finished your lunch, you went away, but Peddler stayed behind and I spoke with him. That poor colored man had so many good things to say about you, he couldn't stop. He told me you have something inside you that's eating you alive. He suggested for me to dig it out. The only place you can hide anything is inside of you. Don't let it stay there too long, it'll turn to poison."

"Look at me!" uttered Erik, going near her, taking her by the shoulders and looking hard into her eyes, "Look at me! Look at me, girl!" he continued, with a soft voice, "Don't you know there something wrong with me? Do you know that my heart wants you?" He stopped for a moment and letting her go he looked downwards, " I wish I could stand before you and say, 'Come here girl! Be lucky and pick me up!' I don't like myself, how can I expect someone else to like me?" exclaimed Erik in a loud voice. "I want you to know it's me, I'm sorry.

"Erik, honey, I'm the one who should be sorry. Do you realize how hard is for me to make a friend and offer him my body? That's probably why I have no one to call my friend. You came to me, not to make love, but only to touch base with the opposite sex. From the first minute we met, I behaved as if I had known you all my life and that made you feel comfortable and you only vented your anger."

There were tears in the eyes of the young girl as her words were spoken and when one fell upon her crimson cheek, glistening brightly, making her face even more beautiful, it seemed as though the outpouring of a fresh young heart claimed a common kindred with the loveliest things in nature.

"Here I am, " said Erik with a grin on his face, "I came here tonight to sing a trapezium song and I'm singing the blues."

"I don't understand, a trapezium song," said Mary Lou, wiping the tears from her eyes with the back of her hand, trying to smile.

"Next time you see Peddler, ask him, he'll tell you, " returned Erik, kindly.

Mary Lou went over to him, reached out and straitened his shirt, "I'm sorry for yelling at you. I'd like you to sit and have the whole cup of coffee with me. Then you can go. I'll leave a light on in the window for you so you'll know you can always come back"

"Good." said Erik bending his steps towards the chair, "guys like me," he rejoined, as he sat down, "need that light. They say, back in Jersey, we always turn up, 'like a bad penny." I hope I've said something you can use for your own good, Erik," said Mary Lou, pouring a fresh cup of coffee.

"Ask Peddler what school I attended, he'll tell you; and then you'll know how much of what you said I'll use."

CHAPTER SEVEN

The Peddler's bargain

Having spent a few hours with Mary Lou, drinking coffee and talking, Erik returned to his motel room, went to sleep and woke up the following morning completely relaxed.

He started for breakfast and, wanting Peddler to accompany him, headed for his truck, parked in a lot, a few minutes' walk from the motel where Erik was staying.

"Peddler!" shouted Erik, looking around and waiting for him to respond.

"Sir?" said Peddler, stepping out from the back of the truck, still trying to tighten his belt.

"Do the words ham, eggs and grits sound good to you or does ham, eggs and potatoes sound better?" asked Erik.

"You sound very cheerful this morning, you must have sung that trapezium song," said Peddler, smiling. The peddler's smile awakened no gleam of mirth in his friend's face.

"As a matter of fact, I sang," said Erik, turning around with a sudden change of mood, "Yesterday When I Was Young. That's the song I sang."

"At your age?" returned Peddler, "what would you sing at my age?"

"If had a hammer."

"You really know how to make somebody's day, don't you?" murmured Peddler, walking around to the passenger's door.

"I suppose I've been elected to drive," said Erik, getting behind the wheel. Erik closed the door, made himself comfortable, started the motor, drove away and plunged into a profound meditation as Peddler looked ahead with a face that seemed especially anxious to hear Erik's story about his date with Mary Lou. The truck hummed along the fine smoothly paved road. The day started nice, cool and bright, with no clouds as mid-morning approached. The sun shone brightly, as brightly as if it looked upon no misery or troubles in the world below. The two friends looked forward to a pleasant breakfast.

The truck reached the summit of a little hill with a commanding view of open green fields in every direction for three or four miles.

"You were out late last night," said Peddler, breaking the long silence.

"How would you know I was out late? You were so drunk you didn't know whether you were standing on you heels or the crown of your head."

"I might have been drunk, but not dead. I know I wasn't on my heels or the crown of my head; I was lying on my back."

Erik stole a glance at him and shook his head, deploring Peddler for admitting his condition.

"You know, I always park my truck outside your motel room to watch out for you."

"What are you, my mother?"

"Hell no! The way you behave, I think your mother dropped you off on some zoo's steps, knowing that only zoo keepers could handle you, like the rest of the animals," said Peddler, looking straight ahead. Erik turned and looked at Peddler with an indifferent smile, then returned to his task of driving, without forming a reply.

"How was she?" asked Peddler, after a thread of long silence.

"Who? My mother?"

"No, stupid, the girl, the girl you spent half the night with. Was she good?"

"What?" exclaimed Erik, in a storm of indignation?

Peddler modestly repeated the question, with more subtlety.

"What kind of question is that?" asked Erik, a little calmer, "I hate it when people ask me that question. Was she good, was she bad, did she scream, did she cry, did she laugh, did she talk, did she moan," responded Erik with controlled madness, "No! She growled like a tiger, then she tore up the furniture," he continued, then, stopping for a moment for his nerves to calm down, he added, "She is a woman, true representative of the opposite sex, Peddler. She stood there before me fully clothed, with her hair done and with delight in her eyes and flair in her manners."

"All right, all right, you made your point. Now shoot me, why don't you?"

"Do you prefer getting shot, or learning some class?"

"You're right, Erik. I apologize," said Peddler, after a minute's thought, embarrassed. "Take a right here. We are going to the town of Hixton. I think the town of Hixton is ready to start reading the Bible."

"Of course," replied Erik with a smile on his face, "new road, Peddler, new way and the inception of a new life. The prospect before us is a brilliant one. All the honors that great talents and powerful characters, like us, deserve are ahead, Peddler, " declared Erik in ardent terms.

"Are you sure you didn't sing that trapezium song last night? You sound as if you were shot full of some magic power," stated Peddler, with a polite and careful tone.

Erik gazed at him and smiled, "There is no pursuit more worthy of me- more worthy of the highest nature that exists, than the struggle to win fame and fortune."

"Are you sure you didn't sing the trapezium song last night?" asked Peddler.

"You'll never know."

"Oh yeah, I forgot, you don't kiss and tell."

A half hour's drive brought the travelers to a little roadside café that sat between two huge willow trees with a vegetable garden on the right side where an old bald headed man was working the soil.

Erik pulled the truck in and stopped in the middle of a driveway, it was the entrance to a fairly large parking lot off the main road and on the left side of the café.

"How far is Hixton from here?" asked Erik, of the old man. The man continued to work in the garden, without raising his head to respond.

"Hey! I said, how far is Hixton from here?"

The old man continued his chores.

"He's either deaf or stupid," said Erik, getting out of the truck and walking towards the man. "How far is Hixton from here?" he asked, in a very normal voice.

The bald-headed man, now suddenly startled, raised his head, straightened his body, shaded his eyes with his hand and looked at Erik but uttered nothing.

Erik advanced closer," How far is Hixton from here?"

"Hello!' replied the man.

"Hello!" said Erik, going closer to the man, "how far is Hixton from here?"

"I'm sorry, I don't know if you noticed or not, but I don't hear very well," said the old boy, taking his hand away from shading his eyes and placing it around his ear. Peddler stepped up next to Erik and stared at the old man.

"He's not stupid, he's worse. He's deaf," murmured Peddler.

"How far is Hixton from here?" shouted Erik, disregarding Peddler's comment.

"Hixton?"

"Yea! Hixton."

"That way," said the old man, pointing the way they were traveling before they entered the driveway.

"I know it's that way," shouted Erik, "but how many miles?"

"Oh! About forty thousand."

"He's also stupid," murmured Peddler again.

"Hush, Peddler," said Erik, looking at the old man, "How many miles, not how many people," yelling so loud, a flock of birds flew for cover.

"Oh!" said the old man breaking into wide smile, "it's about twenty-five miles. But you better get your truck out of the driveway, you are blocking the parking lot entrance. I heard that about ten busses full of people will be here any minute now, they're going to have some kind of memorial picnic."

"Lets go!' said Peddler, turning towards the truck, "I don't know how in the hell he heard it, he's deafer than a rock."

"Where are you going?" asked Erik, grabbing Peddler by the arm. "What are you? Are you deaf, too?"

"What's the matter?" asked Peddler, jerking his arm from Erik's grasp.

"Are you some kind of neophyte?" asked Erik with an emphatic tone.

"What the hell is neophyte? Another word for trapezium song?" asked Peddler with some degree of indignation.

"A neophyte is a new plant that just came out of the ground. Didn't you hear? Over five hundred people will be here for a memorial picnic."

Peddler, from embarrassment, walked away a few paces then stopped and turned to face the two men in conversation, "You know Erik? The more I'm with you the more I find out I don't know shit. Your brain clicks and mine is lingering like an windmill in a weak breeze."

"How's the food in here?" asked Erik, disregarding Peddler's complaint.

"Here we go again," uttered Peddler, moving away towards the truck.

"What did you say? What did you say?" asked the old man, leaning on his spade.

"I said, how is the food in here?"

"Lousy. Lousy. We ain't had no rain for a month and everything is dead. We eat dead stuff now. For the restaurant they bring in vegetables from New Orleans. First time this happened. We used to sell our vegetables down there, now we buy from them," having said that, the old man burst into laughter, "are you going to have breakfast in there?"

Erik nodded vigorously in assent, having no other choice and not wanting to spend another minute with the kind gentleman, lost in misunderstanding.

"Very good food they have in there. Try their sausages. They're good"

"Sausages are good, eh?"

"No sauce, we don't call it sauce here, we call it gravy. The gravy is good too." Having declared this, the old man, apparently satisfied on seeing Erik smiling, resumed his work.

Erik headed for the restaurant and Peddler caught up with him, "even the deaf man knows you're a foreigner."

"How do you know that," asked Erik.

"He said to you, 'we don't call it sauce here, we call it gravy,'" said Peddler.

"For that, you're buying breakfast," said Erik, starting for the door of the restaurant, then he suddenly stopped, "The truck! We have to move the truck otherwise we're bound to lose our Bible buying customers, and because you called me a foreigner, you move it!" said Erik.

They both stood and looked at each other, with looks that showed their thoughts were elsewhere. Erik broke the gaze by suddenly turning and speeding into the restaurant.

He walked to the farthest corner, retired to a booth and remained perfectly mute, waiting for Peddler. He looked out of the back window and saw a white church, standing a half a mile from there, and a pond, surrounded by willow trees. Then he turned his gaze and surveyed the inside of the restaurant. The walls were old and garnished with many pictures of what he assumed were former customers and owners. There were many tables surrounded by leather captain's chairs, enough to accommodate over one hundred and fifty people. The floor, made out of wide planks, shined and sparkled. The bar, on the far side, was attended by a young man with short hair who wore a red long sleeve shirt and a black bowtie, was smoking a cigar and talking to a small group of attentive waitresses. Everyone of that group of lassies was pleasant and pretty and they all tittered and giggled with the boy wearing the bowtie; he laughed out loud until he was red in the face. They all looked at Erik, but they offered no service, as if they had a policy for the customer to call upon them in order to be served. Erik, thinking that it might not be polite for him to go to them just then, decided to stay put in the booth and wait patiently.

Peddler rushed in, looked around for a moment to find Erik and when he saw him rushed over.

"You should see what I've seen," said Peddler, sitting hastily across from Erik and appearing terrified and distressed.

"What have you seen, a ghost?"

"Four buses just pulled in, loaded with people. An old man is in charge of the whole thing, because I heard him saying to the drivers not to open the doors and not to let anybody out until he gives the order," said Peddler, quickly not even taking time to breath.

"Why are you so excited?"

"Why? What did you call me a while a go? Nymph?"

"Neophyte, I called you."

"Are you some kind of neophyte yourself, asking me why? I'll tell you why," said Peddler, standing up, "I'm going to go make some kind of deal for us to sell Bibles." With those words he hurried out, and immediately afterwards was seen on the street, approaching a man who appeared to be in his early sixties, dressed conservatively and monitoring the parking of the buses.

"Excuse me sir," said Peddler, with as much coolness as if had been dispatched on the most ordinary assignment.

"Yes," said the man, keeping his eyes on the performance of the buses.

"What is the occasion, sir?" asked Peddler, of the man, who, in every respect and description, looked and acted as if he were the man in charge of the entire event that was about to unfold.

The man turned to Peddler and smiled, "I'm Rev. Joseph Dupont," he said, offering his hand to Peddler.

"I am very glad to meet you, Reverend, my name is Stephen Spencer," said Peddler, taking the Reverend's hand and shaking it vigorously.

"Today, we are here to celebrate the anniversary of the death of a very important man who died here on this day, in 1955, leaving three hundred thousand dollars to this town of Tilton, to build schools and to rebuild the church behind this restaurant, which he attended when he was a little boy, growing up here, in this house, " said the Reverend, pointing at the restaurant. "Peter Dubois was his name; he was great man. What is your business, Mr. Spencer, may ask, sir?"

"I'm the manager of the Evangelist, Erik Karas," said Peddler, folding his hands as if in prayer and bowing his head with a smile.

"Erik Karas," murmured the Reverend, placing the tip of his index finger on his lips, as most man who think first, before they speak, do. "I think I heard of him. Did I see him on TV?"

"Probably," returned Peddler, "he is from up north, New Jersey to be exact, he is the man with the silver tongue."

"I would like to meet him. Is it possible, Mr. Spencer?"

"Sure, Reverend, he's inside. We were traveling through here," said Peddler, now with an anxious manner, realizing that dreams can come true.

"Good!" returned the Reverend, "give me about fifteen minutes to set up everything here. There is a truck coming with the Mayor of the town of Hixton and the Mayor of Tilton. Excuse me, Mr. Spencer, they are not coming in the truck they are coming in a limousine, but the truck is bringing the platform, the podium, the microphones and speakers."

"Good! It sounds like it's going to be some kind of real important event," said Peddler.

"Oh, yes. The two politicians are going to speak, like most politicians. They are going to announce today that a statue of Peter Dubois is going to be erected, before the end of the year, in front of that church. Oh, listen, Mr. Spencer, do you think the Evangelist Erik Karas could say something?"

"I am sure he is capable,"

"I'm sorry, Mr. Spencer, I didn't mean to offend you or the Evangelist, sir, I'm sure he can, but what I really meant was whether he would like to say a few words." said the Reverend, in an apologetic manner.

"No offence taken, Reverend Dupont, tell him what subject you want him to talk about and he will. After all, he is an Evangelist," said Peddler, with an air of genuine dignity.

"I'm sure," there he stopped to think for a moment. "Do you know?" said the Reverend, touching Peddler's arm gently, "does he have time or you are rushing out?"

"How much time?" asked Peddler.

"Never mind!"

Those words brought the look of disappointment to Peddler's face, a heavy feeling of distress, like the shadow of a sudden cloud, landed on his whole being, changing him to almost deadly pale.

"No! No! Just tell me, I arrange his schedule," said Peddler, giving himself a last shot.

"Did you know," began the Reverend, touching Peddler's arm again with great affection, " that Peter Dubois was in jail for many years?"

"No," replied Peddler, in amazement.

"Yes, and the people don't know his life story, which was very sad. I know it, but I don't think I have the ability to tell it like an Evangelist could."

Peddler was about to throw his arms around that man, in front

of everybody, kiss him twice in each cheek and shake his arm out
of its socket, but he held back his excitement.

"Would you be kind enough to give him a little summary and
the Evangelist Karas will take it from there," suggested Peddler.

"Oh, sure," replied the Reverend, with enthusiasm, "let me
finish here and I will be right in," saying this, he left hastily and
Peddler, with twice the Reverend's speed, ran inside. If the place
weren't empty, there would have been an accident and the Peddler
would have never made to Erik, he would have knocked down at
least two-dozen people trying to get to his partner.

"Do I have some good news for you," exclaimed Peddler, trying
to sit down, his hands trembling with the excitement he felt in his
heart.

"Mary Lou is outside," replied Erik.

"No! Would you get your mind off the garter for one moment?"

"Yes, but just for a moment," replied Erik.

"Let me catch my breath and then I'll tell you the good news,"
said Peddler, taking a deep breath, then he started. "First, I must ask
you, do you think you can do it?"

"Are you crazy?" asked Erik.

"This will make us big. Can you do it?"

"Are you crazy?"

"I beg you, to do it. Can you do it?" pleaded Peddler.

"Are you crazy?" asked Erik, with the same tone in his voice
all three times, "first tell me if you're crazy, then I'll say."

"Yes, I'm crazy, but can you do it?"

"Do what, Peddler? Can I do what?"

The Peddler spoke for three minutes straight without pausing
for air, drink or to swallow his saliva; he only wiped his sweat off
his face and focused on Erik, but even in all that time, he omitted
some vital information.

"They want you to give a speech about the man they are honor-
ing today. Can you do it?"

Erik looked at the Peddler intently and said softly, "Do the bears
shit in the woods?"

"Yes, yes, yes, my God, yes, they do shit in the woods," yelled
Peddler, with as much excitement God allowed any of His children
to experience while still to holding on to their sanity, "yes, they

do," repeated Peddler, in triumph.

The Reverend Dupont joined them, in some time, just when the two had finished their breakfast and were having the last of their coffee. The Reverend told the story in less than fifteen minutes. Erik knew his throwing in an indecisive word, now and then, would induce the Reverent to continue in more detail with the story of Peter Dubois.

"I personally could not spin out the story in the fashion that it should be told," said the Reverend, slowly, "but I think you, Mr. Karas, can do justice to it. There now, Mr. Karas, if you can make it convenient to reduce your eyes to their normal size, because all the while that I was talking they seemed to be wider than normal, and to let me hear what you think, I will feel rather obliged to you."

"You want my opinion on this matter, I suppose?" said Erik, looking from the musing face of Reverend Dupont to the eager face of Peddler and taking a puff from his cigarette.

"I think so," said the Reverend, looking at Erik.

"I also suppose you are looking for donations to complete the project," said Erik bluntly; Peddler, hearing that, swallowed his saliva with a great difficulty. Erik squeezed his cigarette in the ashtray politely, looked straight in the Reverend's eyes and said in a low voice, "I can swing the people in to a favorable mood, but I don't ask for money."

"No! No! You don't have to do that, I will do that, if you put them in the right mood," said the Reverend, in a positive and convincing tone.

"What's in it for us?" asked Peddler, glancing at Erik to see if he asked the right question. Erik remained silent, watching closely for a reaction from the Reverend.

"I suppose this can be arranged," said Dupont, after a long vacant silence. "What do you normally get?"

"I beg your pardon," said Erik, "what did you say? I didn't understand."

"How much do you want?"

"You see, Reverend, we are not fundraisers for other causes. We have the '**The Erik Karas Crusade Foundation,** sir, through which we help people in need," replied the Peddler, with a solemn tone.

"I appreciate that, Mr. Spencer, but tell me what you want," asked the good Reverend. At this inquiry Peddler looked at Erik.

"We want a date at the Hixton auditorium, two weeks from this coming Saturday. And we want the Mayor of Hixton to make the announcement the moment Evangelist Karas is off the stage; of course we will give you a cut of it, for your cause, and we want nothing from this. Remember we are only helping you here," stated Peddler, trying to read the Reverend's mind, "one more thing," continued Peddler, reading the eyes.

"Yes?" asked the Reverend, earnestly.

"A band."

"Done," replied Reverend Dupont, without the slightest consideration. "Incidentally what would be your topic?"

"Thou shall not kill," said Erik softly. "Against capital punishment."

"Capital punishment in the south..." remarked the Reverend, stopping in his narrative.

"What's the matter, Reverend?" asked Peddler, "please go on."

"I was saying capital punishment in the south is usually not opposed," concluded the Reverend.

"You see Reverend, I am not a politician, sir, I am an Evangelist. My job is what my title says sir, revealing. I am a messenger of God's good message," stated Erik, sternly but softly.

"Forgive me, Mr. Karas, sometimes I tend to be a politician, We have an agreement, gentlemen," said the Reverend, getting up," let's shake hands on it and let's go to work. One more thing,"

"Yes?" asked Erik.

"I'll make arraignments for you to have the rest of your breakfast in a private room," said the Reverend, looking around for a hostess, "I think some VIPs may want to join you."

A tall, bleached-blond hostess appeared almost immediately and the Reverend commanded the lady to show the two guests to a private room at once. The command, like all commands of emperors, judges, and other great personalities of the earth was at once obeyed and the hostess, interestingly annoyed, ushered them away. The two guests, Erik and Peddler, and the Reverend followed her close behind. Erik, who was the first behind her and even though he had a great admiration for bright eyes, sweet faces, long legs and nice feet, in short, he was fond of the whole opposite sex, found, on close inspection, that the hostess had all those but didn't appeal to him, for she lacked finesse and a woman's personality; he simply saw her as a walking mannequin. She stood at the side of the door, allowing all three to pass though, before she went away. The private room was rather small but cozy and there was a large round table with about ten chairs around it. The Reverend, satisfied with the accommodations, shook hands with the guests then disappeared with a happy grin.

Erik Karas, Evangelist, and Stephen Spencer, Peddler, sat down and looked at each other with majestic smiles.

"Where in hell did you get that Erik Karas Foundation crap, Peddler?"

"My English ancestry comes out sometimes. Do you like, The Erik Karas Foundation?"

"Are you kidding me?" replied Erik, looking hard into Peddler's eyes, "I love it."

"You didn't tell me you have English blood in your veins. Why do you think I like Yorkshire putting and kidney pie?"

Reverend Dupont returned, ushering in two well-dressed gentlemen, one of whom was a heavy-set man in his early fifties. The second man was taller but stouter and a little older.

"My Lord," cried the second man "How do you do, Mr. Karas, I hope you are well, sir, I didn't think I would ever have the pleasure of meeting you face to face, sir, " said the man, not wishing to waste the time of being introduced and properly presented to Erik, as all serious minded men in a hurry do, when they are meeting their subordinates. He pulled a chair and placed it next to Erik, Peddler's eyes opened wider than giant shrimp's, and Erik, not totally impressed by the man's manner, bent his head slightly in answer to the salutation and saw the first man pulling up a chair for himself next to second man, who rose slowly, thinking that he was about to be introduced properly, but when that didn't happen, he sat down again as slowly as he had risen.

Peddler sat a few chairs away from Erik and the Reverend sat closest to the door.

"I didn't think you looked as healthy or relaxed, as you do now, the last time I saw you," said the second man with a happy grin on his face.

"Possibly not, sir," returned Erik, who was puzzled by that man's comment, without producing the slightest effect, " when did you see me, sir, may I ask?"

"I'd say about two months ago. I saw you on 8 mm film. Some kind and also some unkind comments were made about you, from different people, you know."

"No! I don't know, sir, would you be kind enough to explain them for me," uttered Erik, with a slight degree of indignation.

"Oh! Yes, there was also a newspaper article about that unfortunate incident and you were mentioned at length, you were referred to as the stranger without a name," replied the man.

Erik came to his feet and looked at both men with some clear indignation, "Gentlemen, I must explain to you that I don't like it when people talk in circles, and you, sir, you are like Archimedes, not only do you talk in circles but you also draw them," said Erik, preparing himself to leave. He cast his eye on Peddler, who looked as if he were boiling in misery, he too stood up and walked away, a few paces.

The other man stood still, but broke into natural violent cough. The Reverend sat there bewildered and astonished, thinking, up till now, he had a bird in hand, but he suddenly realized, it was only the bush; so he stood up, "Mr. Karas, I too think the honorable Mayor is speaking in circles."

"Wait a moment!" said Erik, interrupting the good Reverend, "Did you say the honorable Mayor?

"Yes, yes, that's what I said," returned Joseph Dupont, the Reverend.

Erik burst into a loud laugh and when he sat down was still laughing.

"Aren't you the happy wanderer," exclaimed Peddler, coming closer with happy bewilderment on his face. The Mayor and the other man laughed together pleasantly and cheerfully, as men, who are about to receive money, often do.

"I am very sorry," said the Reverend, "this is the honorable Mayor of Hixton, William Dodson," pointing at the second man, "and this is the honorable Mayor of Tilton, James Bridges."

"I know the honorable Mayor, John Lambright from Richville,

Virginia," stated Erik, when the introductions were finished, "Mayor Dodson, do you happen to know John Lambright, the mayor of Richville Virginia."

"Of course, of course, of course I know John Lambright," replied Dodson, with a deep serious voice.

"He is not you favorite candidate, is he?" inquired Erik.

"Not really," replied Dodson, reluctantly.

"You must be with the Democratic party," said Erik.

"I am," said the Mayor, sternly.

"Then you must have heard of Harry Sharkey."

"Yes, he's a friend of mine," said the Mayor, with great disappointment, "and because of you, according to the last polls, he is going to lose the race."

"That's too bad. How did you put the whole thing together? How did you know that it was me who was there?" asked Erik.

"8 mm film" mumbled the Mayor.

"No offence to you, Mayor, you couldn't have remembered me from the film," said Erik, touching the Mayor's arm gently, "unless you looked at it three minutes ago."

"No!" said the Mayor," someone who was there and is here with me now, saw you and recognized you."

"And he doesn't like me," interrupted Erik.

"True!"

"Why doesn't he like me, did he tell you, Your Honor?" asked Erik.

"He was a supporter for Harry. I can say he was Harry's right hand man."

"Don't tell me, it's Bob!" said Erik, smiling.

The Mayor thought for a long moment with his eyes on the table, "Yes, it's Bob. Bob Duncan."

"Small world we live in," said Erik, "Did he tell you that he and I met before?" asked Erik.

"That's why he doesn't like you," replied the Mayor.

"Tell him that I like him. I think he's a nice guy but he talks too loud," said Erik softer than the Mayor.

"Yes, he does have a mouth on him," returned the Mayor, with an apologetic manner.

"Your Honor, we all have mouths to talk and to eat, and speaking of eating, sir, Bob '**Koukia troi, koukia martirai**'," said Erik.

"I am sorry, Mr. Karas, you lost me there," rejoined the Mayor of Hixton.

"That's an old Greek saying and it means that he 'eats beans and beans he talks,'" said Erik.

"I'm still at loss, Mr. Karas. You see, sir, Greek is not my native language."

"I know. What really means is 'One says what he thinks, without thinking.' Is that clear to you now, Your Honor?"

"Not only clear, sir, but I also find your Greek sayings very interesting," said the Mayor earnestly, "and, Mr. Karas, I would like you to write it down and give it to me. Write it in Greek. I know a lot of blabber mouths and I can hit them with that."

"I knew you would like it," said Erik, "later on I will write it down for you in Greek words but English characters."

"Beautiful!" said the Mayor, delighted.

When Rev. Dupont perceived that Erik and Dodson had reached a common plateau, he asked, with some signs of easing anxiety, "do we have a deal?" Looking around at all of them, his eyes stopped when they came to Erik.

"We have a deal," said Erik, winking at Peddler, who returned a smile bigger than the table.

"Let me introduce you, gentlemen, to someone who is my right hand man," said Dodson, turning to the door, saying loudly, "you can come in now." On those words of command, the fat man, Bob, squeezed himself though the half open door, making his face red in the process.

"Bob, let me present to you Mr. Erik Karas and his manager Stephen Spencer," said the Mayor with great delight both in his voice and on his face.

"How do you do, gentlemen," replied Bob, with a smile. Unfortunately the room was too crowded to afford the newcomer a chance to shake Erik's hand, "The first time I saw you, Mr., Karas, you were a waiter, and then you sounded like an English professor and then you turned out to be a bouncer for the restaurant and then a speaker for John Lambright and now you're an Evangelist. Are you going up or coming down?"

"What can I tell you Mr. Duncan? You wouldn't know the difference between going up or coming down, because, sir, if you did, you would not have climbed on the stage after Sharkey's speech; you would have been torn to pieces if you hadn't run," said Erik.

"Mr. Karas, for the first time in my life I'm going to complement someone who's insulting me. I saw you, sir, and I heard you, and you were very good in all the stations you held. Not only good, I would say the best," said Bob earnestly, clearly disregarding the insult that had been thrown at him, "Even Harry Sharkey said that you were good up there and it was too bad you weren't on his side."

"Thank you, Bob, I now realize we all know a good thing when we see it; I hope we can also sense a bad thing coming." Erik's utterance of those words was impressive, well delivered and calculated to strike thought in their minds and spirit in their hearts. He looked to them, a full size larger than them all.

"Incidentally, the newspaper article that was written about you printed a nice phrase; I memorized it verbatim, 'A mysterious stranger stopped here, spoke with a poetic style and sounded as if he came from someplace no one ever came from, on his way to someplace no one had ever gone'," recited Bob with a solemn tone, garnishing his declaration with a smile.

Although both Erik and Bob were men of words and both possessed the talent of persuasion, it was clear up till now, to the eyes of even of the most unskilled beholder, that there was no love lost between Erik and Bob, but Bob, in that small room, on that large table, surrounded by those big men, threw a telling piece of information of the flair that Erik Karas, his perceived adversary, possessed. The whole body of those significant men gazed at each other with alternate allotments of focus, from one to another, with the exception of Erik, who looked downwards and said softly, "Gentlemen, upon hearing those kind words from Bob's mouth, if I were a rich man, I would take my wallet from my pocket and pour out its contents on this table and let my money to do the talking. If I were wise, I would just place my fore-finger on my temple and endeavor to compose a reply to that article, but because I am neither rich nor wise, I will simply allow my face to turn red from the embarrassment of that flattering phrase."

That entire body of men fell into a fit of laughter.

While these resolute and necessary discussions were taking

place around that large table, in that small and private room, between those public figures, more buses arrived and more people poured out of them and the preparation of the stage was being conducted according to plans.

CHAPTER EIGHT

Erik's confession

Two hours after the business negotiations ended, with most satisfying results, the ten acres of ground, designated for the celebration, were filled with spectators. There was a band and four singers, dressed in country-western garb, to provide song and music to enhance the spirit. All the dignitaries stood next to the stage waiting, in prearranged order, to be called upon to enlighten the world with their knowledge, wit and charm; the politicians stood ready to make the attendant crowd feel good with their promises. All the men, women, boys and girls who were assembled there, screamed with ecstasy and applauded with vigor when the music stopped. The bandleader assured the public that the best was yet to come and that was received with an even louder round of applause and another wave of screams. There was no doubt that the preparations were met with the delight of all.

"Ladies and gentlemen may I have your attention please," shouted the Reverend, holding a microphone in one hand and a piece of paper in the other, waiting for the crowd to adjust to some serious business, leaving the music behind for a little while, which was very hard for them to do. "Ladies and gentlemen, he shouted again, waiting patiently, like most good Reverends are trained to do. "Ladies and gentlemen," he repeated, finally gaining some control, "we are here today to celebrate the life and death of the most distinguished citizen of our town of Tilton. Very few of us know about the life and death of Peter Dubois, whose money and love for this town, enabled us to build a beautiful school and remodel our sacred and historic place of worship. But, my friends, in addition to our local dignitaries, who have gathered here today to celebrate with us, we have been lucky to have a man of God, honor and substance, who was just passing through, when he heard about our celebration and is kind enough to share with us the story of Peter Dubois, the man we are celebrating. The man I am speaking about is the Evangelist, Erik Karas, and I must thank him from the bottom of my heart for taking time from his busy schedule to speak to you; I know you are going to enjoy his words very much. Ladies and gentlemen, let's welcome the Evangelist Erik Karas."

Erik walked solemnly across the stage, shook hands with the Reverend, took the microphone in his hand and listened. Never before were heard such sounds as those that greeted him. He only grinned, slightly bowed and walked a few paces, waiting for the crowd to calm while Peddler wiped tears from his eyes; they were the tears of joy.

The hue of Erik's face had changed to bright crimson. Its expression had lost nothing of its attractiveness, but yet it was changed, there was an anxious fresh look about that gentle face, one it had never worn before.

"There was a man, who lived in the house that now is the restaurant," said the Evangelist, pointing in it's direction, "That man, whose tears never found their way into his soul, whose nerves were rendered stronger and more vigorous by the showers of tears that fell down his abused wife's face, eyed his good lady with looks of satisfaction on seeing her crying her hardest. That man was Charles Dubois, the father of the man whom we are here today to celebrate, Peter Dubois. In the year 1925 Charles Dubois, a twenty-five year old man, with a wife and two children, a girl nine years old, named Joan and a boy five, named Peter, came and settled this farm. They lived in this house, the now famous restaurant, The Dubois Café, it has been expanded several times, as you all know, to accommodate its loyal customers.

Charles Dubois, the father and breadwinner, according to his neighbors, was a mean man, cruel to his wife and children, and would drink his own homemade liquor until he reached a stupor. Charles was a parishioner of the small church behind us. He was a savage, full of hate, cruel and ferocious to his wife and children and never allowed them to mingle with the rest of the parishioners. He was heard, by his neighbors, to say to his wife, 'cry my dear, cry tears, my dear, open your lungs, wash the evil from you, exercise your eyes and soften your temper, so cry. Cry hard so I can hear you.' He would clasp her tight around the throat with one hand and inflict a shower of blows on her face with the other. 'Remove yourself from here if you already had enough, if not stay until I give you what you really deserve.' He himself had not a single friend or acquaintance. No one cared to speak to him and everyone feared him. No one ever heard his wife complain, but it has been said, that man, her husband, for many years, methodically and systematically tried to break her heart, but she endured the torture for her children, Joan and Peter. No matter how cruel he was and how brutally he acted towards her, she would not leave him. Regularly, every Sunday, both morning and afternoon, that mother, with her children would attend church and occupy the same seat, with her sitting in the middle of her two beloved children. Although they were poor and dressed in clothes of the lower class, they were high in spirit; they were always neat and clean. They were poor, and many times the good neighbors would go to the family's aid but Charles Dubois would turn back every kindness with scorn on his face and insults from his mouth. It's been said, God forgive me if I' am wrong," said Erik, pausing to gather strength from the dead silence around him and the eager eyes upon him. He then turned his head and stretched his arms towards Heaven, "Please God, please forgive me if I'm wrong," lowering his arms and scanning the spectators, he continued, "People, who passed the house, in the late hours of the night, reported to one another that they heard the moans and sobs of the woman and her children. Sometimes, late at night, the little boy would run to a neighbor's door, looking to escape his father's drunken fury, but he was refused assistance, for fear his father would seek deadly revenge against anyone who offered it to little Peter.

It has also been reported, that at the conclusion of Sunday services, sometimes his wife would stop to exchange a few kindly words with the neighbors outside the church, her husband, Charles, seeing her trying to be social, would push her away violently and if the children looked at him with grimacing faces, he would whip them right there, in front of the parishioners. That went on for seven years. Late one night, a young man was walking on the narrow lane, in front of the house, and noticed the little girl, who was then seventeen years old and beautiful; he befriended the girl. The young man, who was a tall, dark and handsome and came from a good family; he was the man of Joan's dreams. They met secretly, in out of the way places, as forbidden young lovers often do. Peter's frame had grown and his limbs were weak no longer. He began to rebel against his father, began to disrespect his mother and was no longer the little child she adored. He took after his father, in cruelty and crudeness. She would go to church with only her daughter, holding the Bible with the hand that for so many Sundays held her son's.

Shortly thereafter, her soul was summoned by God. Her remains were buried in an unmarked spot near the pond, an unmarked grave in the back of the building, discarded as trash. Not long after that, the girl and the boy she befriended were found shot dead near the pond. The father informed the authorities that his boy, Peter, had killed them. The boy was arrested and sent away to a prison until he became twenty-one years old. At the expiration of his prison term, steadily adhering to his old resolution to make his mother proud of him, he made his way to Chicago where he attended school and became a doctor. Having made some wise and lucky investments, he became wealthy and eventually married a woman of class and even greater wealth.

One Sunday afternoon, in the month of July, on the exact date we are celebrating today, Peter parked his car in the driveway of this house, which was already a small restaurant, and walked through the willow shaded path to the church, knowing no other place to visit. As he was walking, he remembered himself as a young boy, clinging to his mother's hand and his sister clinging to her other, and the three of them finding peace, if only for a few hours. He remembered looking into her pale face as she was crying, having undergone some ferocious treatment by his father, just before. He remembered how often he would run ahead of her to show off and to plant a smile on her face.

He entered the empty church with fear in his heart and looked at the empty seat his mother occupied for such a long time; a tear came down his face. The place looked the same, though smaller than what it used to look to him, before he was sent away. He looked at the old statues and the shabby pulpit with its faded decorations. He went near his mother's old seat; it looked cold and desolate. The kneeling cushion was still there but her Bible was gone. Trembling violently with fear and anxiety, he rushed out of the church, went outside, stood silent and still and looked back one more time, trying desperately to hear his mother's voice, but his memory failed him and his heart sank in despair. He went back to the house of his youth, yet his happiest days, remembering his mother always looking at him with pride, love, care and affection, like no other woman had looked at him since." Erik stopped, reached into his pocket, pulled out a white handkerchief, examine it and then slowly wiped his face.

"He remembered his mother on her deathbed," continued Erik, sighing deeply, "He and his sister stood there helplessly watching her sinking away from life. He remembered her breathing was hard and thick and she moaned painfully as the pain came and went. At her bedside sat a pair of reading glasses and the Bible she hadn't felt strong enough to read for many days. As the two children stood above her, the sick woman drew a hand from each towards her and pressed them affectionately in her own, keeping them in her grasp. He knew that she was in the balance of life and death, fighting with nature. 'May God for give me' she murmured and she fell asleep, only asleep at first, for they saw, after a few minutes, a smile caress her face, as the scale tilted in nature's favor; nature won and their mother crossed over to the next world, she smiled seeing it was a better world.

Peter only hoped that her merciful judge would bear in mind the punishment she endured on earth. He continued standing there looking at that house, he remembered how many times he buried his head under his bed covers, listening to his father's harsh words to his only friend, his mother, hearing his mother's sobs and imagining her pale face covered with tears. He remembered lying there with clenched fists, feeling a fierce and deadly passion. He remembered how his father would whip him and how he would plead with him to stop saying 'please not again, not again.' His father, hearing those words, would stop for a split second and would then continue on with even greater fury. 'Please, not again, not again' were only words of hope for little Peter. His father heard them, but was not affected. Peter carried in his mind a picture of his home and playground for so many years, but when he came back, everything seemed strangely different, but the mental anguish, the memories of physical pain, and his father's exhaling stinking breath with every stroke he imparted, were clear and vivid even twenty-five years later. Peter could still hear his own pleas, 'Please, not again, not again', all that was still the same."

Erik stopped for a moment, wiped sweat and tears from his face and listened to all the quiet that came from that restless sea of life before him, he saw the faces sunken with sorrow.

"The last soft light of the setting sun was falling over the land, casting a rich glow on the cotton fields, as he stood in front of the home of his innocent youth. The garden his mother had taken care of, watered with tears of her sadness and lost dreams, was still there, but the flowers were more beautiful then, than now. He rambled around hoping to find a face to welcome him, or a look of forgiveness, or a door to open for him, or a hand to receive him. But it all was in vain. He had returned to the town he left in shame, and had come back to claim his rightful place in it, with pride. He did not have the courage to speak anyone, so he walked slowly on, like a guilty man. He went about a mile down the road from here and sat on a park bench, next to an old man who was lying down. The old man, who smelled as if he had never taken a bath, and if he had, it was in alcohol, looked up at him from the corners of his eyes.

'What do you want?' asked the old man, with a hoarse voice and ugly manner. The sound of the old man's voice sounded familiar to Peter's ear. He thought it might have been one of the people he knew from church, 'do I know you?' asked Peter.

'Hell no!' responded the old man, coming to a sitting position and looking at the stranger with a weary eye, 'what do you want?'

'Nothing. I thought I knew you,' replied Peter.

'Get out of here!' screamed the old man, with a dreadful oath. He got on his feet and stood before Peter. His garments were tattered, his hair tangled, his face unshaven, his features charged with suffering, his mouth twisted in anger and his eyes fixed upon Peter like burning fire. Peter, suspecting the old man as being one of the people he knew from his childhood days, stood up moved towards him, for a closer look.

'Get out of here, you devil!" screamed the old man, raising his heavy cane, ready to bring it down on his boy's head, at the same time Peter clasped him tightly by the shoulders.

'Give it up! Can't you see you've lost life's battle?' uttered Peter. Awed by those words, the hard look Peter threw at him and quite out of breath, the old man suffered himself to be disarmed. Peter removed the cane from the old man's grasp, placed it at the far end of the bench and set him free, with caution. "Tell me where you live and I'll take you home," said Peter, softly. The old man, not knowing the stranger was his son, stood still for a moment and gazed at him. Peter beheld those symptoms of calmness, took him gently by the arm and began to lead him away. Now, while Peter was preparing to tell the old man who he was, and the old man was thinking he was destined to a nursing home which he had refused before, a demon of discord happened to fly over that scene at that very moment and saw a father and a son walking in harmony. The malicious demon darted down, entered into the head of the old man and prompted the old man, for the demon's own evil purposes to say, 'my cane.' and the old man disengaged himself from his son's gentle grasp went for his cane. While Peter stood and waited, looking away from the old man and to the direction they were about to follow, the old man snatched the cane, and with the demon's evil thought and power and his own anger, raised it as he had done before and charged against Peter. Peter turned to see his father but only saw the cane coming down on him. He felt one powerful hard blow to his head and the blood rushing out as he struggled to stand on his feet. The stranger moved backwards and fell upon the grass, 'please, not again, not again" he mumbled as he hit the ground. The old man screamed, hearing his son's cries and the sound of the word 'again' realizing that he had hit his son. Down on his knees, screaming, he could see that he had ruptured a vessel in his son's head and his son was dead. In the silence of the park the old man stayed on his knees holding his dead son's body across his lap and called upon God to take him also and send him straight to hell for taking his son's life. His words ran high and his voice higher, looking for some one to come to his aid."

Erik stopped there, wiped the sweat from his face and looked out at the crowd. Some were astonished, some visibly saddened and some were crying. Peddler blew his nose and wiped his eyes. The old man was sent to the state prison for the rest of his shameful life. At first he was sent to maximum security but, due to his age and his inability to escape, was later sent to a work farm. It became the old man's habit, in the morning, to go out in the courtyard but he was unable to perform that task alone. A guard would need to fetch, from a peg in the old man's cell, an old coat and a light cane with a smooth handle; the old man would put on the coat very slowly, lean one hand on the cane, the other on the guard's shoulder and walk slowly, with an audible moan, into the court yard where the guard left him to get some fresh air for half an hour, at the end of which time he was conducted back into his cell. He died there some years later and towards his end, age and infirmity deprived him of the power of speech but he showed signs of having the feelings of intense terror. He only uttered shouts with no audible words, pointed at the wall and sometimes would shrink, coiled up in the desolate corner of his cell, covering his eyes and face with his hands as if someone or something dreadful was pursuing him.

Some time before those fits of terror enveloped him and before his death, he confessed that he was the one who had killed his daughter and her young friend," stated Erik, now peering into the crowd intently. "It was the demon that persuaded the old man to hit his son again. It was the demon, who was a constant companion to the old man all throughout his miserable life and forced the old man to be cruel to his wife and children over and over, again and again; it was the demon who pushed the old man to kill his daughter and her friend; it was demon who made the old man call the police and place the blame on his innocent boy, Peter; it was the old man who called upon the demon again and again; it was the demon who made the old man angry enough to hit his son again and again.

There will be no more 'agains,' because the old man, Charles Dubois, finally killed his only son, Peter Dubois.

Ladies and gentlemen, I stand here before you and I confess to you for the first time in my life that the demon was my constant companion for many years too. I lost my son by a gunshot, and my wife, by his death. I lost everything all that I loved. Then, my friends," continued Erik with a rattling and low voice. "I cursed

God. I turned against Heaven. I cursed God with all the fury that the demon had stacked inside of me. I called God selfish and ruthless. I called God cold, deaf and dumb. I condemned God for my self-made catastrophe. Then I asked God, Why me God? Why do you make me suffer? That, my friends, was the big question. Why me God? Am I not one of your children? Then I realized that I wasn't his friend. I was the friend of the devil. Why not me? God went after the devil, and the devil was with me. I made my bed and I lay in it with the devil.

God wasn't about to let me go on hurting people. I chose to be the devil's child. I chose to find joy for myself without thinking of others. The devil whispered in my ears to do things that I knew were wrong, but the pleasure I derived from those things is how the devil used to keep me on his side. I chose the serpentine path leading to my destruction. I did not choose the straight road that leads to life's happiness. I didn't quite understand the path, the devil's path, was a path leading to a dark tunnel. But I knew that it was wrong path and though taking it was risky and exciting, it would lead me to pain and horror.

The devil knew, once he whispered in the old man's ear, 'get your cane' he knew what the old man was going to do with that cane in his hands. The devil was the old man's friend and he was not about to allow the old man to walk down the street in harmony with his son. The devil wasn't about to loose that soul. He snuck in there in his usual way, just as he snuck into my life and stayed there. Ladies and gentlemen, as I was speaking about the old man I was also talking about myself," shouted Erik in triumph, " I realized God took my son away from me, because he wasn't about to let that innocent child be a part of me and a friend of the devil. Oh God, my God, now I know why. Now, ladies and gentlemen, I know why," Erik stopped, placed the microphone on the podium took out his handkerchief and sobbed violently. He went fell to his knees weeping, gasping and weeping.

The crowd was overcome and bewildered. Peddler looked at the Reverend and the Reverend looked at Peddler and then he looked at Erik with as much confusion on his face as Peddler showed on his. Then Peddler motioned to the Reverend to follow him onto the stage, where they both quickly headed. The crowd wailed pitiful lamentations as their hearts went out to him, as Erik rose to his feet, looked back out and planted himself against the podium, as firmly as he could. When he saw the Reverend and Peddler climbing the stage steps, he motioned for them to stay where they were. Then he turned and faced the crowd, "I will spend the rest of my life condemning myself for what I have done to my family and to myself and I will spend the rest of my life fighting the devil. I will search to find a way to keep him off the face of this earth," shouted Erik, and the crowd responded with triumphant applause. "I will seek and I will find him, no matter where he hides. I will arm people with the weapons of goodness, decency and purity with which to destroy him. I will teach people to lock him out of their hearts, their homes and their lives. I will learn all his disguises and I will uncover his existence." Erik stopped for a moment and looked downwards as if he were praying.

"He is good," whispered the Reverend to Peddler, while applauding along vigorously with the crowd."

"He's my main man," replied Peddler, with a visible enthusiasm and a wide smile.

"In Peter's pocket," continued Erik, now contained, "was found a check for three hundred thousand dollars, made out to the town of Tilton. The money was used to build a new school and renovate the church, this according to Peter's written instructions. We are here today, like every year on July twentieth from now on, to celebrate that young man's significant life and not his death. My dear friends, help me say a prayer for those who died and a prayer for all of us who still live." The entire crowd got down on their knees with their heads bowed. Erik looked around him and then he too knelt.

"Lord, you have given us the right to choose between good and the evil. That father and his son chose two different paths; not all was evil, Lord, and not all was good. Please forgive them and forgive us because we are not all evil and we're not all good. Show us the light, dear Lord in Heaven, to fight and keep the devil away from the ones we love. Show us the way to live according to your wishes, to do right, good, and be just and to forsake the evil one. Please, Lord, give us the strength to fight the temptation of the devil. Give us strength to forgive others and ourselves. Give us strength, Oh,

Lord, to face each morning of a new day and see it through as a good day." Erik stood up, looked around at that huge body of faces again and said, "My friends, make it your business from now on to make someone happy everyday and you'll see, you'll be happy too. God bless all of you, now and forever."

Erik placed the microphone on the podium and left the stage in haste as Dodson, James Bridges, Bob Duncan and the other escorts of the local dignitaries applauded feverously. Some of them yelled in triumph, as all the rest of the crowd did, while Erik stood still, gazing at the people. They were obviously deeply impressed with Erik.

Erik, himself, was not only satisfied with his performance, but was somewhat amazed, feeling the people's needs, hearing their cries and seeing their troubled faces, now shining hope. He recognized there are many mortal frailties and weaknesses that ordinary people cannot overcome, without help. After several bows, he waved goodbye and headed for the truck to wait for Peddler. The truck was parked in the middle of the parking lot among buses and the sea of cars. He climbed in and sat on the passenger's side. His first act, once inside the truck, was to lock the door and test it, to see if it was secure; his second was to remove his watch, place it on the dashboard and wipe the sweat from his head and face. Afterwards, looking around to be sure no one could see him, he placed his head in his hands and sobbed violently for several minutes. When completed, he tilted back his head, closed his eyes, and feeling drained, stayed in that position for a few minutes, then opened his eyes, looked straight ahead and noticed the forest. Erik, without any further ceremony or any additional thought, came out of the truck and headed in the woods.

CHAPTER NINE

Erik's Disappearance in the Forest

Erik was hoping to find a place of quiet repose for an hour, to breath the fresh and fragrant air on the ensuing afternoon and to try to recover from the effects, brought on him by the recollection of his recent past. He sauntered deep into the forest. There he paused and contemplated, with calmness, hearing people's voices and the distant inaudible speech of an orator, coming from the direction where he had performed his end of the bargain. Having loitered there for a little while, he began winding his way farther into the forest through a variety of obstacles, small bushes, wide trunk trees, dead branches and other bits and pieces of forest. As he was rambling along, still hearing the human sounds, he suddenly hastened his walk as if he had a purpose in mind. He did that for a short time. He then suddenly stopped, without being able to give himself a reason, and, with his eyes resting on a certain undistinguished medium sized bush, a little more than a hundred feet away, he started in its direction rather hastily. He then saw a young boy, about three tall, burst out from behind that bush with his arms up high, waving him vigorously and jumping as if to attain an elevation that would provide Erik the convenience of a full view. Erik stopped, filled with bewilderment, trying to make out the form of that little boy. Then all natural sound changed into the muffled wailing of a distant choir mixed with an organ peeling forth a lively air, children's screams and laughter coming from a different direction and all were unrelated to one another. Then a faint and translucent image of the face of a young boy with curly blond hair and a pair of wings, and nothing else, lingered a few feet off the ground. It appeared to be watching over the other boy on the ground, who was still waving his arms violently. Erik started to run towards the unnatural scene but was retarded by a sudden strong wind, a brier patch and other obstacles. Unconsciously, he tripped into a running brook; his feet sank into a muddy bottom and his entire body submerged under murky water. He was hit on the head by some flying object in the process. It was impossible for him to go forward.

Men and women, who are not in the habit challenging nature, would have found it difficult if not impossible to survive such a circumstance, they would have panicked in the brook and unskillfully struggled in vain; eventually their bodies would had been discovered, some days later, floating lifeless, in a bigger river. Erik strived with all his might and half of his wits and finally made it to the edge. At that exact moment, the unnatural sounds died out, the sounds of the forest greeted his ears again and the other human sounds and the orators echoes from the gathering were not heard again, only the sounds of the forest, louder, more distinct and undisturbed than ever.

Erik raised his head to see the spot where the two boys were, and much to his surprise he saw nothing there except the bush. Now it was to his far right, encircled with different plants than those he had observed before and was trembling, as if an exclusive gust of strong wind was whipping it. He came out of the brook looking like a man who had undergone a variety of weather for some time and stretched out on his back on the solid land. Feeling exhausted, out of breath and fresh out of thought, he shivered wildly. He remained there until he stopped shivering and his clothes dried, falling in and out of a partial sleep. After some hours, lying still, he gradually began to grow back to his old self, less abstract, more alert, particularly when he saw a young man, standing above him and staring downwards with a sober face.

"Mr.- Mr.-" mumbled the stranger, squatting down next to Erik, "I—I –I haven't had the pleasure of seeing you here before."

He was a full-grown young man in his early twenties. He had a nervous manner and a partial hesitation of the first word of each sentence, it didn't appear to be a natural defect but something that was created during his early days as child growing up in a overly strict environment.

"Who and what are you?" inquired Erik, with a haughty condescension, coming to his feet without any difficulty.

The young man stood up and planted himself a little more than two paces away.

"My—my—my name is Mark. Mark T. Coon. They call me MT for short. I—I—I live a mile down, near the swamp," said the boy, "It's—it's—it's a great pleasure to see you. N—n—not many people come here. We—w—where do you come from?"

"My name is Erik Karas and I have my truck down by the Dubois restaurant," said Erik, dusting himself off.

"Wha—wha—what restaurant?" asked the young man, a surprised look on his face.

"Dubois restaurant down the road," replied Erik.

"Wha—wha—what road? T—t—t—there ain't a road around here. H—h—here is nothing but swamps for fifty miles."

"You're crazy," commented Erik, looking around to show him where he had come from.

"I—I—I ain't crazy," screamed the young man, now with indignation, getting closer to Erik.

"Take it easy, don't get all shook up," warned Erik, waving his forefinger in the direction in which the young man was standing, "it's a figure of speech." Erik, after gazing at the young man for a short time and making certain that he was not advancing, looked around at his surroundings, but he found himself bewildered when he recognized nothing of what he had passed on his way to that place.

"I'll bet you one thousand dollars there's a main road less than two miles from here," said Erik, still looking around.

"D—d—do you have a thousand dollars?" asked the young man, hastily.

"D—d—do you have a thousand dollars? Now you got me to talking like you," returned Erik, with a grin.

"No. But I know there ain't no road anywhere near here."

"How do you know?"

"B—b—b—because I ain't stupid."

"You know nothing about this area then," mumbled Erik, looking away.

"M—m – not, but I ain't lost, like you," responded the young man.

"You're right, young man, I'm lost and stupid," commented Erik, with an involuntary sigh.

"M—m—my name is Mark, I know yours is Erik." uttered the young man.

"I know your name is Mark. You told me that."

"Y—y –you forget it. I—I –I'm going," said that young man, turning abruptly and walking away hastily.

"Hey! Where are you going?" shouted Erik.

The young man turned around and walking backwards said, "b—b—b,"

"By-by?" interrupted Erik.

"No! Be back," returned the young man, turning away again and assuming his hasty walk.

Erik was under the firm impression that he was only a few minutes away from the truck and thought the young man was either not all there or not smart enough to have known the restaurant, so he pressed eagerly forward, to where he thought he had entered the forest.

He did that for half an hour and the farther he went on, the more unfamiliar and tropic the surroundings became. Being unacquainted with those exotic surroundings, that in his wildest imagination, he never thought he would ever stumble upon, he felt desperate, dispossessed, and cut off the main stream of normal life. Then, becoming restless and undecided as to what direction to follow, he sat on a dead log to gather his faculties, planted his elbows on his knees and his face in his hands and thought hard. He identified his feelings as being more puzzled and annoyed, than concerned about his physical welfare.

In the meantime, Peddler, who had summoned the authorities to report his partner's unexplainable disappearance, was surrounded by four plainclothes men and two uniformed state police officers in the private room where the negotiations with the two town Mayors had previously taken place. Each of those lawmen sat around the big table with a cup of coffee in front of them. Peddler however sat a respectful distance from the round table as he explained to them all that had occurred. It was necessary for Peddler to explain it to them, together, for various reasons, but mostly thinking that Erik might be in imminent danger. He explained that Erik had just felt the important rise on his life's flight of steps, which he had taken when he stood in front of hundreds of people confessing his life's story and was received with adoration and enthusiasm and that his future expectations were bright and smooth.

"Therefore, he had no reason to disappear," concluded Peddler, in a most earnest tone.

"We understand all that, Mr. Spencer, but according to you, he was drifting through when you met him a few days ago and he only disappeared twenty four hours ago," said a middle age crimson faced man, sitting there next Peddler with his hands folded on the table, looking calm and cool. "Granted, we ran a sheet on him and found nothing derogatory, but still, according to you, he comes up as a drifter."

"Mr. Foster, your name is Foster?" said Peddler. The man nodded in assent. "Mr. Foster, you are with what agency sir?"

"FBI, New Orleans," replied Foster. "Mr. Foster, wouldn't it sound a little strange to you, if you told yourself that this man, who had everything to look forward to, picked up and took off, leaving his belongings in a motel where he stayed the last four nights and left his gold watch on the dashboard of my truck?"

The man smiled openly, something FBI agents don't often do, "first I would tell myself to wait another day or two. The reason I'm here is because the Mayor of Hixton called my office and urged that somebody get on this case," said Foster, without taking the time to breathe.

"I know. William Dodson, the Hixton Mayor and James Bridges, the Tilton Mayor, were, and still, are very much concerned about Erik. They had police with dogs and a lot of volunteers searching the area last night. You see, Mr. Foster, and the rest of you gentlemen, I went to the truck and when I saw his watch on the dashboard and he wasn't there, something of an uncomfortable feeling came over me, and I walked towards the woods and I thought I heard him screaming, from the top of his lungs, as if some strange animal grabbed him, not too far from where I was standing. That's when I alerted the Mayor and he immediately sent police in there, but they found nothing. We waited a little while, I would say two or three hours, and we started the search again. The sniffing dogs picked up his trail, but they lost it just where I thought I heard him screaming. A very mysterious situation this is," said Peddler.

There were many thoughts around that table, with pros and cons; everybody expressed their feelings and argued their case in their own way and at their own length and Peddler, thinking that Erik was in an imminent danger, argued and remonstrated out of his wits and declared that he regarded Erik with feelings of affection and attachment, and, as his best friend, that he had the good right and title to be considered, and in some degree, his guardian and adviser, he was therefore demanding steps to be taken by the authorities to find him dead or alive.

"You are demanding, you said, Mr. Spencer?" shouted the FBI agent, getting on his feet, breathing short and looking long at Peddler, with great antipathy, "who in the hell are you to demand?"

The excitement, that had cast an wonton light over the man's face, did not subside as he finished his comment, which was uttered as an rhetorical question; he just left his eyes nailed on Peddler for a round minute

"Sir, a man of your profession sees the worst side of human nature. All its disputes, all its ill will and bad blood rise before you. If you, Mr. Foster, are a learned man, as you are required by your profession to be, you know for whom you are working. To remind you, sir, your gun and badge don't scare me like they used to. I just learned it from the man you don't wish to find. Do I make myself clear to you, sir?" replied Peddler calmly, apparently thinking that it was better to be cool but with as much strength and power as the FBI agent, shooting his eyes to him in a piercing manner.

"Clear! It's very clear!' replied the agent, with a much calmer way, after taking some time to stare at Peddler and absorb his sentiments. "Now, there is nothing else we can do for you, so let me and my men plan our search."

"Very good, sir," replied Peddler, complying with the agent's somewhat earnest retreat but still looking very hard at him. "You will see me again, sir, tomorrow. I hope you may live to remember and feel deeply what I have tried to communicate to you, young man, to stay a learned man, which is just the opposite of ignorant," said Peddler, bowing respectfully before Mr. Foster and imparting a hint of a military salute to the rest with a steady hand. He departed immediately, leaving the door open as he left the private and crowded room.

"Learned man," mumbled one of the uniformed state troopers, after he made certain Peddler was out of sight, "who does he think he is?"

"A learned man. That's who he is. Which is the opposite of ignorant. You heard that too," said agent Foster, earnestly taking a sip from his coffee, after a long stare at the trooper who had made that comment.

"I heard it," replied the trooper, arrogantly.

The FBI agent placed his cup in the saucer very carefully and stared at the trooper once again but harder, much harder than before, "Did you understand it?" he asked, with a firm entreaty.

"What is this, a test on Civil Rights?" asked the same uniformed trooper, with the blond hair and shaved sides.

"No! A question of feelings," uttered the FBI agent, calmly, "but you flunked on that subject."

At the sound of those words, all those President's and Governor's men looked at each other with dubious and short alternate allotments of glances, and lastly they took sips from their coffees and then they bent their heads down and gazed at their coffee cups.

Erik, sitting on that dead log, still with his hands on his knees and his face resting on his hands, feeling low and confused, thought it might raise his spirit, perhaps, if he went on to look for an exit out of that jungle. As he went on his chosen way, even though he felt lost, with many vivid and visible indications that he wasn't going to make it out of that weird and unwelcoming place alive, he wasn't stricken with any feeling of panic, misery or anger as one might have guessed; there was a pleasing feeling within him that reflected the satisfaction he derived from his speech. He struggled on, forward, looking back once in a while and taking very little heed of the scanty progress he was making. Suddenly, the young man, Mark, appeared to be coming his way, accompanied by a young woman and another young man. Erik noticed they all carried rifles slung from their shoulders and looked like hunters, returning from a long trip.

"Hey!' shouted Erik, waving at them with delight depicted in his countenance.

"I was wondering what could have happened to you," he exclaimed. By this time, he had found another dead log to sit on, and was looking from Mark to the young woman and from her to the other young man, still with delight on his face as the arrived. All three of them planted themselves near him and looked down at him like three street lampposts.

"Th—th—this here, young lady is my sister, Annabelle Lee, and this here is my brother, Gauguin" said Mark, removing the rifle from his shoulder and resting its butt on the tip of his shoe.

"How are you," returned Erik, raising himself slowly out of civility and sitting back down with the same speed, "my name is Erik."

They both nodded without saying a word but the young woman smiled, flirtingly. "Th—th—this here boy," said Mark, bending his head to the side, "e—e—is a good boy, but sometimes he gets into mischief, and my father says that he has hot blood."

The young man, Gauguin took a warning pinch and shook his head and distorted his face skeptically

"I—I—I am the only one to whom he listens. A—a—ain't it so, Gauguin?"

Gauguin shook his head again, calmed his facial features and winked at Mark, after he imparted a hint of a grin.

"Who gave you those names, your mother or your father?" asked Erik, looking at Mark, "they are significant names of famous people."

"My father," said the young lady with a smile, "my father was born in England and likes books and art and poetry."

"I see," replied Erik, with a faint grin, "Mark Twain, I presume, Gauguin, the French artist and Edgar Allen Poe's, Annabelle Lee."

All three youngsters laughed and looked at each other, perplexed.

"How about you mother?" asked Erik.

"We have no mother," answered the girl, almost abruptly.

"S—s—she died right after she gave birth to Gauguin. T—t—twenty years ago."

"No she didn't die," said Gauguin, almost protesting, "she ran away with another man. Now she lives in New Orleans. I saw her once. She has a big store."

"Department store," interjected Annabelle Lee, unleashing her rifle from her shoulder and letting it rest the same way Mark had.

Erik studied her face and found it to be very pretty, with long, light brown hair combed back and tied in a pony tail and a dimple on each side of her mouth that made her smile attractive, knowing that, she always smiled at the end of a sentence.

Gauguin was a thick set young man with light brown hair, rather short and pale; his round face was embellished with spectacles. Such were the two souls to whom Erik was introduced by their brother and leader, Mark. The arrival of the trio had somewhat lifted Erik's spirits a bit, their earnest openness to Erik's curiosity helped matters to a good extent.

"You look like a good and healthy family in both body and in mind. Your father has done a good job in bringing you up, which wasn't, as you must know, an easy task," said Erik, most earnestly.

That was no comment, no words were spoken but the three looked at each and grinned.

"How old are you, Mark?"

"I—I—I am twenty-four years old, today," remarked Mark with a smile.

"Oh! Happy birthday. You were born July twentieth, how nice," said Erik.

"N—n –no I was born today, July twenty-one," responded the young man.

"Today is his birthday July twenty-one," added the girl.

Turning what he heard over in his mind as he sat there, Erik gradually worked himself to a frenzy; thinking, if the youngsters were playing with him, it was reason to be alarmed, if they weren't it was worse, because somewhere, somehow he had lost his mind, his senses and a day; and overtaken by those reflections, he jumped to his feet, looked at all of them with furious eyes and said with clenched teeth, "You're lying to me. You're liars, all of you. Today is the twentieth of July. Do you hear me?" The trio lifted their rifles to the ready for what they feared to be a mad man.

Erik, paranoid, believed those three rascals were trying to drive him crazy so they could take his thousand dollars. He looked at the girl for a few seconds and was in some doubt as to whether it would be better to snatch the rifle from her and fire at Mark and then to turn and off Gauguin, then finish her, leaving no eyewitness behind. On second thought he abandoned that plan as being a severe punishment for those kids who only wanted his money, so he attempted a new method of solving the problem.

"Are you guys working?" asked Erik in loud voice and in an open unreserved sort of manner hoping to engage the two boys in a conversation. Neither one of them took much notice of him, but they shrank the space between them. They whispered something to each other and scowled at him. The young lady was far to their right and couldn't hear what they were talking about but from the expression on her face she must have understood it had to be something bad, so she ventured to wave her hand as if beseeching Erik. Erik chooses not to make a move, as she seemed to be expecting it; he only looked at her as if he had noticed nothing. Then the two boys advanced a little closer.

"D—d –don't you know that this is a forbidden garden, buddy?" said Mark with his rifle pointing downwards in front of Erik.

"No, I didn't know that, buddy," returned Erik, as if he didn't really understand his meaning. "He said this here land is off limits to everybody, didn't you hear my brother telling you?" said Gauguin, flourishing his rifle in the air showing off his knowledge and confidence in it.

"What?" said Erik, pretending not to comprehend their words.

"Leave or die," cried the younger brother, placing the rifle on Erik's neck.

"Kill him!" shouted the older brother, falling back, as if he didn't wish to be splattered with blood. Erik being a man of courage and great presence of mind and not believing that he was about to die, stood still, appearing so indifferent to what was going on, he astonished the young brother who looked back to see his sibling's reaction. With one bound Erik grabbed the rifle and hit him on the head with the butt of it, he went down face first and never make a move. Erik then jumped forward and hit the other brother in the chest, but he didn't go down. With an acrobatic move, Erik imparted a side-kick hitting Mark's knee with the side of his shoe; he heard the cracking of bones. Mark, hearing and feeling the breaking of his knee, turned white and fell only a few feet from his brother. Erik turned and saw the girl holding the rifle on him with trembling hands. He walked slowly over to her, pushed her rifle aside and placed the muzzle on her firm breast.

The young lady stepped slightly aside and looked at Erik with an alluring smile. Her teeth sparkled and the dimples blossomed, she unbuttoned her blouse, looking at him with her mouth half open, "You don't want to hurt me, you want to make love to me. I'll show you a place in the grass and then we can do it in the water," whispered the girl in an innocent voice, while undoing the top button of her blue jeans with one hand and still holding onto her rifle with the other. She then let the rifle drop and unzipped her jeans halfway down to show her white panties, three inches below her belly button. Erik threw away his rifle, kicked hers out of reach and went close to her. He kissed her forehead, placed his hand underneath her chin, raised her face and kissed her lips.

"Annabelle Lee, she wanted to love and be loved by me'," whispered Erik, softly.

She turned her face up to him and said coquettishly, "I'll bet I'm the youngest you've made love to, for a long time," running her fingers through his hair and still looking at him in the eyes.

"Only if you less than eighteen," said Erik, touching her cheek with his lips. "Then, I'll be the best," said the young lady. "That title is always up for grabs," whispered Erik, touching her lips with his fingers.

Annabelle Lee grabbed his face and pulled his mouth against hers. Her manner was hard, fast and a splendid example of triumph and a strength that was irresistible. But the stars weren't in their favor, track or position for them that day, because the sight and sound of a helicopter flying above them filled the sky.

Erik disengaged himself from her grip, a task that wasn't easy, turned to see the helicopter and let out a scream louder than an air horn. He watched the big bird land a little distance beyond. When he turned back, the girl was over fifty feet away, threading her way through the woods as if a dozen demons were pursuing her, while her two brothers still slept peacefully.

Erik looked around in confusion, and then, turning his eyes towards where he helicopter had landed, spotted two uniformed police and two civilians struggling through the forest hastily heading towards him.

"Mr., Karas!" shouted one civilian, who happened to be the FBI agent Foster, who had conducted the conference with Peddler in the private room.

"Eh?" exclaimed Erik, focusing his eyes beyond them, as he recognized the familiar features of Peddler almost flying towards him.

Peddler passed all of them and was the first to reach Erik and grabbed and hugged him as if he hadn't seen him for years.

"Couldn't you have made it an hour or two later," said Erik, with an ironic smile, pulling away from Peddler.

"Why? Did we interrupt your seven course dinner?"

"Worse."

"A girl?" replied Peddler.

"What girl?"

"It has to be a girl. The only thing better than a seven course dinner for you has to be a girl," said Peddler, looking around.

"How about you?" asked Erik.

"For me its dinner."

"You're that old?"

"Don't worry, you'll be here too one day," remarked Peddler, still looking around anxiously.

"If I get there and dinner comes first, I'll jump in a swamp to be dinner for the alligators," said Erik.

"Just remember, life is sweet no matter what your desires are." replied Peddler, as he waited for the officers of the law to arrive, who after seeing Peddler get there first, slacked off their pace a little. "This is Mr. Erik Karas, the Evangelist," announced Peddler, extending his arms towards Erik as the officers reached the twosome.

The FBI agent first acknowledged Erik then extended his hand to shake; the rest vaguely waved their hands in salutation.

"How do you feel, Reverend?" asked Mr. Foster.

"Please, sir, don't refer to me as a reverend. I'm not an ordained minister, I'm just an orator," answered Erik waving his greeting.

"What happened to these two? Broken necks?" asked the FBI man, pointing at the two bodies sprawled on the ground, one face up and the younger face down.

"No broken necks here," replied Erik, "one has a broken leg and the other just a messed up face."

"Where is the girl?"

"The girl ran away as soon as she saw the helicopter," responded Erik.

"We'll find her soon," answered the agent, " somebody call an ambulance," ordered Foster, turning to his men.

"The girl is innocent. She didn't do anything."

"I am glad to hear that. She has no record. She may learn a lesson from this," returned the FBI man, with an earnest ring to his voice

"Pick up those rifles!" commanded Foster, to his men.

"The rifles are empty," declared Erik.

"How do you know? Did you check them?" asked the same man again.

"No. I didn't check them, but I know they're empty. When the young one held his rifle at my neck, I felt him playing with the trigger," replied Erik.

By the time Erik concluded his statement a uniformed State Police officer handed one rifle to the FBI agent, the agent checked it and founded Erik to be correct.

"How did you find me? I know how, you just flew in here, but why?"

"You partner in crime,"

"I beg you pardon Mr. Foster, sir. Partners in business," interrupted Peddler, kindly. "I'm sorry," began The FBI man, "Your friend here insisted that we run a missing person's report on you on the TV. A man, named Wallace Coon, from Plato, Louisiana, saw the TV and recognized your name. He reported that his two sons and his daughter, convicted petty thieves, found a man fitting your description and said he overheard his kids talking of robbing him. First we spotted their truck parked a couple miles from here and here we are. We knew the rifles were empty. Wallace Coon told us. He said he had hidden the rounds a long time ago."

"Why, Peddler? I'm glad but why? I was only gone less that six hours," said Erik, turning to Peddler.

"Six hours?" questioned Peddler, astonished, "twenty-six you mean."

Erik just looked at Peddler, vacantly, and said nothing.

"Six hours, you said?" asked Peddler again, still surprised and bewildered.

Erik made no reply. He only looked around him. A universal astonishment fell on every soul at that scene. There was something so impressive in that mute astonishment, that each man viewed each other and then Erik and all seemed reluctant to speak.

"Are you all right Mr. Karas?" asked Mr. Foster.

"I haven't gone crazy. Not yet any way," replied Erik, with a smile fixed on his face.

"You are the best judge of that," continued the agent.

"Best judge of what, that I am not crazy?" asked Erik, with another smile.

"No. No, that you're not hurt."

"There is a logical explanation for everything that happens in life," said Erik, "Yesterday afternoon I tried to cross a creek. At first, I thought the creek was shallow and I went in, but I found it to be too deep with mud on the bottom and I slipped; at the time, I felt I was hit on the head with a heavy log and I lost my senses. I probably walked all through the night, suffering from amnesia. When I came to, now I remember, I was lying on the ground and when I opened my eyes I saw the young man standing above me. What happened between the youngsters and me is simple. It was a vile attempt to extort money from me," deduced Erik, "and somehow it got out of hand, as most crimes do, and turned into a violent defense and you're looking at the results."

"You're a very lucky man, Mr. Karas," said Foster, "but if I were you, I'd shy away from swamps."

"How far did I travel, Peddler?" asked Erik, not wanting to elaborate on the subject any further.

"Twenty-five miles from Tilton," Peddler answered.

CHAPTER TEN

Peddler's secret

"Where do we go from here?" asked Peddler, leaning with both elbows on a round table, a half full large pitcher of beer and the two half filled glasses, in front of him.

"Out of town!" said Erik, looking away.

"To do what?"

"Sell Bibles."

"No Good. We introduced you as a mighty Joe Young. And you performed like a mighty Joe Young. How can we have you do the monkey dance now?"

Erik returned no response to that comment; he only gazed around the roadhouse. There was a large bar with a marble vase-like a beer dispenser in the middle, out of which the bartender drew beer into big glass mugs. There were many booths and tables filled with men of the working class, most of them with pumped up bellies as if their only sports were eating and drinking beer in excess.

"I beg your pardon, gentlemen," said a heavy-set waitress standing over them, "did you want anything else? I'm going home now, but I'll bring you whatever you want." With this request, Peddler some money in the waitress' hand and ordered another pitcher of beer.

Erik gave Peddler a corrective look.

"I must confess something to you, Curly."

"Don't waste you confession on me, I'm not wearing a white collar."

"Sometimes you can be very nasty, Erik," remarked Peddler.

"I'm sorry, " was the return.

Peddler returned the gaze with a disappointed countenance.

"Go ahead, Peddler, fire when ready, confess!"

"Liquor is the best way to practice life for me. I carry it with me in a little bottle. It's like a crutch. I haven't met a man who doesn't have some kind of crutch," said Peddler, still looking into Erik's eyes, trying hard to sound sober, which by this time wasn't an easy task, "you have a crutch too, Curly."

"Me?" responded Erik.

Peddler broke into a boisterous laugh as the waitress brought a fresh pitcher of beer; it reduced him to the ignominious necessity of gulping what was left in his glass.

"The Greek philosopher, what's his name. Oh yes, Socrates," recalled Peddler, as soon as the waitress had gone. "He said, that each man caries two bags with him. One hangs in the front and the other hangs on the back. The front one contains all the bad deeds and habits of others; the back one contains his own. Socrates went on to say, that most men never look at the back bag, only at the front. Have you heard that before, Curley?"

"Even the Amazonians heard of it. Go on, say what you have to say and get it off your chest."

"My crutch comes in a little bottle, yours comes as a big bundle of bones and flesh that's stacked in the right places, it's called women. I'd probably walk a mile for a drink but you'd run ten miles just to see some woman."

"Let me tell you something, Peddler," started Erik, in a solemn tone.

"Oh, pray tell, my friend, pray tell!" interrupted Peddler, in a somewhat obliging manner.

"Never mind," said Erik, as if he had wished to change the course of the conversation, " but I think I like you better when you're sober and broke."

"Wait a minute," said Peddler, searching his pockets hastily, "talking about being broke," there he stopped, reached deep in his pocket, brought out a bank check and stretched it flat on the table before Erik, "Here!" said Peddler, pointing at the check, with all his fingers shooting at it.

Peddler winked, shook his head, smiled then winked again, with an expression on his face that clearly denoted he was proud of himself.

"Peddler!" exhaled Erik, as he picked up the check and examined it, "this is a lot of money. Who gave you this?"

"The Mayor of Hixton. That's a down payment for your next revival meeting at the town auditorium"

"Why?"

"You'll find that answer large and complicated," replied Peddler.

"You know, Peddler, I never met a man who doesn't know how to read and write, who goes to the library, except to clean up the place."

"I don't understand what you are trying to say, Erik."

"I don't know anything about politics. What in the hell am I supposed to do there? Maybe those guys want us to clean up their mess."

"No, no, no. It's nothing like that," affirmed Peddler, hammering the table with his fist lightly.

"I hope they're not weaving a sock with us."

"You know, Erik, sometimes you're talking Greek to me. What you just said, it's all Greek to me."

Erik looked at Peddler, "Shakespeare said the same thing, just a little differently, 'What a tangled web we weave when first we practice to deceive'. What bothers me is when you said the answer is large and complicated."

"Things go through my mind like they go through yours. When I saw the check I told them that you're Greek and you know, very well, the old Greek saying, *"Fool me once and I'll be sad. Fool me twice and you'll be sad and sorry.* " Saying this, Peddler smiled as if swimming in pride.

"I've never heard any Greek saying that," returned Erik.

"I know. I made it up and I just signed your name, like Plato did. He made up things and signed Socrates' name."

"Peddler, don't ever allow yourself to get sick and die and never allow yourself to be fatigued beyond your powers. Consider yourself a valuable asset to society. For the sake of your fellow man, keep yourself as healthy as you can, it would be an immense loss to society if something happened to you. Remember the world needs drummers and dancers. Drummers to grab the attention and keep the pace going so the dancers can provide the entertainment."

"I assume you're referring to yourself as a dancer. Then I must be the drummer," reasoned Peddler.

"You beat your drum to bring people around to watch me dance and then we collect."

"Collect their money?"

" What else? Look, you conned those guys out of their money and you're conniving me into getting up there to pull their chestnuts out of the fire. It works. Everybody's happy and everybody can walk into the sunset together holding each other's hands."

"Talking about being healthy and keeping alive, can I confess something to you?"

"Confess again? What is this, Good Friday?" snapped Erik.

"Erik' are you afraid of dying?" asked Peddler, disregarding Erik's response.

"I knew it, I knew it, that check is going to be my death, you must have got it from the Mafia."

"No, Erik, the check came from the politicians," interrupted Peddler.

"I know. They're worse than the Mafia. They can, with the strike of a pen, have the government take care of you, just like with the nod of a head the Mafia will. Any more good news? A nice confession maybe?" quizzed Erik, appearing more indignant than he really was.

"Why are you so excited?" asked Peddler, calmly.

"Why? Why, you're asking? You handed me a bank check for ten times more money than I've ever had at one time, then you are asking me if I'm afraid of dying. Hell yes, I'm afraid of dying, like anybody in his right mind is afraid of dying!" exclaimed Erik, now even more agitated.

Peddler broke into loud laughter and then, once he had finally composed himself asked,

"Erik, I just want to know why we, as human beings, are afraid of dying."

"You mean to say that you weren't trying to tell me that someone was out to get me? returned Erik, calmly now.

"No, Erik. I just wanted to know if you're afraid of dying."

Erik closed his eyes for a moment and smiled, "Peddler, I understood what you were asking me, I just wanted to bust your chops," said Erik, adding a wide smile to his face at the conclusion of his comment.

"You sounded as if you wanted to chop my head off," returned Peddler.

"Well, when we were born, God inserted the fear of death within us so we'd preserve ourselves to accomplish our missions. One of our missions in life is to multiply. None of us knows what our other missions in life are. But there is a mission for each of us and that varies from being the leader of the world to being food for alligators," concluded Erik.

"Erik, you're speaking Greek to me again."

"Okay, okay. Listen to me! A man's mission in this life is not always pleasant. Are you listening?"

"Oh pray tell," responded the peddler.

"Example." Erik stopped, smiled and changed the tone of his voice, "here we are, you're half drunk and I'm half asleep and we're pursuing a topic that great philosophers attempted to solve only with a great deal of mental toil."

"You are a philosopher," said Peddler in an earnest manner.

"No, Peddler, I'm a sophisticated man, which regrettably only means I'm a pseudo-philosopher."

"Go on," said Peddler, reaching down to pick up his glass.

"Don't even think about taking another sip before I finish what I started. I'm not gonna waste a deep thought on a drunk," said Erik. Peddler put down his glass as carefully and as firmly as Erik spoke.

"Like you always say, fire when ready!" said Peddler.

"You said you have a confession to make. Tell me! Be my guest," encouraged Erik

"I forgot," returned Peddler.

"I think I'm going to hit you on the head with that pitcher, then you'll remember."

"Now, I remember what I wanted to confess to you. I'm afraid of dying, not because I have a mission, but because nobody is going to come to my funeral. Nobody was enthused at the event of my arrival on this earth and nobody will be saddened at my departure. Can you imagine, I've lived on this earth for over sixty-five years and there is no one who'll miss me when I'm gone. But I know why, because I loused up my youth and when one louses up his youth he grows up to be a fool and there ain't no fool like an old fool and that's what I am," declared Peddler; lowering his eyes he added," I don't a have mission, Curly, probably a dream, but no mission."

"What's the difference? Missions and dreams, they're all the same," assured Erik.

"No, Curly, a mission is designed by God but dreams are designed by the person. Very few people know what their mission in life is. I know what your mission in life is. Your mission from God is to live until you are one hundred and two and to be shot by some jealous young husband."

Erik smiled, looked at Peddler and replied " from your mouth to God's ears, my friend."

Erik would not hear of passing by that statement without digging a little further, "Is that it?

"That's it."

"That's not a mission, it's a sin, Peddler."

"Wait, I'm not finished yet. I loused up my life, that's all but I'm only hanging onto a dream," said Peddler.

"What's your dream?" asked Erik.

"I'll tell you later," was the answer from Peddler who, looking away, then mumbled, "I just loused up."

"How did you do that?" asked Erik, " I mean, how did you louse up?"

"How?" cried Peddler, taking a long drink from his glass, as if preparing to tell his story, "It's a secret how I loused up. I won't tell anybody that."

"I understand. You must have a secret recipe for screwing up. Very few people louse up their lives, in this world, you must just be a rare species," said Erik, sarcastically.

Peddler turned to Erik, gazed at him for a long moment and said with a broken voice, "Please, Curly, don't make fun of me. When the time comes, I'll tell you."

These tokens of Peddler's feelings, slight as they were, were not lost on Erik. He took a drink from his glass, looked away for a short moment then gazed at his friend, who had already placed his head on the table and was sobbing silently.

Erik thought the beer and other spirits Peddler had consumed attributed to the scene but at the same time he believed there were many roots deeper than a pitcher of beer that had triggered Peddler into his sobbing ceremony.

Peddler, after a few minutes in that attitude, appearing aware of where he was and what was happening, raised his head from the table, looked at Erik from behind the tears and said, rather snappishly, " I want to go to Jackson."

"Jackson?" asked Erik, bewildered and somewhat astonished.

"Yes, Jackson, Jackson Mississippi, and I want to go now," declared Peddler, wiping tears from his eyes with unsteady hands.

"Do you know that it's past midnight? And, do you know how far Jackson is from here?" questioned Erik, with indignation in both his voice and manner.

"Yes I know it's past midnight and Jackson is a few miles away from here," replied

Peddler, attempting to stand.

"A few miles? A few hundred miles, you mean."

"I don't care, a few miles, a few hundred miles, a few hours, days, months or years. I've got to go to Jackson," said Peddler firmly, now standing up and looking down at Erik.

"Jackson it is, Jackson we go," said Erik, getting to his feet without any further delay.

"Can I finish my drink?" asked Peddler, calmly sitting down again.

"I'll wait for you in the truck," responded Erik, turning to leave rather hastily.

"No." said Peddler, grabbing Erik's coat.

"Let go of me."

"Sit down, Curly. Greek, please sit down. I want to talk to you."
"Then talk to me, but first let go of my coat. I don't like to be held back."

"Not until you promise to listen to me."

Erik took a deep breath rolled his eyes towards the sky, sat down, methodically folded his hands on the table and stared at Peddler, "Go ahead, fire when ready!"

"I am sorry you got angry when I mentioned Jackson."

"I am not angry about Jackson," replied Erik.

"I don't know why I said Jackson. I've never been to Jackson."

"Peddler, I am most aware of the inestimable value of your assistance during the last few days as we endeavor to accomplish something worth while, but unless you sincerely believe that I'm incapable of reading people's faces, even though that is a part of my job, as a salesman, I would rather be deprived of your aid and talents unless you are willing to level with me. Now, tell me about Jackson."

"Nothing to tell," replied Peddler.

Erik, who's thoughts had been gradually growing less abstract and more solid on the subject of Jackson, looked and smiled back at Peddler and concluded, "Behind every successful man there is a woman who inspires him and behind every looser stands a woman filled with scorn."

CHAPTER ELEVEN

Peddler's secret uncovered

The truck rolled swiftly past the fields and orchards that skirted the road. Groups of men, women and a few children were just beginning to get to work in the fields. The villages they passed glowed in their full summer glory. The same trees one could imagine as shrunken and bare in the early months of winter, had now burst into life, strong and healthy, and stretched out their green arms over the thirsty ground, transforming open and naked spots into choice places of deep and pleasant shade from where to gaze upon the sun's domain stretched out beyond. It seemed as though Mother Nature had spread her brightest green blanket and her richest perfumes all over that land.

Peddler sat in the passenger seat, nervously fiddling with a whiskey flask he held close to him. He didn't drink but just looked down at it from time to time and then out of the window.

"I'm sorry about last night, Erik," he said.

"Why? For getting drunk," asked Erik.

"Not for getting drunk, or for spilling my guts out to you. I hate to complain and I hate feeling..." he stopped himself.

"For feeling sorry for yourself? Don't think about it. It happens to everybody. It happens from the day we're born, until the day we die. I've written a poem about how lonely I felt when I was young," said Erik.

"When I was a young lad I used to leave home
In the wheat and tobacco fields I used to roam.
I didn't leave home to look for my future, fore I had no past.
My only worry was to make my day's bread to last.

I'd watch the bees feeding the flowers with pollen, flying
    from one to another.
I just waited for someone to call me, particularly my mother.
When nobody called me, I wanted to leave for distant lands
To find new parents, new folks and friends.
But there was a mountain on one side, on the other the sea,
Where could I go with just only me?
Then I would pretend I heard someone calling my name.
I'd go home and find everything to be the same,
My little brother still standing by the fireplace,
My little sister in the courtyard chasing chickens with a
    smiling face,
My mother was preparing the meal of the day.
No one ever missed me when I went away."

Erik concluded, looking away.

"My God, Erik you have a way with words. I can tell you've
been a loner all your life and you're a poet too, aren't you?"
remarked Peddler.

Erik stricken with true emotion lost his power of speech for a
moment, still looking away, he grunted, "Uh! Huh!"

"I must tell you, Erik, in my opinion, you're a whole man," said
Peddler.

"Thank you, Peddler, but how's that?"

"I should have said that you're God's man, not a man of God,
just God's man," said Peddler, earnestly.

"Why?"

"God, according to what I believe, designed man to be with a
woman. You're a romantic man. I saw you how you behaved with
Mary Lou. You must be with a woman. That's how God wants a
man to be. God took a rib from Adam to make the woman. He didn't
have to do that unless he meant for her to be a part of him. He
didn't run out of mud, you know. He simply wanted Adam to know
that the woman was a part of him. A man is only half of a man
without a woman. Now, I know why you like women, Curly. A
man without a woman is a half a being, half man you might say.
I've been half a man all my life," discovered Peddler.

"You don't have a woman? Why in the hell are we going to Jackson? shouted Erik, slowing the truck, "I thought you had a woman down there."

"Curly, don't get excited. There is a woman down there, but it's different. You'll see. Now, pull over here," said Peddler

"Why?" asked Erik

"Never mind why, just do it," ordered Peddler

Erik pulled the truck over onto the side of the road and gazed at his companion with curious eyes. Peddler got out of the cab and headed for the back of the truck. Meanwhile, Erik sat in the driver's seat smoking and thinking. After a few minutes of preparation, Peddler reappeared.

"That's some fancy get-up you have there," remarked Erik, examining Peddler from top to bottom.

It was interesting to observe Peddler, with his hair slicked back, wearing a fancy suit that was at least thirty years out of fashion.

"Just drive, we're almost there." said Peddler, trying to catch his breath.

The truck rolled down a beautiful southern street. The homes were all set back, far off the road, to more proudly display their expansive green lawns.

"Where are we?" asked Erik

"This is Jackson," said Peddler

"Between you and me, Peddler, I think you have a rich broad here, one that you don't want to tell me about. That's why you said that she's different. She's rich; she has to be different. All my women were poor. But I must admit, you're looking good, " teased Erik, with a smile big enough to broaden Peddler's heart to bigger than a cotton field.

"There's a third party involved here, I can't say anything," said Peddler.

"So you're a lover boy! I never thought you had it in you," said Erik.

Peddler pointed at the corner, disregarding Erik's statement. "Turn right here," he said.

The truck turned down a beautiful tree-lined lane.

"It's at the end of the street," exclaimed Peddler, pointing his finger and focusing intently.

"This must be the best part of town," remarked Erik.

"The very best," replied Peddler.

"I'm impressed, Peddler."

"Stop in front of that house, there."

The truck came to a stop in front of a huge white home. Peddler opened the truck door, stepped out, put on his hat in a easy graceful way and looked at Erik with a nervous smile.

"I'll be back, I won't be very long," he said.

"Go! Stay as long as you want! I'll be sleeping," returned Erik, urging Peddler to go.

"No. I'll be right back," replied Peddler, walking away with deliberation.

"What are you going to do? Are you just going to deliver a message? I'll wait, then," shouted Erik

"Good."

Erik watched as Peddler walked the sycamore-lined path, until he reached the

front door; there he paused for a long moment looking at the door, showing symptoms of hesitation. He suddenly turned and headed back towards the truck While walking, he looked only in the direction of the truck, saw Erik glaring at him, stopped, thought for a long moment, gazing at the ground, threw a quick glance at Erik and seeing him gesturing him to go on, he turned around and went back to the house, gave a timid knock on the door, stood back and waited for an answer. While waiting, he took off his hat, dusted it with his hand and then pressed the doorbell. He placed his hat under his arm and stared at the door. Erik, watching Peddler, felt his jaw drop when the door opened and he saw a blond haired, blue- eyed man of about thirty standing in the doorway.

"What the hell?" mumbled Erik, scratching his head with both hands.

"Who are you?" asked the blue-eyed man with curiosity in his eyes and voice.

"I beg your pardon, sir, is Clara Ann in?" asked Peddler.

"Who? You must mean my wife. Clara! There's a man here to see you," he called aside.

"Be right there," yelled a lady, from deep inside the home.

The man didn't take his eyes off Peddler, as if he were at a loss to comprehend what that colored man was doing there, calling on his wife, but Clara's voice snapped him out of any thinking.

"Who is it, Kevin?" asked Clara, approaching.

"I don't know. A colored man is here asking for Clara Ann," replied Kevin, with his eyes still nailed on the stranger.

The young lady came to the door as briskly as she could, having no idea who the uninvited visitor could be. She poked her head out of the door to take a good look at him, then her face underwent a variety of odd contortions, the moment her eyes fell upon the stranger at the door.

Peddler, on seeing that striking and dignified white woman with long dark hair, made an ineffectual attempt to smile at that beautiful creature, but that gesture was terminated by the quivering of his lower lip.

Her husband, who had stepped aside to let her see the visitor, sensing some hesitancy in her manner, was about to make a comment, but she spoke first.

"Why don't you go upstairs and take your shower? We have to start getting ready for tonight," suggested Clara, with her eyes nailed on Peddler.

"Are you going to be long?" asked Kevin.

"Two minutes, that's all. Come in please," said Clara, gesturing Peddler to enter, after only a moment's consideration.

Peddler saw, with his mind's eye, distinctly, that he wasn't welcome there. The thought of turning back and running to his truck came to him, but being a man of great determination, he walked right in, cautiously. The husband cast a quick glance at the visitor just before he disappeared at the top of the stairs. Peddler twirled his hat in his hands as he awkwardly stood in the center of the living room.

"What are you doing here?" whispered Clara, glaring.

"Then, you must know me," replied Peddler, grinning as if he wished to smooth matters.

"I know who you are, that's all," retorted Clara, still looking at him in the same manner.

"How do you know me?" asked Peddler, still spinning his hat.

"I asked you to tell me what you are doing here." demanded Clara, stepping a few paces away from him.

She moved to stand behind a large living room chair, folded her hands before her and stared, silently.

"Something happened to me last night, in my mind that is; I had to come and see you," whispered Peddler. "Incidentally, you have a nice husband."

"You came, you saw me, now leave," said Clara, harshly, disregarding the compliment.

"Ok, I'll leave. But I must admit, I was expecting something a little more tender and softer from you, like I treated you, when you were a little girl. Do you remember?" asked Peddler.

"I remember nothing and I don't wish to remember anything about you," returned the girl.

"If you don't remember anything about me, how do you know me?" asked Peddler, with a wide grin on his face.

"I don't wish to discuss it now or ever."

"That's sad. I traveled hours and hours just to see you. But I have to tell you that when I look at you I see your mother," said Peddler, shaking his head mournfully.

Clara never responded; she just stood there indifferently, staring at him.

"Do you remember your mother?" asked Peddler.

"Yes." Clara said softly.

"Her hair was as silky as yours, her skin was as creamy and pale. Her eyes were very green like yours. When she was looking right at you they sparkled. They were mysterious eyes....." said Peddler.

"And when she married you she got what she deserved?" interrupted Clara, turning her face away. "I'll tell you how I know you." she continued, now in a softer tone of voice and manner, taking a few careful steps towards Peddler, "When I was a little girl my mother would take me out, we would go to where you were working, out of some junky looking truck, peddling stuff. She used to point you out to me and say, 'look at that colored man, how quickly and precisely he moves selling his goods,' recalled Clara, turning away abruptly. "Right before she died she told me who you were and I have not seen you since then," she continued, wiping a tear that ran down her face.

"Do I see a tear?"

"Don't fool yourself. The tear is for my mother who suffered so much on this earth for marrying you," she returned, now with an angry look coming upon her face.

"Wait a moment! Let me tell you my side of the story," exclaimed Peddler.

"I don't want to hear it," retorted Clara, looking into his eyes.

"I want you to....."

"I said I don't want to hear it," retorted the girl, loudly and precisely.

"Listen to me. It's less than two minutes. Your mother knew she was dying, and" confided Peddler, softening his voice to an almost to a whisper, "she came to meet me and that's when she told me. You see she and I were still married to each other. She told me she was going to give you away to a white couple. I got down on my knees and begged her to let me have you but she refused to listen," continued Peddler, wiping his eyes with the back of his trembling hand "You see, Clara, I understood why she was giving you away to a stranger, her folks did not want you. They hated her for marrying me."

"She never told me she had any relatives," was her surprised reply.

"She had a brother and a sister," continued Peddler.

"Do you know them?" she asked.

"Sure, I know them."

"Do they know me?" now with a trembling voice, wiping her tears with both hands.

"They saw you at your mother's funeral when you were there. They didn't know who brought you there, but I knew. You were there with the couple that adopted you," said Peddler.

"How do you know all this?" asked Clara

"I was at your mother's funeral. Nobody saw me, but I saw everybody."

"Why didn't you come to see me after my mother died?"

"Oh, my God, my God, girl, I used to see you, but you didn't see me. I made a promise to your mother that I wouldn't bother you. Besides I'm just a colored peddler. I also knew that you were happy," said Peddler, with a trembling voice.

"Do you see her folks anymore?"

"No, her sister died. You've seen her brother though," said Peddler, with vague smile.

"I've seen her brother? Where is her brother?" asked Clara.

"He is in jail. You've seen him. You were the prosecutor who sent him up the river," said Peddler, smiling.

"Me? What's his name?" asked Clara, with much interest.

"That I will not tell you. He doesn't know you," returned the Peddler.

"What's his crime?"

"That I will not tell you either," replied Peddler.

"It looks like I was born into a family of thieves and liars," mumbled Clara, as if she were talking to herself, "I am glad I wasn't raised by them," she continued, raising her voice with her last statement.

Peddler stood and stared at her for a moment, as if preparing a proper response to her statement and as if he had a contradictory opinion.

"Things and people are not, many the times, what they seem to be," replied Peddler, with an audible sigh. Peddler just stared at Clara with a serious expression on his face and Clara stared back with a most indifferent look on hers, as if nothing of substance was said.

How long that scene might have lasted or how much Peddler might have suffered for not daring to say something in order to set matters straight, no one could tell, had it not been for a little girl who, descending from the top of the stairs, stopped half way down, "who's the man you're talking to, Mommy?" she asked. The little girl, about three years old with dark hair and light eyes, held a raggedy doll with one hand and the stair spindle with the other.

"Nobody, honey, nobody; go upstairs, nanny is coming soon to take you out," answered Clara, looking down at the floor.

The little girl turned and went up the steps without looking back or saying another word.

Peddler looked at the child, put on his hat and started to leave. "Like I said, I'm just a colored peddler, a nobody," he declared, walking towards the door straight and dignified, filled with disappointment and swollen with indignation. He stopped at the door, placed his hand on the doorknob and turned to face Clara.

"I know who you are. You are an attorney and prosecutor and you're also married to an attorney and you are very successful. I'm not only proud of you, but I'm also proud of myself. They say, Clara Ann, that the apple does not fall far from the tree. Did your mother tell you that I am your father, biological father?" asked Peddler.

"Yes," snapped the daughter, "my adopting father told me it was certified by a blood test that you were my father. They did that for medical reasons. You know my birth certificate clearly indicates that I am a Caucasian. I don't know how," said Clara

"I know why and I also know how. Just remember things and people sometimes are not what they seem to be," said Peddler, with a vague smile on his face.

"Good! I'll remember that," she replied, sarcastically, "I don't want you to come back here anymore as if nothing has happened. I have no favorable feelings for you. I don't need a father anymore, particularly someone like you."

"I know. I know, who you and what you are, I said this before and I will say it again, because it gives great pleasure. You are good and smart and I know you are going to go on to high places and, according to you, I'm nothing but a colored peddler." At the point he turned and faced the closed door. He stood in that position for a long moment as if he felt trapped, then he slowly turned and, looking at his daughter, his left hand ran up and down his inner arm, "but my blood runs in your vein." He opened the door abruptly, turned and faced her one more time. "I understand you ma'am and I respect your delicacy, but if I were so damned bad, you couldn't have been so good," cried Peddler, rushing out of the house but carefully closing the door behind him.

Clara sped to the door and seemed as if she were about to call him back, but she froze holding onto the doorknob, while tears again appeared to be forming in her eyes. Peddler, with quick steps, headed for the truck. Erik opened the door for him but saw something unusual in his face.

"That was short. I hope it was sweet," he quipped.

"Move! Get me out of here!" ordered Peddler.

Erik looked at his friend and saw him fixed dead straight ahead with a quivering lip and a tear beginning to roll.

"What's the problem, Peddler?" asked Erik

"Nothing. Move out, man," roared Peddler

"You went in all dolled up like you were on your way to a wedding, now you came out looking like a chewed up cat after a dog fight and you tell me nothing?" retorted Erik, starting the truck and moving away very slowly, his eyes pegged on his friend. Peddler hurriedly opened the glove compartment, came out with a flask of liquor and continued to look straight ahead without a decent or pleasant thought in his head.

"Are you going to tell me or you're going to wait and let the liquor do the talking," asked Erik, changing gears to speed up the truck." I hate people who linger around with bad news."

"What makes you think I have bad news?"

"Because you're crying."

"Tears of joy. Haven't you heard of tears of joy?" replied Peddler softly, taking a long drink. "If you really want to know, I have a daughter who lives there,"

"Is she working in there?"

"No! She is not working in there. She lives there with her husband and my little granddaughter."

"She is different, all right," mumbled Erik

They wanted me to stay there to live with them. But I can't. My little granddaughter, who is only three, touched my face with her tiny fingers and asked me to stay. I don't know if and when I'm coming back. My daughter is still crying. And my son-in-law, you've seen him by the door, he's nice too."

"But he's a blue-eyed blond redneck."

"So?" asked Peddler, "my daughter is white like her mother and I'm not one hundred per cent Negro you know."

"I know you have some Indian blood in you. You told me that," rejoined Erik

"Like I said, my daughter told me she needs her father and my granddaughter needs a grandfather."

Erik turned again to look at Peddler who was drinking as if he wished to put out a fire that burned inside him.

"I'm glad you didn't stay. I need you too, you know. Not as much as they do. Besides, you promised to make me rich and crazy," said Erik, "do you remember?"

"I remember," said Peddler, welcoming Erik's words of comfort.

"They're probably angry with you for not staying," said Erik, lighting a cigarette.

"Why do you say that?"

"Because nobody came out to see you off."

Peddler looked at Erik from the corners of his eyes and said nothing.

"Like they say in Greece, sometimes friends can be like brothers. That's why they named

the city in Pennsylvania, **Philadelphia**. Which means, the city of brotherly love." Peddler looked at Erik with a vague smile, " I always thought that smart people were selfish and not very kind, Curly. I was wrong." Peddler took another sip from his bottle. "You are genuine. I meant to say, Curly, as genuine as the dark of night."

Erik eyed his companion for a few long seconds and seeing him looking straight ahead as if his eyes were following something of great importance, Erik, as if activated by a new thought asked, "Peddler, where do we go from here? Back to Louisiana or are we staying here in Jackson, Mississippi?"

Peddler gradually allowed his face to resume its natural expression and exclaimed "Erik, I came here and I saw what?"

"You were very glad to see your daughter, weren't you?"

"Glad!" cried out Peddler, "oh, Erik, my dear friend, if you had any idea how I looked forward to making this trip for so long now." And with those words Peddler gave way to a shower of tears.

"Take it easy, Peddler, take it easy, buddy! Things never are as bad as they seem," said Erik, soothingly.

"I'm sorry, I can't keep my feelings inside any more," said Peddler, after a short pause, "I know you suspected the conversation I had with my daughter. She's probably very sweet, to others, not to me. That sweet girl, my own flesh and blood, said to me in no uncertain terms that I am not worthy of being her father. She judged me on the basis of the testimony of her adopted folks. That's the way it went. But, Erik, I have a place on this earth, I have Philadelphia, not Pennsylvania, just Philadelphia. Erik, it's not the liquor that's talking now, it's my heart. The liquor never talks, it only cries."

They rode through the smooth avenues of Jackson and jolted

over some rough paved streets and, at length, reached the wide and open countryside. The wheels sang their monotonous song rolling over the hot highway; the wind whistled as it pushed on by and the engine purred along tirelessly as if the chicken wire, the picks and shovels, the boxes of Bibles and all the other numerous items that Peddler sold to make a living were but a feather on it's heels. The truck, driven by Erik, sped as if pulled by a team of smart, healthy galloping horses and rattled on as if excited at the rapidity of it's own motion.

Erik slowed down once he crossed the State line and entered a small town in Louisiana. Modest homes were scattered on either side of the road. The day had gone and the night came, adorned with her usual streets lights. A motel's flickering sign appeared up ahead and Erik pulled into the parking lot and stopped near the registration office

He opened the door and went into the office to register. He signed in, paid the bill and hurried out straight for the truck. Peddler was curled up asleep, his head leaning against the door, the empty flask clutched in his hand.

Time to get up," shouted Erik, banging on the truck door.

Peddler remained in that position and was not moving a hand or a foot.

"Do something, if you have it in your power to produce any evidence that will alter the low opinion I hold regarding liquor or those that drink it in great amounts," said Erik.

"You're talking Greek again," replied Peddler, without opening his eyes or moving a muscle.

Erik was no less surprised, although his astonishment, hearing Peddler awake, was not expressed in the same eccentric manner. "I'm glad you're awake," he returned.

Peddler never made a move.

"You can go to sleep once we get you to your room," said Erik, louder than before.

The Peddler still didn't move.

"This is wonderful," mumbled Erik, "I don't understand this, I just heard you speaking."

The words no sooner escaped his lips, than Erik opened the truck door, put his arm around Peddler and realized his friend had lost the use of his limbs from imprudently drinking the entire bottle of liquor. Erik pulled Peddler out of the truck and stood him upright on his feet, resting his body on the truck. He then positioned him on his shoulder and carried him, with much effort, into a room on the first floor, almost in front of the parked truck. He then slowly and gently stretched him out on the bed. Erik, being greatly disturbed by Peddler's remorse, state of mind and condition, stared at him for a full minute, then turned slowly and left the room after shutting the lights and closing the door behind him, gently.

PART IV

CHAPTER ONE

Erik encounters the image of his son

Streaks of dim light shot into Erik's room, through the edges of the drapes, while he lay half-asleep on the bed, tossing fitfully in the late morning following Peddler's night of disenchantment.

Suddenly violence struck and he shot up in bed, his eyes opened wide and wandered fearfully around the room as if looking for a familiar place to recognize. It was with a great effort that he tried to catch his breath while wiping a cold sweat from his face.

After a short while, when he finally emerged from what was evidently a bad dream and returned to his normal state of mind, he stealthily descended from the bed, with about as much difficulty as he would have experienced in climbing up onto it. He slowly meandered to the bathroom.

After the short time it took Erik to shower and dress himself to his satisfaction, he came out of his room and, for all who might see him, appeared to be in excellent physical and mental shape. He walked along the front of the motel, in a first-rate military manner, and stopped in front of Peddler's room. Without any delay or hesitation, he knocked on Peddler's door and after a little time, hearing no sound from the inside and thinking Peddler was still asleep, pushed the door open without the slightest difficulty. Dismay and anguish were immediately planted on Erik's face when he realized his friend and partner, Peddler, was gone. He observed the bed covers were wrinkled, but the bed didn't really look slept in. The drapes were open and the bright midmorning sun threw a stream of light into the room. Erik hastily went to the window and looked at the space where he had parked the truck, the space was also empty. He paused, not an instant, and ran until he was standing in the spot where the truck had been parked. Standing there, more puzzled than concerned, searching with his eyes up and down the street, he saw no sign of the man or his truck. He stood there and thought for a moment and then he began to walk away, ill at his ease but still with the remarkable dignity that was in keeping with his character.

A ten minute walk brought the traveler to a little road where he came upon an old building, resembling a court house, with two huge live oak trees on one side and a parking lot, filled to its capacity of thirty cars or so, on the other. An old colored man was working in the flower garden under the elm trees.

Erik stopped and called hastily, "Hello there"

The workman raised his body and shaded his eyes with his hand to stare long and calmly at Erik.

"Hello!" repeated Erik.

"Hello" replied the man.

"Is there a shopping area or Main street in this town?" asked Erik, in a lower voice.

"Yes, straight ahead about ten minutes, you'll run into a shopping area, if you want to call it that," having uttered the brief reply and apparently satisfying himself with his scrutiny of the stranger, the colored man resumed his work.

"Excuse me, sir," said Erik, approaching the man with cautious steps, "that hoe you have, is it new? It looks very new."

"Why are you asking, stranger, did you lose one?" asked the man, in a serious manner.

"When did you get?"

"Why, did you lose one?" repeated the man, with a little more emphasis, leaning on the hoe.

"No, I didn't lose one," replied Erik, who had advanced by this time to the garden's fence.

"Then, why are you asking me all these questions," roared the man, emerging from the garden and looking very hard into Erik's eyes, "why?"

"Why are you so angry?" asked Erik, approaching him calmly.

"Why?" asked the man.

"Yes, why?"

"Because I just realized that the man who sold it to me about two hours ago, didn't give me a receipt and anybody can claim it," responded the workman, softly.

"This man who sold it to you, did he have a truck?" inquired Erik

"Yes," replied the man.

"A big milk truck with the lettering on it THE PEDDLER?" asked Erik.

"Yeah, that's him, do you know him?" asked the man, smiling.

"Yeah, I know him. He's my partner," mumbled Erik

"Your partner?' asked the man, with a great delight.

"Yup."

"Your partner?" exclaimed the man, with a boisterous laugh, "You must be the odd couple. The odd partners, I mean to say," laughing harder than before.

"Why are you laughing?" asked Erik

"I think its funny. Salt and pepper, partners. What's the matter, you lost your sense of humor?"

"That's what happened when I got up this morning. I saw that my partner was gone, that's when I lost my sense of humor," mumbled Erik

"Your partner took the truck, your money and your sense of humor and left," shouted the man, still shuddering with laughter.

"I am glad you're laughing at your own jokes; I do that too sometimes," responded Erik and turning to leave, "Laughing is good for. You'll probably live to be a hundred."

"A hundred?" shouted the old man, "hell, man, I am already ninety six," chimed the old man, with another burst of laughter.

Erik tuned his face and smiled, "God bless you."

"I am blessed," shouted the man, "I had five wives. Four died before me and every time I get a new wife, she's younger than the last one. The one I have now, she's half my age."

"I think you are eventually going to get shot by some jealous husband," said Erik walking away, waving his hand.

"That's not my dream," yelled the old man.

"What is your dream then?" asked Erik.

"I want my young wife to catch me in bed with a younger woman, and shoot me. What a way to go. That's my dream," replied the old man.

"Mine too," whispered Erik, "Ill see you," replied Erik a little louder.

"I'll see you in Heaven," yelled the man.

Erik stopped for a moment, turned slowly, looked at the laughing happy old man for one last time, waved and left.

Winding his way towards the shopping area through a variety of side streets, past small front yards, he sauntered away, never stopped and never took the time to pause or look at any objects he passed, which was unusual for him. In his mind there was no anxiety, worry or displeasure at being left by Peddler. He walked on with calmness and the positive attitude that he had plenty of time at his disposal to saunter as far as his legs could carry him. When he reached the Main Street of that town, he stopped, paused and contemplated his options. Numerous cars, small trucks and station wagons were assembled in great confusion in front of a big mansion that looked like one of the first structures that had been built at the founding of the town, more than a century ago. Having loitered there for a quarter of an hour, he began walking again along the Main Street, hoping to see or hear something of Peddler and his truck.

He noticed that no buildings were more than two stories tall. Everything was a little unreal. No shop looked any newer than twenty years old; it would not have been difficult for a visitor to lose the sense of where he was or what the year might be. He walked along, looking in shop windows and stopped in front of a jewelry store, where reflections of jewels and watches flashed across his face. His expression became serious when, in the window's reflection, his eyes fell upon a long dark limousine parked behind him, across the street. He stared at the reflection of the car and while he did that, suddenly, a little boy appeared sitting in the back seat, smiling at Erik. Instantly he was stricken with apprehension and anxiety when he realized that the boy that was sitting there was the true image of his son, Randy. "My God." whispered Erik, turning his head abruptly to face the phenomenon. Without any hesitation or further pause he ran towards it but, at that precise moment, the car intentionally moved out into the traffic and sped away.

"Randy?" yelled Erik, running to catch up with the limousine.

The car turned the corner and Erik ran in the direction the car took but, by the time he reached the next corner, the car had turned and disappeared. He got to the corner and spun a full ways around, looked and saw nothing. The street was narrow and filthy with only a second hand clothing shop on the left and on the right, a wooden house in ruinous condition. On its door was nailed a cardboard sign stating that the house was for rent; the cardboard sign looked as if it had hung there for many years. Erik, struggling to catch his breath, stricken with anxiety and hopelessness, leaned against a building and held his face in his hands. He remained silent for a few minutes and then, as he was removing his hands from his face, he saw the car at the end of the block, driving slowly in his direction. Erik, seeing and feeling an imminent danger coming his way, lost the ability to think, turned and began to run towards the Main street, while the car rolled at his heels, without making any attempt to either stop or slow down. Knowing he was about to be run over by the car and blinded with fear, he jumped backwards and fell, tripping against the curb. He looked at the passing car and saw the driver, who was a young man, not stopping to bestow any other mark of recognition upon Erik other than a humorous grin, as if the whole incident was a staged act of comedy. As Erik stood up, he caught a glimpse of the boy staring dispassionately at him from the rear window. He saw a living copy of his son, the eyes, the hair, the mouth; every feature was the same. The expression was, for an instant, so precisely alike, that the minutest line seemed copied with accuracy; it all was perfectly unearthly.

"Randy?" whispered Erik.

He stayed in that position looking after the car as it drove further down Main Street until it finally disappeared in the distance.

"Randy! Come back" screamed the father.

With those words, voiced with the energy of passionate grief, Erik fell upon his knees and clutched his skull with both hands, as if something was trying to escape from inside his head.

Several puzzled pedestrians stopped to stare at him with merciful looks on their faces. He came to his feet and, with some common gestures, assured them that he was all right. Then, without waiting for the pedestrians to disperse, he walked away, crossed the street in haste and bent his steps to a narrow street leading away from the town's center of activity and traffic. He went on, passing some narrow streets and alleys, at length his wander was terminated in a large open space, where, scattered about, were pens for beasts and other indications of a stockyard. He hurried for a few steps when he heard a deep church bell strike the hour, turning his head in the direction of the bell's toll; he curved his steps and proceeded in its direction.

After a brisk ten-minute walk, Erik found himself in front of a church, a huge old building that seemed to guard the park in front of. As he walked by the church in a daze, his eyes fell upon a young priest who stood on the church steps. He was strikingly handsome, so much so that his collar looked out of place; he possessed a conspicuous resemblance to the limousine driver, but Erik didn't pay much attention to that detail.

He gestured to Erik as he walked by and said, "Come on up."

Erik looked up at the young man in the priest's attire and asked, "Me?"

"You," said the priest

"Forgive me, Father, but is my need to talk with someone that evident on my face?" asked Erik.

"I'm sorry if I offended you, I thought you might want to see the inside of the church," replied the priest.

"No, no, Father, you didn't offend me at all. I would like to go inside to pray," said Erik

"Of course," said priest.

He opened the door to the church. Erik poked his head inside and saw the church was vast, empty, dark, and cold. He left the priest standing at the door and walked slowly and quietly to an elaborately carved pew. He knelt, bowed his head, closed his eyes and whispered a prayer. Suddenly a hand appeared out of nowhere. It reached out and firmly grasped Erik's shoulder. Feeling the hand on his shoulder, Erik turned around alarmed, then relieved, when he saw it was Peddler kneeling next to him.

"Where did you go?" whispered Erik

"To get some more Bibles," said Peddler.

"How did you find me here?" asked Erik, coming to his feet.

"A little boy told me," said Peddler

"What little boy?" questioned Erik, with an alarmed voice, while assisting Peddler to stand.

"Take it easy, Curly," said Peddler.

"What little boy, I asked?"

"It was just a boy who probably saw you coming in here. He was standing in front of the church," said Peddler.

"How did he know you were looking for me?" asked Erik, in an even more alarmed voice.

"I must have asked him," said Peddler, a bit confused with Erik's concern about a little boy.

Peddler took Erik's arm and began to lead him out of the church but Erik broke away and advanced to the vestibule where he turned to the priest and asked, "excuse me Father, have you seen a little boy out here?"

"Me? I haven't seen any boy here," replied the priest sounding somewhat confused.

To Erik, the reply sounded false. He looked sternly at the priest's face, but it was impossible to doubt him, as it was the beauty of truth that filled every line of the vicar's face.

"My mistake. The reason I asked is because my partner saw a little boy around here and he thought the little boy knew me," said Erik. Although his motive for eying the priest no longer existed, the nagging resemblance between the priest's features and those of the limousine driver's persisted so strongly that he could not withdraw his gaze.

"Would you excuse me for a moment?" asked the priest, in a beseeching manner, as he hurried into the church.

"What was that all about? Who were you talking to," asked Peddler.

"The priest," replied Erik.

"What priest?" puzzled Peddler.

"The priest who went inside when you came out," replied Erik, with no small amount of alarm in his voice.

"Wait, Peddler," said Erik in a tone half way between a sneer and a scowl. He advanced to the doorway and looked inside the church for a along time. "You must be blind, didn't you see the handsome priest I was speaking to; or am I really going crazy?"

"Please, don't go crazy before I make you rich," returned Peddler. "You do realize that we have a truck load of Bibles out there, and you're going to sell them? Yes sir, we're going to make a lot of money together," said Peddler

"I don't want to make a lot of money," said Erik, walking away from the church hastily and pushing Peddler aside.

Peddler shot after him. "Don't say that, Curly. I have no respect for any man who doesn't like money or women," said Peddler, as he followed him to the truck that was parked a few spaces from the church steps.

"Peddler," said Erik, holding the passenger side door handle, "I only mean at this time my goal in life is not to make a lot of money. So, my friend, I want you to send back the ten thousand dollar check to the Mayor of Hixton. Hixton is not the right place to start and those fellows are not the right people to get mixed up with. I'm always involving myself in one scrape or another, by acting on somebody else's impulses. Today I may be a little out of sorts and that has nothing to do with you, but the fact still remains that I want you to send the money back. I feel that if we do what they want us to do, we'll be involved in their troubles and misfortunes."

"Your manner, not your actions, assures me that you've given this some thought and that something like this has happened to you before," said Peddler.

"I have nothing more to tell you," rejoined Erik, getting in the truck and closing the door as if he wished to end the conversation. He sat there looking straight ahead until Peddler took the driver's seat. When they were on their way, Erik looked back and saw the priest standing by the church doorway, waving; a vague grin was on his face.

"I saw a sign on the interstate about a revival meeting a few miles north of here. What do you say we go up there, sell a few Bibles?" asked Peddler.

Erik nodded his head absent-mindedly; Peddler looked over at his friend, but didn't say another word.

CHAPTER TWO

Reverend Butler's sudden illness

The truck rolled along, down an isolated country road. After some time, Peddler stopped and pulled over to look at a house, not with amazement but seemingly with nostalgia, as if he had seen the structure before. It was a huge mass of cream-colored stone topped with crenulated turrets; it was set off in the distance. There was one high pointed gilded spire. The house was too far away, though, to make out its other many details.

"Yes sir, that house has a story to tell," said Peddler, pointing it out to Erik. He drove much closer and stopped on the shoulder.

Erik got out of the truck and walked on, doggedly, a little distance for a better view. Looking at it from a closer perspective he heard shouting and a roar of noise. Alarm, wonder and a peculiar terror shot through him causing a tremble in his every limb and a cold sweat from every pore. Erik saw, in the front yard, three tall oak trees laden with moss. They made the house very dark and he could hear the wind moan its way through them with a dismal wail. He remained standing in the road, perplexed by what he saw and heard and agitated by no stronger feeling than the doubt of what to do; he rushed back to the truck.

Peddler looked at Erik and seeing him weak and pale, as if his blood had been drained, asked, "What's the matter, Curly?"

"Nothing," replied Erik, staring straight ahead and appearing to have begun to regain his composure, "very interesting illusion though, like a phantom."

"Phantom? Why did you call it Phantom?" asked Peddler, unable to comprehend the statement.

"Look at it! It's sitting there like an old man, dead and waiting for somebody to bury him."

"I'd bet if that house could talk it would tell some interesting stories," observed Peddler, driving away as he glanced at Erik for a reply.

"How's that?" asked Erik, now quiet and reserved.

"There was a lady who lived in that house in the year 1910. Lady Ann, they called her.

She was a mean, bad and nasty woman, never satisfied. She had a wealthy, handsome and devoted husband, by the name of Richard Adams. She cheated on him. She had a five year old son with another women's husband," said Peddler.

Erik threw an interesting glance at Peddler, urging him to continue.

"Well," continued Peddler "one day, this quiet, devoted man went a few hundred yards from the house, all by himself and dug a large hole. It took him two or three days to do it.

One Sunday morning, he told everybody he was going to church by himself, but he didn't go to church, he took an axe, and sharpened it. Went hid in the attic and stayed there until two o clock in the morning. He came downstairs and he told the cook to fry him a big steak. He finished the steak, burped, took two bottles of beer with him and went back to the attic. Later on about six o clock in the morning he came down and woke everyone up, including his wife and the five-year-old son and told everyone he was going away for three days. He went out through the front door and eight o clock that evening he came back through the back door. He went straight to his bedroom, where his wife was sleeping with some salesman. Then, unnoticed, he went upstairs to the attic. He got the axe, came down to the bedroom, axed his cheating wife and the poor stupid salesman. Then he went to the boy's bedroom, raised the axe, looked the innocent boy straight in the eyes and said, 'from a bad plant not even a seed;' he came down with the axe on the boy's head. He took all of them to the hole that he had dug, buried them, then he put a gun in his mouth and pulled the trigger," concluded Peddler.

"Who told you that story?" asked Erik.

"I was there. Their cook was my mother. My mother told me later on what I hadn't seen with my own eyes," responded Peddler.

They both sat quietly for a moment, reflecting on the house and the horrible crime that took place in that neglected mansion.

"Nobody's been able to live there since the tragedy," added Peddler " some say the house is haunted."

It was some time later, after they left the scene of the alleged haunted house, when they arrived at their destination, the gathering of many people to hear the preaching of Rev Butler.

The daylight was drawing to a close when they drove into the park. A great multitude had already assembled. The two partners parked the truck and walked to the entrance of the park. They stood there and took in the sights and sounds of that chaotic gathering place. The bleachers were filled with people and more were standing around. Workers ran from place to place carrying tables and chairs as the mounted police paraded their horses up and down the park looking like knights protecting the order, shielding the array, and still the crowds were pushing, quarreling and joking. All those people were linked together with a single common notion - to find, to see and to touch God. There was a sign pitched at the entrance to the park: "THE WORLD FAMOUS EVANGELIST, REV. ROBERT BUTLER." Clusters of people had gathered at the entrance, waiting their turn to enter the park.

"This is our night, eh, Curly?" asked Peddler.

"If you want to sell Bibles, go ahead. I'm going to be in there, close to the preacher," said Erik.

Peddler stood there, confused, as Erik walked into the park. He watched Erik leave then started to work the crowd himself, without him. Erik moved through a group of people who were mulling around and took a seat near the stage. Rev. Butler suddenly came onto the platform. The band played his theme song, as he stood silent, on that platform, holding a Bible in one hand, the other resting on the podium. He was a powerful-looking white haired man. He fixed his eyes on the crowd, took the microphone in his hand and after a short while, motioned for the band to stop. He cleared his throat gently.

"God bless you! God bless all of you!" said Rev. Butler, walking around the podium, to allow the crowd a better view of him.

People were shouting and sent up scream upon scream that penetrated the air and rang in their ears until reaching open space.

The people pressed against each other to be near the white haired man.

"Seeing you before me, shouting and cheering and welcoming God into your hearts, proclaiming His name and His love with all your senses, makes me tremble with joy," said Rev. Butler.

The crowd shouted ALLELUIA! and PRAISE GOD! Alleluia! Alleluia! Erik looked up at the Reverend. He was transfixed. Rev. Butler closed his eyes and shook his head a few times. His hands clutched his chest; he paused for a moment. Then he threw his arms toward heaven. Suddenly, he pulled the microphone closer to him and continued, lowering his voice and looking down at the ground.

"Dr. Joseph Parker, the Pastor of the City Temple of London," said Rev. Butler,

as his voice became almost a whisper. The crowd began to murmur, "was crossing the Atlantic, coming to North America. A group of young men," he continued …

The Reverend fell to his knees clutching his chest. He almost looked as though he was in prayer. The crowd was still shouting. Erik stood up alarmed by the scene. Sensing that something wrong, he started to push forward through the people who were ringing the platform. The Reverend fell forward. A few people began to scream. The bandleader, having some sense about him, started to play an Old Gospel Hymn. Erik climbed onto the stage, fell on his knees next to the Reverend, gently turned on him on his back and placed his ear close to the Reverend's mouth to hear fading mumbling. Some of the crowd came to their feet, astonished; others recognized Rev. Butler's grave condition and started to cry. A neatly dressed, middle-aged man made his way to the Reverend.

"Give me some room to work, come on. I'm a doctor," said the man.

The circle of people around Rev. Butler cleared back a little.

"What can I do?" asked Erik

"You can give me some room to work," exclaimed the doctor, taking out his stethoscope and placing it on the Reverend's chest.

Rev. Butler's eyes opened wide, as if he were stricken by fear and with his lips, barely he muttered, "minister to my people;" he weakly handed the microphone to Erik.

"Do, as he says! Take over to avoid chaos. He seems to know you," said the doctor.

Erik got up slowly, still staring at the Reverend and then he moved cautiously but deliberately to the center of the stage.

The sunset was blinding. He first shaded his eyes with his hand and then tapped the microphone with his finger, but no sound came out. He gestured to the soundman to increase the volume while the band was playing, tested the sound again and he then looked over at the band.

"Cut the music! Cut it!" shouted Erik; the band stopped playing and Erik shouted at the crowd to quiet down, straightened his posture and when the noise subsided, he undertook the Reverend's wish, beginning in a reverent tone.

"Every man has a mission in this life." The crowed settled down and listened intently. "When his mission is accomplished, God will send the spirit to claim him. Rev. Butler's mission has not been finished. Rev. Butler is a fighting man. He has been fighting for justice, fighting for the rights of man and striving constantly to bring the word of God to the ears of mankind; now he is fighting for his life and he will win." These remarks were received, by the troubled crowd, with much favor and applause.

Erik looked over at the doctor working on Reverend Butler. Emergency Technicians, with a stretcher, made their way to the stage. Then he turned and looked around the crowd for a pregnant moment, partly to think but mostly to give the crowd time to settle down. He stood there, looked and saw the park paved with human faces. Erik stood frozen, in all the glare of that living light, with one hand resting on the podium and the other holding the Bible. Inquisitive and eager eyes peered back from every inch before him. Every eye was fixed only on his form. Every eye of every man, every woman and every child, was fixed upon a man who had fallen, who had stumbled and had lost it all for doing what God forbade. Beaming faces surrounded him; before him, behind him, above and below, on the right and on the left and he remained completely still, readying for their challenge.

He didn't stir a limb. He could see some people come to their feet, to better see his face. He had scarcely moved since that trial began. It was a significant trial. He felt he was being judged. Judged;

not on performance, not on attitude, not n charisma, but on his character. He thrust his head forward to better read the thoughts of the presiding judge and jury. In time he turned his eyes sharply upon them to observe the effect of his presence. He looked wistfully into their faces. He saw and felt their emotion, returned to his bewildered glance.

"Brothers and sisters, let us pray. Let me say the prayer. Not a prayer spoken on the verge of death but a prayer to celebrate the glory of life, a prayer for the love of God. Let us all kneel and pray for the recovery of this great evangelist," said Erik.

He then cast his eyes on the unconscious Reverend being carried off the stage by the technicians, the doctor in close pursuit, while the entire crowd feel to their knees.

"Dear Lord, you know Reverend Butler's mission and his struggles. Now, Lord, he is in the arena fighting for his life. Lord, he's on the scale of life and death, please, allow the scale to tilt in his favor. Thank you, Lord, Amen," closed Erik.

He rose, saw that the crowd still focused intently on him, and continued,

"Ladies and gentlemen, I said before, that was not a prayer on the verge of death.

"God doesn't want to hear our prayers when we are dying, asking to be forgiven and accepted in Heaven; rather we should pray to God to show us the way to help others who need us; we should pray for God to help us live the right way so to avoid suffering on this earth and then we will take our rightful place after death. It is a scientific truth that people who help other people live longer. God needs you to be good; He needs you to help other people live the right way." Erik stopped for a moment and listened to the silence. There was a complete and profound silence

Peddler stood there with his mouth open, his face filled with excitement, holding a number of Bibles in one hand and a bucket for the money in the other.

"I knew a man who was condemned to die in the gas chamber," continued Erik. " I went to him and I spoke to him and I spent time with him in his cell. He was a judge, who all his life judged others, but because he was living a hypocrite's life, he committed a crime for money and glory. He had sent many to prison unjustly and had sent many to their deaths. So at the end, as a just reward, he was condemned to die. I sat in his cell the last hours of his life and listened to him speaking and I listened to him thinking. I remember him. Oh, how well I remember him. I remember he sat on the bench in his cell, which also served as his bed; he cast his bloodshot eyes upon me, as if he were seeking mercy. He was trying to recollect his past. After a while he began to remember a few disjointed fragments of what he had done. He began to think of all the men he knew who had died in the chamber. Some of them were innocent but died as a result of his condemnation. He confessed to me, that those men kept appearing in his mind's eye, ever since he was placed on death row. He recalled that he had often seen them dying and he secretly joked and laughed because they died with prayers on their lips. He also told me that he could not sleep at night, thinking that some of them might have slept on the very bench on which he was to sleep, in that same cell. Ladies and gentlemen when we are born we know it marks the beginning of our death. Most of us don't know when or how we are going to die. But that man said to me that he lived in hell, for the ten years after his conviction, knowing he was going to die any day and worst of all, he knew how he was going to die and where. He practiced his death, he told me, by holding his breath but nature was stronger than his determination. He begged me to get on my knees and say a prayer for him. That man, who had laughed at others who prayed at their time of death, it was that man who took my hand and, trembling, squeezed it as hard as he could to bring me down on my knees; he was finally ready to pray. That was a prayer on the verge of death," declared Erik, stopping for a moment to replenish his lungs, "a prayer on the verge of death is a common thing. How God receives those prayers, I don't know. But, my friends, a prayer for the glory of life, a prayer to God to show us the way to live is always answered."

Saying this Erik stopped once again with a sullen look on his face and continued, "If that judge would have prayed to God before, he would have known right from wrong. He would have known that if one does something right he is rewarded and he would have known that one who does something wrong is punished."

Erik took a piece of white paper from his pocket and continued.

"Reverend Butler handed this to me and asked that I take over his mission until he returns. I know, my friends, I will never be big enough to walk in the Reverend's shoes, but my beliefs, my thoughts and my feelings are the same as his," said Erik, unfolding the paper.

How far is home from where I live?
How much is mine of what I give?
Does all of me cry when I cry?
Will all me die when I die?
Is there a mission for me on this earth?
Shall I find it or was it written at birth?
Is the clock hour one hour long?
If something is not right is it always wrong?

"These are the thoughts that Reverend Butler must have wanted to share with you. He had the answers to these questions; I must confess to you that I don't. The other place the answers can be found is in that book, the book called the HOLY BIBLE. Coming to a gathering such as this, you must all have a Bible in your hands, like I do in mine. If you don't have one, I saw a Christian somewhere in the crowd who is passing them out. Take one from him; just leave a small donation so he can buy more," said Erik.

Peddler was passing out Bibles to the crowed cheerfully and the money was dropped into the bucket faithfully. Peddler was in high spirits, and however fatigued or saddened he was from the disappointed meeting with his daughter, the day before, he was still able to display his good humor with a righteous smile while alternating the words thank you, God Bless you and praise the Lord.

Erik walked over to the bandleader and after a moment spent in whispers, he made vague bow and returned to the podium. Evidently the subject matter of the conference was not disclosed to the crowd but was understood, because immediately thereafter the band began to play a song familiar to Erik, and Erik began to sing. In song, he descended the platform and walked down an aisle, a microphone in one hand, the Bible in the other. Everyone joined along in singing with their arms high in the air and their bodies swaying with the music. Erik reached the back of the crowd, turned to regain a full view and continued his song.

Busy recollections of hopes and dreams, cherished since he

was a young man, crowded into his mind that evening, as he made his evangelistic debut. They brought tears with them, as old dreams often do when they come back from the lockers of our memories to be resurrected. Before the song was over, he strode back to the podium, took his place behind it and waited for the music to prepare the next act. He then opened the Bible with steady hands.

"In the beginning was the word, and the word was with God, and the word was God," declared Erik, closing the Bible cautiously. He stared at the crowd, paused for impact and uttered in a low voice, "today is the beginning."

With the next morning came a rumor that Reverend Butler had died. Peddler rushed to where Reverend Butler was to be laid for view and there met the Reverend's widow, who was gracious, but too sad to speak at length. She referred him to the ones who were in charge of the Reverend's business. In short order, after some examination and a great deal more conversation with the Right Reverend's serious minded men of business, Peddler and they reached a meeting of the minds that served the purpose of all concerned. A business arrangement was struck and they shook hands, vigorously, at the satisfactory conclusion. Peddler believed, at that moment, that ardent prayers, coming from kind hearts filled with gratitude, would be heard in heaven, and if not, then what were prayers for? He left that party of movers and shakers and went out, hurriedly, to put the finishing touches on their deal, before he picked up Erik.

It was mid morning, the sunlight struggled through the dark clouds that covered most of the sky as Peddler drove the truck, with Erik sitting silently on the passenger's side, looking straight ahead. Peddler, knowing where he was gong but not knowing what he should say to Erik, drove slowly through the village. All the stores were closed, the doors were locked and the streets noiseless and empty, without a soul awakened to the business of that Sunday.

After a while, the sun began to chase the clouds away, except for the few most stubborn and brave ones that had clustered together, to the west side of the village, showing their true colors of threatening gray. As Peddler drove, he threw quick glances at Erik from time to time, trying to detect his mood.

" All my life I wanted to be a king maker," said Peddler, bringing the truck to a stop in a half filled parking lot, "but I never found a man who would be king. Last night, I damn near cried from excitement when I heard you preaching. I don't give a damn what you believe, as long as the people believe in what you say, and I believe in what you're doing." said Peddler, "wait right here, I'll be right back, he continued."

Peddler left and Erik remained there, in the passenger seat, looking straight ahead at the park, as if he were expecting to see something. Suddenly, from that spot, he saw his son on the other side of the park, running away. Erik jumped from the truck and ran towards his boy, but the boy was gone, out of sight. Erik tripped into the park and at that moment the park changed to a livestock yard. The ground was covered, nearly ankle-deep, with filth and mire, restraining him Erik from running. A thick steam was rising from the bodies of the enclosed cattle. There were pens, in that sea of animals, filled with sheep, cattle, goats, pigs and every sort of beast suitable for human consumption. There were countrymen, butchers, drovers, thieves, idlers, vagabonds of every kind and grade of human being, all mingled together in a dense mass – unlike any Erik had ever seen or imagined. There were shouts and oaths, ringing of bells, the roar of voices, and all the unwashed, the unshaven seamy filthy figures constantly ran to and fro rendering it a stunning scene, as never seen before, and confounding to his senses. Erik became further bewildered when his eyes encountered, across this jumbled mess, on an elevated plane, the handsome Priest, carrying a stray lamb and beckoning him, with a kindly wave.

Erik was still in that world of illusion when Peddler found him, took him by the elbow, and attempted to escort him from the park, unaware of his vision of the Divine.

"Lets go, I want to show you something. We can come to the park later," said Peddler, completely unaware of Erik's dilemma.

Erik collapsed, in a breathless state, on a nearby bench, and covering his eyes with one hand, placing the other on his chest, he grasped for air.

"What's the matter, Erik?" asked Peddler, stooping over his friend, "what happened?"

Erik, in his alarm, could not find the words to answer, so he said,

"Do you smell this place?"

"Yeah, it does smell nice. All these beautiful flowers are in their prime," returned Peddler.

"I felt dizzy, for a moment," said Erik, coming to his feet and looking away from Peddler.

"I can understand that. A lot of people are allergic to the flowers - some of the flowers anyway."

"Maybe," replied Erik, as he unsteadily ambled from the park.

"It's a good thing you're not allergic to women, you'd die," joked Peddler, catching up and escorting him by the elbow, "Erik, I want you to remember something. Never allow glory get into your head or defeat to touch your heart."

"Peddler, you're a genuine walking philosophical encyclopedia this morning," remarked Erik.

"Come on, there's something around the corner I want you to see," said Peddler, pulling Erik by the elbow and directing him to the left."

"I don't feel like seeing anything right now," said Erik, shying away from him.

Peddler broke away and shot towards another bench and sat there, angry and silent, with his head drooping.

Erik followed him there and drooped his head, so as to get a better view of Peddler's face. Peddler, with great propriety, turned his head away. Erik sat next to him and looked in the other direction.

Nothing was said on either side for a minute or two, afterwards, at the expiration of that time, Peddler turned his whole body away from Erik.

"We are all weak and brittle creatures, Peddler. We get shattered inside, if we don't have our own way," mumbled Erik.

"Look who's talking,' returned Peddler, turning to face Erik, " Most people would kill to see what I was about to show you."

"And now, I'm dying to see it, " responded Erik.

'Come on, come on," said Peddler, getting to his feet and pulling Erik by the arm.

"Look! Look!" said Peddler, bursting with excitement, once they had turned the corner, pointing to a sign. The name Reverend ROBERT BUTLER had been white washed over, a workman was in the process of replacing it with ERIK KARAS.

"We don't have to sell Bibles anymore," said Peddler, looking straight at the sign with a sense of accomplishment, "are you ready to do it?"

"Do what?" asked Erik, with a look of curiosity on his face.

"Be the evangelist."

"Do the bears shit in the woods?" returned Erik, after a moment's consideration.

Peddler turned abruptly, hurried back to the same bench and sat there, with his head drooping, as it did before. Erik followed, drooped his head to view Peddler's face, as he did before, and this time heard Peddler mumbling, "They do shit in the woods, they do," He then raised his head and looked at Erik and Erik saw a tear drop rolling down Peddler's cheek, "If angels, for God's good purpose, were created in human likeness, then you are my angel. I'm glad you finally arrived, but I'm crying because, instead of coming in the spring-time of my manhood, you grace the autumn of my life; however, Erik at last, I can be a king maker and I know you will be my king."

"From your mouth, to God's ears, my humble subject," said Erik, seriously.

"Don't let that get too far inside your head, your majesty."

The next night, in accordance with the terms of the agreement Peddler had made with the representatives of the late Reverend Butler, Erik stood on the podium, a microphone in one hand and a Bible in the other, listening to the band. He outstretched his arms and gestured to the bandleader to stop the music. He cleared his throat gently, stepped forward and began to read from a white page of paper.

Have you been on top of the mountain and never seen the view?

Have you been to a beautiful place but have seen nothing new"

Have you ever sung and never heard your sound?

Have you ever fallen and you never hit the ground?

Erik folded the paper cautiously, placed it in his pocket and took his place behind the lectern.

"My beloved friends, I am happy to see you sitting here tonight, and some of you standing, before me with respect and love in your hearts. Before I go on with my sermon that I have already begun with the poem I've just read, I must tell you a short story. Two ladies, having made an application for employment at a local firm, were called upon to be interviewed for the position, but the interviewer had an unusual method of determining the best candidate for the job.

One of the two ladies, slightly advanced in years, was dressed with the utmost nicety and precision, in an appealing mixture of bygone styles, with just a slight concession to the current taste. She sat in a stately manner with her hands folded on the table before her and her eyes attentively fixed upon an open magazine while waiting to be called. The other lady was young, in the lovely bloom of her early years of womanhood. She was so pure and beautiful, that the earth seemed neither her element, nor its rough creatures her fit companions. Deep blue eyes were stamped on her noble head and alternating expressions of sweetness and intelligence brightened her face with a happy smile.

With purpose, both ladies were left to wait, but were monitored from the inside office through a one-way mirror by the interviewer.

After a long while, though not being called, the older lady continued with her reading. The younger lady became very edgy. She drew her chair closer to the table and began hammering it with her elbow. First this was done softly then, after a bit longer the hammering became harder and finally she stood up and began to walk around the room, as if looking for something to vent her anger on.

Suddenly, the interviewer appeared at the door and the young lady rushed to him, now with a wide smile on her face, saying softly, "I'm ready for my interview."

"You've been interviewed already. You may go home and we'll call you if we need you," said the interviewer as he watched her march capriciously out of the door. He then turned to the older lady and asked her to follow him inside.

Ladies and gentlemen, the young lady had everything. She was on top of the mountain but she couldn't see the view, she was beautiful but couldn't see anything new. God is like that young lady's beauty. When things don't go our way we lose sight of God. She had all the right stuff to make it though the interview, but she lost sight.

We have all the right stuff, my friends, to make it, but we must believe in God and we must never lose sight of Him and we must always keep in mind that we are constantly monitored by an all knowing and all seeing God, by Him," concluded Erik.

CHAPTER THREE

Mary Lou comes home to Erik

On the side of a busy highway, not far from the city of New Orleans, stood a two story Motor Inn with a flaring sign, closer to the road, announcing its name, **LIVE OAK INN.** On the second floor of that appealing structure was a room occupied by Erik Karas, who, in the midmorning hours, was still sleeping on a king sized bed covered with a dark green comforter. Suddenly a gentle but audible knock on the door was heard. Erik opened his eyes slowly, raised his head and looked around as if trying to recognize where he was. The knock was repeated in the same manner.

"Just a moment," yelled Erik, getting off the bed as briskly as he could. After he put on a dark blue robe, he went to the door, stood there with his ear near it, and asked, "Who is it?" He waited to hear an answer from the outside. Erik, though roused from sleep by the first knock on the door, was not thoroughly awake.

"Who is it?" he repeated, coming closer to his normal senses. He waited a moment and hearing no answer, opened the door abruptly, poked his head out and found Mary Lou standing a few feet away from the door, with a large suitcase on the floor next to her.

She was standing with her weight thrown on one foot and a hand on her hip, "Darling, there are two things in life. Either you love me or you don't," stated Mary Lou, shaking her body with peculiar rhythm.

"Anything between?" asked Erik, smiling.

"Darling, if you love me, I'll make you a night like no night has been or will be again. I'll sail on the moon, I'll ride on your touch, I'll talk to your eyes that I love so much," declared Mary Lou.

She extended her hand, but Erik caught her by the shoulder, brought close her to him and imprinted one kiss on her beautiful forehead, "You have your favorite song and I have mine."

"What 's your song?"

"Take me to the moon, " said Erik, taking her suitcase and a short survey of her as she swung into the room.

She looked around with an examining eye and a happy face. She sat herself down on the bed he had just left.

"Don't you know, Erik, it's a sin for a man to spend the whole night alone on a big bed like this" said Mary Lou, bouncing up and down gently.

"They have no single beds in this hotel. Besides, it's not bad when you're waiting for the right one to come along," said Erik

"Am I the right one, Erik?"

"I don't know," he replied, walking towards her, "you are the right size and you're blond."

"Blonds are your weakness, eh, Erik?" interrupted Mary Lou.

"I can't help that weakness, but it makes my purpose stronger," he returned.

"And your purpose is? As if I don't know."

"To see if you're the right one," he replied.

"To see? Erik, or to find out?"

"First is seeing then comes believing," he answered.

"How many have you tried, up till now, Erik?"

"Four hundred and sixty-six," he stated, matter of factly, with a serious face.

"You've been counting them, Erik?" she asked.

"Yes,"

"Not only have you been counting them, I think you kept records on them. Did they all count, Erik?" asked Mary Lou, making her eyes smaller and distorting her face, as if scrutinizing the man before her.

"Not all. Look, I kept records on a lot of them; I have a diary two feet thick. Are you happy now?" he asked.

"Am I going to be in your diary?" asked Mary Lou.

"I don't know. There's an old Greek saying. "Don't judge a woman before she is done.""

"You creep!" yelled Mary Lou, throwing her purse at him.

Erik ducked; the purse missed him but hit a lamp. With the sound of broken glass, he shot across the room, threw his arms around her and together they flew onto the bed. They kissed passionately.

"Four hundred and sixty-six, you said?" asked Mary Lou, pulling away from him.

"No! Silly girl. Not that many."

"How many, then?" she demanded.

"What are you, my priest?"

"No, but I heard you're some kind of a priest. I've seen you on T.V.," stated Mary Lou.

"Okay. What do you want? You want to confess?" asked Erik.

"If I confess, will you bless me?"

"That depends on your confession," he said, with a smile.

"Okay, I'll confess," returned Mary Lou.

"Go on! Confess, little girl," said Erik, touching her face gently.

"I confess. Since I met you, almost a year ago, I haven't stopped thinking of you. Now, are you going to bless me?" asked Mary Lou, waiting to see what was going to happen next.

After finding complete satisfaction in her answer, he pulled her tenderly close to him.

"Kiss me, silly," he said, softly.

It was early next morning when Erik awoke and saw that beautiful creature sleeping in his arms with her head resting on his chest, her hand locked in his. He fell back on his pillow and turned his eyes to her face. His eyes closed, opened again, closed once more, then opened again as if just to make sure it was Mary Lou, sleeping. He shifted his position restlessly, and, after dozing again for three or four minutes, finally fell back into a deep and heavy sleep. The grasp of his hand relaxed, his arm fell languidly by his side and he lay there in a profound trance. He suddenly sprung up, as if overcome with terror and restlessly gazed around the room. The sound of a knock on the door brought him to reality once again.

"I think its Peddler," whispered Erik

"Talk to him or do whatever you have to do, but get rid of him," cried Mary Lou, hastily.

Mary Lou, naked as she jumped out of bed, hurried to gather

her things and flew into the bathroom. The knock on the door was repeated again and again. Erik made his way to the door, opened it abruptly and found, as he expected, Peddler standing there. "You knock on a door like I shoot a pistol," uttered Erik, gesturing for Peddler to come in.

"I don't understand what you're saying Curly, how do you shoot a pistol?" asked Peddler, as he entered the room.

"I don't stop until somebody's dead?"

"How many have you killed up till now, Curley?" asked Peddler, looking around

and knowing, by the condition of the bed, that more than one had spent the night there.

"None, but if you keep on knocking like that, you'll be the first," returned Erik, reaching for a cigarette.

"Why is it, Erik, that no matter how light we travel, we always bring our old selves with us?" asked Peddler, looking towards the bathroom and seeing someone moving around in there, through a crack.

"Tell me, Peddler who would I be if I left myself behind?" asked Erik.

"Curly, I said we always bring our old selves with us. Can we acquire a new self?"

That question produced an effect on Erik, who then strolled towards Peddler and said, "That reminds of a poem that a good friend mine, Larry Quick, wrote some years back.

Self, you and I should face
Our mutual problems in life's long distance race.
If one could imagine,
The waiting often is stretched to the point of uncaring.
That I sit wanting, waiting, showing courage and daring.
Should I wait caring,
Wanting, straining and bearing,
The thought that I might see you for the first time,
Or should I forget
And forfeit?
Should I forget
And forfeit
Our meeting and seek another day,

with our mutual problems coping?
To find out who you are, I wait.
I kept the date,
Today.
Tell me self, should it ever be so?
Tell me yes or no?

"I'm sure you know who you brought with you, Erik," said Peddler, going to the door of the bathroom.

"Whoever you are, you can come out now," shouted Peddler, facing Erik.

"Are you my sergeant or my bodyguard?" yelled Mary Lou, from inside the bathroom.

"A familiar voice," said Peddler, to Erik.

"Mary Lou, the waitress, from Choctawville. You remember her," responded Erik, taking a seat.

"I thought she was nuts, but now I know you're both nuts," said Peddler.

"Young love. Haven't you heard of young love?" asked Erik.

"Yeah, I heard of young love, but I also heard that youth is wasted on the young," he replied.

"Yeah, and I say that wisdom is wasted on the old," returned Erik.

"Tell me, Curly, isn't she kind of young for you. She must be at least twenty years younger than you," said Peddler.

"I like them young. They're what I call geriatric food," said Erik.

"Oh? How's that?" asked Peddler

"Simple. Women who are my age or older talk about baking cookies. Young women talk about making whoopee. I don't only hate cookies but cookies are bad for me," explained Erik, pausing for a moment as he looked at Peddler seriously.

"I have a little problem. Maybe you can help," he said, lowing his voice to almost a whisper.

"Go ahead, tell me what's the problem?" asked Peddler, in the same conspirational tone.

"Her mother's name is Helen and she's younger than I am. Do I call her Mom? Or do I call her Helen, Peddler?" asked Erik, with the pretence of a serious look on his face.

"Call her Helen, because you might end up with the mother

once the daughter finds out how old you really are," said Peddler, looking at Erik while donning a wide smile.

"Peddler, it's not how old you are, it's how young you feel," said Erik, in a louder voice.

"That feeling will eventually go away. Don't worry. Go on, put some street clothes on, you have another problem Curley."

"Oh, yes?"

"Most of the young women have two men and are looking for a third," whispered Peddler.

"Tell me about it," said Erik, devoting his full attention to Peddler.

"They have one man they love, but don't like him, the second man they like but they don't love him, and they are looking for a third man, hoping to find one that they like and love," concluded Peddler, with a smile bigger than the door. "I must speak with you. Just remember I am a wise old man. Don't let my wisdom be wasted," said Peddler.

Erik, without additional words, picked up some clothes and headed for the bathroom, as soon as he saw Mary Lou coming out fully dressed.

"Hi Peddler, I see you're still in need of a bodyguard," said Mary Lou.

"Hi, Mary Lou, I see you're still nuts," replied Peddler, looking at her with a grin on his face.

CHAPTER FOUR

Erik visits the haunted house

One particular night came, after many nights had passed since Erik undertook the task of preaching and many words were uttered by him and after some more sightings of the mysterious boy, accompanied the handsome priest.

It was beautiful evening and the first shades of twilight were beginning to form upon the earth. Eric had been driving on a lonely dirt road without a purpose or destination, reflecting on what was behind him and what lay ahead; with so many conflicting thoughts occupying his mind, he felt fatigued. The ensuing darkness was shutting the gates of his open consciousness drawing him to pull over to the side of the winding lane, partly to think and partly to rest for a while. In spite of his stupor, he noticed the moon was full and starting to bathe the road in soft light. He climbed out of the truck, moved off into the indistinct atmosphere, gradually acquiring energy, and decidedly marched with deliberate steps, as if, all of a sudden, he knew where he was going and what he had to do.

He reached a bend in the road and came to a halt when he saw, across a secluded overgrown pasture, a structure silhouetted in front of the rising full moon. The image forced him to draw closer, his having recognized the shape as being that of the haunted house. He stood only several feet away from the dilapidated place when suddenly the moonlit night became a black void, the air chilled and oppressive. Erik felt perplexed, terror-stricken and disoriented, lost and enveloped in the changing phenomenon. He stared at the tall turret that projected into the sky and noticed some movement of drapes that obscured the interior. Not knowing if an individual or the night wind, whispering through the house, caused the movement, posed a mystery. He sat on the warm earth in front of the house, pulled up his knees against the chin and stared, in anticipation of finding an answer. He raised his eyes to the window, and saw, once again, the heavy drapes sway; he noticed that there was not even the faintest draft, therefore, he reasoned the fabric had moved by intentional purpose and upon further observation he was able to make out the figure of a little boy standing by the window, looking down at him. Could it be the same boy he had seen in the limousine, waving and beckoning him to follow? As that thought was passing through his mind, another figure appeared and stood beside the boy. It was the image of a man that from the distance resembled both the limousine driver and the priest. He jumped to his feet trying to get a closer look at the faint apparition and was able to distinguish that it was the priest who he had met before, in the church and in the park holding a lamb. The shock of that sight jolted his senses and sent a surge of blood through his veins that deprived him of speech and left him unable to move. A twitch, a blink of his eyes and in a flash, the boy and priest had vanished. Erik remained transfixed for a moment, then gathering his wits and composure, ran for the truck, sped away from that place and headed for home.

While driving, he tried to rationalize the striking phenomenon and separate the real from his imagination. He felt sometimes reality and imagination become so strangely blended that afterwards it is almost a impossible to separate the two. It was dawn when Erik finally managed to get home. It was less than one hour later when Erik walked out of his room and headed for the conference center of the motor lodge that served as his and Peddler's office. Erik rubbed his eyes while walking into the office to find Peddler sitting behind a desk.

"Good morning, Peddler," said Erik.

"Good morning, Erik. Are you all right?" asked Peddler.

"I'm fine, I just didn't get much sleep last night. Mary Lou said you wanted to talk to me," replied Erik.

"Do you know what's happened?" asked Peddler.

Erik shook his head.

"Two things have happened. A lot of people sent in donations," said Peddler.

"Good, just keep track of them. I don't want to go to jail," said Erik, laughing.

"Don't be silly. I'm hiring a bookkeeper. The other thing, which is very important, we have been offered the auditorium. We have to pay a high rent, but I got a big T.V. deal."

"I thought we had a T.V. deal. People have been seeing me on T.V." returned Erik.

"No. You're right, but I said, a big T.V. deal," said Peddler, smiling with an immeasurable delight and proud manner. "Curly, I told you that I would make you a king," said Peddler.

"I don't care if you make me a king or a pauper. Just don't make me an inmate in some prison. I'll see you later, kingmaker," said Erik, leaving by the side door as he set off on a morning walk.

"Good morning, Peddler," said Mary Lou, coming in from the same door that Erik had.

"Mary Lou, you just missed Erik," said Peddler.

"Good. I just wanted to talk to you,"said Mary Lou, softly.

"Why? Don't tell me you're pregnant," returned Peddler.

"Why would I tell you if I were pregnant, Peddler?" asked Mary Lou.

"I'm sorry. I was only trying to be funny," he rejoined.

"Erik did not come home last night. And when he did get in this morning, I noticed his suit was soiled with grass stains on it," said Mary Lou.

"There must be an explanation," said Peddler, after leaning back on his chair and thinking seriously. " Don't worry about it. One thing you must have already figured out, I think you'll be able to control him just like any local boy. If you love him, try to understand him. If you don't, leave him now," said Peddler.

"I love him, Peddler," exclaimed Mary Lou.

"Mary Lou, I'm really happy for you," returned Peddler.

Erik, having decided that he had found his mission in life and believing in what he was doing, remained so unassuming that Mary Lou felt quite grateful to him for not getting overcome by his own self importance. Erik never knew how devoted Mary Lou was to him and she didn't know how grateful he was to see her standing behind the curtains listening to his performance. It had never entered her mind to control or even advise him on his sermons or other business.

She had all the good sense and all the good feelings possible for him; she felt at ease with him, and he was at ease and in love with her.

They shared long talks together after supper and hours of physical love after they returned from work in the afternoon and again in the early morning hours.

She often told him, how quick and bright she thought he was at his work, and he heard her say, many times, when one shot a complementary word about him to her, 'you ain't seen nothing yet.'

CHAPTER FIVE

Erik finds Jonas

Erik, alone on the podium, sized up the audience with his eyes and signaled for the band to stop playing.

"The dew seems to sparkle more brightly on the green leaves, the air rustles among them with a sweeter music and the sky itself looks more blue and bright" said Erik, stopping for one moment, as all orators do, partly to catch his breath, partly to change his tone and partly to give some time for the audience to think. "Such is the influence of our own thoughts and attitude over the appearance of external objects. Men who look on nature and their fellow men and cry that all is dark and gloomy are right; but the dull colors are reflections of their own pessimistic eyes and hearts. The brilliance of colors is delicate and requires a clear vision," there he stopped and smiled as if he had brought his point across in a most satisfying manner. " What I am trying to convey to you is that, things sometimes are not what they seem to be." Saying this Erik, took the Bible in his hand, opened it and began to read.

"If you had faith as large as a grain of mustard seed, ye might say unto this sycamore tree, be thou plucked up by the root and be thou planted in the sea, and it should obey you." Luke 17:6 What "Luke" in 17:6 is saying here is that faith will move mountains. This doesn't mean with faith you can move the mountains from Colorado to New Jersey. It only says that you can cross the mountain. Many mountains in our lives stand before us; most of those mountains are created by our own selves, because we have no faith. Sickness is a mountain," declared Erik as he closed the Bible. "I believe that every sore and every ill spot in our body is where the devil has harbored himself in us. How was the devil allowed to enter my body, you may ask, and you may answer that, I have faith and I believe in God, how did the devil enter my body? My friends, it's not enough to tell the world that you believe in God; you must also act upon His advice and follow God's advice. God has given you the body to shelter your soul. It is under your absolute control. For what you do to your body and what you do to other bodies, your soul will be rewarded or punished. God made this world. God made you. We are designed to eat. Common sense will tell us what is good for us eat and what is bad. We were each given the right to eat one swimming pool full of food in our life. The sooner we eat that amount of food the sooner we pass away. God is good and will give you a warning. The devil is also a creator. He creates the bad. If you allow him to come into your body, he'll do his job and create more pains, more sores and more sickness. If you allow him to enter your body he will affect your thoughts, your beliefs and your common sense. There are many of God's advices that you haven't or don't follow. My beloved friends, according to my belief, God's only wish is that you follow His advice. You must have heard the saying that 'God will punish you'. God doesn't punish he only advises. If God told you to make a right turn and you made a left and you fell over a cliff, He didn't punish you; you punished yourself. The devil, on the other hand, wants you make that left turn so you can get in trouble and will be angry with God. When you become angry with God you are siding with the devil and the devil is constantly looking for a way into you, so he can eventfully penetrate your mind, your thoughts and your deeds and then your actions will be controlled by his horrible influence.

Erik walked around, placed the Bible on the podium, took the microphone, held it in his two hands and scanned the audience for a longer time than normal.

"Not too long ago I was invited to visit and speak to large group of people who had gone skiing in the mountains of Vermont. I finished my speech and went to dinner afterwards with some of the new friends I had made there. Later, it was ten o'clock according to my watch on the lamp table, I was reading the Bible and listening to the wind. The lodge consisted of many wooden, chalet type, houses and I was given the top floor of the last house on the row.

The weather was stormy and nasty; it was a bad night to be

anywhere else except inside. I listened to the wind howling and heard trees being torn and coming down, some against the exterior walls of the house. As the wind came up from the valley, blowing through the forest of naked trees and curving the evergreens with its power, it sounded like the discharge of a cannon or the breaking of the sea. I felt I might be spending the night in a storm-beaten lighthouse. I saw the lights blinking, as if they were signaling each other to break their chains, leave and run away to hide somewhere. Recollecting then, that on my arrival, when a college boy conducted me to the house, three days before, he took the time to show me the kerosene lamps placed around the rooms and instructed me how to light them in the event the electric power should fail. I eyed one, and just as I stood and went for it, suddenly the lights went out. I lit the lamp, went to the window, looked out and saw that everything was dark and dismal. I sat down on a chair, next to a writing table, but I wasn't in that position long when I heard the unmistakable sound of footsteps on the stairs, sounding as though they were caused by one laden with a heavy load. I listened again and heard them approaching. Remembering then, the staircase lights were out, I took the lamp in my hands, reluctantly opened the door and walked to the top of the stairs. Whoever or whatever was down below had stopped, on seeing the light of my lamp. All was quiet, except for the gusts of wind blowing, moaning and screeching one after the other as if racing in competition. I shaded my eyes with my hand, looked down, saw nothing and heard nothing.

'Is anyone down there?' I yelled, believing whoever it was had to know only I was there, because the rooms below me were vacant as of the second day after I arrived.

'Is anyone there?' I repeated, again with the same voice.

'Yes, I am here,' yelled back a man's voice, from the darkness beneath me.

'What do you want?' I asked.

'I'll tell you when I come up,' said the voice, as he began the trip up to me.

I stood with the lamp held over the stairs and he came slowly within its light. The lamp's circle of light was tapered; he was in it but a brief moment and then, as he turned the twist of the stairs,

I saw a face I had never seen before.

Moving the lamp as the man was approached, I made out he was between fifty and fifty-five years old and dressed elegantly. He wore a gentleman's hat and his hair was short, wavy and gray; his face was clean-shaven and healthy. He was a muscular man, strong and heavy on his legs. As he ascended the last step and the light of my lamp shone brightly on him, I saw him hold out his hand for me to shake, but I didn't.

'Now tell me, what is it you want' I said, rather sternly.

'I will tell you what I want inside, if I may come in?'

'Do you want to come in?' I asked him, unreceptively. I resented the assurance that glowed on his face and rang in the words that came from his mouth. I took him into the room that I had just left, and, having set the lamp on the table, I stared ahead, as I had a remote suspicion of his purpose in coming there.

'I know you but you don't me.'

'That is true,' I said 'a lot of people know me, but regrettably, I don't know them.'

As I turned to face him, my suspicion came to pass; I saw him standing by the door holding a pistol directed towards me.

My heart began to beat like a heavy hammer.

'I want you to know I'm an ex-convict and that I've come hear to thank you for the big favor you did for my mother, while I was away,' said the man.

'Are you going to thank me by shooting me?'

'I said, I was a convict not insane,' returned the man, with a smile that looked somewhat like a frown. 'Now I live in Boston and I heard you were up here,' continued the man, 'I came to ask you to do me a favor,' said the man in a soft voice; he then stopped, looked at his pistol and placed it on the table. When he put the gun on the table, I saw, with amazement, that his eyes were filled with tears.

Up to this time, I had remained standing and all the while wished he was gone, something I don't often feel about people, but seeing his tears, I was softened by that aspect of the man.

He then came to where I was standing and held out both his hands. Not knowing what to do, for, in my astonishment, I had lost my self-possession; I reluctantly gave him my hands.

He grasped them heartily and shook them, as if pumping a well, then dropped my hands, stretched out his arms and went to embrace me; I laid my hand upon his breast and pushed him away, gently.

'When I a young boy I started to cheat in school; I didn't get caught,' the man began to speak with a somewhat melancholy voice, taking a seat by the table, 'then I began to steal small things and realizing I wasn't going to heaven, I did bigger and nastier things. Soon, I was traveling the streets of crime and to the criminal element, I had become as familiar as the mailman to a neighborhood. Once in a great while I would to church, not to pray, because I was afraid of praying to God. While in church I would recognize the frequent attendants and wondered how those people could be so happy. Eventually, like most criminals, I got caught and sent to prison. I finally came out a few months ago and I got sick; I went to the doctor and he told me I have very little time left. Brother Karas, I don't want to go though a lingering death, I want you to do me a favor. I want you to something for me that I don't have the courage to do myself,' said the man as he stood up hastily, turned, went back to take the gun and returned. Without letting any time lapse, he pointed the gun at me and said, 'I want you to kill me.' He glanced at me with the look of insolent triumph on his face.

'No!' I said loudly and sternly.

One thing was manifest to both of us, but until relief could come from some unknown source or spirit, neither one of us could say a word. There we stood, face-to-face, eye-to-eye and foot-to-foot; he with his pistol in his hand and I with my hands wrapped around the chair ready to use it in my own defense. Neither one of us, was about to budge an inch or retreat a step.

I was struck by the horror of the idea that had weighed upon me from the moment I heard his words and saw the look on his face. I knew then, that his plan was to tempt me to kill him in self-defense.

'If you have come here to thank me,' I decided to speak first, 'you have found me, there must be something good in your mind that has brought you to me, but what you're asking me to do is all bad.'

My attention was so glued to his fixation on me, I almost swallowed my tongue in speaking my own words.

'I must tell you,' I continued, 'that from what I have seen with my eyes and heard with my ears, you have repented. You want to come back to God's ways, but you have been accustomed to acting with malicious thoughts in your head, a threat on your face and a gun in your hands.

He looked at me with the strangest air, one of wandering pleasure, as if he had liked some part of what I had said; he then put the gun on the table, removed his hat and covered the pistol with it.

'Now I know,' he said, in coarse broken voice, 'the moment I realized I wasn't going to go to heaven, I turned away from God and the devil sided with me. I traveled on down that road until I reached the point of no return. I know the road back to God's side will be a hard one. I hope I will eventually develop conscience, something I never had before. I know God will forgive me, from what I've heard you say. God will forgive me but my conscience will never allow me to forget all the bad things I've done. That is my punishment, but I can endure it, knowing that I'll be traveling on God's side of the road.'

My dear ladies and gentlemen, that man, being in my company, felt the presence of God. I assured him that I was going to help him and I did. He now lives in Westfield, New Jersey, where I lived. He lives with his family and is a frequent attendant of church. He calls me very often, just to tell me how happy he is. He feels that he is in heaven. My dearly beloved friends, most evangelists try to pave your way to heaven, but I am trying to make a heaven for you here on earth. If you can find heaven here on earth, chances are, your road to God's heaven will be a joyous one.

I must confess to you that, right now, I feel the presence of God in this place. I feel that I am in heaven. Please close your eyes and feel the living Jesus Christ sitting next to you. Now I know," yelled Erik "Now I know you feel the presence of God! Now I know you feel the presence Of Jesus Christ next to you! Do you feel what I feel? Please answer me!" he yelled again, louder. The crowd screamed in ecstasy. Some cried, some mumbled a prayer and some yelled out in response.

Erik fell to his knees and in a broken voice, whispered a prayer with tears in his eyes. He then slowly stood up and walked behind the podium. "While I was praying," he continued in a softer tone,

" I didn't hear God speak to me, but I felt His holy spirit enter and find a place way down deep inside of me and I felt a heavy weight lifted away from there. I felt as if the devil were waiting to get in," his voice became more vivid and louder, " I felt as if something that was lingering in a corner of my mind, something unkind, something evil, was chased away. Now, tonight, I sense I can do something that I have never done before. I want anyone of you who has a sore, an ache, or a disability to come forward. I will not cure you, I don't have that power, but you have that power. If you believe in God and if you promise God that you will, from now on, follow His guidance and act only upon His advice, God will enter your body and the devil will run back into his hellhole," shouted Erik.

Many from the crowd, prompted by his words and comforted by his assurance began to line up in front of him. At the head of the line was a lady on crutches. Erik went over to her, placed his hands on her forehead, turned towards heaven, closed his eyes and prayed in silence. The lady, supported by her crutches, stood still, with all of her limbs trembling to the core and sweat, mingled with tears, running down her face; she too prayed in silence.

"Please, lady, help me. I'm not a magician. Please believe in him and asked him to forgive you, let Him know you believe in Him," shouted Erik.

"God, dear God, help me!" screamed the lady, "Help me to walk again, my God, I believe, I believe, I believe."

"Throw away your crutches, dear lady. Throw away you crutches! You need them no more. The devil is gone," shouted Erik, "God is with you now. I can sense it in my heart, I can feel it in my hands," he screamed. Sweat, mingled with tears of joy, poured down from every pore of his face; he remained still, touching her forehead with his left hand. The lady's eyes were closed, her face turned to heaven and, as she mumbled a prayer, she let her crutches fall to the floor. She stood there for a moment, free, shaking from head to toe, wobbling back and forth and then she fell down in a faint. Her husband rushed to her aid but Erik gestured to him to stay away.

"Come on dear lady, get up and walk! God wants you to walk, get up and walk! Walk! You can walk! Walk with God! Walk with

Him!" Erik stood above her and yelled, with all the power God had given him, his words echoed through the crowd.

She opened her eyes, came to her feet slowly, scanned the faces focused on her, then slowly turned her head, looked at Erik and smiled. Erik gave her his hand, she took two steps and let Erik's hand go and she continued. There were tears of joy flowing down every face in the assemblage on seeing that lady walk away, without her crutches, empowered with a new found faith in God. She reached out and threw her trembling arms around husband.

It was as if all God's angels fluttered around that lady, at that instant, as she joined the world of the walking, leaving behind her all the sorrow and calamity she was accustomed to half of her life. She passed through the crowd like a soft shadow on her way to take up life again, among the healthy.

Suddenly a change came to Erik's expression; he saw Leroy, the young man who had attacked him in front of Mary Lou's trailer, standing motionless in back of the auditorium, unmoved by what he had just witnessed, but visibly agitated. Erik recalled the young man's promise on the night of their confrontation.

Leroy, although witnessing a miracle take place before his eyes, had not improved his disposition. He appeared to have the nervous manner of one on the eve of some bold and hazardous step, one that required no common struggle to resolve.

Erik stood and watched him exit through the rear door.

Once Leroy reached the street, he paused and considered for a moment whether to go back or to leave, but he went on doggedly. As he left the auditorium behind him and plunged further and further into the solitude of darkness, he envisioned, with the eye of his warped mind, Erik making love to his girl, Mary Lou. Those thoughts, of course, shook him to the core. In order to shake them from his mind, he ran for the parking lot where his car was parked, he flew into it and remained there, panting like a running dog. He could hear her panting, her voice softly speaking, not to him, but to Erik; every breath of the passing wind brought a new horrible image to his mind. Feeling helpless, emasculated and overtaken by frustration, he began pounding his head with both hands and burst into a violent fit of sobbing.

Erik, in the auditorium, completely unaffected by the sight of

Leroy, nodded at the chorus who began to sing a slow hymn. He walked back to his podium and raised his head towards heaven.

"Thank you, Lord. I too believe," he whispered, bringing his head down slowly. While he was doing that, his eyes opened and were filled with ecstasy as he looked straight back at the crowd and saw a little boy, resembling Randy, rush out, away from the crowd, while keeping eye contact with him on the podium. Erik closed his eyes, shook his head a few times, to chase out the vision, but when he realized he couldn't, he darted out, following the path the boy had taken. The crowd stood still, applauding, watching in confusion as Erik ran down the aisle and out the door.

Eventually he found himself standing alone in front of the auditorium, looking, panting and sweating.

The familiar black limousine rolled in front of him; while it slowly passed, Erik looked into rear window and caught a quick glimpse of the mysterious boy staring and waving at him, as he had done before. Erik, not knowing what to do, loudly called out Randy's name and finding that action totally ineffective, he remained there confused and lost, looking after the car until it disappeared in the distance. He decided to run after it. As he was running into the darkness where the limousine had vanished, another vision came before him, as constant and more terrible than that from which he had escaped. He saw two eyes staring at him, lustrous and glassy, having a light within themselves that shown onto nothing. Erik then began to hear shouting and a sort of roaring, looking to see the origin of those sounds, he saw the distant sky on fire, the fire was coming from the direction of the haunted house; he ran in that direction with all his might. As he was running, his face drained of color and there would have been considerable difficulty in recognizing him as the man, who, a short while before, stood in front of thousands of people and performed, as if he were one of God's chosen on this earth.

He finally reached the haunted house, the fire had vanished and he was alone, standing in front of it, staring at the same window in the turret. He stood without moving, but could make out again, the movement of an indefinite form. Suddenly, a figure became clear, it was the young boy, and appeared as if lit from within, waving and beckoning; the priest was standing close behind..

"Randy! Randy!" screamed Erik, running towards the house.

As he threw the door open, he looked both ways and ran up the stairs taking two steps at a time. The stairs creaked and shook under his feet as he pounded on them with his heavy steps.

Everything was dank, filthy, covered with dust, ashes and hanging cobwebs. A row of closed doors lined an eerie hallway.

"Randy!" Erik screamed, kicking one door open. The room was empty, cold, and dark.

He kicked a second door open. It was the room from which he had seen the boy waving. He looked around anxiously. The room was lit by a single gaslight; its beam was prevented, by shutters and closely drawn curtains of faded red, from being clearly seen on the outside. Those tattered drapes swung back and forth, as if someone had just touched them.

Erik stood there, waiting for his eyes to grow more accustomed to the darkness, hoping to see anything that would make some sense to him. Standing there in silence and in wrath, he saw nothing. He then ran to open the window and wrapping his hands on the side of its frame, he leaned forward and looked out. He ran back into the hallway when he heard cries and moaning coming from the lower level of the house, then there were more, coming from the attic; they echoed throughout the entire dismayed structure. Suddenly the cries and the moaning stopped; Erik stood on the top of the stairs, looking down, searching for an exit.

A gossamer white figure stood at the foot of the stairs, it bore a definite resemblance to his son. He rushed down the stairs taking two steps at a time. Each time his foot hit a step, the stairs creaked and almost broke. Halfway down, a step finally gave way. Erik plunged into the darkness below. He reached up with his hands as he fell and succeeded in grabbing onto the last remaining stair tread, under the weight of his body it creaked but stayed; Erik hung on by his fingers. Looking down, the darkness made the distance to the bottom indefinite, and therefore more frightening. Suddenly everything became quiet and he heard footsteps, a series of heavy thuds accompanied by heavy breathing.

"Please help me. Somebody help me! Randy?" cried Erik, still hanging on by his nails.

The sound of the footsteps stopped directly above him. Erik

was tried to look up, but he couldn't.

"Please, help me, whoever you are. I think my leg is broken," uttered Erik, in a soft pleading voice.

"Oh!" shouted a man.

A huge arm hung down, and Erik, wrapping his arms around it tightly, was lifted up. He saw a big man with a long full-faced beard, seeming, in the darkness, more like a phantom than a man. The man, with only a slight effort, lifted Erik and carried him, in silence, into large ill lit room where he was laid down on something that vaguely resembled a mattress. Erik passed out.

The next morning, the sun snuck through some openings and shot its rays in, lighting up the house, as much as was possible. Erik, still lying on the same spot where the big man had placed him, opened up his eyes slowly and looked around at his surroundings, trying find something familiar. He was covered with a clean white sheet and seemed no worse off the past night's ordeal. He realized he was there, all alone, in the same large room, and after he came to his senses, began examining the room very carefully. He could now comprehend its beauty hidden by layers of dust and dirt. The furniture was a strange mixture of opulent but filthy antiques, as decrepit as the house, with stuffing falling out of the chair cushions. There was a Queen Anne sofa, with an improvised leg made from a piece of raw wood.

On one wall leaned a mattress that was evidently dragged from one of the beds. On the other side was a fireplace that looked as if it had seen its last glowing days quite some time ago. On another was a hallway, leading to another room, probably a dining room or kitchen.

"What are you doing here, Mr. Karas?" asked a man's voice, coming from another room.

"Where are you?" shouted Erik.

"I'm making coffee for us," replied the man.

"Who are you? I recognize your voice. Your voice sounds familiar," returned Erik, looking to the direction the voice came from.

"You'll know me when you see me shaved," replied the man, and then he appeared at the door, scratching his short beard, "Half shaved, anyway."

Recognizing the man standing in the doorway, Erik couldn't

contain the excitement he felt and shrieked, "Jonas! Jonas! Is that you?"

"It's me, Mr. Karas," said Jonas, smiling and approaching Erik, with a tray of coffee and cookies, "How do you feel?"

"I feel as weak as water to whiskey drinker," replied Erik, coming to sitting position.

"Why here, Jonas? From the looks of you, you've been here for a long time," said Erik.

"I lost my wife, Mr. Karas," said Jonas, placing the tray near Erik on a nearby table and taking a seat on tattered old chair across from his guest.

"I'm sorry. I'm very sorry," said Erik.

"No, Mr. Karas, she didn't die, she left. She packed up and went," muttered Jonas.

"That's too bad," said Erik.

"It was bad. I don't blame her. She couldn't take my drinking anymore. She sold the house and went back to Indiana. Selling my house was bad. It hurt me more than anyone could tell or know. I had no place to go. I stopped drinking, but too late for her and me; it was as meaningful as a loser's post- election cry. I found this place, and now, I live like a hermit. I haven't seen or spoken to anyone for almost a year. Somebody drops some stuff off at the door," said Jonas.

"Who drops stuff at your door?" asked Erik.

"I don't know, I haven't seen anybody. These here cookies, and the coffee, and the bread and other things are from some kind soul. You know, I hear sounds once in a while, as if somebody is walking around. I looked around a couple of times, but I found nobody. Besides, I don't care. What can happen? Somebody kill me? I'm already dead," uttered Jonas.

The speech, accompanied by his expressive glance at his surroundings, as if he dreaded spending another night in that filthy oversized trap, instilled pity in Erik's heart.

"You must have heard, that the sins of the parents fall on their children?" continued Jonas. "I think, I was my own parent, and now I'm paying for his sins. I don't know if you can understand that. You probably do, you're a smart man, Mr. Karas."

"I understand," said Erik, after a brief meditation.

"What are you doing here?" asked Jonas

"I am chasing my past, or my past is haunting me," said Erik.

"We all have our own problems," returned Jonas, shaking his head, mournfully.

"I must be getting back home," said Erik, getting to his feet with great difficulty,

"What prevents you from leaving this place?" he asked.

"Pride, my fellow man, pride," exhaled Jonas, in a very firm tone, taking pleasure in the sound of his words.

"Pride, you said, pride?" asked Erik, with an astonished tone in his voice, "you're living all alone, in a dilapidated house, and you say pride? I don't understand."

"I don't compete with anyone in here. Going out in the world I must constantly compete. If I compete and lose, then I lose my pride. Why do you think I was drunkard? The liquor restored my pride," retorted Jonas, standing up to be noticed by his visitor. "I don't drink anymore, I have no reason to. I also want you to know that I dislike the police who take it upon themselves to run the world, according to laws they don't understand, creating more chaos than if a real law was broken, I must compete with them in order to stay out of trouble. Second are lawyers, in their scattered nooks and offices of the legal profession, where summons are issued, judgments signed, declarations filed and numerous other ingenious machines are put in motion for the torture and torment of the layman and for the benefit and comfort of the practitioners of the law. Licenses to drive a car, a boat or a motorcycle, licenses for dog, insurance for all the catastrophes that men could put together...." Thus rambled Jonas, looking around with a winning smile. "That's what prevents me from leaving this place and these living conditions."

"I sense your animosity and grudge against the police and the lawyers. How did they harm you Jonas? How did they cause you to lose your pride?" asked Erik, sternly as if Jonas was mad at the world for no good reason.

"Just because I choose to live like this, you think I'm crazy, the way you asked me," said Jonas. Turning away, he walked a few steps. "Animosity? Grudge, you said Mr. Karas? I'll tell you. The lawyers got together with my wife and took my house away from me, a house I was paying the mortgage on. The police came with the new owners came; they had a signed order from some judge who never saw me and they told that I had twenty minutes to get out, otherwise they would lock me up. I went in my car and they came over, the police, I am saying to you, and asked me for my driver's license and I couldn't find it right there and then. They asked me to leave and leave the car there, because I couldn't drive it on a public road without my license, but the new owner said the car must go. Was there any loss of pride, Mr. Karas? The car went. The police called a tow truck and towed my car away. It took me a week to get my license and the charge for car storage was too high and my wife had taken all my money because I had it all in her account at the bank. I left my home with only my jacket. Was there any loss of pride? I fled from there and plunged into the thickest recesses of the neighboring woods. On and on and on, I wandered night and day, beneath the burning sun and the cold moon and I finally came upon this place and I stayed here ever since then. No one to talk to and no shoulder to cry on, but I got used to it," exclaimed Jonas, with flooded eyes and a trembling lower lip. " There is one thing that I will never forget. I had a small chicken roasting in the oven and I asked the peace officers to allow me enough time for the chicken to be done and they said they were in a hurry and I had to go. I even lost my chicken in the bargain. Was there any loss of pride, besides the loss of my chicken?"

"I understand and I believe everything you told me and it breaks my heart; you living here, under these conditions, breaks my heart more."

"My father told me one time that there is more pride in riding a mule than to ride in car you can't afford. Can you understand that too, Mr. Karas? The mule needs no license, registration, insurance, oil, gas and thousand other things," said Jonas, looking at Erik with a wide smile, "only a little love and a little grass," he concluded, stretching his legs out like an independent gentleman. "As you can see Mr. Karas, I haven't a worry in the world."

"I understand that too, but," said Erik softly, going close to him, placing his hand on his shoulder and looking deeply at him with true concern, "Jonas, let me help you".

"Mr. Karas, I meant to ask you something when we met at the

funeral. What kind of work do you do? I mean, what do you do to make a living?" asked Jonas, lowering his voice to a confidential whisper.

"I am an evangelist," replied Erik, with a wide smile.

"My God," said Jonas, no longer stretching out his legs; he coiled them up as well as he could, under his chair. " I knew it the very first time I heard you speak; you were a man of God."

"That is why, I told you I think I can help you, Jonas," said Erik. "I have a friend I think can help you in the right way. You can take whatever job in our business you think will suit you best at first, and then be taught all the others. I promise you that we'll never cause you to lose your pride. Get ready," said Erik getting on his feet with some difficulty, "I'll tell you more on the way there. Come on get ready," repeated Erik, seeing Jonas still sitting even though he was already standing.

"Get ready, Mr. Karas?" replied Jonas, coming onto his feet. "I only have one suit to pack. It won't take me more than three minutes to get ready."

In due time the two arrived at the office and Erik, on his way out of the taxi, asked Jonas to wait outside for a moment.

"Jonas, " said Erik, once he paid the cab driver and the cab was gone, " you will eventually be associated with what I do, you will read the Bible. In the Bible you will read, 'Pride goeth before destruction and a haughty spirit before the fall.' Think about it. Stay here until I call you," said Erik as he walked into the office.

Jonas, without a doubt, being a man of pride and perhaps a haughty spirit, realizing that we always get change back if we hand out a bigger bill that is necessary, stood there and watched Erik go in.

It was fortunate for Peddler that his acquiring success and the possession of money occasioned so much employment in running the business he had neither the time nor the inclination to occupy himself with anything else. He was sitting in his swivel chair, behind a pile of papers, when Erik walked into his office.

"Good morning Peddler" said Erik, as he stood at the door.

"Good afternoon Mr. Karas. I suppose if you woke up alone this morning you wouldn't be truly telling me good morning," said Peddler, getting onto his feet out of respect.

"If you sleep alone during the night then you wake up all-alone, Peddler. Allow me to show you something of interest," said Erik, gesturing for Jonas, who was out of Peddler's view, to enter.

Appearing at the door, Jonas, with a wide smile on his face, wearing a suit that was at least twenty years old, slowly entered Peddler's office.

Peddler saw Jonas, jumped up and down and howled with excitement.

"What the hell. Look what the cat dragged in, a man from the past. What are you doing here?" asked Peddler, shaking Jonas' hand with vigorous freedom.

"Peddler, you look better than ever. You must be eating regular," remarked Jonas, still maintaining a smile.

"I've never been hungry, Jonas. Lonely yes," returned Peddler. "I hate to interrupt this intelligent conversation, but I have to go. Peddler, remember I am not a cat. I am a lion. My father told me once, never shake your ass before a lion's mouth; you may lose part of it. Jonas is going to be with us for a while, find something for him to do. Incidentally, he doesn't drink anymore," with that, Erik left in a hurry.

"That I have to see," said Peddler.

Jonas looked after Erik until he turned the corner.

"Have a seat, Jonas," said Peddler.

Jonas sat on a chair, across from Peddler, with a hand on each knee, holding them tight, as if he had inside information that they intended to take off and go back to the haunted house. He meditated at first on the probable consequences and his own feelings on being able to adapt to a new life. He promptly dismissed the subject from his mind, released his knees, folded his arms in front of him, sat back, looked at Peddler and smiled.

CHAPTER SIX

A change in Erik's attitude

By a moderate computation, it was a few months over a year since Erik had taken over the late Reverend Butler's mission.

Erik, Mary Lou and Peddler were assembled on the lawn of a large, dignified house in mid November, two weeks before Thanksgiving. It was the beginning of the season of hospitality, merriment and open-heartedness. The old year was preparing, with feasting and revelry, to pass gently and calmly away. Happy and merry was the season, as happy and merry as were the three hearts that stood in front of that serious house.

"Well, Curly, it looks like you're doing pretty well for yourself. You bought yourself a nice house here," remarked Peddler.

Erik shot him a cool glance. "This is not the occasion for an apology, on my part, Peddler, for buying a house. Do you see the need for one?"

"No, oh no, my friend, it just makes me happy seeing you doing pretty well for yourself," returned Peddler.

"I'm doing pretty well for others too," said Erik, giving Peddler the eye of a hawk, "it's a house, nothing more than that, a house that I want to be my home."

"I'm happy for you, like I said, my dear friends. I wish you luck and happiness, to both of you," said Peddler, catching a glimpse of Mary Lou taking Erik's arm.

"Whatever you say, Peddler," said Erik, as he walked away from them both.

Peddler didn't show that he was affected by his partner's scowl rather, to the contrary, he treated it with reverence and even raised a laugh, that sounded as though it were genuine. He looked at Erik as he walked away and asked, "Mary Lou, you know him well, why did he walk away like that?"

"Peddler, haven't you seen people who were laughing heartily and then suddenly stopped and became serious?" she asked.

"Yes, but why, Mary Lou?"

"They feel guilty for being happy," she replied.

"How do you know all that?"

"Peddler, I was a waitress. Do you remember? I used to see and talk to more people than a priest."

With those words she led the way to the door, opened it and went in with Peddler following close behind.

Erik had already advanced to the side of the house, where he stopped and looked fixedly at it. He did not withdraw his eyes for some time afterwards; his gaze gradually became vacant and abstracted, seemingly lost in thought. For some time he appeared doubtful whether he ought to be happy or disappointed for buying of the house, but at length he breathed more freely, withdrew his eyes and observed it was a happy occasion then turned around and followed the others inside.

Many days had passed since Erik bought the house; he and Mary Lou had settled down with a cheerful serenity prevailing between them.

One beautiful night they took a longer walk than was their custom. The day had been unusually warm for the beginning of December, there was a brilliant moon and the light wind that sprang from the gulf was refreshing. Mary Lou had been in high spirits, but Erik was more pensive and less talkative than ever before. They walked on until they exceeded their normal boundaries and then turned, heading for home. Even though Mary Lou seemed at ease, her brain was engaged in different thoughts. She had conceived a suspicion that Erik had found and attached himself to somebody new, not only because of his quiet attitude that night, though it helped to confirm what she was thinking. His altered manner, his repeated absences from home, his loss of interest in her, his desperate impatience to leave home some nights and not return until the early hours of the morning, all favored her supposition, and rendered it, to her, almost a matter of certainty.

They returned home slowly; Erik removed his jacket and placed it on a chair, instead of hanging in the closet as he usually would, then proceeded to the living room couch. He sat there with a hand holding each knee. Mary Lou sat in a nearby chair that perfectly matched the couch and looked at Erik intently while she did some needlework, a handicraft she often occupied her spare time with. The more she studied him the more incapable she became of concentrating on her craft; the longer the silence lasted the more unable she felt to speak. She seemed rather confused, pausing her knitting for a moment with her eyes upon him and then going on, unable to allay her fears.

At length she stood up, placed her needlework on the chair, slowly walked to Erik and sat before him, face to face.

"What are you thinking, Erik? You seem to be in deep thought," she asked.

"I was just thinking of where I've been and where I am now," he replied, gazing down at her, a serious look on his face, "when things go my way and I'm happy, my mind reverts back to my old life, when I lived in Westfield, New Jersey, with my wife and son. I'm thinking how unfair I was to them then and how I could have been gentle and fair, as I am with you now. These are the pains of my yesterday and I can't shake them loose. They're like the shadows of the night, they get stronger and deeper when the Moon is at its brightest. Please, understand sweetheart, I love you and can live happily with only you for the rest of my natural life. You're like a solid wall to me, one I can lean on without the fear it may collapse. You're like a sycamore tree I can lie under, your branches giving shade to my exhausted body and tired soul. Even, with all the love I feel for you, I resent your being happy because I'm the one who makes you that way and there were others in line in front of you and I let them down," confessed Erik, holding a lingering stare towards her. " When I'm away and these feelings enter my heart, they tell me, 'don't go home. Erik, don't go home." I know how much my wife and son loved me. I was a part of their thoughts, a part of their existence. I was in my son's heart, his poor little heart that was wounded so many times before it stopped beating. I was in every prospect and every plan that my wife and son ever had. They saw me everywhere they looked, in the river, on the bridge, on the sails of the boats, in the wind, in the clouds, in the blue sky, in the light and in the dark. I was there, everywhere they looked. I was the bedrock of their thoughts, as solid as the rock that keeps the mountains up. Now I know what they were. I didn't know it then. They were the biggest part of the little good that's in me. Like I said, sometimes in those horrible moments, I resent you as being the only good that's left in me. I resent the fact I will always know that you have done far more good for me than I can ever do for you." concluded Erik, bending his head down, ashamed.

In what ecstasy of misery he shaped these last sentences, from within, he didn't know. It was if a rhapsody of memories, welled up within him, found an open wound from which to gush and spill upon his ill-fated companion.

Mary Lou reached up and held her hand to his lips, for a lingering moment, looking at him with a stare filled with pity and remorse. "Erik, my love. I'm not wise enough to say anything that would make sense to you. I know how you feel, but I can't feel what you feel because God and fate have been kind to me; I have never had the taste of tragedy you have. I want to be to you, what you feel I am. If it were possible to take a part of my heart and use it to mend yours, I would gladly do that. Whatever I know, I learned from listening to you, on stage and off stage, in your sermons. I can never forget the story of the man who came to you in Vermont. He said, I'm sure you remember, coming back from the road of the devil and finding God, he would develop a conscience and his conscience would never allow him to forget all the bad things he had done in the past. He said that was his punishment and he was ready to endure it. Erik, I'm not saying you sided with the devil, you're the only one who knows that, but what I am telling you is, don't let the devil take your tomorrow just because tonight you need a friend. In the past you needed a friend. You have one now." She removed her hand from his lips and placed on her heart, "God is your friend" she concluded.

Erik looked back at her; he found no reason to reply, had no statement to make and nothing more to confess. They exchanged gazes and felt, what was said was enough. The truth was spoken without forming another syllable.

Mary Lou was the first to make a move. She stood up, went to her chair, took her needle-word in her hands and when she felt comfortable, said with a sigh, "Who knows where the road may lead us."

"That's a song that Frank Sinatra used to sing," said Erik, enthusiastically getting onto his feet. He crossed the room, picked up his guitar, sat down on a chair and began strumming. Keeping his eyes on Mary Lou, he sang, "Who knows where the road may lead us, only a fool could say."

Mary Lou, hearing these words, understood he was consciously making a point with his singing, she jumped in and began to answer, her voice joined in song, "When somebody loves you, it's no good unless she loves you, all the way." Her pitch and tone and tone were perfect.

"My God! Oh, my God!" burst Erik, filled with excitement, coming to his feet to get closer to her.

She put down her needlework and looked at him with astonishment resembling anger or anger resembling astonishment and said, " Erik, have I been so cold that I've never told you the love I have for you? Is this the first time you realized it; is that why you're so excited?"

"No, no, I'm excited to hear you sing. You can sing," he yelled.

"Yes, I think I can sing," replied Mary Lou, with a loud laugh.

"You think you can sing? You have a beautiful voice," he declared, "wait, I have an idea, a beautiful idea. I want you to sing with me on stage, I want you to sing with the band."

"I'm not sure I want to do that," responded Mary Lou.

Looking at Mary Lou with the phone to his ear, "you'll sing with me tomorrow tonight," he then continued, into the phone, "Peddler! Come over to my house right now. I have a big surprise for you," he exclaimed, and after a short pause, "you'll see when you get here.

The following morning, when Erik and Mary Lou left their home, it appeared his idea had made a considerable difference in his general outlook on life; he scarcely appeared to be the same person.

They both entered the car. Erik looked at his face in the review mirror, Mary Lou looked at hers in the sun visor's. He looked at her face and she looked at his; they both smiled at the same time and said nothing.

Erik removed his eyes from Mary Lou and gave his attention to driving.

The day came creeping on, haltering, whimpering, shivering, wrapped in patches of clouds and rags of mist.

"This looks like the proper day for all the flies from the butcher's, the snakes from the fields and the bugs from the countryside to go find a place somewhere to hide until next summer," said Erik.

"What a strange observation," remarked Mary Lou, "Is that a notice to them or a warning?"

"It's a simple suggestion; a warning is nature's job."

"I often wondered how long those creatures live," said Mary Lou.

"The mosquito lives twenty-four hours, the turtle, over two hundred years. The concept of time is different for each of the creatures on God's earth. We don't know how long a year is. Is it a long time or is it the blink of an eye? Experts shaped some theories and formed some opinions, but nothing is definite. I know that nature's process is a long process," said Erik.

"You told me that before, Erik."

"When and why?" he asked.

"When I told you that I fell in love with you the first time I met you, you told me that was impossible, because of nature's process of love, and love, being one of nature's passions, takes a year to mature and ripen. Whose time clock were you using then, the mosquito's or the turtle's?"

"You getting to be too smart,' said Erik, taking his eyes off the road to look at her. "Smarter than I, and according to Kipling, a woman should not be smarter than her man."

"Was it Kipling who is to be blamed for that or Theophylus, who refused to marry Kasandra, thinking she was smarter than he? But why should a woman be dumber than her man," asked Mary Lou.

"In my opinion, a man is like a kitchen utensil, when it loses its use, it's should be set aside, to be thrown out at the first opportune moment, or it should be placed in solitary confinement at the bottom of the last kitchen drawer."

Mary Lou looked at Erik and laughed out loud, but before she was able to ask a question or give a reply, the office came to view.

Erik pulled the car up in front of the office and saw Peddler, waiting inside the door.

"Are you ready to start your new singing career," asked Erik, looking at Mary Lou with one hand resting on the car door handle and the other on her shoulder. "One more important thing," he continued, still having one hand on the handle, but the door now was half way open, "sing the song the way you like to hear it, if you like it, the whole world will and I'll love it as much as I love you."

Mary Lou threw her arms around Erik, kissed him and whispered in his ear that she loved him.

"Sing you heart out, sweetheart," said Erik, disengaging himself from her. He jumped out of the car, walked to the office entrance door and held it open for her to enter.

"How are you Peddler?" asked Mary Lou, as she slowed down to hear from him on her way to her office, down the corridor.

"Some days I feel young and some days I feel old," responded Peddler.

"How do you feel today?"

"Today I feel as old as I really am, older than some of my friends and relatives who already have died," replied Peddler.

"Don't worry about it, Peddler, you're going to live long enough to see me all wrinkled up," said Mary Lou; she kept going.

As Erik and Peddler were conversing in low tones, Erik's office door opened and a very pretty blond lady of thirty or so came in, holding a small suitcase in her hand. Peddler gently relieved her of the case and placed it on a nearby chair. The girl looked so pretty she might have passed for a character in a fairy tale. It seemed as if she had timed her visit to correspond with Erik's arrival.

"Mr. Karas, may I have a word with you, sir, in private," requested the girl.

"Please, miss, have a seat," suggested Erik, pointing to a chair next to where her suit case was placed, "What can I do for you?" he asked, sitting behind his huge mahogany desk, on a high-back black leather chair.

The lady looked about with an uneasy air, "Please, privately," she said.

"I'll see you later, Erik," said Peddler, taking a hint. Before he left the room he threw another glance at the lady and closed the door behind him.

Erik noticed that there was something unusual in the lady's resigned way of looking around her in detail and yet loving and innocent, in her modest and gentle manner.

Before any words were exchanged, there was a knock on the door, it opened and Peddler's head appeared, "I just wanted to remind you that we don't need anymore singers. Mary Lou will do just fine," said Peddler.

"Have you heard her already?" asked Erik.

"No, but you did. I'll take your word for it," said Peddler, closing the door immediately afterwards.

"I have watched you on TV a number of times and you always conclude your program with a very kind message, saying that you're willing to help the needy," said the lady, breathlessly.

Erik nodded in assent, with a smile.

"I just left my husband and I'm in desperate need of shelter. I have no money now," said the woman, with a forced smile and a tear drop accompanying it.

Erik, whose eyes had seen many needy people and whose ears had heard many sad stories, sitting behind his high chair, was never able to avoid the feelings of pity and concern, so he sighed involuntarily, although he was never presented with one who looked more like a patron rather than the needy.

"I detect an accent in your speech, where are you from?" asked Erik.

"I'm from Ireland"

"Oh, Ireland. How well I remember the song, summer is gone and all the leaves have fallen, tis, tis you must go and I must bide," he recited with a smile.

"Oh, you know the song, " remarked the Irish lass, proudly.

"Of course, I know the song. I love Irish ballads."

"I love Greek music," said the lady, looking to her right at the hanging guitar.

"You see how the world is. It's a world of give and take. Anyway, talking about giving, the money we give out to the needy is not ours. People give the money to us to hand out to the needy at our discretion. I must ask you some questions; you don't have to answer them. I will make some suggestions, you don't have to take them and I will give you some advice you may or may not act on," said Erik.

"I understand perfectly," returned the lady, wiping tears from her face with a tissue.

"What is you name? First name, you don't have to give me your last name.

"Patricia."

"Patricia, how long have you been in this country?" asked Erik.

"A little more than three years."

"How long have you been married?"

"A little less than three years."

"Are you working?"

"No, sir."

"Do you have any children?" asked Erik.

"No. I have no children," she replied, with a slight annoyance in her tone.

"Do you have any money, at all?" asked Erik, in the same tone she responded to his last question.

The lady suddenly stood up grabbed her suitcase, placed it on his desk, unzipped it, threw the flap open and said firmly. "This is my accumulation in this country, since I've come here"

Erik just glanced at the contents very briefly, then raised his eyes to her and left them there for much longer than the time he took to see her personal belongings.

"These are items you have chosen to take from the house," said Erik, flipping the flap over, as if to hide the contents from his eyes.

The lady hastily zipped up her little suitcase, picked it up and headed for the door, without saying another word or throwing another glance at him.

Erik monitored her actions and said nothing until she placed her hand on the doorknob, he then said, "Wait a moment, please."

The lady stopped and waited, without turning around.

"How much money do you need? he asked, getting onto his feet.

The lady considered for a moment, still facing the door. Then she turned and said, "I should tell you the truth. I need protection more than money."

"Please, sit and tell me," said Erik.

The lady sat on the same chair as before, after having placed her little suitcase on the other, dropped her face into her hands and remained quiet for some time, while Erik sat down.

When she raised her face again there was such concern upon Erik's, she felt relieved even in her passionate grief.

"I am not here to connive you out of any money. As you can see, Mr. Karas, I couldn't hide anything from you, even if I desired to. If you have any doubts as to my identity or my state of need, please tell me. Just don't toy with me."

"Please, Patricia, remember, you're angry with your husband, not with me," said Erik, focusing his attention on her. "Here you are. You have come to America, like most immigrants with a pure desire to work and better yourself. You are very attractive, intelligent and educated. I think you look, in every respect, like a winner but you come across like a loser, and you expect me not to have my doubts?" said Erik, in a clear tone and purposeful style.

"I am sorry," replied Patricia, lowering her head, "Whatever I am, is because of my husband. I was a schoolteacher in my home country, Ireland. I have come here with the same intention as most immigrants, searching for the American dream. But I fell short by leaps and bounds, for I fell for my husband, and he turned out to be a rich attractive mystery."

"You're placing all the blame on him. Tell me a little bit about him. What kind of work does he do?"

"I know he is Italian, was born in Italy but educated in England. I know nothing of what he does for living; he keeps everything a secret, he is an enigma. I have met his brother who is an engineer and his sister who is an educator. They are both successful with good jobs and houses, spouses and children. My husband and they may be of the same blood, but not of the same nature," said Patricia. She stopped to blow her nose with a tissue she all along carried in her hand. "He is charismatic, he is intelligent and I found him irresistible. I told you before that it turned into mystery, a rich attractive mystery of which I was the heroine and he, Leo, that's his name, was the inspiration and the heart of. He had taken such strong possession of me, please understand, I surrendered to him, all my hopes were set upon him. His influence on my girlish character was so powerful that I was led into a mental labyrinth.

I loved Leo, although I now realize that the conventional notion of love cannot be always true. I loved him against any reason, against promise, against logic, against peace and hope, against discouragement from others, including my dear Mother. I did not love him because of his influence in restraining me, as she said, I wouldn't have loved him one penny less if he hadn't restrained me. I believed that he was the perfection of man, the man for me. I have toiled with my thoughts and struggled with myself to stay and be a good wife to him, but I have slipped hopelessly back into being a coarse and simple girl, with no thoughts of my own and no self to defend any more. I lived with a sense of distance and disparity coming between us."

"I am sorry to interrupt you, Patricia, I'm not in a rush because of limited time, but I am in a hurry because of the anxiety you have created, as to how and why you need protection. You're sending me mixed signals. The bad and good feelings you're harboring within you, towards him, are not old and gone, they're fresh and present. The sense of distance and disparity that has come upon you because of his inaccessibility are thoughts created by passion, those I cannot alter, my dear, I am neither a psychologist nor a psychiatrist, I am a simple man who uses the Holy Bible to show to the world the difference between good and evil. Show me why and how you need protection because, I assume, your life is in danger, that I can probably remedy."

"Mr. Karas, I am not in need of having my head straightened or my thoughts corrected, I am in need for someone to listen to me and take the time to analyze my dilemma. I feel as though I have been abandoned in the solitude and darkness of the path I am walking. I have changed so much since I have come in this country, this land of dreams and prosperity, not only in the course of nature, but I am so differently dressed and so differently conditioned, that it is not likely anyone who had known me at home, could recognize me now, without some outside help. My life is in danger because I m contemplating suicide. This is not a new feeling that has come upon me, it's an old one, but now it is stronger than ever; unless I'm shown a solution for the confused state of mind that I'm trapped in," she continued with effort, "I must escape and the only route of escape I can think of is suicide. Thinking about it constantly, I've come to realize, committing suicide serves three purposes, one is escape, another is it saddens the ones close to you, who refuse to believe you or raise a finger to help and the third is it punishes the one who placed you in the tormented state of mind. Is committing suicide covered in the Holy Bible, Mr. Karas?" Does the Holy Bible cover that, sir?"

"Taking a life, no matter whose life, is a sin, I'm certain you know that. Preventing one from sinning is a part of my calling. Seeing a mind expert, who I am not, doesn't necessarily mean that one who does is insane. As you well know, the brain is very complicated; therefore love and marriage are complicated. I will not lift a finger or move a muscle to tell you or anyone else what to do when it comes to a marital relationship. How to love one another is different from telling one to abandon or stay with a relationship, and those who try to tell, unless they're experts, are wrong. The head is the house is thought. That house, at times, for many reasons, becomes desolate. Experts try to restore the desolate house, admit the sunshine into the dark rooms, set the clocks on going and the cold hearts blazing; they know how to tear down the cobwebs and destroy the vermin. They know what to do, with the patient's help and willingness and sometimes with medication. I know that we all act according to what we see and hear. Sometimes seeing is more powerful than hearing. If you were to bring your husband here and sit him in that chair and I looked at him for six days and six nights, I would not see him the way you do; so how can I tell you what to do about your life with him?"

When Erik finished his short monologue, he studied Patricia's reaction and realized she had understood his message. He waited to hear a response from her, but the very last words he heard in his head were his own, 'so how can I tell you what to do about your life with your him.'

Looking at her, Erik sensed she had left the solitude and darkness of the path she had traveled on and was about to enter, with a small doze of assertion, another path, a lighted path. He realized that she wanted to, but was unable to, voice what fears and doubts were left in her mind, for her fears and doubts were altogether undefined and vague. To dispel her fears, Erik decided to proceed with his explanation. Intentionally, he dropped his pen on the floor, got down after it and delayed his surfacing, to give her enough time to digest what he had said. When he came up, he looked at her intently again and observed more of what he had seen before. "I want to tell you that I'm happy to see a little change for the better on you face, but I'm not convinced that you have chased from your mind all your anguish. In order to explain myself in saying that I cannot tell you to stay with your husband or to leave him, I will tell you a short and true story, " said Erik getting onto his feet, walking around his desk and standing in front of Patricia. She raised her head and looked at him, showing eagerness to hear his story. Returning the glance, Erik smiled and placed his hand on her right shoulder. She remained unmoved and unaltered.

"During WWII," he began, while he pulled his hand from her shoulder and returned to his desk, "There were many soldiers stationed around the world," he continued, as he sat, "and most were station in Europe. David O'Brien was the name of one soldier, from Kansas, who was stationed in a small town, in France, near the German border. David fell in love with a pretty French girl named Michelle. In his off duty time, David would go into town, register in a small hotel, named the Bonsoir and sit outside, on the patio at small round table; there would wait for Michelle, who was always on time to meet him. From there they would go off to paint the town or have dinner in a small restaurant. Sometimes they would attend a dance or other social gathering. They had no close friends, just one another; Michelle was an orphan. They decided to get married. David, following American army regulations, went to his company commander to ask for permission to marry Michelle. The company commander, whose name I'll withhold for the time being, refused to give him the necessary permission. David pleaded and begged but his requests fell on deaf ears. They decided, David and Michelle, to get married and to keep the marriage a secret until after the war. But David, excited by the upcoming event, told the news to one of his soldier friends who he asked to be his best man. Finally the day of the wedding arrived and David was walking along a narrow street on his way to the church where he was to meet his bride to be and his friend. There came a touch on his shoulder. He stopped and turned, only to find himself confronted by two MPs, military police. They were the last people he expected to see in that small French town on his way to church. He was then escorted back to the base, presented to the company commander, who, in turn, immediately transferred David to the front lines without giving him the time to notify Michelle. Eight months later he was transferred back to another unit not far from Michelle. At the first opportune moment, he rushed into town, registered at the same hotel, and went downstairs waiting and hoping for Michelle to show up, not knowing where else to look for her. Michelle never came to him. Disappointed and angry at the world and somehow Michelle, he left the hotel and returned to the army base. David, for the remainder of his tour of duty, almost four months, would spend his every off duty hour at that hotel, waiting for Michelle; but she never returned. He was finally sent back to America, discharged and found a job. For the next twenty years, on his vacation time, David would return to France, check in at the same small hotel and wait for Michelle. One morning he got up, got ready, went downstairs for breakfast and began a conversation with the manager of the hotel, with whom he had become acquainted over the years. He told the manager, who was by now familiar with David's problem, that he had a dream that night of an old man who came to speak with him about Michelle. In the dream, the old man had showed him a big wooden box that was sticking out of the trunk of his car. David told the manger that he woke up before the man got to show him the contents.

'I have a good feeling about that dream,' said David to the manager as he went away with a smile.

Some hours later, while David was sitting at his usual table, looking down the hill, was his habit, he heard a man's imposed mild cough coming from behind him, as though someone were trying to attract his attention. He turned and saw an old Frenchman approaching him.

"Pardon, Monsieur, Are you American?" asked the old man, timidly.

"Yes, yes," responded David enthusiastically, remembering an old man in the previous night's dream.

"Weren't you Michelle's boy friend?"

"Yes, yes," replied David, more enthusiastically than before.

"Oh, I remember you and Michelle. I had a restaurant down the street from here, where you two used to often come for dinner. I used to see you from the kitchen and envied you young lovers. Have you come here to visit Michelle?"

"Yes, yes, but I don't know where she is. Do you know where I can find her?"

The old Frenchman looked hesitant and sad, but quite charming, "Let me take you to her."

The two went down the hill in silence. Some hours later, David came back all alone, sat on the chair, planted his elbows on the table, rested his head on his hands and stared at the ground. After a little while, an older lady and gentlemen took the table next to him.

Suddenly the man, who seemed to be an American turned to David enthusiastically and asked him loudly, "Hey! Aren't you an American? I think I know you."

David, recognizing the voice, turned his face and looked at the man with distorted features, "I think I know you too," he replied, in a low voice.

"Now I remember you. Your name is O'Brien, David O'Brien, you were in my company."

"Yes, I was one of your soldiers," said David, with the manner of contempt.

"Small world. Imagine meeting you back here again after twenty years. Honey," said the man, turning to his lady, "this man was in my company, I was his captain," then turning to David "this beautiful lady is the love of my life, my wife, Alexandra."

The wife and the soldier exchanged brief cordialities.

"Are you here with your family?" asked the captain.

"No, sir, I have no family,"

"Oh, now I remember. Honey, he was in love with a French girl; what was her name?" asked the captain, turning to David, whose face was turned away from both of them.

"Michelle," returned David.

"Oh, yes, Michelle. He came to me," continued the captain, " to ask permission to marry her and I didn't give it. In fact, now I recall, David, being a young red blooded American, made plans to go on with the wedding anyhow, I was notified of what was about to take place and ordered the MPs to find him and bring him to me,' said the captain, with a tone of pride and accomplishment. 'They picked him up and I immediately transferred him to the front lines, figuring that fear might chase out his love for Michelle."

'Well, that didn't happen.' remarked David. 'In fact, I never stopped loving her.'

"What ever happened to her? Have you seen her since then?"

David looked at the Captain with scorn, "Yes, I just came from her. You see Captain, the day I was to marry her and I was taken away, without you giving me the opportunity to let her know, she waited for me, at the church for over three hours, holding her wedding flowers in her hands. She had bought those flowers and a pretty dress for our wedding with the last little money she had. I have been coming here every year, for the last twenty years, looking for her and I just found her, today. When she left the church that day, twenty years ago, she went home, cut her wrists, she killed herself. I just visited her place of rest.'

Everything became as quiet as if the world stopped turning. The wife looked away, clearly saddened, the husband looked at his wife and then looked at David who continued to stare at the ground.

"I'm sorry," returned the captain.

"I bet you are," said David, and with that, he stood up, bid both of them goodbye, with a slight imitation of a bow, dusted him his pants and went into the hotel.

The captain's wife, Alexandra, stood up, looked at her husband with disdain and walked away. The captain followed, hoping to justify his actions to her by convincing her to listen to his reasonable explanation.

"The following morning," continued Erik, " The captain and his wife, came out of their hotel, heading for the little restaurant, when they noticed a commotion and an ambulance parked in front of David's hotel. They rushed to the scene and found that David O'Brien had committed suicide; he had left an envelope with close to two thousand dollars and a note asking to be buried next to Michelle.

"That captain was my uncle, who had come to America when he was only fourteen years old. My aunt Alexandra, who was related to my mother, told me later on, that after that day things had changed between her and my uncle. 'She said to me that she once told him, that she didn't know how many people he had killed during the war, but she knew that he had murdered two innocent ones, David and Michelle. She continued telling me not to ever intervene between two lovers, 'They will always find their way without any outside interference,' she said."

"Mr. Karas, David's and Michelle's story is different from mine, I feel sorry for them, taking their lives. I don't wish anybody to feel sorry for me and or my husband," said Patricia, coming onto her feet, "I will go home and I'll find something good in my relationship with my husband. I know I will find many good things in him.

No other words were exchanged between Erik and Patricia, only a few kind glances of understanding; Patricia took her suitcase and went away.

Erik leaned back in his swivel chair, listening while Mary Lou, on stage, sang a rousing gospel number. She was well received. During the song, Peddler walked into Erik's with a thought and a smile.

"Do you know what? She's TV material. We're going to put her on T.V. with you," said Peddler, "For a moment, after seeing you spending so much time with woman, I thought we were to have another secretary or another singer."

"Peddler, I've changed. I don't know whether to be glad or sorry about it, but I'm not the man I used to be."

CHAPTER SEVEN

Leroy is back

Leroy had been squandering his time and life in the streets and in the most raucous bars in town. He was looking to find love or temporary affection from any girl who turned, if even for only a moment, to greet him. Mary was Lou was the only girl in whom he had evidently placed his confidence and fallen in love with, by just watching her as she worked as a waitress. He longed for that magic moment, when she would greet him with a smile. He was under the illusion that because Mary Lou felt sorry for him and treated him with human decency and with a touch of womanly tenderness, it communicated something more than what it was, that she was his girl.

Mary Lou never had a reason to discourage Leroy from leaning so heavily on her. He hung around her, hoping that she, some day, would tell him that she loved him. Erik's dropping into town and Mary Lou being attracted to him caused Leroy to lose his hope. The love he felt for her was transformed into jealousy, a by-product of pride. The thoughts, the fearful acute thoughts, of being powerless while the love he had counted on was trembling in the balance, between staying or going. It was these thoughts that crowded his mind, made his heart gallop and his breath thick. These thoughts combined with the force of the perverted images his mind had conjured fueled his desperate anxiety to do something to lessen his pain and lift his spirit; they pushed him over the edge.

It was a Sunday night; Leroy found a room in a motor lodge in the same town where Mary Lou and Erik lived, close to the auditorium. He sat in his room and watched Mary Lou singing alongside of Erik on the television. Every once in a while, as evil thoughts traveled through his mind, he would turn and look at the rifle with a telescopic sight attached to it, leaning on the wall.

He suddenly reached over, turned up the sound and screamed harshly and loudly, "Howling, are you? Come on girl, don't stand there barking like a bitch in heat. If you can't do better than that, drop it altogether. Do you hear me?" He stopped there for a while, as if to catch his breath, "Don't mind me, it'll be over soon, real soon. What's the matter, babe?" continued Leroy, peering into the TV.

"Lend her a hand, can't you? You stupid Greek," said Leroy impatiently, "and don't stand chattering and grinning at me!" he concluded, reaching over to turn it off, at that precise moment, Erik's words rang, "Upon my honor."

Hearing those words, Leroy turned off the sound, "Upon what? Upon what?" growled Leroy, with disgust. He reached over and grabbed a half full jug of a whiskey, flipped the cap off quickly, raised the jug to his mouth and before he lushed feverishly, said, "Here, I've got to have a drink on that, Erik, to take away the taste of what you just said, or it'll choke me to death, you goddamned hypocritical Greek," he drank hard, and then continued with a bitter grin, "You've been conniving and plotting away every minute that I laid here, shivering and burning." He looked at the rifle with a careless levity, withdrew his eyes then turned back to the TV, threw another look, so kin and searching and full of purpose, if there had been any bystander to observe the change, he would hardly have believed the two looks to have come from the same person.

Leroy didn't look as scared as he had the last time he confronted Erik. There were newspaper photos of Mary Lou and of Erik taped to his wall. Now and then, while he was watching that recorded program, he would throw a quick glance at the photos and then another, again, at the rifle.

Mary Lou's life, in the mean time, was filled with happiness, with Erik, their work and their home.

Twilight was beginning to close in when Peddler pulled his truck into Erik and Mary Lou's circle driveway. He got out, walked up the three stone steps and knocked softly; the door opened and Mary Lou stood there with a smile, inviting him to come in and leading the way to the kitchen. In the large kitchen, Jonas and Erik were seated at the table and welcomed Peddler with broad smiles.

"I have to tell you that I don't have the inclination or the power to palaver, until I get something to eat," declared Peddler.

"Sit yourself down without a word. The chair has been waiting for you for hours now. Dinner will be ready in a few minutes," announced Mary Lou who was busy preparing a dinner meal.

A few minutes later, just as she had announced, dinner was on the table and Erik, Mary Lou, Peddler and Jonas sat around the dining room table enjoying it. Suddenly, Erik threw a glance at Peddler, whose teeth were gleefully tearing apart a chicken leg.

"Peddler haven't you learned how to eat yet?" asked Erik.

"Why?" returned Peddler, stopping that process of eating and looking at Erik as if he were waiting for further instructions.

"You make noise when you eat," replied Erik.

Peddler paused to look at Erik to make certain he wasn't joking and Erik looked seriously back at his partner.

"Now you're going to teach me how to eat?" asked Peddler, putting his fork down.

"Somebody should have taught you how to eat!" yelled Erik.

"Do you think you know everything?" inquired Peddler, with a soft   voice,   attempting   to   avoid   a   confrontation.
"Maybe I don't know everything, but at least I know how to eat," returned Erik, throwing his fork on the plate.

"Maybe. But nobody is watching you. Nobody is trying to find something wrong with you," retorted Peddler, staring at Erik with anxiety and reading in his face nothing but indignation.

"That's because I am the king. Don't you remember, you are the kingmaker," declared Erik, looking around as if he was expecting applause.

"I told you, don't let glory go to your head. Don't you remember that?" stated Peddler, with a soft voice.

"Excuse me," interrupted Jonas, getting on to his feet.

"No, Jonas, you stay where you are," said Erik, getting on his feet and looking at Peddler with a peculiar annoyance.

Mary Lou put her hand on Erik's arm but he shook it away vigorously; his eyes were still nailed on Peddler.

"You seem to remember everything, Peddler. Do you remember where you lived when I met you? Do you remember your wife and your daughter?" yelled Erik, hammering the table with his hand, to place more emphasis on his last words.

Peddler stood up and looked at him with a subdued anger showing; after a long silence, during which he had placed himself in sullen defiance, he walked towards the door, turned back to see Erik, and said civilly, "all my trials and errors that I passed through in my young life haunted me until now that I am old and all the things that moved me made me treat you gently. I disclosed a part of my life to you, its something I've never done before to anyone; your manner, no less your actions, assures me that you've taken it wrong and you evidently never ceased to think of it with bitterness. You know where I was when you met me, but that's not where I am now. Erik, I thought I was a king maker, but I turned out to be Dr. Frankenstein. I have nothing left to disclose to you," said Peddler, looking at Erik a little longer after his words were finished.

At this point Mary Lou and Jonas held their breath and listened with eagerness, though their eyes were not directed on the speaker, but towards Erik.

Erik stood up, looked at Peddler with an unnatural disdain, grabbed the table cloth with both hands, pulled it with vigorously and the food flew everywhere, hitting everything, including Mary Lou and Jonas.

"If you think, I'm a monster, you're right," hollered Erik.

Both Mary Lou and Jonas stood while they attempted to clean up the food and their clothes. They looked at Erik as much with pity as contempt.

The following evening, after the incident at Mary Lou and Erik's home, Erik walked up the stairs heading for the stage, with Peddler following close behind; they did not speak. At the top of the stairs, Peddler, who ascended with evident reluctance, stopped where Erik was standing. The two men looked at each other, as if it were the first time they met.

"Peddler, I must tell you something," said Erik, "by all I hold most solemn and most sacred, the instant I behave again, the way I behaved towards you last night, that instant, you must promise me that you will apprehend me as a disorderly person, drag me into the street, call the police and have me arrested," said Erik, pointing at Peddler with his index finger, to add emphasis to his statement.

"How dare you say that to me. How dare you underestimate me, how dare you think that my heart is hardened and unmovable when it comes to the man who I've come to know, and learned to love like a brother. I felt pity for you last night, Erik, feeling how you must have been suffering, turning on me, while you knew, that I am the last person on this earth who wishes any harm to come to you," said Peddler, displaying a indignation on his face as he continued. "You're Greek, you must have read the Illiad. When Achilles dearest friend, Patroclus, was overcome by the god Apollo and then killed by Hector, Achilles went into his tent and cried, although he was a hero and a feared warrior, he cried. He eventually killed Hector who was a fierce warrior too, the strongest of all the Trojans. I feel that I am to you, a dearest friend, just like Patroclus was to Achilles, and that one day you'll cry over me."

Erik, after contemplating Peddler's words for some seconds with evident enchantment, stepped onto the stage, picked up his guitar and planted himself in front of the sign, THE ERIK KARAS CRUSADE—LET GOD KNOW YOU'RE THERE.

Mary Lou came out, singing a gospel number. Everyone in the audience began applauding and stomping their feet; Erik accompanied her on the guitar and the band played along.

Leroy, in the motor lodge room where he was staying, on hearing Mary Lou's voice coming from the TV, thrust his head out of the bathroom door, shook in an unbridled manner, clenched his fists, muttered a vulgar curse and then, with a horrible grin, walked into the room, picked up the rifle, sat on a chair, placed rifle across his lap and began, methodically, cleaning the firing mechanism and scope. He remained transfixed on the TV with his jaw formed into that sadistic grin.

Mary Lou finished her number and the audience broke into another round of applause. Erik put down his guitar and picked up the Bible; the crowd grew quiet. Erik stood in the center of the stage and stared back at the crowd. He clutched his Bible and said nothing. There was pure silence with the exception of an occasional cough or clearing of a throat.

Erik fixed his piercing eyes on the crowd and Jonas, in the

wings, stared at Erik with eagerness.

"My beloved people, I am here today to tell you that Christianity is the religion of love. Christianity is the religion of giving. Christianity is the religion of helping one another.

"How great are His signs, and how mighty are His wonders! His kingdom is an everlasting kingdom, and His domination is from generation to generation." Daniel 4:2," said Erik.

"I said that Christianity is the religion of love. If you look in the dictionary you will find that there are several types of love, the love of parents for their children, the love of brothers and sisters, the love of one for their homeland, but the most important love is that between a man and a woman. A man and a woman fall in love and begin their regeneration, a new generation. The love between a man and a woman is like a river. Nobody knows for sure where or when a river starts. We know it starts, somewhere in the mountains and hills, from tiny drips and drops of water and grows gradually forming a trickle, then a stream and then a mighty flow. It finishes its life when it flows into an ocean or sea. We don't realize when there is no longer a river, when it becomes brine, mixed with the salt of the sea. Where did it go? I wrote a poem and I will read a small part of it now.

'What happened to the tears of love that ran down our faces?
Did they mix with dust leaving only faded traces?
When that river of love found its way to the sea,
What happened to the couple we called we?'

My dearly beloved friends, keep that river flowing. Don't let it touch the sea. Keep that river flowing, until death due us part."

Leroy, who now was standing in the middle of his room, watching, still grinning and holding the rifle with both hands, as if its purpose had now been destined, shouted, "Yes! Yes! Till death due us part," he raised the rifle high, arms fully extended, crossed the room and pulled the television's plug from it's socket.

CHAPTER EIGHT

Peddler collapses

It was midmorning; the atmosphere was damp, the ground wet and the rain continued with force. Erik stood by a pond, in the back of his house, looking into the circles formed by every drop of rain that fell on the green water.

Peddler stood inside the house and, by chance, threw a glance out the window. Seeing Erik standing still in the middle of that landscape, soaking wet, he rushed out, taking an umbrella with him. The sound of the rain, though muffled, was almost deafening. Peddler ran to where Erik was standing, stopped and gazed at the same spot, with his arms crossed.

"What are you doing here, Erik? You're going to catch a cold," shouted Peddler, while placing the umbrella above his friend and brushing water from his head.

"I'm just thinking," replied Erik, still looking into the water.

"In the rain? Or you don't know it's raining?" shouted Peddler, partly to overcome the sound of the downpour and partly to bring Erik back to the present place and time.

"You're right, Peddler. I don't know it's raining, I don't know if the sun is shining, I don't know who loves or cares for me. Look what I did and said to you the other night, Peddler. If I behaved that way to you, with no feelings, do you think I can feel the lousy rain?" asked Erik, in a voice mingled with the echo of the rain's fury.

"Don't think about it. I've forgotten it; I know you too well." returned Peddler, brushing more water off Erik's suit.

"Peddler, you're not Dr. Frankenstein, but I'm a monster, and have always been a monster. I am a self-made monster. I lost my son and my wife. I let her go. I could have stopped her, but I didn't, I shot my only son, Peddler," cried Erik.

"You didn't shoot your son, Erik. It wasn't your fault, Erik, it was an accident."

"I lost my son, Peddler. I see him everywhere I go. I see his beautiful face in every corner I turn. I lost my wife and son and I'm still laughing. I lost my wife and son and I'm still shaving my face every morning, as though I have no feelings. And you think I'm going to feel the rain Peddler? Instead of shaving, I should stand in front of the mirror and scratch my lousy face with my fingernails, so I can see my flesh torn apart," retorted Erik, with a thunderous voice, venting his anger and eyeing Peddler with an expression of disgust. Then, changing his gaze, he looked anxiously around as if contemplating running away.

He might have attempted to do so if it weren't for a sudden violent cough from Peddler, who immediately collapsed at Erik's feet and struggled to catch his breath.

"Peddler! Peddler!" screamed Erik, falling to his knees, grabbing his friend's head and rubbing his face.

"Get an ambulance! Can't someone get an ambulance?" cried Erik, rubbing Peddler's hands and wrists. He screamed for assistance over and over again until an ambulance came.

Two men jumped from the ambulance and ran to where Peddler was lying with Erik holding the umbrella over him. They lifted Peddler, placed him on a stretcher and rushed him away to the hospital.

Peddler remained still for hours in a hospital bed with a number of tubes leading from various monitors to his peaceful body. When life, look and speech returned, his senses followed and he smiled when he saw Erik standing over him. Peddler realized that if it hadn't been for Erik's being there during his attack, his troubled life would have been shortened and he would most likely have been dead.

"Curly, did I make you smart, rich or crazy?" asked Peddler, in a withered voice, with a vague grin on his face.

"For certain, all of the above," said Erik, straightening out his friend's blanket.

"Curly, do you remember how we started. We started with an

ugly duckling and then it grew into a duck, a big duck, Curly. Our duck became so big it grew goose bumps." Peddler laughed with a full heart, then he stopped suddenly, "I am going to die soon, Curly," he said, matter of factly.

"Don't talk stupid. You'll be okay, you just have a lousy case of pneumonia," said Erik.

"Did I also make you a liar? Or were you one, before you met me?"

"Would I lie?" asked Erik

"Do bears shit in the woods?" saying this, Peddler began to cough violently.

"Get a doctor here!" yelled Erik, looking around, as though one was hiding nearby.

"No!" whispered Peddler, gesturing Erik to relax.

"You know why we became good friends?" continued Peddler, when the fit of coughing subsided. "When we first met we were opposites. Then I became a little bit like you and you became a little bit like me. You know that I'm dying, don't you know?" asked Peddler, lowering his voice with the last sentence

"Who told you that?"

"Nobody has to tell me. I know it. Erik, dying is not bad. Everybody is doing it. Some of the smartest and richest men in the world did it, and more are waiting to do it. Arizona and Florida are loaded with them. They call themselves retirees. I call them waiters. They are waiting for the bus of death to come by, pick them up and take them to the other side," declared Peddler, "how did you say it once, in a poem?

'I wanted to leave for distant lands
To find new folks, new relatives, new friends
But there was a big mountain on one side
On the other, was the sea,
Where could I go, with just only me?'
Do you remember when you told me that, Curly?"

"I remember. You think you're the only one who remembers things? I recited that the night you got stinking drunk," said Erik.

"Yeah! Yeah! That's when I told you that I was afraid of dying, because nobody would come to my funeral. I'm not afraid of that anymore, because now I have a lot of friends. When the time comes,

Curly, I want you to do two things for me. First, tell my daughter so she wouldn't expect me to come back and then take me to my truck, so I can die there. It's been my home for almost my whole life," whispered Peddler.

"Don't talk stupid! Partner!"

Peddler reached over and touched Erik's hand. "The big mountain on one side, on the other was the sea, where could I go with just only me? Curly, I'm not going with just only me. God is going to send a spirit to show me the way to my final place of rest," continued Peddler, turning his face away, trying to hide the tear that had escaped and ran down his face, "then you went on, Curly,

Finally I thought I heard somebody calling my name
I went home and found everything was still the same
My brother was standing in front of the fireplace
My sister in the courtyard, chasing chickens with a smiling face
My mother in the kitchen, preparing the meal of the day
Nobody ever missed me when I went away.

Erik, I know you are going to miss me when I go away," concluded Peddler, with a grin.

"Oh, yes? Who told you that?"

"When I passed out, I heard you screaming. You screamed so loud, you roused all the dogs and frightened all the chickens in town; then you scared the hell out of all the birds, so they flew away."

"Peddler, do you know you have oral diarrhea today?" retorted Erik.

Jonas rose next morning with a saddened heart and went about his usual early habit of visiting the office, with a bit less hope, and a tad more discontent, thinking that Peddler was a sick man who had very little chance of getting better. The Erik Karas office was in a freestanding building, with a parking lot in front, designed to accommodate about fifty cars; it was situated on one of the large boulevards that lead in and out of the city. Jonas went into the office and sat awkwardly behind a desk, playing with a pencil. A woman walked in and went straight to him, disregarding the young secretary sitting near the entrance, in front of his desk.

"I saw brother Erik on the TV and heard him say that you could help," said the woman.

"What do you need?" asked Jonas.

"There's this car dealer called Smiling Sonny's down on route #1. My son got himself a job, but he needed a car to go to work. I gave this Smiling Sonny a down payment on a car, but later when we went to get the car, he said my son's credit wasn't good and he couldn't get the car, and the down payment was non-refundable," explained the woman.

Jonas, without any additional questions, turned to the secretary, "can you give her two hundred dollars? Is that how we do it?" asked Jonas.

"No! No! I don't want the money from you, I just thought, maybe, you can call him up, and tell him to give it back to me," said the woman.

"Jonas, we must have paid out over three thousand dollars to people who Smiling Sonny bilked," said the secretary.

"Ok. Give this lady two hundred dollars and give me the list of all the people we paid money to because of this Sonny Smiling guy," ordered Jonas.

"It's not Sonny Smiling it's Smiling Sonny," stated the secretary.

"Ok. Ok. Give me his address and when I get through with him, he'll be Grieving Gregory," said Jonas.

"SMILING SONNY is a good ol' boy," read the sign in front of a building, in the middle of a used car lot that was filled to capacity. Jonas walked up to that building and before entering, looked inside, through the glass window of the showroom. He saw one man sitting behind a desk, wearing a loud polyester suit; a larger man stood behind him. Jonas, being perfectly informed and satisfied with that brief survey, walked right in, went over and leaned, with both hands, on the desk and stared at the man who was sitting there; he looked back at Jonas and smiled.

Jonas then placed a file folder down and a Bible on top of that car dealer's desk.

"What can I do for you, preacher?" asked the man, seeing Jonas dressed in a conservative suit, with a Bible in hand.

"I am looking for Sonny Smiling."

"It's Smiling Sonny, and that's me you're looking for."

"I am glad that I found you," returned Jonas.

"I'm sure the pleasure is mine," said Sonny, with a polite smile.

"No it ain't, " replied Jonas, standing back a little.

"Everybody who comes in here with money is my pleasure;" said Sonny.

"You must like money," returned Jonas.

"I love money. I love George Washington and all the dead presidents," said Sonny, bursting into laughter.

"If George didn't have so many loyal friends like you, he wouldn't be worth two shits today, not alone ten silver dimes," said Jonas. "Now that we have established your love for George Washington, I have something else to tell you."

"Go ahead!"

"Listen to me; I have a list of people who paid you three thousand and two hundred dollars to buy cars. They didn't get their cars and they didn't get their money back. These are all poor people, we gave them their money back," said Jonas.

"Who do you think you are?" retorted Sonny, standing up in wrath, "read their contracts, the down payment is non-refundable. They lied to me about their credit."

"I can't read, you see, I can only read the Bible. I will come back here tomorrow and I would like to have the money back. Do you understand, sir?" said Jonas, calmly.

"Well, sir let me tell you. My dealings are with those people, they are not with you," returned Sonny, who looked like an old experienced hand in the art of fraud.

"Oh no, sir, you have to deal with me now. This money came out of the Erik Karas Crusade, do you understand?" asked Jonas, still calmly.

"Who in the hell is this Karas Crusade character?" asked Sonny. That question sounded more like a remark.

"Boss, you know him. He's that guitar-playing preacher on TV, " reported the salesman.

"Oh yeah, the preacher with that blond broad, who sings with him. Well sir..."

"I said, do you understand?" asked Jonas, with a shout.

"Yes, I understand," replied Sonny, coolly.

" No, you don't understand. Where I come from, people can

get very mean. So tomorrow, I will come back here, and at that time I would like you to give me the money. Do you understand? asked Jonas, showing a little more indignation than before.

"Yes, I understand," said Sonny, in the same style, as though he were not affected by Jonas' intimidating manner.

Jonas, pretending to be troubled by Sonny's response, shook his head pitifully and heaved a sigh, "You see, again you don't understand, I was born in the mountains of West Virginia, " stated Jonas, with a controlled voice and temper, "and when you're born in those mountains of West Virginia, you're born naked and stupid and before you learn how to dress, you learn how to use a knife. I'll show you tomorrow what I'm talking about, when I come back here and you don't have the money ready. Do you understand, now?" asked Jonas.

Smiling Sonny gestured to the thug behind him, "Get him out of here," he ordered, with contempt.

The thug started towards Jonas, his features distorted and fists clinched, "are you going to leave now or do I have to throw you out?"

Jonas, without any kind of ritual, cordial or otherwise, threw a blow at the thug's face and sent him flying into Sunny, knocking him down too. Jonas rushed to the thug, grabbed him firmly by the collar, restored him to a standing position and pounded the wall with his head. The thug went down like a lifeless bundle of clothes. Jonas bent down and said softly, "when you want to hit, you hit, you don't talk." He then stood up, keeping his eyes on the thug who lay there in what might have been a deep sleep.

"I said, do you understand?" hissed Jonas, turning to Sonny and panting with anger.

"Yes, sir, yes, sir, I understand, "cried Sonny, coming onto his feet, not to protest as one may think, but to serve, "You killed my salesman. Please, mister, no more violence. I'm a man of peace, the sight of blood makes me sick."

"Only if it's yours."

"Is my salesman dead?"

"No, not really. I only shook his brain a little bit," said Jonas. "He just whispered to me."

"He talked?"

"Yes. I asked him how he felt, and at first I thought he started speaking in tongues," said Jonas, trying to catch his breath; then he added, "He must have visited South Carolina.

"Why, what did he say?"

"He said, 'dum spiro, spero,' It's the State Motto, it's Latin and means, as long as I breath I hope. That should tell you a lot, my brother," uttered Jonas with a smile, looking down at Sunny. "On second thought, I don't think I want to come back tomorrow, I want the money now. Some times the devil does a favor for his friends. If I come back tomorrow, I may do something real bad. Today, the devil is doing you a favor by telling me to collect the money from you right now"

"Now? Right now?" asked Sonny, in a high pitched voice.

"Now! I said; I told you what the devil said, don't you have no respect for your friends?" shouted the big man, looking at Sonny with fierce eyes.

Sunny, understandably stricken with fear, moved quickly to the safe in the back room, so fast that he was back with the money before Jonas could catch his breath. "Here's your money. Count it," cried Sonny, laying out the greenbacks, with a scowl.

"No need to count it," remarked Jonas, with a mocking smile," I trust you." He put the money in his pants pocket, picked up the Bible and the file folder, went over to where the thug was still laid out and squatted next to him. The salesman was moving slowly and wiping blood from his mouth when Jonas whispered, "your boss understands me now." He then stood up and still looking down at his victim, "incidentally, while your were taking a nap your boss gave me the money. What a nice man you work for. It took him no more than thirty seconds to get from here to the safe and back; if his legs weren't so short he would have made in half that time." Jonas turned and methodically walked away towards the main door.

"You only pretended to be a Bible man," barked Sonny.

"I go by the Bible. It says here, " said Jonas, pointing at the Bible with his index finger, "It says right in here, a tooth for a tooth and an eye for an eye. Next time, if I have to come back here, it will be for your tooth and your eye!"

"I have some friends in heaven too," shouted Sonny.

"Yeah, I know, in crook's heaven," replied the Bible man,

pushing the big glass door with his shoulder, exiting with a triumphant smile.

Sonny tripped over to his salesman, who had just gotten up and was dusting his cloths, "I was counting on your strength, not on your brains."

"Did you see him? He was bigger than a garage and meaner than a junk yard dog," said the salesman. .

Sonny, aggravated by the entire incident, including his salesman's statement, took a seat behind his desk, planted his two elbows on the desktop and looked off in the direction Jonas took.

CHAPTER NINE

Peddler's daughter reveals the truth

It was late afternoon and the truck was zooming along a two-lane highway. Peddler, the driver of the truck, was alone in the cab. He wiped some perspiration from his face and forehead and smiled, as if getting away with some kind of a mischief. It was almost dark by the time he reached Clara's house There he stopped at the curb in front of the house, and, while still in the cab, looked in the truck's rearview mirror to straighten his hat. He opened the truck door and stepped out slowly, as if aches and pains affected him. The front of the house was brilliantly lit and his walk up the level sycamore-lined path was an easy one.

He stopped when he reached the front of the house, paused, partly to catch his breath and partly to gather his courage. Tastefully dressed, in a suit of the latest fashion, he stood in a stately manner with his hands folded before him and a new Stetson hat hanging from his fingers. He then placed his hat under his arm, pressed the doorbell, took a back step and waited.

Clara opened the door, saw him and smiled, "Hi, come in," she said, in a most gracious manner.

Peddler bowed respectfully, looked at her for a long moment and proceeded in the house, with timid and cautious steps.

"How are you?" asked Clara, kindly.

Peddler was apparently considering the decency of indulging in a respectful smile himself, but when he thought of the way his daughter had treated him the last time he paid her a visit, he just remained respectful and serious.

"I feel that I'm getting old," responded Peddler.

"We're all getting old, " said Clara, awkwardly.

"You know that's funny," said Peddler, "your grandmother, your mother's mother, she was the only one who liked me out of the whole family. Anyway, right before she died, I went to see her in the old folk's home. I remember, she raised her hand and hammered the table with all the strength that the Lord had left her with, which wasn't too much. 'You know, Stephen,' she said, 'I am getting old and there is nothing I can do about it.' 'Stephanie,' I said, 'we're all getting old.' Then she looked at me, smiled and said, 'you don't have anything to worry about, at your age.' And I remember, I agreed with her. How little did I know, back then I felt I would never get old. So, I will not correct you," said Peddler.

"Her name was Stephanie?" asked Clara, apparently somewhat astonished.

"Didn't you know that?" asked Peddler, surprised at her question.

"No, I didn't know. Who would tell me? But I know your name is Stephen and everybody calls you Peddler."

"I thought you knew her name. Then why is your daughter's name Stephanie?" asked Peddler.

"Do you like it?"

"It isn't for the likes of me to judge that," he returned, respectfully.

Clara looked at him for a short time and, not knowing how to respond to that statement, walked away into the kitchen.

"I am going to make some coffee. You want some, don't you? shouted Clara from the kitchen.

"No thank you."

Clara appeared at the hallway holding a coffee can in her hands. "How did you know that my daughter's name is Stephanie?"

"I read it in the newspaper when she was born. But I thought you named her after your grandmother," replied Peddler.

"No, Stephanie is a girl's name for Stephen," replied his daughter, walking back in the kitchen after a short pause.

Peddler turned his head to the sky, partly smiling, partly astonished and partly crying.

"Thank you, God, for knowing that I didn't do everything wrong in my life," he mumbled, as if he were only talking to himself. "You think you can find it in your heart to let me see my granddaughter before I leave?" he asked, loud enough for his daughter to hear.

"I'm sorry," replied Clara, coming out of the kitchen, "she's not here and I really must have some time to think about it."

"I'm sorry, I understand," he said, bending his head down, "I always have high hopes." After those words, he paused, still looking downwards, then raised his head and gazed at her, with a grin, "but today, what you told me, it was more than I ever hoped. I really came to say good-by to you, because of my health, I am compelled to go to high places," said Peddler.

"High places?" asked Clara, without any alarm in her voice.

"Yes, very high."

"I know nothing about you and yet, you are my father. Are you alone?" asked Clara.

"I am your father but I haven't been a father to you," exclaimed Peddler, looking downwards. He stayed in that attitude for a long moment, then raised his head, looked at her and smiled, "I still live in New Orleans, where you were born and where all three of us lived in a nice house," then continued, "I am sorry for jumping into a serious matter so soon, but I'm afraid you'll tell me to get out, like you did the last time I was here, without giving me the opportunity to say something in my own defense."

"No, please, do go on, I asked you to tell me something about yourself. The last time you were here I had a completely different thought in mind. So, please, do go on, for my sake."

Peddler, delighted with her statement, allowed his face to explode into a huge smile. He displayed the smile briefly he then drew serious and began, "Your mother took you and left. I was alone, with nothing. I'm still alone and have been most of my life. I have never made a home for myself. I never felt that I belonged with anyone. I lived like a Gypsy, in the back of my truck. I lived like I was trying to punish myself. My life can be referred to as a tale of grief, and sorrow and guilt, my dear. For what, I don't really know. Wives and women came and went. They came in like lambs and they went out like lions. I was never a good husband and not a good father to my only child, you. So I failed the only missions that God gives to a man, father and husband, and I failed at both of them. That's probably the reason I live like I do."

Peddler's sincere confession was in a sullen tone then a lengthy silence prevailed in the room. Peddler turned away, as if to hide the sadness he felt in his heart that might have been visible on his face.

Clara stood there and watched her father, with misty eyes and quivering lips, "I cannot describe the state of mind into which I'm thrown by this circumstance, the shock of you coming here, after so long and yet so suddenly and for some mysterious reason, I expected the door to open and you to appear standing there, straight and healthy as I always remembered you," said Clara, wiping the tears from her eyes with the edge of her hand. "Those thoughts created an empty space in my heart, an appalling vacancy I couldn't fill. I felt, everywhere I lived, that I saw a room where there was a chair, table and a single bed waiting for you. I felt an indefinable impossibility of separating you from that room.

"My God, girl, there was a room in our house. A room with a chair and a table and single bed, where I used go to eat and sleep when I came home very late and didn't want to disturb your mother!" exclaimed Peddler, excitedly.

"Oh, Lord," said Clara, with tears coming down her face, "I had been in agony trying to obtain some hint or knowledge of the circumstance of that vision. There were times when I thought of going to see a psychologist. Can you believe that?" she concluded and ran into kitchen.

Peddler looked at the kitchen door and now began to turn his hat around as he had done the first time he visited his daughter.

"Is the house still there?" asked Clara, coming out of the kitchen, wiping her eyes with a tissue.

"It's still there and it looks the same to me," responded Peddler.

"I wish I could go there, just to see the house and walk through the old streets, to calm my spirits and ease my heart. I remember going to kindergarten there. Funny, I was a schoolgirl there, now I wonder if the place has changed as much as I have."

"It still looks the same," returned Peddler, with a wide smile.

"Strange to say, that quiet influence, inseparable in my mind from you, seemed to pervade even the cities where I lived. I remember, I remember everything now. The row houses, the battered gateways, I remember them and the ancient buildings in the city, the urban landscape, and I can still feel their calm softening spirit," said the daughter with a nostalgic tone. "I must tell you that I lied when I told you, the first time you came here, that my mother told me who you were, right before she died. I knew who you were; in fact, I wanted to marry somebody who looked like you. When I was in college, I fell in love with Kevin. But I must confess that I was raised as white. Actually there are only three people who knew that I was your daughter besides me. One of the three is dead, one is you and the third is still around."

"How about your husband, doesn't he know?"

"Know what, that I'm a colored man's daughter? No, my God, no, he's filled up with bigotry, like most white people down here," she said, with worried features and a hint of guilt.

"What would happen if and when he finds out?" asked Peddler.

"I don't think about it, Stephen," said Clara. Immediately she threw her hand to cover her mouth at the mention of 'Stephen.' "I'm sorry I called you by your first name,"

"That's okay, Clara, you always called me Stephen," replied Peddler.

"Why?"

"I told you to. One of the reasons is sad. When you, me and your mother went out, people looked at us with hate in their eyes, but when they heard you calling me Stephen, their features were softened, thinking I was a hired hand. If they knew that I was your father I would had been lynched on the spot," concluded Peddler, with an involuntary sigh.

"Things, were that bad?" asked Clara.

With this, Clara stood in the middle of the room, looking like a little girl, lost.

Peddler, seeing her in that manner, went close to her and said with a trembling voice,

"Please, come to me and give me a hug, like you used to when you were a little girl and didn't know the difference between black and white."

Clara, without any delay, but with certain caution, stepped towards her father, then froze on a spot, a few inches away from him, upon hearing the front door open.

Her husband and an older, distinguished, well-dressed man came in. She quickly backed away from her father and wiped the traces of tears that had emerged below her eyes. Both men stopped at the door. The older man's gaze fell on Peddler. The man stared at Clara's father with a grimacing look on his face; Peddler returned the look in the same manner.

"Hello!" said Kevin, with a smile bigger than a lake.

"Hello, Honey. Hello, Judge Miller" said Clara, hurrying to them, kissing her husband on the lips and the Judge on the cheek, but the judge's eyes were still pegged on Peddler.

"I'm just finishing with a client," said Clara to her husband.

"Search around and look to find my granddaughter before I leave for the high place," said Peddler, turning to leave.

"I will do my best," said Clara, with much grace, pausing for a moment, "I promise." Peddler, without any further ceremony, departed, closing the door behind him, very gently; the Judge's eyes were still nailed to his direction. Clara walked to the door, stood there with her back to it, as if to keep it shut and gazed at the Judge, a trace of contempt in her eyes.

"Honey!" uttered the husband, going to his wife," I have some wonderful news to tell you."

"Kevin, don't you want to wait?" rejoined the Judge.

"Don't be silly, Judge. I have to tell her now. The news is too good to hold in, besides my wife and I have no secrets. Do we, honey?" said Kevin, looking at his wife who just nodded and said nothing.

The Judge's eyes fell upon her at the precise moment she turned to him; he grew uneasy with her contemptuous stare, maybe, he thought, it was for the grimacing look he had given Peddler. The contempt turned to disdain and he became almost certain that if she were allowed to charge against him, she would probably leave the signal marks of her fury on his face and body.

"Honey," screamed her husband, filled with excitement, " I was selected by the party to run for Congress, Isn't that wonderful? Aren't you excited?" and with those words, he rushed to his wife and threw his arms around her.

Clara just stood there, with quivering lips and tear filled eyes, without moving a hand or a foot, as if some invisible spirit restrained her.

"There are a lot more things to be considered," stated the Judge, as if to hint he were the fittest person to pursue the dialogue.

"Nonsense," yelled Kevin, letting his wife loose and facing the Judge, "they said I will be elected, unless something scandalous takes place between now and then. Judge, you need not worry about anything, my wife and I live clean lives; we have no skeletons in any of our closets. They said they've already started the ball rolling. Judge, you know that, you're one of the bosses."

"Isn't your wife allowed to say anything? She hasn't said a word," declared the Judge.

"Look at her, " said Kevin, putting his hands around his wife and pointing at her with his index finger, "she's so happy she's crying. She is really crying, " said Kevin, wiping the tears off her face with his hand, "she was the one who was pushing me all these years. Who knows, she may be the first lady some day. First Congress, then the Senate and then, of course, the Presidency."

"Judge Miller is right," said Clara, softly touching her husband's face with both hands, "let's talk."

"Talk?" complained the husband loudly "we have been talking about this for years."

"Kevin, go upstairs and let me have a moment with your wife," said the Judge, softly.

"What am I, a child? I have to go upstairs? Maybe one of you wants to read me a bedtime story so I can go to sleep."

"Get used to it. That's political life, kid," said the Judge, now with a stronger voice, "members of the party, the serious minded people, have meetings behind closed doors and the candidate or the elected official waits outside for their decision. Do you understand, young man?"

Kevin stood there and divided his glance between the Judge and Clara, and then, without any further delay, though still with hesitation, he turned and slowly disappeared up the stairs.

"You heard him," said the Judge, when he made certain they would not be overheard.

" I heard, I heard, " said Clara, rubbing her head and walking away to another spot.

"You heard and I saw. I saw that Negro here," said the Judge, in a low voice, "what was he doing here? You know, this is Mississippi, not New York. You cannot represent colored folks and be the wife of a GOP congressman. You cannot bring colored folks here. You hear? No colored folks for clients."

"Why don't you stop the act? hissed Clara, " he is no client of mine, and you know it."

"Who is he then?"

"Stop it! Stop it, before I start screaming, " screeched Clara.

Judge Miller knew that there was something to fear about a roused woman, especially if she added to all her other passions, the fierce impulses of recklessness and despair, those which very few men dare to provoke.

" I thought that son-of-a-bitch died," uttered the Judge, with anger in his voice, "but I see he still lives in the streets, like a bum."

"You're the wretch that drove him to live in the streets, in the cold, wet, dirty streets where he made his home, you're the wretch who pushed him there and there he will stay, until he dies."

"Watch your mouth, woman!" ordered the Judge, " I have done nothing wrong."

Clara looked at him for a long moment, "a poor man you are, Judge. You stand here, before me, and tell me you have not done anything wrong as if I were a fool who would believe your story. I know you fixed my birth certificate to say I was born in Mississippi, instead of New Orleans. I know you trumped up charges against my father and blackmailed my mother with those charges, saying you were going to throw my father in jail for years, if she didn't leave him. My poor mother loved my father and she left him, so he would stay out of jail for a crime he never committed. You know why you did all that, because you were in love with her and my mother didn't want anything to do with you. You are the one who told my mother, when you found out she was dying, not to let me go with my father and if she did, you would reopen the case against him. You're the one who ordered her to allow your brother to adopt me, even though he knew I was half colored. Lord knows how you blackmailed him to adopt me."

"Who told you all that, that Negro?" asked the Judge with anger in his voice.

"God Almighty help me," cried Clara passionately. "No Judge, my father told me nothing." She paused for a minute, as if something had entered her mind, "one thing I do remember is when I told him that although I was born into a family of thieves and liars, I was glad I was raised by decent folks, he said that sometimes things and people are not what they seem to be. At that time, I knew nothing about your dirty double dealings and scams."

"Come on now, Clara, we must use civil words in our private conversation," interjected the Judge.

"Civil words?" exclaimed the girl, whose passion was frightful to see, "civil words you said! Yes, civil words, you deserve them from me, making me believe, all these years, that my father was a thief and a criminal. I believed in you since I was child. As a prosecutor, I did my best to impose stiff sentences on the colored thieves and criminals, thinking I was punishing my father. Don't you know that? Don't you know it? Speak up, didn't you know it."

"Well, my dear," returned the Judge, in an attempt to pacify her, "if you did all that, it was because it was your duty to bestow justice."

"Ah, so it's all in the name of justice. Then wrongful punishment to you is justice," retorted Clara, shivering from head to toe with anger, "the only way justice can be served now is to turn you in and for you to pay for your double dealings and scams. But unfortunately, I don't have it in me."

"You keep repeating the words double dealings and scams. Who told you all that if it wasn't that colored man?"

"Your secretary, Miss Dixon," replied the girl, abruptly, as if she were waiting to hear that question, "she told me all that, and plenty more, three months ago, on her deathbed. I taped her last words, her last testament."

The Judge made no reply, he only looked at Clara and saw her face had turned colorless from the passion of the rage into which she had gradually worked herself.

"Tell your husband all that, and see how far he'll go in his political career," replied the Judge, now smiling, as if it were a relief to throw the ball in her court, " and I, my dear lady, I will do such mischief as will ruin everything for him faster than you can spell Mississippi."

"You're too smart to do that, you won't cut off your lip, just to get rid of your mustache. One thing I will tell you, you better hope and pray there is no God, because if there is one, I'd hate to see the price you'll pay for what you did to that colored man, my father," said the girl, in a soft voice, as if she had just decided on the proper punishment for Judge Miller.

"Put all that bitterness aside, girl. Let's think of the future, your future and your husband's future. Just don't let that colored man open his mouth," said the Judge, gently as, though he were trying to smooth matters over with Clara. There's a lot at stake here." he continued, pausing for a moment, "aren't you happy with your life?"

"I am very happy, Judge. I am white. I see colored people the way you see them, but I see my father like you saw yours."

"If I lied, I lied for you, Clara."

"No, Your Honor, you lied because you hated my father, not for being colored, but for marrying the woman you loved, my mother," said Clara, looking towards the stairs. Upon seeing her husband coming down, she softened her features.

"What's this? I only heard the tail end of your conversation. Was the Judge in love with your mother before or after your father was killed in Korea?" he asked, looking and grinning at them both.

"Don't be silly, Honey. Judge Miller is as pure as the driven snow in Canada," quipped Clara, staring at the Judge, who in turn, gave out a practiced smile.

CHAPTER TEN

The death of the corrupt

A few weeks after his meeting with Clara, Peddler felt sick again and drove himself to the hospital, leaving his truck near the emergency entrance. The truck stayed and waited there, like a domestic pet, while Peddler checked in and was tucked away in a small room down the farthest corridor. Jonas, standing close to Peddler, his hat in his hand, looking and pitying, thought how much he would have given to see Peddler healthy again.

Peddler was hooked up to a ganglion of tubes and wires, his limbs were wasted, his face drawn, his lips parched and cracked, his dry skin almost glowed. There was a glistering layer of sweat on the dying man's forehead; his fever was uncontrolled.

Jonas went to the bed, pulled up a chair and sat next to him, his eyes nailed on the sick and his face masked with sorrow. Peddler stirred, feeling Jonas' presence, he became restless, tossed to the side away from Jonas and then rolled back towards him; his hand fell out of the bed. Jonas caught it and held it close. Peddler began to think of all the people that had died in that town over the years, how many had inhabited that very same bed in that very same room in which he was now. He thought that scores of them must have passed their last hours here. He saw, in his weary mind's eye, himself, sitting in the middle of a graveyard where dead bodies were rising to surface to face him, welcome him and show him his place of rest beneath the cold soil.

"Jonas?" mumbled Peddler, with a quickened breath. He had barely looked up to see Jonas.

"Yes," replied Jonas, caressing Peddler's hand.

"Don't go, stay with me, please."

"I will, I will," returned Jonas.

Peddler, with great difficulty, turned his head and eyes to the direction where Jonas was seated and saw a slim dark haired Nurse, standing by the door, watching. Peddler muttered something unintelligible and pointed at the door with a weak and trembling hand.

"What?" asked Jonas.

"Don't let her come near me. Get her out of my room. My daughter and my granddaughter will be here very soon, Jonas. They'll take care of me; I can't stand that nurse watching me," said Peddler, with a withering voice.

"I think I hear your daughter talking to the doctor now. She wants to take you home. Do you want to go?" asked Jonas.

"Yes, yes, I want to go. If I stay here, Jonas, that nurse will kill me. She knows I have done bad things in my life. She wants me dead. She's a killer!" screamed Peddler, weakly.

"You go to sleep now, I'll watch out for you until your daughter comes in. You have to rest if you want to go home with your daughter," urged Jonas.

The nurse went to Peddler and checked him thoroughly.

"Go now, he's delirious from the high fever. You won't be any good to him now. He'll calm down when his fever subsides. I just gave him medication."

"Jonas!" called out Peddler, with as much strength as the good Lord allows a dying man to have.

"Look at her, Jonas! Look how fast she's moving her fingers as if she's knitting a sock."

The nurse, hearing this, glided out of the room. Only twice more did she appear at the door and both times her stay was short but all the while Peddler kept reciting,

"Look at her hands," but the nurse was not around, "look at those eyes! I have seen those eyes before, Jonas. Look at her flowing hair! Those eyes, Jonas, belong to a woman who has been brutalized by a husband for twenty years. Those eyes belong to a woman who has lived a stormy life. I am looking again at those hands and I still see them moving; when I look again, I see those eyes. She is all-alone in this life, Jonas; she has nobody to love her and she never loved anybody, that's why she turned into a killer. Listen, look at her, she cringes and growls. Jonas, are you still here?"

"Yes Peddler I am still here," responded Jonas, awkwardly.

"Jonas, why didn't they turn on the lights in here? It's very dark. Jonas, when the night comes, it's a dark, dismal and silent night and then day comes and is gone again and the night comes back; the night is so long and yet so short. Long in its dreadful silence and short in its brief hours. Jonas, I saw her the other day,"

"Who did you see, Peddler?" asked Jonas, soothingly, as if to pacify him.

"My wife, Clara's mother. I started to speak to her and many moments passed before she showed me she was aware of the fact that I was speaking to her. She showed me what I knew but didn't understand. I didn't know what I had done. She never told me what I had done, except she told me that I had done something horrible. What have I done? What have I done? What have I done? I asked fifty times, what have I done?" uttered Peddler, tears now filling his eyes.

Many miles north of New Orleans, Louisiana in Jackson, Mississippi, Clara was in her home the precise moment her father, Peddler, saw her mother from his deathbed. The phone rang, it was Erik Karas, he was asked, by her father, to do so and to give her the news about her loving father's last hours on this earth. While on the phone, her husband, Kevin, walked into their bedroom. Clara turned, at the conclusion of her conversation with Erik, and looked at her husband with tears pouring down her face. Muted with bewilderment, Kevin walked close to her. Clara dropped to her knees at his feet, looked at the floor and sobbed violently. Seeing her in such a state sent a shock wave through his entire frame.

He urged her to come sit and got his arms around her to help her up, but she only pressed the hand that was nearest, hung her head on it and wept. Kevin had never seen her shed so many tears before and thinking that anything he might offer would only upset her more, he chose to be silent and bent over her without speaking. She was no longer kneeling; she sprawled herself on the floor.

"Why? Why?" cried Clara, despairingly, "Why does he have to go now? Why does he have to go now that I found him. What have I done? What have I done?"

The word, he, brought many unwholesome messages to Kevin's

mind, but the only thought that remained with him was that he should find a way to comfort her and continue to love her under any circumstances – he was married to her and they had a child together. He sat beside her on the floor and waited for her sobbing to subside, caressing her hair and studying her form. He looked at her with compassion and confusion.

After a while, the sobbing subsided. She stood up, wiped the tears from her face, looked up at Kevin and said softly, "My dear husband, just hold me. I promise not to cry anymore."

"What's the matter, honey," cried her husband, wrapping his arms around her.

"Just hold me, Kevin; I'll tell you in a moment."

"Okay, honey, okay," he returned.

It was a long moment later that Clara softly disengaged herself from her husband's arms and slowly walked to sit on the bed. She turned her face to see the two beautifully framed photos positioned on her bedside table, one of an attractive lady and the other of a distinguished looking air force officer.

"What's the matter, honey? "questioned Kevin, sitting next to her." It can't be that bad."

"My father is dying, "replied Clara, without any delay in her response.

"Your father? You kidding me," said Kevin, astonished.

Clara nodded. "No, Kevin, I'm not kidding," she said.

"What father? I thought your father was Judge Miller's brother, the air force colonel whose plane was shot down in Korea when you were sixteen, " rejoined Kevin.

"That was my adoptive father. My real father lives in New Orleans and is alive, and now they just called from the hospital. He's dying. Until the other day, I hadn't seen him for over twenty years. That meeting we had renewed the tender feelings I had for him when I was child," returned Clara.

"I can understand that. Let's go to him!" stated Kevin, offering what any good husband would. She shook her head, negatively. "Why didn't you tell me your real father was alive?" he asked, sitting close to her and showing the deepest concern.

"I didn't want to lose you," answered Clara, turning and looking back with quivering lips.

"Lose me? Why? I don't care if your father is the head of the Mafia or Jack the Ripper. I married you, not your father. Tell me, why you didn't say anything?" he questioned.

"Do you remember a colored man who came to the house some time ago?" said Clara, softly.

"Yes, I do remember him" replied Kevin.

"That was my father," retorted Clara.

"You're kidding me? You've got to be kidding," said Kevin, in disbelief.

"No, I'm not kidding. I am a colored man's daughter," stated Clara, sternly.

Kevin stood up, stared at her in disgust and said, softly, in a loathing manner.

"Do you mean to tell me you're a Negro? You're a goddamned nigger? Why, why, why, why didn't you tell me you're a colored girl?" after those injurious words, Kevin got down on his knees, with tears in his eyes, grabbed her by the shoulders and shook her violently.

"Why, Clara, why didn't you tell me? Why, why Goddamn it? Clara, why couldn't you stay white, like you were? Tell me! Tell me!!!

He stopped shaking her and slowly got to his feet. He was lost, filled with anger and searching for someplace, something or someone to vent it on. He turned, with desperate determination, to see what was in his path that could be destroyed. He saw a glass lamp table, ran to it, smashed it with a kick, and began, in a rage, throwing and kicking everything in the bedroom. In minutes the room was destroyed, draperies torn, drawers toppled, bedding disheveled, furniture broken. Clara never moved. She no longer cried. She seemed to be insensitive to everything he did, as if in a trance. After ruining his home and his marriage in a matter of minutes and causing irreparable injury to his wife's heart, he stood there by the door, his hand on the doorknob, panting like a wild animal, looking like a vicious beast and surveying the damage, breathed deeply, noting his accomplishment.

"Does Judge Miller know what you are?" he asked, looking straight at her.

"Of course he knows. He is the only one alive, besides my father, who knows.

Kevin turned his head away, distorted his features, clenched his teeth and declared, "I am leaving you. I'm leaving this house. I'm leaving you and I'm leaving behind everything here. I cannot stand being the husband of a nigger."

"How about our daughter? Are you leaving her behind too?" asked Clara, getting on her feet and going closer to him.

"She's a nigger too, isn't she?" retorted Kevin.

Clara, with a protective mother's strength, speed and scorn charged against her husband, screaming "You bastard! You animal!" Flailing out with both hands, connecting on the face and the chest, with every blow she yelled, "You bastard. She is not a nigger She is not white. She is not colored. She is my daughter; she is a human being, like I am." Kevin never made an attempt to protect himself from her hammering but seemed agitated by no stronger feelings than the doubt what else to do and where else to go.

"Maybe I fooled you all these years I passed myself off as white," said Clara with the tone of anger and disappointment. "You fooled me too and passed yourself off as a human being, instead of what you really are, a beast. Get out of my house! You beast! Get out of here!" she screamed, bellowing the last phrases.

Kevin slowly turned the handle, opened the door and left their home, closing the door behind him, gently. Clara set on the bed, sobbing hysterically. She could here his footsteps on the steps and when she they stopped, she raised her head and listen keenly.

On the way out of the house, Kevin stopped, as his pistol, sitting on the fireplace mantel, caught his attention. He stood and considered it for a moment, then went, took the pistol in his hands, balanced it, checked its readiness, put it in his pocket and departed, hurriedly.

Clara, hearing his footsteps fade in the distance, placed her face in her hands again and listened. She heard only the rustling of the trees outside and the wind that echoed a low moan; she then proceeded with her sobbing.

Kevin, on exiting the house, found the light of day darker than when he went in; it wasn't that long before. In a precise and orderly fashion, he stopped and reviewed his house, his car in the driveway, his daughter's toys scattered around the yard, the trees he used to trim, all that bore his personal touch were now but distant memories. Although he stared steadily at all these things, they were no longer his, but whose? His confusion gathered.

After a long pause he walked away from everything. He marched along the neighborhood's quiet lanes and ways then struck off to walk all the way to his downtown Jackson office.

Resembling a man who was about to have his portrait painted, posed in a chair besides his library's fireplace, Judge Miller was about to drop off to sleep. He was awakened by the entrance of a middle-aged lady, the maid.

"Judge, excuse me, sir, would you like your tea now?" she asked, respectfully.

"First, remove your cleaning bag from my leather couch! That couch was expensive and is very dear to me. When are you ever going to learn that?" muttered the Judge, coming out of a nap, "Just make my tea, bring it here and you can go home. I will not need you anymore tonight," he continued, without taking his eyes away from the fire. The faintness of his voice was pitiful and dreadful, but his unusual eyes were bright and sparkled, even in the ill lit room. The hollowness and thinness of his face would have made them appear even larger but the thickness of his dark eyebrows overshadowed their power.

"Don't you want a little more light in here," asked the maid, walking away towards the window with the clear intention of pulling open the curtains, before removing her bag or making his tea.

"No!" said the Judge, "I am expecting another visitor tonight."

"Another visitor or another prowler?" asked the maid, cutting her trip to the window short.

"Another intruder," said the Judge, who had not removed his gaze from the fire, "Nobody believes there is someone out there who's after me."

"If you feel that way, let me stay here tonight," said the maid, removing her bag from the couch.

"No! I must face him alone," said the Judge, placing stress on the last word.

"You know best," said the maid, making her way out of that room, to proceed with her mission.

By the time the maid returned with tea, Judge Miller had on his robe and was back in his favorite chair. She bid him goodnight and left.

Judge Miller leaned back and fell into a train of rambling meditations. First he thought of his friends in the political party; then his mind traveled to Clara, her father and mother, then his mind went to Kevin who had become the center of his concerns and worries. He thought how he duped his brother to adopt Clara by telling him that was Clara his daughter, how he blackmailed Clara's mother into leaving her husband, Clara's father. He thought of all the scams and double-dealing he had done while he was a prosecutor, and before and after, when he became a judge. Thinking of all these bad deeds, he smiled, as if he believed they were smart accomplishments and glorious triumphs. Then everything stopped turning in his head as his thoughts went to a pistol that had become his constant companion through the nights. The pistol had become his favorite security blanket; he often carried it around under his coat during the past months. The possibility of going to sleep without his pistol under his pillow had never entered Judge Miller's mind. He stood up and hurried upstairs where he had left it when he went for his robe. He opened the door to his bedroom, searched where he thought he had placed it but he couldn't find it anywhere in that room.

He began to search frantically all over the second floor of the house; at length, he was about to blame the maid and was ready to call her when he opened one last door of a bedroom and beheld his missing friend on a lamp table.

Judge Miller seized the pistol in triumph, went downstairs and sat again on the same chair, leaning forward towards the fire as if he were expecting something to rise from the flames.

After a few minutes resting in that manner, he rolled back in the chair laughing so loudly and heartily, that any witness of that peculiar phenomenon would be so delighted and amused he would follow suit and begin laughing along with him.

He laughed, remembering Clara's words, 'Judge, you better hope and pray there is no God, if there is one, I'd hate to see what He's going to do to you for what you did to my father.'

"What God?" asked the Judge out loud, as if he was in the habit of mumbling to himself.

"God must be stupid. He makes people then he kills them. He's either stupid or crazy. What would anyone say if I'd built a house and then burnt it down? They'd say that I'm crazy."

He suddenly stopped laughing, took the pistol in his hand, wrapped his fingers around it and said, "I'll wait here. I'll wait and they'll see that I may be old but my heart is young and bold."

Kevin was still walking along on the opposite side of the town from where Judge Miller lived. He had, by that time, come to his senses, so far as to consider, that he could not go back home to face his wife and he certainly could never bear to sit on the parlor couch and speak to her. All done, he thought to himself, all gone. He had done it all in; he made it all gone. His wife, his daughter, his home, his future, had all vanished with the day's light as that night marched in. What a doleful night. What a long, dismal and inhospitable night it turned out to be. Whatever night-images and night-noises crowded his mind, they never scratched away the thought of 'you can't go back home.' That thought planted itself in his brain and lingered like a bodily pain that would not go away. It was almost past-midnight when, muddied, weary, wretched and footsore, he found himself nearing a traffic free bridge. His plan had been to enter town quietly and undetected by means of the unfrequented ways and to get into his office in the same manner, but he suddenly realized that he had no keys.

In that desolate place and at that ungodly hour of the night, he walked on without feeling any danger, although danger was there, near and active.

There was a lingering mist in all the hollows and on the bridge ahead of him. It was a clammy cold mist that made its slow way through the night air in ripples that followed and overspread one another like waves of a silent sea, looking like evil spirits in search of a place to rest. As he ascended the bridge his heart beat loud enough to be heard but its drum was lost in the symphony of sounds coming from the city.

Nearing the end of the bridge, he felt a peculiar fear coming over him; he heard something rolling, quietly, some distance behind him, like a ghost. He could not make out what the figure was, but he was certain it was following him. Was it there because he was or was it a mere coincidence? He bent his steps to the right and quickened his pace. The rolling object turned out to be a car, keeping its speed down to that of his steps. The cat and mouse game lasted long enough for Kevin to get off the bridge, then suddenly the car rushed in front of him, turned and stopped to block his way.

The car's front doors opened simultaneously and two well-dressed men, each holding a flashlight, jumped out.

Kevin felt an eerie sensation on seeing them approach cautiously and slowly.

"What are you doing here? Pal," questioned the first man who came out of the driver's side. "What are you doing here?" he repeated, in a commanding tone. He was tall and slender and shined his light directly into Kevin's face.

"Why do you want to know that?" asked Kevin, striking the best pose he could of being unafraid and unaffected. He put his hand in his jacket pocket and felt for his pistol.

"We got ourselves a wise guy," exclaimed the man, turning to look at his companion.

The second man, who was a little older and heavier, just smiled and was resolved not to say anything.

"You want me to tell you why?" asked the same man, beating his chest lightly with his flashlight, as if he were accustomed to the question.

At first a chill crept over Kevin then, feeling the gun in his pocket and knowing he was prepared to use it, he settled into a calm conversational tone. "Yeah. Tell me why, and tell me what and who you are and what you want," returned Kevin firmly.

Hearing these words from someone who looked like a vagrant and in need of a hot meal, the first man burst into hearty laughter and turned to the other man saying, " I told you he's a wise guy."

"He's a real genius," replied the other man, more seriously.

"Okay wise guy, I'll tell you who we are," said the driver, coming close to him and opening his sport coat with his left hand while the other was occupied holding the flashlight that he kept pointed in Kevin's face.

"Hold it!" warned Kevin, shading his eyes with his left hand, his right holding the grip of his concealed pistol. "The only thing I want to see in your hands is the flashlight, otherwise I'll think I'm about to be robbed and I'm prepared to defend myself."

"We're the police," replied the man, in the quiet tone of law enforcement authority.

Having many reasons suspicion, Kevin backed off two steps and ordered, "Show me a badge. But first, no matter how I look, I want you to know my name is Kevin Barley and I'm a Madison County prosecutor."

"We'll see if that's so," said the same man who, without any consideration, put his hand on his lapel and pulled his jacket to the side, exposing a badge clipped on his belt and the pistol that hung in a shoulder holster.

"Okay, I'm detective Cornelius Lord and my partner is Richard Ray," said the second man, not waiting for a response or a comment from Kevin. "Now that you know who and what we are, let's have some sort of ID from you, Mr. Barley" he continued, coming closer to Kevin.

"I unfortunately don't have any ID with me, having gotten into an argument with my wife; I left the house abruptly," stated Kevin, in a confident manner.

"Where do you live?" asked Cornelius Lord.

"80 Sycamore Tree Lane, Jackson, in the East Over section," responded Kevin.

"I'm sure, and I am not going to hold that against you, but can we call your house, sir?" asked detective Lord, knowing that the East Over section was one of the best areas in Jackson, where only an affluent family would live.

"I wish you wouldn't do that, detective," requested Kevin.

"Let's take his ass in," shouted Richard Ray.

"On what charge?" asked Kevin. "Don't forget, I am also a lawyer, Mr. Ray. If you were to do that, some other officer will be reading you your rites three minutes after we arrive at the station."

"Shut up Ray, he's a college boy!" said Lord, "Do you know Clara Miller?"

"Yes...,"

Kevin moved away in the mist and darkness, not only to think how to complete his answer, but to shake off some of the mud and wet from his clothes. After sitting on the knee-high wall, that was an extension of the bridge, he put his hands on his face, rubbed it for a moment or two and said, "She's my wife."

"Judge Miller's niece?"

"Yes."

"She's very good."

"She was good."

"What do you mean?" asked Lord, as he had learned, being a cop for many years, every human being has a secret they unknowingly want to reveal and by that by listening closely one can often pick up hints that are thrown in passing.

"She's not the prosecutor any longer. That's what I meant." answered Kevin.

"Oh, yeah I know. I meant to say that she is a good person," said officer Lord. "I heard of Kevin Barley. In fact you were the prosecutor in the trial of a Jackson policeman who was charged with police brutality; I was supposed to be a witness."

"Oh, yes. That's Henry Temple. He went to trial and was convicted of beating an escaped convict. You were going to be called as a witness for the defense."

"Let me tell you what has happened, Mr. Barley," said the detective, as if he found an audience to listen to something that was bothering him.

"Yes! Please tell me something that may help ease my mind. I hate to prosecute a member of the force," exclaimed Kevin.

"I also wish to ease my own mind," interjected detective Lord. "As you know, these two convicts escaped from the County Jail, stole a car and headed out of town, driving erratically. We came to find out after, that the car they had stolen had a manual transmission and neither of the two knew how drive a stick shift. My partner, Henry Temple and I followed that car through the streets of Jackson. It was a miracle they didn't kill somebody. They zigged and zagged and zoomed out of the city and finally made it into Madison County. We saw that the car had run off the road and the two convicts took off on foot into the fields. I saw the convicts disappear into a ditch. My partner, who was much younger and lighter than me, left me way behind, but I ran after them too. When I was coming up on them, I heard loud punches breaking on, what sounded like, human flesh. My partner was in the ditch with them.

Suddenly I heard a loud scream, I then got to the ditch and jumped in and saw one of the convicts bleeding out of one eye. I checked and saw that the other one had a lot of bruises and cuts on his face and his knuckles were cut up and bleeding too. I checked Henry's hands, which he didn't take too kindly, and found that his knuckles were all bruised and cut too. That's what I saw and heard and that is what I was about to tell the court. A lot of people tried to change what I was going to say, but they weren't very successful, that's why I wasn't called to testify."

"What do you think? Do you think he was the one who poked out the convict's eye?" asked Kevin.

The detective considered his answer for a moment, looked downwards, then turned his face up and said softly, "Henry was my partner for almost six months. He was young and eager. He wasn't a trouble maker, he was a trouble hunter."

Kevin shook his head mournfully and said nothing.

"That's why he only lasted in prison less than three months. The one who killed him, didn't kill Henry because he was a cop, he killed him because he kept hassling him and others too."

The two men stood and stared at each other with somber looks on their faces.

"I hate to interrupt story hour for you two, but it's cold out here, when are we going to shove off? Let the prosecutor go on to his merry way," said the younger officer, Richard Ray.

"Where are you going counselor, can we give you a lift?" asked Cornelius Lord.

"You heard that the road to hell is paved with good intentions. I'm on my way to find out whether some were good or bad to start with and only Judge Miller can tell me," said Kevin. "First take me to my office. The janitor has a key to let me in."

When all three got in the car, it began to roll down the street at a modest speed with detective Lord driving, Kevin sitting in the front and the younger officer in back.

"Talking about the Judge, I must tell you the other day Judge Miller called the police saying he had seen a prowler around his house. Two patrolmen were sent there and later, when I was in the area, I went there too. Judge Miller followed the patrolmen around, with a pistol in his hand, while they searched the house and the outside area. The peculiar thing was that at the slightest noise, he'd turn and face that direction like he was ready to shoot. I'm not saying that he's loosing it; I'm saying that he's upset about something. After the search was over and nothing was found, he spoke with me. All the time he spoke, it sounded as if he were talking to himself. He said that he had told her, that he was going to ruin them before she could spell Mississippi," recounted the detective, while driving, "Who the 'her' was, he never told me and I didn't ask."

"You see, Mr. Lord, he's a Criminal Court Judge and with all the years he spent on the bench, he must have made a lot of enemies. Judges don't have many friends, some business acquaintances, but a lot of enemies," said Kevin.

"But he gets a lot of respect,"

"A Judge is like the sea that does what it likes and what it likes is to conquer and destroy the earth. All the strong and devastating winds come from the sea, yet most people love to live by it. People say that you must have respect for the sea, just like they say about the Judge" said Kevin. As he uttered the words, he looked down with pity, as if he had just pictured himself being swallowed by the sea.

At length, a tall building came into view, "That's where my office is," said Kevin, pointing at the building.

"I know," said Lord, as he pulled in front of the building, stopped and looked at Kevin, "Are you going to be ok?"

Kevin did not answer; he jumped out of the car, nodded to the detectives and went into the well-lit lobby. The two officers watched him turn the corner at the deep end of the corridor.

"Let's go get some coffee and we'll figure out what we're going to do next," said Lord, pulling away from the building.

It was at least two hours past midnight. Judge Miller's house looked sleepy but not dead, mysterious but not strange, lonely but not alone. The Judge, after sundry thoughts of accounts of his past, his connections and his business, dozed off but was suddenly aroused and alarmed by a slight noise at the back door and the creaking of the wood plank floor as someone stepped upon it. Hearing these sounds, he was reduced to the verge of despair, particularly when he felt a cold draft, knowing there was no open door or window. He tiptoed upstairs and into his bedroom.

Having carefully drawn the curtains of his bedroom to the side, he peeped out and saw the driveway empty and the street deserted. He felt the gun in his hand and sat on the edge of the bed to collect his thoughts and calm his anxiety. The anxiety played out on his features was lost in a look of unbounded fear. The person, he thought, whoever it was, has come into my home so suddenly and so quietly, I'd no time to block his entrance. Who could he be? A burglar? An armed robber? Or, some crazy convict recently released from prison, out for revenge? What can I do?

The only way in which he could fathom saving himself from the wrath of the mysterious visitor was to creep under his high bed. It was this maneuver to which he accordingly resorted.

Whatever grounds for self-confidence he might have entertained, for having escaped so neatly and smartly from an awkward situation, were dispelled on the consideration of his present position. He was all alone, under his bed, trembling and if he made the slightest noise, he stood a good chance of getting shot and killed, under his own bed, that which he had enjoyed so many times in the company of some of the most beautiful women of Jackson.

There he was, under the bed, coiled like a rattle snake, overtaken by fear derived from a subconscious guilt of a long career of evil deeds, injustices, threats and the destruction of others' lives for his own comfort, personal satisfaction, money and glory. There he lay, shivering, with his knees rubbing against each other, as if trying to reduce themselves to dust and he, thinking he never imagined his life would end under his bed instead of in it; he was afraid of death. How could he have been so brave and bold, sitting to pronounce judgment on the bench and so fearful and weak in his own bedroom? How could he have portrayed himself to the world as one high and mighty, but feel so frightened and frail, there, hiding under his bed? When he could no longer stand these thoughts and feelings, he backed out from under the bed, stood up, but not erect, softly walked to the bedroom door, opened it a little more than half, poked his head out and scanned the dark hallway. Seeing nothing and hearing less, he pulled in his head, went to the window, drew back the curtains, then saw, much to his surprise, a black car parked in his circular driveway, where none had stood, when last he looked, after the maid had left for the night. He then tiptoed to the lamp table on the left side of the bed, opened the drawer carefully, took out a flashlight, tuned it on then off, to test its working ability and satisfied with his findings, went to the wall and turned off the light. He stood in the middle of the bedroom floor, in the darkness, took the gun in his left hand and held the flashlight with his right, swung both hands around, in practice, and not liking the feel of the flashlight in his right hand and the gun in his left, reversed them. Not knowing what else to do or where else to hide, he sat on the edge of the bed, listened intently and heard nothing. Some minutes of complete silence had passed when his haggard eyes looked around the dark room. A sudden creak of the floor brought shivers to his spine so intense that he began to visibly shake from the first hair of his head to the last toenail of his foot.

He then bent over and stealthfully made his way, in a crouch, to a tight nook between the lamp table and the wall and thought to stay there, in that position, until the next day's light. He had not long been entrenched in his concealment when, to his horror, a man, bearing a flashlight in his hand, appeared, standing at the bedroom's threshold. The Judge's face took on long strong frown lines, those of anger emerged on his forehead but they all gradually faded away once he recognized the figure of the intruder, Kevin.

In anger and in haste, without saying a word, Judge Miller placed the flashlight back in the lamp table drawer, turned on the light and sped down the stairs into his well lit library, while Kevin followed close behind, in silence.

"What are you doing here in the middle of the night?" asked the Judge, as he placed the pistol on the table next to the chair he had occupied earlier. He then sat down on the same chair and studied Kevin, keeping steady and angry features.

"You're a snake, Judge Miller," said Kevin, with clenched teeth, "you've been a snake your whole life."

"Who do you think you are? calling me a snake, you little piece of shit," yelled the Judge, getting on to his feet in wrath.

"You're a snake!" yelled Kevin, "and I'll make you pay for it." Looking hard at the Judge, he repeatedly punched the knuckles of his right hand into the palm of his left, as anger welled up in his face and form.

"I'll show you," growled Judge Miller; he turned quickly, picked up his pistol, aimed at Kevin and paused for an instant, laboring for breath.

Kevin, seeing the pistol and realizing the Judge's intent, threw the flashlight at him. The Judge ducked and at the same instant fired at Kevin, who dove behind the leather couch. Kevin, squatted, withdrew his pistol from his pocket and held it tight in his hand.

The Judge, not realizing Kevin was armed, moved slowly and defiantly towards the couch, holding and aiming the pistol steady and straight. He then stopped when Kevin came into view, behind the couch. Judge Miller raised his pistol and prepared to fire at almost point blank range, saying "Goodbye, punk!" A sudden shot rang out; the Judge's features froze, with evident pain. Kevin stood up as the Judge went down on the couch, landing on it with the upper part of his body while his lower portion fell to the floor, still gripping his pistol, tightly, in his right hand. Kevin, confused, stood in silence on the Judge's left side, looking down with a feeling of accomplishment, as blood poured from the villain's left leg.

"Who in the hell shot me?" asked the Judge. His voice was crackling, wretched and dreadful. Kevin understood that tone wasn't entirely caused by the wound, but partly from the anger and disappointment of not accomplishing his mission.

"It wasn't me, Judge," replied Kevin, squatting down a few feet from him.

"There is somebody else in this house, find him and kill the bastard." The sound of his voice was sunken, suppressed and echoed, as if it had lost the quality and pitch of that which was human. He then moved slowly to the left, still tightly holding the pistol, "Go! Get the bastard, " urged the Judge, with the same pain filled voice, as if he were endeavoring to throw Kevin onto a false scent. Kevin gazed about vacantly, not moving to see where the gunshot had come from, as if he had already known. While his head was turned away, the Judge raised the shaking hand that held the pistol, squeezed the trigger, it went off and the bullet that was most likely intended for Kevin, lodged into the top of Judge's head, for the pistol was not raised high enough to clear his temple. Blood rushed out; his body began to shake vigorously, with his legs on the floor, the rest of him on the couch and his friend, the pistol, next to him.

Suddenly, the two detectives, Lord and Ray, burst in and sped to Judge Miller's shivering body. They stood above the Judge and looked down, breathlessly.

Some moments of silence passed while all three looked down on the dead Judge. Part of his face was covered with blood; the rest had turned pale. His lips and his nails had taken on the same color, his body had stopped shaking, the hand that held the gun was empty and idle, his eyes remained open, still looking up at the three, but seeing no one.

The Judge's ill-blessed life ended there and there he lay, cold and unfeeling. He hadn't ended under his bed, as he had feared a few minutes earlier; he ended on his prized leather couch, not at the hand of an intruder, but by his best friend, the friend that kept him company for such a long time, his own pistol, thus proving true the proverb 'you have a gun for a friend, you need no more enemies.'

"He's dead," pronounced Lord, holding his eyes on the body, as if waiting for the Judge to move.

"I didn't kill him," said Kevin, sadly.

"I know; he killed himself. I suppose he shot himself in trying to kill you." said Lord.

"Why do you suppose that?" asked Kevin.

"Ahem, a man who wants to kill himself, shoots himself on the side of the temple, not the top, like the Judge did."

The experts, who based their opinion on facts, confirmed that supposition on information they gathered after his death. The Judge had a stronger reason to kill Kevin than to kill himself. Kevin posed a threat to expose him and all his double-dealings, mischief and scams with which he was familiar, but not a participant. Kevin, over the years simply turned a blind eye, in exchange for access to the Judge's connections and his support, for his political hopes and his future. But as the barber knows, as does the butcher, the baker, the court clerk, and all the fair-minded housewives and every decent sister of every man and woman, the simple fact that no one will go to heaven holding onto the devil's hand. So Kevin, in accordance with the laws of nature, was back to—-all gone —— it was all gone.

After a while, "I shot him, to stop him from shooting you," said Lord.

"I know, I saw you storming in the side door of the house, right after I lunged behind the couch."

"Now he's dead," mumbled the younger officer, Richard Ray, "He can't do any more harm or any more good to anyone any more. He's dead,"

"Everything died inside him, a long time ago, his love, his hate, his pride and passion; everything died except his deal making," said Lord, shaking his head mournfully.

"He must have known you well," said officer Ray.

A concerned expression settled upon Lord's face, he seemed to become more conscious of Kevin's connection to the newly departed and said, "Kevin, you and I knew him better than he knew us."

"That's sad," returned the prosecutor, shaking his head mournfully, looking down at the dead, "His grand oddity was that he seemed to be too big for any place or space, big or small. How many men he squeezed out of a room where his was standing and how many men he carried under his wings when he was going places, is unfathomable. Look at him now! Even though he's stretched out, he looks coiled. When death touched him, he shrank and he'll dissolve into nothing, like all men, big or small. Why?" continued the lawyer, "Why, why do we place ourselves under life's grind wheel, why do we put our skin and bones in harms way, to save what? We can save our own skin and bones for the time being, we have little else to save, but we loose our souls forever. That's what I meant when I said, that's sad." He hesitated then asked, "How come you're here? Who called you?" as he turned to the detective.

"Nobody called. We came here because of you," said Lord.

"Because of me? Why because of me?"

"After we dropped you off, we went for coffee. Then, Ray and I were on our way to the station; we stopped at your office to see if you'd made out all right. The janitor told us he didn't have a key and you called a cab and left. I thought you'd pay a visit to the Judge because you were angry with your wife and didn't want to go home. Knowing the Judge's state of mind, I got concerned about your coming here and getting shot. The Judge had been suspicious of intruders and we knew he had a handgun; he might have mistaken you for a prowler. We got here a few minutes after you had arrived. We sneaked up on the house and saw you and the Judge in the room downstairs, talking. An instant later I saw the Judge pick up a pistol and you fly behind the couch. I shot at the Judge to stop him from killing you, the rest is history," said Detective Cornelius Lord, scanning the room with a vacant look and scratching his chin to lessen the importance of his story.

"Why did you think the Judge would shoot me? The prowler story doesn't amount to a hill of beans. You're using it as fairy cloak, thinking it would fit anything, but it doesn't," said Kevin.

"Well, he did shoot at you, didn't he? You see, counselor, I know some things about you and the Judge and some of the other political heads around here. I've been around guys like you for the biggest part of my life. I know you were the Judge's favorite boy, but he wasn't your favorite patron," replied the officer, stopping to look down at the Judge's body. He then raised his eyes and said to his partner, Ray, "Go out to the car and call for a coroner, we'll make out a report later." Lord turned, walked towards the smoldering fireplace and took a seat on the Judge's reading chair.

When Ray was out of sight and earshot, Kevin took a seat across from Lord and stared into the fire.

"As we happen to be alone for the moment," said the detective, "and we're both in the law enforcement business, let me ask you something."

"Go ahead."

"After spending only a few minutes with the Judge, why would he try to kill you? Don't give me a fairy cloak answer, like you called my prowler motive," said Lord.

"Now, officer, you sound like a cop and I'm going to sound like a lawyer. It's irrelevant and it's private. But you could say, like you said before, he was losing it," returned Kevin, with a hint of amusement.

"I beg your pardon, sir, I never said that. What I did say was that I didn't want you to think that I believed he was losing it," returned the cop.

"So it had entered your mind, that he was losing it. Then, case closed."

"Not by a long shot, it ain't, counselor. There are two possible answers. Judge Miller was about to withdraw you name as a candidate for Congress, you found out from your wife and came here to convince him otherwise. The other is you had gotten into an argument with your wife, you were going to spend the night in your office but you left your keys at home so you came here looking for a shoulder to cry on and a place to spend the night. You must have told him something to make him mad; he was already angry and took a shot at you. That's why I came back and as you can see, I was right, somebody died. I might have been able to stop him if I got here earlier. Do I feel bad? I feel like hell. If my eyes hadn't seen so many deaths, starting with the Korean War, I would be crying my heart out now because the Judge was my friend; we had many talks and broke bread many times. Somewhere along the line I began to rationalize death to avoid its effects on me, but my job as a police officer tells me to dig for the truth. Tell me, what happened here this morning?"

"In essence, I alluded to the fact that I was going to divorce my wife and if he tried one of his old tricks on me, I would destroy him," said Kevin. "I know how you feel, officer. I should be crying, but I'm in shock, when that wears off, I'll probably cry like little boy. He was like a father to me, but I couldn't bring myself to be like a son to him," responded Kevin, getting on his feet and, without any further consideration, starting to make his way out of the room.

"Are you going to, for real, divorce your wife? Just remember, Kevin, one tragedy does not deserve another. You divorcing your wife would be another tragedy," said Lord in a sullen tone.

There were no other words spoken, as Kevin disappeared into another part of the house.

CHAPTER ELEVEN

The death of the Drummer

A few hours after the Judge's death and many miles away, Peddler was still in his hospital bed. Erik approached the room and stood silently at the door. Peddler, having regained some strength and energy on the sight of the object of his personal accomplishment, struggled onto his feet and attempted to walk away from his deathbed.

"Help me, Curly. Help me to the window," begged Peddler, with a withered voice, as he sat on the edge of the bed and attempted to remove the oxygen tube that was in his nose. The nurse suddenly appeared at the door and rushed to him.

"What are you doing Mr. Spencer?" she yelled, trying to undo what he had done.

"Take me to the window!" screamed Peddler, with the little force that the good Lord allowed him during his last hours.

"Help me get him to the window," said Erik, softly, preparing him for the short trip to fulfill his request. "He wants to look outside."

The nurse nodded with hesitation. The task of taking him to the window wasn't an easy one, tubes had to be adjusted and wires redirected, but all were done, to the nurse's satisfaction and Peddler was assisted to a standing position. He was pale and weak. Leaning on Erik, he stared out the window and said, "It's really dark out there; I don't know which is thicker, the darkness or the air I'm breathing."

"Will you be OK with him? I'll be back in a few minutes with his medication," said the nurse.

Erik nodded and the nurse glided out of the room.

"Let's leave, Curly, lets go," said Peddler, turning to face his friend.

"Where do you want to go now, Peddler?" asked Erik, in amazement.

"I want to go to my truck. Take me to my truck," he answered, looking straight ahead, leaning his head on Erik's shoulder.

"Hey Peddler, are you okay?" Recalling him from the trance into which he had fallen was like reviving the faint from a swoon, or endeavoring to hold onto the spirit of a dying man.

"First take me back to my bed, so I can get dressed," mumbled Peddler.

"This is crazy," said Erik, helping Peddler to sit on the edge of the bed.

"Now, get my clothes," requested Peddler, with a little more life in him.

"Stop this for God's sake, be sensible!" pleaded Erik.

"I am sensible. I don't want to stay here; I don't feel safe in this room. Erik, don't you understand that? I want to go back to my truck, lock the doors, close the shade and put cotton in the keyholes. That's where I feel safe. Can't you understand that?"

Erik, without uttering another word, began, hurriedly, to gather Peddler's clothes from the drawers and closet.

"Let me help you get dressed and I'll take you to your truck. We'll close the shade, lock the door and put cotton in the keyholes so nobody can get you."

"God bless you, Erik, bless you for your goodness," rejoined Peddler, putting on his shirt, "if you only knew how I felt, you'd take pity on me," he continued, sliding his pants up over his white boxer shorts. "Thank heaven, upon your knees, for still having your strength."

He struggled to stand on his weak and trembling legs while attempting to hold up his trousers. Having lost so much flesh because of his illness, they were too big. "We always criticize someone who gets too big for his britches, will you criticize me for getting too small for mine? asked Peddler, letting his pants go and looking down at them as they landed around his knees.

"You'll be okay, once you'll start eating again."

"Haven't you heard, Erik? I'm dying," said Peddler, kindly, as he sat on the bed, holding up his pants while trying to catch his breath.

"We're all going to die," returned Erik, occupying himself with the task of getting the rest of Peddler's belongings together.

"Curly, I'm dying now," cried Peddler, getting onto his feet again, still plagued with the task of keeping his pants up. "You know that I am dying, that's why you're getting my things together.

"Nassos, Nassos, stop reading between the lines!" yelled Erik.

"Thank you, Erik. You're still calling me by your brother's name," said Peddler, with as much delight as he could find the strength to express.

"What can I tell you? You're both the same; you both claim you can read the future," uttered Erik, looking at Peddler.

"You don't know how true those words are about me right now. I really can read my future. Come tomorrow, I won't be here. I'll be at rest somewhere, away from here, far away," responded Peddler, with a frail grin.

"Nonsense."

"But you know, Curly? All my life I wanted to be a kingmaker and I finally made it. Finally I made it. It's not bad enough that I'm dying now, after finally making it, but the worse thing is, I can't even keep my damn pants up," said Peddler, with a dim laugh. Erik remained serious and just looked back at his friend.

"That's what I call a stroke of bad luck," continued Peddler, gazing around the room as if to find an answer. "Tell me Curly! You're a man of God, tell me why God is doing this to me?" Peddler stopped, posed, as if he were listening and then continued in a different tone of voice, " No, no, hell no! It's not a stroke of bad luck. No, hell no! It's not a stroke of bad luck. Curly, my friend, God dealt me a good hand of cards when I was born, but I took too damn long to play it," said Peddler, looking fixedly, in turns, at Erik and the ceiling. "But I made you a king of the ministry, didn't I, Erik?"

"Yes, Peddler you did."

"Curly, I want to tell you something you said to me, when we first met, that gave me the courage to become a king maker."

"Fire when ready," said Erik.

"One night, I was feeling bad; my insecurities showed, like you always said, like the donkey's ears. You read that feeling in my face and you said, 'Peddler just remember, no matter how much smarter the smart people are than you, they can always learn something from you, if they're smart.' I think you told me that when I said I didn't feel comfortable talking to smart people, because I wasn't that smart."

Erik looked at Peddler in surprise and in silence, finding himself at a loss for words.

"Let me go find you a belt to keep your pants up," said Erik, breaking the uncomfortable silence, "before you piss in them," he continued, rushing out of the room without delay.

In the pursuit of a belt Erik, rushed to the nurse's station; it was less than fifty feet from Peddler's room. It took a few minutes, but the good nurse found a black leather belt. Erik hurried back and while walking, examined the quality of the belt by stretching it with both hands.

"Peddler you're lucky," announced Erik, entering the room. He stopped in his tracks when he saw Peddler stretched out, with his eyes wide open, on the floor. Erik fell down on his knees, shook his friend, hard, but got no response.

"Peddler! Peddler! Peddler! Peddler, wake up, you son-of-a-bitch! Wake up Peddler. Peddler, wake up, we're going to your truck."

The nurse and two doctors rushed in after they heard Erik's screams. No one said a word but they did what they knew best. Both doctors stooped down, gently picked Peddler up and placed him on the bed. Erik backed away, with tears streaming down his face, put his two hands to his lips, as if to hide their trembling, then clasped them on his breast, as if to mend his ruined heart.

One doctor took his stethoscope and placed it on Peddler's chest. Erik looked on, with a frightful sadness, then slowly walked out from the room into the hallway, placed his arm on the wall, leaned his head on it and cried. Shortly thereafter the doctor, who had examined Peddler, walked out of the room, went to where Erik was standing, crying and said in a quiet voice, "I'm sorry Mr. Karas, he's gone."

"I know, I know, doctor. You all did everything you could. He was my best friend and I was his only friend," returned Erik, facing the doctor.

"I know Mr. Karas. I've seen you on TV, you're a good man."

"A good man, but I let my friend down."

Mary Lou, who just arrived at the hospital, saw that Peddler had died. She rushed to Erik with tears in her eyes and threw her arms around him, "I'm sorry, I'm sorry, Erik. Peddler is gone and we're all going to miss him, terribly," she cried.

"I didn't believe he was going to die, I thought he only wanted to go to his truck," said Erik, " I didn't believe he was going to die. No, I didn't believe it," continued Erik, with his eyes wandering from place to place, eventually they came upon Mary Lou and rested on her face. Suddenly, releasing himself from her grip, he rushed back to Peddler's room and in the process pushed aside doctors, nurses and everyone else he found in his way. He stopped above Peddler and stared at his pale and lifeless face.

Not a word was spoken, not a sound was made. He stood, like a spirit, above him, then knelt before Peddler's torso, brought his hands to his face in a praying manner and softly began a prayer. It was a nurse who knelt beside him first, then another nurse, then an aide, then one doctor, then the other doctor and then everyone in the room followed suit and prayed in their own separate way, but they all prayed. Erik and everyone there stood up after their prayers and he said, in a low voice, "I plead with you good ladies and gentlemen, do not come near me, do not speak, do not move. I only wish one or two of you to help me take him to his truck. That was his last wish and I must fulfill it."

He then stood there and listened with his eyes, for a just longer than an instant. Hearing no one speak and seeing no one move, he grabbed the wheel chair from the corner, opened it and said gently, "Somebody, please help me. I repeat, I'm going to take him to his truck, that's where he wanted to go." Erik looked around eagerly and seeing no one come to his aid, said again, "Somebody, help me put him in the wheel chair."

"We can't do that. It' against hospital policy," said one of doctors.

"To hell with policies," bellowed Erik, authoritatively.

The good doctor, seeing Erik's determination, gestured to the nurses to help him with his request. Mary Lou, the doctor and several others followed Erik who pushed the wheel chair with Peddler in it, covered. Half way down the corridor, a woman's scream was heard. It was Clara, Peddler's daughter. She was dragging her daughter by the hand as the nanny followed close behind. Once Clara reached the wheelchair, she let her daughter's hand go, fell on her knees in front of the chair and placed her hands on those of the corpse.

"She must be Clara, his daughter, "said Erik to Mary Lou.

Mary Lou took the child by the hand and walked down the hall, with the nanny following.

"I want to see my father," said Clara, as she gently reached over and lifted the sheet. "Father please wake up, wake up and see Stephanie, your granddaughter. I'm sorry I'm late, father. I promised I would bring her to see you. Father, please wake up. Wake up and talk to me, " continued the girl softly as endless streaks of tears came down her face. "I'm sorry."

"If I tell you, Stephen, that your agonies are over, that I've come to take you home with me, would you forgive me? I'm kneeling before you, in your honor, if I tell you that I love you and I have secretly loved you my whole life through, even though I didn't see you, would you let your spirit hear me, so I too can be at peace and rest. I know I caused you to think of your life as being wasted, for not coming to find you."

Seeing her state of mind, Erik walked around the wheelchair and made an attempt to assist her. Clara pushed her shiny black hair aside and buried her face into the torso of the corpse and, as Erik tried to lift her off, she screamed, "No! No, I want to be with him."

"Take him back to the room," said Erik to the aide, and then to Clara, "I'm his friend, Erik. Please, let him go, you'll see him back in his room."

As the aide tried to push the wheelchair, Clara threw herself in front of it, as if to freeze time and motion. Erik pulled her up and held her with his arms.

"Erik, I never told him that I love him. Erik, did you tell your father that you loved him before he died? I never had the chance to say goodbye. Erik, did you tell your father goodbye, before he died? You told me on the phone that your father had died a few years ago, but you still feel his presence," she cried, looking up at Erik, while his arms were wrapped around her.

Erik did not respond; he remained in such sorrow as none but he could know. Clara looked up at him and saw tears in his eyes.

"He lived like he was a nobody," she cried, looking at her father as he was being wheeled away, covered with a white sheet. "He lived like he was a nobody but he was truly a somebody. I hope he'll get to his high places and be appreciated for what he was."

If the sun had shone anywhere around the earth, it certainly didn't shine the day of Peddler's funeral, which took place with all the reverence and ceremony becoming a man of dignity. A hearse and two flower cars were parked in front of a large church, they headed a line of limousines. A gospel song poured out of the church's open doors where clusters of people were gathered, standing, for lack of enough room inside. In the church, the pews were filled and hundreds more stood in the aisles and listened to Mary Lou's mournful song. Clara was seated in the front row dressed in black; her face, covered with a veil, pointed downwards.

At the end of the song, Clara looked up at the casket, burst into sobs and drew her shawl around her, as if it would bring her to a place of solitude.

Erik stepped to the pulpit, gazed over the congregation and then motioned for them to be seated. He waited in silence, listening to the toll of the church bell, and then began, "If I were given the chance to live my life over, there many things that I would change. I would, no doubt, alter some parts of my character so to become a better person, a different person. The one thing I would not change would be my all too brief association with my business partner, Stephen Spencer, whom you all knew as Peddler. He fought all life's battles with courage and honesty. He had fallen from the heights, to the lowest depths of ridicule. He blamed no one. He never failed to admonish himself, claiming his descent was his fault and did not attribute it to others. He was universally known as one of the best even-tempered creatures on God's earth. For the last year or so, being his business partner, I had seen Peddler in health and in sickness, but health or sickness made no difference in his warm feelings to those about him; he was still the same gentle, affectionate creature that he had been even when pain and suffering had wasted his strength. Even then, he was still on hand and accessible for anyone who asked for his attention.

"Peddler's mission has been completed. Of all the people that I have known, he is the one who most deserves a place in heaven, next to God. Peddler is gone and his voice will be heard no more on this earth but his name will remain in the hearts of all who knew him. I am very proud to say that he knew he was my best friend. If I could wake him, I would tell him how blessed I was, to be his friend." Erik walked to the casket, stood and stared at Peddler for one long moment. "Peddler, I am going to miss you. If there was ever a time that I disappointed you or hurt you or got you angry, I am truly sorry. Peddler, as I told you before, I am sorry if I ever did anything to hurt you and I want you to know that I never did anything with malice in my heart. I know that wherever I go, wherever I turn, your thoughts, your sayings and your deeds will always be with me. Peddler, you gave me hope when I lacked belief, when I had no faith you gave me purpose, you were always there, on my fallings, to revive me. You kept me alive and I am what you made me, a light in a world of shadows. You were the drummer and I was the dancer. Wherever you go, keep on drumming and I promise you, here, behind, where you left me, I will keep on dancing. Peddler, I thank you. I've told you before that the world needs both drummers and dancers and that one can't succeed without the other. I take comfort in believing your struggles, here on earth, have gone for something good and I know, in my heart, that you will find peace, wherever you are.

In and around the church, the crowd watched the casket being carried down the steps. Clara and Erik followed. Jonas and Mary Lou were next in the line of mourners.

Standing at the foot of the steps was Kevin, looking up at Clara coming down behind her father's casket. He had been there for the entire funeral, but his caring for his wife was overshadowed with such fatal darkness, that even if the sun were out, it could not brighten it. He watched his wife, led by Erik, reach the long black limousine that was waiting behind the hearse. Kevin suddenly charged forward, pushing his way through the crowd and reaching his wife just as she entered the limousine.

Clara opened the car window, glanced at her husband and noticed how nervous, sad and out breath seemed to be. Looking up at his face, she observed a change in him.

"Clara, can you forgive me for being so blind? I would like to ride with you to the cemetery, if I may. From there we can go home together," said Kevin with a trembling voice.

She sat there, stared and said nothing, as if she had lost her power of speech. She then began to cry. Kevin, with a compassionate expression, waited for her sobbing to subside. She then raised her head and said "I see a change in your face. I hope, for the others who are still alive and vulnerable, it corresponds with your character." Without waiting for a response, she opened the door, exited her seat and threw her arms around her husband. They both remained in that stance long enough to give and take their loving feelings.

"Kevin, I have told you that I love you, many times," said Clara, bringing her face close to his ear, "I never told my father that I loved him. Kevin, when we get home I want you to call your father tell him that you love him. You promise?" cried Clara.

"I promise, I will."

CHAPTER TWELVE

Jonas' last stand

Three months had glided by since Peddler passed away, three months that, in the life of the blessed and most favored of mortals as Erik's was, because of his station in life, should have been filled with happiness and joy, but in Erik's world, everyday brought a troubled and clouded dawn. On one hand was the glory he felt and the good he did in a troubled society and on the other lingered the fervent attachment to his son in his sensitive heart and the loss of his friend, Peddler. Every day brought more confusion.

One evening he stood, holding the Bible, looking around the audience, in his usual style; the crowd was focused on him and waited intently to hear his words.

"Please, Lord," he began, opening the Bible, "lead us out of the darkness and the shadow of death.

"These may have been the words of the lost, pleading to God to show them the way back. They were lost. They were ready to be guided out of the darkness and the shadow of death. When sheep get lost, a good shepherd goes out to find them; he brings them back to the flock. Isn't God our good shepherd? Wasn't He smart enough to know and realize that group of people was lost? Yes, God knew they were lost. Was God going to let them walk into the darkness and the shadow of death for the rest of their lives, without lifting a finger to help them? Was God prepared to allow those mortals to fall off a cliff or to plunge into a river of and drown? Would a good shepherd allow his sheep to disappear? Would a good shepherd let his sheep be eaten by wolves? My friends, there is one big difference between people and sheep. The lost sheep in the Greek language are referred to as '**Apolwlon probaton,** lost sheep, innocently lost sheep. The sheep have no knowledge of good or evil. We humans, since the time the serpent convinced Eve to eat the fruit of the forbidden tree, have acquired the knowledge of the opposite side of the good, evil. God then gave us the ability to choose between good and evil. Before Eve and Adam ate the fruit of the forbidden tree, they were like sheep, innocent. The only difference between them and the animals was they spoke a transcribable language. So my friends, if these people were lost, it only meant that they chose the evil way. Maybe they didn't know they chose to side with Satan. Many have lived and died walking along Satan's path of evil. Many have fallen over the cliff and many have drowned in the river. Some of them felt lost but didn't admit it. Some who were lost and realized it, called upon God to accept their repentance and to save them. The sheep were physically lost, but people may be physically at ease, earning their living, watching TV or playing canasta with their neighbors, but their souls are lost, off playing footsies with Satan. God was ready to save and forgive those people for whatever they had done to enter that place of darkness and death. So God is a good shepherd. Some say that Satan has more power than God. That's not true. That's not true, though Satan has many tricks up his sleeve. When those people asked God to be shown out of the darkness, God took them by the hand and delivered them into the light of truth and onto the way of the just. Satan stood back and watched helplessly, seeing his friends, or those who used to be his friends, abandoning him. That is an example of what we call the Glory of God."

While Erik was speaking in the auditorium, Leroy was sitting and watching him on the television set in his motel room, holding his rifle in his hands, as if he were ready to fire at a moment's notice.

At a pause, Erik turned his head to the right and then to the left; suddenly the features of his face changed. He believed he had seen his son, in the back of the crowd, smiling and waving slowly. He looked again and saw again the boy suddenly stand up and run out of the auditorium. Erik closed his eyes, shook his head violently, and abruptly opened them, thinking the sighting was just an illusion that could be shaken off. The crowd noticed the change in Erik's attitude but was neither alarmed nor concerned because everyone there, who was a frequent attendant, knew that Erik, to bring a relevant point across, often moved about the stage in a restless manner, changing his face expressions to correspond with the meaning of his words. Erik blinked again and concentrated on the seat where he had seen his son; the seat was empty.

His sermon lasted one hour more, after which time Erik left the auditorium and headed for his car, parked nearby. On his way to the parking lot, Erik, still thinking of his son's appearance in the auditorium, sensed a slow moving car following him; he rushed into his car and drove hastily in its direction. He was not confused, rather angered on realizing the strange car that followed him was not an illusion, it was real. The car turned and sped away with Erik in pursuit. It was a dark night; the day had been unfavorable and at that late hour there were few people in the streets. However many there were, Erik passed in haste, without recognition. There was a little doubt he would carry out his angry intentions if he were to catch up with the speeding car. Passing other cars and running through red lights, the pursued car left Erik with no doubt he was either being led into an ambush or it was trying to evade him. As the pursuer and pursued passed the city limits, the chase accelerated to a reckless speed. Erik, incensed, caught up with the car and drove along side of it, twisting and turning, trying to catch a glimpse of the driver, but he was unable. The pursued car suddenly slammed on its brakes, Erik swerved to the left and kept on going while the other car turned to the right, heading uphill. Erik made a hasty U-turn and then an immediate left and sped to follow, but the car had disappeared. Erik pulled of the road, shifted into park with his motor still running, jumped out, looked around and realized he was by the haunted house. He advanced with swift and rapid steps, looking eagerly about, as though in quest of an expected object. Thinking again, the car he chased was not an illusion, rather, it was real, he considered the thought that the sightings of his son were not figments of his imagination, but designed with the intent to drive him insane. He suddenly felt as though he was being observed, he turned to the right and saw a figure of a man, at some distance. As Erik kept moving towards the house, he astutely monitored the man who slunk along in the deepest shadows, creeping stealthily, but never allowing himself to gain on Erik's foot steps.

When Erik finally reached the front of the house, he stopped and gazed at it for a second or two, then hastily turned back to see the figure. The movement was sudden, but whoever was watching Erik was not thrown off by it; he didn't panic, he only shrunk deeper into the bushes and leaned into them to conceal his figure. Erik hastily moved around the house and with the same speed but on a different path, headed for his car. He opened the passenger door, reached into the glove compartment and came out with his handgun. Holding the pistol in his hand he looked, listened and waited for the figure to appear, but there wasn't any trace of him. It was logical that any human sound in that desolate place was a cause for alarm. With his pistol in hand and his eyes roaming around, he noticed, a few hundred feet to his rear, a car, hidden behind the bushes. He squatted down, searching and listening for any movement. The trees rose heavy and dull from the dense mass of bushes. The haunted house was visible from where Erik was positioned; it stood, in dreariness, dark and lonely like a forgotten tombstone in the middle of an ancient graveyard. From nowhere came the sound of thunder; the wind began to moan and the leaves turned and rustled on their trees as if they sought to flee that unholy place. A peal of thunder echoed in the sky and sent down burning arrows that nearly pierced the rooftop of the haunted house. Erik was startled when his eyes caught a glimpse of a man's figure running down the hill, away from him, holding a rifle with both hands. Squatting in the same place and waiting for another flash of lighting to illuminate the figure once again; he more than once thought of giving the matter up for lost, but reconsidered, thinking the man was somewhere near, waiting for him to go to his car and would find him an easy target. The thought of becoming the hunter rather than the hunted crossed his mind, but the odds of finding him in the dark, were far too long. The likelihood of finishing the ordeal that night seemed improbable. Postponing the drama for another day, on his own terms, he thought, would be the best possible solution, believing the pursuer would strike again. He snuck behind the hidden car, carefully looked inside and when he found nothing of interest, backed off a few paces, aimed his pistol and shot twice, hitting two different tires and flattening them. He then rushed into his car and sped away.

Seeing Erik pull away, the mystery man came out into the open. Another round of thunder exploded in the darkness and more streaks of lighting shot from the sky, illuminating the man's face; it was Leroy. Running to the wounded vehicle and seeing it disabled, Leroy was unable to control his emotions. He kicked the tires, opened and slammed the doors several times, cursed his heart out and yelled his throat to shreds; and to make matters worse, the clouds burst with a vicious force and the winds blew with a vigorous freedom. Leroy, finally exhausted in vain, sat in the mud with his back leaning on a flattened tire and said loudly, "The preacher has a gun. The preacher has a Bible and a gun."

Erik found himself driving at an excessive speed through the deserted streets with unbridled emotions rushing though his confused mind. He arrived at the conclusion that he was being persecuted in a most unusual way; he had come to envision a struggling current of angry faces, illuminated with glaring torches, marching into a holy battle. It was as if an entire city poured its population, filled with wrath and passion, out into the streets with no other purpose and intent than to curse and punish him.

After speeding recklessly down the road for twenty minutes, he managed to pull his car into his home's circular driveway. He existed his car, with his mind still clouded, approached the door and suddenly froze. He pressed his ear to the door and, as though he heard a frightening ruckus inside, jumped back and just stood there, helpless, hopeless and bewildered. Deciding, after several moments, to face whatever lay on the other side, he pressed the doorbell several times, one after the other, without waiting for a response, began to pound on the door with his fists and kick it with his foot. He saw a light come on inside the front hallway, then stepped aside and watched the doorknob turning. On seeing Mary Lou come to the door in her nightgown, his heart settled and he smiled.

"What happened? Did something happen to you? Is something wrong?" asked Mary Lou, excited and confused.

"Nothing is wrong," replied Erik, forcefully, as he barged in. "Don't try to tell me there's something wrong with me, there's nothing wrong with me," he shouted, grabbing her by the nightgown and dragging her into the living room. "I said, there is nothing wrong with me." He threw her on the couch. "There is nothing wrong with me, I told you! Why don't you listen to me," he shouted.

His hands wrapped themselves around her neck and his angry face came nose to nose with hers. With wild eyes, clenched teeth and such emotion as to distort face, he exclaimed, "Tell all your friends and lovers that I am indestructible! Tell them that I will destroy them, every one of them!"

"Erik! Erik," squeaked Mary Lou, not having enough air in her lungs to scream.

He shook her violently. Suddenly he stopped; he realized what he was doing. His sudden change from cruel to timid was with no less speed than that of restrained to rage. He crawled away, as if he were escaping from harms way.

Seeing her love in a truly visible state of suffering, Mary Lou rose with regained strength and energy and following her compassionate heart, ran to where Erik had crawled. She found him curled, in a fetal position, beneath the kitchen table. Grabbing his arm with her left hand, she stroked his hair and caressed his face, forsaking any fear that he would turn and strike again.

"Erik, you 're burning up with fever. Sweetheart, I love you; let me help you. Honey, I love you so very much," she whispered, running her fingers through his hair, in an effort to soothe and calm him.

"I, I'm cold. I'm scared." He spoke faintly; his face had turned a deep crimson; he gasped for breath.

"I know, I know, honey. You'll be okay, it's alright sweetheart."

Erik's physical ailments were slight, but not so his mental condition. Haunted by the frequent visions of his son, the death of his closest friend, Peddler and the pressures of running a revival and healing ministry, his mind had reached a boiling point; it had bubbled over into fever and illusions that hung on for days and reduced him, sadly. At length, he began to recover with the kindness, caring and love of Mary Lou being the primary antidote for the poison that had overcome his mind. Although not completely recovered, but eager and anxious to get back to his normal routine, as well as to release Mary Lou from the responsibility of his care, he returned to his ministry in less than a week's time.

Standing in the wings of the TV studio, Erik was studying the new stage setting when Jonas approached with a wide smile and handed him an envelope filled with cash.

"What's this? " asked Erik, looking at the bundle of money.

"It a contribution from Smiling Sonny, the car dealer; it's thirty-two hundred. I've been carrying this around and didn't know what to do with it," replied the big man, now with an even wider smile. He stood, shifting his weight from one foot to the other as if he were waiting for a reward.

"How did you do it, Jonas?"

"I just made him understand about us folks."

Erik nodded, smiled and patted Jonas on the back.

"Now I understand," replied Erik, coolly.

"No! You don't understand," retorted Jonas, changing his features in pretence.

"Don't mess with me, Jonas, I said I understand," returned Erik, putting the money in his pocket and walking onto the stage where he took his chair.

"There's still something wrong with him," whispered Mary Lou to Jonas, after she watched Erik take his position on center stage.

"Nothing's wrong with him. I just talked to him; he's fine. It's just a little pressure," said Jonas in the same tone of voice as Mary Lou.

"One minute to show time," announced a voice over the speaker.

"I have to get out there," said Mary Lou, primping in preparedness.

"Don't worry, everything will be okay with Erik," whispered Jonas, taking a reassuring hold of her sleeve.

She looked squarely at him and nodded a hopeful smile.

Mary Lou stood at stage left, her eyes pinned on the floor director. The man with the headphone and clipboard pointed at her and nodded. She looked back at the band, gestured them to begin and as the introduction played, walked over to Erik and asked him if he'd like to sing along with her; he shook his head, negatively. The fact was that, throughout his life, Erik had never acted on anything other than impulse and, having a quick mind, this almost always was to his benefit, but now, truth be told, Erik was less than his usual self.

Mary Lou took up the joyful song. Erik, who was positioned directly behind her, didn't even look at her as she sang; he just looked down.

Delighted with her singing, the audience clapped their hands and swayed their bodies. There were heads of every color from floor to ceiling and smiles from wall to wall, most of them looked alike but none looked the same.

Among those many people, far to the rear, stood Leroy, a grimacing look molded on his face. He stood there watching Mary Lou sing. Her song style and phrasing led her to make eye contact with the entire audience, which she accomplished by turning her head gracefully and holding her eyes wide. Leroy saw that, and when her eyes were about to turn his way, he would shrink down and hide, just long enough for her eyes to pass.

Leroy's mussed and tangled blond hair rose plainly above the dense mass of heads as he frowned austerely upon Mary Lou and alternatively, Erik.

The singing girl took a few quick steps to and fro, in rhythm with the song, while Leroy closely watched her.

Jonas clapped and swayed and gradually approached Erik.

Suddenly, Leroy emerged standing, peering out over the seated crowd, his eyes fixed on the stage, a disturbed look on his face and a rifle in his hands. Without any delay, hesitation or further consideration, he broke away from the ranks and ran towards the objects of his scorn. A woman's loud scream pierced the air, but Mary Lou heard nothing, totally emerged in song. Another scream burst from the crowd, more piercing than the previous one. Jonas, hearing the scream, sprang forward towards the audience, as if to quell a disturbance. Leroy raised his rifle and aimed at the stage; the rifle jumped in his hands as he pulled the trigger. Jonas clutched his chest. Mary Lou, turning in time to see Jonas fall, screamed and fell to her knees beside Jonas' body. Erik rushed to Jonas' side, squatted next to him, looked down and said nothing. Leroy, in the confusion, ran towards the rear exit without being spotted or suspected by anyone. A roar of voices mingled in alarm and terror echoed from the panicked crowd. Uncertain where to go and what to do, bewildered by the fleeing crowd, Erik stood up, ran to the microphone, held it in his hand and froze, unable to speak a single word. The sounds of heavy footsteps, bodies falling, chairs cracking, the cries of children, the screams of women and the moaning of men combined to a din that had left him speechless. There were people everywhere, men, women and children, some standing and a few lying on the floor. Erik rushed to the band and told them to play Glory Glory Alleluia. The band started to play that familiar strain and the sound and inspiration of music overcame the fear and roar of those that remained.

"My dear friends," shouted Erik with the microphone close to him, "There has been an accident," said Erik, gesturing the band to stop, once he felt the chaos had subsided. He stood still, monitoring the crowd with a cool look.

"Lets confine ourselves to that one accident. Let us not make it a disaster. I beg of you to take your seats; listen to me and everything will be all right.'

After the lapse of nearly two minutes, the crowd's fear began to diminish, visibly. A rumor began that a firecracker, left over from the 4th of July, had been thrown on the stage as a practical joke.

Like a good shepard, feeling responsible for the well being of his flock, and for the time, oblivious of any but benevolent thoughts, Erik, who always counted on his ability to communicate with large crowds, continued his sermon.

CHAPTER THIRTEEN

Erik loses himself and Mary Lou

A few weeks after the shooting, Mary Lou sat at the kitchen table, drinking coffee, her mind overcome by unhealthy thoughts. She had conceived an idea, that had grown, not just from the shooting, but from other clues, as well. She perceived Erik as having detached himself from her. His past feelings of love had been distorted and were as a dead flower in the cold winter, only vaguely enlightening the beholder of its past glory and beauty. In Mary Lou's imagination, there was something hollow in Erik's manner, a shaded emptiness that she observed in a dusky silence. His altered manner, his frequent absences from home, his indifference towards the work for which he had once been so passionate, his desperate eagerness to leave home in the middle of the night, all favored her suspicions, but the suspicion of his dying love bore no solid support for her to act upon.

Being young and still untouched by life's trials and tribulations, she was like a craft that had never encountered gale winds or rough seas, but was only the sport of small waves and undercurrents, ones she could easily deal with. Falling in love with someone such as Erik was akin to setting a course into merciless winds and treacherous seas where even a seasoned craft could be dragged under and tossed about until it was a shattered hull.

These were the thoughts that ran through her mind. She stood up abruptly, as if she wished to escape the world of reality, went to the window, gazed out towards the pond to see Erik standing there, staring into the blue water. She thought it might be the right time to confront him and set off on the short walk.

"How much longer are you going to be like this?" asked Mary

Lou, the very moment she arrived at his side, "you've changed so much since I first met you, it scares me."

"I lost my son, then Peddler and now Jonas," said Erik, still staring into the pond; "is God trying to tell me something, Mary Lou?" asked Erik turning to face her. "Is God trying to tell me something? Is He telling me He'll take away anyone who loves me? Who killed Jonas, Mary Lou?"

Mary Lou shook her head helplessly and said, "The police will find whoever did it; I know they will."

"Am I destined to live alone? My two friends, first Peddler and then Jonas, are gone," continued Erik, "Mary Lou, if it's true that God will take anyone who loves me? What is going to happen to you? Do you know where and how I've been spending my nights?"

Mary Lou shook her head negatively, looking into his eyes with hers, flooded.

"There's a dilapidated abandoned house, a few miles from here; I go there to spend time because I've seen my son there, waving at me. Maybe it's an illusion, I can't tell, I don't know what it is" cried Erik.

She held an expression of surprise, hearing something beyond her imagination, so different than her assumptions. Mary Lou was unable to understand all the images and scenes that he spoke of, but what parts she had understood, abolished all ill thoughts and suspicions from her mind.

"Is God trying to tell me that it was my fault for everything that happened to me and I am to blame for all the people I have lost?"

"No! It's not your fault, Erik. Stop punishing yourself!" returned Mary Lou, caressing his face with a trembling hand.

"Mary Lou, I caused them to die. I've done so many things in my life that started out with good intentions but somehow they turned out all wrong."

As he said those words, his face turned half around, as to be visible to her; he seemed, by his expression, to hint he was desirous of hearing her answer.

"Stop it! Stop it!" shouted Mary Lou " you can't blame yourself for any of your losses."

She tried, in compassion and with her deepest love, to ease his troubled mind, to free him from dreadful thoughts of himself, but her efforts were in vain.

"There is something in me," cried Erik, as if he hadn't heard a word she said; he began to recite.

"Who is inside of me that makes me sing the wrong song,
Who is inside of me that does not know the right from wrong,
Who is inside of me that makes me fall in love with the wrong one,
When things don't work out, he laughs as if nothing was done.
Who is inside of me that makes my kinfolks and friends cry.
Half of him wants me to live, the other half wants me to die."
Erik stopped there.

Mary Lou, trembling with impatience, cried, "Yes! Yes, yes, now you're on the right track, honey. Go on! Erik, finish your poem."

Erik stared back at her with vacant look on his face.

Then Mary Lou began reciting the end of his poem.

"I am going to search and find him, there is no doubt.
I am going to chase him until he is completely out.
Will I be dry and empty when he goes away?
Will all my days be the same as if only one day?
What happens if he is right and I happen to be wrong?
Then I should go on and keep singing the same song.
Because whether he's wrong or whether he's right,
At least I know singing his song, I'll make it through the night," concluded Mary Lou, looking at him with a grin of accomplishment.

"You know my poem," returned Erik, surprised.

"I know and love all your poems Erik. Stay as you are. You can't change," said Mary Lou, touching his face. Filled with uneasiness on seeing his fixation, all Mary Lou could think of was to lead him to another subject that might serve to dismiss his feelings of guilt. "Come on, let's have an old fashioned Greek party, the kind you've told me about. I know you'll love it and I will too."

It was some days later and nearly three hours before daybreak, the time which, in the winter of the year, may be truly called the dead of night; when the streets are silent and deserted, when even sound appears to slumber, and recklessness, revolt, turbulence and unrest have staggered off somewhere to sleep. Erik's home had been turned into a place of frolicking, skipping, hopping and cavorting where over thirty people let down their hair and kicked up their heels to a five-piece band playing Greek music. It was a party of cheerful voices and merry laughter that some would dream of for many nights to come and would recall, in conversation, for many months. As every good thing in life must finally come to an end, the party was beginning to wind down. Erik, having not been the center of the group's attention, felt that he had purposely been pushed aside, so, at the conclusion of the band's last number and in the midst of vigorous applause, he went over to the young dark-haired Greek singer and asked her to dance, alone on the floor.

"I'm paid to be a singer, not a dancer," responded the young woman, rebelliously.

"You're paid to be what I want you to be," retorted Erik, pulling out a roll of bills from his pocket, "come on, take your singing clothes off and belly dance. Come on!" shouted Erik, throwing bills at her by the bunch, "I said come on!"

She stood there, gazed at Erik, with a vague grin, then nodded at the band. The musicians struck up a traditional Greek dance song; she started moving her hips, gyrating with the music and began to unbutton her blouse until her bra and naval were exposed. Erik began to move along, dancing close to her. After two or three choruses, she slid off her blouse and threw it in Erik's face; he grabbed it and wrapped it around his neck. The guests watched her dance around the room with Erik close behind, shoving bills in her bra. Mary Lou stood there, petrified, watching sadly. The Bouzouki was the main instrument of that particular tune and suddenly the player stopped strumming in the middle of the song and the rest of the band followed suit. Erik, alarmed and confused, ran to them.

"What are you doing? You're not done yet!" he shouted, looking at them one by one with furious features.

"We are finished," said the bouzouki player, softly, preparing to put his instrument into its case.

"You're finished when I say you're finished," shouted Erik, getting closer to the music man and with indignation. With the sense of having gone too far to be forgiven, Erik was about to go further by charging against the musician. Seeing what was about to happen, Mary Lou dashed to his side, grabbed Erik by the arm and pulled him away with the help of two other guests.

"Now calm down, Erik," said Mary Lou, caressing his face as if to smooth his rumpled feathers.

Finding himself staring at Mary Lou for too long a moment, Erik directed his attention, for an instant, at the hapless bouzouki player then brought his eyes back to Mary Lou. "Go ahead! Let the bastards go!" he shouted, walking away.

The musicians and the singer, come dancer, hurried out the front door.

Finding himself in the middle of the floor, Erik looked down, raised his right hand to his lips, as if he were absorbed in deep thought, then turned and faced Mary Lou, who was on the opposite side of the room.

"Turn on the record player Mary Lou, turn the record player on!" he yelled.

"Erik, calm down!" she returned.

"I said turn it on!" shouted Erik, with the strongest voice he had.

"No!" yelled Mary Lou back; she looked back at him in fury, as if she wished she could knit her fingers into his hair, shake him, pull him, drag him for a half a mile in the street and beat him until he was too weak to move and too scared to speak.

Hearing these words and not taking a notice of the fire in her eyes as most men, in control of their senses, would have, he walked across to where she standing and spoke as if there were a lump in his throat. "No? Mary Lou, you said, no, to me?" overtaken by surprise.

"You can't control everybody all the time, Erik."

Without saying anything else or thinking of anything else to do or say, he ran to the front door and threw the lock. He then sped from window to window and repeated the process of locking them, while his guests watched, amused and astonished. Erik then stood in the middle of the room, looked around without changing his attitude in the least, and declared, in an oratorical voice and style, "When Moses stood on top of the mountain holding the Ten Commandments in his hands, he said, 'if you don't wish to live with these commandments, with them you shall die.' He glanced inquisitively around the room, and again facing sharply towards

Mary Lou, grasped his guitar that was leaning near the door, as if taking it up to play and smashed it against the wall. If he had any thoughts of not being the center of attention, they were speedily dispelled by the demeanor of all present. Oaths, threats and exclamations were not vented, but contempt and abhorrence were exhibited on the face of every man and every woman in the room. He saw it, felt it and was puzzled and confused.

Seeing the hurt on his face, Mary Lou ran to him and threw her arms around him in a clear effort to tell him that she forgave his actions, but he pushed her away and stood dauntlessly, scanning his guests.

"Go ahead!" yelled Erik, suddenly taking on a new attitude, with distorted features, "Let them out of my coral!" After a long pause, he realized that he had gone far enough and couldn't go any further, so he retreated and sank down on the floor.

A complete silence overtook the house. There was no clamor to subside, no music to stop, no playing and no speaking, only the sound of rushing footsteps as the guests dashed out the door. When the rooms became empty, Erik stood up, without dusting himself, without looking for anything or anybody and walked away, as if in the pursuit of a different agenda.

"Erik, where are you going?" asked Mary Lou.

Erik stopped, turned around very slowly and stared at her with a vague smile, "I, my dear lady, have been treated by all of you as an apprentice, not as a master, as a slave, not as the victim of your tyrannical behavior, as a home breaker, not the mender of problems, not as the healer of wounds but as one afflicted, and you, you my dear love, behold in me as an enslaver, not as a lover."

"Erik, you're wrong about that. We all know and see the greatness in you," said Mary Lou, who by now knew it was a high time for him to seek help, to be brought back to reality and to stop punishing himself out of guilt.

Erik heard nothing, as if he had rented out his ears, exclusively, to his own thoughts.

"You asked me where I am going. I am too old to go find myself, so my only hope is to lose myself."

"Erik! Please!" said Mary Lou, rushing towards him.

"Shh! Stay away for one more moment. I must go and loose

myself in the densest forest I can find. I won't stop until I come to the most out of way spot I can set my eyes on and I'll stay there until whoever is inside of me dies and sets me free," he said, as if voicing a real plan.

Staring at him and seeing he showed every sign of one who was dangling over the precipice of reality, Mary Lou ran to him, threw her arms around and begged him not to leave, not just yet, she emphasized.

Erik capitulated and without spitting out another word, sigh or blink of an eye, went upstairs to their bedroom.

She was both pleased and surprised with his sudden change of demeanor and his not storming out into the night, but whether he was overtaken with common sense or had made different plans, was yet to be seen.

CHAPTER FOURTEEN

A voice from Heaven—
The final chapter

The following night, Mary Lou entered their bedroom and found Erik in bed, fully clothed, dressed in the same suit he had on the day before, laying on his back and staring at the ceiling. She noticed an unusual paleness in his cheeks and fire in his eyes. That sight sent chills up and down her spine. She planted a tender kiss on his forehead, but it was ignored.

Erik sat up on the edge of the bed, resting his elbows on his knees and his chin on his hands; he remained that way, as if frozen in thought. Mary Lou, a few paces away, watched him and tried to read his mind. Although she could not determine his thoughts, she was certain that each one contained the sense of guilt, the fear of losing and the dread of living. These thoughts, in any mortal's mind, could gnaw at the heart of all pleasure, blur all beauty, dilute all music, dull the tastes and blacken all dreams. Guilt, fear and dread can invade ones mind and be constant companions, not only in the dark of night, but in broad sunny days, in the twilight and in the light of fire, in the dullness of smoke, in company and in solitude. These thoughts bear no glory, only criticism, no victory, only defeat, no respect, only persecution.

Mary Lou turned a wistful and inquisitive face towards him, but he continued to meditate, without acknowledging her presence.

"Erik, my love, what can I do to make you feel better? Should I go down on my knees and pray to heaven for help, in our hour of need? Would you feel better if I go down on my knees and ask you to forgive me for whatever you think I've done wrong. Tell me, Erik, what can I do?"

"I want you to leave this house," replied Erik, in a deep and horrifying voice, without raising his face to hers.

"Why? Because I love you? That's crazy," said Mary Lou, taken by surprise.

Suddenly, Erik got up, rushed out of the room and ran to the kitchen table where her purse was placed, grabbed it angrily and then grabbed Mary Lou, who had followed him. Holding her tightly, he forcefully escorted her out the front door, throwing her purse behind her. When she was completely out of the house, he slammed the door and locked it from inside.

"Erik, Erik. I didn't say you're crazy," said Mary Lou, pounding the door weakly. Erik stood inside the door, confused and silent, as if he had lost his ability to think.

"Erik. Erik I'm sorry. Please, Erik. I don't want to live without you," she cried.

Hearing her pleas, he turned, looked at the closed door, checked its lock again and headed for the kitchen where he took a chair at the table, only to stare straight ahead. From the kitchen, he was still able to hear Mary Lou's pleadings. He stared straight ahead with smooth features, a look that might have indicated his heart was softened by her distress, or it might have been he felt, to some degree, indignant in that the woman he loved was struggling while he remained in the grasp of madness. In any event, he still remained unchanged, unmoved, unaffected and silent.

Mary Lou who, after pleading, sat down in front of the door with her head resting against it, sobbed loudly.

"Erik, please let me in," she begged, faintly.

It was a beautiful evening when the first shades of twilight were beginning to settle upon the earth and Mary Lou, exhausted, with her head still resting on the door, pleading faintly now and then, gradually and by slow degrees, fell asleep, in a true effort to escape from that dreadful hour. It was the kind of sleep that fell upon her that, while it held the body prisoner, did not free the mind from trouble and worry. She mumbled on, sometime in whispers, and although nothing of her ramblings was distinguishable, beyond a few disjointed words here and there, they seemed a blend of reality and imagination.

She remained in that state of mind and body until darkness set in, then opened her eyes and realized where she was and what she was doing. Standing up, she dusted herself timidly, with trembling hands, and headed for her car. She sat in the car, shivering and crying for a while longer, desperately trying to get her thoughts together, then started the car, leaned back for a moment, sighed deeply and wiped her tears with a tissue. The car slid as she pulled back then skidded onto the main road; she drove away. The moment the car had gained the momentum of a regular speed, another car, following behind, turned on its headlights and took up the pursuit of Mary Lou, to wherever her destination might be. After a few minutes, she pulled into the parking lot of a motor lodge; the car that had been following did the same, but kept a monitoring distance away. Mary Lou checked in at office. There were a great number of cars in the lot, but one older black car, evidently the one that followed her, was parked further back and stood out from the others. Leroy sat there, smoking and watching, as she came from the Motor Lodge's office. She was about to turn her room's key in the lock when Leroy appeared besides her, discreetly concealing a rifle under a raincoat.

"Get in there! Go on!" whispered Leroy, pushing her into the room.

Not knowing or what to do or where to go, Mary Lou, once she entered the room with Leroy right behind her, broke away and went behind the dresser, clinging onto its side. She felt her face flush and she began to sob, while Leroy paced around the room, holding the rifle, as if waiting for something to happen. He then suddenly stopped, threw a glance at Mary Lou and moved close to her. Turning the rifle on her, he spoke, angrily, "you shouldn't have done this to me, Mary Lou; you shouldn't have done this. Why did you do it? Why did you leave me, knowing that I love you? You knew I loved you. I tried to forget you, but I can't. So if I can't have you, nobody will. I promised that I would kill you and your lover boy. Do you remember that promise I made to both of you?"

"I still love you, Leroy. He doesn't mean anything to me," cried Mary Lou, reaching to touch Leroy, but he turned and walked away, slowly.

"Do you know how long I've waited for this moment to come?" questioned Leroy, laying his hand upon her arm, "a long time, since the first day I saw you with that lover boy walking you home. Up to that time, I had never thought of killing any man or woman. I had never been placed in a situation that it made it worth my while. Killing your boy friend though will make me happy for the rest of my life."

"Leroy!" exclaimed Mary Lou.

"Shut up!" he ordered, tightening his hand under her chin, "I'm talking. I'll tell you what I want to do, before I kill you, I want to kill him, with my knife. I want to see him scared of me, I want to see him looking at the knife he knows is gonna kill him. I'll go closer and closer to him with my knife in my hand. Do I want to see him die? Oh, yeah, I can see it now. After I put my knife in his belly, he'll stagger back into the wall, bleeding inside; he'll stand there, not fall, dying inside, but not dead yet. Then I'm gonna drag him out back, to the pond. I'll roll him in, hold his face in the water and listen to the bubbles that'll mark his last breath. Then, Will I go home? No, hell no, I'll come back here and repeat the same thing on you. I'll look in your eyes, while you're losing hope for life and I'll hear your last breath, coming up in bubbles."

"Leroy, I love you," tried Mary Lou.

"You lying bitch," exclaimed Leroy, turning and walking away in almost a trance. He suddenly stopped, glanced back at Mary Lou, as if he had just remembered something he had forgotten.

"Wait a minute. I'm thinking; for the first time since you went away, I'm beginning to think for myself. I'll kill you and then I'll fasten your murder on him. I'll kill him too. I'm gonna put the gun in your hand, to make the cops think that you killed each other after he caught me in this room with you. And I'll live happily ever after, knowing that both of you died, like I told you."

"I love you Leroy," pleaded Mary Lou, desperately trying to pacify him until some miracle might happen.

"You love me?"

"Yes I do."

"Oh, sure, you just kept it a secret," returned Leroy, disgusted with what he was hearing.

"It was no secret, darling, I always wanted to marry you. I told everybody. Everybody knew it, including Erik. There was no secret."

"You lying bitch, you even tell stories, like your lover boy," said Leroy, surveying her from head to foot with a lofty scorn. "Now you love me, now that you're about to die you love me. Now you're coming up with words of love. They're all four letter words at this stage of the game," continued Leroy, raising his right hand to shake a trembling finger at her.

Seemingly, he wanted to continue talking, but his passion was so great that the power of speech escaped him. Mary Lou then realized there were no words left for her to say. There were no more words that could remodel Leroy's mind that lay in ruin.

Without conscious thought, but as a natural reaction to dire fear she exclaimed, "don't do anything stupid, Leroy. Don't lose me now that you found me. If you kill him they'll put you in jail for the rest of your life. What will I do without you, Leroy?" she cried.

"You're too late to give advice, bitch; I'm a gonner. I'm the one who killed Jonas, so my life is over. I didn't mean to kill him," he stopped for a moment to renew his anger, "I meant to kill your lover boy."

With his nostrils flaring and chest heaving, he grabbed her by the hair, dragged her into the middle of the room and placed the barrel of the rifle against her skull.

"Please Leroy, spare my life and. I will always be with you, forever," gasped the girl, wrestling, with the strength of mortal fear. "Leroy, I left him for you. Why do you think I'm here? I knew you killed Jonas. The police asked me and I didn't tell them in order to spare your life, now please, Leroy, spare mine," cried the girl.

"It's too late, Mary Lou. It's way too late for both of us. Lady luck is gone for me and you," said Leroy with a drowned voice and quivering lip, "your lover boy will die, you will die and I will die, one after the other, and in a very short time. I've changed my mind about living."

Erik drove up slowly and scanned parking lot of the motel where Mary Lou was held hostage. He looked at room 105, the one he and Mary Lou had shared, and saw her car in front of it. With his radio blasting Greek songs, he pulled his car in next to hers. Mary Lou, from inside, heard the familiar tunes, but Leroy didn't seem to notice them. Erik seemed to have returned to the world of the sane. He was dressed and ready for his performance at the auditorium, not far from the motor lodge. He exited the car, leaving the door open, and walked to room 105, where he stood for a moment, his right hand ready to knock. He then changed his mind, returned to his car, closed the door and sat there wondering what he should do.

Leroy suddenly became aware of Mary Lou's change in demeanor, looked once towards the door then quickly wrapped his rough hand over her mouth. She bit the hand of her captor; Leroy screamed and held his injured hand with the other, fixed in disbelief. That instant gave her just long enough to spring to her feet. She ran to the door and pounded it with both hands, screaming Erik's name. Erik, still sitting there, wondering, heard nothing; he pulled away with reckless abandon.

"You bitch! I'll kill you," shouted Leroy, striking her on the head with his fist. Mary Lou went down. He dragged her by the hair and sprawled her on a couch. He then leaned his rifle on the wall a few feet from her, stood back, took a pistol from his belt and aimed it at the girl.

"Go ahead and say you prayers, bitch; reach for the rifle, and shoot me before I shoot you. I know you'll never love me; I don't want to live. You don't want to live with me, then, die with me! But first, say your prayers." shouted Leroy, looking at his left hand where she had bitten him. "I heard your lover boy say once, in one of his phony TV sermons, 'a prayer on the verge of death is not answered. Go ahead and pray to God to save you from me. Maybe your lover boy was lying."

Erik approached the auditorium. The car stopped, he got out and an attendant drove the car away while Erik went inside. He strode onto the stage, looked at the audience and listened to the band playing a familiar gospel hymn, 'Nearer My God To Thee.' He took the microphone in his hands and looked at the band.

"Stop the music! Stop the music!" He stood there staring at the band as if he were counting its members. Do you want to see a monster come to life? Do you? Well, do you want to see a monster come take me?" shouted Erik with his eyes still aimed towards the band. "Look, listen, see him," he said, as he remained motionless, thoughtless and staring at the band. He then turned away from the band and cast his eyes on the crowd.

"I'm overjoyed to see over a thousand eyes aimed at me and over a thousand ears perked in my direction to hear what I have to say. Ladies and gentlemen, I stand before you, here today, to tell you something about myself. I am a spiteful man; I am a man who seeks revenge; I am a man who never finishes anything, because nothing turns out right. I destroy everything I start and everyone I hold dear. I am a man who derives pleasure from being sick as long as others are aggravated by my sickness, so I refuse medical treatment out of spite. I believe that I am a man with too much consciousness and consciousness is a disease. The more conscious I become of goodness, the more I sink into evil. I'm a man who believes that all that has happened to him, and is still happening, was caused by outside interference from others, like you. I want you to see my infirmities if only to upset you. All of you suffer with infirmities, but most of you hide them away, not boast of them. You may not even acknowledge them, because you have never taken the time to consider what they are. I used to think that it was I, who had created my unhappiness, until I met you. No matter how many sons God sends down, or how many daughters, he will never be able to remodel or reform your world. God is not wasting his wrath with words; He acts upon his wrath. He tried once, with the flood, to abolish evil, and then with plagues and natural disasters, all to make you repent, but you're incorrigible. God sent you Moses. He sent down his only son. He enlightened and then posted, throughout the world, evangelists like me. Yet you continue to beat the same drum and sing the same song, from generation to generation. All your lives, from cradle to grave, you have lived among liars, and liars you have become. All your lives you have lived among thieves, and you have learned to be as them. All your lives you have lived among the greedy, and avarice has overcome you. You have been raised and live with violence, and have grown into violent creatures. Every one of you has been raised by non-believers and you have turned out just like them. Them, them, I say again are your parents. You are all hopeless sinful animals. You have all sided with Satan and you have become worse than he. At least Satan sits quietly in the presence of God. When God walks away from Satan's corner with one of you in hand, Satan sits back and says nothing. You see me as a man of God, that I am, but because I am one of you, I have infirmities. When I tried to remove you from Satan's corner, to show you the way to God's side, you turned against me; now it's time for me to turn against you. I told you before when I begin something and if it doesn't turn out the way I envisioned it, I destroy it. Today, I will prove one of your infirmities, violence. As I look at your eyes, I see them as small, harmless spots in the middle of your ugly faces..."

The audience, hearing this, but not completely comprehending the meaning of his rage, were growing restless. Erik turned and faced the band again. "Do you want to hear the monster growl? Listen to the monster come alive." He placed a hand on his ear, pretending to listen. "Hear the monster getting ready to strike out at me," he said softly.

The musicians looked back and forth at one another, astounded; some shrugged their shoulders in disbelief, all remained wordless.

He turned to the crowd again. "Your eyes are small, but when they unite for the kill, they become one big eye, belonging to one huge, harmful, heartless monster. I can see it now; it's growing and growing. Come on, monster! I am a man of God, but I am just like you, a monster." Then, from that moment on, everything changed. The audience was transfixed, stupefied. Erik pulled out his pistol from its holster and started waving it in the air and pointing it at the crowd. He then declared, loudly, "I am like Moses. This pistol is the enforcer of the Ten Commandments. If you don't wish to live according to the Commandments, with this pistol, you shall die. His face turning red with rage, he continued, "Come on! I said, come on monster! Come and get me! I want to see you grow and grow, come on I said, yelled the Evangelist.

Security guards rushed onto the stage. Erik jumped onto the rail around the musicians' platform. The musicians scattered. Erik was screaming and waving his pistol. At first a current of people had been confined to the pathways exiting the auditorium; after a while the passages were completely blocked by the eager stragglers and the outside had become just as chaotic. The crowd was roaring.

Some people were running out, some were heading towards him and some just watched him swagger on the rail, waiting for him to fall. Finally he slipped. A policeman grabbed him from behind, restored him to a standing position and pulled his arms behind him. Erik was still raving and uttering curses and threats. The roaring crowd charged after him. The police and security guards pushed them away, while Erik managed to slide out of their hold. He mingled with the people, threw away his jacket, put on a hat, snatched off someone's head, and sped, unnoticed, out of the auditorium. Some forty or fifty of the most violent and trouble prone men, without the slightest preparation, ventured out into the streets where they gathered, planned, and designed the further pandemonium that was to follow. Their numbers were rapidly increasing with newcomers, who had gone there, as spectators. They soon divided up into posses, agreeing to hunt down the imposter, and scoured the town in various directions. When Erik reached the outside and ran about one hundred yards from the main entrance, he slunk down against a closed door and looked on as the crowd poured out, in droves. He then turned to the right, began to run and didn't stop until he felt safely far enough away from the near riot he had created. He looked back and saw that some were running behind him without paying him the slightest attention. After a while, he slowed down, began to walk normally and stepped aside to allow other to pass. One posse, of about fifty angry men, crossed to the other side of a small bridge where a shopping area began, but the shops were closed because it was Sunday. Some shopkeepers who lived in the immediate area, alarmed and scared on seeing the crowd, rushed to protect their doors and windows. In the upper stories, all the inhabitants looked down from their windows into the packed streets, below. The pursuers all claimed they were after the blaspheming evangelist and were banded together to fight whoever opposed the religion of their country. Erik walked stealthily among them, unrecognized, listening in silence.

As time went on, the accounts of what had happened became more dire and mysterious. Quite often, someone would fly by and yell to inform the innocent public of additional groups of rioters heading their way, not far behind. Property owners began to shut and bar their property with whatever means were available to them. In short, the city was as if invaded by a foreign army. Erik walked into an open door, ran up a staircase to a window and peered out over the crowd. Some of the rioters held flashlights, some lit torches that made their faces distinctly visible in the flames. It became apparent the crowd was intent on destruction; their target was the Church of Saint Andrews. Many other rioters began to break doors and windows; the looting began. Fifty trained men could have stopped them or a single platoon of soldiers could have dispersed them, but not even one man interposed, there was no authority to restrain the agitated. It was apparent that every law and civil order had vanished. Divided into parties that swelled as they went along, the crowd was not unlike a river, out of control but still winding its way to the sea, though not before leaving a wake of destruction. Stricken with another thought, Erik began to run, alone, in a different direction and didn't stop running until he reached the motor lodge where May Lou's car was parked. When he reached the door of room 105, he screamed her name.

Hearing Erik's screams and disregarding Leroy, Mary Lou ran for the door. Leroy grabbed her from behind and struggled to keep her back. Unable to hold her, he grabbed his pistol from his belt. Mary Lou, seeing the pistol aimed at her, let out a piercing scream, calling Erik's name. She did not know Erik was but a few feet from the door, and he, lost in thought, heard nothing. Leroy tackled Mary Lou, overpowered her and came down mercilessly on her face with the grip of his pistol. On impact, blood rushed out as if waiting for a place and time to exit. To reassure himself of having done her in, he imparted another blow to the other side of her head. Her body lay collapsed at his feet. Erik knocked on the door again, stood back, waited calmly, but on hearing no response, walked away again. Cracking open the door, Leroy saw Erik walking slowly to his car. He hastily closed the door, swallowed his saliva and peered down at bloodied female form at his feet. He held his pistol, pointed, as if expecting her to come to life and fight back.

Shortly thereafter, there was another knock. On hearing it, Leroy turned pale and desperate, feeling a confrontation was at hand. He spun in turns around the room with no purpose in mind, but realized his end was near.

"Mary Lou sweetheart, open the door. I have something to tell you. I need to tell you something terrible has happened in town and all the people have turned on one another," began Erik, with his mouth close to the door. "Mary Lou I want to tell you this place is being watched, they're out to get us. I'll protect you; I'll stand her by the door and keep them away. I'll keep you safe; don't worry. Don't stand by the window or the door, they may see you and if you're not one of them, they'll hurt you. They just burned down Saint Andrews Church."

Hearing those words, Leroy became more confused and said loudly, "You're crazy, I know how to handle drunks, but not nuts." He rushed around the room, as if looking for a place to hide. He ran into the bathroom, looked around for a moment and backed out into the room; he placed his pistol on the lamp table, took hold of Mary Lou's feet, dragged her into the bathroom, closed the door, firmly grasped his pistol and stood ready by the door.

Knocking gently on the door, Erik said again, "Mary Lou, I'll stand guard here, I'll protect you, honey, do you hear me? All the town's people have gone crazy, they're wild, they out to hang all the preachers. Boy, am I glad I'm not a preacher, Mary Lou." He paused for an instant, then took a seat on the doorstep, placed his elbows on his knees and looked off in the direction from which he had come.

Loud shouts and the singing of psalms posted the advance of a great body of men. A large number of people, by this time, had taken to singing and when their self-appointed leader passed proudly between the ranks, his followers raised their voices to their utmost, obviously to curry his favor. Many of those who pledged to fight, even to their death, had never sung a hymn or read a psalm in all their lives and most had never laid eyes on their leader before, but they followed him and sang their songs. And so they went on, breaking shop windows, smashing down doors, going in empty-handed and existing laden with merchandise, some of which they had no conceivable use for, but claimed as the spoils of a holy war. Eventually, they became an organized body of rioters and looters; their sounds echoed through the air and could not have failed to further stir the hearts of the enthusiasts, however wrong or mistaken their actions might have been.

Erik stood up and knocked on the door. "Mary Lou, please open the door, I need you to forgive me," he said, sullenly. Suddenly the opened half way and Leroy's face appeared.

"Who are you? Asked Erik, curiously, "Where is Mary Lou? I'm sorry, I must have knocked on the wrong door," he continued, turning to leave.

"No you don't, she's in here," mumbled Leroy, shoving his pistol in his belt and wrapping his raincoat around him. He paused, looked at Erik, open the door wide and allowed Erik to enter.

"Where is Mary Lou?" asked Erik, scanning the room. His eyes focused on Leroy, whom he did not recognize, "Where is Mary Lou? I've come to save her from Satan's flock."

"What are you talking about? Whose flock? Man, you're nuts," was Leroy's response.

"Eh cowboy, what's the matter; haven't you heard? Ha, ha, ha," joked Erik.

"What do you think you're laughing at, jerk?" replied Leroy.

Erik stared at Leroy long enough to realize he was serious and finally declared, "I know you, you're Leroy. How have you been, Leroy?" continued Erik, offering his hand to shake. Leroy stepped back, more confused than ever. "I am Erik Karas, you may not remember me, but we had a little squabble some time ago, outside Mary Lou's trailer home," explained Erik, now embarrassed and pulling his hand back.

"I remember you," returned Leroy, through clenched teeth.

"Good, I'd like to ask you to forgive me and now tell me where's she hiding," stated Erik, heading for the bathroom door.

"Hold it!" shouted Leroy.

Erik looked back at him and seeing the pistol aimed at his torso, asked, "What's that? You have a gun? Disregarding both Leroy and the pistol, Erik opened the bathroom door, rushed to Mary Lou, lifted her hand, checked her pulse and then slowly stood. He came from the bathroom, dazed, with more sadness than anger on his face.

"You killed her! You killed her! May God strike you dead, Leroy," said Erik, shaking his finger at him, as if it were a match for a gun.

"I'm not proud of anything I ever done, but I'm gonna be proud when I kill you," said Leroy, spitting out the words while holding aim on Erik.

Seeming not to comprehend Leroy's response, Erik moved closer to him and said, in a sullen manner, "you're in big trouble now, Leroy. You're in trouble with God!"

They stood there, face to face, glaring at each other, equally insane. Leroy was the first to speak. "You're nuts," he declared, simply.

Erik suddenly became infuriated, struck out with his fist and caught Leroy on the jaw. Leroy jerked back and held the pistol even tighter, pointed at Erik's chest. Erik hit the floor just as Leroy pulled the trigger; the bullet missed but hit a mirror, shattering it into tiny pieces that flew around the room. Leroy turned and was ready to shoot again, but Erik jumped forward and grabbed onto his arm. Leroy still managed to hold the pistol. Ignoring the gun, Erik grabbed him by the throat with both hands and shook him, violently, while kneeing his groin again and again. Panting for breath, Leroy stammered for a word with his opponent and in that one instant saw the torrent of Erik's wrath unleashed upon him.

Leroy, who only a moment earlier, with a gun in his hand, felt powerful and unbeatable, wished there was a way to hide from Erik's madness. Erik beat him, unmercifully, kicking his legs and body while pounding his head against the wall. Blood began to run from Leroy's mouth and nose, his face turned pale then white, but Erik kept pounding until the body grew heavy against his fists and there was no longer a sign of life. Leroy's body slumped to the floor, a broken sack of blood and bones.

"I told you, you were in trouble with God, but you didn't listen to me," said Erik, panting over Leroy's lifeless carcass. He slowly moved to the bathroom where Mary Lou lay. He lifted her gently and placed her on the bed. Standing above, his eyes a blur, he could only think enough to say, "you're in heaven now, darling."

While Leroy was being beaten to death, back at the auditorium, a large crowd, separate from the ones that had taken to the streets to loot and destroy everything in their way, had gathered around the Sheriff. That officer of the law, now challenged with the prospect of the community being destroyed under his watch, conversed with other policemen, some of who were on radiophones.

"We have a report from the Holiday Inn, there's been gunshots and Karas's car was spotted in the parking lot. The shots were reported in room 105, a Mary Lou something was registered there," reported one officer, with his radio still at his ear.

"Good report, let's go check it out. The only way to stop the riot is to get Karas, he's what they want," declared the Sheriff. He then took his car's microphone in his hand, turned the loudspeakers up and proceeded to address the crowd.

"Calm down! Calm down! It's over," yelled the Sheriff, gesturing with his free hand, in case the listeners weren't sure what he meant. The crowd continued to roar. The Sheriff had no choice but to fire his service revolver in the air to get their attention. The shot had the effect he desired. He continued, "I want you all to go back to your homes, lock your doors and stay inside until we apprehend the Evangelist. We received a report that gunshots were heard not far from here. The man is armed and dangerous. We need you all to stay out of the way, let us do our jobs. We don't need your help; we don't want any more people hurt. Those crowds on the streets will be broken up very soon. We don't want to have to arrest any more people. Just go home." The crowd, though hearing his words, did not leave, just grew angrier than before. The police got into their cars, turned on their sirens and sped away. The crowd followed, some in cars, some on foot.

It could not be known if his brutal murder of Leroy had any effect on Erik, his mind was so twisted that the only feelings left in him were those of self-preservation. He calmly moved the drape aside, to see if his car was still in the lot, where he left it. His face bore neither a sign of remorse nor a hint of the consideration of his crime and likely punishment. The bright moonlight shone through window and landed on the bodies, one of the woman carefully placed on the bed and the other of a man, contorted in a ghastly fashion, on the floor. Erik could hear sirens in the distance; they were approaching. Understanding the pursuers he had eluded were not far off, he bolted through the door and took off, at full speed, for the wooded area, across the road from the motel. Once he reached the darkness of the woods, he felt safe, hidden and out of danger. He looked back and saw police cars pull into the lot and his room lit by their spotlights. He ran swiftly up a hill and down the other side. He crossed a wooden bridge. He remained steady of purpose and sure of his destination. He took a footpath that ended in front of a dilapidated shed; he became confused, fear etched into his features as the wind came up in gusts, behind him. It sounded like a human, moaning. He threw a quick glance behind him, just to make sure, but the wind caught his ear and drilled its way into his brain. He began to run, in a circle, around the shed, looking for a place to hide from the excruciating sounds, holding his ears with his hands, screaming. He looked down and saw a child's sweater tangled around his feet. He fell to his knees, buried his face in the dirt and tightened his body, hoping the moans, the wind and the vision would end. As suddenly as it came on, the wind stopped, all became as silent as death.

He slowly raised his head and saw before him, a gravestone. His son's name was on it, etched in fresh, red, running blood. He sprang to his feet, ran for the shed, squatted in a corner, wrapped his arms around his knees, buried his head and stayed there, shivering. More than a few minutes later he stopped trembling and unraveled himself. Gaining what could be mistaken for a normal composure, he said aloud, " It's safe here now, it's nice and safe. The Lord wants me to stay here, to keep away from Satan and his people. When the Lord tells me they are gone, I will leave and go back home."

No sooner had he uttered those words, than the wind began to moan again. The dismal wail poured in through every crack and open board in the shed, rattling tools that had not been touched in half a century. A white misty cloud crept in, under the door; it lingered over the dirt floor. In a feeble attempt to hide, he covered his eyes with his arm, but peeked out to see, in the middle of the mist, his son, standing there, looking back at him. The wind's moan was coming from Randy's figure, and his eyes were more pronounced than any feature of his body.

"Daddy, I'm going to heaven, I'm going to heaven," moaned the wind emitted from Randy's form.

The image suddenly disappeared, along with the mist. Erik followed it, with his eyes, as it made its way towards the hill. He hastily came to his feet and went to the door, but before he reached the handle, he saw Randy's body, placed in a coffin, set on the floor. In his desperate attempt to touch it, Erik tripped. He struggled to get up, only to find the coffin and his son were gone, but looking out, ahead, he saw the mist heading slowly up the hill and behind it, the priest, in a black robe. The white spirit beckoned him to follow. He ran to it, trembling, cold, with sweat dripping from every pore. When he reached the top of the hill, he lost sight of the mist and the priest but, to his surprise, found himself only a few hundred feet from the haunted house. The moaning had stopped, but he heard a distant roar, angry voices, filled with fury, coming fast. Gathering his strength, he ran for the haunted house. He bounded up its steps, threw open the door and scurried for a place to hide. Without any hesitation, he impulsively ran to the top of the stairs, entered a room and lay down on a single bed, empty save a mattress and pillow. As he curled himself on the bed, shivering and hoping to escape the oncoming crowd, he felt a thousand spirits haunting him. Then the mist faintly appeared, on the side of his pillow, rising from the floor, white, becoming more and more visible at the head of the bed, at the foot of the bed, behind the half-opened closet door, on the floor, the ceiling and everywhere he looked. He jumped up and ran down the hallway, to a window, looked out and saw the crowd coming towards him. Somehow they knew he was there; they reached the front door, some still carrying torches, some with flashlights. They hesitated on entering the house because the word had spread that it might collapse from the weight of too many intruders. Some chose to stay outside, running back and forth as if to stir the pot of agitation. Of all the shouts that had ever fallen on mortal ears, the most dreadful were from those who had come for vengeance that night, not surprisingly, they were the same ones who earlier had gone to hear the Evangelist pour forth the word of God, indeed they were the ones who felt deceived and cheated by God himself. The nearest voices took up the cry and hundreds echoed it. Some called for ladders, some for sledges, some suggested to shoot and others to set the house afire. Among them all, there was not one mortal that held in his mind, any goodness, compassion or pity for the man who was their Evangelist.

Erik, gaining new strength and courage, stimulated by the roaring crowd, threw open the door and stepped onto the balcony. He moved slowly around the turret, shouting curses and threats to the crowd below, "Damn you; damn you to hell, all of you. Go with Satan, follow him; he's what you want."

There was confusion on the ground, some tried to get closer to the door, others tried only to extricate themselves from the mass of humanity, hungry for blood. Voices drifted up to Erik. He heard the shouts, "set the house on fire; burn him out." Others only hoped to get a clean shot at him. A man on horseback burst through the crowd and, as his horse reared below the turret, yelled "come down you bastard." Another man shook his fist and shouted, "get out of there, yeah, get out of there, you come down here." The crowd started to take up the cry "come down, come down, come down," as torches waved back and forth. A few, possessed with the ecstasy of mad men, attempted to scale the drainpipe, but the pipe broke before they were six feet off the ground. To Erik, the torches looked like a field of corn swaying in an angry wind. Then, a flicker in the corner of his eye, turned him around to see flames spreading up the stairway. He looked to his side and saw flames rolling out the windows. Pieces of burnt wood and wasted lumber were beginning to fall to further feed the fire; its flames became fatter and taller and broadened the sky, all around. Tongues of fire shot from the house and licked the sky, followed by the horrible breath of gray smoke. The broad sky itself seemed to be on fire. Rising into the air were showers of sparks and rolling sheets of flames, lighting the earth for miles around. In the distance, above the crowd's roar, fire sirens could be heard, approaching. Yet the shouts grew louder as new voices joined in.

"Go to hell! Go live with Satan, the lot of you!" yelled Erik, standing on the turret, which, itself, was beginning to give way. Erik, seeing what was about to happen, clutched onto the sidewall. That entire section of the house, as though it were breaking free of the dying structure it was a part of, began to tilt forward, with Erik riding it. In seconds it crashed to the ground and flames consumed it. The crowd grew hushed. Some men rushed forward to pull out their Evangelist. The crowd raised a cry of triumph. Erik was carried from those fires of hell to a safe spot where he knelt on the ground, surrounded and protected by his rescuers and the police. People pressed around him from all sides, a current of angry faces, illuminated by an occasional torch, struggled for a glimpse of their fallen hero. Suddenly several shots echoed through the air and all became silent. The only sound that could be heard was the feeding flames and the crackling tinder being consumed by the fire. The Sheriff, who had fired the shots, broke the silence as he quickly moved through the crowd with Mary Lou at his heels. Holding her bandaged head, Mary Lou rushed ahead of the Sheriff and fell to her knees besides Erik. Immediately she began to care for him.

"Move back, give me room," yelled the Sheriff.

As the Sheriff approached, Erik, in a sitting position, shrunk back, as if to hide. "I want to go to heaven, I want to go to heaven" he moaned, rocking back and forth, holding his knees.

Mary Lou continued to wipe his face and comfort him.

"I want to go the heaven," he cried again, this time louder.

"How is he?" asked the Sheriff, bending down for a better look.

"That's all he says," whispered Mary Lou.

"I want to go to heaven," Erik repeated.

"Hush sweetheart, hush," said Mary Lou, still wiping his face, trying to ease his pain.

"He's my whole life, he saved my life, if it wasn't for him, I'd be dead now. He's sweeter than my home and bigger than my country," cried Mary Lou to the Sheriff, with a stream of tears pouring down her crimson face.

"I know," returned the Sheriff, standing up, "but he's a sick man and it breaks my heart to see him that way. He was a great man. Most great men are not self-made. Society makes them and society breaks them," said the Sheriff to another officer who stood besides him.

"I want to go to heaven," repeated Erik, again and again, monotonously, as the light of a torch shone on his face. "I want to go to heaven, I want to go to heaven," he repeated, with a silver necklace of tears ringing the face stained with soot, sweat and soil.

THE END

About the Author

Frank Elias Georgalis was born in Astakos Greece, a small fishing village on the Ionian coast, twenty miles from Ithaca, the home of Homer's Ulysses. His childhood in the late years of the Second World War and the Civil War that followed inspires much of his writing. When Frank was a teenager, his parents, with their three children, immigrated to the United States and settled in Danville, Illinois. Attending high school and college in the mid-west, Frank developed a love of the English language and public speaking. After college, he entered the US Army and was attached to Army Intelligence. Being multilingual and a trained paratrooper, he was assigned to reconnaissance on the German-Czechoslovakian border where he served more than a year at the peak of the Cold War. Injured and incapacitated behind the Iron Curtain for several days, he was eventually rescued and carried five miles on the back of a fellow officer before being airlifted to Walter Reed Army Hospital. There he spent many months honing his writing skills while in rehabilitation, before being discharged. Shortly thereafter, seeking a career, he moved to the New York area and became involved in real estate, building and finance. His employers often called on his speaking skills for sales presentations and motivational seminars; it was at these public speaking events that "The Evangelist" was born. He eventually married his childhood sweetheart from Astakos and has one son, a physician who practices in Greece.

During the past thirty-five years he has written three novels, many short stories and several screenplays. Most of his writings are based on true-life experiences garnished with humor, philosophy, love, romance and mystery. No longer married, he now lives in New Jersey and has devoted himself to his writing. His works reflect his admiration of Greek mythology, which he identifies as the basis for all modern religion and western civilization. Those who know him well often refer to him as a philosopher but he labels himself merely as an observer of nature and a libertarian. His trust and belief is in God; he does not glorify or worship celebrities, officials or other dignitaries and feels that those who do are expressing a natural craving for a deity but are unsure where to find one.

His first novel, set in the Second World War, "Eagles Don't Rest," a second contemporary novel, "The Other Side of Love," a book of short stories, "Tales of the Unexpected" that includes "Tsika and I," "An Eye for a Tooth," and "The Wind May Blow," are pending publication.